Th

Strawberry Fields

Katie Flynn

arrow books

This edition published by Arrow Books in 2008

Arrow Books
Random House, 20 Vauxhall Bridge Road,
London SW1V 2SA

www.rbooks.co.uk

Addresses for companies within The Random House Group Limited
can be found at:
www.randomhouse.co.uk/offices.htm

The Random House Group Limited Reg. No. 954009

A CIP catalogue record for this book
is available from the British Library

ISBN 9780099527725

The Random House Group Limited supports The Forest Stewardship
Council (FSC), the leading international forest certification organisation.
All our titles that are printed on Greenpeace approved FSC certified paper
carry the FSC logo. Our paper procurement policy can be found at:
www.rbooks.co.uk/environment

Printed and bound in Great Britain by
CPI Cox & Wyman, Reading, RG1 8EX

The Mersey Girls

It would have been nice to take Lucy, though Maeve thought rather wistfully, heaving the sheet up over her shoulders. Nice for Linnet to meet her sister at last, nice for Maeve herself to have the company. But no point in even considering it. Lucy was doing well at school, she was useful on the farm, sensible and helpful. Padraig would do very well with Lucy and with one of his other daughters to keep an eye on things, and the twins would meet up again soon enough, for Maeve was determined to bring Linnet back with her. She hugged herself at the thought of that other fourteen-year-old, waiting in New York, about to get the surprise of her life when her Auntie Maeve turned up to rescue her.

And still smiling at the thought, Maeve fell asleep at last.

Katie Flynn has lived for many years in the Northwest. A compulsive writer, she started with short stories and articles and many of her early stories were broadcast on Radio Mersey. She decided to write her Liverpool series after hearing the reminiscences of family members about life in the city in the early years of the century. She also writes as Judith Saxton.

Also by Katie Flynn

A Liverpool Lass
The Girl from Penny Lane
Liverpool Taffy
Strawberry Fields
Rainbow's End
Rose of Tralee
No Silver Spoon
Polly's Angel
The Girl from Seaforth Sands
The Liverpool Rose

For Olive Edwards, because she has
promised to enjoy it!

As always, the staff of the Liverpool Local History Library on William Brown Street were both patient and helpful in finding me the material I needed, and Rosemarie Hague told me what Exchange Flags had looked like many years ago – and how to find it now!

And in Ireland, Elaine Walsh of Waterford was enormously helpful, telling us how to get where, and advising us not simply to head for one particular place but to wander, which is the best way to enjoy the country and to meet the people. We accordingly wandered down to Kerry and on to Cahersiveen, with its half-a-dozen different spellings, its fascinating sea-lough-cum-river, its gently rolling countryside and its weird, Eastern-looking barracks, to say nothing of the stump of a castle which I 'borrowed' for Lucy, Caitlin, Finn and Granny Mogg. Even the views are all there as described – and so is the delightful Evelyn Brennan, who, with her daughter, runs Brennan's Restaurant in the town and not only introduced us to brack, which is absolutely delicious, but told me a great deal about her town and the surrounding countryside – and put me straight on the state of the railways in the thirties.

And thanks to Maggie O'Driscoll and Nick Evans, who shared their knowledge of Irish tinkers in the thirties with me and helped me with the language of the travellers and their ways.

Chapter One

May 1913

As the faint chimes from the church clock stole across the dark waters of the lough, Maeve Murphy sat up on one elbow, struggling out of the depths of sleep. She did not know what had woken her, only that something had. A sound? A voice, perhaps? She turned her head cautiously and checked that Nora, with whom she shared her bed, was still fast asleep, then glanced across the small attic room towards the bed shared by two of her three younger sisters. Had one of them stirred, called out? But the girls slept, Clodagh curled up into a tight little ball, Éanna sprawled on her back, her beautiful lips just parted, a tiny snore curling rhythmically from her mouth. Maeve listened again. Yes, there had been a sound – a creak, and not just the usual creak of an old house settling either. This was the sort of creak, lively yet furtive, which meant that someone was awake and trying to move about the house without disturbing others.

Was it time to get up, then? Maeve glanced towards the uncurtained window; the sky was still dark, she could see stars twinkling, and there was not a sound from outside, not even a bird cheeped, forestalling the dawn chorus. Later the farmyard cock would start to clear his throat ready for his first cock-a-doodle, but right now the household should be wrapped in slumber, not prowling around. The last creak, Maeve was fairly sure, had come as a foot landed gently on the last stair but one.

Still, it was probably only a cat having a snoop round whilst the rest of the house slept. Maeve was about to lie down again when it occurred to her that her sister, Evie, who had slept in the small bedroom next door to their father's room ever since her twin daughters had been born, might be up and doing. Immediately Maeve swung her feet out of bed, listening more intently than ever. Evie was barely seventeen and Maeve, the oldest of the five Murphy girls, had taken upon herself the care of the smallest, frailest twin. If Evie had gone down to feed them or change them she would appreciate Maeve's presence.

Maeve shuffled a bit further down the bed and reached for her shawl, draped across the bedpost. She wrapped it firmly around her shoulders, glad of its soft, woolly warmth. Although the month was May it was still chilly in the early hours and her flannel petticoat wasn't much protection against the cold. Then she stood up, carefully tucked her side of the bed in – Nora did not even stir – and tiptoed over to the door. It opened silently, because when five lively young girls share a house with an elderly father it behoves them to keep their door-hinges well-oiled, and Maeve slid out on to the steps which, ladderlike, descended to the upper landing.

Outside Evie's room she hesitated; should she peep inside, just make sure? No one would burgle the Murphys because there was nothing to steal, but there was usually food in the pantry and there were always gipsies and tramps eager to fill their bellies. She put a hand on the door knob, then drew it back as a sound from downstairs reached her ears; there was definitely someone in the kitchen, she could hear quiet footsteps padding across the hard earth floor!

That settled it: they either had an intruder, in which case two people were better than one, or Evie had got up. Quickly, before she could change her mind, she opened Evie's door. One glance at the bed showed her that it was empty, the covers pushed back, the pillow still dented from the impression of Evie's head.

Relief washed over Maeve in waves. She turned away from her sister's room and ran down the stairs, not bothering to go particularly quietly. At the bottom, in the small, square hall, she turned at once to the kitchen, though she opened the door softly enough.

At first she thought the room was empty: moonlight streamed through the two low windows overlooking the farmyard, turning the room into a symphony of black and silver. Puzzled, Maeve took a step into the room . . . then stopped short, a hand flying to her heart.

By the fireplace, something moved. A figure stood there, on tiptoe, reaching up for the battered teapot which stood directly under the grandmother clock. A hand, white in the moonlight, was already curled round the blackened pewter pot.

'Evie! What on earth . . . ?'

Evie spun round, leaving the teapot still rocking from her touch. Her face looked white as a ghost, her eyes black pits. She gasped, then relaxed. 'Maeve! Dear God, girl, I nearly died. What are you doing down here at this time of night? I thought everyone was asleep, so I did.'

Maeve walked over to the fire and took a taper from the box by the hearth. She lit it, then held the flame to the candle on the end of the dresser. Her mind was working furiously; Evie was fully dressed, this was no trip downstairs to fetch something for one of her babies, this was . . .

'What are *you* doing, Evie?' she said evenly. 'I came down because I heard you creepin' down the stairs. Where's the babies?'

'In bed, Maeve, me love, it's the middle of the night; where else would me darlin's be but in their bed?'

In the candlelight, Maeve looked hard and long at her

younger sister. Evie was so beautiful, that was the trouble, it became difficult not to believe every word uttered by those pink, perfect lips!

'Evie, you're fully dressed,' Maeve said, changing tack. 'Where were you going?'

'Were going, Maeve?' Evie sighed and turned back to the mantelpiece. She reached up and took the teapot down, then stood there cradling it. And when she spoke again it was with more than a touch of defiance. 'I *am* going. In ten minutes or so a cart'll pull in off the main road. I arranged it a day or so ago, it'll take me down to the station. Oh, Maeve, you know I can't stay here for the rest of me life – you wouldn't want it for me, would you? The disapproval's enough to break my heart, and besides, I'm wasted here. I'll never get anywhere, do anything . . . *be* anyone, come to that, whilst I stay in Cahersiveen. So I'm leaving, going to – to seek me fortune, you could say.'

'And you're taking the housekeeping money,' Maeve stated calmly, jerking her head at the pewter teapot. 'That's stealing, Evie, no matter how you justify it. And what about your little girls, then?'

'I'm taking Linnet with me, but I can't burden meself with two of them,' Evie said defensively. 'Besides, what'ud you do, Maeve me darlin', if I took Lucy as well? You'd miss them both sore, you know you would. And leaving Lucy shows I mean to come back – but I can't take 'em both or I'll never get rich and famous!'

The last words were almost a wail. Despite herself, Maeve smiled.

'Oh, Evie, what does rich and famous matter, after all? Isn't it better to be happy here, with your two little girls? To live a good life?'

Evie shrugged her shoulders and set the teapot down on the table. She took the lid off it and tipped the contents very gently out onto a cloth she had already placed there to receive it. Then she wrapped the money in the cloth and pushed the small bundle down into the shabby bag which Maeve now saw at her sister's feet.

'I can't settle to it and never could,' she said honestly. 'Country living's always drove me mad . . . I should've gone a year back, only it seemed a big thing to do. And then Jan didn't want me to leave, said to wait a while, so I stayed . . . and look what happened!'

'Jan Wilde's a good feller and would have taken you and the babies on, if only you'd let him,' Maeve reminded her sister. 'But if you don't want Jan why in God's name didn't you marry the Ronald feller from England? You let him give you the babies, so you must have liked him. Or at least you could've got his address, so our Dad could have sent someone looking for him, told him what he'd done.'

'I don't want to marry anyone,' Evie said pettishly. 'You don't understand about babies, Maeve, that Englishman was dull as ditchwater; if I hadn't been so bored I'd never have let him do more than kiss me, so there!'

'Indeed, madam? Then why not marry Jan Wilde if you weren't in love with that blackhearted English? He'd be good to you, treat you right.'

'Because I can't bear the thought of scratching a living from a poor little place all me life, because I know there's more to me than Jan could possibly appreciate. I'm a good actress; I sing like an angel and dance like a . . . a dervish, and I can imitate voices so folk don't know it's me,' Evie said definitely. 'And it isn't just me that thinks so, Maeve me love; that Ronald feller knew a thing or two and he said I was talented, in the right hands he said I'd go far.'

'He was a big-mouth,' Maeve said bitterly. 'He comes

for a holiday after an illness, turns your head, gets you pregnant and then leaves, never realising the harm he's done. I hope the good God has shown him the error of his ways, even if 'tis too late for you to come to your senses.'

'Well, I am talented, and I shall go far despite all of you,' Evie said hotly. 'Did you think I'd stay here for ever, rotting away, while other girls went to Dublin, to England, and had all the fun and excitement?'

'Once you'd had the babies . . .' Maeve began patiently, only to be briskly interrupted.

'Oh, the babies, the babies! One little slip from grace and you'd condemn me for the rest of me life! You're as bad as the others, Maeve Murphy, and I always thought you understood!'

'I do understand, alanna, and I know you're a good actress and beautiful, too. But how can you go back to Dublin with a child under each arm? Who'll take you seriously as an actress when you're hung about with babies? Leave it a few years, until they're older . . .'

'Until I'm older you mean,' Evie snapped. 'I've got to strike whilst the iron's hot, Maeve – I've got to! And it'll work, I promise you, because I've learned me lesson. This time I'll steer clear of the fellers and be single-minded and really work at my career, I won't listen to any man, no matter how sweetly he talks. I'll make a name for myself and then . . . then you and little Lucy can come and visit me in London, or Paris, or – or New York, and I'll buy a mansion and we'll all live happily ever after!'

'They're just daydreams, alanna,' Maeve said gently. 'Put the money back like a good girl and go and get into your bed. I'll make us a cup of tea and by the time you've drunk it you'll be sleepy again and tomorrow you'll realise that there's a good life for you here – a good man, too. Why, half the young men in the town would give their eye-teeth for a smile from Miss Evie Murphy!'

'I don't care about local fellers and that's no more'n the truth. I'm going, Maeve, and if you try to stop me then I promise you'll never set eyes on me again, as long as I live,' Evie said hysterically. 'I can't stay here and rot – I won't! You can stop me tonight, but you can't stand guard over me for the rest of my life. I'll get away, and if I do it that way I'll never come back, I swear it.'

The two girls stood on opposite sides of the table, the teapot between them, the candle casting its flickering shadows over the smooth oval of Evie's face and the rich glory of her thickly curling wheat-coloured locks. Maeve knew that the same shadows danced over her own plain and bony visage, over tear-filled eyes and lank, dust-coloured hair; but right now it was not Evie's beauty nor her own ugliness which was in question, it was whose will would prove stronger.

For what seemed like an eternity they stood there, eyes locked, then Maeve sighed and let her glance drop before the icy determination in her little sister's gaze. If she held out, she knew, she would lose Evie and she could not bear that.

'All right. If you must go, you must. Take Linnet and come back for Lucy when you're able,' Maeve said in a small, colourless voice. 'Remember, Evie, that we love you. Don't forget us, whatever happens. We'll always be here for you.'

The ice in Evie's glance melted and tears brimmed over and trickled down her cheeks. She ran round to her sister and put her arms round her, giving her a hard hug.

'Maeve, me darling, as if I could ever forget you. You're the best thing that happened to me, you've been like a mother to me – better than most mothers from what I've seen. And I'll come back to you, I swear it, when I'm rich and famous. And – and I'll take great care of Linnet ... I'll write to you every week. Oh, darling Maeve, you'll never regret what you've done tonight.'

'Don't wait till you're rich and famous,' Maeve said with a slight smile. 'I'll fetch Linnet for you, shall I?'

'She's already in the sling you made for me, sleepin' like a little angel,' Evie said with a sparkling look towards the big fireside chair. 'Did you not see her, in the shadows? Oh, Maeve, look at the time – give me a kiss, dear, then I must run. I dare not lose me lift into town.'

The sisters kissed, Evie clinging for a moment, then Maeve went over to the big fireside chair and lifted the sling and its rosy, sleeping occupant, helping Evie to arrange the sling so that the baby lay comfortably against her breast, leaving the young mother's hands free.

'Now isn't that grand?' Evie murmured. 'I've got a bag with a few things in ...'

'The bag's awful light,' Maeve said uneasily, picking the shabby little holdall up from the floor. 'Are you not taking food and drink for your journey?'

'No need,' Evie assured her. She took the bag and put a hand on the back door latch. 'I've got me best dress and some stuff for Linnet ... hark, can you hear that rumbling? It's me lift coming across the river-bridge. Oh, Maeve, I do love you; hold onto that! And take care of Lucy for me.'

'I will alanna, but I wish ...' Maeve began, but her sister had slipped out of the doorway and was crossing the dark farmyard on quick, light feet. Maeve went and stood on the big, cold flags, watching the younger girl while tears ran down her cheeks, but Evie did not look back. She turned out of the yard and into the lane and Maeve strained her eyes but could see only Evie's hair, pale as the moon's glow, and her slim ankles beneath the dark coat. She watched, a hand pressed to her mouth, until a bend in the lane hid Evie from her view. Only then did she turn back into the candlelit kitchen.

Gone! Maeve doused the candle and crossed the dark room, suddenly aware of ice-cold feet and a heavy heart. She had let Evie go – but how could she have stopped her? She could have insisted that Evie take both babies but it would have been wickedly unfair on little Lucy. The smaller of the twins was not a bouncing, rosy-cheeked child like her sister, she was pale and frail. At four months old Linnet had not seemed at all bothered when her mother had weaned her from the breast onto bottled cow's milk, whereas little Lucy had not taken to the bottle at all. She cried a lot, drank a small quantity from her bottle very slowly and reluctantly and then sicked half of it up again, usually all over whoever was bringing up her wind. Placid, fat Linnet seldom cried, played with her pink toes and chuckled and cooed. But Lucy suffered from colic, bringing her pointed knees hard up into her small stomach whilst she screamed with pain. Maeve had noticed that even the slightest change in her routine brought about an attack, and weaning the smaller twin was a painful process which Evie had left almost entirely to Maeve.

I should thank the good Lord that Evie didn't suggest taking Lucy, Maeve told herself, wearily climbing the stairs on her ice-cold feet. Evie could never manage the smaller twin – at least with a healthy, happy child like Linnet she has a head start, and I can manage Lucy meself, no problem.

Outside Evie's bedroom door, she paused. If she left Lucy to slumber on undisturbed the child would not waken until six or so, but then, with Maeve having had such a disturbed night, would she herself wake before Lucy's howls had aroused the entire household? Their father was not a particularly patient man and had been heartbroken when his favourite daughter had produced twin girls and no husband to go with them. Indeed, Padraig Murphy had been deeply disappointed when the wife of his bosom had presented him with no fewer than five daughters and not one single son, though he had grieved over her death for they had been a fond couple. Nevertheless, he felt that fate had dealt unfairly with him.

'Fine it is for herself, a-choirin' wi' the angels on high,' he had observed sourly in the hearing of the eleven-year-old Maeve. 'And here am I, left lit'rally holdin' the babby.'

But it had been Maeve who had brought Evie up, with very little help from her other sisters, and even less from Padraig, though he had adored his youngest daughter and revelled in her pretty, loving ways. Plain old Maeve, the only Murphy girl that no man ever looked at twice, had also adored – and spoiled – the little sister who looked on her as the only mother she had ever known, and now she adored that little sister's children. Especially Lucy. There was no getting away from it, Lucy's pale little face and wistful blue eyes had wound their way firmly into Maeve's susceptible heart. Perhaps, Maeve thought, tiptoeing into Evie's bedroom and over to the stout wooden cradle in which young Murphys had slumbered for generations, perhaps I'm the sort of person who needs to be needed even more than I need to be loved. Or perhaps someone who needs you automatically loves you. Whatever the reason, though, I couldn't have borne it if Evie had taken Lucy.

She leaned over the cot. Lucy was awake, her thumb wedged into her small mouth, her eyes fixed on the ceiling above her head. She was bald but for a quiff of lint-white hair and she had lately developed a rash around her mouth and chin, but to Maeve she was the most beautiful thing on this earth. She smiled at the baby, a smile full of all the stored up, imprisoned love in her heart and the baby smiled back, her eyes lighting up with pleasure, her mouth curving into that most trustful of expressions, a beam of pure, unselfish love.

'Oh, Lucy, you're going to be my little girl until your mammy comes home,' Maeve whispered, picking the child out of the cot and cuddling her against her breast. 'No man'll ever want me – why should they, indeed? – but you do don't you, me darlin'? You'll want your Maeve for – oh, for years and years and years!'

And the baby sighed and nuzzled against her, seeming to listen when Maeve told her that it was not time for a feed yet, not for a couple of hours at least, but that there was plenty of time for a cuddle.

She climbed carefully into Evie's little bed with the child still held against her breast, and presently she had the satisfaction of seeing Lucy's lids droop, of hearing her breathing become slow and regular.

She's always been dear to me, but she's dearer than ever now, because she's as good as me own, Maeve thought, letting her cheek rest gently against the baby's silky hair. Oh Evie, Evie, I'll miss you sore every day that I live . . . but I'll be a good mammy to your little one. You can trust old Maeve to take as much care of her as you would yourself. No, I'll take more care of her, she added, letting her lips caress the child's soft crown. She'll be my little princess for she's all I've got, until you come home and take her from me. And then there'll be the four of us, in your grand big house, all happy as – as queens!

And on the thought, Maeve Murphy slid into dreams and slept soundly, with Lucy in her arms, until the new day dawned.

There was no waiting room at the small station in the

town, so Evie sat on a wooden bench in a sheltered corner and watched the stars pale in the sky and breast-fed a sleepy but compliant Linnet. She had weaned Lucy off the breast but had continued to feed Linnet, though secretly, knowing that if Maeve knew she would put two-and-two together and make four. Because Evie's plan, to leave the farm and her family far behind her and seek fame and fortune in the big city, had been in her head for two long years. She would have gone before had it not been for Jan.

Jan was the son of a neighbouring farmer, a dark, handsome young man in his early twenties, much sought after by local girls. But he had ignored them all until he came across Evie one bright April day, with her hands tangled in the mane of the new colt their father had bought from Killarney market, being pulled off her feet.

He had rescued her, talked to her – kissed her. Evie, white and gold, sixteen years old, on the threshold of womanhood, had needed little persuading to go with him into the nearby haybarn, where they had fallen on each other like love-starved animals and conceived the twins.

'I'll marry you,' he said when she told him she was going to have a baby, but Evie had shaken her head, feeling the bars of the cage close round her on the words. She had enjoyed making love, feeling his strong arms round her, she regretted that she would have to forgo it, once her child was born. But she wanted more freedom, a life of her own, fame and fortune, and she would not get any of those things once Jan had roped and tied her to his smallholding. Not even the pleasure of making love in a soft bed every night could make up for the loss of her dreams.

The baby finished, burped, was returned to her place in the sling, and very soon afterwards the train came chuffing lazily into the station. I've done all right for myself so far, Evie thought as she climbed into the carriage of the small train which would take her right across Ireland to the magic city of Dublin. She had managed to let everyone assume that the Englishman had been her lover, so that Jan had not lost face over the affair. And there was no ill-feeling between herself and Maeve, for if she had succeeded in her attempt to run away without a word to anyone, leaving Lucy behind, Maeve might well have felt some justifiable annoyance. As it was, Evie had got just what she wanted – escape from the farm – and had remained on good terms with her sister.

The train, which had waited for several moments in the station while goods and a few passengers were put aboard, sounded its whistle, but mutedly because of the early hour, and pulled out of the station. Evie settled herself comfortably in her window seat and looked down at her sleeping child. Dear little, good little Linnet, she would be no trouble, Evie was bound to find someone who wanted to look after her during the day while she sought her fortune. And the child was company, in an odd sort of way. I won't feel lonely whilst I've got Linnet, Evie thought contentedly, letting her gaze wander over the rich green of Ireland as the train chugged along. She was sure Linnet would be beautiful and would have a lovely singing voice, so perhaps they could do an act together when the child was a little older. Evie sat back in her seat and dreamed out of the window, and went back in her mind over what had happened at Ivy Farm that morning.

It was very good of Maeve to let me take the housekeeping money out of the pewter teapot, she reminded herself, because it means I shall be able to live quite well for the first month or so. And I'm sure Daddy won't give Maeve any cash to replace what I've taken until the month's end because he's tight-fisted and mean. A shame it is that he doesn't like me any more just because I fell for the twins, but when he sees I'm gone he'll probably be nicer to the others. He might even be nicer to Maeve, because although she's not pretty, she works harder than most.

The train chugged on and a plume of smoke swept by the window. There was grit on the surfaces and, although the sun was well up now bathing the countryside in gold, it was chilly in the half-empty carriage. A woman with two children, who had got aboard at Killarney, got out a bag of sandwiches and some apples. The woman offered Evie a ham sandwich and Evie accepted graciously and when it was eaten, leaned her head on the window and snoozed.

The children told each other stores in loud voices but the sound scarcely entered Evie's dreams, certainly did not wake her. With the baby snug against her breast, Evie slumbered on.

'She'll come back, Da, when she discovers that life isn't as easy as she thinks,' Maeve said next morning, expertly frying bacon and eggs in the big black pan whilst her father and the farmhands, Tom Flanagan and his son Kellach, sat with their big mugs of dark tea at the breakfast table. 'Inside six months she'll be back home, I'm sure.'

'She'll not be welcome here,' Padraig said at once. 'A wicked girl she is, and a bad example to her sisters. She's gone, now she can stay away.'

Clodagh, cutting bread at one end of the table, smiled at her sister, Éanna, who was making the bread into sandwiches and packing them into two lunch-tins. Both girls were tall, buxom and blonde. Clodagh taught at the local school and Éanna worked behind the counter in the town's only drapery shop, so they usually walked into town together, though Clodagh finished at four while Éanna was not finished until six or later. They were good friends, only a year separating them in age, and Maeve used to wonder whether the twins would be like them when they were older, for the twins, too, were fair-haired.

'If little Evie does come home she can come to my place, alanna, when Niall and I are wed,' Clodagh said, cutting a thick slice and handing it to Maeve for frying. 'Will she come back for the weddin', I wonder? She could be me attendant and welcome.'

'She'll not be welcome here,' Padraig repeated obstinately. 'At your own house, Clodagh, I shall have no say, but I won't have her here.'

'That's all right, Father,' Clodagh said peaceably. She smiled across at Éanna and her sister smiled back. They were placid, pleasant girls, much sought after by the young men of Cahersiveen. Whilst neither was strictly beautiful, as Evie was, the two girls nearest to Maeve in age were acknowledged to be pretty and sweet-natured, and both were engaged to be married to neighbouring farmers' sons.

'If she writes with her address, you must tell her to come back for our weddings, Maeve,' Éanna said comfortably. 'Sure and I wouldn't have little Evie missed out for the world.'

Padraig ground his teeth and Tom, drinking tea, looked from one girl to the other over the top of his mug and grinned.

'Sure an' you'll never get the better of a woman, Paddy,' he said, eyes twinkling. 'Your Evie'll be back home in a twelvemonth, mark me words.'

Kellach was a big, quiet young man of about Maeve's age. He had admired her once, walking her home from school, stopping to chat with her as she worked around the house, but her steadfast refusal to go out with him whilst her sisters needed her had resulted in his looking elsewhere and now it was commonly believed that he had an understanding with a widow who lived six miles away, on the other side of the town. She was ten years older than Kellach if she was a day, but she had a decent farm and at thirty-eight she probably still needed a man. Maeve knew one day she would be sorry that she had not snapped Kellach up whilst she had the chance, but that day was not yet. First it was Clodagh and Éanna who needed her, then Nora and Evie; now she had Lucy to think of. There was simply no time in her busy life to worry about men.

Maeve dished up the breakfasts and watched her father eating with the speed he always showed. He shovelled the food in, packing his mouth with bacon until the grease ran down his chin, wiping spilt yolk with a slice of bread, drinking his tea in big gulps between mouthfuls. The pity of it was, she reflected, that though he was a good farmer, none better, he was always rushing, hurrying to get on. So he seldom praised her meals, though perhaps as the bacon came from the pigs he reared, the eggs from the poultry strutting in the yard outside, even the bread from their own wheat, he might think that to say that the food was good was a form of self-appreciation.

It would have been nice to have been appreciated by her father, but to Padraig Murphy, Maeve was simply a work-horse. A good one, yes, but not valued as she ought to be. It isn't really fair, because if I were pretty then I'd marry and leave and he wouldn't like that, Maeve told herself, putting a piece of fried bread and an egg onto her own plate and taking it to her place at the end of the table. Her father was ashamed of her because she had no man sniffing after her, yet he resented the men who came calling after Clodagh, Éanna and Nora, was continually critical of them and obviously more than a little jealous.

'More tea, Maeve.'

She had only just sat down; Kellach made a half-move, but Clodagh was quicker. She took her father's mug without a word, refilled it, put it down before him. Once again, Padraig showed by neither word nor gesture that he had been given the tea he had demanded.

'Get the honey.'

This time Maeve reached the jar down from the dresser without having to move from her chair and stood it with a crack on the table before him. He reached for it, dug his knife into the smooth, amber sweetness, spread it thickly on a round of buttered bread.

'Lovely manners, Daddy,' Nora said. She had come into the kitchen softly and reached round her sister for the teapot. 'Don't worry, Maeve, I'm not eating breakfast this morning, I'll just have me a nice, hot cup of tea. Oh, and some bread and honey because I mustn't be fainting behind the till.'

Nora worked in the town's only dining rooms and was already clad in her working uniform – a black dress with white collar and cuffs, a rustling white apron and neat low-heeled black shoes. She was golden-haired, like three of her four sisters, and was currently walking out with the schoolmaster, a pleasant, scholarly man in his forties who had never been married and who probably never would be, unless Nora nudged him a little.

Padraig looked up and gave Nora a half-grin; she was his favourite daughter, now that Evie had fallen from favour with such a crash. I was never a favourite, nor ever will be, Maeve thought sadly, though I'm the only one that works at home, slaving to keep the place halfway decent. Still, I've no charm, no pretty ways. How can I expect to be anyone's favourite?

But then she remembered Lucy, sleeping in the cradle upstairs, and a smile curved her lips. Her sisters were lovely and beloved, but she – she had a baby who was as good as her own. She would see that Lucy got the best of everything and when Evie came back, or grew famous, there would be the four of them, closer than friends, staying together for the rest of their lives.

Me Da can be as grumpy as he pleases, and Kellach can court his old widow and go and live in her rich little farm, she told herself, eating her fried bread. The girls can marry their young men and Nora can flirt with the schoolmaster and get prettier and more sought-after by the day together. But what does it matter to us Murphy girls, Maeve and Evie, Lucy and Linnet? We'll manage fine so we shall, Maeve told herself blissfully. And did not even hear her father's voice as it ordered her to cut more bread and look lively, woman, we men have got work to do even if you haven't!

Chapter Two

1924

'Hey, watch out, watch out! Gerrout me wa-a-a-ay!'

Linnet, who had been walking carefully down the snowy pavement on Havelock Street, clutching her messages and thinking wistfully of the hot cup of tea which would await her on her return home, was unwise enough to turn round to see who was shouting, which was how she came to find herself travelling, very fast, along the pavement with a pair of arms clutching her and her bum slithering at incredible speed along the steeply sloping snow-covered flagstones.

The unexpected trip finished with equal suddenness. One moment she and her assailant and a small tin tea-tray were hurtling down Havelock Street, the next they had burst into Netherfield Road and were trying to untangle themselves from a lamp-post whilst a small boy sat on the pavement howling and clutching his knees and a very fat woman belaboured them indiscriminately with a large umbrella.

'Bleedin' gipsies!' the woman shouted, swishing the umbrella in a half-circle and catching Linnet and the would-be tobogganer around their unprotected shoulders. ''Ow dare youse ruffians come into a decent neighbourhood like this, a-playin' your wicked games! As if it ain't bad enough living 'alfway up Havelock Street, which is a rare danger in this sorta weather, without bein' knocked off our feet by kids on bleedin' tea-trays!'

'Sorry, missus,' the boy said, trying to get away from

the flailing umbrella. 'We din't do it on purpose, it were an accident, we're hurt, too, me and the little gal, we din't mean to . . . ouch!'

Linnet struggled to her feet as the woman gave her companion one last, valedictory thump with the umbrella and began to cluck over her small son, leading him up the steep street which she and her companion had just left. Bleakly, Linnet surveyed her string bag and its mangled contents. She had come all this way because Mammy had told her to fetch the new frock Miss Spelman, the dressmaker, had just completed for her, and now look at it! The brown paper was torn and beneath it, the tissue which Miss Spelman had carefully wrapped around it was torn, too, and wet. And she had visited Mammy's favourite confectionery shop first because the owner had promised to obtain for them some rather special crystallised fruit – Mammy loved crystallised fruit – and now the pretty white package tied with pink ribbon was looking decidedly the worse for wear.

'Oh me darling, whatever has happened to my parcels?' Mammy would say, examining the dirty wrapping paper. 'Did you fall over now in all this miserable snow and slush? I scarcely know how to bear the weather we've been having lately, I'm truly tempted to take my friend up on his invitation and go to Paris in the spring, just to get away from Liverpool snow and fogs.'

Mammy never shouted when it wasn't your fault, that was one good thing. And they were really flush at the moment because Mammy had a good part in the pantomime and her latest admirer, Mr Jackie Osborne, liked to buy special treats and to take Mammy out to dinner after the show. So perhaps it wasn't terribly serious that the messages had got a little snow and slush on them – by the time she got home the wrapping paper would, in all probability, have dried out and be as good as ever.

So there was no point in standing here wondering what Mammy would say. The fat woman and her son were labouring up Havelock Street now, the woman heaving herself along by clutching at the house-walls whilst the child's howls had turned to hiccups, but the boy with the tea-tray stood there still, rubbing a scarlet ear and scowling after his attacker.

'Well, as if I meant to do it!' he muttered crossly, turning to Linnet. 'As for you, you wasn't even on the bloody tray, was you? I should think your knickers is probably ripped to shreds though, comin' down Havey at that speed.'

Linnet frowned at him. It was rude to talk about knickers, a boy his age should know better. He looked quite a bit older than she, he must be twelve or thirteen she supposed, so he could not pretend that knickers were a suitable subject of conversation between them.

'I was just walking down the road with my messages,' she pointed out coldly, 'when you knocked me off my feet. You could have spoiled my Mammy's new dress and squashed her crystallised fruit. I think I'd better go now, before anything else happens.'

'Where d'you live?' The boy said, falling companionably into step beside her and ignoring her critical tone. 'I think I might have seen you before somewhere . . . live round these parts, do you?'

Linnet turned her head and surveyed him carefully. Mammy had said not to fall into conversation with strangers, but she had not meant *boys*, surely? Linnet went to a small private school run by the nuns, but boys were everywhere, as common and numerous as the raindrops which spotted the flagstones or the snowflakes which had made all this nasty slush. You could no more avoid boys than you could the rain or the snow, and when one actually spoke to you, you could scarcely pretend not to have heard. That would be rude and Mammy did not like rudeness.

'Well, will you know me again?' the boy said, but not nastily, because he was grinning at her as he spoke. He had a nice face, not clean or handsome or anything like that, just nice. He was thin and brown, with a wide grin and grey eyes and there was something about him, some quality of friendliness and concern for others – he had apologised to the woman and had not tried to blame Linnet for the accident, something a less honest boy might well have done – which made Linnet decide to forgive him for knocking her down and muddying her messages.

'Yes, I'll know you again,' she said seriously. 'I don't live round here, though. I live on Juvenal Street, in rooms over a shop opposite the back of the fruit market. My name's Linnet Murphy, what's yours?'

'I'm Roddy Sullivan,' the boy said readily. He stuck out a grimy hand. 'Well, we're neighbours, Linnet, 'cos I live in Peel Square; that's off Cazneau and right near Juvenal. So we'll walk back together, shall us? Come on, lemme give you a hand with them messages.'

'It's all right, I can manage,' Linnet said, clutching her string bag defensively close. He seemed nice, but you never let a stranger get his hands on your possessions, no matter how friendly he was; she already knew *that* much. 'Where did you get that tray from, though, and what were you doing coming down Havey like that?'

Havelock Street was famous for its steep slope; the elderly and infirm heaved themselves up it with great difficulty, clutching the walls as they went, but Linnet always felt sorry for coalmen's horses, who had no hands to help them along and had to risk a tumble and broken knees every time they delivered on Havelock Street.

'I were sledging, of course, and the tray's me mam's ... well, she works for James Blackledge, on Derby Road, and the tray comes from there ... an' Havey's steeper'n it oughter be when you're on a tray,' Roddy explained a trifle defensively. 'Good thing you and the old woman was there, come to think, or I'd ha' charged straight out into the middle of the carriageway. Why, I could of been killed stone dead!'

'It was a mad thing to do,' Linnet pointed out primly. 'I daresay you might have been killed, but you might have killed us and all – me, the old lady and the little lad. What'ud you have done then, eh?'

'I'd've run like the divil,' Roddy said cheerfully. He delved into the pocket of his ragged trousers. 'Here, want a licky stick?'

He produced two liquorice sticks. They were shaped like tiny walking sticks and were liberally covered in fluff but Linnet accepted one graciously and bit off the curved end.

'Thanks,' she said. 'Where d'you nick 'em?'

Roddy grinned, not taking offence at the question though her mam, Linnet knew, would have been shocked at her rudeness. The trouble with Mammy is that she thinks Liverpool's just like Cahersiveen, and it isn't, Linnet thought defensively. In Cahersiveen, when Mammy was a little girl, you never stole anything, 'cos there wasn't no need. But when you lived in rooms over a chandler's shop three doors down from the Clock public house, you soon realised that a great many people had little choice but to take what they could when they could – and that included the kids.

I'm lucky, though, Linnet reminded herself, blissfully sucking liquorice. My mam's got her lovely job in the theatre so she's hardly ever out of work, she earns good money and doesn't blue it on drink, so I get all the food

I want and decent togs, not like some. Roddy's thin grey jersey had huge holes all over and his shirt was torn as well so you could see his bare skin in places. As for his trousers – oh well, they cover most of him, Linnet thought charitably. And he had boots, though they were pretty ancient ones, with cracked uppers and almost certainly holes in the soles. Probably, Roddy was one of a big family, whereas Linnet, as her mam often told her, was a lucky only child.

'Got it legal, like,' Roddy said in reply to her question, speaking through a mouthful of his own liquorice stick. 'Payment for takin' a tray of iced cakes from Peely to Havey. Me mam made 'em for a party . . . made 'em in her own time, like. So she give me a penny for delivery an' the old gal on Havey give me the licky sticks. So it's all square, honest to God.'

'Good,' Linnet said politely. Not that she cared. Mammy would be horrified, but Linnet knew that it was a lot easier to be honest if you had a good job and no brothers and sisters. Mammy had told her to steer clear of street kids, but that didn't mean don't watch them. Linnet watched, and had seen with wonder tinged with envy, that the poor kids stuck by one another even in their thieving. One kid would hoist another over the wall and into the back of the market when the stallholders had gone home, then they would share whatever spoils came their way. Another would keep cavey when a friend was after a few toffees and the resultant booty would be religiously divided. What was more, she knew that some kids would never see an orange or a liquorice stick if they didn't prig one now and then. No point in sticking your nose in the air and coming all Holy Joe about it; so far as Linnet could see, it was all right for her to be honest, because she ate well anyway. Others were not so fortunate.

'When you play out, Linnet, where d'you play?' Roddy asked presently, as they trudged through the filthy slush which, two days ago, had been great heaps of white snow. 'I ain't never seen you up our way.'

'No, you wouldn't. I'm not allowed to play in the street,' Linnet said. 'My mam's an actress, though, so when it's school holidays I go to the Playhouse with her, mostly.'

Roddy's eyes rounded. 'An actress! Is she famous?'

'She's Miss Evaline Murphy,' Linnet said cautiously. She had been told to keep her mother's identity a secret – but surely not from this friendly boy? 'I dunno if she's famous, but she does lovely acting, honest to God.'

'Not the one wi' the long yaller curls, the one they calls little Evie?' Roddy said incredulously. 'Cor, my mam saw her in a play last summer, she thought little Evie were a cracker! Blackledge's took their workers to the theaytre instead of on a seaside trip. Ooh, she can't be that Evie, can she?'

'Yes, she's that one,' Linnet said proudly. 'She's ever so beautiful and a very good actress, too, your mam was right. She's played all sorts . . . she's in the panto now, you know . . . she's the lady who gets sawed in half in the Giant's castle.'

'Cor,' Roddy said again, suitably impressed. 'My mam said little Evie come on the stage wi' a white, floaty gown you could see right through, she said there weren't nothing left to . . .'

'Oh well, you have to do all sorts of things if you want to be a star,' Linnet said. Her cheeks felt hot and she wished – not for the first time – that she hadn't started boasting. Not everyone understood that Mammy, who was so strict at home, sometimes had to do things which weren't quite . . . quite nice. 'Mammy sings lovely, too. She sings to me when she puts me to bed.'

'Puts you . . . how old are you, Linnie?' Roddy said. 'You looks about twelve, same's me.'

'I'm eleven,' Linnet told him. 'Eleven years and ten days, 'cos I was born on New Year's Day. Why?'

'Well, me mam puts the baby an' Freddy to bed, an' me brother Matt gives little Bert an 'and, but the rest of us gets ourselves there, some'ow,' Roddy said. 'Can't you git to your buttons, eh?'

'I only meant that I get into bed and then Mam comes along an' tucks me in,' Linnet explained hastily. 'Then she sits on the side of my bed and sings a song or tells me stories about the old days in Ireland. That's what I meant, I didn't mean she undressed me or put my nightgown on – I do that for myself, of course.'

'You're a right 'un. A nightgown!' Roddy said. 'What's wrong wi' your shirt, or knickers or whatever gals wear?'

'Well, you see . . . but let's not talk about it, it's just Mammy's ways are different,' Linnet said. She could just imagine how involved the conversation would become if they started talking about the dangers of catching fleas or lice if you wore the same garments day and night for a week. 'You've got quite a lot of brothers and sisters, haven't you? There's only me and Mam in our rooms.'

'What about your da?' Roddy said. Linnet tried not to glower at him. She was already realising that Roddy would always pick on the difficult subjects, ask the awkward questions, unless he was carefully guided away from them.

'My da's back in Ireland,' Linnet told him, mentally crossing her fingers though not doing so in fact, since he would undoubtedly notice. 'Mam left him there. He – he wasn't the sort of man she wanted to live with, you see.'

Roddy nodded knowingly. 'Aye, I know what you mean. Me mam's sister, Auntie Prue, she lives not far from Peely. She's got two brats, Simmy an' Sukey. She din't like either one o' the fellers she went with, she told me mam so.'

'Well, there you are then,' Linnet said bracingly, thanking God for Prue and her brats. 'Tell you what, Roddy, it'll be dark quite soon. If you come home wi' me, Mammy'll give us buttered toast an' fruit cake. We could play Snap, or Beggar your Neighbour if you'd like to.'

'But she don't know me,' Roddy said doubtfully. 'She won't want a kid she don't know in her place.'

'Yes she will, she likes me to have friends,' Linnet said.

The remark was not strictly truthful but Linnet had noticed lately that Mammy, who at one time had frequently told her to steer clear of what she called 'street kids' and had made it plain that she did not want Linnet to bring school friends home, was beginning to change her tune. A year ago, when Linnet was nine, she had decided that her daughter was now old enough to have friends back to their rooms or to visit their homes, when she was invited. And on Linnet's tenth birthday, when Mammy had come, pale-faced and heavy-eyed, into the living room, complaining bitterly that she had a champagne headache, she had reminded Linnet that she still had not brought any friends home, nor visited her classmates.

'You're old enough to find your own friends now,' she had said, accepting the cup of tea her daughter had poured her and using both hands to lift it to her mouth. 'Dear God, my head's about to take off and float round the room! You're to bring a couple of girls home to tea when you start school next week; do you hear me, now?'

But after holding aloof from them for so long, it was strangely difficult to infiltrate the little groups of girls, all in similar circumstances, who went to the small private school in Rodney Street. They had fathers as well as mothers and they lived in the smart houses surrounding the school, whereas Linnet caught the tram morning and evening and seldom talked about her home circumstances. Mammy had impressed upon her that she should not mention that her parent was little Evie, the actress, not to her schoolmates nor to the nuns who taught them. And Linnet had speedily seen that not talking about one's mother also made friendships difficult.

But today Linnet knew at once that this boy, this Roddy Sullivan, was different. He was from their own neighbourhood and despite her mother's dismissive remarks about 'street kids' Linnet felt sure that he would be a friend worth having, if friendship were on offer. And if she had someone tough enough to take care of her and befriend her, someone who could take her round to Peel Square occasionally, then Mammy would be able to go off with her gentleman friend without a qualm.

Because that, of course, was what it was all about. Linnet loved her mother dearly but she was quite shrewd enough to realise that there were times when she was a drag on her mother's career. And Evie's career was tremendously important to her. Linnet knew that it was her fault that her mother had not already reached stardom, and always felt guilty when she found Mammy in tears, staring at her face in the mirror, lamenting an imaginary line or a tiny wrinkle, reminding herself that she was not getting any younger, that the years were passing.

I hold her back, Linnet told herself sorrowfully now, as Roddy considered her invitation. If it hadn't been for me she'd have been a star by now, but having a big daughter of eleven puts a lot of people off. So if this latest gentleman friend means what he says and helps Mammy's career, I must keep out of the way a bit more, learn to amuse myself. And with Roddy as my friend that will be very much easier.

'Finished the licky? Well, if you means it, if you're really a-going to take me back to meet your mam, we'd best clean ourselves up a bit,' Roddy said as they crossed Homer Street and waited on the pavement's edge at Juvenal whilst a huge dray dragged by two immense carthorses thundered past. 'There's a tap in Peely – want to go there first?'

'There's taps in our rooms,' Linnet said, puzzled. 'We can wash there.'

'Ye-es, but your mam . . .'

'Oh, yes, we're a bit lickyish round the mouths,' Linnet said, light dawning. Truth to tell, both their faces were now dirty and sticky, she guessed. Roddy's certainly was and she knew it would be best if her new friend was at least clean. 'But won't your mam mind us going in?'

'Where was you born?' Roddy exclaimed. 'The tap's at one end of the bleedin' square, gal! We can clean up wi'out anyone being any the wiser. Well, 'cept for the kids,' he amended. 'They're everywhere, but they won't care what we does, they'll be playing some game or other.'

'All right, we'll go to your place first, then,' Linnet said. 'I – I don't know where Peel Square is, though. It's not far, is it?'

'No, nobbut a step,' Roddy said reassuringly. 'It's right instead of left, though – you get to Peely down Cazneau.'

'Oh, I see,' Linnet said, following close behind Roddy. Trams thundered along Cazneau Street with the horsedrawn traffic keeping well clear of them, and despite the snow and the cold there was considerable bustle as shoppers made their way along the pavements, trying to get back home before darkness fell. 'We don't often come down this way, me and Mam.'

'No need, I don't 'spect,' Roddy said cheerfully. 'Here we are . . . come on in.'

He dived under a shabby brick archway and abruptly, as though it was the transformation scene in a pantomime, the street noises were muted, even the light seemed dimmer, softer. It was as though, in walking under the archway, the two children had entered a different world.

It did not seem, Linnet thought rather apprehensively, a very nice world. The oblong which was Peel Square was completely surrounded by sooty houses, each one attached to the next so that the only glimmer of daylight came from the sky above and from the archway under which they had just passed. The square was paved with large, uneven flagstones, each narrow house had a set of three steep steps which ended on the flags, and there was one gas lamp, as yet unlit, though in the enclosed space it seemed as though dusk had already fallen.

But the space was not quiet, because it was crowded with children. Small girls played hopscotch on the paving stones, shouting out to one another, small boys kicked a ball about or squatted on the ground, playing fives. Bigger girls and boys were moving purposefully about, filling enamel jugs and buckets at the tap or coming and going on messages, Linnet supposed, since they mostly carried bags or bundles of some description.

'Roddy!' A small, tow-headed boy carrying a blue-and-white enamel bucket with a lid came bounding down the step of the nearest house and caught Linnet's companion by the sleeve. 'We're havin' a treat – our mam was goin' to make blind scouse but Aunty Prue got some scrag-end cheap off o' Mr Perkins in the Scottie so we'll have a good supper tonight. Where you been?'

'Deliverin' for Mam,' Roddy said briefly. 'All you ever think about is grub, our Freddy! Now gi's the bucket a mo, we'll have a splash an' then bring it over for you. That's me little brother,' he added in a quiet aside to

Linnet as the small boy nodded his agreement and went back into the house from which he had just emerged. 'He ain't a bad kid.' He jangled the lidded enamel bucket at her. 'Let's stand in line for the tap, then.'

Most of the people queueing for the tap were children, but one or two were much older women. Linnet eyed them curiously. Seldom had she seen such weary, defeated looking faces, and why were they waiting here? She whispered the query to Roddy, who answered equally quietly.

'Their kids is all working, so there's no one to get water in but them. Most of the old gals will pay a kid a farthing or so to fetch 'em water and that, but some just ain't got the gelt. Ah, us is next.'

They reached the tap, ran it until their bucket was full, then Roddy, disdaining Linnet's offered help, carried it across the yard once more and stood it down near the stained doorstep of No 16.

'The water won't be very nice for your mam, though, after we've washed our hands and faces in it,' Linnet said as Roddy began washing with a good deal of unnecessary splashing. 'What's she going to use it for, anyway?'

Roddy finished splashing water on his face and the front of his hair and wiped himself dry with a grimy sleeve. He shrugged. 'Dunno, everything, I guess. She'll boil the spuds with it, mash the tea, wash up the pots . . .'

'But we've washed in it,' Linnet protested again. She wet her hanky and wiped round her face, then washed her hands, patting herself dry on her warm little jacket. 'You can't drink water you've washed in, we'd better get her another bucketful.'

'Don't be daft, look at that line o' kids,' Roddy said with the sort of affectionate tolerance for her odd ways which Linnet was beginning to expect from him. 'Me mam wants the bucket now, norrin a week's time. Come on.'

He lugged the bucket to the top of the steps, waving Linnet away in a lordly fashion once again when she tried to help, hollered through the door for 'Freddy!' and then came down the steps towards Linnet, grinning brightly.

'All right, are you? Off we goes, then, to your mam's! Now what did you say your name was?'

'Linnet Murphy,' Linnet said patiently. 'You should be able to remember that; I can remember you're Roddy Sullivan!'

'I couldn't forget a name like Linnet, could I?' Roddy said, chuckling. 'It's the Murphy bit – I gorra remember to say, "Evenin', Mrs Murphy, ma'am, how are you today?" ' Roddy laughed at his own words and caught Linnet's elbow as they emerged from under the arch. 'Careful, there's a lorra traffic at this time o' night. We *are* late, here comes Jimmy Winkup to light the street lamps. We'd best hurry.'

'Yes, I don't want my mother worrying,' Linnet said seriously. 'I usually go straight home with my messages. Still, she'll be so pleased I've brought a fr – I mean another friend home that she won't mind me being a bit late, I daresay.'

Chapter Three

1925

It had been a brilliantly hot and sunny day but now the sun was sinking in the west and long shadows striped the dusty road. A small group of schoolchildren, with Lucy Murphy in their midst, were making their way home across Barry's Bridge. They had passed the burnt-out barracks and had stopped for a moment by the big willow near the water so that the boys, Daniel, Peder and Garvan, might cut themselves willow wands, though what they wanted with them no girl, Lucy thought disdainfully, would ever understand. As they walked now, the three boys belaboured the hedges, talking in loud and boastful tones of how they would spend the coming holiday, for it was the last day of the summer term which meant – Lucy hugged herself – two whole months at home, with neither school nor teachers to bother them.

'What'll we do tomorrow, Caitlin?' Lucy asked as they began to cross the river. She paused for a moment when they were a few yards out from the bank and looked down into the water; sinuous silver-bodied fish could sometimes be seen gliding in the depths and Lucy always secretly hoped that, because this was one of those strange and magical spots where the River Fertha and the sea lough joined, she might one day spy the shadowy form of a small mermaid, combing her hair with a golden comb, moving easily with the swirl and sway of the sparkling water. And anyway, she reassured herself, looking never did anyone any harm. 'What'll we do after we've done our messages, I mean?'

Caitlin Kelly was thirteen years old and lived in the cottage nearest to the Murphys' farm. Her father worked on Murphy land and her mother gave a hand in the farmhouse, doing the washing on a Monday and what she called 'cleaning through' on a Wednesday, whilst on a Friday she and Maeve baked and baked until the house roared with heat and the sweet smell of cooking. Though there were large families of children on surrounding farms they were all much further off, so Lucy and Caitlin had been friends ever since Lucy was old enough to toddle and Caitlin's attitude, at first protective since she was the elder, had subtly changed over the years until now they were simply best friends and almost always together.

Fortunately, furthermore, Maeve, who was the most important person in Lucy's life, approved of Caitlin.

'She's a clever girl, that one; she'll go far I wouldn't wonder,' she would say when Caitlin's name came up. 'She'll do our Lucy nothing but good. Big families are all very well, but with only the one to worry over the Kellys can give her the best and make sure she minds them.'

'Tomorrow?' Caitlin said thoughtfully, now. 'Well, we'll be busy till dinner time, that's for sure, but when I've done me chores an' fettled me room I t'ought we'd go on a picnic. We could start out by two o'clock I daresay. Will your Maeve put us up a bite o' tea?'

'Course she will.' Lucy did a little jig, bouncing her bulging satchel up and down in the dusty road and doing it no good at all. But it's time I had a new one, she told herself virtuously, seeing that a red arithmetic book was poking out of a hole in the corner which she did not remember seeing before.

'You were twelve last January; it's time you saw life,' Caitlin was saying thoughtfully. 'And seeing life isn't much good unless it's a bit frightening, wouldn't you say?'

Lucy agreed with enthusiasm. She and Caitlin were great believers in magic as a whole and witches and the little folk in particular and Kerry was a great place to live for all those things. She said as much to Caitlin, dancing along beside her whilst the boys strolled on ahead.

'Sure and wouldn't we be after findin' a mermaid, if we went right down to the shore? We could fish for tiddlers and we'd mebbe find a mermaid – just a little one, you understand – in our bucket by the end of the day. You can't keep sea-folk,' she added righteously, 'Maeve says so. But we could put her back when we'd had a wish or two.'

'Oh, you! There's nothing frightening about mermaids,' Caitlin said with some scorn. 'No, I'd more witches in mind.'

'Oh, I see,' Lucy said rather more doubtfully. There were Irish witches, everyone knew that, and several doubtful characters lived in the area who might fit the bill. There was old Mrs O'Rourke, who lived in the tiny, teeny squeezed up house between two quite ordinary ones in the town, and there was Liam's gran, who was over one hundred years old, bald as a coot, and managed to eat frogs, toads and raw rabbits which she caught with her hands, though they only had Liam's word for that, of course. 'Were you thinkin' of Liam's grandmother, Cait?'

But at this point the boys dropped back to walk with them, mostly in order to tease, and both girls had more sense than to continue the conversation. Instead, they kicked a stone along from one to the other so that the boys could rush at them and try to tackle it away, then they made up riddles, discussed their holiday tasks and, at the end of the deep little lane with its high banks and arching hazel trees, they told each other to enjoy their holidays and promised to meet up some time.

'I dunno why we bother to say all that when we'll see them in church every Sunday and at the Stations, wherever they're held,' Caitlin said as the boys shouted and jostled off down the road. 'I wonder what Mammy's got for my tea?'

'I'm going to start my holiday task this very evening,' Lucy said. 'Why don't you come round later, Cait, then we could do them together. We could work in my room – or in the hayloft, come to that. It's nice up there, all quiet and dusty and the hay smells so sweet.'

Lucy had slept with Maeve until the previous January, when she had qualified for a room of her own because all her aunties were married now, even Nora.

'I might come round,' Caitlin said cautiously. 'What'll you do first? Your arithmetic or the English essay or the history one? I thought I'd do arithmetic, get it out of the way.'

'I shan't, I'll leave my sums till last, in the hopes my brain'll have grown bigger by the end of the holidays,' Lucy said, earning a crow of laughter from Caitlin. 'You may mock, girl, but I'm growing all the time, Maeve keeps grumbling about it, so surely my brain's growing, too? Oh, I do hate sums and I do wish I was like my Auntie Nora who can do a sum without even a wrinkle coming on her forehead – and she doesn't add on her fingers, either,' she finished triumphantly.

'Brains don't grow so's you'd notice, though,' Caitlin pointed out as they turned into the even narrower lane which led directly into the farmyard. 'And they're slow doers, Lu, rare slow doers. You'll do the sums by thinking about 'em and working them out in your head when you're sitting quiet, not by waiting for your brain to expand.'

Lucy sighed deeply and broke into a trot; from here she could see the small kitchen window and Maeve, standing before it, cleaning something in the low stone sink. If she hurried she might persuade Maeve to hand out a bite of bread and cheese and a drink of milk before she began laying up for the family's tea, because Lucy was starving hungry, she realised, almost dead with it.

'All right, I'll do a bit of each,' she called as Caitlin continued past the end of the yard, heading for the Kelly cottage. 'And I'll see you later, shall I?'

'Maybe,' Caitlin called back. 'Ask Maeve for some carry-out, will you?'

'I said I would, didn't I?' Lucy shrieked. 'Where are you now, Caitlin?'

'Passing the cabbage patch,' Caitlin yelled. 'Where's you, Lu?'

'Halfway across the haggard,' Lucy bellowed. This was a nightly ritual which drove the other members of both families mad, but she and Caitlin loved it. 'I've got me foot on the back doorstep now – where's you?'

'Ducking under the lintel . . .'

The slam of the Kellys' door told the rest of the story. Lucy threw open her own back door and hurled her satchel across the kitchen, watching it collide with the sturdy legs of the big kitchen table with a certain satisfaction. 'No more school for two months!' she shouted.

Maeve, scrubbing a sinkful of potatoes which she would bake presently in the ashes, said automatically, 'Shut the door, don't slam it, and pick up that satchel for goodness sake, we aren't made o' money, Lucy Murphy. What do you think your grandad would say if he saw you wearing out your good bag on the old earth floor? He'd want to know why in the name of God you have to hurl your books about, that's what, and by the same token I'd like to know why you have to tell the whole of Kerry your whereabouts each afternoon?'

'Shan't have to for another eight weeks,' Lucy said, begging the question since Maeve knew the answer as well as she herself did. 'As for me satchel, it's full of holiday tasks and they ought to be slung in the river, not just across the floor. It isn't fair is it, Maeve, to give you a holiday with one hand and take it back with the other? That's what holiday tasks are, they're trying to make you be at school even when you aren't.'

'They're to make sure you use your brain during the summer and don't just leave it lie and rust,' Maeve said. She put the last potato on the draining board and turned away from the sink, beginning to dry her hands on a scrap of blue and white striped towelling. 'Well? How did today go, and aren't you going to give me a kiss?'

Lucy struggled out of her school jacket, not without difficulty for it was shrunk from many washes, and slung it across the kitchen table, then hurled herself at Maeve and gave her a squeeze, burrowing her face into Maeve's flowered wrap-around pinny as she did so.

'Today went great . . . oh, I do love you, Maeve! Do you know you smell of new-baked bread? I love that smell – is there a wee bit to spare? I'm so hungry me belly's flapping against me backbone, I could murder a slice of bread and some cheese so I could!'

'You've a clever nose on you to smell fresh bread when the larder door's shut and the loaves came out of the bake-oven first thing this morning, I'll say that for you,' Maeve said with a chuckle. She dropped a kiss on the top of Lucy's head and gave her a hug. 'But since you're starving to death there's a loaf cooling on the marble slab in the larder and some cheese in the meat safe. Can you help yourself while I get these potatoes on to cook?'

'Helping meself is what I'm best at,' Lucy said eagerly.

'Shall I cut you a slice an' all, alanna? Can I have some milk, too?'

'It's a surprise to me you can still do up your school jacket,' Maeve said. 'Go on, then, there's a jug of milk in the safe, you won't want to go trudging over to the dairy when you're worn out from hollerin' at young Caitlin and sweating over your school books. And close the safe door properly,' she added as Lucy danced across to the larder, emerging presently with a large hunk of bread and cheese and a mug of creamy milk.

Maeve was kneeling in front of the oven, pushing her clean potatoes down its hot black throat. 'And now, young woman, where's your report?'

The air immediately became electric. Lucy had no idea what Miss Carruthers had said about her this year, but it was bound to be something horrible, or at least critical. Miss Carruthers had sharp eyes, a sharp voice and an extremely sharp tongue – her pen would no doubt resemble the rest of her. But it would not do to say so; Lucy affected extreme nonchalance.

'Oh, that. It's in the bottom of me satchel, under the red arithmetic book. And I haven't opened the envelope, either. Want it now?'

'Yes, I think so. Get it out of the way before Grandad comes in, shall we? He'll remember it later and probably read it, but we don't want to spoil his tea!'

Maeve was smiling as she spoke and Lucy stooped and picked up her satchel, rummaged her way through the books and produced the long white envelope. If Miss Carruthers has given me a hard time I'll put a live mouse in her desk and a dead one in her outdoor shoes next year, Lucy vowed grimly. Or she can have the plague of frogs next spring; take your choice, Miss C.

Maeve slit the envelope open and pulled out the report form. She sat in a chair and began to read, one finger following the line across. 'Hmm . . . hmm . . . hmm . . .' She looked up at Lucy, anxiously hovering, still trying to pretend indifference but not making such a good job of it now the moment had come. 'Well, she's given you top marks for English, both language and literature, anyway. Which isn't surprising, considering you came top of the class in the English exam.'

'Good,' Lucy said. Even to herself her voice sounded somewhat strained. English was no problem . . . but what about history, geography and the hated arithmetic? And then there was conduct, and the strangely named attitude. She'll say something horrid, Lucy thought, and Maeve will be upset and she'll keep me in tomorrow to think about things and . . . and . . .

Maeve was laying the sheet down on the table, pushing it across to Lucy. 'You have done well, alanna! I t'ought you said Miss Carruthers didn't like you – if she doesn't, she certainly likes your work. She says you try hard at everything, even your sums, and she says a bit of after-class tutoring would bring you up to date with arithmetic, even. Now that's what I call a good report, a real little beauty! When your grandaddy sees it he'll be pleased, he couldn't fail to be.'

'What about conduct? And attitude?' Lucy whispered, staring at the sheet of paper.

'She says you've behaved pretty well on the whole and have the right attitude to work and to your fellow pupils,' Maeve said. 'Go on, take a look for yourself.'

Lucy looked and decided that Miss Carruthers was a saint so she was and she, Lucy, would make sure that no one ever tried the dead mouse trick on her, or the tadpole soup torture.

'I'll take on the after-class tutoring,' Lucy said, dazed by the A grades which marched neatly alongside each subject on the report sheet, scarcely marred at all by the

B for arithmetic. No one can be perfect, she told herself, beginning to smile. Well and haven't I misjudged the woman after all? I almost wish I hadn't tied her stockings into a knot the day she came and played hockey with us – though she couldn't have known it was me or that conduct mark would have been a bit different!

'Well, alanna, so you're not wasting your time at school after all.' Maeve pushed back her chair and smiled across at Lucy. 'Now how about laying the table for me, if you've finished your bread and cheese?'

Because of the good report Lucy had no difficulty in abandoning the rest of her tasks once she had helped to clear away the tea things. Hurrying round to the Kellys' cottage she found Mrs Kelly scrubbing the kitchen floor whilst Mr Kelly dozed in a chair.

'Caitlin's out the back,' Mrs Kelly said before Lucy could so much as open her mouth. 'Give her a shout, alanna, she's givin' me a bit of a hand cuttin' mint, that's all.' Mrs Kelly was a great one for bottling and preserving, drying and jellying, and Lucy quite envied Caitlin, who would be somewhere out in the garden cutting the mint which would be hung in bunches from the kitchen ceiling beams throughout the summer and allowed to dry. Once it was like tinder it would be crushed, sugared, vinegared and packed into small jars which would last for the whole of next winter, enlivening mutton dishes and giving an added piquancy to vegetable stews.

'Caitlin, is that you?' Lucy said to a patch of vigorously shaking cabbage plants, but it was only Mrs Kelly's one-eyed cat, who was sharpening his claws on a woody cabbage stalk. He gave her a mean look out of his one eye and stalked away from her, tail straight up, feet turned out, fur well fluffed, outrage in every line of his body.

'Lucy?' Caitlin's head appeared from the middle of

what looked like currant bushes. 'Want to give me a hand?'

'I don't mind,' Lucy said, pushing her way through the vegetables until she reached her friend's side. 'Your mammy said you were cutting mint. Shall I bunch them for you?'

'Sure,' Caitlin said, cutting another stalk and handing it to Lucy. 'You're early, aren't you?'

'It was me report,' Lucy told her. 'Me knees fair shook – 'member the stockings? And the bits of chalk I nicked to make indigestion medicine? But she was really nice, she gave me all A grades except for sums, and she couldn't have give me higher than a B for that, not without perjuring her soul, as the priest would say.'

Caitlin sat back on her heels and pushed her lank brown hair out of her eyes. She grinned up at Lucy. 'Told you she wasn't a bad woman,' she said righteously. 'I got mostly A grades as well, Mammy's ever so pleased and Daddy, too. So d'you want to ask if we can go off for the whole day, tomorrow, instead of waiting until after our dinners? We could really cover some distance in a whole day.'

'That's why I came round,' Lucy admitted. 'I've already asked; Maeve said she was sure it would be all right. Go on, if Mrs Kelly's in a good mood she'll likely say yes as well.'

And so it proved. 'But no drownin' yourselves in the lough or gettin' into bad company,' Mrs Kelly warned. 'Is Miss Maeve puttin' up enough dinner for the both of you? Right, then you can have a bag of me dried apple pieces and a bottle of me lemon barley water.'

Polite thanks were chorused and then, as the sun was setting, Caitlin, as the elder, offered to see Lucy home.

'It's funny how your mammy always tells us not to drown ourselves or get into bad company, and Maeve always says to take care of each other and not to play with fire, isn't it?' Lucy said as they ambled across the farmyard in the dying sunset. 'Yet it's my mammy who got into bad company, and my daddy who was drowned. I don't really understand grownups at all, do *you*?'

'I don't want to understand 'em; we'll be grownup ourselves quite soon enough – too soon,' Caitlin said promptly. 'There's your back door, alanna; get indoors, then I'll run home and we can light our lamps and wave.'

This was another tried and true activity. Lucy had a little room up under the eaves of the old stone farmhouse with ivy constantly trying to block out her light. Caitlin was in an even smaller room in her parents' cottage with a tiny window cut into the thatch. But when they lit their lamps the glow could be seen from both homes, and if Caitlin leaned out of her window and looked very hard to the left and Lucy leaned out of hers and looked downwards and to the right they could each see the lit-up square and the head and shoulders of the other.

Signals were many, including ones which needed a bit of curtain, some cardboard and a lamp held close to the window, but shouting beat them as a means of communication which could be immediately understood.

'Night, Cait!'

'Night, Lu!'

'Where's your cat, Cait?'

'On the bottom of me bed, Lu . . . why?'

'He pulled a rude face at me in the cabbages this evening. He's a funny old devil, your cat.'

'I know. As funny as your old Shep.'

'My old Shep's all right, but they won't let him sleep on my bed, worse luck. Wish I had a cat, Cait. If I could have a kitten . . .' there was a short scuffle and then a wail.

'Oh, Maeve, you are mean to me! Don't you love me? There's something real urgent I've got to tell Caitlin before I close me window and get into bed!'

Caitlin heard mutterings which she guessed were being made by Maeve, then the slam of a window shutting. Presently, it opened again, with extreme caution, as she had known it would.

'Sorry about that – see you in the morning, Cait!'

'Aye, see you in the morning, Lu!'

It isn't unknown for it to rain in Kerry in July and when Lucy woke at daybreak the following day, with the birds kicking up enough row to deafen you, especially in a room right under the eaves, she opened her eyes on the soft and misty rain which so often continues all day and ruins the best laid plans of mice and men.

'Oh, not rain!' Lucy muttered to herself. 'It's the first day of me summer holidays, God, you can't mean to ruin it all with rain!' She sat up on her elbow and peered out through the window once more. Rain was pattering against the window panes and a row of fat raindrops clung to the slate roof-edge, just waiting to drop. Outside, the big red cockerel, who was not above giving you a nip if you went near his harem of hens, cleared his throat and cock-a-doodle-doed; he sounded uncertain, as though he wasn't perfectly sure whether day was really breaking, but was prepared to give it a go anyhow.

'We were going to have a picnic,' Lucy reminded her Maker, snuggling down the bed again. 'It's the first day of everyone's summer holidays, Lord, so you're punishing everyone by sending rain! I do wish you'd think again and give us some blue sky instead.'

With that she fell asleep once more and when she woke because Maeve was slamming about in the kitchen and Grandad was shouting to one of the men and Shep was barking, the sun was streaming in through her window and the sky was so blue it hurt her sleepy eyes.

'Thank you, dear Lord, thank you,' Lucy burbled, jumping out of bed. Ah, it wouldn't do to leap into her clothes without a wash, not when God had been so obliging as to change the rain to sun just for her! She said a couple of Hail Marys under her breath as she washed and dressed, then ran downstairs, humming beneath her breath.

In the kitchen, Maeve had made Lucy's breakfast; two fried eggs, a round of fried bread and a rasher of bacon, crisped just as she liked it. The tea in the pot steamed merrily and on the dresser were two greaseproof packets and a blue cloth bag which bulged in a satisfactory sort of way.

'There's your dinners,' Maeve said, dishing up the food and jerking her head towards the bag and the greaseproof wrapped packets. 'I've done your sandwiches in the greaseproof and you can get some water to drink, and there's apples and some of my rich fruit cake in the bag.'

'Oh, Maeve, you are kind to me,' Lucy said rapturously. 'This is the best breakfast in the world!'

She ate fast and very soon was poised in the doorway, bag in hand, looking rather guiltily back at Maeve.

'Are you sure I can go? That you can manage without me?'

'I'm sure; don't I manage every day of the week and you in school?' Maeve demanded. 'Just go out and enjoy yourself, alanna, tomorrow we'll talk about your house-jobs.'

It was a glorious day. Lucy and Caitlin strolled down the lane, wondering aloud which way to go.

'I vote for the shore,' Lucy said, but Caitlin shook her head.

'No, not the shore, exactly. I've a better idea. How brave are you feeling, Lucy?'

'Very brave,' Lucy said stoutly, though a little shiver of unease ran along her backbone at the words. Hadn't Caitlin said something the previous day about witches? But it was hard to believe in anything evil under a cloudless blue sky with the sun warm on your back so she smiled across at her friend with a fair degree of confidence. 'Why? What'll we do, Cait?'

'We're going to the castle,' Caitlin said at once. 'There's a boat pulled up on the shingle, which means someone's home. What do you say?'

The castle had long been an object of great curiosity not just for the two girls but for most of the children in the area. It stood in a commanding position beside a creek which ran into the lough, and from a distance it still looked impressive. To the left of it was a stand of trees, old and crabbed now and bent all one way by the prevailing wind, and all round it stretched that mixture of meadow and marsh which prevailed near the sea lough. Once, it had been a real castle, no doubt the towers had been manned by archers and men-at-arms had guarded the battlements against pirates and other invaders, but now it was a ruin and almost all that was left was a tower, part of the keep and a peat hut which crouched against the tower like a lamb against a ewe, as though seeking shelter from the old, old stones. Now it looked lonely and sad rather than sinister, Lucy told herself, so there was no need to feel afraid of it. Only it was a well-known fact that it was haunted, probably by the spirits of its one-time occupants, and not even the big boys went near if they could help it.

And there was the boat. If no one lived in the black hut or the old ruin, then why was the boat so often drawn up on the shingly strand of the creek? It was a curragh, made of willow wands and canvas and tarred to keep out the sea, not a proper, modern boat, but even so, who would leave it there, far from any proper habitation? No, the boys were right; someone was living in the tower – someone who did not want to meet his neighbours or want them to meet him.

'Well, Lu?' Caitlin said impatiently now, as Lucy did not immediately answer her query. 'What do you say to visiting the castle?'

'No one else does,' Lucy said. 'Not even the big boys. Not even Kellach has been to the castle.'

'That's why we ought to go, wouldn't you say? Perhaps there's a witch living in the peat hut,' Caitlin said in her spookiest tone. 'But if you're afraid . . .'

'On a day like today? I'd go anywhere in sunshine,' Lucy said stoutly, though with fast-beating heart. 'Tis just at night I'd not go near the castle for a thousand pounds.'

'Nor me,' Caitlin said quickly. 'Will we take your Shep with us, then? For company, like,' she added.

At the words, Lucy realised that Caitlin, though a year the older, was as afraid as she and wanted Shep along just in case. Immediately she felt better about the whole thing, though quite determined that Shep should stay at home.

'Shep's working,' she said. 'But never mind, Cait, there's you and me. If anything scares us we can run faster than most. And if one of us is grabbed the other can make off like the wind and bring help.'

'Sure we can,' Caitlin said, looking anything but reassured. 'Will we have our dinners first, though, down by the stream?'

But Lucy, sensing that she had the upper hand, pressed home her advantage. 'No, let's go straight along there now; we can have our dinners later, when we've seen whatever there is to see,' she said decidedly. 'If there's a stair that's safe we can climb up and eat on top of the tower, perhaps. Come on, let's hurry.'

If the look Caitlin gave her was less than friendly she did not care, for she sensed the underlying admiration. So the two of them set off along the winding little lane, dreaming along in the sunshine, with their eyes every now and then unwillingly drawn to the tower ahead whilst Lucy, at least, kept her imagination firmly under lock and key. But despite their wanderings in the soft, summery air, the castle got nearer and nearer, until at last only the marsh separated them from it.

'We'll go down to the creek first and have a good look at the boat,' Caitlin said at this point. 'Suppose it was a fairy boat, fancy missing it!'

'Even an ordinary boat would be good,' Lucy panted, following her longer-legged friend down onto the marsh. 'I don't suppose anyone would mind if we just sat in it?'

'We could go to sea,' Caitlin said. 'It's just an old, abandoned boat; nobody would care, probably.'

But when they reached the pebbly beach they could see for themselves that the boat was by no means abandoned. It was a curragh as they had guessed and it had been tarred fairly recently judging by the sharp smell of it and the gleam of the fresh tar. It was lying bottom up and the girls prowled round it, trying to assess just when it had last been used.

'The tar may be shining because of the sun,' Caitlin said at length. 'Give me a hand, we'll turn it over.'

It didn't take much strength for it was a light, handy little craft.

'Just right for two girls,' Lucy said wistfully. 'The inside isn't too clean, but it's a dear little boat. No oars, though.'

Caitlin wrinkled her nose. 'It smells fishy, but who cares for that? We could paddle up the creek using our hands, I should think. And further up, where there's trees, we'd probably find something we could use for oars.'

'Shall we just push it on the water a little way?' Lucy suggested, rocking the boat on its shingly bed with one wistful finger. 'Sure and no one would want to keep it on land all the while, the poor little curragh; it's longing for a dip, I can tell.'

'Well, I suppose we could . . . but let's take a look at the castle first. We might even find the oars there – who knows?'

The girls turned and surveyed the castle once more. It looked a lot bigger from here, but still not too dangerous; not with the sun shining.

'It's on a little hill; I don't think I've ever noticed that before,' Lucy said at last. 'It's well above the marsh now, but in winter, when the sea backs up, I've seen it surrounded by water more than once.'

'Who owns it, I wonder?' Caitlin said as they began to jump from tussock to tussock, carefully avoiding the brackish pools. 'Your grandad's beasts graze on the marsh but I don't think he's got anything to do with the castle, has he?'

'Our cattle graze all over,' Lucy pointed out. 'But they're not fools and it's much wetter here than it is to either side because of the creek, I suppose.'

'We're almost there,' Caitlin panted.

'True,' Lucy said. She reached the little hillock and hauled herself up on it, sitting down and breathing hard.

Caitlin came up out of the marsh dragging the bottle of lemon barley water. She sank onto the grass beside Lucy.

'I wonder if this castle ever had a moat and if that's why the marsh is marshier around it?'

'I wouldn't be surprised,' Lucy said. She found that

she did not much want to go on sitting here, talking about the castle, with her back towards it, though. Just supposed there was someone . . . She turned and stared up at it. Close to, like this, what you noticed most was the dilapidation, the air of quiet but lengthy neglect. It must have been lived in once, but if so it was a long time ago. Lucy got to her feet and dumped her bag of food unceremoniously on the grass.

'Sure and we've come all this way so I'm not going home wit'out taking a look,' she announced firmly. 'You coming, Cait?'

'Of course I'm coming,' Caitlin said, getting to her feet in her turn. 'Castle or hut first?'

'Oh, hut, because it'll probably be easier to get in.'

It was true that, now they were so close to the castle, they could see all manner of rubbish piled up in the entrance. It would be the floods, Lucy thought wisely. Bits of branches, what looked horribly like a dead sheep, half a hen coop, there were all sorts in the wide stone archway, but the hut, because its doorway faced a different direction, might well be easier of access.

The two girls climbed the short distance to the turf hut and bent to peer inside. It was very dark in there, but reassuringly empty. There was a fireplace thick with ashes opposite the low entrance, a couple of what looked like bracken couches and a lopsided, short-legged wooden table, so old that it had actually sunk into the earth floor, and nothing else, unless you counted the smell which was almost thick enough to touch.

'Someone's eaten a lot of fish in here,' Caitlin said. 'Doesn't it stink?'

'Yes, it does. And they've kept hens, too,' Lucy decided. 'That's chicken dirt by the bracken. Phew, let's go before we're gassed!'

Giggling, the two of them abandoned the hut and

made for the castle entrance. Working briskly, they cleared it in ten minutes, then peered cautiously in – and were pleasantly surprised.

The small part of the castle which still stood and was referred to locally as the 'keep' had no roof of any description, so it wasn't dark. The walls towered up and up on three sides but the wall facing the lough was no more than six feet high. And despite the fact that the walls were patently inside walls, they had, over the passage of time, taken on many of the attributes of outside walls. Little ferns and wild flowers grew on them, a honeysuckle had seeded itself in the shelter and had climbed the ten feet necessary and now it let its sprays of pink and gold sweetness cascade over the grey stones. To their right an enormous stone fireplace was crammed and crowded with wild roses which fought for space with tall foxgloves and with more honeysuckle, all anxious to seed themselves in this strangely sheltered spot.

'It's beautiful,' Caitlin said slowly. 'It's like the secret garden in that book your Maeve read us when we had measles last winter. Where's the door to the tower, then?'

They knew from their observation of the castle that the tower had no outside door and for a moment they thought it had no inside one either, then Lucy spotted it. In the near corner was a narrow wooden door, tightly closed, in silvery grey wood. Oddly, it looked in quite good repair. She pointed.

'There's the door. Shall we go up?'

'Might as well,' Caitlin said with a nonchalance which, this time, was only partly assumed. The sheer beauty of the castle keep and its wonderful collection of sheltered wild flowers had made the entire expedition suddenly less frightening. Witches, Lucy was sure, did not live in bowers!

'I wonder if it's locked?' Lucy said, and gave the door

a shove. It opened immediately, and the pair of them almost tumbled into a small, round room with a narrow slit window in the wall far higher than their heads and a set of curling stone steps which led up, and up, and up . . .

'Come on, we might as well take a look,' Lucy said. She led the way up the stairs and when she reached the slit window, stopped for a moment to peer out. 'It's a lovely view,' she said. 'Take a look, Caitlin. You can see the sea!'

'I will,' Caitlin said, following her. 'Why does the staircase just stop? I always thought you could get out at the top, I don't know why.'

'You can, there's a door,' Lucy said, following the stairs round. She pushed and, like the door downstairs, it opened at once, though it gave a rather horrid creak. She found herself in a small, round room with four window slits, all giving views over different parts of the countryside. It was, she decided, a nice little room, with wooden boarding on the floor, the stone walls clean and dry . . . and a short wooden ladder which led up to what looked like a trapdoor in the ceiling. Someone at some time had dumped a good deal of hay here, it was piled up high to her right, but it neither smelled unpleasant nor straggled about; unlike the turf hut this seemed simply a pleasant, dry little room which nobody knew about but them. She was standing directly beneath the ladder looking curiously up when Caitlin appeared.

'Phew – a secret garden downstairs and a secret room up,' Caitlin said with considerable satisfaction, coming right into the room and looking curiously around her. 'I don't think witches come here, do you? Now there might be one or two on top of the tower, though – what a place to fly a broomstick from! Just wait till we tell the big boys what we've found! I don't think we need go right up to the tower-top though, do you?'

Lucy already had a foot on the ladder. She turned and stared at her friend 'Not go up? We've got to, and we won't tell the big boys, or it won't be our secret – in fact it won't be ours at all if they ever get their hands on it. Stay if you like, but I'm going!'

She mounted the ladder and shoved hard at the trapdoor. It did not give an inch. She was going to shove again when Caitlin, staring up, gave a muffled exclamation.

'Lu, you eejit! There's a bolt – slide it back first.'

Lucy looked, saw the bolt, and complied, then pushed again. The trap door opened easily and she pushed it right back and then hauled herself through the gap, looking round her as she did so.

It was a round roof, of course, surrounded by spiky battlements and because the trapdoor was right in the middle of it, she was able to take a good look in all directions before climbing any further. It looked safe enough so she clambered out and onto a stone roof with some sort of tarry stuff spread on it, and when she looked back at the trapdoor she found that it, too, had been treated with tar, undoubtedly to keep the rain from penetrating the wood and soaking the room beneath. Having satisfied her curiosity on that score she crossed to the battlements, then looked over the edge.

The view was splendid, the best she had ever seen, though she soon found that if she looked down to the ground her stomach turned over in a rather nasty manner and a strange buzzing filled her head. But if she looked straight across she could see to one side of her the sea lough with Cahersiveen beyond it, every detail perfect in the clear summer air. The bridge, the burnt-out barracks, the church and every house, shop and building spread out before her like a living map.

Lucy shuffled round a bit further, still being careful not to lean on the battlements. She could see ferns and tiny plants growing between the stones and she could not help thinking of all the storms and gales the tower must have known, for Grandad said it was as old as time. But when she looked out there was the sea, with what she guessed must be the island of Valentia, looking like a relief map from here. And if she moved round further still she could see, though trees hid the finer detail, both the ivy-covered farm and the Kellys' cottage, whilst above and behind them the hills stretched, golden gorsed, up to the brilliant blue sky.

'What's up there?' Caitlin's voice echoed hollowly round the room below. Lucy walked over and peered down at her, surprised to see that Caitlin's face looked both pale and worried.

'Nothing much, just battlements. But you can see for miles, Cait – want to come up and see Valentia Island? It looks like that map Miss Carruthers showed us when she took us to the museum in Killarney. And I can see your cottage and the farm . . . come on up.'

But this Caitlin refused to do. 'Not today, Lu,' she called. 'We've got to get down yet, and those stone stairs look awful bare when you're going down and it's a long way to fall. Do come back here, then we can have our dinners.'

'I thought we were going to have our dinners on top of the tower?' Lucy said plaintively. She had climbed a long way and now she was hungry – whatever was the matter with Caitlin all of a sudden?

'Our dinners are at the bottom of the stairs,' Caitlin said. 'I couldn't carry the lemon barley water, it's far too heavy, and you dumped your bag. Oh, do come on, Lu, I'm starving so I am!'

And Lucy soon realised that Caitlin had a perfectly valid point; going up the spiral stone steps had been easy, because you were looking up. But going down! It was a nightmare if you weren't too keen on heights and Lucy suddenly discovered that heights, in fact, were not her favourite thing. She clung to the wall and tried not to look down, but she was in a sweat of fear until her feet touched solid ground once more and even then she felt, suddenly, that she wanted to eat her dinner in the bright, clean sunshine and not in this weirdly beautiful place.

'Let's go back to the curragh,' she said as soon as they were in the fresh air once more. 'We've conquered the castle, now let us be rowing off a way in the boat – we'll use two bits of planks as oars.' She seized two short lengths of plank and tucked them under her arm and in five minutes they were across the marsh and making their way over the sandy, gravelly strand to where the boat waited.

Had waited.

'It's gone!' Caitlin's shrill cry was disbelieving. 'Sure and it was a fairy boat, Lucy Murphy, for hasn't it gone entirely?'

'It can't have gone,' Lucy said, though she had the evidence of her own eyes to give the lie to the statement. The little strand was empty, there wasn't a sign of their small craft. 'Wasn't it further down the creek, Cait – or further up?'

'No indeed, it was right here,' Caitlin said. She gave an exaggerated shiver. 'Oh, Lu, it was magic, and we touched it – turned it over! Oh, what'll become of us?'

'We'll have to have our picnic on dry land,' Lucy said prosaically. 'Well, I never would have believed it – who can have come and taken it in the little while we were exploring the castle and climbing the tower?'

'Only someone who was magic,' Caitlin said. 'A good thing they didn't come back for it when we'd got it out in five fathoms of water, that's all I can say.'

'I don't *think* it was anyone particularly magic,' Lucy

said cautiously. She had no urge to upset the little people, particularly if one was hovering nearby, eager to sink his sharp little teeth into someone's unprotected calf. But she was a practical child in her way. 'There's footprints.'

'Where?' Caitlin said, having given the beach a quick glance. 'I can't see any footprints.'

'There, right on the very edge of the sandy bit just where the tide's coming over . . . look, quick, or it'll be too late, the water'll cover it.'

Caitlin looked in the right direction but even as she did so the tide gave a triumphant little hiss and water lapped where, a moment earlier, Lucy had distinctly seen the print of a bare foot, with the toes well splayed . . . no doubt the owner of the foot which made the print had been pulling his curragh into the water, Lucy told herself, whilst her friend triumphantly asserted that there was no footprint.

'Oh well, the curragh's gone anyway and I'm still hungry,' Lucy said soothingly. 'Whoever took it, it's still not here. Do you want to share dinners? Only I guess Maeve will have put the same in for both.'

'You're not thinking of eating here, on this enchanted beach, are you?' Caitlin said incredulously. 'Why *she* might suddenly appear and magic the sandwiches from our very hands so she might.'

'She'll have her work cut out to get a sandwich off me, I'm so hungry I could eat grass,' Lucy said. 'And if she tried I'd kick her straight back into the water . . . suppose it was mermaids? Suppose they swam up the creek and fancied the boat and pulled it into the water . . .' But her tone lacked conviction; she had, after all, seen the footprint.

'Or the sea-king, as big as the tower and lying on his belly to get up the creek, and opening his mouth and crunching the curragh down,' Caitlin suggested cheerfully. 'He probably t'ought it was a stranded whale.'

'Small whale,' Lucy pointed out through a mouthful of sandwich. Despite Caitlin's strictures she had unwrapped the greaseproof to disclose ham sandwiches – her favourite – with Maeve's own mustard pickle. 'He could've thought it was a seal, or a walrus, I suppose.'

'Oh, you!' Caitlin sat down on the grass at the edge of the creek with her feet dangling over the beach and opened her own packet. 'When we've eaten our dinners and drunk me mammy's barley water we must be sure not to sleep, though. It doesn't do to sleep in enchanted places.'

'Whenever do we sleep except in our beds of a night?' Lucy scoffed. 'But I think you were right, we ought to explore the creek now we're here. We can follow it up as far as it goes.'

She did not want to say so to her friend, but she thought that if they went up the creek they might well come upon the curragh and whoever had taken it away. Because the view of the lough from here was a good one, and we'd have noticed a boat, I'm sure we would, she told herself, tucking into ham sandwiches. But if I say that to Caitlin she'll go on about witches and the sea-king until I'm afraid to look round the next bend . . . better just pretend it's to explore.

'I wonder what the time is?' Caitlin said presently, as they passed the lemon barley water from one to the other. They had decided to save the fruit cake for later.

'Dunno; mid afternoon, I guess,' Lucy said. 'We've got plenty of time to explore the creek, especially if we go now.'

'Right.' Caitlin corked the empty bottle and put it into the blue cloth bag. 'Off we go, then.'

It was great exploring the creek. The sun continued to shine and when they got further inland, to where trees leaned over the water, they moved slowly and dreamily along in the dappled shade, watching their feet and legs made green by the ripples, scarcely talking at all save to draw each other's attention to a fish, a particularly fine shell, an unusual wild flower on the bank.

It took them longer than they had thought to reach the head of the creek and both girls were secretly glad to turn back; it had been a long day.

'I'm starved,' Caitlin said, pushing damp hair out of her eyes. 'Let's go back to the castle now and eat your Maeve's fruit cake!'

Oddly enough it did not take them very long to go down the creek, nowhere near as long as it had taken them in the opposite direction. But even so the sun was low in the sky when they reached the little beach, with the castle very black against the red-streaked heavens.

The first thing they noticed was the curragh, of course. Drawn up precisely where they had seen it earlier, lying innocently upon the shingle.

'I don't believe it!' Caitlin gasped. 'Oh Lucy, it *is* a fairy boat – can you see any footprints now?'

Lucy went over the beach with a fine-tooth comb, but this time could see no signs of human interference. She looked uneasily across at Caitlin who was standing on the grassy bank looking smug. 'I don't think there are any footprints this time,' she admitted. 'Suppose – suppose there *is* a witch up there, looking down at us?'

'Do you not want to go back to the castle, then, fraidy cat?'

'We-ell . . .'

'We won't if you'd rather not,' Caitlin said, suddenly all concern. 'It's been quite a long day . . . we can go straight home across the marsh if you'd rather.'

But past experience told Lucy that if she agreed to go straight home, Caitlin would never let her forget it, so she shook her head until her sun-bleached curls bounced on her shoulders.

'No, we'll go back to the castle. Come on, because I want to be home before dark.'

They set off at once, though their leaps from tuft to tuft certainly lacked the enthusiasm of earlier in the day, and reached the castle breathless but on Lucy's part, at least, determined to scotch any idea that she was afraid.

'Come on then, let's take a look round,' she said. 'Are you coming up to the roof this time?'

It was a below-the-belt remark and Caitlin didn't bother to answer. Instead, she said, 'Tell you what; let's hide in the secret room and watch through the window-slits, see if anything out there moves.'

It was, Lucy decided, a good idea. Agreeing, she dumped her blue bag on the ground outside the keep entrance and the two of them went in, far more cautiously this time. Even if Caitlin pretended to believe that a witch or a leprechaun had moved the curragh, she must realise, as Lucy did, that it was far likelier to have been moved by human intervention and, since the boat was now back on its beach, that must surely mean that someone was lurking in or around the castle?

So up the horrible steps they toiled, neither keen if the truth were known, Lucy decided, but both determined not to be the one who said so.

They reached the top of the stair and the blandly empty little room met their gaze. Was the hay more rumpled, as though a body had been lying on it? She didn't really think so, but put the question anyway. Caitlin sniffed.

'Course not, it's just the same. You go to that slit and I'll keep guard on this one.'

'It'll be sunset soon,' Lucy said when they'd been watching – and mildly squabbling – for what seemed like hours but was probably only ten minutes. 'We've got a good walk, Cait. And we've not eaten the fruit cake yet.'

'Oh well, if you're fed up . . . no, don't start, I'm fed up, too,' Caitlin said at once. 'You go down first, though . . . I really hate those stairs.'

'Oh . . . perhaps I should've gone up to the top of the tower, in case there was someone hiding there,' Lucy said belatedly, halfway down the stone steps. She was descending with her eyes shut and one hand clutching grimly at the stone wall. 'Don't you fall on me, Caitlin Kelly, or you'll kill the both of us for sure.'

But no one fell on anyone and within six feet of the ground Lucy opened her eyes and found that she wasn't quite so scared this time. She finished the steps at a gallop, just to prove it, and then turned and told Caitlin to jump, holding out her arms to catch her.

'No, I'm too heavy for you,' Caitlin said. 'Get out of the way, I'm coming down like a ton of bricks!'

She hurtled down the last few steps, cannoned into Lucy, and the pair of them, winded and giggling, rolled around on the floor, clutching their stomachs, until they could breathe properly again.

'Come on, then,' Caitlin said, struggling to her feet. 'Let's have that cake.'

They galloped good-naturedly out of the castle and Caitlin grabbed the blue bag and swung it at Lucy, who promptly tried to wrestle it away from her. They fought amicably over the bag for five minutes, then there was an ominous tearing noise.

'It's all right, it's only a bit of stitching,' Lucy said, having anxiously examined the bag. 'Phew, and isn't that a relief? Maeve wouldn't have taken kindly to another bag going west. My satchel sprang a hole when I tossed it across the floor as I got back from school yesterday afternoon.'

'I'll mend it for you,' Caitlin said. She was good with

her needle, Lucy was hopeless. 'Give it here, you can have it back before bedtime.'

'Thanks, Cait,' Lucy said gratefully. 'Now let's eat the fruit cake.' She opened the bag, rummaged around for a moment, then stared at her friend, her eyes rounding.

'Cait, the cake's gone,' she said in a whisper. 'I swear to God it was there when we came in but it's gone now – there isn't a crumb of it left!'

Later that night, when the hens, pigs and ducks had been fed, tea had been eaten, and the washing up and clearing away done, Maeve sat down by the hearth with her knitting whilst her father settled himself in his chair opposite her and got out his favourite pipe and the farming quarterly which he favoured. When they were all settled, Lucy with her English books spread around her, Lucy cleared her throat and looked up at her aunt.

'Maeve, do witches eat fruit cake?'

Maeve put her knitting down and stared, plainly astonished. 'What a question! There's no such t'ing as witches and well you know it, young lady. But most people like fruit cake I'm thinking, so if there were such things as witches, and they were offered fruit cake, I daresay they'd eat it and enjoy it.'

'Umm . . . would they steal it, though? Would they take it from – from a person's box, or bag, or whatever?'

'Now where's all this leading, alanna? No more answers unless I get some questions in, first. Who stole your fruit cake? And what makes you think it was a witch when it was far more likely to have been a wandering child, or a dog even, if you put it down somewhere.'

Lucy looked thoughtfully around the room. She did not intend to tell Maeve any lies, but she had no intention of admitting they had been playing at the castle, either.

As she had told Caitlin, a secret place of your own was only a secret so long as you told nobody, especially an adult who would feel bound to check out that you were safe and the play-place suitable. And if Maeve ever saw those stone steps – well, Lucy could almost hear the words: *You'll not go there again, alanna, tis far too dangerous. There's a million places you can play so stay away from the castle, and that's an order.*

'We did lay the bag down for a moment,' she admitted, therefore. 'And when we got back the cake had gone, clean disappeared, and Caitlin said probably a witch had taken it. I expect it was a dog or perhaps even the cattle, because they like sweet things, don't they? I didn't really think it was a witch, but I just wondered whether they had a fondness for sweet things, that's all.'

'Hmm,' Maeve said. She looked rather piercingly at Lucy, then picked up her knitting once again. 'Well, don't go handing me good fruit cake to a cow another time, ástor.'

'I won't, don't you worry,' Lucy said fervently. 'I'll keep me bag fastened tight.' As she said the words she was remembering the fastening – tied tight. She sighed and opened her English book. It was a mystery and no mistake, not that they'd tried to solve it, mind. The truth was they had taken one quick look behind them to where the castle loomed, and they had run as if their lives depended on it, bounding from tussock to tussock, letting the lemon barley water bottle fall and not stopping to pick it up, whilst behind them they seemed to hear a cackle of mocking laughter.

Once safely in the sloping meadow where the Murphy sheep grazed, however, they had thrown themselves down on the soft grass and looked at one another a trifle shamefacedly.

'Someone played a trick on us,' Lucy said. 'There *is*

someone in that old castle no matter what anyone says. After all, we know the boat was moved, don't we? And we know the cake was eaten. Someone had to do both those things and don't you say "witches" again, Caitlin Kelly, or I'll scream and hit you, so I will!'

'Witches, undoubtedly witches,' Caitlin said with great promptitude, and ducked Lucy's half-hearted swipe with ease. 'Well, that settles it; we'll go back as soon as we finish our work tomorrow and search the place from top to bottom. Or we'll hide in the nice little room and watch the curragh through the window-slits and see who moves it. And if it's an old woman with a pointy hat, or a little feller in green, about so high . . .' she held a hand six inches from the ground on which they lay, 'then you may tell me how sorry you are you called me a liar.'

'I never did!'

'You did so! Well, not in so many words, but you meant it, you t'ought I'd imagined the witches, did you not?'

'Well, you certainly did not see them,' Lucy pointed out. 'Look, let's not argue, alanna. Tomorrow we'll find out, hey?'

'Tomorrow. Give me your hand on it, then.'

Solemnly, they spat in their palms, then shook hands. The handshake started out as a pact and speedily became a trial of strength, then went to the sort of wrestling which Maeve disapproved of because she said girls didn't need to fight and besides, it was unfeminine.

'So's planting spuds and carting manure,' Lucy had said and Maeve laughed and tutted and said that work was a different matter altogether, bless the child, and when a farmer didn't have sons his daughters – and granddaughters – have to do all sorts.

But now, sitting by the fire and knitting, Maeve was a

picture of feminine domesticity, and indeed, these past couple of years, with Mr Murphy taking on extra help outside, she worked mostly in the house, apart from those times of year when all hands were needed outside. When the sheep lambed, the cows calved and the pigs had their litters, then both Maeve and Lucy were needed to help. And when potatoes, wheat or barley were being sown then again it was all hands to the fields, as it was when the crops were harvested.

And the housework, come to that, was no sinecure; the Murphy home was a big, old-fashioned farmhouse with four bedrooms on the first floor and two attic rooms above, and Maeve, her father and Lucy rattled round in it like peas in a half-empty pod.

'What are you studying, alanna? You look more as though you're dreaming, again. As I said, the sooner you get your holiday tasks out of the way the sooner you'll be able to enjoy some freedom.'

'It's holiday reading, this,' Lucy said, flourishing the book. 'It's quite good . . . I thought if I read a chapter a night . . .'

'Then read, girl,' her grandfather growled. 'And stop this chatterin' before you drive me mad as you are yourself.'

Lucy sighed, then got up and dropped a kiss on her grandfather's brow. He pretended to rub it off and scowled at her, but she could see he was pleased, really.

'Sorry, Grandad; I'll stop chattering now, I promise.'

'You'd better, or you'll find yourself weedin' the vegetable garden tomorrow afternoon instead of jauntin' off wit' young Caitlin.'

'I like weeding,' Lucy said. 'I'll do some tomorrow evening, so I will.' She read for a while in silence, then closed her book. 'I'm off to bed now; goodnight, Maeve me love, goodnight Grandad.'

Her grandfather grunted and Maeve glanced up at

the clock above the mantel. 'You'll be wanting to holler to Caitlin I suppose,' she said drily. 'Well, try not to crack all the eggs before the hens have laid 'em.'

'I'll try,' Lucy said blithely. 'Can I take a candle?'

'God have patience, it's as light as midday so it is,' her grandfather exploded, putting down his paper. 'Why the candle?'

'Because if Maeve doesn't want me to holler then I could signal to Caitlin if I had a candle and a bit of cardboard . . .'

'Dear God, will you go to bed and stop your chatterin'?' her grandfather said. 'Oh go on, go on, take a candle, pauperise me before me time, don't you worry about your poor grandad's purse, always more where that came from . . .'

'Thanks, Grandad,' said the unrepentant Lucy, kissing his head as she passed him. 'See you in the morning!'

But later, in her own bed, Lucy fell to wondering once more about the cake. *Someone* had taken it, either an animal or a person, and there weren't many animals, in Lucy's experience, which could extract cake from a person's bag, and devour it without leaving so much as a crumb.

Unless it was a rat? Rats are cunning, and ingenious with their paws and teeth . . . I suppose it must have been a rat, Lucy concluded, and began to drift towards sleep, but in her heart, she was not convinced. Someone had taken the cake, someone had moved the curragh . . . but it had been a long day. Soon, she slept.

Maeve sat on for a while, finishing her row, then she rolled up her work and put it up on the mantelpiece and yawned.

'Want a cup of cocoa before you go to bed, Father?'

'Might as well. Got any soda bread?'

'I'll butter you a piece.'

Maeve went through to the kitchen, reflecting how Lucy had mellowed her grandfather these past few years. He had begun by resenting the child and had ended up doting on her – not that he would ever admit it, mind. It was strange, really, that he seemed only able to love one person at a time, unlike the rest of humanity, who had affection and to spare. First, years ago, it had been his wife, then his daughter Evie. When Evie had gone Nora had become his favourite and reigned supreme for a couple of years . . . but gradually, even before Nora's marriage, Lucy's star had begun to be in the ascendant and by the time Nora left her father had scarcely missed her at all.

'Time they were gone,' he had said gruffly to Maeve. 'The three of us will do very nicely, very nicely.'

He still doesn't love me, Maeve told herself now, bustling round the kitchen and making the cocoa, buttering the soda bread. But he tolerates me much better than he did – and he dotes on Lucy, so he does. And he's a good farmer, very much better than most in these parts, so whatever he may say the money's there to keep the child in comfort when he's gone.

And there was Evie. Not that they heard from her much, especially lately. But she sent money regularly, and Maeve put it all away in the post office so that Lucy would have something of her own one day.

Maeve wrote, though always to a theatre or a post restante address since Evie assured her sister she was always moving around. Maeve asked about the other baby, Lucy's twin sister, in every letter, but apart from saying that Linnet was well, growing out of her clothes and eating her out of house and home, Evie never really gave details.

Still, if Evie was really doing well, and it seemed that

she was, then it surely could be only a matter of time before she came back for a visit? England isn't the ends of the earth, Maeve told herself sometimes. It was more than twelve years since Evie had left Ireland, so wasn't it about time that she came back, if only for a visit? And how lovely it would be for Lucy and Linnet to meet! Lucy knew all about her sister, of course, but had long ago stopped asking about her. She was more bound up with Caitlin and her life on the farm than with a mother who had abandoned her at four months old and a sister she had never seen. It was all right for Maeve, because she only had to close her eyes to see Linnet, who would be the spitting image of Lucy, only a bit bigger since she had been the stronger, stouter baby. But because she had not liked to tell Lucy that she had a double, she had never mentioned the likeness, nor even the fact that they were twins. Lucy had somehow got the impression that Linnet was older than she, which was why Evie had taken her sister and left Lucy, and Maeve thought it was better that way. To explain why a mother would abandon one twin and take the other was too complex for Maeve, and besides such an explanation might not show Evie in a good light, and Maeve loved Evie still and always thought and spoke of her with affection.

Maeve had a vague idea that Lucy might sometimes hear her mother talked of – possibly even slightingly – by other children whose parents were in no doubt that Evie Murphy had been no better than she should be, but she continued to believe that Lucy regarded her absent mother with fondness and her sister with interest. In fact, though, it was far simpler than that. Lucy simply never thought of her mother or sister at all.

Chapter Four

When Linnet was thirteen, she was asked to make a big decision: to go or to stay? She came home from school on a bright but windy October day to find Mammy in a state, sitting on the green silk sofa she was so proud of and weeping buckets into a small, lace-edged hanky.

'What's the matter, Mammy? Are you ill?' she had asked, very dismayed at this sudden change of tack, for her mother had been on top of the world for the best part of a week, singing around the flat, taking Linnet out for fish and chip dinners, buying herself pretty hats and elegant shoes.

Her mother looked up. Her face was quite swollen with tears and her eyes were red-rimmed from weeping. 'Oh, Linnet, my little darling, the most distressing thing! Th-they don't want me to take you with me when I go off in a month's time!'

Mammy had been touring several times, ever since Linnet was eight, in fact. 'You can take care of yourself, a big girl of eight,' Mammy had said persuasively, and though at first Linnet hadn't liked it much she had soon grown accustomed. It wasn't nearly as hard as it sounded since Mrs Roberts in the flat downstairs had Linnet in for her tea each day and saw to her washing and came up and did any big housework that Linnet could not tackle. And later Mrs Sullivan, Roddy's mam, had been equally eager to help out – for a price, of course. So Roddy and Linnet had roamed the city to their hearts' content all through the long summer holidays and Linnet had helped Roddy to sell wood-chips, to run errands, to hang round the people coming off the ships at the docks, offering to carry their cases for tuppence and, alas, to prig vegetables from St Martin's market when Mrs Sullivan fancied blind scouse but had somehow run out of money.

So what was different this time? Linnet said as much, taking the sopping wet hanky from her mother's hands and replacing it with a dry one.

'This time it-it's further, and for l-l-longer,' her mother had wailed. 'This time it's Am-Am-America, alanna. And it's my b-big chance!'

'Then you must go,' Linnet said stoutly, though her heart failed her a little. America! That was a long way off, further even than the Glasgow Empire, she believed, where Mammy had played to packed houses only a few short months ago. 'It's your career, after all,' she added. 'Your whole future, Mammy!'

She was well-trained; she had said the words a dozen times before, but had never meant them less, because she would have been a fool had she not realised that Mr Terence Beatty, her mother's latest impresario, did not like her, resented her in fact.

Other impresarios had come and gone, and there had been one or two who found her a nuisance, but never had there been one who showed it more constantly than Terence Beatty. He wasn't elderly, for a start, which she thought a great shame; elderly admirers were usually very generous, both to the object of their admiration and to her small daughter. Younger men, though they might lavish gifts on little Evie, were more inclined to give Linnet a sixpence and tell her to go and see a film-show and then grumble when she came home.

The odd thing was that Terence was beautiful by anyone's standards. He had richly curling black hair, dark, flashing eyes and a mobile mouth which smiled easily and often. Women adored him, and Linnet had been totally taken in by his beauty and willing to fall at his feet, but he had not wanted her. From the outset he had made it clear that Linnet was nothing but a nuisance, though he had fallen head over heels in love with little Evie the very first time he had seen her on stage.

'In the raw?' Roddy asked with interest when Linnet told him this tale, and got a clip round the ear for his pains. Linnet might occasionally dislike an impresario – she very soon hated Terence – but she was too loyal to her mother to let it show. Roddy, as her dearest friend, was allowed a good deal of licence, but he should know better than to make a remark critical of little Evie!

'Why should it matter what she was wearing?' Linnet had said when the subsequent insults – and a few rapid blows – had been exchanged. 'Me mam's ever so lovely, and you know it, Roddy Sullivan!'

'Oh aye, she's pretty,' Roddy agreed. 'But you don't much like Mr Beatty, do you, chuck?'

Linnet had never lied to Roddy and she was not about to start now, especially over Terence Beatty.

'No,' she said shortly. 'But he's a big impresario in the United States of America; Mammy says he may ask her to star on Broadway!'

Every small cinema-goer knew about Broadway, where unknown girls became stars overnight. And then there was Hollywood, where even little girls and boys could become stars – look at Jackie Coogan! At her words even Roddy looked impressed.

'Cor! But would you like that, our Linnet? All them traffic cops an' cowboys an' Injun braves? Suppose 'e *marries* your mam? Then you'd be 'is kid and you'd live over there for always!'

'Oh, I'd get used to it, I suppose,' Linnet had said airily. 'I've never tasted an ice-cream soda.'

And now the crunch had come and Terence Beatty, it appeared, had put his foot down. He wanted, needed, adored Evie, but he neither wanted nor needed, far less adored, her daughter.

'I *told* him I couldn't think of leaving you,' her mother sobbed now, sitting on the little green sofa and filling yet another hanky with her tears. 'What'll I do, oh, what'll I do? Me big chance . . . if only you'd been a little sweeter to him, alanna, if only you'd tried a little harder!'

'I *did*,' Linnet said, stung for once by her mother's blatant unfairness. 'I've done everything, Mammy, run his errands, polished his shoes, made that beastly, sickly pudding he's so fond of . . .'

'There you are!' Evie said triumphantly through her tears. 'You resented him from the first or you wouldn't call Italian trifle a beastly, sickly pudding! And now look what's happened. He simply won't get you a ticket and when I said I'd buy it he looked at me with flashing eyes and said if I did he'd see I lived to regret it. Oh, Linnet, I'm so very, very unhappy.'

Even at thirteen, Linnet was quite old enough to see that if her mother turned down this opportunity she would blame Linnet for it for the rest of her days. And she would be right, Linnet told herself stoutly, putting the kettle on to make a cup of tea and assuring Evie, in motherly tones, that she must not think of losing the chance of stardom. She, Linnet, would manage just as well with her in America as she had managed when Evie was starring at the Glasgow Empire, or in the summer show on the pier at Scarborough, or up in Blackpool at the wonderful Winter Garden Theatre.

'But what will people *say*?' Evie wailed at last, taking the cup of tea Linnet held out to her with a trembling hand. 'They'll think I'm a monster of selfishness to leave my little girl and go off to New York with Mr Beatty! I can't bear that folk will think ill of me, and I'd sooner die than let you down, ástor.'

'Mam, what else can I say?' Linnet said at last, when Evie had poured out her feelings ten times over, interlacing them, unfortunately, with reproaches to Linnet for not being nicer to Mr Beatty. 'I'm happy to stay here – I don't want to go to New York – so why shouldn't everyone accept that? My schooling's important,' she added cunningly. 'You've said so over and over indeed, so why not simply say I'm staying in Liverpool until I leave the convent?'

'We-ell now . . . d'you think folk would believe me if I said that, alanna? Every word is true as I stand here, mind, for 'tis an excellent school and I'd not be happy taking you away from the good nuns over to a land where for all I know they may have shockingly bad schools.' Even as she said the words, a little smile spread across her face and her cheeks began to glow again. Evie was about to convince herself she was doing the right thing and that will at least mean some peace until she goes, Linnet told herself. So be happy with that – and anyway, it'll stop her remembering she's thirty years old now. And when she starts crying in front of the mirror because she's seen a wrinkle and demanding asses' milk for her skin, at least it'll be darling Terence who gets sent out for it and not me . . . asses' milk indeed! How Roddy had laughed when she told him, and how she had jumped at his suggestion that they went round to Ward's dairy on Limekiln Lane and bought a gallon or so of skim.

'She won't know whether it's from an ass or an ox, just so's it's fresh milk,' he said cheerfully, dragging Linnet through the streets with a clanking bucket in both hands. 'What did she give you?'

'Four whole shillings,' Linnet had said, cheering up.

'What'll they charge us for two buckets o' skim, d'you suppose?'

' 'Bout tenpence, probably. And this time, young Linnet, don't you go handin' the change over, meek as – as milk. You hold onto it for the next time she buggers off.'

She had felt mean, but she saw the point of Roddy's advice, because though her mother always did send money, it was often very late indeed and harsh words were apt to be said before the money orders turned up. With some savings of her own tucked away, therefore, she could appease Mrs Roberts' strident demands with the odd bob or two.

'You really mean it, then, Linnet acushla? You truly don't want to come to New York? You'd really rather stay here, with your school friends and Roddy?'

'I truly would,' Linnet said steadily. And then decided that, if she was to be left, she might as well say a word or two of warning. 'But I really don't like Mr Beatty, Mammy, and I just hope he means well by you.'

Evie, sipping tea, laughed and leaned over to stroke her daughter's cheek. 'Darling, of course he means well by me,' she said indulgently. 'He's going to make me a star – I *told* you.'

'Yes, but . . . other impresarios have said that, and it hasn't quite come off, has it?'

It was extremely brave of Linnet to say this since it was a forbidden subject, but though her mother frowned and looked reproachful, she did not start to cry, or tell Linnet that she was cruel and unjust and simply did not understand show business.

'Ah, but Terence is rather special, alanna. He has connections with the highest in the land, he's going to introduce me to everyone . . . he could've been a star himself with his looks, but he's chosen to scout for talent all over Europe instead, because he so loves to travel.'

'But, Mam, suppose something goes wrong and you don't – don't *take*? What'll he do then?'

Evie gave a soft, triumphant laugh and set down her cup of tea; then she jumped to her feet and began to dance, whirling and twirling, with her arms round herself in an ecstasy of excitement.

'Ah, then, what do you think? You'll never, ever guess!'

'He'll bring you home?' Linnet suggested, and saw her mother's brow momentarily marred by a frown.

'No, alanna, what a dreary thing to say – he'll marry me, of course!'

Evie left for New York in November and although Linnet wept and at times felt both lonely and vulnerable, she very soon settled into a routine. It was no different really from her pantomime routine – except that when January and February, both miserably cold and snowy months, had passed, there was still no sign of her mother's return. Her letters had been few and somehow guarded, as though she did not want to talk about her life, and this worried Linnet, but Roddy cheered her up by reminding her that it was early days, that her mother had already been in some famous revue on Broadway and that the money, at least, came regular.

'Which it didn't always do when she were in panto, as we both know,' he reminded her. 'I reckon your mam's doin' all right. She'll send for you one of these days, just you see.'

'I don't want her to send for me,' Linnet pointed out. 'I want her to come home!'

'Oh, well, send for you or come home, what difference does it make, so long as you's together? And anyway, you're with friends and old Ma Roberts is all right to you, ain't she?'

Mrs Roberts was all right and continued all right until just after Easter, when she came up to 'have a chat' as she phrased it. It was just after they had finished the hot meal she had served downstairs for herself, Linnet and her elderly and apologetic husband and Linnet, answering the door to her, had to hastily shove out of sight the large bar of Nestlés chocolate which she was using to fill the chinks left by Mrs Roberts' rather uninspired cooking.

'Come in, Mrs R,' she said, however. 'Make yourself at home.'

Mrs Roberts settled herself on the little sofa with its pale green silk upholstery, looking very out of place, Linnet thought privately, and cleared her throat a couple of times before she spoke. And when she did speak, she did not once look at Linnet but allowed her eyes to rove around the living room, now alighting on the little walnut wood piano, now on the fancy what-nots with their burden of pretty china ladies and gentlemen, now on the tasteful watercolours in their gilded frames which hung on the walls.

'Well, queen, this is a snug little place an' no error,' she said at last. 'And your mam sends the rent regular, I'll give 'er that.'

'Yes, I know she does,' Linnet said politely. 'I bring it round, don't I, Mrs Roberts?'

'Oh aye, indeed you does. Yes, indeed. The only trouble is, queen, that prices 'ave riz. Oh aye, they've riz somethin' shockin'.'

'Butter is a little dear,' Linnet said cautiously. She had not actually noticed much change in prices, but it was usually politic to agree with grownups. 'Margarine is nearly as nice, though.'

Mrs Roberts began to bridle and Linnet realised that she had been a bit tactless. Mrs Roberts had indeed begun to make Linnet's butties for school with margarine, but perhaps she should have gone on pretending that it was butter? Grownups are so weird, Linnet thought despairingly, how was one ever to learn how to treat them?

'I wouldn't know about that, being as 'ow I allus buys butter,' Mrs Roberts said untruthfully but with such conviction that Linnet wondered if she could have been mistaken. 'But things *is* a price, chuck, so I wondered whether . . .'

'Whether what, Mrs Roberts?' Linnet asked when the silence began to stretch uncomfortably. 'Do you want an errand running?'

'No, norran errand. I was wonderin', queen, whether it wouldn't be a good scheme for you to share this flat, which is plenty big enough for two. Then I wouldn't 'ave to write to your mam askin' for more money, you see.'

'I could eat less,' Linnet offered after a moment's thought. 'I don't need butties for school, I'll wait for me tea. Mrs Sullivan usually gets me a hot meal.'

'But sharin' would be company, like,' Mrs Roberts wheedled. 'You're only a child, if the authorities knew you lived 'ere alone . . .'

Danger, said a little voice in Linnet's head. She's right, they wouldn't like it, people like schoolteachers and attendance officers and doctors. Mam meant them when she said 'People won't like it,' and now this old terror is going to tell on me just so's she can get more money out of Mam!

'I'll write to my mother, Mrs Roberts,' Linnet said, suddenly seeing that in prevarication lay her salvation. The longer she made Mrs Roberts wait for a reply the more likely the old girl was to forget the whole business. 'It's for her to decide, but I don't think she'd like someone else living here when she's gone to such trouble to keep the place nice, do you? I mean there's all the ornaments and the knick-knacks, to say nothing of the pictures. Some of them are valuable, you know.'

'Oh aye, but if it were another gairl from 'er very own theaytre?' Mrs Roberts said, almost pleadingly, Linnet thought. 'Norra rough type o' woman but a nice little actress, say? A decent gairl what 'ud tek good care o' you, for your mam?'

Oddly enough, the thought of company made Linnet hesitate before reiterating firmly, 'I'll have to write to my mother, Mrs Roberts.' She had sat herself down on the little round chair with the tassels, now she stood up as she had seen her mother do when she wanted to end an interview. 'Thank you for calling,' she said with great formality. 'As soon as I hear from my mother I'll let you know.'

She watched Mrs Roberts out of the door and down the stairs, then she settled herself at the table with a pot of ink, a scratchy pen, and a pad of paper. She would write to her mother immediately, and then she would nip round and see Roddy. He would have an opinion on the matter, she was sure of it – and Mrs Sullivan, though her home was threadbare and money tight, had her head screwed on right in certain directions. She would soon tell Linnet whether she was being taken advantage of or not!

Roddy was having his tea when Linnet knocked on the door and then entered, as she always did. The whole family were there, with Mrs Sullivan presiding over them all in her wrap-around apron and scuffed, down-at-heel shoes. When she saw who their visitor was she grinned at Linnet, revealing bare pink gums save for one defiant front tooth.

'Well, if it ain't our Linnet! Want some grub, chuck?'

'Please, Miz Sullivan. And some advice, if you don't mind.'

The arrangement was that Mrs Sullivan would feed Linnet during the school holidays and at weekends and Mrs Roberts would do so the rest of the time, so since this was a holiday Linnet felt entitled to slip onto one of the broken wooden chairs, square her elbows, and begin to eat, whilst explaining, rather thickly, that she was having a problem with her landlady.

Mrs Sullivan was a first-rate cook and could, as she was fond of saying, make a meal fit for a prince out of what others threw away. Her dumplings swimming in a rich mutton gravy had to be tasted to be believed and Linnet wished her present hostess might teach Mrs Roberts how to cook cabbage so that there was still flavour left in it, and potatoes so they didn't just mysteriously disappear into the water. But of course she could not possibly say so, or not to Mrs Roberts at any rate.

'More spuds?' Mrs Sullivan said when Linnet's plate was mysteriously cleared – it was mysterious, Linnet thought guiltily, when you considered that she had eaten what Mrs Roberts would no doubt think of as 'a good, hot dinner', not half an hour ago. 'Eh, you're one for your vittles, our Linnie, an' no mistake.'

Liverpudlians dearly liked to shorten names and Mrs Sullivan was no exception. Roddy's real name was Roderick, Freddy's Frederick, Bert was Albert and Matt was Matthew. So Linnet did not object to being called Linnie but regarded it as a love-word, like alanna or acushla on Mam's lips.

'You mean I'm greedy, Mrs Sullivan,' she said now, holding out her plate. 'Just a couple then, if you can spare 'em. And now, what do you think? Mrs Roberts says prices have riz . . . risen, I mean, and she wants me to share my flat with someone else!'

'Ow much rent'll you get?' Mrs Sullivan said at once. 'If you're short of a bob it ain't a bad idea. There's always someone wantin' a roof over their 'ead in the city an' Roddy says you've gorra nice little place there.'

'Oh! Well, I think Mrs Roberts means to keep the rent,' Linnet said doubtfully. 'I'm pretty sure that's what she meant. She said if I'd share it would mean she wouldn't have to ask Mammy for more money.'

Mrs Sullivan shook her head decisively. She was a small woman, flat-bosomed but blessed with a large bottom and very large grey eyes which twinkled across at Linnet now with a touch of reproach in their gaze. 'She can't do that, you pay a fair rent an' I'll tell anyone who asks it's norra penny too little. If you rents out, that's one thing. If she's tryin' to do you outer your place, that's another. What did you say to 'er?'

'I said I'd write to my mam,' Linnet said. She popped the last piece of potato into her mouth, chewed and swallowed. 'Eh, that was great, Mrs Sullivan; I wish old Ma Roberts could cook like you can.'

'It's nice as someone appreciates me,' Mrs Sullivan said. She winked at Roddy. 'Don't you lerrer push you around, chuck. She's doin' very well out o' you, let's make no mistake.'

'Right. I'll tell her my mam says I'm not to share, then,' Linnet said. Mrs Sullivan shook her head at her.

'Don't say that, say your mam might think of sub-lettin', but you'll lerrer know when,' Mrs Sullivan said. 'If you need a bit o' extry money one day, chuck, that's a better way 'n most to earn it. I'm not sayin' Mrs Roberts might not get 'er claws on some of it,' she added generously. 'But not all, by no means. Lerrer put tharrin 'er pipe an' smoke it.'

'You comin' out, queen?' Roddy said presently, when Linnet had helped his mother wash up and clear away.

The boys usually gave a hand but Linnet enjoyed it and the boys, who often lamented their lack of a sister, enjoyed a break from housework. 'We could go down to the pier'ead.'

'Don't mind if I do,' Linnet said cheerfully. 'Will you come back with me, afterwards, Roddy? I'll read you me letter.'

'Sure,' Roddy said easily. 'And me mam's right; you don't wanna let that old crow do you down.'

'No-oo. Except that sometimes I do get scared, by myself at nights,' Linnet admitted as they strolled along Byrom Street, looking in shop windows as they passed. 'To tell you the truth I've always been a bit scared, like, at nights when me mam's away. It's no worse now, so I can put up with it, but in a way I wouldn't mind someone living with me. If it was someone nice, that is,' she added hastily.

'You've never telled me that before,' Roddy said, staring at her. 'You've always said you liked it fine, bein' alone.'

'Yes, well, it's never gone on for so long before,' Linnet said lamely. 'It's better in the summer, with the lighter evenings. Are we catching a tram or not?'

'Not,' Roddy decided, turning out his pockets. 'Let's go down to the docks, instead, eh? Tain't so far.'

'Right,' Linnet said cheerfully. 'Race you to the next tram stop!'

The letter to Evie had been finished off when Linnet and Roddy got back from their stroll by the river and Linnet had finally gone off to bed quite satisfied with what she should do. She did not hold out much hope of her mother replying quickly – it took weeks for a letter to get to New York and if Mammy was off touring, as she said she might be, then it would be some while before she actually read it, let alone got round to answering. But Mrs Sullivan was a sensible woman, and she had undoubtedly given the same advice that Linnet's mother would give, particularly as, under Roddy's instructions, Linnet had assured her mother that Mrs Roberts would take the extra money for herself.

'No point in your mam thinkin' she could send you less rent money,' Roddy said, ignoring Linnet's objections that her mam would not do anything so unkind. 'That would put the cat amongst the bleedin' pigeons, 'specially if old Ma Roberts couldn't find no one to take it on. No, chuck, play it safe an' just mention it, like.'

So Linnet had heeded the advice and gone off to bed satisfied that she had done her best to keep herself – and her mam's beautiful rooms – safe until Evie's return. But in the very back of her mind there was a warmness, a security, which had not been there before; if Mammy really did not come back, if she intended to stay in America and did not send Linnet the ticket which, at first, she had promised in every letter, then at least her daughter did have a means to make a living, of sorts. Whilst the rent continued to come regularly she would live in the flat alone, but if prices really did rise, and Mam found herself unable to send more, than she could always sub-let, as Mrs Sullivan had called it.

And in the very very back of her mind, where nightmares lurked, Linnet also told herself that if she was ever threatened for living alone, then she would take a lodger, a nice young woman not many years older than herself, who would provide her with the respectability which, she knew, she would lack in the eyes of authority if they knew her mother was away.

Happier in her mind than she had been since her mother's departure, Linnet slept well that night.

*

It was about the same time – the Easter holidays after the twins' fourteenth birthday – Lucy and Caitlin finally discovered who had stolen their fruit cake the previous summer.

After that first visit to the castle, and the mysterious theft, they had decided they would make a point of visiting the old castle at least once a week, and at first they actually did so. But after a couple of visits the curragh wasn't there, and it did not appear again. After that they went because they enjoyed having a place of their own, one which nobody else knew about, but it gradually palled because it was a long walk, because the marsh grew next to impassable as the summer rains swelled its puddles into small ponds, and because nothing much happened when they went over there.

'We ought to have gone over in winter, because whoever was living there likely wouldn't be watching for visitors in winter,' Lucy remarked on Easter Sunday as they stopped by the gate to the meadows and the marsh. They leaned on the mossy top bar, looking across at the black finger of the tower pointing up at the pale blue sky. 'What's more, whoever lives there would have needed a fire, and newly dead fires leave traces . . . oh, why didn't we go over in the winter?'

But they had not gone because they were busy with other, indoor activities and also because as the weather worsened so the lure of the castle had palled. It no longer seemed mysterious when the rain sheeted across the marsh but just lonely and dilapidated, and when the snow came, and the howling gales, both girls found plenty to occupy them in the old farmhouse with its empty rooms and crowded attics, or in the sheds and barns which abounded around the farmyard.

'But this holiday, now that we're fourteen and past, we'll go back again and do all sorts,' Caitlin announced.

'This year, we'll do all the things we didn't do last year, starting off by nagging our daddies to make us a curragh of our own.'

'I don't have a daddy,' Lucy reminded her. 'Is it my grandad you're meaning?'

'Yes, of course. I do forget,' apologised Caitlin. 'Your grandad will help my daddy to build us a curragh, won't he?'

'I doubt it; he'll say there's easier ways of gettin' rid o' the pair of us than be drowning,' Lucy said placidly. 'They're against boats, the Murphys. They say they're farmers, not fishermen.'

'Oh well, we'll have to find the magic curragh, then,' Caitlin said. It was a fine day and she was in a good mood and besides, school had broken up which meant that though they would be busy about the farm they would not have to go off to school each day. 'Are we plantin' spuds tomorrow?'

'We are. I'm going to get the thickest sack out of the barn for me poor knees, you'd better do likewise.'

On Easter Sunday itself, of course, they had been too busy with church services, visiting the graves and being lugged here and there by their respective families to go anywhere or do anything, but finally, after tea, Caitlin came over and the two of them agreed to plant potatoes all the following day in return for a picnic the day after that.

'Fair enough, though if the rain holds off your grandad will expect you to finish the big field,' Maeve warned Lucy. 'It's half done, mind, but there's still a power of plantin' left to do.'

As it happened, the next day started off chilly and overcast and it seemed that it had rained most of the night – at any rate, as the children, Maeve and the farmhands squelched across the half-sown field every step was a battle.

'If it had rained *now* then they'd likely have put the plantin' off till tomorrow,' Caitlin moaned, as they reached the end of the rows and dumped their sacks on the cold, wet ploughland. 'As it is, we've got to put a good face on it and start, at least.'

Lucy said nothing but threw her own sack down and knelt on it. Oh, the pain of the sharp little pebbles digging into her kneecaps, the discomfort of hands gone numb from the cold and wet, trying to delve into the claggy soil, oh the misery when, presently, the nippy wind brought a gust of cold rain with it, not enough rain so that they might give up, just enough to fur their lashes with wet and to soak their hair into rats' tails.

'At least the best part of the field's done,' Maeve called over her shoulder at one point. 'And Kellach's such a worker, look at the rate of him, shootin' up his furrow like a racin' greyhound!'

The simile made Lucy smile – her first that morning. Kellach was a beefy young man and his broad behind, moving stolidly along his furrow, resembled a greyhound about as much as Clara Bow, the mournful old mule who had done the ploughing, resembled a racehorse.

'Sure an' it's nice to see you smile,' Maeve said encouragingly. 'Let's see if we can keep pace wi' one another, shall we? Then at least we can talk.'

'I don't feel like talkin', Caitlin grumbled. 'Sure an' isn't the inside of me mouth the only warm bit of me? I'm not after gettin' that cold by openin' me gob more'n I have to.'

That made Maeve and Lucy laugh and Maeve said that since they were all working like Trojans now, she'd offer them a bit of a prize . . . Kellach would undoubtedly finish his row first, and probably be halfway down his second before any of the females had reached the hedge, but whoever came second to Kellach at the end of the field would get a bag of Maeve's cinder toffee and a threepenny piece to spend.

It definitely gave a point to the work, Lucy thought, seizing her bag of spuds and heaving herself further along the row. She planted two likely looking potatoes, eyes up, and entombed them, banged the earth flat, moved on. Maeve was a little ahead of her still, Caitlin a long way behind. But Caitlin had heard, and was rapidly brightening up despite the rain which was starting in earnest now.

'We should've started off evens, though,' she panted at Lucy's heels. 'What's the prize for whoever comes in third?'

'A clip round the ear,' Kellach shouted from way up front. 'Delivered be the all-time winner, Kellach Flanagan, and am't I the best spud-planter in all of Ireland, now?'

'First isn't important today, Kellach,' Lucy shouted. 'The race is a ladies' race with just me an' Cait competin', and I'm in the lead as they round the bend!'

'Neck and neck!' Caitlin screamed, drawing level with Lucy. 'Put your money on the Kelly filly, ladies an' gentlemen, sure an' she's got the stamina an' the speed, what more can you ask?'

'The Murphy mare's drawin' ahead,' countered Lucy, planting like mad. 'The Murphy mare's got the legs on the filly, she's used to heavy going, she's got a light foot on her so she has!'

Maeve was laughing so hard that they caught her up, both now ignoring the dreadful weather conditions, not even bothering to lift up their kneeling sacks but bending and straightening, slamming the seed potatoes into place, covering them up, stamping them down and dragging their equipment on to the next bit of trench.

'Sure and if old Tom was out here he'd be puttin' a bob each way on the pair of ye,' she called after them. 'Mind them spuds don't get planted upside down, we don't want to have to dig six foot down to get 'em when they're ready.'

'Australians would get them,' Lucy said, pushing her hair back from her forehead with a muddy hand. 'Good Irish potatoes, gone all that way... oh, oh, you distracted me, Maeve, now the poor Murphy mare's handicapped!'

By evening the race was won and the field finished. Mud to their eyebrows, the children went to their own homes, almost too tired to shout a goodnight; almost, but not quite. Lucy reached the haven of her little room under the eaves, opened the window into the downpour, and leaned out, but only a little way, out of deference to her clean white nightgown.

'Caitlin, are you in your room?' She shouted needlessly, since she could see both Caitlin's candle and her head and shoulders against the light. 'Have you had a bath? Maeve said when she emptied my bathwater she might as well have taken it straight along to the nine acre, for 'twas all good, rich loam. I washed me hair, though I didn't see the point; it 'ud been rinsed in rainwater all day so it had.'

'I'm bathed,' Caitlin answered. 'And I'm dog-tired, so I am. If I live the night out shall we go over to the castle tomorrow? For I'm damned if I'll set another potato until next year.'

'There aren't any more to set, thank the good Lord,' Lucy said piously. 'If the sun shines I want to go a picnic tomorrow. If it's rainy again we might go into Cahersiveen with Maeve in the donkey-cart. She's got shoppin' to do, she says.'

'We could go to the cinema,' Caitlin said eagerly. 'Honest to God, Lu, your Maeve knows a t'ing or two –

we earned those threepenny bits twice over so we did.'

'Aye, you're right there, she's a psychia . . . whatsit, isn't she just?'

'A cunning old mavoureen, you mean,' Caitlin called. 'See you in the morning then, alanna. Goodniiiiiiight!'

'See you in the morning,' Lucy shouted back. 'Goodniiiiiiight!'

She shut the window, causing drops to fly into the room and speckle the floorboards, and took a flying jump into her bed. The bed cannoned into the wall and the metal head rail squealed and scattered flakes as it rammed against the whitewash.

Lucy cuddled down the bed and dragged the blankets up over her shoulders. Tomorrow they would . . . they would . . .

She slept.

'Well, me prayers were answered,' Caitlin said with a good deal of satisfaction next afternoon as they set out for their picnic. 'Didn't we work like a couple of Irish navvies all morning so as to get our legs loose this afternoon, and aren't we rewarded? Isn't it just the sort of day we wanted, alanna? A bit windy, I'll grant you, and wit' the odd cloud floating along, but it's sunny, that you cannot deny.'

Lucy looked dubiously up at the sky above them. It was sunny, that was certainly true, but there was a great deal of cloud above and there was an oddness in the weather, something she described to herself as a sort of brassiness, which she did not much like.

'Well, I don't know,' she said heavily. 'The air tastes odd, don't you think? Perhaps we'd better stick close to home, eh, Cait?'

But Caitlin was having none of it. 'For a start off, if we stick close to home then your Maeve and my mammy will see us and hand out jobs, sure as me name's Kelly,' she said. 'And for another start off, it's sunny and you can't be too sure of sunshine in April. And for *another* start . . .'

'You can only have one start, the rest isn't,' Lucy said pedantically. And then, when Caitlin pulled a face and fell silent, 'Well then? What's the next start?'

'How can air taste funny?'

'It can,' Lucy said, after a short pause to consider. 'It tastes of metal polish.'

'Smells of it, d'you mean? Because sure I can understand a smell of metal polish, but a taste of the stuff? Air can't taste, it's not water!'

By now they were across the long meadow and climbing the gate onto the marsh so Lucy just shrugged and wrinkled her nose.

'I don't know how it can taste, I just know it does. I can taste it in my mouth. Are you saying you cannot?'

They crossed some more marsh, leaping from tussock to tussock and avoiding the brackish, sky-reflecting pools.

'I know what you mean,' Caitlin said at last. 'Only I don't think it tastes so much of metal polish as torch batteries. D'you want to turn back, then?'

It was a good question since, as Caitlin spoke, they could see blowing across the lough towards them a rain-shower, fine as cobweb, colourful as a rainbow as it caught the sunshine. And looking across at it, Lucy could feel the tingle in the air, the strange stillness, which presages exceptionally bad weather.

'Too late,' she said, however. 'We'll never get home before the rain reaches us; let's make for the castle.'

They ran on, but very soon the rain was upon them, misty and cool on their skins, not at all unpleasant. They reached the edge of the mound in good order and were about to pull themselves up when from the rapidly gathering clouds overhead came an ominous rumble and almost at the same moment, a vivid fork of lightning arrowed down into the lough.

'God help us!' Caitlin gasped.

Lucy, fervently echoing her friend's words, bounded the last couple of yards, hit the grass running, and made straight for the castle, Caitlin close on her heels.

'It's an electric storm,' she gasped as they ran in under the arch. 'I'm scared, Cait, we shouldn't be out, we should be indoors . . . aargh!'

She had shrieked because at that moment the thunder cracked overhead so loud that it pained the ears, and the narrow space in the castle keep was lit up by a brilliant flash which completely swamped the afternoon light.

'Oh, oh, *oh*!' Caitlin squeaked as the thunder cracked a second time. 'It's right overhead, we'll be killed stone dead! The bloody castle will fall on us and Mammy and Maeve will skin us alive!'

'It's stood for a thousand years, so no reason why it should keel over now,' Lucy said stoutly, but perspiration was trickling down the sides of her face and her heart was thumping like a trip-hammer. 'You made a poem just now, Cait – *It's right overhead, we'll be killed stone dead*! That's a p . . . oh, oh!'

Even as she spoke a tongue of lightning struck the sapling growing out of the highest wall and licked down the stones towards them, causing both girls to shriek and Caitlin to cover her head with both hands in a gesture as instinctive as it was futile.

'Get through the door, for divil a hope have we got here,' Lucy said briskly, giving her friend a shove. 'Go on . . . at least there'll be a roof over our heads.'

They dived through the door just as another great, hollow clang of thunder echoed around them so that the slam of the door was noiseless. And just before it closed they saw more lightning flicker horribly around the keep.

'Phew,' panted Lucy, leaning against the door. 'That was the most frightening thing ever! But what a storm, Cait! Shall we go up to the secret room?'

'Climb those terrible stairs in a storm I will not, and you would be mad to do so, Luceen, with the place liable to tumble around your ears any second,' Caitlin said roundly. 'Let's sit on the floor under the table and say a Hail Mary.'

'I'm going up; think of the *view*, Cait,' Lucy said, though she did not much fancy climbing the stone steps whilst the thunder continued to crash right overhead. 'If the stairs shake though, divil a bit further will I climb, you may be sure of that.'

'Don't leave me down here alone,' Caitlin said, clutching her friend's sleeve. 'Oh stay, Luceen, your Maeve will kill me if I let you get into mischief.'

'Come with me, then,' Lucy said stoutly, heading for the stairs. 'I need to be doing, Cait, I can't stay here shaking like a lily leaf, I'm better doing.'

So when Lucy started to climb Caitlin was close on her heels and presently both girls realised something which made them feel a good deal safer.

'The stairs don't shake, not even a tiddy bit,' Lucy said. 'I told you these old stones had lasted a thousand years and would go on for a bit yet.'

'Aye, they're steady so they are,' Caitlin agreed. 'Are we nearly at the door, alanna?'

Glancing back, Lucy discovered that Caitlin was climbing with both eyes squeezed tightly closed and that her own brief skirt was clutched in Caitlin's paw. For the first time ever she was the leader and she liked it. She gave her friend's shoulder a reassuring pat.

'We're there,' she said, stopping in front of the door. 'And I think the storm's moving away at last. Let's hope the door doesn't stick or we won't get a good view at all at all.'

As if the thunder had heard and wanted to make a liar of her it crashed again, sharply, right overhead, just as Lucy pushed the door and it swung obediently open. She and Caitlin stepped into the secret room – and stopped short.

They were not alone. Leaning half out of the window was a small and shabby figure with a shock of white hair. Dressed in an ankle length black skirt, cracked black boots and a tattered shawl which was more hole than pattern, the person – a woman, presumably – had not heard them for the sounds of the storm, or possibly for the sounds that she herself was uttering, for she was shrieking like a banshee and cackling first with laughter and then with what sounded like annoyance, though it was difficult to tell without being able to see her face.

'Who is it?' Caitlin whispered. She had obviously opened her eyes, the journey up the stairs having been accomplished. 'What's she doing?'

'Watching the storm,' Lucy whispered back. 'I don't want to startle her in case she falls out . . . we'd better just stand still until she turns back into the room.'

But Caitlin had not suffered the terrors of the stairs for nothing. She shook her head obstinately. 'I want to look out,' she hissed. 'Come on, the old woman won't notice us moving round.'

And Caitlin was right. The small female continued to shriek, to swear, and to laugh whilst the two girls moved round to the nearest window-slit and peered out.

And it was worth doing so. Lucy watched, awed, as first the rain came sheeting across the lough like a veil, then the sun would peep out from behind a black cloud making rainbows, then the thunder, rumbling sullenly, would crack and the lightning would flicker across the blackness, looking not gold or silver, but a sort of electric lavender blue.

'It is moving off,' Caitlin breathed against Lucy's ear. 'I never did see such a storm, me. Oh, look at the rainbows!'

'Look at the big one will you, stretching right across the lough . . . ah, here comes the rain in earnest.'

They stood back from the window as the wind, which had dropped whilst the storm raged, drove the rain straight at them, or so it seemed, and at the same moment the little creature gave one last squawk and turned towards them.

She was very old and very, very dirty. Her snow white hair was laced liberally with dirt and bits of hay, and her skin was soft and dark, crumpled and cobwebbed with tiny lines. She was thin as a thread, and bent like the moorland trees, and she was no bigger than a child of six or seven. But, astonishingly, Lucy saw that she was still pretty, with eyes as black and sparkling as a young girl's, a haughty little nose and a firm and pointed chin beneath a mouth sunken through age and toothlessness.

They didn't get much chance to look at her though. She shrieked again, revealing that she didn't have so much as a tooth in her head, and dived head-first into the piled up hay, disappearing so fast that the girls did not have a chance to stop her.

'Well, did you see that?' Caitlin gasped. 'Why did she go in there?'

'Scared,' Lucy said briefly. 'She didn't know we were here, so we frightened her, I suppose.' She leaned down over the pile of hay. 'Come out do, alanna,' she said coaxingly. 'Sure and we'd never hurt you, this is your own little room, I daresay? Come out and say good afternoon like a Christian.'

The hay remained unmoving.

'Who were you shouting at?' Lucy wheedled. 'Wasn't the storm great, then? Ah, come on, we're only a couple o' kids, we wouldn't hurt you, grandma.'

Several more remarks failed to get the hay to stir and Lucy was about to give up when Caitlin sat down on the floor with a thump and addressed her friend, whilst keeping a wary eye on the hay-tump.

'Amn't I glad we brought so many delicious hard-boiled eggs and so much of your Maeve's new-baked bread, Lu?' she said innocently. 'Enough there is for an army and we'd share willingly, wouldn't we, Luceen? And the chocolate cake with the butter icing that melts in the mouth – enough for five or six my mammy did pack in our old blue bag. And it isn't everyone who can make lemon barley like Mammy, to quench your thirst and make you want more at one and the same time.'

The hay definitely stirred. Both girls held their breath.

'It's the drink I'm longing for,' Lucy said, her eyes on the hay. 'Sure it'll slide down me dry t'roat like a trout slipping along the stream bed. Why, if there's a drink I do love it's your mammy's lemon barley.'

A small and dirty face could be dimly seen through the hay, whilst two large, dark eyes burned out at them. Caitlin opened the blue bag and peered inside as though unaware she had an audience. She brought forth rustling parcels and laid them tenderly on the dusty boards between herself and Lucy. The watching face emerged altogether from the hay and the owner heaved herself right out and crouched there, staring at them, half hopeful, half wary.

Lucy leaned forward and picked up a slice of chocolate cake.

'Would you like some of this, missus?' she asked politely. 'Or would you rather start with a sandwich or two, and a drink?'

'Sure an' we've not been interduced,' the old lady said

in a voice creaky with age and lack of use. 'Will ye not give me your names before we share a crust?'

But her bright eyes did not seem able to move from the cake and when Lucy held it out a grimy paw with blackened nails reached out and grabbed it, though she did not immediately carry it to her mouth.

'Sorry, missus,' Caitlin said humbly. 'I'm Caitlin Kelly and me friend's Lucy Murphy. And your name?'

'Moggy, Granny Mogg,' the old woman said thickly; the cake had at last reached her mouth, crammed in by an impatient hand. 'I'm Granny Mogg so I am, Moggy to me pals.' She cackled briefly, spraying crumbs. 'Tis good cake,' she added, swallowing the last mouthful. 'Tis rare tasty, Caitlin. Ah, wouldn't it be grand if I had cake like t'at every day, now?'

'We don't get chocolate cake every day, Granny Mogg,' Lucy said hastily. 'Only for a special picnic. Would you be having a drink of the barley water now?'

The old woman looked curiously at the bottle, but shook her head. 'I'm thinkin' I'd best stick wit' tay,' she said. 'A cup o' tay goes down well wi' cake.'

Silently, Lucy leaned forward and picked up the remaining piece of cake; it was taken from her hand – almost snatched – at once and despite her toothlessness the old lady made short work of it. Then she sat back on her heels and gazed expectantly at the girls. Lucy broke the silence.

'The storm's moving away, thank the Lord,' she said. 'But would you look at that rain? We'll be here for a while yet.'

It was true that the rain was falling steadily but Lucy did not think it would last all that long, she had merely made the remark for something to say, and now she sat down and began to unwrap the rest of their picnic.

'A sandwich, Mrs Mogg?' she said presently and, after

some rather unconvincing remarks that 'I shouldn't take your food, indeed indeed,' the sandwich disappeared inside Granny Mogg, who smacked her lips and said it was 'a fair treat, so it was'.

'Have you lived here long?' Lucy asked presently, when the first edge of their hunger was dulled. 'Where do you do your shopping? I can't remember seeing you in Cahersiveen.'

Granny Mogg stared reflectively out at the steadily falling rain. 'I've lived 'ere a whiles,' she said after a moment. 'I doesn't do no shoppin', though, child. How would I pay for shoppin' eh? I lives off the land, I does.'

'Do you eat rabbits? And raw corn, and blackberries, and nuts?' Caitlin asked, letting her incredulity show. 'We've got a friend at school, his gran's a hundred years old and she eats rabbits wit' their fur and all still on.'

'I skins 'em,' Granny Mogg said with disdain. 'Eatin' fur's mortal dirty, an' bad for ye. I dunna tek to raw flesh, either. Why, your friend's gran must have a set o' teeth on 'er like a farmer's dog if she kin eat raw flesh.'

'Oh, it's only what they say,' Lucy said comfortably, taking a pull out of the bottle. She swallowed, then handed the drink on to Caitlin. 'Do you eat fish, cooked over a fire?'

Granny Mogg thought for a moment, giving Lucy quick, bright little glances out of her shrewd and sparkling eyes, then nodded. 'Aye; I'm fond of a nice piece of fish.'

'The trout in the lough are good,' Lucy said, nodding, too. 'Do you fish from the curragh beside the creek?'

This time there was a distinct pause whilst Granny Mogg's brow wrinkled in cogitation. Then, with some reluctance, she shook her head. 'No indeed, for if I got into t'at tippery shell wouldn't I be drowneded dead in a moment? Girls can't swim, childer, it ain't for females, not swimmin' ain't. No, I gets fish give be – be a friend.'

'He's a very shy friend, the one who fishes from the curragh, for never have we set eyes on him,' Caitlin remarked. 'What does he use for oars, Granny?'

The old woman shook her head. 'Ne'er mind,' she said. 'If it hadn't been for the young devil I'd not be here. And you'd best forget you met me,' she added. 'We're hidin' up, see? Not hurtin' no one, just hidin' up.' She dropped her voice and made the sign of the cross, first to her left, then to her right, then on the bony ridge of her breast bone. 'Sure an' they t'ought I was dead,' she whispered. 'They meant me to die, they put me out on a turble night, with the snow sweepin' in across the mountains . . . if it hadn't been for the young devil . . .'

The girls leaned closer to catch her words, Lucy uneasily aware of a thrill of fear running through her. Was the old woman mad, or had someone really tried to kill her? And if so, was that person even now approaching the castle with evil in his heart – evil which might spread to encompass two defenceless girls as well as the old woman?

'Who did it, Granny?' Lucy asked, unconsciously whispering in her turn. 'Who tried to kill you? And why?'

But before Granny Mogg could say a word the door to their retreat shot open, causing all three of them to give a shriek of sheer shock and terror, before Granny Mogg dived into the tump of hay and Caitlin and Lucy, hearts thumping, turned to face the doorway.

A boy stood there, framed by the silvery wood. His mouth was opened on an 'o' of surprise and his eyes, black as night, rounded with disbelief when they met Lucy's before narrowing again to slide quickly round the room. Then he stepped in and Lucy noticed the string of trout in one hand and the spoon-shaped oar in the other. It was undoubtedly the curragh owner, the giver of fish . . . the young devil himself!

Chapter Five

For a moment no one said a word; the hay stopped quivering, the boy's stare ceased to roam the room and fixed itself with unnerving steadiness on Lucy, and outside the rain seemed to give a little sigh before continuing to fall whilst the thunder rumbled away into the distance and a long finger of golden sunlight slid through the western window-slit and fell across the dusty floor.

'And just what've you done wi' the old woman?'

The accent was strange – Lucy found herself wondering what part of Kerry the boy hailed from – but the meaning perfectly clear. Lucy pointed to the hay. The boy nodded.

'Sure and she's the nervous one, isn't she? No wonder, either, after last summer – and now tell me, will you, just where you two beauties sprang from?'

Out of the corner of her eye Lucy saw Caitlin bridle and drop her eyes so that she could look up at the boy through her lashes; it made Lucy smile since she was absolutely certain of one thing – that when the 'young devil' used the expression 'two beauties', the last thing on his mind was their looks. And Caitlin suddenly seemed to realise the same thing, for she stopped looking coquettish and looked worried, instead.

The boy sighed, then laid his fish carefully down on the board floor and propped his oddly shaped oar against the wall. Then he took two steps into the room and Lucy shrank back, suddenly aware of menace in his dark-eyed glance. He was older than she and Caitlin, taller, stronger

. . . and he seemed to be angry with them, though why this should be she had not yet worked out.

'Well? You, the little fair one, where d'you come from and what are you doin' in this old castle, where no one comes?'

'We came for a picnic,' Lucy said. She stood her ground but could not help her glance shooting towards the hay-tump. It was moving again, not much but enough to make her realise that Granny Mogg, having realised who the boy was, was definitely considering emerging. This made her feel better, though she could not have said why. 'Only there was the storm . . . so we came into the castle and climbed up here and . . . and there was Mrs Mogg, watching the lightning through the window.'

'Aye; leppin' like a – a leprechaun and swearin' like a trooper and cacklin' like a hen going to lay an egg,' the boy said, suddenly good-humoured. He grinned at Lucy and she saw that he was good to look at when he grinned, with the very dark eyes narrowed into shining slits and a long laughter dimple in one thin brown cheek. 'Scare you, did she?'

'Only for a moment,' Lucy said stoutly. 'It was the shock – we'd got used to thinking there was no one here, you see.'

He nodded, then bent down and picked up his string of fish. He walked over to the pile of hay and swung the fish ruminatively, then bent down and spoke. His voice, which had seemed harsh and rather angry to Lucy, went very soft and deep.

'Come along out wit' you, Gran, tis meself out here, wit' the younglings.'

The hay shook and Granny Mogg emerged. She was grinning, showing her pink gums and her tooth, but there was a wariness about her, as though she secretly doubted her welcome.

'Twaren't my fault they finded me,' she squeaked. 'They come on me sudden like, when the thunder was roarin' too loud to hear a scream o' mortal terror. You shouldn't ha' leaved me, you should ha' stayed by me.'

'I've got six trout,' the boy said ruminatively. 'Two each for you an' me, Gran, and one each for these spratleens. Shall we tek 'em down to the fireplace and fry 'em?'

I just hope he means the trout and not us, Lucy thought fervently, whilst the old lady nodded, grinned, and shook the hay off herself, then began to hobble at a fair speed across the floor towards the open door.

Lucy went to follow her, but the boy put an arm across the doorway, barring her.

'Not so fast, girleen; now you can tell me, slow and quiet-like, what you're doing here and how you came to find me gran.'

'We live over there,' Lucy said, waving a vague hand in the direction of the farm. 'My grandad owns all this land, though not the castle, of course. He grazes his cattle on the sea marsh and the meadows leading down to it. We came down here last summer and we thought then that there was someone here, but we couldn't find you. Only the curragh.'

He nodded, thoughtful now, gazing absently past her, his eyes fixed on the window-slit behind her head.

'Aye, last summer . . . there was someone, I remember Gran saying. But she's kept well hid, until now.'

'Why does it matter if anyone sees her?' Caitlin said from behind, giving Lucy quite a surprise. So involved had she become with the boy that she had almost forgotten her friend. 'No one would really hurt an old lady.'

The black eyes left Lucy's face for a moment and fastened on Caitlin's, with a mocking look in their depths.

'Would they not? Have you never met an Irish tinker, girleen? There's good and bad amongst them but Granny Mogg was with the Duveen tribe, and they're rough, real rough. A year gone she sickened and Vorth, the boss, decided she was dying. He left her, wrapped in a soaking wet blanket, under a hedge. She should've been dead by morning but Mogg's a tough old bird. I found her and carried her to where she'd be safe, gave her water to drink, put her deep in the hay and waited. She slept and snored for two days, half-waking to drink, and on the third day she sat up and demanded food. You could say she's never looked back since.'

'But why should the tinkers care whether she's alive or dead?' Lucy demanded. 'She's just an old woman, she can't hurt anyone.'

'True. But she'd make a liar of Vorth, she would indeed, and he'd never stand for that. Told the tribe she was dead, see? So as far as Vorth's concerned Granny Mogg's dead and should stay so. Which is why she dives into the hay and keeps out of sight most of the time, though I tell her the tinkers may not come this way again for many a long year.'

'Or they may come back tomorrow,' Lucy said in a hollow tone. 'Scared I am at the thought – they might kill us all!'

'Not me,' the youth said. 'Nor the old'un whilst I've breath in me body to defend her. She's a good old gal, no one shall hurt her. But the Duveen tribe's a bad lot, I don't mind tellin' you, and Vorth – he'd murther the lot of yez if he took it into his head so he would. And come to that, if either of you say a word about Granny Mogg to your mammies and daddies, sure and won't Finn Delaney slit your little t'roatsies for you from ear to ear?'

'Are you Finn Delaney?' That was Caitlin again, peering out from behind Lucy's shoulder. The boy nodded.

'That's me. And who are you two? Not sisters – friends? In the same class at school, mebbe?'

'That's right,' Lucy said since Caitlin simply mumbled something beneath her breath. 'I'm Lucy Murphy and me friend's Caitlin Kelly. So now we all know each other can we go down to your gran? I'm longing to see where she puts the fire, so I am, for divil a sign of new ash did we see.'

The boy chuckled but stopped barring the door and went ahead of them to the top of the stone stair. 'And see you shall. Now I'll go first so's if you fall you'll have a soft landin' on me back, though I hope you won't fall – you're neither of you feather-weights by the looks.'

'You're heavier than the both of us,' Lucy said stoutly, eyeing the broad back and shoulders before her as they began to descend the stairs. 'A nice dint in the ground you'd make if you fell.'

He turned to grin at her. 'Aye, but Finn Delaney's never been known to fall – I climb like a goat, run like a racehorse and fight like a tiger, so show me respect and you won't go far wrong.' He glanced past Lucy to Caitlin, clinging once more to her friend's skirt. 'What's wrong wi' you, Caitlin? Open your eyes, woman, or you could kill the t'ree of us.'

'She doesn't like heights,' Lucy said calmly. 'If she looks she freezes and divil a down will she go. And if you keep turning round . . .'

She said nothing more since Finn, still staring at Caitlin, bounced a shoulder on the wall, staggered and fell off the step five but one from the ground. Being a feller he pretended he'd done it on purpose, of course, and held out both hands to Lucy to jump as well, but Lucy knew it had startled him and gave him a told-you-so smirk before ignoring his outstretched hands and going demurely down the rest of the flight.

'We're there,' she told Caitlin, preventing her friend from continuing to grope for the next step with one foot, and Caitlin opened her eyes and gazed round in a dazed sort of way.

'So we are indeed; where's Granny Mogg, though?'

'In the sod hut,' Finn said briefly. 'Come on.'

He led the way out into the now tenderly falling spring rain and dived into the turf hut. Sure enough, there was Granny Mogg lighting her fire which she had set right in the middle of the long-dead ashes. She blew on it, and ash floated into the air, making her sneeze, but even as the girls watched a steady red glow began to invade the peat and Granny Mogg reached into the pile of dead bracken and produced a frying pan, blackened and heavy but obviously still very much in use, an ancient iron trivet and a kettle.

'Never saw 'em, did you?' she cackled, turning to grin at the girls. 'Ah, younglings never look beyond their little noses, never!' She picked up the kettle and began to fill it with water from an old milk churn pushed well into a corner and disguised by a pile of ancient turves, then she hung it over the fire. 'We'll eat an' drink when the kettle boils,' she stated calmly. 'I'll make us a wet o' tay.'

'Where do you get the tea from?' Lucy asked as Finn, hunkering down, began to gut the fish and throw them into the blackened pan. 'You can't find tea, you have to buy it!'

'I get it for her, sometimes from O'Rorke's in Cahersiveen or from a nice little shop I know in Caherdaniel village,' Finn put in. 'Granny Mogg stays here when I'm away, so she has to have supplies to keep her goin'.' He looked speculatively at the two girls, but his eyes rested longest on Lucy. 'Ye wouldn't like to look in on her from time to time?' he wheedled. 'She hates to be left so she does, but I've our livings to make.'

'What do you do?' Caitlin asked inquisitively. 'You don't work on any of the farms round here or we'd have recognised you. And you don't work in the shops in Caher, either, I'm sure. Well, it isn't everybody who would . . .'

She stopped short. Finn finished the sentence for her. 'It isn't everybody who would employ a tinker, Caitlin, is that what you were goin' to say?' he asked softly. 'Sure and you're right, but they'd take a one-legged Protestant negro on the fishing boats if he could haul a line and trim a sail and pull an oar. And I can look as respectable as – as a farmer when the harvest needs all hands.'

'But not round here,' Caitlin persisted. 'You don't work round here, do you, Finn? Because Lu and me, we go round the other farms when they have the Stations, or when they need help with the harvest, and we've never seen you, have we, Luceen?'

'Divil a once,' Lucy said cheerfully. She picked up the panful of fish and pushed it into the heart of the red-hot turves. 'I'll see to the fish, Finn, whilst you find us something to drink out of – you don't take your tay from the kettle, do you?'

Finn laughed. 'We've two tin billies which do duty for all,' he said cheerfully. 'But you'll have to sup hot tay from your cupped hands and eat fried fish with your finger-ends. Unless there's something in the blue bag?'

'Of course!' Caitlin said. They had left the bag in the castle and she turned and went out of the hut. 'I'll fetch our bottle, Lu, that should do for us.'

As soon as she had gone Finn turned to Lucy. He put a strong brown hand on her upper arm and gripped it, urgently but with care and gentleness. 'Lucy, I want speech apart. Where can we meet where Caitlin won't follow?'

Lucy stared at him, a frown knitting her brow. 'You

could come to my house,' she said slowly. 'When it's evening time. But whether Maeve or Grandad would let you in I can't say.'

He laughed with a trace of bitterness. 'Let a tinker into a farmhouse for to visit the farmer's daughter? Is it likely, alanna? Can you not come out, say you want to be private? Pay a visit?'

'Oh, I don't know,' Lucy said doubtfully. 'For why don't you want to see Caitlin at the same time, Finn? She's me best friend.'

'I've got something for you,' Finn said after a short pause. 'Only one I do have, Luceen, so none for Caitlin there is. And soon I'll be gone from here. Where shall we meet?'

'Tonight, do you mean? After it's dark?' She was tempted to say she did not dare, did not know him well enough, but then she heard Caitlin's step returning. He seized her hand, his fingers hard now, and urgent.

'Your home?'

'The big farm built of pale stones with the ivy round the front,' Lucy whispered rapidly.

He nodded, the dark eyes still fixed on her face. 'I know it. In the big barn just inside the gate . . . tonight.'

He moved away from her but she followed, anxious. 'What time, Finn?'

He shrugged. 'I don't go by clocks. When the moon is high . . . when all the eyes in your house are closed and the windows of your farm are in darkness. I'll wait for you.'

She barely had time to nod, to say she would do her best to be there, before Caitlin was back, the blue bag in her hand. They shared out the sandwiches, drank the lemonade between them, then had the fish, so hot that Lucy and Caitlin wrapped theirs in their sandwich paper and even then squealed whenever they took a bite. Granny Mogg and Finn ate theirs unconcernedly with their fingers, and drank the tay from their tin billy cans, so hot that it hurt Lucy to watch them. And presently Finn took them down to the lough to see the curragh whilst Granny Mogg had a snooze in the sun and then it was time to go, because though the soft rain had not ceased to fall all day, it came down from a darkening sky.

'Shall we see you tomorrow, Finn?' Caitlin asked, as he waved them off.

He shrugged. 'Mebbe. But I'll be gone before long; you'll visit the old 'un for me? And say no word, for fear of Vorth comin' to know she's alive?'

Both girls promised they would, then began to cross the marsh, scampering through the puddles and pools, intent now on getting back home before they were late for their tea. But Lucy, at least, did not forget Finn for a moment; whether he was good or bad she did not yet know, but he fascinated her. She knew she would meet him tonight, if it was humanly possible, even if it meant lying to Grandad and deceiving Maeve. After all, there's the old 'un to consider, she told herself righteously. You can't let an old lady down. But inside her head it was Finn's dark eyes which danced, Finn's curving mouth which smiled . . . and the recollection of the feel of Finn's hard brown hand on her arm which brought that shivering pang of excitement darting through her.

Finn stared after them until they were just dots crossing the lushness of the distant meadows. What luck that they should have come today, when he was beginning to think that he must leave Granny Mogg alone here whilst he went foraging for food! They would look out for the old 'un, he had no doubt of that, and because they were now thoroughly frightened of Vorth, whatever they might pretend, they would give neither Granny nor himself away.

Not that they had any idea that he, too, was in hiding of a sort. But when all was said and done they were only a couple of children, and you couldn't tell children too much or they would get in a panic and tell their parents and then where would he be?

He liked the little fair one, though. There was something about her, he did not know what it was, which made him want to look at her and go on looking. It was strange really, because she had fair hair and he liked dark women, and she had grey-blue eyes and he admired a passionate, dark-brown gaze. What was more she was a child, no more than thirteen or fourteen, and he was a man – sixteen at least and not interested in children.

Finn had had his first woman over a year earlier, after his mother had died and his father had remarried, choosing Eilis of the Duveen tribe, a woman as voluptuous as his mother had been slender, as bawdy as his mother had been gentle.

The marriage had been a success in that Eilis had made Paddy happy, but she resented having a stepson only half a dozen years younger than she and made no secret of it. And the Tuam people did not take to Eilis and did not trouble to hide their feelings, which was why the Delaneys had moved in with the Duveen tribe and why Finn had come across Brónach one fine April morning just after Easter. The two young people had seen each other often enough before, but had never so much as spoken until they had chanced to meet on Church Island, in Caherdaniel Bay. It was a small island almost completely taken over by the local churchyard and Finn had been digging cockles on the long sea strand and had come up to the island to sit on the grass and drink from his bottle of cold tea. He came over the ridge, his cockles in a bucket, sweat beading his brow, and the first thing he saw was Brónach, with a mass of flowers by her side, sitting on the green spring grass between the graves. He could see she had been stealing the Easter flowers to sell in the nearby town, an activity of which he disapproved, but she smiled at him so he walked over to her and, as he felt courtesy demanded, wished her top of the morning.

One reason that Finn had not mixed much with the Duveen young was that they were very different from the Tuam tribe, who were horse dealers, donkey barterers and lace-makers. In fact, the Tuams worked for their living in every possible way. Children cut hazel-wands and the women wove them into baskets which the men sold to the villagers and townsfolk. Old men cut rushes and mended chair seats. Others searched for the lucky white heather and wheedled pennies out of superstitious housewives. They lived, by their own standards, fairly enough. The Duveens, however, lived not on the country, but on the people. They preyed on villagers and townsfolk alike. They were thieves for a living and stole hens, eggs and farm stock without compunction. They took the flowers from the graves, the butter from the churn, the milk from cows in the meadows, and seemed to believe they had a God-given right to do so. They would pull down an isolated cattle shelter and burn it on their fires, or untie the dog from his kennel and demand a ransom for his return, or steal the washing from the line or the bicycle from the shed. They were able-bodied but idle and feckless in the extreme, with a streak of real viciousness if things did not seem to be going their way.

So Finn's feelings upon seeing Brónach were not exactly of unalloyed joy but were laced with considerable caution. She was a year older than he and a naughty girl, even his stepmam said so. However, one could not be rude, particularly to a member of the opposite sex, his real mother had taught him that.

So after cautious greetings had been exchanged he had sat down next to her and, after a quick glance at him, she had pushed her skirt back so that her long, slender brown legs could enjoy the warmth of a rare day's sunshine. Finn had looked at the legs – he swallowed now at the recollection – and then at Brón, looked at her properly for the first time. She had a small face, almond-shaped dark eyes and ripe red lips, the lower one bee-stung, fat and tempting, reminding him of some exotic fruit. And when she laughed she showed teeth which were small and perfectly white, and the tip of a scarlet-strawberry tongue.

He had never felt the urge to touch a girl before but suddenly it was upon him, hot and strong and irresistible. He glanced sideways at her and she was laughing at him, eyeing him coquettishly through the long, curly lashes which fringed her big brown eyes. Though a year younger, he was both taller and broader than she, and suddenly the surge of desire in him peaked, could no longer be denied. He took hold of her shoulders and pushed her back onto the sweet spring grass.

'Brónach, you're a beautiful crathur.'

She smiled sleepily up at him and her tongue flickered out and ran across her lower lip. 'Sure, sure,' she murmured. 'And what are you goin' to do about it, Finn Delaney?'

He smiled, too, suddenly sure of himself, suddenly seeing where the conversation was heading – if you could call it a conversation, that was. He had been born in a tinker's tent and bred in the sod huts they built to over-winter, and in the wooden caravans which were the palaces of his tribe. No child could be brought up in such circumstances ignorant of the facts of life. Many a night when he was very small he had lain awake wondering what made his mother cry out softly and his father groan with pleasure, and as he grew so did his understanding of such nightly activities. So now, in the quiet graveyard with the water lapping at the little strip of golden sand which would presently be covered as the tide rose, he put his hands on beautiful Brónach's beautiful body and gently pulled the dress down over her rounded shoulders and began to stroke her smooth skin and make much of her. And in a little while he had made love to her and laughed at her when she screamed like a vixen in spring and clung to him and vowed she would love him for ever.

By then he had heard it all before, knew it was the way of a tinker's woman to scream when she was aroused, though his mother had been a gentle soul who took her pleasures gently, too. But Eilis was uninhibited in bed and he had lived in the same small wooden caravan as she and his father for six months.

Parting company with his father had happened easily in the end, almost painlessly. Finn had been eating his share of a pan of sausages when his father had come up to him, cleared his throat and delivered what was, in effect, an ultimatum.

'We're goin' across the water, Finn me boyo, to feed on the fat lands of the English,' Paddy Delaney had said. 'The Tuams didn't like me beautiful Eilis and to be frank, boy, the Duveens are trouble. So we're gettin' right away from the both of 'em. Are you with us?'

Finn had looked at his father and had read in the older man's face enough to realise that it would be a mistake to accompany them. His father loved him, but his loyalty, now, lay with Eilis and his new marriage, the babe which would come to Eilis when autumn coloured the trees. Finn had been fifteen, near enough a man in his own right, so he shook his head and tried not to be hurt by the relief in his father's dark eyes.

'No, I'm for stayin',' he had said simply. 'I'll move out from here and I'll work for meself, so I will.'

He had meant to do so, meant to search out the Tuams and move back in with the tribe. Finn would have been happy with them and might have gone back indeed, but he stayed partly from laziness, partly because of Brónach. He took his shabby little tent and parked it near Granny Mogg's old wooden van and told anyone who would listen that he would be gone by winter. And though he had held aloof from the stealing and general wickedness of the other lads his age, he had not got himself a job but had idled the summer away, meaning to move away but doing nothing about it. And he had thought himself a man, pleasuring Brónach and being pleasured by her whenever they could sneak away from the others, and had swaggered around the camp like the man he so nearly was, looking down on the lads who stole and boasted because they didn't know how good it was, to lie in the heather with a beautiful woman and make love to her.

Granny Mogg wasn't a true Duveen, though, and looked down on those who were. She was Vorth's mother-in-law, the mother of his first wife, who had been older than he and very beautiful, and she told Finn she would never have moved back in with the Duveens except that she was too old, any longer, to keep herself, and the tribe to which she had belonged were all old too.

'An old 'oman waren't good for nothin', an' Vorth's the nearest t'ing I've got to kin,' she told Finn. 'But he's a bad'un, so don't you take him as a sample of how to live. Work for what ye want, me laddo, because tinkers don't have to steal, there's good work on the land for the likes of us. I'd not have brought my old nag and my old shack over to the Duveens if I'd known how low they'd fallen since my darter died.'

But then she had got ill and one night Vorth had come quietly past Finn's sacking tent and stolen into the creaking wooden caravan. Finn thought he was just looking in to see the old lady but next day he guessed, when he found the caravan empty, that Vorth had picked her up like the bag of dry old sticks which she so closely resembled and carried her off for reasons of his own. Not good reasons, he was sure of that. If someone died in a van no self-respecting tinker would live there for fear of the ghost of the departed; instead they would set fire to the caravan or tent or sod hut, turning it into a funeral pyre, and Finn knew that Vorth wanted the old wooden van for his sullen, mean-eyed eldest daughter and her new husband. Vorth was sick of sharing space with newly weds who made sheep's eyes at each other and never helped with the cooking, he'd been saying so for a month. Granny Mogg's caravan was clean and relatively spacious, and fully furnished with all that was necessary for life on the road – what more could a daughter ask?

So Vorth had gone off in the dead of night and next day, when Finn asked where the old lady was, he told the tribe that Granny Mogg had known she was going to die and had begged him to take her some distance away for her final moments so that he might take over her caravan when her soul had departed this life. He said he had put her in a curragh and set fire to it, pushing it out to sea so that her bones might rest in the deep, as she had requested. Whether the tribe believed or not Finn did not know, he just knew they accepted it. Easier, they would think, than questioning their leader who, in a rage, could kill a man with a single blow – not only could, but had done.

So Finn had pretended to believe, too, and had left the camp as soon as he could and tracked Vorth's passage of the previous night with all the skill and persistence which had been born in him. He had followed Vorth's footsteps across the wet field, through the mud at the gate where the cattle had poached the ground, along the lane, through a copse. And his eyes on the ground had seen every step, noted the deeper marks of the heels because of the burden the man carried, seen where he paused, how he laid the old woman down to open a gate, saw in his head a picture of Vorth's doings of the previous night as clear as though he was seeing it all in a crystal ball.

He had guessed what he would find in the ditch before he reached it, because the footsteps going out were deep still but here they crossed with footsteps coming away which were shallower and with the gaps between them longer, too. An unburdened man had made those prints. Finn ran, then, suddenly afraid. If she was in truth dead why leave her in the ditch, why not build her a funeral pyre from dry branches, or turves, and send her body cleanly on its way? Vorth had told everyone she'd wanted her mortal remains to be carried out to sea in a curragh and there burnt, but the footsteps stopped by the ditch . . . if her body lay there still, then Vorth was the liar and the murderer Finn had always thought him.

He dived into the ditch and there she was – his heart jumped when he bent over her though; her breathing was stertorous, her face blotched white and purple. She was alive still despite Vorth's treatment; he must have hesitated to deliver the *coup de grâce*, believing she would die anyway if abandoned in the ditch. Finn said her name softly, then picked her gently up in his arms. The blanket in which she was wrapped was soaking wet and as he held her he realised she was shuddering and shaking as though with an ague. But she was still alive and would remain so if he moved swiftly. Granny Mogg, who had been kind to him when his father had left him with the Duveens, was in his charge now, and needing him. And Finn Delaney, Finn told himself as he walked steadily away from the ditch, was not the man to let her down.

He carried her, still wrapped in the stinking wet blanket, to the only dry spot he could find – a haystack. He buried her deep in the heart of it and stayed with her, feeding her water from a cracked old cup when she stirred and cried out for a drink, stealing eggs from the birds' nests and feeding her with them, too. For three days she had not known him, had burned with fever, had cried out and cackled, putting him in mortal fear that she would bring the Duveen tribe, or at least Vorth, down upon them. But she was a strong and wiry old bird, and she had recovered. Her mind was not as sharp and quick as it had been, but her body was healthy once more and she remembered Vorth and what he had tried to do to her.

She had woken that night to find him bending over her, a look of such evil on his fat, dirty face that she had thought her last moment had come. So when Finn told her that they must lie low for a while she had nodded anxiously, understanding the necessity, and had followed him trustingly to the castle, which he had found when she had been so ill that she had not known whether he was with her or away.

For a whole year they had lived there, hiding away. He had found the curragh washed ashore with a hole in its outer canvas and made it his own. He had fashioned the oar, patched and tarred the little craft to make it watertight, and then he had gone into Cahersiveen and bartered for a net so that he might catch fish in quantity. He dared not work on any of the nearby farms, however, for fear a Duveen might come there and guess what he had done, might let it be known that the old 'un lived and that he, Finn, was taking care of her. So he left the old 'un for as much as a month at a time in the summer and tramped until he found work on a distant farm. He went out with the fishing boats further along the lough in winter and earned money to see them through . . . and sometimes, he fretted a little for the feel of a strong, supple girl like Brónach in his arms, and the soft whicker of a horse as he tacked it up before riding it along the country lanes. But mostly he enjoyed his freedom, Granny Mogg's strangely restful company, and the sensation of being entirely his own master.

Until now. Until a fair-haired, blue-eyed scrap of a girl had looked him in the eye and he had felt his stomach clench, not with any sort of sexual desire but with a sort of *knowingness*, as though he and Lucy Murphy meant something to each other, as though their fates were, in some way, entwined.

And he wanted to see her again, wanted to see her so much that he could not resist making a rendezvous, even though it wasn't wise to mix with buffers, not if you were a tinker born and bred.

But perhaps it was different for him, because his mam had not been a tinker, she had been a respectable girl from a respectable farm just outside Roscrea, and she had fallen in love with the dark-eyed, curly-haired tinker who came to the farm to visit her father, wheeling and dealing, promising his fine grey mare, with a foal at heel, for the farmer's broken-down old plough horse – new lamps for old, his mam had said with a small, secret smile.

So the respectable girl had run away with the handsome tinker, only to find the travelling life was no very wonderful thing – but she had stuck with Paddy Delaney through hell and high water, and she had loved her son and taught him to read and write and given him a love of books and stories, though it was few enough of the first that came his way.

But . . . Lucy Murphy, thrown in his path by chance, too young for him, too innocent, too indifferent, even. She had laughed at him when he fell off the stairs, it was her friend who had slanted looks at him through her lashes, looks which told him that one of the little birds was on the threshold of womanhood – but it wasn't the one he wanted.

'Tis not right nor fair to meet the girleen in her father's barn when she's as unawakened as a day old kitten, he told himself severely. If you're so mad for a woman then go into Caher and find a willing lass – the barmaid from Tom's Tavern on Main Street, or the plump and laughing beauty who gave you a startled, admiring glance as she came out of the O'Connell Memorial Church last Sunday fortnight. Stand Lucy Murphy up, give her the go-by, Finn Delaney, he ordered himself; she'll be disillusioned, sure, but that way she'll be far less hurt than if you let her believe the two of you have a future together. Not that she would believe any such thing, not a child like her. So I won't go, she can wait in the barn until morning comes, but Finn Delaney will be long gone about his own business.

So he fed Granny Mogg and himself and tucked the old 'un up in her bed of hay halfway up the castle tower and went down and stood beside the curragh in the gathering dusk and watched the stars prick out one by one over the lough and the distant sea – and knew he would go to the farm, and stand just inside the barn door, and wait for her to come to him.

'Lucy, where's your appetite? Didn't I make pancakes especially for you, and aren't you pushin' them round and round your plate and scarcely a bite have you taken?

If you're ill, alanna, then it's in bed you should be and not sittin' at the table playin' with your good food.'

Lucy hastily took a mouthful of her pancake and brought her mind back to the job in hand – eating her tea. A pleasant job enough, too, when Maeve had made pancakes with honey over them and a squeeze of lemon.

'Sorry, Maeve. I was thinking so I was,' she said humbly, swallowing her mouthful and giving her aunt a reassuring smile. 'There's nothing wrong with me at all at all, only I was dreaming. When I've had me supper, shall I be after collecting the eggs? I saw the hen with the ragged comb going into the big barn as I come up with Caitlin for me tea, and the speckled hen likes to lay right up against the orchard hedge – I could look there.'

'I got them earlier,' Maeve said, looking surprised, as well she might, Lucy reflected guiltily. Maeve knew too well that Lucy hated being sent out at dusk to search for eggs and right now dusk was rapidly turning into darkness. 'Besides, you've some darning to do, young lady.'

Lucy groaned. She absolutely hated any form of needlework and was dreadfully bad at it, but Maeve was adamant. She must be able to darn and to sew a little because farmers' wives – and she was obviously going to be a farmer's wife – made their children's clothing if not their own.

'Oh, Maeve, I'm ever so careful now about me socks, I hardly ever make a hole in the heel, and . . .'

Grandad was sitting at the head of the table reading a farming journal and eating a round of bread and cheese with a pickled onion. He did not care for pancakes. Now he looked at Lucy over the top of his pince nez and shook his head sadly. 'You'd sooner plant an acre of spuds than darn one,' he said placidly. 'I've said it before and I'll say it again – you should have been a lad, Lucy Murphy.'

'There's a hole in your fawn socks and a rent in your

checkered pinafore,' Maeve said inexorably, ignoring her father's words. 'Might as well get it over, alanna, but first we'll wash up if you've done pushing that pancake round your plate.'

'I'll eat it, I'll eat it,' Lucy squeaked, gobbling pancake. She cleared her plate and pushed it away, then slid her chair back. 'Come on, then, let's get on with the washing up.'

'There's something up with that young lady,' Maeve said to her father when Lucy had done her tasks to the best of her ability – a cobbled up sock and a torn apron now boasted her huge, untidy stitches – and gone off up to bed. 'Never have I known her so vague, nor so willing to go to her bed. No doubt we'll hear her raisin' the echoes presently, bawlin' out to Caitlin how misunderstood she is.' Maeve put her own sewing down in her lap and rubbed at her tired eyes. 'She'll need a new school skirt come the autumn, she's growing so fast. I'll go into Caher tomorrow, see if I can pick up some material, cheap.' She glanced sideways at her father, smoking his pipe now and gazing reflectively at the empty fireplace, for in summer they no longer lit the fire even in the late evening. 'I wouldn't mind catching the train up to Dublin for a nice day out, and there'll be material cheaper there than I can get in Caher. The child might enjoy it, too. I could ask Mrs Kelly if I could take Caitlin along.'

The farmhouse was old, its walls a foot thick, its ceilings substantial, but because it was a warm evening the parlour window was flung wide and the door leading into the hall was open, too, letting the gentle evening breeze freshen the rather stuffy room. Through the window they heard Lucy's window shoot open.

'Caitliiiiiiin!'

'Oh dear God preserve us, here they go,' Padraig Murphy said resignedly, but there was a twinkle in his eye nevertheless: 'One of these days that voice'll crack every pane of glass in the house so it will.'

'I'm here, Luuuuuuuucy!'

'I'm rare tired, Cait. Goodniiiiiiiight.'

'Oh but Lucy, we've not . . .'

Crash. The firm closing of Lucy's window was only just short of a slam. Padraig looked across at Maeve and raised his grizzled brows. 'A row have they had, Maeve? Never have I heard the whores' chorus come to a more abrupt end!'

'Hush Dad, you mustn't talk like that,' Maeve admonished. 'Now I wonder what's up with those young devils tonight? I *knew* something had upset Lucy earlier, when she wasn't eating her tea. I wonder, should I go up?'

Padraig yawned, stretched, and tapped his pipe out on the empty fire grate. 'It's time we both went up, but not to interfere with the childer,' he said decisively. 'If they've had a fight they'll make up, if the child's ill we shall fetch the doctor in the morning. But right now, Maeveen, you and I need all the sleep we can get, for tomorrow, all being well, we've got those young heifers to drive down to the market.'

Lucy thought it would never get dark, or not dark enough, and then she thought Grandad and Maeve would never douse the lamp and come up to bed. And then, of course, after her vigorous and exciting day, she began to fear she would simply fall asleep and slumber straight through the night until Maeve woke her for her breakfast next morning.

But she was in luck. She was down the covers with her window closed and her lamp out when her bedroom door creaked open; it was Maeve, looking in on her to give her a goodnight kiss. She tiptoed over to the bed and Lucy felt gentle fingers caress her cheek and then land, featherlight, on her brow for an instant. She thinks I'm maybe not well, Lucy thought, instantly remorseful. She knows me so well, she could read my troubled mind. But with a bit of luck she would put it down to a tiff with Caitlin or a slight stomach upset and go to bed now herself and leave Lucy to sleep whatever it was off till morning.

And she was right, for presently Maeve tiptoed over and opened the window, then left the room, closing the door gently behind her.

Lucy lay very still for what felt like an hour but was probably more like five minutes. Then she jumped out of bed and, with infinite care, opened her door a crack. She could see the line of light from Maeve's lamp shining under her aunt's bedroom door. As soon as the light goes out I'm off, she told herself, reaching her dark coat down off the back of the door and pulling on her fawn socks, complete with cobbled heel where her darning had grown slipshod. It's a mild night, I don't need anything but the coat and me socks and wellingtons – and they're in the kitchen, of course.

But the stairs creaked, and Maeve would probably take a few minutes to actually go off to sleep. Maeve had told her so many times about how she had woken in the middle of the night and just kind of known that little Evie, Lucy's mother, had been downstairs, preparing to leave the farm. Suppose such second sight leapt into being again tonight and Maeve turned up just as Lucy was halfway down the stairs, or worse, tiptoeing across to the barn? She'd be mad as fire, Lucy thought fearfully, just as Maeve put out her lamp and, judging by the sighs and creaks, settled down in her bed. Oh mercy, what'll I say if she catches me outside in me nightie, jabbering away to a tinker, when she's always telling me how they kidnap little girls and take them away to work for them?

The thought was almost enough to have her climbing back into bed and pulling the covers up over her ears. Almost, but not quite. As it was she tiptoed down the stairs, light as a feather and almost without breathing, and into the kitchen.

It was dark in here, but it smelled nice. Maeve's baking, the pancakes, even the lemon which had been used to flavour them, were all still here, in the warmed kitchen air. And there stood her boots, like a couple of soldiers on parade, right by the back door.

Lucy put the boots on – she was already wearing her coat and socks – and gently turned the key in the back door lock. It squeaked, but only as a mouse might squeak; even to Lucy's senses, heightened by fear, the squeak was a small one. Then the door was unlocked, she turned the knob and opened it and there was the yard, bathed in moonlight, with that air of other-worldliness which comes over any familiar place seen in unfamiliar circumstances.

Out I go, Lucy said to herself, remaining frozen to the spot. Out I go and across the yard and into the comforting shadows of the big barn. I'm not scared, I know who's waiting for me there . . . I'm fourteen and a half years old, almost a woman grown, I'm sensible and I'm good at me schoolwork and I love writing essays and the history of me country and – and I'm scared witless and I don't think I'll walk out into all that enchantment and danger and excitement, I think I'll go back to bed instead, the same as Maeve would want me to do if she knew about all this.

But . . . that would mean letting Finn down. I don't know him, not properly, Lucy argued to herself, all I do know is that he's a tinker and tinkers do dreadful things to little girls, they steal them away and make them work in big houses in Dublin and pinch their bottoms to make them scrub faster. This was the nearest Maeve had ever got to explaining that there were men in the world who exploited young girls for their own ends but it was quite enough to put Lucy off – she thought that having a man pinch your bottom without so much as a by-your-leave was quite the most horrible thing which could happen to a girl, and did not intend that it should happen to her if she could possibly prevent it.

Therefore, her sensible mind told her now, you don't go out to a black-shadowed barn through enchanted silvery moonlight, because that's how they get you. For all you know Finn may be false, she told her shivering, cowardly self, he may have a whole band of tinkers waiting in that barn to carry you off to Dublin, shut you in a blackbeetle-ridden kitchen and pinch your bottom until you've peeled a ton or two of potatoes and scrubbed several miles of filthy floor.

So right then and there, whilst her whole body was shouting at her to turn back, relock the door and make for her warm, safe bed, Lucy marched – but quietly – out of the kitchen, leaving the door gaping open behind her though in case she needed a quick retreat, and across the moonlit yard. She did not know that the moonlight silvered her hair and made her skin shine with a soft pearly glow, or that the moon-shadows made her eyes look huge, enhanced the small curves of her budding breasts beneath her nightgown, turned her, for that short walk, into the woman she would one day become.

But the watcher knew. He saw her coming steadily across the yard, saw the dog in its kennel glance up, then lie down again, secure in the knowledge that his little mistress was in command of the situation.

Lucy came on steadily, then slid into the shadowy barn and there was Finn, smiling at her, taking both her hands in his warm, safe clasp.

'And aren't you a fine, brave girl?' he said softly, and

the touch of his hand excited her less than the warm commendation in his voice. 'Oh little Luceen, I'm glad you weren't scared that the tinker meant you harm, for I swear by Jesus and Mary and by all the holy saints that I wouldn't hurt a hair of your head, nor let anyone else do so. Will you come up with me, into the hay?'

With his hand in hers, all her hesitations and doubts were lost. She nodded and followed him closely as he loped across the barn floor and began to climb the short wooden ladder which led to the hayloft. He was neat and quick, she no less so, and a moment later he made a nest in the hay, using his body, then held out his hands to her.

'Sit down, alanna; then we can talk.'

Afterwards, Lucy could not remember much of what they had talked about; she could remember far more easily the feel of his hand in hers, the smell of his skin, the way he would give a sudden crack of laughter, hastily muffled, over something she said.

At one point they talked about Granny Mogg and he told her he was going away, probably for as long as a month, and would be obliged if she would keep an eye on the old 'un.

'Her mind isn't always her own,' he said carefully. 'Most of the time she's great, but then something seems to slip in her head and she's – she's not so good. But if you can take her a bit of bread and cheese, some milk, make sure she drinks each day, then she ought to be all right until I get back.'

'Where are you going?' Lucy asked. She stroked his arm very gently, as one might stroke a wild cat who might run at your touch. 'Is it far? Can I get in touch with you, Finn?'

'I'm going fishing, then I'll join in the harvest of some crop or other,' Finn said. 'I don't know where I'll be though – anywhere I can get work, I guess.'

'And you'll come back?'

He laughed, then caught at the hand which was stroking his arm and kissed the palm, his lips warm and somehow intimate against her skin, the small gesture sending odd shivers down her spine.

'Of course I'll come back, little eejit,' he teased. 'Would I leave Granny Mogg to your tender mercies? Or you to hers, for the matter of that? I'll come back with me pockets bulgin' with good t'ings, and a host of stories and tales.'

'Good,' Lucy said. She was getting tired but had no desire whatsoever to leave her nest in the hay. She leaned her head against Finn's shoulder. 'I do love a story, Finn. Shall you tell me one now?'

'If I do you'll go to sleep and then where will we be?' Finn said. But he looped an arm round her shoulders and drew her close. 'What tale would you like, then? A story of witches and wizards in old Ireland, or leprechauns and the fairy folk? Or shall I tell you about me travels with the Tuam tribe, before I met up with Vorth and his band?'

'Tell me about your travels,' Lucy begged sleepily. 'I'd love to hear where you've been and what you've done, Finn.'

Finn knew himself to be a fine story-teller and began in time honoured fashion with 'Once upon a time . . .' but he had barely got to the bit where he rode his first horse and got thrown into his first gorse bush when he felt an extra heaviness in the head leaning on his shoulder and glanced down at her, tenderness mixing with something wild and sweet which he had never felt before.

She slept, trusting him totally. And she's right so to do, Finn told himself, for no safer could she ever be than she is this night. Ah, but this girleen will be safe with me for the rest of her life – and special to me, also. One of these days, Lucy Murphy, you'll be all mine, but until that day dawns, I'll not touch a hair of your head, and nor shall any man.

He woke her when the stars were beginning to pale in the sky and Lucy, alarmed, sat up in the rustling hay and apologised for falling asleep and promised, in a flurried whisper, that she would see the old 'un lacked for nothing.

'If she's ill, I'll get Maeve to her, and a doctor,' she hissed. 'But only if she's rare bad, Finn. You – you won't be away longer than a month, will you? I'll miss you sore.'

She saw his teeth flash in the dark as he grinned down at her.

'You scarcely know me, alanna! But I'll miss you more than ever you could miss me. Now you'd best get back to your bed before day dawns. I'll help you down the ladder.'

He scrambled down ahead of her, then turned, hands held out. 'Jump!'

She jumped; he caught her, held her for one breathless moment against his heart before putting her away from him and then, with a suddenness which startled them both, snatching her back and dropping three kisses on her upturned face – one on her brow, one on the tip of her nose, the last on her chin. Featherlight kisses they were, almost casual, almost teasing . . . so why did the touch of his lips burn on her skin for what was left of the night?

'Off you run now, alanna. I'll see you again as soon as I can get my business done.'

He took her to the barn doorway and from its shadows they surveyed the house. All was in darkness, the kitchen door gaped open still, the room behind it black.

They crossed the yard like a couple of shadows and Lucy slipped into the kitchen. She glanced around and was at once reassured: no one had stirred, everything was as she left it.

Finn must have been able to tell that the tension had left her, for he gave her hand a quick squeeze and turned away.

'Goodbye for now, Lucy. Take care, and – and don't forget me.'

'I never could,' Lucy whispered vehemently. 'Oh, Finn, I never could forget you! I like you better than anyone else I know.'

He was gliding away from her when the dog in the kennel looked up again, his muzzle turning from Lucy to Finn and back as though questioning whether he should not, perhaps, bark a bit at this stranger?

'Friend, Shep,' Lucy whispered. 'Best friend, dearest friend. Don't you bark, Shep, or I'll give you a clout, so I will.' And she stood in the doorway and waved until Finn was out of sight and the pre-dawn dark was still again, save for the wind stirring the leaves on the tall old elms and the scuttle of a mouse behind the corn bins.

Only then did she turn and make her way back, undetected, to her cold little bed.

Chapter Six

At first, when the money stopped coming, Linnet thought it was just that her mother hadn't remembered, or had had a bad few weeks. Then she thought it must be the post, notoriously unreliable for a long distance letter. She was sure, of course, that Evie would not let her down and besides, she had her savings; so for the first few weeks she continued to pay the rent and keep herself from the money she had salted away during the pantomime season when she had taken in two chorus girls as lodgers. Mrs Roberts had not liked it, but Linnet had given her some of her rent and the landlady had taken the money, though not with a very good grace.

'I'll 'old you responsible if there's any trouble from them gairls,' she had said. 'And tell 'em no fellers or they'll be out on their ears before you can blink.'

So Linnet, though worried by Evie's apparent defection, had at least been able to support herself for the first month, though she had confided to Roddy that her money would not last for ever.

'If only me mam would write,' she said miserably. 'Then at least I'd know what had gone wrong for her.'

'You're fifteen years old, our Linnie,' Roddy reminded her. 'Most gals are workin' be the time they're your age. Perhaps your mam just got fed up wi' feedin' a chick which oughter 'ave flown the bleedin' nest months agone!'

'She knows I'd work if she wanted me to, only she said to stay on at school until she give the word,' Linnet reminded her friend. 'Mammy wouldn't just forget all about me, even though she's been doing awful well – she says so, in her letters. No, something's gone wrong, I can feel it in my heart.'

She clasped her hands to her chest and Roddy jeered at such a theatrical gesture and got a clout round the ear for his cheek.

'You don't know nothing, Roddy Sullivan,' Linnet shouted at him. 'My mammy says education is terrible important – I don't want to work in a match factory and come home all yellow-faced like your Auntie Prue, nor do I want to get all filthy and bloody like you get when you help in that butcher's shop! Mammy will write to me soon, just you see!'

Roddy never got cross with her because he understood that she was upset and worried, but he did scowl. 'You needn't come near me when I've been workin' if you're so high and mighty,' he muttered. 'You're glad enough of a loan of the spondooleys, though.'

It was true that Roddy had lent her money for her various needs when he had the cash to spare and Linnet immediately felt guilty. 'I'm sorry, that was a horrible thing to say,' she said remorsefully. 'Oh, Roddy, if only she'd write!'

But the truth of the matter was that Evie's letters had speedily degenerated from chatty epistles to a couple of lines, and that in the first six months of her absence, too. So now, after nearly two years, Linnet did not expect much in the way of news or information – but she did expect the money.

When the letter came at last, whilst Mrs Roberts was muttering darkly about the selfishness of theatricals, as she called them, in not paying her rent for two months, Linnet was so relieved that she couldn't even open it for a minute. She just held it in her hands and breathed deeply and thanked God, as well as little Evie, that she was about to receive proof that she'd not been forgotten, after all. The writing on the envelope did not look much like Evie's bold and confident hand, but it was her writing, nevertheless. Rosy with relief and anticipation, Linnet opened the letter. And it was just a letter, there was no money, not so much as a penny piece. But the letter would explain, Linnet knew that, so she had best read it immediately.

Dear Linnet, it said in a spidery hand which Linnet could scarcely recognise as her mother's. *I have been very ill and unable to earn money, which is why I'm afraid you've had to go short. I don't know when I shall be able to return to the stage, so I want you to go back to Ireland, to your Auntie Maeve, and ask her to take care of you for me until I'm well again. Don't think too harshly of me, alanna, Mammy.*

Linnet stared down at the blotched page and the thin, wobbly writing. Little Evie must have been very ill indeed to write so for the nicest piece of the letter was missing, the bit where Evie always said, *With much love from your very own Mammy.* And how could Evie expect her daughter to go back to Ireland? Linnet knew her aunt's name was Maeve Murphy and she knew Evie had gone to school in the town of Cahersiveen, but she did not know the name of the farm, nor whereabouts in Ireland Cahersiveen might be . . . and she had no money now, not so much as a penny piece. She could scarcely buy a tram ticket to the docks, far less her passage to Ireland!

She stood in her mother's neat living room whilst black despair washed over her. What on earth was she to do? The month was June, which meant that the next pantomime season was six months away and in any event, though the money her lodgers paid her was a help, it could scarcely keep her and pay the rent, too. Right now she had no money at all, no prospect of money from what her mother said, and no idea what to do next. But one thing she did know – she must run round to Roddy at once and tell him what had happened. She thought now, going back over his attitude these past couple of weeks, that he would not be entirely surprised to hear that little Evie was penniless and far from sending the rent, was actually advising her daughter to go back to Ireland. But Roddy was a realist. He would see at once that this was impossible and would suggest an alternative means of keeping body and soul together. Roddy was resourceful and intelligent, he would advise her on her best course of action.

It was a Saturday morning which meant no school, but when Linnet ran down the stairs, Mrs Roberts popped out of her own quarters.

'When can I 'ave me rent?' she said belligerently. 'Or weren't there no money? It were a skinny sort o' letter, weren't it?'

'The money's following,' Linnet said quickly. 'I've got to go out now, Mrs Roberts, I'm fetching the shopping for Roddy's mam.'

Mrs Roberts started to say something but Linnet just ignored her, flying down the hall and out of the door, turning at once in the direction of Peel Square. She had crammed the letter into the pocket of her jacket and it burned there like a guilty conscience. What on earth was she to do? Even nice Mrs Sullivan had mentioned mildly that times was 'ard and she didn't like to grumble but feedin' one extra every day . . .

Roddy was coming out of the square just as Linnet rounded the corner at a gallop. She must have looked pretty desperate because he stopped short and put a soothing hand on her arm.

'Wharrever's the marrer, chuck? Come on, tell your pal.'

'Mam's written; she's not got any money,' Linnet gabbled, clutching Roddy's hand. 'She says to go back to Ireland, but I can't do that, our Roddy! I dunno where me mam's sisters live, I only know the name of the town, and I haven't got any money at all, honest to God. Oh, Roddy, you should see her writing – she must be real bad, real ill.'

'Show me later,' Roddy said when Linnet tried to press the crumpled page into his hand. 'I've gorra deliver this lot.'

For the first time Linnet realised that her friend was wearing a long blue-and-white striped apron and carrying what looked like a very heavy basket.

'Oh, you're working; I'm sorry,' she said humbly. 'Can I help, Roddy? Only I can't go back to old Ma Roberts, she'll say things . . . I've got to think.'

'You can walk along o' me and tek some o' the parcels into the 'ouses,' Roddy said. 'We're goin' right along to Tenterden Street for the next delivery though, so you'll 'ave plenty of time to talk. Tell you what, you'd best read me the letter as we go.'

This seemed like a good idea so as they plodded along – for the basket was heavy – Linnet read the pitifully brief letter aloud and then looked hopefully at Roddy.

'Well? What d'you think? Will some money come, Roddy?'

Roddy began to shrug, hesitated, then shook his head. 'It's no good lyin' to you, chuck. I reckon your mam's real ill an' I don't see 'ow she can earn if she's ill. You've gorra give up any idea of help from that quarter; you've gorra get yourself out o' this mess.'

'How?' Linnet said bluntly. 'I can't think straight!'

'We'll sell some o' that posh furniture, for a start off,' Roddy said, changing his basket to the other arm. 'You'd gerra pretty penny for that walnut pianny, and there's the oil paintin' over the mantel; that oughter make a bit.'

'I can't take furniture without Mrs Roberts finding out,' Linnet pointed out, trying very hard not to let Roddy see that she was crying. The letter for which she had longed had turned out to be the final straw. She felt completely at the end of her tether and incapable, any longer, of being brave. 'If she finds out there's no money coming then she'll kick me out and take everything for herself.'

'Yeah, I can see that,' Roddy said thoughtfully. 'Wharrabout smaller stuff, though? Some of them ornaments is worth a mint, we'll run 'em down to Uncle's, see what 'e'll cough up.'

'Yes, we could do that,' Linnet said rather reluctantly. She had visited T J Cookson, the pawnbroker on Scotland Road, more than once, accompanying Roddy when he took his mam's hat and his own Sunday suit in on a Monday morning, and thought it an odd way of getting money, particularly as it had to be paid back in time for church so the clothing could be worn once more for Sunday services. 'Some of the little china things are valuable, Mammy said so. But that won't pay everything, you know. There's the rent and what I owe your mam, and soon it'll be school fees . . .'

Roddy looked at her, then stood his basket down alongside the plate glass window of a flower shop with beautiful carnations, roses and lilies pressing close to the glass and buckets full of blooms on either side of the doorway. 'John Tart, Florist', ran the legend over the door, and Linnet sniffed appreciatively as the most wonderful scent came to them from the lavish array of blooms. But Roddy seemed indifferent to their beauty. He took hold of both Linnet's hands and shook them to emphasise his words.

'You've gorra gerra job,' he said forcefully. 'The

money your mam sent covered your school fees, your rent an' your food, but now it's stopped. So you'll 'ave to leave school, chuck. I left school long ago, our Linnie, an' most of me class did the same. You've gorra be practical, gel, you'll 'ave to work.'

'Yes . . . but what can I *do*?' Linnet said, her voice rising to a wail. 'It's awful hard to get a job unless you're trained, and the nuns don't teach you how to be a shop girl or a factory hand. And those are the only jobs I know!'

'You're pretty, clever and well-dressed,' Roddy said, rubbing a dirty hand across his sweaty face. 'You'll gerra job awright, chuck. But I dunno whether it'll run to payin' Mrs Roberts' rent, 'cos she charges your mam a deal o' money, from what you've said. I think you'll have to move, Linnie.'

Linnet stared. 'Move? But what about all me mammy's lovely things?'

'You'll be eatin' them,' Roddy said. 'Linnet Murphy, you've lived amongst us for the past two or three years an' you still 'aven't learned, 'ave you? Folk like us can't afford pretty china wozzits an' nice furniture. Think on, our Linnie.'

Linnet thought. Mrs Sullivan was grand, she worked very hard for her kids and her husband worked hard, too, when he could get the work, that was. But they had almost no furniture save for the big kitchen table and some broken-down chairs, they slept on straw mattresses on the floor, and with six kids to feed Mrs Sullivan thought herself lucky to have fuel for the fire – it never occurred to her that a mantelshelf might have contained ornaments or a clock, so long as there was a bit of coal and some kindling sticks she was well satisfied.

Thinking back now, Linnet remembered that when she'd first known the Sullivans Roddy's mother had worked for Blackledge's, the baker on Derby Road, and

Roddy's father had been at sea. But then he'd had an accident – he'd been below, fastening a couple of loose barrels during a storm when a whole ruck of them had broken loose and crushed both his legs. Now he walked oddly, a bit like one of the little yellowy crabs which lurked in the thick, smooth black mud down by the Pier Head, and they wouldn't let him go to sea any more. Instead, he did bits and pieces of work when he could get someone to employ him, and for the rest they survived on what the kids and Mrs Sullivan could earn and on what Linnet's mother paid for her keep during the school holidays.

'Have you thought, queen?'

That was Roddy, massaging the arm which had been carrying the basket, looking thoughtfully into the window behind them with its brilliant and tempting display of something which, surely, few of the shoppers thronging the street could possibly afford to buy? Flowers, Linnet found herself thinking defensively, are even more useless than china – you can't eat them and you can't look at them for long, either, because they die. Was that why Roddy had chosen to stop outside the florist's, to prove something? But if so, she was no nearer understanding, not really. Except that she was a bit like one of those roses or lilies herself – she didn't work, she just looked pretty, and what good was that when the odds were against her? Precious little, it seemed. And poor Mrs Sullivan had scarcely said anything when Linnet had mumbled that the money still hadn't come, she'd gone on feeding one extra. I've been horribly selfish, Linnet thought humbly, but all that's over. I'll do just what Roddy says and at least I'll be able to pay his mam for all the food I've eaten these past couple of months. She turned to Roddy.

'Yes, I've thought. What I'll do, I'll sell some of the little things and pay the last month's rent and your mam as soon as I get enough money. Then I'll sell something like a picture, or that small green velvet chair, and look round for somewhere cheaper.' She hesitated. 'I suppose your mam wouldn't like a lodger, Roddy?'

'She'd like one, but where'd we put you?' Roddy said with all his usual frankness. 'There's too many of us crammed into the 'ouse already and you wouldn't want four inches o' straw mattress an' young Freddy an' little Toddy breathin' into your face all night, would you? 'Cos Mam wouldn't want you sharin' wi' us big lads!'

'There wouldn't be room, not with the four of you all fighting for space,' Linnet said. The thought had given her her first smile that morning and now she seized the handle of the big, heavy basket. 'All right, now let's get this lot delivered, then I'll go home and start taking stuff out – are you sure Uncle's the best one to go to, though?'

'If you think your mam might want to buy the stuff back one day a pawnbroker's the only place what'll hang onto it for 'er,' Roddy said, taking the basket firmly away from her. 'Just keep your tickets somewhere safe. But if you think your mam will just buy new, then you'd get a better price, I guess, from a shop what sells such things. We'll go round and ask when I've done me deliveries. Now let's 'urry, queen, or I'll get into trouble for bein' too late for their Sat'day dinner.'

The plan worked well for the first week. It might have gone on working well, too, but for one of those wretched, silly little accidents which can happen to anyone. Linnet discovered a kind man in a shop on Church Street, a very smart area of the city, who remembered little Evie and was happy to give her daughter a fair price for ornaments which had been lovingly dusted daily and washed in soap and warm water weekly, so that they looked as good as new.

Linnet took sufficient to pay Mrs Roberts the rent owed, pretending to have received a letter whilst her landlady was otherwise engaged. She sold a few more china shepherdesses, goose girls and a child with an apron full of chicks and paid Mrs Sullivan, too. And then she decided to take the picture next.

There were lots of pictures, but the one over the mantelpiece, with its rich, dark colours and the elaborate gilded frame, seemed likeliest to raise a decent sum, so Linnet waited until the Robertses were eating their midday dinner and then stole carefully down the stairs, with the picture none too well concealed in the folds of her winter coat. And halfway down the flight, the door to the basement where the Robertses lived shot open and Mrs Roberts emerged into the small, dark hallway, saying at the top of her voice that she'd heard that dratted boy rattlin' on the front door again and she'd give him sauce.

Linnet dropped the picture. Mrs Roberts looked up. There was a moment of ghastly silence before Linnet said, 'I'm taking it to be cleaned, I do hope dropping it didn't do much damage. You startled me, Mrs Roberts.'

Mrs Roberts said nothing. She simply stared very hard at the picture, and then at Linnet, whilst you could almost see the rusty wheels inside her head start to whirr until the answer she sought finally clicked into place.

'I . . . see . . .' she said at last, in a menacing sort of voice. 'Ho, yes, I see indeed!'

Linnet shot down the rest of the stairs, across the hall and out of the door but as she told Roddy later, she feared she'd given the game away. Now the old girl would be watching her all the time.

But she was wrong. Mrs Roberts did not bother to watch her at all. When Linnet got back that night, rather later than usual in the hope of not having to explain anything to Mrs Roberts, she found the lock on her door had been changed. She tried her key again and again, but it would not turn. Finally she had no choice but to go downstairs and confront Mrs Roberts.

'You was goin' to do a moonlight, owin' me a small fortune in unpaid rent,' Mrs Roberts said coldly, her mean eyes gleaming in the gaslight. 'So I've took your stuff in lieu of rent and you're out, madam. Don't you come botherin' me again or I'll 'ave the scuffers round 'ere before you can say knife.'

'But I paid your rent, every penny,' Linnet said indignantly. 'The furniture in the flat belongs to me mam and to me, too. You can't take it, that's stealing!'

At the mention of stealing, Mrs Roberts' face went a dark and ugly shade of red and she shot out a hand, gripped Linnet's shoulder, and shook her vigorously. 'That's done it! I might 'ave felt sorry for you before, let you 'ave a bed for the night, but not any more, not now you've accused me of stealin' your stuff when it's mine by right. Gerrout of this place, you saucy little bleeder, an' don't you never come back no more!'

'I'm going to the police station in the morning,' Linnet said when she went round to Peel Square to tell Roddy and give him a hand with his deliveries. Roddy's job was badly paid but at least the money was regular and Roddy was delighted to be a wage-earner, though it cut down his time with Linnet. 'I'll tell them what's happened and they'll put Mrs Roberts in prison, I'm sure they will.'

'Ye-es . . . but suppose they put you in one of them orphan asylums?' Roddy said uneasily. 'Or even the work-'ouse, chuck? You wouldn't want that, would you?'

'You can kip down on our kitchen floor if you can gerra blanket from the market,' Mrs Sullivan said. 'Just till you get somewhere of your own, like. I'll come wi' you to the cop-shop tomorrow, 'ow's that?'

Linnet was delighted and, the next day, trotted down to the police station beside Mrs Sullivan feeling that at last she was to be vindicated. The policeman was a fatherly man who listened seriously to her story, wrote in his little notebook, and promised her that they would all visit Mrs Roberts together, right now, and find out just what she was playing at.

'When I see you at teatime we'll have sorted it all out, and I'll have me mam's stuff, if not the flat,' Linnet told Roddy joyously. 'I can't wait to see her face.'

Over the teatable, Linnet gnawed on her disappointment like a dog with a bone, scarcely able to eat for her rage against Mrs Roberts.

'She'd cleared the whole place,' she said furiously, whilst the Sullivans listened and ate boiled spuds and scrag end of mutton. Mrs Sullivan, almost as upset as Linnet, was in the kitchen, boiling the kettle for a fresh pot of tea. 'Not a single ornament was left, not a carpet, not a rag of curtain. The sergeant was ever so nice, too, I never knew a scuffer could be so kind. But there weren't anything he could do, only say he was sorry to me and warn Mrs Roberts that if she'd lied to him she'd find herself in big trouble.'

'What did she say, Linnie?' little Freddy piped up, taking a pull at his weak tea and then putting his mug down on the table with a bang. 'She must ha' telled lies, o' course.'

'She did,' Linnet said heavily, fighting back tears. She toyed with the food on her plate, pushing a boiled potato round and round until it collapsed into the gravy. 'She said I'd sold everything in the flat meself and that and she'd got proof . . . she'd found a couple of receipts or whatever they call them under the clock. The sergeant said sure I'd sold a few ornaments, and hadn't I already told him so indeed? And then she produced a receipt for the chair to prove I'd sold it as well as all the other things. She'd only got a bob for it – a bob for me mam's lovely antique chair – and she'd sold it to the little feller in Paddy's market, a black-hearted little bugger the sergeant called him. She said he'd swear he'd bought it from a small, fair-haired girl and the sergeant said Finkel – that's his name, Jeremiah Finkel – would swear black was white if someone paid him, and Mrs Roberts said she wasn't the only one who wanted to watch what they said and that there was a law of libel whether you was a scuffer or just a poor woman trying to make ends meet. Honest to God, I do hate that old woman!'

'So you should,' Roddy said, but he didn't look anywhere near as miserable as Linnet felt. 'So tomorrer, queen, we'll go lookin' for a job for you, right? For tonight you can lend me blanket, it's a warm night, I'll be awright with me coat.'

'She sold all me clothes, too,' Linnet said broodingly. 'Oh, I'll get back on her one of these days, you see if I don't.' She turned to Roddy. 'Your mam's the best person in the world, next to me own mam,' she said. 'That scuffer really liked her, he said she had a heart of gold and I was all right whilst I had Janice on my side. And he give me two lovely thick blankets and another pair of shoes, so at least I'll look respectable enough when I try the shops for work tomorrow.'

'Letter for you, Maeve,' Lucy said, coming into the kitchen and throwing the envelope down on the table. She and Grandad had been taking the milk churns down to the gate for the lorry to collect and she had spotted the postman coming up the lane just as her grandfather had turned the cart round to return to the farm. 'It's probably from *her*; it's a foreign stamp, anyroad.'

'If you mean your mother, you should say so,' Maeve

said mildly, but Lucy didn't bother to answer. What sort of a mother just went off, taking your sister and turning you into an only child, and then scarcely ever wrote? 'No, it isn't from Evie, it's . . .'

'What's the matter, girl?' Grandad said, pausing with a forkful of bacon halfway to his mouth. 'What's happened?'

Maeve looked up at him but Lucy did not think she saw either the old man or indeed the farm kitchen, for her eyes had a dazed, faraway look. But she suddenly gave herself a little shake and spoke.

'Oh, Daddy, it's from a feller in New York – our little Evie . . . she died ten days ago. He – the feller – didn't ever know her, he says, but he took her room over after she – she left, and found a letter for me and guessed we'd not been told. He's enclosed the letter, if you can call it that – it's just a couple of lines. All she says is: *Maeve, love, take care of Linnet, I've been a bad mammy to her* . . .' Maeve's voice broke and she laid the sheets of paper carefully down on the kitchen table and turned her face away from them, looking out across the yard.

'Evie, dead? But she was the youngest of you . . . there must be some mistake, you say the feller didn't know her . . . we must bring her home, Maeve, she can't stay out there! I'd go meself, though I'd be no use, no use at all, but at least we've got the money so's you can go for me, alanna. At least we've got money in the bank.'

Maeve nodded, swallowed, then turned back to the table. 'And there's the child, Linnet, alone in New York . . . you're right, Daddy, I must go to her. I'll fetch Clodagh back before I leave, though, to keep house whilst I'm gone – she has no children, she could manage it – and for the rest, you've grand, reliable workers who'll give an eye to things if you need them.' Maeve turned to Lucy. 'You'll be a good girl whilst I'm gone, Lu? You'll help

Auntie Clo in the house and do your usual work on the farm, won't you? And think how nice it will be for you, to have your sister living back here again.'

'I don't know her,' Lucy said slowly. 'Is she nice? I wish I could come with you, Maeve, and see New York for meself, but of course I'll take care of Grandad for you,' she smiled across at her grandfather. 'We'll take care of each other, won't we, Gramps?'

'We will so,' her grandfather said. 'As for nice – are you not nice yourself, Luceen?'

'People change,' Lucy said quietly, but she said it beneath her breath. She found that she had no desire for an unknown sister to turn up here to boss her about and tell her what she should and should not do – older sisters always bossed you about, she had heard the girls at school say so many a time – and she could not squeeze out a tear for a mother who had abandoned her when she was only a couple of months old. 'When will you leave, Maeve?'

'As soon as I can buy me ticket,' Maeve said distractedly. 'Oh my poor darling, to die so far from home!' She jumped to her feet on the words and ran out of the kitchen and when Lucy would have followed, Grandad caught her arm and held her back.

'You didn't know your mammy, child,' he said gruffly. 'And no doubt you feel you have a good reason not to love her. But Evie was a sweet girl once, and it's that Evie that Maeve and I are after remembering. You must respect our tears, alanna.'

And Lucy, turning to throw her arms round the old man's neck, saw that he was indeed weeping.

In her bed that night, Maeve planned her journey. She would go across to Liverpool and catch a ship to New York from there. She thanked God that there was money saved which could be spared both for the journey and for her keep whilst she was in America. The farm was doing well, her father was a shrewd judge of what would sell and what would not. And her sisters were good, they would take it in turns to keep an eye on the farm and on the child, too.

It was a long way, though, especially for someone who had never left Ireland before. But Maeve had seen too many friends and relatives go off to America – and come back, too – to worry unduly about the journey. It took a couple of weeks, but modern ships were comfortable, the crews kind to bewildered passengers. And when you got there, sure and didn't you meet nearly as many Irish as you did in Ireland, now? Evie had gone when she was a good deal younger than Maeve – so had Maeve's old school friend, a couple of cousins and Maeve's Aunt Maria.

It would have been nice to take Lucy, though, Maeve thought rather wistfully, heaving the sheet up over her shoulders. Nice for Linnet to meet her sister at last, nice for Maeve herself to have the company. But no point in even considering it. Lucy was doing well at school, she was useful on the farm, sensible and helpful. Padraig would do very well with Lucy and with one of his other daughters to keep an eye on things, and the twins would meet up again soon enough, for Maeve was determined to bring Linnet back with her. She hugged herself at the thought of that other fifteen-year-old, waiting in New York, about to get the surprise of her life when her Auntie Maeve turned up to rescue her.

And still smiling at the thought, Maeve fell asleep at last.

'Are you well, Granny Mogg? A pity it is that Finn's gone off to the fishing, because I've news for you both. Me mam, the one I telled you about, has died in America and Maeve's gone off to New York to bring me sister back here to live. Now, what d'you think of that?'

Granny Mogg was sitting in the evening sunshine with a bowl in her lap, gutting fish. Lucy had set her up a line and if she felt in the mood she would pull the line in, detach any fish they had caught from it, and bring them back to the sod hut to be prepared for her evening meal. Now she smiled very sweetly at Lucy and beckoned her over.

'Did you bring me bread an' milk, so? Oh, I do love me bread an' milk warmed over me fire before I go to me bed. What's that you say?'

Lucy squatted down beside her and produced half a loaf and a covered jug full of milk. Maeve had found out about Granny Mogg a long while ago but Maeve was kind and generous; she simply gave the girls food for the old lady and sometimes a soft shawl she did not need, or a blanket, and let them get on with it. So Granny Mogg thought herself undiscovered and was happier so.

Lucy had never once regretted her decision to take on the responsibility for seeing to Granny Mogg . It meant that she saw Finn whenever he could spare time from earning a living to come and see Granny, and as the old woman grew stronger with the good food which Lucy and Caitlin brought over to her so she grew stronger in her mind, too. She told the girls stories of her life with the tinkers, of her love for her husband who had died . . . oh, a lifetime ago . . . and older stories, too, folk tales, legends, stories of the days when dragons roamed the hills of Ireland and knights on horseback fought and conquered them, drove them away from the enchanted hills.

'I said my mammy has died in New York and Maeve, who has been like a mother to me all me life, has gone off to bring home a sister of mine called Linnet, to keep me company,' Lucy repeated. 'Maeve thinks I should be glad, but divil a bit o' gladness can I find in me heart. Mammy took her and left me, why should I be glad she's coming home?'

Granny Mogg considered the question for a moment, head cocked, bright eyes fixed on infinity. Then she put the fish down beside her and heaved herself to her feet. 'I'll take a look,' she muttered. 'Fetch me water, girl, dear.'

'Bossy, bossy, bossy,' Lucy said, smiling. 'Do this, do that – what do I want with a sister when I've a Granny Mogg always on at me?' But she picked up the old bucket and went down to the creek and half-filled it, brought it back to where Granny sat outside the sod hut, and poured it with great care into what Granny called her 'seeing bowl', though Lucy knew perfectly well that it was only a fat glass jar with well-rounded sides and a narrow opening at the top. When it was full she put it down carefully on the grass near the old woman and sat back. She was a complete sceptic so far as Granny's second sight was concerned, but she loved watching the old woman going through her ritual, nevertheless. Once, she knew, Granny had told fortunes on the fairs, and she still went through the same mumbo jumbo even though Lucy, this evening, was her only audience.

Granny took off her darned black shawl first and threw it over the sweetie jar. Then she leaned forward and began to sing; she didn't use any words but just sang in a deep, hypnotic, thrumming hum which, Caitlin had once said, sounded right across the marsh on a still evening.

Lucy sat back on her heels and watched. The sun was sinking in the west, casting a glorious red-gold glow over lough and marsh, meadow and mountain, and as Granny removed the shawl with a quite unnecessary flourish Lucy nearly jumped, for the water was blood-red.

But only for a moment. It was the reflection from the sunset, Lucy told herself, leaning forward to see what would happen next. The water in the jar was clear and dancing again so Granny must have moved it. Not that it looked as though it had been moved, so still it lay, but there had to be an explanation for the water seeming red one minute and clear the next, and Lucy was far too sensible to think that there was anything in Granny Mogg's forecasting of the future.

'She died violently,' Granny Mogg said. She sounded surprised, as indeed Lucy would have been had she believed a word of it. 'But she's at peace now. Pretty t'ing, pretty t'ing, she's leavin' all the noise an' fuss behind an' driftin', like the good white mist of autumn, back to the places she loved an' left.'

'Sure she is,' Lucy murmured wickedly. 'Sure and haven't I seen her, comin' over the marsh towards the house, with her head tucked underneath her arm?'

Granny Mogg had closed her eyes and was rocking herself gently backwards and forwards, but at Lucy's words her eyes flew open and she scowled at her companion. 'Shut your gob, young Morphy,' she said, very rudely Lucy thought. 'And listen whiles I tell ye what is to come.'

'Sorry, Granny. I'm listening,' Lucy said contritely. She produced a chunk of bread from one pocket and the bottle of milk from the other and began to crumble the bread into one of the billy cans whilst Granny Mogg continued to regard her jar of water as though it was doing something a lot more interesting than sitting on the grass and reflecting, in miniature, the world of castle, marsh and lough.

'Ah, here it comes,' Granny said at last, when the bread

and milk were ready for warming. 'Give the fire a poke and blow on the ashes, alanna; there's enough heat left in it to warm me bread an' milk.'

Lucy turned to stare at Granny Mogg's fire, which looked like dead ashes but would, she realised, come to life again with a bit of a stir. She found the stick which Granny used as a poker and then blew life into an ember, then another, until the fire burned up brightly once more.

'Give us the billy can, Granny,' she said at length. 'Have you finished with your seeing bowl?'

'Sure an' didn't I say so?' Granny muttered. She tipped the jar sideways and a flood of water poured out, sank in the grass and vanished. 'I've seen, haven't I?'

'I don't know. You just said me mam died violently which . . . which . . .' she decided, quite suddenly, not to say as she had intended, 'which I do not believe for one minute,' partly because it was rude but also, she realised, because she was not sure at all how her mother had died. 'Which is rather upsetting,' she finished instead, feeling a fraud, because she had no feelings one way or t'other, for her mother. 'Have you got a screw of sugar handy?'

Granny Mogg produced a spoonful of sugar in a screw of blue paper and Lucy shook it into the billy can, then stirred it and waited for the bubbles to start. Granny, meanwhile, hunkered down beside her, staring into the blue and gold flames.

'She won't come back,' she remarked at last, as Lucy brought the can off the fire and stood it on the grass to cool. 'Not this time – no, not this time. Poor gel, poor gel.'

'Who, my sister? But Maeve's gone 'specially to bring her back and she can't be more than sixteen or seventeen, a year or so older than me, so I suppose she'll have to do what Maeve says, won't she?'

'Oh aye, she would . . . only your Maeve won't find her,' Granny Mogg said with a quiet certainty which

Lucy found rather unnerving. Honestly, the old woman really believed she could see all sorts, and in an old sweetie jar full of water at that! 'She'll search and search, she'll come closer'n she knows, but she won't find her.'

What nonsense it all is, Lucy told herself, pretending to agree with Granny Mogg that if she saw it in the seeing bowl of course she must be right. When Maeve comes back with my horrid sister with the silly name which isn't a name at all I'll bring her over here and make Granny Mogg eat her words. Not find her indeed, and Maeve as persistent as any old sheep when she sees a hole in the hedge and decides to cram herself through it. I just hope she's not long away, though; Clodagh will drive me mad before the first week's end with her pernickety ways.

Maeve arrived in New York after a long and trying journey, only to find that the theatre, where she had hoped to get news of Evie's child, was inhabited by a touring company who did not even know Evie's name.

'But you can find up the manager; he's not gone with them,' the girl in the box-office drawled when Maeve explained that she only had a limited time in the United States of America and had hoped to accomplish her mission in that time. 'He lives on West 52nd Street – that's on the West Side, near the docks. If you'll hold on here, I'll find up the number for you.'

She did so and Maeve ventured onto the subway system, terrified of the speed at which the trains moved, the black faces amongst the passengers, and the awful sameness of the dead straight streets and their fringes of identical buildings. And it did her no good. The manager was a nice man, eager to help, but although he had a vague recollection of a girl in the chorus who had been called little Evie, he assured Maeve that she had not worked at the theatre for a long, long time.

'And she's dead, you say? Well, I don't like to upset you, Miss Murphy, but hadn't you better look in a burial ground? There are a great number of them, but if you go to the department of . . .'

'My sister left a child, a girl of fifteen,' Maeve said, when the man paused for breath. 'I'll want a copy of my sister's death certificate but I see little point in searching for an unmarked grave. Why, we didn't even know she was ill until a perfect stranger wrote to me to tell me he had taken over her flat after her death and found a letter, half-written, addressed to me.'

'Flat?'

'Oh, I think you call them apartments,' Maeve said. 'Thank you for your help, but I think I'd better search out Mr Caleb Zowkoughski and see what else he can tell me. You don't remember my niece at all, then?'

'I daresay the girl I thought might be your sister was someone altogether different,' the man said with a weary smile. 'An English accent is rare and therefore memorable, but an Irish one – forgive me – is commonplace. Our city is full of such immigrants, some of them of many years' standing.'

Maeve, who had been sitting on a long sofa in the window of the manager's apartment, rose to her feet. 'Thank you for your time,' she said formally. 'But I must not waste any more of it. I have a farm and a family at home who need me.'

Next, Maeve visited Mr Zowkoughski. She rang the doorbell and listened with considerable trepidation to the footsteps approaching the front door. Suppose he had been lying to her? Suppose he had Evie trussed up inside – her heart rose at the thought that her sister might still be alive – what would she do then? But Mr Zowkoughski turned out to be a man of around Maeve's own age with an open, friendly face, tufty, toffee-coloured hair and matching eyes. He guessed who she was before she had opened her mouth and asked her in.

It was a nice apartment, though extremely high, with a view over the masses of shipping in the enormous docks. Maeve accepted his offer of a cup of coffee and a doughnut and sat on a long windowseat, almost afraid to look down at the ant-like figures of people in the street below.

'Miss Murphy, I'm real sorry to have brought you here on a fool's errand, but from what I've managed to discover, your sister didn't have a child here in New York. Most folk think the kid lived in the country round about, since Miss Murphy went away most weekends, probably to visit her. But all my asking has got me nowhere, so far. And – and I do earnestly suggest that too many questions ... I don't know what sort of a man your sister was mixed up with, but I – I do have reason to believe that – well, she didn't die in her bed, Miss Murphy.'

Maeve was so shocked that she couldn't speak. She just stared at Caleb Zowkoughski whilst all the blood drained out of her face, leaving her feeling sick and lightheaded.

'Didn't you know? I feared you didn't, but I felt I had to write ... I have acquired a copy of the death certificate, if you would like to see it ...'

Maeve took hold of the certificate by one corner, and managed to take in what was written without once actually looking straight at it. Little Evie had bled to death as a result of multiple wounds caused by being struck repeatedly by a knife.

'I saw the police,' Caleb murmured, when she had recovered from the dreadful shock and the storm of weeping which had shaken her after reading the certificate. 'She wasn't in this apartment, she'd gone to – to someone's place in Brooklyn Heights. The police think it was a case of – of friends falling out. She had been very ill, it seems, but had felt well enough, on that particular afternoon, to – to visit her friend. I don't know the circumstances, of course, but the police surgeon said your sister would not have lived long, in any case. She was a sick woman, Miss Murphy. Perhaps that was why she decided to try to talk to the man who killed her, instead of steering well clear of him.'

'I don't understand,' poor Maeve said, thoroughly bewildered. 'My sister was on the stage, she was doing very well, she'd said nothing to us of an illness. When she first came over here she spoke of a man called Guiseppe Fuego who was going to make her rich and famous, and I thought, reading between the lines, that he was in love with her and planned to marry her. Did it have anything to do with Mr Fuego, this business?'

Caleb, who had been understanding and kind but perfectly at ease, began to show signs of considerable perturbation at the mention of Mr Fuego's name.

'Yes . . . no . . . I'm not sure,' he stammered. 'You'd do best not to mention Mr Fuego, Miss Murphy, neither to the cops – the police, that is – nor to any of Evie's acquaintance. How old did you say the child was?'

'Only fourteen. You aren't going to tell me . . . '

Caleb moved closer to her. He took both her hands and spoke urgently, his voice low.

'Miss Murphy, this is a dangerous city and your sister mixed with dangerous people, very dangerous people. I don't think for one moment that she would have involved her child with those people but the best thing you can do is go away from here. Leave New York, go back to Ireland, and wait. If your niece needs you she'll get in touch. If she doesn't, if she's living with good people and happy with them, then the best thing she can do is to mourn her mother quietly, and then forget the whole business. Believe me, this is a dangerous city.'

'But my niece . . . I must find her,' stammered Maeve. 'She's got to be here somewhere – her name's Linnet Murphy, surely I can trace her from that?'

Caleb looked doubtful. 'Without an address, ma'am? With no idea where she might be? Well, you can try, I guess, and I'll do my best to help you. But I can't guarantee that we'll get so much as a sniff of her.'

Maeve smiled at him, immensely cheered to hear him say 'we' and not 'you'.

'Thank you, and God bless you,' she said fervently. 'I'd be most grateful for any help, so I would. Can we start looking tomorrow?'

It was that same autumn that Granny Mogg began to show her age. She took longer to climb the long stone stairs to her upper room and scarcely ever ascended the ladder which led out onto the roof. She had always had a healthy appetite but now it gradually shrank as food interested her less and became less important. And she hardly ever looked into her seeing bowl, nor did she cross-question Lucy about her comings and goings. She simply accepted Lucy's absence and rejoiced in her presence and when she was left alone she slept a lot. It was not Lucy who noticed first that something was wrong because she was with Granny, on and off, most of the time, but Finn spotted it the moment he strolled into the upper room at the castle.

'She just smiled at me, so she did, and not a moan about her aching bones nor a question as to where I'd been hidin' meself this time,' he said helplessly. 'So meek and quiet she was that I knew all wasn't well. It's as if she's lost her zest of late, and I'm sure she's shrunk, too, got physically smaller since I was here last.'

'We've had enough rain to shrink a six foot giant down to a two foot pigmy,' Lucy said gloomily. 'She's had a nasty cough, mind, but I gave her honey an' lemon which seemed to help. Only then she got her feet wet going down to pull in our fishing lines, and the cough came back and a headcold with it. She's over both now, but with every cough and sneeze she seems to get a bit weaker, a bit less quick to get over the next one.'

'I wonder should she see a doctor?' Finn said uneasily. 'I've got the money; sure and haven't I had the good season this time? Aye, there's a penny or two to be spent over the hard months.'

'I don't think a doctor would say much except that she was getting old, wearing out,' Lucy said. 'Caitlin's grandaddy's the same age as Granny Mogg and he's wearing out, the doctor says so. But there are things we might do which could help a bit; if it wasn't for the stairs I'd say she should give the old turf hut the go-by and stick to the upper room. It's healthier, I think.'

'But she likes her summer home, as she calls it,' Finn said. 'I can understand it, 'specially now she finds the stairs hurt her poor ole knees. Aw heck, I knew this would come one day, but I didn't know it would be so soon. What'll we do, alanna?'

Lucy felt a lovely warm glow at that 'we', but it didn't solve the problem, of course. The marsh was damp, the lough was downright wet, and the rheumatics were in Granny's bones something cruel. Getting her away from the low-lying ground, she supposed, would probably be best. She voiced the thought aloud and Finn, to her surprise, jumped at the idea.

'You're right, Luceen. Where'll I take her, then?'

'Well, she needs a proper roof over her head,' Lucy said slowly. 'There's turf huts in plenty high in the mountains but when it rains she'd be wetter than she is down here, or at least as wet. I suppose you couldn't build her something?'

'I could,' Finn said with a grin. 'But be the time I finished it I'd be pushin' me own century so I would. What would your grandaddy say to a lodger, eh, just for the winter? With Maeve still gone you must have the room and to spare.'

'Well, we have, and Maeve doesn't look like coming back yet awhile,' Lucy admitted. 'But Finn, if I could persuade me grandad, and Clodagh, because she's still up there standin' in for Maeve, would Granny come with me? A barn she might enjoy, but someone else's house, where she'd have to ask before she fried herself a trout . . . I don't know. And I don't think Grandad would let you live with us as well. I wish he would,' she added with the candour which Finn found so delightful, 'but he'd say it wasn't right to have a young man and a young girl in the house together and them not even relatives.'

'You're probably right and Granny wouldn't stand for it,' Finn said, after some thought. 'She's never had a proper roof over her head, not a house roof which belongs to someone else. I'd think about a caravan, only we've got along fine and no trouble from the Duveens for so long it seems mad to tempt fate. If your Maeve was here you could ask her what best to do; you always say she's sensible.'

'She is, and I wish she'd come back,' Lucy admitted with a sigh. 'She's been gone so long – that wretched sister of mine's disappeared, you know, they can't find her anywhere, but Maeve's stubborn. She won't give up, and America's a huge country.'

'They? Who's they?'

'Oh, didn't I tell you? She's met a feller called Caleb Zowkoughski, he's an att-attorney and I think he's sweet on Maeve, so I do. Her letters are full of him and in the last one she said she might bring him back home when she does come, since his ancestors were from County Kerry and he'd like to see the old country.'

'Well, that 'ud be nice,' Finn said. 'Nice for Maeve, anyway.'

'Yes. And nice for Caleb, too.'

They stared at each other with unrelieved gloom for a moment, both sunk in their own thoughts. Then Lucy spoke.

'We ought to get Granny to get out her seeing bowl; if Maeve's going to marry Caleb I'd like to be prepared.'

'Gran's gettin' too old for seein' things,' Finn said. 'Besides, we'll know for ourselves soon enough. She wouldn't stay away for Christmas, surely?'

'I dunno. She really does like Caleb, Finn, I can tell from her letters. If she does marry him then I don't suppose she'll ever come home.'

If Linnet had expected getting a job would be easy, she was to be disappointed. Day after day she washed carefully, brushed her hair, put on her best winter coat (only just beginning to be a little small) and sallied forth. Every evening she came back to Peel Square with less of a spring in her step as the weeks became months and still she was reliant on the Sullivans.

'It's the weather, chuck,' Mrs Sullivan said in mid-January, when the snow was a couple of feet deep around the sides of the square, though the constant passage of many boots kept it to slush in the middle. 'Folk aren't doin' much shoppin', there ain't much money about . . . you'll do better when the warmer weather comes.'

Linnet said she was sure she would and set off next morning, with great determination, to try the factories.

'I know I said I wouldn't work in one and get a yellow face, but I'll do anything to help your mam out,' Linnet told Roddy as they walked up Scotland Road together in the dark and early morning. 'You work for that beastly butcher and I know you don't like it, our Roddy.'

'Oh, it could be worse,' Roddy said. 'I 'ates the smell o' blood an' the feel o' carcasses on a cold mornin', but it's a job, queen. Look, it's early, come into Cobble's canny house wi' me an' I'll buy you a wet nellie to set you up for the day.'

Linnet squeezed his hand, her mouth watering at the thought of the doughy roll soaked in syrup. She had not eaten any breakfast because she felt so guilty, taking from Mrs Sullivan all the time, when that good lady had her work cut out to feed and clothe her own brood. Trust Roddy to notice, though, and he was always slipping her the odd copper to see her through the day and heaven knew he earned little enough from that old skinflint!

'Oh, you are kind, Roddy! But I shouldn't let you spend your money on me, you don't get much to spare.'

'Wet nellies don't cost a fortune,' Roddy said grandly. 'I'll mug you a cuppa tea an' all if you're good.'

They reached the canny house, which was really only a room which faced onto the pavement, and went inside. Immediately the noise hit them; the porters from the market shouted across to one another, a delivery boy with a box of bread rolls was trying to get someone to take them out of his wooden tray and even at this early hour there were women shoppers, eyeing the food on sale with critical interest, reading the chalk board or peering over the top of the high wooden counter to the shelf at the back which held Mrs Cobble's collection of cakes and prepared sandwiches. There was also a line of would-be customers standing by the counter, none of them looking too happy at being kept waiting.

'Mrs Cobble does a nice cuppa,' Roddy said, catching hold of Linnet's elbow. He raised his voice to a bellow, for there was no sign of Mrs Cobble behind the counter.

'Come on, Ma Cobble, gerra move on or I'll be late. The old feller wants me to clear the snow before I start an' our Linnie 'ere is goin' job-huntin' agin.'

'I can clear the old feller's doorway for free,' Linnet said, delighted to be able to pay Roddy back for once. 'I can, honest, I'm strong, I can shovel snow.'

Roddy laughed and leaned over the counter. 'Two wet nellies an' two cuppas, Mrs Cobble,' he shouted. 'Shift yourself, Auntie!'

Mrs Cobble emerged from her tiny, steamy slit of a kitchen and grinned across at Roddy. She was a fat little woman with thinning grey hair screwed into a tiny bun on top of her head, small grey eyes which twinkled at the world beneath bushy grey brows, and a laugh as raucous as a crow, only a good deal louder.

'Good Lor', it's the butcher's boy, wantin' service,' she announced to the world at large, slapping the tray she held down on the counter. 'Gorrany pennies, Roddy?'

'Enough for two wet nellies an' two cups o' tea, Auntie,' Roddy said promptly. He slapped the coins on the counter. 'Gerron wi' it, queen, or we'll be in trouble, our Linnie an' me. What's gone wrong this mornin', hey? Be this time you're usually servin' like a mad thing!'

'Four cups o' tea an' eight toasts,' Mrs Cobble said, removing tea and toast from her tray and pushing them over to the customers. 'An' you was a breakfuss, weren't you?' The man she addressed said he was indeed and Mrs Cobble piled a plate with fried food, handed it to her customer, and then turned back to Roddy. 'Ain't you got eyes in your 'ead, young feller?' she said, reaching for the wet nellies and sticking them onto a couple of white pot plates. 'Wharrabout your ear'oles, then, eh? Don't you listen to gossip, chuck?'

'Dunno what you're talkin' about,' Roddy said.

'Butchers' lads know everything there is to know; well-known fact.'

A fish porter, smelling strongly of his wares, pushed past Linnet and dumped a box of fish on the counter. He leaned across it and spoke right into Mrs Cobble's flushed face. 'Ere, I can't wait all mornin', gi's me money an' I'll be orf. Ten pun' o' cod you said an' ten pun' o' cod you've gorrin this box.'

'Ta, love,' Mrs Cobble said, fishing money out of the till and pushing it across the counter. 'God ha' mercy on me, where's that bleedin' baker's boy?'

'He's gone, but he left the bread,' Linnet volunteered. 'He's coming back for his money later, he said. And he wants his tray back, too.'

'And two teas,' Mrs Cobble said, pouring tea from a big black pot into two chipped cups. 'I'm short-'anded, Roddy me lad, which is why I'm buyin' bread in instead o' makin' me own. You must ha' heard about Millie, the gal what worked 'ere?'

'Who? No, 'aven't 'eard nothin',' Roddy said, picking up the two cups. 'What's she done, then?'

'Oh, nothin' much, only 'ad a baby, that's all,' Mrs Cobble said heavily. 'I didn't even know she were in the fam'ly way, like. So me right-'and woman's out o' the picture for a bit, 'cos I won't 'ave a squallin' brat in 'ere, upsettin' me customers.'

Roddy was carrying the cups over to the nearest table; he stopped short, put the cups down so hastily that he splashed tea on the table's plain deal top, and turned back to the counter. 'You need someone like our Linnie 'ere,' he said. 'Me mam swears by 'er – she's a dream of a cook, our Linnie, an' that fast on 'er feet . . .'

'Hold 'ard a moment, young Roddy,' Mrs Cobble said. She stared at Linnet across the counter. 'Your mam don't 'ave no gels!'

'No, our Linnie's a – a cousin,' Roddy said quickly. 'She's been livin' with us for a while, ain't you, Linnie? Real quick, is Linnie – why don't you let 'er give you an 'and just for this mornin', eh?'

Linnet looked from one face to the other. The possibility of a job loomed suddenly, and this – this was a nice place! Little Evie would have thought it low, but Linnet had stopped taking little Evie's word for things like that long before she left for America. So she smiled hopefully at Mrs Cobble, and to her pleasure Mrs Cobble smiled straight back.

'Well, gel? Gorra tongue in your 'ead, 'ave you?'

'Yes, Mrs C-Cobble,' Linnet stammered. 'I'd like to give you a hand.'

Mrs Cobble nodded slowly. 'Convent schooled?' she hazarded. 'Mam Irish, father missin'?'

'More or less, Mrs Cobble,' Linnet agreed. 'My mam died a while ago and I never did meet my dad, but Mrs Sullivan's been very good to me.'

'Aye, Janice is a good woman,' Mrs Cobble said, still staring thoughtfully at Linnet whilst leaning her elbows and a large bosom heavily on the counter. She suddenly seemed to make up her mind and stood up straight. 'Awright, queen, you're on. Come round 'ere an' get the overall off of the kitchen door. You can start servin', I'll explain as we goes on.'

Linnet came out of Cobble's at eight that night, almost dizzy with tiredness but with a big smile from ear to ear. It was snowing again and as she left the shelter of the doorway someone fell into step beside her. It was Roddy, his striped butcher's overall filthy, his boots clagged with slush.

'Hello, chuck,' he said, taking her arm and tucking it through his. 'How did it go?'

'Oh, Roddy, I can't ever thank you enough – she's going to keep me on and it's a grand job, I love it! She's already taught me how to cook scouse for twenty people, to bake a huge flat loaf of bread – she cuts it in pieces to go with the soup – and to make a sandwich so fast you wouldn't believe. And I serve the customers . . . they give you the odd ha'penny, too . . . and get to bring leftovers home . . .'

'What's the money like?' Roddy said. 'Twon't be great, but work's so scarce any job's a good job.'

'It's all right; ten bob a week, and it's only eight till eight because Mr Cobble helps early and late. What d'you think?'

'It's bleedin' good,' Roddy said admiringly. 'I only get twelve an' a kick meself. Well, you're made up, I can see. So'll me mam be when we tell 'er. When does Ma Cobble pay you, eh?'

'Saturday night, but because today was just a trial she gave me two bob in my hand – wasn't that kind? And she gave me half a fruit cake, I've got it in under me coat.'

'Coo,' Roddy said reverently when Linnet showed him the cake, nestling in her apron pocket. 'The kids'll go barmy – it ain't often they get cake mid-week.'

'They're welcome to it,' Linnet said. 'Mrs Cobble gave me a big dinner at noon and a big tea an' all. Me stomach's tight as a drum, you won't see me eating cake.'

'No? All the more for the rest of us, then,' Roddy said. He squeezed her arm. 'I'm that glad for you, queen, because I knowed you was miserable, feelin' you were a charge on me mam.'

'Well, I was,' Linnet pointed out as they turned the corner and plunged under the arch into Peel Square. 'I've helped her in the house of course, and done the ironing when she's washed sheets and stuff, but I couldn't pay for me keep, though I know you handed over extra, often and often. You Sullivans have been very good to me, Roddy.'

'Oh well, you can pay us back some day,' Roddy said obscurely. 'Want to go in first and tell me mam about Cobble's? Or shall I go first an' make trumpet noises for your entrance?'

Linnet laughed delightedly. She thought she had never felt so happy, not even when Mammy had been alive to share her pleasure.

'You go first,' she urged. 'Get 'em all in the kitchen, so's I only have to tell me story once!'

Lying rolled up in her blankets on the floor by the kitchen fire that night, Linnet reviewed her day. It had been the best of days, and she could not imagine ever being more excited by a job than she had been as what Mrs Cobble called 'me gofer'.

'What's that?' Linnet had asked, and Mrs Cobble told her that it meant a sort of dogsbody, a do-everything, called a gofer because she would be told to 'go for this and go for that'.

But the best part had been marching proudly into the kitchen whilst Roddy made a trumpet of his hands and blared triumphant music through them and Bert did wonderful things with a comb and a bit of paper.

'Here comes the conquering 'ero!' Freddy shrilled. 'Wharrever 'ave you done, our Linnie, to make Roddy play 'is trumpets?'

'She's gorra job!' Mrs Sullivan had hazarded. 'Oh, queen, I couldn't be 'appier for you an' it ain't the money, neither. Wharra you doin', eh? Clearin' snow? They pay a bob a week some firms, to 'ave snow cleared away.'

'No, Auntie Sullivan, it's a real job,' Linnet had said, her voice shrill with excitement. 'I'm waiting on at the Cobble's canny house, for ten bob a week and the left-overs.'

The hugs, the kisses, the excitement which followed! Mr Sullivan, who had a bad heart as well as crippled legs, gave her a big hug and told her she was a good girl and deserved some good luck. Mrs Sullivan danced her round the kitchen and promised to make her a nice apron to wear for work just as soon as she could get some sewing done. The younger boys were delighted with the news and enjoyed the cake to the full and Roddy, of course, was more pleased than anyone except Linnet herself.

'You're a good kid, our Linnie,' he said affectionately when the fire had been banked down and everyone was going off to bed. 'Now you won't need to worry that you stayin' 'ere ain't fair on me mam.'

'Well, it isn't,' Linnet said. She was spreading her blankets out preparatory to rolling up in them. All she did when she went to bed at night was to take off her skirt, jumper and shoes. Her neat cotton nightgowns had disappeared with the horrid Mrs Roberts and though Mrs Sullivan had bought her a second skirt and some cheap shoes, she was still very short of clothing. 'I shouldn't expect your mam to let me sleep on her kitchen floor for ever; and though I try ever so hard, I do take up room, Roddy. Your mam used to spread the washing out here at nights so it would dry in the fire's warmth, but now she can't, and that isn't fair either. As soon as I can afford it, I'll have to move out.'

Upstairs, the boys were already asleep and Mr and Mrs Sullivan were settling down, their voices rumbling slower and slower. Roddy caught hold of both of Linnet's hands, then drew her towards him.

'Our Linnie, I want you to stay 'ere for always,' he said hoarsely. 'You're the best thing what ever 'appened to me, honest to God you are! We all love 'avin' you in our 'ouse, me most of all, so don't you talk about movin' out, 'cos we'd miss you somethin' cruel.'

'I won't go far, Roddy,' Linnet promised. She felt rather uneasy as Roddy pulled her hard against his chest. 'Do stop it, you're squashing me!'

'No I ain't, I'm cuddlin' you,' Roddy said and put both arms round her tightly. He gave a sort of moan under his breath and then he began to kiss any bit of her face which he could reach despite Linnet squiggling away like mad – and giggling, as well, for this was not how she thought of Roddy at all, he was usually so sensible. 'Oh Linnet, Linnet, you don't know 'ow I feel about you, you're just the best, the prettiest . . .'

'Roddy, your mam . . .' Linnet was beginning, when the kitchen door opened. Mrs Sullivan stood there.

'Ah, Roddy, I were just about to call down to you to bring me up that bit o' darnin' I were doin' before supper. But I'll fetch it meself, now I'm 'ere.'

Roddy, scarlet as a lobster, had let Linnet go as soon as he saw his mother standing there, and now, shifting from foot to foot, he said loudly, 'I'm sorry, Mam. I were just – just showin' our Linnie 'ow pleased I am she's gorra job.'

'I daresay. But there's other ways of showin' you're pleased about a job, without pullin' the gel about,' Mrs Sullivan said severely. 'You didn't oughter stay down 'ere after we's gone up, Roddy. It ain't decent.'

'But Mam, I weren't doin' nothin' . . .' Roddy began, to be firmly interrupted.

'I should think not, indeed, when Linnie's in your mam's care! Off wit' you, son, we'll talk in the morning.'

She smiled at Linnet, tipped her a wink, and followed her son out of the room and Linnet removed her outer clothing and rolled herself up in her blankets. And now she was thinking over her day and wondering how long it would take her to save a decent sum.

Because no matter what Roddy said she knew she

would have to go. She was sixteen, Roddy eighteen, and when Roddy had squeezed her just now there had only been a part of her complaining and giggling. The other part, the part which was conscious of a burgeoning figure and her increasing interest in young men, had known a strange, guilty excitement, a desire for his caresses to continue, to take her further along that road which led to womanhood.

So I'd best flit when I can manage it, Linnet told herself half sadly. I can get a cheap room when I'm settled at Cobble's – and that won't stop me coming back as often as possible, because there's no family I love more than the Sullivans, and no place I've been happier than Peel Square.

'My life's going back to normal so it is, after months and months of being strange,' Lucy said joyfully to Caitlin as they walked across Barry's Bridge, heading for school. 'We got a letter from Maeve yesterday and she's coming home and bringing that feller, Caleb, with her. She's sad because she's given up; she doesn't think she'll ever find me sister, but I don't mind that because I never knew her. So she's coming back to us, Cait, and aren't I glad? That Clodagh's very nearly driven me mad with her "do this, do that", and never even a thank you from her.'

'She'll be back just in time to see you leave school,' Caitlin said rather gloomily. 'Then you'll be after gettin' a job, unless you stay on the farm, of course. Are you goin' to tell Maeve what you really want to do, Luceen?'

'What? Acting on the stage, you mean? Well, it might upset her,' Lucy said thoughtfully. 'When I mentioned it to Grandad he was so cross I pretended I was only teasing, but Maeve's not like that. Still, I won't say anything yet.'

'When I said how good you were in the school play

my mam said you'd get ideas like your mam, Evie, did, and look what come o' that,' Caitlin said. 'You never said your mam was an actress, Lu.'

'I didn't know she was until Grandad said, when I talked about the play,' Lucy admitted. 'And anyway, from what I've managed to find out she wasn't ever an actress, precisely.'

Caitlin smiled and patted her hair which had recently been cut in a bob. The new hairstyle suited Caitlin very much better than Lucy had imagined it would, and sometimes Lucy looked at Caitlin's shining dark cap of hair which was cut to show the nice shape of her head and which complimented her round, rosy face, and wished that she, too, might have a bob or a shingle. But if she was really going to be an actress she might need her long hair, so she kept the scissors in their place and did not even try to cut herself a fringe, tempting though it was.

'If your mam wasn't an actress, but she was on the stage, what was she?' Caitlin asked now. She stopped to lean over the bridge and Lucy knew she was trying to see her reflection in the smoothly rushing water below. 'Was she a stage manager or something?'

'No, not really. She danced and sang, she didn't act,' Lucy said rather shortly. She did not want Caitlin, or indeed anyone, to know that during Maeve's long absence she had done a very sneaky thing.

If it hadn't rained and rained and kept her indoors, she told herself defensively now, she might never have gone wandering into Maeve's room and pulled open the bottom drawer of the big old chest which stood against the sloping eaves. Once it had been full of sheets and pillowcases, with Maeve's initials embroidered in the corners, jostling for position with six lacy nightgowns, six pairs of silk knickers, petticoats, bust bodices, all the paraphernalia of a girl's bottom drawer, her trousseau, carefully stitched so that she did not go empty-handed to her bridegroom.

But over the years the other girls had married and Maeve had not and Maeve's generous spirit had refused to hoard all the beautiful things she had so lovingly made. So she had given away the bedding, the clothing, everything the drawer had once contained. Now it contained some material, the last pair of embroidered sheets which Lucy knew without having to think about it would be given to her when she married, and, right at the bottom, where the lavender bags and the pot pourri of rose petals were kept, letters.

They were not love letters, she knew that. Maeve didn't receive love letters. Besides, they weren't wrapped in pink ribbon and they didn't have flowers pressed between the pages, two things which, Lucy knew, were obligatory in love letters. They were just kept in big brown paper bags, and when she looked at the signature on the first one and saw it was her own mother . . . well, surely it was her right to read on?

Reading them, starting with little Evie's very first letter home, had been a pleasurable business at first. Her mother had been interested in baby Lucy, had talked about her Career – always with a capital initial letter – and her other child, the oddly named Linnet. She had touched on the beautiful rooms over the fine emporium on a street convenient to the theatre, on her social life, which was apparently lively and very much of the champagne-in-slipper variety, and on her admirers, who were many and various and all, it seemed, rich and adoring. But as she read on, even Lucy noticed the change in little Evie's attitude. There was defiance, a repeatedly reiterated conviction that Stardom and Acceptance (more capitals) were just around the corner, were kept from Evie by a malignant fate, by ill-luck, by the sheer vindictiveness of others. There were opportunities missed by a hair's breadth, evil acts by fellow Thespians which had caused her apparent downfall, misunderstandings galore. In short, Evie had not succeeded and did not intend to let those at home believe she was in any way to blame.

And, of course, it also came out, in those rather ingenuous letters, that little Evie posed on stage clad in nothing but feathers, or fans, or a large hat strategically wafted, that she sang songs and danced exotically, but that she had never acted a part.

And, inevitably, Lucy concluded, as just by reading on she began to build up a picture of her mother, the letters got shorter and shorter, the intervals between their arrival at the farm longer and longer. Very soon they were scarcely more than notes, particularly after little Evie had reached New York, though there was one letter where she spoke of her wonderful admirer, Mr Fuego, who was going to see her a 'Star' at any cost.

'He's crazy for me, Maeve me darling,' she had written exultantly. 'Nothing's too good for your little Evie – you should see the apartment he's bought for me, the view over the river alone must be worth thousands of dollars.'

Only after that there was no more mention of Mr Fuego – and neither, Lucy slowly began to realise, of the other child. Well, there were mentions, but they were what you might call off-hand, almost as though – almost as though Linnet wasn't with little Evie after all.

I do believe, Lucy told herself incredulously as she tucked the last letter guiltily back into its big brown envelope, I do believe that the reason why Maeve hasn't found Linnet is because she's not in America at all. I think little Evie left her in Liverpool all those years ago and simply dared not confess it to Maeve!

But it was guesswork, so she didn't tell anyone, not Caitlin, not Granny Mogg, not Finn. Why should I? she thought. I'm not really interested in that other girl, it doesn't matter to me whether she's in New York or – or Timbuktu for that matter. But if Maeve really wants to find Linnet I suppose I'll have to admit I read the letters, and then perhaps I ought to tell her what I think. And if Maeve agrees and thinks it's important then I suppose the two of us could go over to Liverpool together and find the girl with the silly name.

But despite herself the letters had, at last, stirred a degree of interest in this sister that she could not remember. A girl a year or two older than me, but maybe very like me, she thought. A girl who's lived with the theatre all her life, who must have met most of the great actors and actresses, played in their dressing rooms, run about on the stage whilst they rehearsed! Knowing her might be quite useful if I do decide I want to be an actress, she decided; she could give me all sorts of tips and advice. Probably she would know just how one would go about getting a job on the stage. Think of that, Lucy Murphy, think of that!

Linnet guessed that Mrs Sullivan had had words with Roddy because the next day she received an incoherent and mumbled apology from a young gentleman very red about the gills.

'Mam said it weren't fair, I put you in an awkward position,' he muttered, staring fixedly at the table, for he had chosen to make his apology in his dinner break whilst Linnet, naturally, was at her busiest, flying round the small room sliding platefuls of scouse and dumplings, apple pie and steak pudding, before the customers. 'I din't think, Linnie, I din't mean no 'arm. Only you're me pal, an . . .'

'It's all right, Roddy, honest to God it is,' Linnet said distractedly, trying to move on to the next table without seeming rude, but Roddy had drawn her attention by grabbing her apron and he still held a corner of it, crumpled up in one large fist. 'Look, what do you want to eat?'

'Oh . . .' Roddy looked round vaguely as though he would find a plateful of something nice on the floor or the walls. 'Oh . . . anything, you choose.'

'Right, scouse and dumplings,' Linnet said briskly. 'Let go me pinny, there's a good feller.'

'Oh . . . sorry, I didn't know I were still 'angin' on,' Roddy said. 'Linnie, can I meet you after work?'

'Course you can; we're still pals, our Roddy,' Linnet said, moving to the next table. 'Why, you're like a brother to me and I wouldn't stop meeting me brother because of a bit of a tiff, like, would I?'

Roddy scowled but made no comment and Linnet continued with her work but the whole episode had made her think. She loved living in the square with the Sullivans but she knew she would have to move out and it looked as though sooner might be better than later. The trouble was she couldn't possibly afford a room, or even a bit of a room, on ten bob a week.

And later that evening, when Roddy, after a significant glare from his mother, had gone off up to bed muttering about gettin' an early night, she and Mrs Sullivan sat down and talked it through.

'We loves 'avin' you, queen, not only for yourself but because I ain't never 'ad a daughter an' I've always wanted one,' Mrs Sullivan said frankly. 'But Roddy's mortal fond o' you, an' he's growin' up, same's you are for that matter. An' we're bleedin' short o' space so you don't get no privacy. An' you're a sight too young for marryin', an' besides that would only solve one o' the problems.'

Linnet, who had no intention of marrying anyway, let alone at the tender age of sixteen, did not understand at all what problem marrying would solve but she did not like to say so. 'If I could earn a bit extra in the evenings ...' she said hopefully. 'I'm free by eight most nights. Isn't there someone round here with daughters who might let me have a mattress on the floor?'

Mrs Sullivan threw both hands in the air. 'Well, you've an 'ead on your shoulders, Linnet Murphy, why din't I think o' that?' she declared. 'Me cousin Myrtle's gorra daughter an' they're always short of the readies. They live a ways from 'ere, but you'd manage. It's a back to back up on Lawrence Street. Want me to 'ave a word?'

'I suppose you'd better,' Linnet said sadly. 'Oh Auntie Sullivan, I'll miss you, and the others, something cruel, but I know you're right and it's only fair. What's your cousin Myrtle's daughter called?'

'Bessie. Bessie Brinton. She's a year or so older'n you but you'll gerron together. A nice gel, Bessie.'

They got on and Linnet, handing over eight bob a week to the Brinton family, was grateful for a roof over her head and cheerful company, but wished, wistfully, that Mrs Sullivan had managed to pass on to her feckless cousin Myrtle some tips about housekeeping in general and cleanliness in particular.

The Brintons had bed bugs and accepted them as a fact of life, whereas the Sullivans, who also had bed bugs, fought them with fire and brimstone, soap and water, much boiling of sheets and hanging out of mattresses. And fleas marched off Tammy Brinton's four large, half-witted mongrel dogs when they grew tired of eating nothing but dog and had many a good meal on poor Linnet's white skin.

'I don't mind for meself so much,' Linnet told Roddy, scratching furtively as they sat in the cinema watching Agnes Ayres rolling her eyes and pouting at her leading man. 'It's passing them on I hate – and if Ma Cobble were to see a fleabite on me neck, what d'you suppose she'd think?'

'Norra lot,' Roddy said rather gloomily. In a moment of cinematic passion he had tried, personally, to mark Linnet's neck and had received an eyewatering clout on the nose for his pains. She did not know what he was up to she had informed him crossly, but she didn't fancy trying to explain to Mrs Cobble that she had been attacked by a leech. 'Everyone 'as fleas, chuck. We does our best, but in summer they're everywhere.'

'The Brintons' fleas are as big as their bed bugs,' Linnet said. 'You know I'm doing shorthand and typewriting in me evening classes, Roddy? Well, one day I'm going to get an office job and I tell you, people in offices don't like fleas one little bit.'

'Well, the answer's there awright – move back in wi' us,' Roddy said joyfully. Linnet giggled and dug him in the ribs.

'So you can sneak down in the night and bite me neck and make 'em think I'm living with Dracula?' she said derisively. 'I should just say so, Roddy Sullivan!'

Linnet's job with Mrs Cobble lasted a year, until the delinquent Millie's child was old enough to be left with Millie's mam.

'I'm that sorry to lose ye, chuck,' Mrs Cobble told Linnet when she explained that Millie was returning. 'But you'll do well, I'll give ye a good reference, tell anyone what asks that they couldn't tek on a better gel. Honest, 'ard-working, clean . . .'

'I do understand, really I do, Mrs Cobble,' Linnet

assured her fat and friendly little employer. 'And I'll never forget you because you've been so good to me. But you know I've been doing night-classes? Well, I'm a fast typist now, and me shorthand's not bad either. I think I'll go for an office job, if I can get one – and there's one advertised in the *Echo* this very week.'

And within a few days, before she had really digested the information that she would be out of work the following week, Roddy had called for her after work, taken her arm, and suggested a trip to the cinema to see her all-time favourite, Gary Cooper, who was starring in a film called *Lilac Time*.

'Because I miss you, now you don't live at our 'ouse no more,' he told her, only half teasingly. 'We can sit an' 'old 'ands an' 'ave a bit of a cuddle, eh?'

'Can't, it's night-school,' Linnet told him, tucking her hand into his arm nevertheless and walking along beside him. 'But I'm out of Cobble's as from Monday. Millie's coming back.'

Roddy stared down at her, lively dismay changing, abruptly, to hope. 'You'll move back in wi' us, of course?' he said ingenuously. 'I won't muck about like when I kissed you in the kitchen an' me mam walked in, but it 'ud be nice to 'ave you near, again.'

But Linnet, who was happy enough with the Brintons, apart from the bugs, made noncommittal noises. Though she had missed the Sullivans and Peel Square horribly at first, she knew that when the time came for her to move on it would not be to return to the Sullivans, much though she loved them. She was beginning to realise that independence, once gained, is important and not to be willingly given up. And though there were drawbacks in Lawrence Street, at least the Brintons never asked her where she was going or who with. Linnet, who had accepted an invitation from an Irish fish porter to go to the Rotunda with him, knew that she would never have got away with the outing had she been living in Peely. It hadn't been a particularly good evening – the smell of fish had seen to that – but at least she had gone, discovered that the fish porter wasn't her Mr Right, and returned to Lawrence Street with no one the wiser. The fact that Mrs Sullivan would have worried in case she was taken advantage of she dismissed with the insouciance of youth. Linnet Murphy could take care of herself!

'Well, if you've got no gelt, queen, I don't see as you've much choice,' Roddy said presently. 'Wish you an' me could 'ave a place between us . . . but full-time butcherin' ain't all that well-paid and me mam needs wharrever I can spare.' He sighed deeply. 'If you ever feel like makin' an honest feller of me, our Linnie, you've only gorra say the word.'

Linnet laughed. 'It 'ud take more than me to make an honest feller out of you, Roddy Sullivan! But what I meant to tell you was that I've got an interview for a job – an office job! It's in one of the big insurance offices on Exchange Flags and it's for an office girl with good prospects for advancement the advertisement says. What about that?'

'You won't want to go around wi' a butcher's boy when you're in an office,' Roddy muttered after a moment. 'I 'ates butcherin', but what else is there? You get a couple o' hundred fellers after every bleedin' job what comes up, what chance 'ave I got? At one time I used to think I'd leave the Pool, go down south, but it's as bad there as 'ere, so they say. I dunno, queen, I'm sure.'

'You're me best friend, our Roddy, and I wouldn't want to go out with anyone else. Well, not unless you count Gary Cooper or Mr Miles Guest, that lovely man who stars at the Playhouse when they do dramas.'

Roddy snorted. 'Bleedin' fillum stars! Well, if they're

the only fellers you've got an eye to I guess I'm awright for a bit. But if you get that job, an' I'm sure I 'ope you will, then you'll be off wi' some bleedin' insurance clerk or other an' not a glance for a butcher's boy, I tell you.'

'Then don't stay a butcher's boy,' Linnet shouted, losing patience and jerking her arm out of his. 'You do talk so big, Roddy Sullivan, but you've not applied for a job for ages, so how d'you know you can't get one? Look, you'd best push off now, 'cos I'm going to me class and it's all I can do not to fall asleep at me desk without you upsetting me. See you tomorrow.'

'I'll walk to the school with you,' Roddy began, but Linnet shook her head impatiently.

'No point, we're nearly there and you've not had your tea yet. Get off home there's a good feller – I'll see you tomorrow, all right?'

Roddy sighed. 'All right,' he agreed resignedly. 'See you tomorrer, then. Same time, same place?'

'That's it. And by then I'll know whether I've got the job, because the interview's in the morning.' Linnet paused in her onward flight and turned her face towards him. 'Wish me luck, our Roddy!'

'Oh, dammit, good luck, our Linnie,' Roddy called back. 'Good luck for the mornin'.'

Roddy watched her out of sight and then turned back towards Peel Square. She was the loveliest thing, his Linnet, but he was so scared of losing her! The trouble was, they'd known each other for too long so she took him for granted, never thought of him as a man but only as the boy who had teased her and taken care of her, alternately bullied and spoilt her. But he didn't know how to change things, that was the rub. His mam, bless her, was always giving him advice, mostly on the lines that Linnet would take him seriously one day, when there was a bit of distance between them.

So what to do? Linnet made no secret of the fact that she hated his butchering, the smell which hung round him, his whole job, in fact. She had as good as told him to do something different today and of course she was absolutely right, he'd not tried for a job for a year or more. Never, in fact, since Sampson the butcher had taken him on, agreed to train him as a proper, time-served butcher, and begun to pay him a halfway decent wage.

And there were jobs. His father had been a seaman and his reputation had been good. More than once Da had said, almost wistfully, that his lads could do worse than follow in his footsteps. And they always wanted seamen – stokers, deckhands, all sorts – but he'd not looked in that direction because he was afraid of leaving Linnet even for a few weeks, afraid of what he might find when he came back.

Oh, well. Butchering wasn't that bad, and he was able to meet Linnet out of work two or three times a week, he took her home, dancing on a Saturday night, to the flicks, even to New Brighton to hang around the amusement arcades and paddle in the water.

And an office girl wasn't such a marvellous job, after all. It was a bit better than being Mrs Cobble's gofer, perhaps, but it wasn't as though she was a proper secretary. Roddy turned in under the brick arch, crossed the paving in a couple of strides, and pushed open the front door.

'I'm home, Mam,' he called. 'Gorrany tea on the go?'

Linnet got the job as office girl and found, to her delight, that it paid better than the job at Mrs Cobble's and finished earlier, too.

'And I'm also teaching a beginners' evening class in typewriting and they pay me a bob a session, and I can manage four sessions a week,' she told Roddy triumphantly as he walked her back to Lawrence Street when she finished at Mrs Cobble's for the last time. 'And I may be getting a room of me own! I like Mrs Brinton, she's awful nice, but . . . oh, Roddy, a room of me own! D'you want to come and see it with me? It's on the Boulevard – you know, that big, wide street with the trees and the grass. Do come, then you can tell your mam what it's like.'

Roddy, secretly thrilled to be asked, pretended reluctance but allowed himself to be persuaded, so next evening found the two of them mounting the stairs at number 8, The Boulevard, Roddy cautiously, Linnet eagerly, whilst ahead of them a young woman with a couple of kids clinging to her skirt led the way, calling remarks back over her shoulder as she climbed the stairs.

'It's ri' at the perishin' top, Miss Murphy,' she said cheerfully. 'Still, your legs is younger than mine . . . an' you ain't carryin', either.'

'Carryin' what?' Linnet hissed and Roddy, grinning, tapped his own stomach significantly.

'She's 'avin' another kid,' he whispered hoarsely. 'I tell you what, our Linnet, a week of livin' 'ere an' you'll think Havelock Street's flat as St George's Plain!'

'It's a long way up,' Linnet agreed, 'but think of the view, our Roddy! Ah, we're there.'

The young woman pushed open a lopsided, creaking door and gestured them to go ahead of her. The reason was soon clear; the room was so tiny that a narrow bed, Linnet and Roddy filled it completely. An expectant mother would have had great difficulty in simply getting through the doorway.

'It ain't a room, it's a bleedin' cupboard,' Roddy announced, looking round him. 'You'll 'ave to undress on the landing, queen, or you'll skin your elbows on the walls.'

'It's very nice, really,' Linnet murmured. 'It is a bit small, but I'm not very big myself.'

A bell sounded below them and the young woman's large and untidy head appeared in the doorway. 'Gorra go,' she said cheerfully. 'That's the doorbell. Look all you want, then come down an' tell me if you're takin' it.'

She lumbered down the stairs and Linnet turned to Roddy. 'Don't say it, I know it's tiny, but there's a bed and a window . . . and she said I could use the kitchen to cook me meals. She said all the rooms are small, Roddy, and it is cheap, honest.'

'And you like this better than me Aunt Brinton's? Well, I can see you might,' Roddy said handsomely. 'It looks clean an' at least you won't 'ave to share a bed wi' Bessie. Wharrabout visitors?' he leered at her. 'You've gorra be really pally to 'ave a visitor in 'ere. I mean you go to scratch your – your elbow and you'll find yourself scratchin' someone else's kneecap.'

'Oh, ha ha,' Linnet said crossly. 'She's only asking eight bob, Roddy, and that's about what I can afford, so I'm going to take it.'

'Who's next door?' Roddy asked suddenly. He tapped on the wall; the sound echoed hollowly back at them. 'This ain't a wall, Linnet, it's a partition, just a piece o' wood. Dear Gawd, you could get through it wi' a toothpick . . . you could wake up one mornin' an' find an eye glarin' down at you through an 'ole in the wall!'

Linnet giggled. 'It's all girls so what would it matter? There's a married couple with two little boys but all the rest of us are girls. That's another reason why I like it,' she added honestly, 'because we're all about the same age and none of us will have much money. I'm going to take it, so I just hope you'll give Auntie Sullivan a good report about it.'

'She'll be up 'ere inspectin' the day you move in,'

Roddy assured her. 'You know me mam – she worries about you, queen.'

'Yes, I know. But – but Roddy . . . it's me own place!'

'Yeah, I know. An' it's a decent little room,' Roddy said, suddenly magnanimous. It was the thought of a houseful of girls, Linnet imagined. 'You'll be awright 'ere, our Linnie, though you've a powerful trek to work.'

'I'll catch a tram; or leave early,' Linnet assured him. 'Let's go down and tell the lady "yes" then, shall we? Oh, Roddy, a place of me own!'

Chapter Seven

Mrs Sullivan was at the low stone sink, up to her elbows in suds, when Roddy came into the kitchen with a bounce in his step and a sparkle in his eye. He had taken pains over his appearance that morning and felt very much the young man about town, with his hair Brylcreemed and a clean white shirt on under his best suit. And at this precise moment he was so happy it was all he could do not to burst into song. He was carrying a big, newspaper-wrapped parcel which he put down on the kitchen table with a thump.

'Present for you, Mam,' he said laconically and then, unable to contain himself a moment longer: 'I got the job, they told me straight off I'd gorrit.'

'The job? You got the job? Well, son, I won't pretend I'm not glad because we could do wi' the money, but we'll miss you, me an' your dad.' Mrs Sullivan turned impulsively from the sink and gave her son a kiss on the cheek, her pink, water-wrinkled hands held carefully clear of the suit. 'When d'you start?'

'It's sail, Mam, you should say, when do you sail? And it's Tuesday morning, wi' the tide.' He heaved a sigh and a grin spread slowly across his face. 'Eh, it's good to be doing a proper job again and it'll be good to 'ave money in me pocket, an' all. First t'ing I did once I knew was go round to the market an' give in me notice to old Sampson an' he let me 'ave a leg o' pork, cheap.' He unwrapped the newspaper and displayed the meat. 'See? That'll mek a meal or two, eh?'

'It's a grand piece o' meat,' Mrs Sullivan said, turning back to the sink and plunging her arms into the suds once more. 'It'll do us for the best part of a week, hot an' cold. I tell you someone who won't be too pleased that you're goin' to sea, though, an' that's young Linnet. She's rare fond o' you, lad, for all she pretends otherwise. She'll miss you turble bad.'

'I wish I believed that,' Roddy said gloomily. 'She's that keen on 'er bloomin' job, she talks about nothin' else when we go out. I met 'er out of work the other day an' she were talkin' to a feller.' He snorted disdainfully. 'A bleedin' insurance clerk, whatever that may be – not quite like a seaman on the SS *Mary Rose*.'

'Well, I hope you haven't signed on because of the things Linnie said about butchering,' Mrs Sullivan said absently, pulling a sheet out of the water and beginning to wring it viciously. She had lost her job at the bakery on Derby Road when they started to cut down on staff and now she took in washing, a miserable, badly-paid business much hated by her family. 'She only said butcherin' were a low business to get a rise out of you, son. She knew it were a decent trade, really. Only the money weren't so good, I'm bound to admit that.'

'The money went down as soon as jobs began to get scarce,' her son pointed out. He crossed the kitchen and opened the back door into the noisome little yard in which the mangle stood. 'Old Sampson weren't a bad boss, but when folk start askin' for smaller and smaller parcels of meat something's gorra go. And I'd been there a good while. Lemme give you an 'and with them sheets, Mam, they're too 'eavy for you.'

'Oh go on wi' you – not that I'm not grateful for your young arms,' Mrs Sullivan said breathlessly, heaving the sheet out of the cooling water. 'Grab a hold o' this, then!'

'You go on wi' the washing, whilst I mangle,' Roddy

advised her. He went into the yard, dunked the sheet in the big rainwater barrel which his mother used as a rinse and then fed it through the mangle twice to get the last drop of water out. Then he shook it, pegged it on a section of the washing line and returned to the kitchen. 'I wonder what Linnie's doin' tonight? I might pop round, later.'

'Go sooner,' Mrs Sullivan advised, wringing a second sheet over the suds and then handing it to her son. 'No point in not tellin' her as soon as you can. Get yourself some bread an' scrape an' a cuppa – you can make me one, as well – then go round to Exchange Flags. They don't finish till six, you've plenty of time.'

'Right, I will.' Roddy rinsed the next sheet, mangled it, pegged it on the line, then rubbed a hand thoughtfully across his chin and heard the resultant rasp with mixed feelings. Seamen could have beards, and it would be grand not to have to shave each day, but Linnet liked a feller to be tidy. Perhaps he'd have a shave before he left, dazzle her with a smooth chin as well as with the news that he had joined the merchant service as a deckhand and would be off the following week.

'All done?' Mrs Sullivan appeared in the doorway with an armful of pillowcases. 'My, I'll be glad when these are done, that Mrs Pedham from the Angel on Dale Street believes in gettin' value for money – still, once they're ironed young Jack delivers 'em and she pays up prompt, I'll give 'er that.'

'I wish you didn't have to do it, though,' Roddy said. 'When I send my allotment home, perhaps you'll be able to ease off a bit. Or you might get another cleaning job.'

'Aye, an' pigs might fly,' Mrs Sullivan said. She wiped sweat off her forehead with the back of her arm and decorated herself with soapsuds. 'Never mind, eh? You don't hear me complainin'.'

'Oh you, you never moan,' Roddy said affectionately.

He went over to the fire and pulled the kettle over the flame, then went to the cupboard and got out a screw of tea, a tin of condensed milk, a half loaf of bread and a packet of margarine. 'What d'you want on your bread and scrape? Can we spare some conny onny?'

'There's nothin' I like better on a buttie than conny onny,' Mrs Sullivan admitted. 'But will there be enough to wet the tea? I don't fancy me tea black an' I've no fresh milk.'

Her son peered into the opened tin of condensed milk.

'Aye, plenty for both,' he decided, standing the tin to one side and beginning to saw at the loaf with the ancient bread-knife. 'Soon have a feast ready, our Mam. Then I'll be off to see Linnet.'

Linnet was finishing off a letter for Mr Cowan, typing away as fast as she could, when he came into the pool and looked around in the rather helpless way men often did when they found themselves amongst so many women – and all working away like mad things, of course, since there were many more shorthand typists in the city than there were jobs. She smiled at him, then waved a hand.

'If it's the letter to General Accident you're after, Mr Cowan, it's over here,' she called. 'I've all but finished it . . . just got the last para to go.'

Mr Cowan looked relieved. He was a bespectacled, dark-haired man in his forties who prided himself, Linnet imagined, on always being spotlessly turned out. He had patent-leather hair – well, it shone like patent-leather – an impeccable dark suit, a severe navy-blue tie with tiny red dots on it and a pencil-line moustache. He was also one of the shy ones.

Linnet had realised soon after starting her first job that the men in the office could be divided into two types: those who were shy with girls and those who felt it obligatory on all occasions to flirt with everything female, even the likes of stout Miss Harper and stringy Miss Elphinstone, who ran the typing pool between them. On the whole, she preferred the shy ones. Rude jokes whispered in one's ear were bad enough, but a squeeze in the confines of the jerky old lift or a hand lingering too long on shoulder or hip could lead to all sorts of trouble. Or so she believed, for she had not been with the Eagle and General Life Insurance Company long enough to be sure how her superiors would behave towards a girl who forgot herself sufficiently to allow a young man to take liberties.

But Mr Cowan was definitely diffident, which was strange because he was married, with a child, and married men, in Linnet's experience, were not generally shy with girls.

But now Mr Cowan was making his way through the desks to Linnet's side and Linnet, with great panache, was finishing off the letter, checking it with a swift glance, and ripping all four copies out of the machine. The top copy was to be sent to the customer, in this case to another insurance company, the second would be added to the fat file, the third would go back with Mr Cowan for his personal file and the fourth, the pink one, would go in Linnet's desk drawer so that any errors, discovered later, could be traced back to her.

'Nearly ready, sir,' Linnet said cheerfully as Mr Cowan bent over her desk and began to read the letter across the top of her head. 'I'll just do you an envelope.'

She took a suitably sized envelope out of her desk drawer, typed the name and address swiftly onto the front of it, and slid the envelope into place. She dealt quickly with the flimsies, then turned to Mr Cowan, who seemed to have finished reading and was fiddling in his pocket, no doubt for the fountain pen with which to add his impressively curly signature at the end of the page.

'Is it all right, sir? Only if so, it can be sent straight down with the rest of our post rather than going back to your office for checking and signature and then coming back here.'

'It seems to be correct,' Mr Cowan said rather stiffly. Linnet was just thinking that he was a bit mean with his praise when he added, 'You type very nicely, Miss er... er. I've yet to find an erasure on a letter sent up by you.'

He could tell who had typed each letter by the initials at the top of the page, of course. LM for Linnet Murphy and AC for... well, for Mr Cowan was the best she could do since she had no idea what his first name was. So now she turned in her chair and smiled up at him, glad to feel that she was a little bit appreciated in this huge firm she had so recently joined.

'Thank you, sir,' she said eagerly. 'I do try not to make mistakes because rubbing out looks so messy.'

It was not precisely what she had meant to say – it sounded rather smug put into words like that – but it pleased Mr Cowan.

'Exactly what I always think,' he said. 'I must have a word with your supervisor.'

When he had taken the letter and gone Miss Everett, who sat next to Linnet and was the nearest thing to a friend she had in the new offices, leaned across the narrow aisle between them. 'Well, you've made a conquest,' she said archly. 'Our Mr Cowan seldom speaks to the typists. Ever so shy he is – he's been worse since his wife died.'

'Died? But she couldn't have been all that old,' Linnet said, beginning to tidy her desk in preparation for going home when Miss Harper or Miss Elphinstone rang the bell. The Eagle and General was very like school if you discounted the number of young men prowling around.

'How old is he, forty-two or three? How did she die?'

'You sound like Cock Robin,' Miss Everett said, giggling. 'Oh no, it's who saw her die, I said the fly with my little eye, I saw her die.'

'Oh don't be silly, Miss Everett,' Linnet said, carrying an armful of files over to the filing tray for the office girls to take back to the basement presently. 'It was a perfectly ordinary question.'

'Yes, of course. Sorry. She died of a fever . . .'

'And no one could save her, and that was the end of sweet Mollie Malone,' sang Linnet under her breath, returning to her desk. 'There you are, I can be silly as well. And it did rather fit in with the song, wouldn't you say?'

'You're a card, Miss Murphy,' Miss Everett said, rather as though she meant something much ruder, though. 'She died of milk fever, I should have said. It was awfully sad. She'd just had a little baby girl, you see, so Mr Cowan was left with the kid, to manage as best he could.'

'Heavens. And how does he manage?'

'Oh, I don't know; I believe he has a mother,' Miss Everett said vaguely. 'I say, did he say he wanted a word with our supervisor?'

'I believe he did,' Linnet said. She put her shorthand notebook into her top drawer and arranged her pencils alongside it, then she straightened her typewriter, which would move sideways, crablike, across her desk as the day wore on, and unfolded her leatherette typewriter cover. 'I expect he was going to tell her she'd done a good job getting me to work here.'

'Oh, the conceit! No, but you see, Mr Cowan's just been upgraded. Mr Smith retired ten days or so ago and Mr Cowan will be doing his job. And that means he'll need a secretary and won't be using the pool any more.'

'Oh, that's a pity,' Linnet said, just as the bell tinkled for the end of the day. All over the long room with its lines of desks and its myriad young ladies, typewriter covers were slammed down over the machines in almost perfect unison, as though the girls had been practising for weeks. 'Just when he's noticed my work . . .'

'You *are* slow,' Miss Everett said in a superior tone. She picked up her handbag and headed for the door, speaking over her shoulder as she went. 'He's looking for a secretary, Miss Murphy, and at least half the typing pool are hoping he's looking at them!'

All the way along the corridor and down the stairs, Linnet mulled over the remark. She could see why Miss Everett had said it but she was sensible enough to attach very little importance to it. Had she not worked like anything at her first job, at the Majestic Assurance Company, staying late, arriving early? First as an office girl, then a junior typist, finally as a trainee shorthand typist? And despite two years' service, had she not been told to pick up her cards when the bosses decided to cut down on staff? There's a depression on, the remaining girls had said wearily as they waved goodbye to half the staff and prepared to do twice the amount of work for rather less wages. You can't even complain when there's a hundred people fighting for every job – you dare not complain. She knew she had been lucky to get this new job.

Still, unlikely though it was that she would be given preferment, she could dream, couldn't she? She stood at her tram stop and stood, also, on the tram when it finally came clattering along, because it was crowded with homegoing workers, all as eager to get away from the city centre as she. She was pressed and pushed and pulled, but at last they reached The Boulevard and she dismounted, sighed and began to walk towards her home.

The sound of someone running along the pavement and shouting breathlessly wasn't all that unusual, but she glanced back anyway, just in case she had left her handbag on the bus or missed a friend – and she had. It was Roddy.

'Hello, our Roddy,' Linnet said as he panted up beside her. She remembered that he had been for an interview for a job on board a ship and guessed from his whole manner that he had been successful, but knew he would want to tell her himself. 'What happened? Any luck?'

There had been other jobs, other interviews; she could still remember the droop of his shoulders when someone had turned him down. But that had been when he had been kicked out of his previous job, before Sampsons on St John's market had taken him on. Then he had been unemployed and beginning to believe himself unemployable. This time he had a job, a steady one, and simply wanted to change from one wage packet to another, or that was how she saw it. And going to sea could be dangerous – she did not know if she approved.

'I gorr . . . I mean I got it.' She had nagged him to improve his speech and now she patted his cheek affectionately, grateful that he realised she was doing it for his own good and did not laugh at her or ignore her advice. 'We sail on Tuesday, at high tide, queen – I'm a deckhand on the SS *Mary Rose*.'

'That's wonderful, Roddy . . . but I'll miss you very much, you know. How long will your voyages be? Is she a liner, or a cargo ship? I bet you're excited . . . how do you know you won't be seasick?'

'She's a cargo ship, a sizeable coaster, in fact. She's out of Liverpool and carries timber, bricks, all sorts, up and down the coast and across to the Scottish islands, sometimes over to Sweden, and to Ireland, as well. Which means we could be away a week, or six, depending. But I don't mind, me Dad was on cargo ships, he says they're all right provided you keep out of the holds. How about comin' out wi' me tonight, to celebrate, like? I shaved on purpose an' I'm still wearin' me best kecks!'

'We-ell . . . were you thinking of going to the flicks?' Linnet asked hopefully. She did love the cinema, particularly the talkies, which had put the old silent films completely in the shade. 'I've not been to the Rotunda for absolutely ages.'

'I thought a dance; then we could cuddle,' Roddy said with all his usual forthrightness. 'I like to get me arms round you, Linnet Murphy, an' hold you to me manly bosom!'

It made Linnet laugh but she took hold of his arm and gave it a pinch, then stood on tiptoe to kiss his cheek.

'Roddy Sullivan, you are a darlin',' she said vigorously. 'Tell you what, though I know it's not at all the thing, come back to my room and I'll make us a little supper, then we can decide where to go later. What do you say?'

'Gee whizz,' Roddy said in true cinema fashion. 'You say the cutest things, Miss Murphy – sure I'll come to your place!'

'Well, I know people might talk, but you're like a brother to me, always have been,' Linnet pointed out righteously. 'And whilst I do the cooking you can tell me all about your new job. Now, why are you pulling that long face, our Roddy?'

'I am not your bleedin' brother,' Roddy shouted, causing several heads to turn accusingly in their direction. 'Nor I don't want to be. I want . . . I want . . .'

'I want never got; do you remember how your mam used to say that to us when we were kids?' Linnet said diplomatically. She caught his hand and squeezed his fingers hard, then smiled up into his face. 'She says it to Freddy and Jack still, I expect. Oh Roddy, don't scowl, it spoils your nice, friendly face. Come on, I'll race you to No 8!'

In all the excitement of going round to the Sullivans' and helping Roddy decide what he should pack for his first voyage, Linnet completely forgot the brief visit of Mr Cowan to the typing pool and Miss Everett's remarks. In fact, when she went up to Canning dock to wave Roddy off very early on Tuesday morning, with a light mist hovering over the face of the Mersey and the streets strangely hushed, she found herself crying so hard that work scarcely seemed important at all. Roddy was her childhood companion, her dearest friend, and he was going away, into danger, where she could not follow!

'The lad'll only be away five or six weeks, aren't we daft?' Mrs Sullivan said through her tears, clutching Linnet's arm. 'Why, when 'e comes 'ome it'll be like me 'olidays, that's all!'

'I know, but I like seeing him on a Sunday, I like talkin' to him,' Linnet said, rubbing her eyes with the backs of her hands. 'He's grand to talk to, is your Roddy.'

The two women stared out across the shining flagstones of the dock as the SS *Mary Rose*, siren sounding forlornly across the oily water, disappeared into the mist. Then they dried their eyes, blew their noses, said six weeks would soon go and wasn't it a great chance for him, and went to a canny house nearby to eat bacon and eggs and drink strong tea before departing, Roddy's mother back to her home and Linnet to the insurance office on Exchange Flags.

'Miss Murphy? Miss Harper wants a word with you. Go to her room at once, please.'

'Of course, Miss Elphinstone. I'll go right away.'

Linnet felt her cheeks grow hot with apprehension but

she typed to the end of the line anyway, then stood up. Summonses to the office usually meant that you had done something wrong but though she racked her brains as she walked sedately across the typing pool she could think of nothing. She had been in early this morning because of seeing Roddy off, she had started work immediately, however, and had not waited until her normal arrival time. What could it be? And did she look neat and tidy, because Miss Harper was always nagging them about personal appearance? She would have liked to rush along to the ladies' cloaks to check her hair, make sure that her nose wasn't shiny and that she hadn't managed to transfer the ink from her typewriter ribbon to her cheeks or chin, but she would have to take a chance. Miss Harper disliked being kept waiting even more than she disliked a slapdash appearance.

Miss Elphinstone, being the junior of the two supervisors, usually worked at her machine at the long desk in the typing pool, opposite the door, whilst Miss Harper, as senior supervisor, could mostly be found in a tiny cell of an office just up the corridor. Here she checked the work going in and coming out, took calls from members of staff who wanted a shorthand writer to take dictation, chose who should go where and generally made sure that the pool ran smoothly. Linnet had only worked here for five weeks but already she knew that Miss Harper also brewed coffee in the office, sent out for sandwiches which she munched whilst hiding behind a large sheet of legal paper, and took personal calls on the telephone which stood on the right-hand side of her desk. Miss Elphinstone, who helped out when the typing pool was frantically busy and never let 'her girls' down if she could avoid it, was popular amongst them, to an extent at least, but Miss Harper was much disliked.

'She can be vindictive,' Linnet had been warned. 'If she takes agin you she can make trouble. It's best to be very, very polite to Miss Harper and don't you ever call her just "Miss", 'cos that's asking for trouble; she likes us to use her full name.'

So Linnet tapped on the door, waited a moment, and then walked in.

Miss Harper was sitting behind her desk, apparently writing in a large ledger. There was a strong smell of coffee in the air and an empty cup stood beside the streamlined white typewriter which was a sign of Miss Harper's power and influence – everyone else, including Miss Elphinstone, had a black machine. There was talk, of course, about how she got the machine; but I don't believe a word of it, Linnet told herself, she's too fat and spiteful and although Mr Cripps, the manager, is old and has bad breath, he surely wouldn't . . .

'Good morning, Miss Harper. Miss Elphinstone said you wanted to see me.'

Linnet stood as the nuns had taught her; feet demurely side by side, hands clasped before her, eyes on the ground. Then she looked up, because she knew people thought you were sly if you didn't look them in the face and saw Miss Harper was staring at her. She was looking at Linnet as though she couldn't understand something; her eyes were going up and down, up and down . . .

'Ah, yes. So you're Murphy, I couldn't quite recall. You've not been with us long I believe, Miss Murphy.'

'Just five weeks, Miss Harper,' Linnet murmured. What was this all about? And why was the wretched woman staring at her like that, as though she was searching for a pair of horns growing out of Linnet's newly shingled head?

'So short a time? And already you've managed to catch a gentleman's eye. Tell me, just how did you do it? I can't say your looks are in any way exceptional – I'm not saying you're plain, precisely, but you certainly aren't as eye-catching as, say, Miss Franchini, yet no one's approached me about her, yet.'

Miss Franchini was a flashing-eyed brunette, the result of a liaison between an Italian seaman and an Irish barmaid from a waterside pub. She was very beautiful but liable to throw tantrums – and typewriter rubbers – when things annoyed her. Perplexed, Linnet tried to remember whether she herself had ever lost her temper whilst working for the company, and decided she had not. So what on earth was Miss Harper going on about?

'I'm sorry, I don't quite . . .'

'You don't quite what, Miss Murphy? What have I said that has puzzled you so? Surely you must realise why I've called you into my office?'

Linnet shook her head. There seemed little point in pretending; she was completely in the dark. 'No, I'm afraid . . .'

'Oh, come now! Mr Cowan came to me a fortnight ago and said he would like you to do his work for a while. Since then, he's been over to your desk on at least two occasions – at least! Surely you did not imagine that he was so enamoured of your work that he had to see you personally on two occasions, when he could just as easily have telephoned through to me that the work was urgent? I don't know what you said to him, Miss Murphy, or what you offered . . .'

'I said nothing, except that his letters were in my "out" tray,' Linnet said firmly. 'As for offering . . .'

Miss Harper cut in at once, and Linnet saw that her cheeks were faintly flushed. 'No, that was badly put. Anyway, you'd best pack your personal belongings; you're leaving us.'

'Today? Without working out any notice? But I don't

understand, I've done nothing wrong, there have been no complaints . . .'

'Yes, you're leaving us. But only, you little simpleton, to move up to the second floor as Mr Cowan's secretary. As if you didn't know!' Miss Harper hissed, her eyes narrowing. 'Why, you must think I was born yesterday!'

A dozen retorts, all of them unkind, danced into Linnet's head, but she banished them firmly. This was a good job, and a secretarial job was beyond her wildest dreams. She would not put it past Miss Harper to be saying all this as some form of nasty practical joke, but just in case . . .

'Thank you, Miss Harper,' she said, instead. 'I'll go and get my things together.' And before the older woman could say another word she had turned and left the room.

Back in the typing pool, it was a nine days' wonder, of course. Only Miss Everett said that she had known all along and that wasn't Miss Murphy a dark horse?

'Come back and see us,' the girls begged as she emptied her desk drawers and filled the large paper sack which Miss Elphinstone had given her. 'Don't go all snobby on us, come back and have your sandwiches with us now and then.'

'Of course I will,' Linnet said stoutly. 'Besides, I probably won't be a secretary for long, not once they realise I've never been one before and don't know the ropes. Oh, I'll be back in the pool before you can say knife, see if I'm not.'

And she might have been, but for two people.

Mr Cowan was the first, and he was on her side from the start. He made it plain that he had chosen her out of the typing pool because he thought she would suit him, and suit him she did. He explained, slowly and carefully, what he wanted her to do and was always quick to congratulate her when she got things right – a very different attitude from that of Miss Harper, who took rightness for granted and grew furiously angry over the tiniest mistake.

The other was Miss Beasley, whose room she shared, for even someone as important as Mr Cowan did not have a private room for his secretary. Miss Beasley was twenty-four, engaged to be married to a successful plumber called Joseph Cartwright, and very elegant. She was tall and slim, with white-blonde hair and large light-blue eyes. She dressed in impeccable dark suits and crisp light-coloured blouses and had a pleasant manner though rather a strident voice. She talked in a very posh way when her boss, Mr Griseworth, was about, and with a local accent when she and Linnet were by themselves. And she was the epitome of secretarial efficiency. She told Linnet she was, using those very words, and when Linnet said, half-laughing, that she didn't know what an epitome was, she threw over a worn copy of Nuttalls's Dictionary and told her new colleague to look it up.

'You've gorra be good at your work, queen,' she said on Linnet's first day, "cos if you get sent back to the pool old Harps'll make your life a misery. Still, I reckon you must be good or old Cowie wouldn't have got you to work for him, but there's good an' good, if you understand me. This job ain't just shorthand an' typing, not once they make you a secretary it ain't. It's book his ticket on the train, get seats at the theatre, take his best suit in for cleaning, buy flowers for his wife on her birthday – remember her birthday come to that, when sure as eggs he's clean forgot. Oh aye, you'll be mam and dad to the feller, you'll all but wipe his bum for him, and if he thanks you a couple of times a year you'll be walking on air, ready to lay down your life for the bugger.'

The bad language, coming from such an unlikely source, made Linnet giggle. 'Is that all true, or are you kidding me?' she asked incredulously. 'I wouldn't know where to start – I've never even used a telephone, you know, and the thought of doing that scares me, let alone booking tickets.'

'Stick with me, honey,' Miss Beasley said, imitating the latest American star to hit the silver screen. 'And you won't go far wrong. By the way, I'm Rose. You?'

'Oh . . . I'm Linnet. Hello, Rose.'

'Hello, Linnet. First names are friendlier, I always say, but we'll only use them when we're by ourselves or out o' the office, because it sounds unbusinesslike. Now come over here and I'll show you how to make a telephone call.'

Linnet was perched on the windowsill in the communal kitchen of No 8, eating toast and looking out at the backyard criss-crossed with laden washing lines, when the door burst open and one of the other residents came in, backwards, having opened the door by butting it with her bottom. She was carrying a heavily laden tray.

'Morning, Margaret; what've you got there?' Linnet asked, eyeing her fellow resident as Margaret thumped the tray down on the wooden draining board. 'It looks like a year's washing up to me.'

'Cheeky mare – it's only a week's,' Margaret said. She was a square, muscular girl of Linnet's own age, clad, today, in a black skirt with stains down the front and a faded gingham blouse. Her substantial legs were bare and she wore down-at-heel pumps on her feet. 'I don't see the point of washin' up while there's a clean cup in the 'ouse. Ain't it a grand day, though? You're workin' this morning, I suppose, but I'm catchin' the tram an' goin' up to the market. Anything I can get you whiles I'm there?'

'Oh, Margaret, you're a pal – Rose and I thought we

might go out this afternoon as it's so sunny so I shan't get a chance to do me shopping. I could do wi' some veggies – spuds and a cabbage would be grand, though if they're selling something nicer, like peas, I wouldn't mind a pound of 'em. And a bit of meat, enough for two, in case I have a visitor.'

'Oh, aye? Roddy in port, then?' Margaret tried to look arch but only succeeded in looking nosy, her black eyes glittering with curiosity and a hopeful smile curving her mouth. She did like to be first with the news did Margaret!

'No. Not for another week.'

'Oh? Then who might you be cookin' for, come Sunday?'

'Honestly Margaret, it could be anyone, I know enough people! There's Roddy's mum, she pops round from time to time, and then there's me friend Rose from work, and Anita, me old school pal . . .'

'Which? Which one will you be entertainin', come Sunday?'

'None of 'em, so far as I know. It's just that a bit of meat for two can be eaten cold on Monday, or, if I *do* have an unexpected visitor . . . see what I'm getting at?'

'You're tellin' me loud ones, that's what,' Margaret said with unimpaired cheerfulness. 'Makin' me think you was entertainin' someone! I thought it might be the feller you work for – I'd be made up if I could just set eyes on him – but no, you was havin' me on. So it's peas if they've gorrem, cabbage if they ain't, an' a bit o' meat for two. Want some wet nellies for your afters?'

'I don't think they'd keep all that well,' Linnet said, wrinkling her nose. 'Get me some fruit for a pie, would you, chuck? Anything they're selling.'

'Right. Where's your chink?'

'Oh, hang on.' Linnet slid off the windowsill and went

over to her handbag hanging on the back of the door with her jacket; there was no point in climbing the stairs more than you had to each day, so she usually left for work as soon as she'd eaten her breakfast. She fished around in the bag and produced a shilling. 'Will this do?'

'That'll do,' Margaret allowed. She took the money and slid it into her apron pocket. 'If you're out when I get back I'll hang onto the stuff, awright?'

'Grand. Thanks, love,' Linnet said as Margaret disappeared, slamming the door behind her. She liked most of the other residents in the big, once-grand old house, and Margaret was no exception, though some of the other girls said she was no better than she ought to be and that the young men she brought home were not, as she claimed, cousins but customers. It could have been true; Margaret was sloppy to the point of sluttishness in the house but dressed up to the nines just to walk down to the corner shop. But whatever her occupation, Margaret was kind, generous when able to be so and good company, and who could ask for more?

Not me, certainly, Linnet thought now, washing up her cup and plate and standing them on the stained dresser beside the rest of her kitchen utensils. Again, with a kitchen on the ground floor and a flat under the eaves there was little point in lugging pots, pans and cutlery up and down and everyone in the house did the same so things rarely went missing.

I don't mind Auntie Sullivan and Roddy coming round, Linnet told herself now, automatically tidying the kitchen and rinsing out the tea-towel before hanging it on the piece of string which the girls had looped across the sink for just that purpose. But I wouldn't like Rose to come. She is so nice, but she wouldn't think much of it, though she would have liked Mammy's rooms.

The thought of little Evie brought a lump to her

daughter's throat, for the previous year she had at long last had definite proof of her mother's death. A friend of Mr Sullivan's, a seaman on the Atlantic run, had volunteered to make some enquiries next time he docked at Staten Island and had come home with an old newspaper cutting telling of the death of Evie Murphy, whom theatre-goers might remember as the little Evie of a few years back.

He had even bought flowers and put them on the grave, and had refused Linnet's offer of payment.

'I remember little Evie when she played at the Royal Court,' he said gruffly. 'Mebbe you'll go over yourself, one day. Put the money towards that.'

Linnet thanked him, but she knew she would never go to New York herself. She had been left, more or less forgotten, and though she bore little Evie no grudge, neither was she foolishly sentimental. She had loved her mammy and her mammy, she believed, had loved her, but with little Evie's death Linnet had been cast even more on her own resources and now it took her all her time and energy just to keep herself respectable and fed with a roof over her head. And no one would blame me for not missing someone who I'd not seen for so long, Linnet told herself a trifle defensively. Our lives were running on different tracks long before Mammy died.

She picked up the mop and went swiftly over the floor, then glanced up at the clock which had been Roddy's gift when he came ashore for his first leave. She had put it in the kitchen because they all needed a reminder of the time down here and there was simply no space in her tiny room. But there was no hurry, it was still only half past seven in the morning. She and the other girls got up very early in the summer because the attic rooms in particular grew both warm and airless as the day went on. So they did their housework whilst it was still quite cool and then, when they returned from work, they could sit outside on the strip of grass between them and the road, play games, call out, and relax until darkness fell and their rooms were losing their heat once more.

Time for one more quick cup of tea, then I really must get going, Linnet told herself, bustling across to her teapot and testing the side of it with the backs of her fingers. It was still hot enough for one more cup. She poured the tea and then sat on the windowsill once more, dreaming away to herself and sipping lukewarm tea carefully; it would not do to have a teastain on her cream-coloured blouse nor on the green cotton skirt which was so elegantly long that it brushed her ankles as she walked.

She had to be smart for work. Rose said it was important and anyway, what was the point in having some decent clothes if they were only worn once in a blue moon? Roddy took her out when he was home but the SS *Mary Rose* had a quick turn-round and he sometimes said jokingly that their lips barely met in their first kiss before they were wrenched apart again and he was off once more.

And Linnet was beginning to suspect that Roddy really enjoyed the life, that he would be a seaman, from choice, for ever if he could. Oh he kept declaring that he wanted to marry her and settle down, but settling down meant, presumably, getting a shore-job, and there was so much unemployment in Liverpool that no one with any sense would advise him to do anything so risky. Especially when he was good at what he did now and enjoyed it and had thoroughly disliked butchery.

But she must stop dreaming and get ready for work. Linnet rinsed her cup, emptied her teapot, then stood back and checked her reflection in the window pane. It wasn't ideal but she could at least see if she had a droopy hem or a bad mark on her blouse. But the most careful check did not reveal anything particularly wrong, and since she and Rose intended to go on the overhead railway right along to Seaforth Sands, she would do her best to look neat and pretty – Rose certainly would. In the summer months Rose favoured cotton skirts and tops or well cut summer dresses with white piping at neck and hem. She had a real flair for clothes and Linnet was happy to take her advice when buying a new garment of any description. Rose had been with her when she chose her green cotton skirt and she had great faith in its ability to make her look nice.

Having checked her appearance Linnet reached for her long cream linen jacket and handbag, slid her feet into her sensible walking shoes, cast a last glance around the room and set off. Her step was light and she felt like singing as she crossed the rather dingy hallway. She let herself out into the morning and saw Mr Proud, from next door, tapping his way along the pavement. He would be on his way to the tram stop and since he was blind Linnet hurried to give him a hand. Not in an obvious sort of way, of course, since Mr Proud had his pride, ha ha, but unobtrusively, to ensure he wasn't pushed or jostled at the stop and that he got a seat when the tram arrived.

'Morning, Mr Proud,' Linnet said rather breathlessly when she reached him. He walked fast despite his disability. 'You don't work on a Saturday morning, do you?'

Mr Proud was a piano tuner in one of the biggest music shops in the city; Linnet, who had learned to play to a fair standard on her mother's little upright, often talked wistfully to him of how she had enjoyed using the instrument, and he had promised to find her a good, cheap secondhand model when she had saved up. She knew she could not have it whilst she remained in her tiny room at No 8, but Linnet was an optimist. One day, she told herself, she would get a better job and move to a room where, if she wished, she might entertain a guest now and then, or even swing a cat! But now Mr Proud turned towards her, smiling.

'Ah, it's Miss Murphy, I never mistake a voice. You're quite right, I don't go round to people's homes to tune their instruments on a Saturday morning, but I do play in the store. People who can't play a note buy pianos, you know, but they all fancy themselves experts on tone and touch when they hear someone else play. So I sit down and tickle the ivories for them and if they buy I get a small – very small – bonus. Now have we reached the tram stop? My stick says we have.'

'Your stick says right,' Linnet assured him. 'You're magic, Mr Proud, I don't know how you tell where you are, I'm sure.'

'Sounds reflect differently off different objects,' Mr Proud told her. 'A tram makes different sounds on corners, you must have noticed, and then there's the paving-edge. There's quite a big piece of kerb missing just before you reach the stop.'

'I think you must be the most observant person I've ever met,' Linnet said humbly. 'And I won't tell you that the tram's coming, because I'm sure you know, nor that we've about a dozen people in the queue before us.'

'Thirteen,' Mr Proud said gravely, then chuckled as though he could see Linnet's astonished look. 'Just teasing, Miss Murphy!'

Linnet had been in a happy frame of mind when she got on the tram and arriving at the office to find their small room full of sunshine and flower-scents lifted her spirits even further. She was first in and hung her jacket on the peg behind the door, then turned to take the covers off the typewriters – and simply stared.

On her desk, laid carefully across her machine, was the source of the lovely scent. It was a positive sheaf of pink and red roses – there must have been a couple of dozen lying there, their stems wrapped in the pale pink and silver paper used, Linnet knew, by a very superior flower shop indeed.

A passing messenger boy, peering in through the doorway, whistled. 'Cor, 'oo's gerrin' wed, then, eh? If that's Miss Beasley's feller 'e's splashin' out ain't 'e? That little lot cost a bob or three!'

'I don't think it can be Mr Cartwright, since he sent Miss Beasley a bouquet of pinks and cornflowers only yesterday,' Linnet said cautiously. She approached the flowers as though they might bite her, touching the nearest head with one forefinger. 'And they're on *my* typewriter; it must be a mistake.'

'Well, I didn't deliver 'em,' the messenger boy said positively. 'Ain't there a card, Miss M?'

'No, I don't think . . . oh yes, there is,' Linnet said, considerably relieved. The nightmare of having to lug the flowers around three floors, each one of which contained countless rooms, had just occurred to her. 'Let me see . . .'

It wasn't a card, in fact, but a tiny white envelope. It had no name on, which made her hesitate for a moment, but she slit it open and pulled out the card, turning it over to read the carefully scripted note on the other side.

Miss Murphy; would you do me the honour of lunching with me today? she read, though not out loud. *I should be most grateful for your company and also for some advice. Yours sincerely, A. Cowan.*

'Oo's it from, then?' the messenger boy asked. He was still standing in the doorway but so curious was he that his neck had stretched out like a giraffe and his eyes, apparently on stalks, seemed to start from their sockets. 'Come on, gel, are they for you?'

'Yes, they're mine. From a – a gentleman friend,' Linnet said, picking the bouquet up and burying her nose thankfully in the scented blossoms. She had no intention of telling anyone – anyone at all – that the flowers came from Mr Cowan! 'Do go away, Frankie, and shut my door!'

'Some gentleman! Guess 'e's rollin' in the readies,' Frankie said enviously. 'Bet 'e's old as the 'ills an' ugly, too. Fellers wi' that much money always is.'

'Go away,' Linnet said nervously. Suppose Mr Cowan had come out of his office up the corridor and heard that unflattering view! 'I would like to do some work this morning if it's all the same to you, young man.'

Frankie shrugged and began to withdraw. 'Awright, awright, keep your bleedin' 'air on,' he said airily. 'It ain't nine o'clock yet, nowhere near, so if I want to . . . oh! Sorry, miss, I didn't see you standin' there.'

'I imagine you did not,' Rose said frostily, rubbing her elbow where Frankie had backed into her. She waited until Frankie, crestfallen, had taken himself off, then came in, shut the door, and began to take her jacket off. 'What a crowd on the tram – you don't know how much I'm longing for Seaforth sands – good Lord above, where did you get them from?'

'From Mr Cowan,' Linnet said in hollow tones, completely forgetting her resolve of two minutes earlier. 'Just read the note, Rose! He wants to take me out to lunch today . . . oh Miss Beasley, what on earth am I to do?'

'Goodbye, Seaforth Sands,' Rose said regretfully, then came across the office and took the flowers and the note from Linnet's unresisting hands. She read the note, then looked up and smiled encouragingly at her friend. 'You must go, queen. He's a nice feller is Mr Cowan, he won't eat you. But he might feel like doing so if you turn him down.'

'Turn him *down*? You make it sound like a date, a proper date,' Linnet gasped. 'He's married . . . well, he's a widow, then. Widows don't take their secretaries on *dates*!'

'He's a widower, not a widow, and of course widowers take girls on dates,' Rose said bracingly. 'How else would they ever re-marry?'

'*Re-marry*? Oh, but-but-but-'

'Do stop stuttering, Miss Murphy, and listen for a minute. Mr Cowan is a widower but he isn't an old man despite what you seem to think. Do I seem like an old woman to you?'

'Honest to God, I've never thought . . . never said . . .' stammered Linnet, much embarrassed. When she had first met Rose she had indeed thought her somewhat long in the tooth, but that had not lasted. Now, she and Rose were just two girls, neither of whom was yet wed. 'You're only half-a-dozen years older than me, Rose! Oh, I'm sorry, I mean Miss Beasley. But Mr Cowan must be . . . well, I don't know how old he is, precisely, but he seems . . .'

'He's probably only in his early forties, not even twenty years older than me and not so much older than you, either,' Rose said. 'So stop thinking of him as an elderly man, because he isn't. Why, he couldn't even be your father, not unless he started awful young. And start practising saying, "*Thank you, Mr Cowan, I would be delighted to lunch with you today,*" because that's what you mean and that's what you are jolly well going to do!'

'I can't! I couldn't possibly! What about Roddy? Oh how I would like to throw these *bloody* roses straight out o' the *bloody* window and forget they ever came!'

Now it was Rose's turn to giggle; she had never heard Linnet swear before. 'Yes, all right, I can see you're embarrassed by the whole business, but you mustn't be foolish, queen. Just you read that note again, careful like. Go on, do it now, whilst I put the roses in water for you.' She buried her own face in the blossoms, inhaling luxuriously. 'Now that's what I call a good scent,' she said, turning to leave the room. 'We'll be swooning wi' it by lunchtime, see if we aren't!'

When she had gone, Linnet got out the little card and read it again. And gradually, her fears began to subside. It was not a lover-like note, it was quite a sensible one. Mr Cowan wanted company; well, that was understandable, he had a little girl and no wife, he must have problems which he thought another woman might be able to solve. *But why didn't he ask a woman, in that case?* a little voice in her head demanded querulously. *Why ask a girl who's only nineteen?*

Perhaps, Linnet told herself, he simply doesn't know many women. But he does know me, I've been working as his secretary for three whole months and we've always got on very well. When I go through to take dictation we quite often have a little chat. The fact that the chat usually consisted of an enquiry as to her state of health, a polite rejoinder and then a request that she might bring him in coffee and biscuits for two people at eleven o'clock since he would have the general manager in his office at around that time was, she told herself, neither here nor there. Her boss was far too conscientious to indulge in light chat in the firm's time. And besides, on a Monday, when he enquired after her weekend, she often told him what she had done at some length, and he did the same. He had gone to New Brighton and sat on the sands, his daughter – her name was Mollie – had tasted her first ice-cream cone, they had come home with pink and peeling noses.

It wasn't much, but it was something. So when Rose came back with the flowers in a rather nice cut glass vase borrowed from the Claims Department, Linnet, pink-faced but determined, was about to set off for Mr Cowan's room.

'What was I to say?' she hissed as Rose sailed into the room with the flowers held out before her. 'Go on, tell me again or I'll make a pig's ear of it.'

'Thank you for the flowers, they're lovely, and I'd be delighted to have lunch with you,' Rose said, giving a mock curtsy and squealing as water tipped from the vase and splashed onto the floor. 'Go on, off with you!'

Linnet hurried down the corridor, repeating the words Rose had just said under her breath. She tapped on Mr Cowan's door and entered, and for a moment sheer terror rooted her to the spot, just inside the door, whilst she stared at her boss like a sparrow mesmerised by a snake.

She might have stood there for ever, until she dropped dead she thought later, but then she looked – really looked – at Mr Cowan, who had risen to his feet and was staring across at her, his eyes eager yet anxious; 'Like a kid waiting for a pat on the head but fearing a slap,' she told Rose later. He didn't look old any longer, either. He looked quite human, really, considering he was a head of department in a large insurance company.

Linnet cleared her throat. 'Thank you very much for the roses; they're really beautiful,' she said, departing from the script but not minding, now. 'And I'd be delighted to have lunch with you today.'

He smiled at her. He had smiled at her before, often, but not like this. Not a frank, broad smile which showed his teeth and made her smile back at him.

'I'm glad you didn't think I was being – well, fresh,' he said. 'We'll go somewhere nice – d'you fancy the Lawrence Hotel, on Mount Pleasant? The food's very good and the service is excellent. Or would you prefer somewhere smaller, more . . . well, smaller?'

'I'd like somewhere smaller, really,' Linnet said shyly. 'I don't know much about restaurants though – you choose.'

'Well, why don't we go to the Albany on Oldhall Street?' Mr Cowan suggested. 'The surroundings are pleasant and it's quiet, too. The offices close at 12.30 today so I'll order a taxi for one o'clock – or do you need more time to make arrangements?'

'No, because R . . . Miss Beasley and I had planned to go to Seaforth Sands this afternoon,' Linnet said, and found she did not regret her missed outing now because she could see she would enjoy herself with Mr Cowan, though differently, of course. 'So a friend's doing my shopping. And I live by myself, of course, so there's no one at home I should tell.'

'Of course. Mollie's nanny usually leaves at two o'clock on a Saturday – she has the weekend off – but she's staying on today until teatime.' He glanced down at the desk, then across at her again. 'I thought, perhaps, we might – might go back to my place and take – take Mollie out with us, for some tea?'

'I'd love to meet her,' Linnet said warmly, and truthfully, too. She liked children but had very little to do with them, apart from two boys of eight and ten who lived in the rooms beneath hers and made the weekends hideous with their fights and quarrels when their parents were out.

Mr Cowan smiled again; well, beamed, really. He looked happy and relieved – and all I did was agree to go out to lunch and then to meet his little girl, Linnet thought with amazement.

'Good, good. And now, Miss Murphy, perhaps we had better get down to business. I've got half-a-dozen letters which should really go this morning . . . if you could fetch your pad and pencil?'

*

Lunch was a rare treat for Linnet, who had never been into a restaurant as smart and discreet as the Albany, let alone eaten such food. Mr Cowan had reserved a table and though there were other diners they took no notice of the quiet couple in the corner and very soon Linnet was chattering away to Mr Cowan as though she had known him all her life.

'Let me pour you some wine, Miss Murphy,' Mr Cowan said when the wine arrived, and Linnet felt her face grow hot. Her mother had warned her that gentlemen who pressed ladies to take drink might, occasionally, mean them harm. But how to refuse without giving offence?

'I've never drunk wine, but I d-don't think I shall care for it, Mr Cowan,' Linnet said, and then added, highly daring, 'I wonder whether I might, if – if it wouldn't inconvenience anyone, perhaps have some water, instead? Only I know that strong drink sometimes makes girls tiddly, and since I'm not used to it . . .'

Mr Cowan laughed. 'The last thing I want is a tiddly secretary, Miss Murphy! Of course you can have water but I'll order you a glass of fruit juice, or some lemonade, if you wish. I'm sorry I didn't think of it, because naturally a girl of your age wouldn't fancy – er – strong drink,' Mr Cowan said. 'Now let me help you to some of this excellent sole, and some of the shrimp sauce, too.'

Linnet was much relieved that she was not about to be pressed into drinking wine, though it looked innocent enough as it was poured into Mr Cowan's glass. It was a light golden colour and little bubbles formed on the bottom of the glass and then rose to the top, behaviour very similar to that of ginger beer, a beverage which Linnet much enjoyed. She watched Mr Cowan taking several glasses of the bubbly golden liquid without any ill effect and halfway through the meal, to her own tremendous surprise, Linnet heard her voice saying, 'The fruit juice is very nice, Mr Cowan, but I – I wonder if I might try just a little wine?' She waited for the sky to fall on her – having refused his early offer to now turn round and ask for wine seemed very daring indeed – but he just said, gravely, that it was a vintage of which most ladies he knew approved and poured her half a glass.

Linnet tasted it; it was absolutely delicious and the little bubbles fizzed pleasantly on her tongue. What was more, when she told Mr Cowan that it was really very nice he poured her a proper glass, and when she finished that the waiter, who had been hovering, brought a whole fresh bottle to the table and poured a little into a fresh glass. Mr Cowan tasted it and nodded, then told the waiter to pour his guest another glass.

'I don't think I'd better,' Linnet said regretfully. She had concluded that the beautiful glow and the warm self-confidence which had enveloped her might well be the work of the wine. Heaven knew what she might do if she drank yet more of the exciting beverage. 'Oh, do look at the trolley, Mr Cowan! What wonderful jellies and trifles and cakes!'

He smiled at her indulgently, fondly almost. 'I like to see you enjoying your food with such gusto,' he murmured. 'So many girls just pick at their plates – I hate that.'

'I'm greedy,' Linnet said, regretfully but without shame. 'I do so like nice food!'

'So do I,' Mr Cowan agreed. 'Ah, here comes the trolley – now you may choose whatever pudding you like best. And I'll have a nice cup of coffee and some cheese and biscuits.'

'I'll have . . . that one, please,' Linnet said, pointing to a concoction in which cream, strawberries and meringues seemed to play a large part. 'No thank you, I don't think I'll need any extra cream. And I'd like a coffee, too, please.'

As she dug her spoon into her pudding, Linnet reflected that, if her mother could have seen her now, she would have been most impressed. It had taken Linnet quite a long time, but eventually she had realised that the admirers and impresarios who had thronged little Evie's life had, in fact, been her mother's lovers. They had bought both little Evie and her daughter nice presents and had taken them out for meals very similar to this one – had given them a gay old time, in fact. Yet I, Linnet thought complacently, have got all this not by agreeing to go to bed with Mr Cowan, but by typing his letters nicely! It seemed a far better bargain than Evie's, to Evie's practical daughter.

Chapter Eight

On Monday morning, Rose was all agog to hear how her friend had got on with Mr Cowan. Linnet would have liked to keep her in suspense for a little, but since she was dying to talk about it and Rose was dying to listen, they very soon settled down to a good gossip, though they waited until their lunch-hour, since both spent busy mornings taking dictation and typing up the resultant letters.

'Well?' Rose said at last, as the two of them set off for the Nelson memorial where, on sunny days, they liked to sit to eat their sandwiches. 'Come on, what happened? Where did he take you?'

'We went to the Albany and had a lovely dinner – lunch, I mean; then we caught a taxi and went right to the other side of the city, to Mr Cowan's house. He lives in the most beautiful street, it's called Sunnyside, and the gardens all have trees and grass and that. The house is awfully smart and huge, Rose, bigger than any house I've ever been in before. And I met Mollie, that's his daughter, and Nanny Peters, and then Nanny Peters went off for the weekend and Mr Cowan and I took Mollie to the park and we fed the ducks and Mollie went on the swings. And then we had a delicious tea with buttered toast first and then cream cakes at ever such a nice little café on Smithdown Road, and after that Mr Cowan took me home in his huge car – I bet you didn't know he had a motor, did you, Rose? – and took me right to my front door. I was afraid he might suggest coming in with me, but he didn't, so I waved him off and trotted upstairs... it was a lovely day, honest to God it was.'

'And what did he want to talk to you about?' Rose enquired archly as they trotted down Exchange Passage and headed for the memorial. 'You've not mentioned that, I notice!'

'I don't actually know,' Linnet said slowly. 'I've just realised, he never asked my advice about anything, anything at all. We just had a really nice time, honest to God we did.'

'Perhaps it was a ruse to get you to go out with him,' Rose said shrewdly. 'He's got a private income, you know, as well as his salary. He may be afraid a girl is after his money, but he'd like to know you weren't like that. Besides he's really quite shy when he's not talking about insurance, wouldn't you say? Perhaps he just wanted to meet you outside the office and didn't know how else to persuade you.'

'He was nice, and we had a nice time,' Linnet repeated thoughtfully. 'And Mollie is a darling. There was only one thing which seemed odd...'

'What? Was it about the kid or about Mr Cowan?' Rose asked at once. 'Let's sit down quickly, though, queen. I spy a group of tatty 'eaded office clerks headin' for our favourite seat.'

They hurried across to the statue and got to the seats before the young men, who pretended they had never wanted to sit down anyway, and started to throw bits of bread at the pigeons whilst covertly eyeing the two girls sitting on the seat with their heads close.

'Any minute now one of 'em will come across and ask if we've got a light, or the time, or some such,' Rose said gloomily. 'Go on then, chuck. What was odd?'

'Well, it was Mollie. I don't know an awful lot about kids, any more than you do, Rose, but I've helped

Roddy's mam with his little brothers, and I don't think any kid should be as good as Mollie was. She's only just two and a half but she stood by her father and threw bread when he handed her a piece, never shouted out or tried to get near the ducks, never went near the water, even. I thought I'd better hold her skirt, but there was no need. She stayed where she was told to stand.'

'Isn't that good?' Rose said doubtfully. 'I'd ha' thought it were.'

'Oh, it's good, all right, it just isn't natural,' Linnet said. 'And it was the same at teatime. Mr Cowan lifted her onto a chair and there she sat. She drank milk out of a mug, no slopping it around, and then she ate a shortbread biscuit. There were lovely cakes but she never asked for one or reached out, even. I took a little round cake with marzipan leaves and a yellow flower on top and offered it to her and she looked scared . . . she put her hand out a little way, then snatched it back, then looked up at her daddy so – so doubtfully. And when I said, go on love, you take it, she didn't attempt to do so until he'd said the same.'

'Hmm. Do you think he's cruel to her? Is that what you're saying?'

'I don't think so. I don't know him very well, except in the office, but he seems proud of her, and I think he'd be affectionate to her if he knew how, but he doesn't seem to. To tell you the truth, Rose, I didn't take to Nanny Peters, good though she may be.'

'Ah ha, I thought there must be a snag somewhere,' Rose said with a smirk. 'How old is she?'

'Oh, young. In her early twenties, I should think. And pretty, too. But . . . there was something about her . . .'

'Do you think Mr Cowan was angling for her and asked you over to show her that he had other female friends?' Rose asked after a moment, when Linnet had done nothing but stare into space. 'Was that what it was?'

'Oh, Rose, all you ever think about is *that*,' Linnet said, not bothering to elaborate further. 'I don't think it was that, though I suppose it's perfectly possible. Nanny Peters didn't like me; I could tell. And I'm not sure she likes Mollie much either, for all she made a great fuss of her and kept tweaking her curls and straightening her skirts.'

'I see. Well, there's nothin' you can do about it, queen, unless he asks you to go round there again, of course.'

'No, but . . .'

'Excuse me, but has either of you young ladies got such a t'ing as a match about you? Me pal an' I are dyin' for a fag but neither of us thought to bring a box o' matches out wi' us.'

The girls had finished their sandwiches. Rose got to her feet and Linnet followed suit. 'No, we've not got matches, nor don't we know the time,' Rose said, bestowing a false and treacly smile upon the hapless youth. 'Come on, Miss Murphy, these fellers is only after our seats.'

This proved an unfortunate remark leading to many guffaws and a number of rude innuendoes, but the girls had to be back in their office dead on the hour so they ignored the young men and hurried back to the enormous Eagle and General building and their desks.

But all the way back to the office, Linnet was wondering just why Mollie was so extremely – unnaturally – quiet and good, and what she ought to do about it.

The warm and summery days passed pleasantly now for Linnet. Roddy came home and they had a couple of days out. They went off on the ferry, caught a bus at Woodside and picnicked in a wood where Linnet paddled in a stream and Roddy lay on his back on the grassy bank and slept – and snored, too. Roddy still insisted that she was his girl, but Linnet could not stop treating him like a brother which, in a way, she felt he was. This led to several hot arguments and once to a fight because Roddy tried to get amorous when they emerged from the cinema, where they had watched Greta Garbo in *Anna Christie*. Linnet, suddenly finding herself in a doorway with her friend Roddy horribly transformed into a hugging, grabbing octopus with eight hands, most of which were in places she preferred to keep to herself, fought back so successfully that Roddy nursed a hacked shin, trampled feet and the beginnings of a black eye for a week.

Roddy said he was sorry for frightening her, but he said it unconvincingly, with a martyred air, and Linnet, who had really been very scared, moved back from him a little. People, she felt, should stick to their roles in life and since she had cast Roddy as her friend and brother, her friend and brother he should remain. If he wanted to behave like the octopus she had called him – and that had been easily the most polite of the many descriptions she had used – then he should choose as a partner someone who liked that sort of behaviour, someone who did not think of him as a friend and a brother, in short.

So there was a certain coolness between Roddy and Linnet which might have made her very unhappy, had it not been for her steadily growing friendship with her boss. At work, Mr Cowan was much easier with Linnet and she with him. He began to take her around quite a lot, without once trying to hold her hand, let alone do anything more intimate. They went all over the place in Mr Cowan's lovely motor, though he did not take it to work but preferred to use a taxi or even the tram. So it was in a car, the very first one she had ridden in, that Linnet saw the Wirral, Lancashire, and even the Welsh countryside. Mr Cowan was a pleasant and undemanding companion – unlike Roddy, Linnet thought crossly – and seemed content just to have her with him so that he could enjoy her enjoyment as much as her company.

And naturally, when they went out in the car, they took Mollie with them. Mollie would sit on the back seat on a pile of cushions, holding onto the strap and watching the passing scene. When they stopped she would slide down from her throne and get into her push-chair, or sometimes she would walk between them, and she would scarcely ever speak and seldom did any expression other than solemn wonder, cross her small, rosy face. And somehow, no matter how she tried to tell herself that Mollie was simply an unusually good child, this worried Linnet more and more.

On one particular occasion, Nanny Peters had gone out for her afternoon off and the planned trip, to see the shops in Chester, came to nothing because the car sprang a puncture as they were going down the drive. So Mollie and Linnet went to the park to feed the ducks and dabble in the lake whilst Mr Cowan dealt with the puncture and the housekeeper, Mrs Eddis, prepared tea at home.

'We'll have it in the garden,' Mr Cowan had instructed her. 'The raspberries are ripe so perhaps we could have some of them, with some cream? I don't suppose Mollie's ever tasted raspberries.'

And since they were alone, Linnet really put herself out to put Mollie at her ease. She persuaded the child to play ring o' roses, and when they came to the end and they both fell down she made a great fuss, saying, 'Oh, Linnet went bump and now look at her skirt! Did Mollie go bump? Up we get, Mollie-Pollie, let's have a race to the big flower-bed. Racing each other means running to see who goes fastest.'

Mollie looked frightened. 'Mustn't,' she murmured. 'Mustn't run. Mollie sit quiet.'

'Yes, Mollie is very good, but now isn't the time for being good, now's the time for play,' Linnet said encouragingly. 'More ring o' roses, then, Mollie?'

Mollie glanced back at the house. Her eyes went very big and dark when she looked at the house. Then she looked up at Linnet. 'Play? Mollie play?'

'That's right. Now take my hands and we'll dance in a ring until we get to the tishoo bit, and then what do you do?'

Mollie thought about it, and then smiled. She wasn't a particularly fetching child but when she smiled . . . oh, poor baby, Linnet thought, to smile so rarely when she has so much! 'Mollie falls down,' she said. 'Linnet falls down too – bump!'

And then, just when Mollie was pink-cheeked, breathless, laughing, Nanny Peters came out of the house. She stood for one moment on the terrace, watching them, and then in a voice which cracked like a whiplash she said, 'Mollie! Here!'

'The kid might have been a dog,' Linnet said afterwards, telling Rose about the incident. 'And she didn't hesitate, or glance at me or anything. She put her head down and walked very quickly up to the terrace and stood by Nanny Peters. And when I went up too and said Mollie and I were just playing a game until tea, Miss Peters said, "Mollie doesn't like rough games. Her skirt's got grass stains on, we can't have that," and she took hold of Mollie's shoulder and the two of them disappeared into the house.'

'What did her father say?' Rose asked, clearly fascinated. 'Did he not ask for Mollie when he came back?'

'Yes. And I said Nanny Peters had taken her away and he gave me a very odd, hunted sort of look and said he supposed that was all right then. But neither of us had much appetite for tea.'

'And what'll you do?' Rose asked. 'Surely you ought to do something, Linnie? You're fond of the kid, I can tell.'

It was one thing to be fond of the child, though, and another to interfere, particularly as all she had to go on was Mollie's extraordinary goodness. It was not natural and she knew it, but she also realised that, unless Mr Cowan said something about it, she had no right whatsoever to do anything other than mention it from time to time. She and Rose talked it over constantly, worrying over it like dogs with a bone, but although Nanny Peters continued to treat poor Mollie with a degree of firmness which worried Linnet whenever Mr Cowan was not present, that was scarcely something about which she could complain. The children of the wealthy, Linnet knew, were brought up to be seen and not heard and her worries over the child seemed trivial when you considered that Mollie was prettily behaved, well nourished, had a wonderful home and a loving father. In short, she was living in the lap of luxury and was a very fortunate little girl when compared with many that Linnet saw in the streets each day.

And then, one Friday morning, when Linnet and Mr Cowan had been seeing each other regularly for six weeks or so, he came into her office and shut the door behind him with what Linnet thought was a definitely furtive air. She was alone since Rose was taking dictation from Mr Griseworth and had been gone almost half an hour already.

'Miss Murphy – are you busy this weekend?'

'Not 'specially,' Linnet said. She had been round to the Sullivans' place the previous day and had learned from Roddy's mother that his ship had docked in Southampton for repairs and would be there for a while, perhaps for as long as three weeks. But Roddy, it seemed, had decided he would be too busy to take time off to come home. He was probably still smarting from their quarrel, but even so Linnet thought he should have got in touch with her himself to tell her their usual meeting was off. He had sent a telegram, but had addressed it to the Sullivan family, obviously assuming that his mother would get in touch with Linnet and let her know. However, because Linnet was smouldering under a definite sense of grievance about what she thought of as 'the octopus affair', she took offence at his behaviour. But, truthfully, she was not looking forward to what she suspected would be yet another confrontation with Roddy, so probably he was wise to stay in Southampton. For all I know he may have a girl there, she told herself, and was surprised at the pang of sheer pain which arrowed through her at the thought. So one way and another, she jolly well hoped that Mr Cowan was going to ask her out this weekend. If Roddy chose to stay with his ship in a port hundreds of miles away rather than come home to Liverpool, then she would go out with Mr Cowan and it would serve Roddy blooming well right!

'I wondered if – if we might go over to New Brighton for – for – for Saturday, Miss Murphy, and – and – and –'

'For the afternoon?' Linnet guessed. 'For the whole afternoon, Mr Cowan?'

He was very pink and flustered, quite different from how he had been with her over the past few weeks; she could not help noticing that a fine film of perspiration dewed his forehead and that he kept pushing his glasses up with one finger with a nervous, almost irritable, gesture.

'Well, yes, and – and – and –'

Linnet took a deep breath. 'Is it Mollie, Mr Cowan? Shall you bring her, too? I'd like that.'

He muttered something; it sounded like 'weekend', but that didn't seem to make sense, so Linnet smiled encouragingly once more.

'Was it Nanny Peters, Mr Cowan? Did you want her to come, as well?'

He looked positively hunted. 'No, no, I don't think . . .' he was beginning when the door opened behind him and Rose entered the room. Talking, of course.

'Well, I dunno, there's enough letters in me book to keep me busy . . .' she broke off. 'Oh, sorry, Mr Cowan, I didn't realise you were in here.'

'I'm just going, Miss Beasley,' Mr Cowan said rather stiffly. 'Miss Murphy, I'd be obliged if you'd come along to my office in five minutes. Bring your pad.'

'He sounded cross,' Rose observed, sitting at her desk and throwing her shorthand pad down beside her typewriter. 'Did I come in at a bad moment, chuck? Was he asking you out again? My goodness, if folk knew about you and 'im they'd start puttin' two an' two together and makin' five! Still, you gerron well, I know. Did you say he was asking you out this weekend? 'Cos your feller isn't home after all, is he?'

'Roddy isn't my feller, he's a friend, and yes, I think Mr Cowan was meaning to ask me out, only he kept stuttering and stammering; but he'll probably tell me easier in his own office,' Linnet said calmly, picking up her own pad and selecting a couple of well-sharpened pencils. 'I'll soon know, anyhow.'

She went straight to Mr Cowan's room and sat down at the chair beside his desk. She put her pad on her lap, opened it, poised her pencil above it. Mr Cowan stared down at her pad but said nothing. After a moment's silence Linnet said, 'Dear Sir, in reply to your letter of the 9th instant . . .'

Mr Cowan looked up and tried to smile, but it was a

poor attempt. 'Sorry, Miss Murphy, it's just that . . . I find it very difficult . . .'

'Mr Cowan, do you bring butties – sandwiches – for your lunch?' Linnet said, struck by an idea. 'If so, why don't you and I take our sandwiches somewhere quiet and talk then?' It had occurred to her that her boss seemed to find it easier to talk away from the office. 'We can't go to the Nelson memorial but there's other places . . .'

'I don't bring sandwiches,' Mr Cowan said, and this time his smile was a real one. 'But if you would join me in a quick snack, we might indeed discuss the matter which is on my mind whilst we eat.'

'Oh, but I didn't mean . . . I've got butties,' Linnet said, wishing she had not made the suggestion. Now he would think her a gold-digger, a girl out for the main chance! 'It doesn't matter . . .'

'It does matter,' Mr Cowan said firmly. 'We'll save your sandwiches for the seagulls, shall we? That is, if you'll really come to New Brighton with me tomorrow. And we'll have our talk over lunch; nothing elaborate, just a nice chop and a roast potato or two – Sainsbury's Café do a businessmen's special which is quite good.'

'I'm not a businessman,' Linnet said feebly. How she wished she had kept her silly mouth shut, now look what she had got herself into! 'People will think it very odd if I go to Sainsbury's, sir, that's where all the managerial staff go. Us girls don't go out much at lunchtime, but if we did we'd never go to Sainsbury's.'

'True,' Mr Cowan said thoughtfully. 'How about Anderson's Snackerie, on Exchange Street, up by the National Provincial? The men go to Anderson's Luncheon Bar because they can get a beer there, but the Snackerie is more for women, I imagine!'

'I've heard of it because Miss Harper and Miss Elphinstone and some of the other supervisory staff go there, so you might find yourself the only feller,' Linnet said with a twinkle. 'Still, if you don't mind, I don't mind either!'

'Oh . . . yes, I see what you mean.' Mr Cowan's hunted look was back. 'Well, we'll get a taxi, go further afield. Yes, that's the idea, a taxi.'

'I am *not* getting into a taxi with you whilst everyone in the office giggles and gawps,' Linnet said firmly. 'There's no point in causing talk, sir. When you've been kind enough to ask me out before it's always been at weekends, and because we work Saturday mornings and by the time we leave nearly all the staff have gone, no one knows. But if you want us to have lunch together then we'll just have to be careful. You wouldn't want to be gossiped about, Mr Cowan, I know that much! Oh, I know! We'll sneak out separately and catch the same tram, that way no one will suspect anything.'

This time he really did laugh, the laugh which made his face almost attractive Linnet thought appreciatively, smiling herself. 'Miss Murphy, are you ashamed of me? Look, you walk down to the corner of Dale Street and I'll pick you up in a taxi. Will that suit your sense of propriety?'

'That's a *good* idea,' Linnet said, much relieved. 'Where will we go for our lunch, though?'

'There's a place on North John Street – Cottle's, it's called. It's a fair way from here, so we're unlikely to bump into anyone from the Eagle and General. Will that suit you?'

'That sounds just right,' Linnet said thankfully. 'And now, sir, to your letters!'

They had a pleasant lunch in the half-empty restaurant and Mr Cowan at last unburdened himself of the worry which, Linnet realised, had caused him to ask her out for the first time so many weeks ago.

'I don't think Mollie's happy, yet I can't tell why not,' he said. 'She scarcely ever cries now, though she cried a lot as a baby. But she doesn't laugh much, or run about, or do the things I see other small children doing, either. I've mentioned the matter to Nanny Peters and she's much more experienced than I, but she simply dismisses my fears, says the child is a good, quiet child and I should be grateful. To tell the truth, Miss Murphy, it has crossed my mind that a child whose mother dies within days of her birth might be affected mentally by the loss. I was – I was distraught at the time and paid very little attention to the baby, and who can say what such neglect can do to a child's mind? I did have a word with our family practitioner, an elderly man who's known me all my life, but he said I was worrying unduly and that little Mollie, so far as he can tell, is a perfectly normal child. But I noticed, three or four weeks ago, that she winces away if I make a sudden movement, which seems very odd. However, I told Nanny Peters that the habit worried me and soon after that she stopped, but . . .'

'Who stopped? Nanny Peters or the child?'

'Why, Mollie, of course. She stopped wincing when I moved towards her. She scarcely moves when I'm with her, now. I'm sure I'm doing something wrong, but I don't know precisely what and Nanny just says everything's as it should be and not to worry. And I can scarcely ask Mollie herself if I frighten her!'

'The trouble is, Mollie's too young to explain how she feels,' Linnet said thoughtfully. 'I suppose you could ask her, but I don't think she'd be able at her age to explain how she felt. And frankly, Mr Cowan, Mollie worries me, and for exactly the same reason. She's good and quiet, but much too good and quiet, if you understand me. And if you mentioned the wincing to Nanny Peters and Mollie promptly stopped wincing, don't you think that it may be your nanny who is at fault?'

'Because she stopped the child doing something which upset me? Surely, Miss Murphy, that shows she's taking my feelings into account?'

'It could also show she can frighten Mollie into obedience,' Linnet said cautiously. 'I can't think how you stop someone from wincing back, which is an instinctive movement, other than by a threat so terrible that even a child of Mollie's age remembers it. You didn't ask Miss Peters how she worked the miracle?'

'No. To tell you the truth, Miss Murphy, Miss Peters starts talking about psychology and some strange American doctor who's an authority on small children, and she even said, once, that it's right and proper for a child to be in awe of its male parent... I feel very helpless, I really do. Upon my word of honour, Miss Murphy, I would never harm a hair of my daughter's head, but from her attitude anyone could be forgiven for believing that I thrash her twice daily.'

'And it hadn't occurred to you that the only person she sees enough of to be genuinely frightened by her is Nanny Peters?' Linnet asked incredulously. 'Mr Cowan, who else could scare Mollie?'

Mr Cowan shrugged helplessly. 'Who am I to say? Dr Davies recommended Miss Peters personally, which makes it difficult, because when I have a worry about Mollie and take it to him he simply says that Nurse Peters will see to it and that I may trust her absolutely. Only just lately, I felt I must get someone else's opinion, preferably a woman's, who could put me right if it was my attitude which was at fault.'

'Well, you aren't very loving towards her, but it isn't possible for you to show her affection when it only frightens her more,' Linnet said gently, pushing her plate away. 'That was a delicious meal, sir, much nicer than sandwiches. But once you've sorted out Mollie's problem you will have to learn to cuddle her, Mr Cowan. Children need to be cuddled. My mam was a great one to cuddle, and she couldn't be called a particularly good mother, I don't think.'

'If I even hold her hand she pulls back,' Mr Cowan said miserably. 'If I pick her up she goes stiff . . . it's quite frightening. She's not speaking as she ought, either, or not when I'm around, though Nanny says she chatters away happily when I'm out at work or when I'm downstairs, having my dinner.'

'Did Mollie never run to you?' Linnet asked, remembering her own childhood and how she would run to her mother the moment little Evie returned to their rooms from a show or a shopping trip. 'Just run to you, with her arms out?'

Mr Cowan shook his head once more. 'No, never. Right from the time she could toddle – and she walked before she was a year old – she was very quiet. Never ran or shouted, never made demands. To tell you the truth, Miss Murphy, of late I've wondered whether her mind was affected at birth because I understand my – my late wife had a difficult time. Yet if Mollie had been damaged, in short if she was simple, she would not, surely, respond to instruction the way she does?'

Linnet, who had wondered the same thing when she had first met Mollie, shook her head decisively. 'She's as bright as any kid I've met,' she said. 'You don't want to worry on that score. But . . . if I may be frank?'

Mr Cowan looked hunted, but nodded his head with the air of one determined, if necessary, to go to the stake in a good cause. 'Yes, Miss Murphy. If it's something I've done I'd rather know.'

'I think it's possible that, all unknowing, you've employed a nanny who is rather too strict, rather too keen to have a perfect charge,' Linnet said, weighing her words as carefully as she could whilst, at the same time, getting her message across. 'I think that if you sent Miss Peters away for a week or two and took charge of the child yourself, you'd see a marked improvement quite quickly.'

Mr Cowan looked shocked. 'Take care of her myself? But I couldn't possibly do that, Miss Murphy. I'm a man!'

'Yes, that is a disadvantage,' Linnet said, quick to see his point of view, for men, naturally, had nothing to do with small children save to beget them, and though she knew very little about that side of things she did realise that begetting was one of man's pleasures whereas upbringing was very much a woman's job. 'Well, how about bringing in a friend or relative to take care of Mollie for a week or two? You might even employ someone else, just for a couple of weeks,' she added, highly daring, for she longed to say *sack her and watch Mollie improve*, but realised such a suggestion would not, at this stage, be politic. Mr Cowan was still not sure that his 'perfect nanny' was in any way to blame for his daughter's behaviour.

'But I don't have any female relatives or close friends,' Mr Cowan pointed out, having given the matter some thought. 'And suppose I did employ someone else and they proved equally unsatisfactory? No, no, I don't mean that,' he added hastily, clearly seeing the trap into which he was about to fall. 'I mean I might choose wrongly and be forced to ask Miss Peters to return. And that really could be hard on Mollie; I don't think Miss Peters is the type of young lady to forgive such a slight.'

All Linnet's frank and forthright soul begged to be allowed to tell Mr Cowan that it was about time Miss Peters was subjected to the sort of pressure she was clearly putting his child under, but by now, Linnet's sympathy for Mollie was sufficiently strong to make her see that she simply had to remove Nanny Peters by stealth, for a couple of weeks, at least.

'Mr Cowan, you must have female relatives, or friends, anyway,' she urged. 'You mentioned your mother . . .'

'My mother likes a disciplined child; she holds Mollie up as an example to others and thinks the sun shines out of Nanny Peters' . . . out of Nanny Peters,' Mr Cowan said drily. 'No help there, I'm afraid.' He looked long and hard at Linnet. 'Actually, Miss Murphy, I was wondering whether you . . .'

'Me, Mr Cowan? But I'm like you, I'm at work all day. And besides . . .'

'You have a fortnight's holiday due to you at the end of the year which, I am sure, I can bring forward. It's paid leave, Miss Murphy, and naturally, I would pay you Miss Peters' salary for those two weeks as well. Now I want you to believe me when I say that when I first asked you to come out with me I had no intention of taking advantage of you – of expecting you to help me with Mollie on a personal basis, I mean – but simply wanted your advice. Only we did get on rather well, wouldn't you say? And Mollie obviously likes you, and I let things slide and slide. Is it asking too much, Miss Murphy? Only I'm at my wits' end and that's the truth.'

Linnet glanced across to the window of the snackerie; outside, the sun shone from a clear blue sky and there were smiles on the faces of passersby. It would be really nice to have a couple of weeks' break from the office, to sit in the beautiful garden of the house in Sunnyside, backing onto Prince's Park, or to take Mollie on the tram and the overhead railway to Seaforth Sands, to feed the ducks, go rowing on the lake, visit the orangery and the aviary . . . why, it would be like a proper holiday! She watched a girl in a primrose coloured frock and sandals, with a straw hat perched on her dark hair, walking past hand in hand with a handsome young man and envied her her freedom. She herself could never stroll, not on a weekday. It would be fun, and she did like little Mollie. She turned back to Mr Cowan. He was still staring anxiously, pleadingly, across at her.

'If you really can arrange for me to have the time off, I'd like to do it,' she said slowly. 'But what about putting Mollie to bed and so on, Mr Cowan? And getting her up, come to that? If she's an early riser, could I get there in time?'

Mr Cowan's smile spread, slowly, across his face. He looked as though an enormous weight had been taken off his mind, he even sat up straighter, or so it seemed to Linnet.

'My dear Miss Murphy . . . you would stay in the house, of course. Why, Nanny Peters lives in and there's no breath of scandal because my housekeeper lives in as well and two of the maids. Besides, you'd sleep, as Nanny Peters does, in the little room attached to the nursery. If you mean it . . . well, I should be – I should be eternally grateful.'

'I do mean it,' Linnet said. She wanted to help Mollie and besides, to be paid simply to stay for two weeks in a beautiful house, to have your meals made for you and delivered to you, to go out when you wished, to enjoy all the advantages of wealth without any strings . . . it was an opportunity given to few young girls in her position. 'When do I start?'

'I'll tell Miss Peters that I'm going away and taking Mollie with me; I'll say I'm going to visit a cousin with several children and shan't be needing her services for two weeks. I'll tell her she can have a holiday with pay,' Mr Cowan said. Linnet realised that he must have been planning this all along, hoping she would come up with some such suggestion. He might have come straight out with it, she thought, but without resentment. A worried father, who loved his daughter and wanted what was best for her, could be forgiven many things. 'If you could start your holiday at lunchtime a week on Saturday, Miss Murphy?'

'If you can arrange it, Mr Cowan,' Linnet said happily. 'I can't wait to see Mollie's face when we wave Nanny Peters off!'

Roddy was annoyed with himself, almost as annoyed as he had been with Linnet. Brother and sister, indeed! He had never thought of her in that way and doubted whether Linnet, an only child to all intents and purposes, had the faintest idea of the way in which brothers and sisters regarded each other. Roddy, cursed with two older brothers and three younger ones but no sisters at all, was still sure that what he felt for Linnet – and what she undoubtedly felt for him – was a very different emotion to the mixture of exasperation and downright dislike which was how he often regarded his brothers.

But you can't bleedin' tell a woman anything, 'cos they know it all, Roddy told himself, crossing East Street to have a look in Edwin Jones' windows. A look was sufficient, however; the windows were full of mouthwatering things, but the prices! Roddy moved on, glumly, further down the street, still looking in windows as he went.

He would have thoroughly enjoyed Southampton and window-shopping if it hadn't been for the fact that he was missing Linnet, and sorely tempted to simply go down to the station, jump on a train, and storm up the Boulevard to her door. He could imagine the scene; himself at the door, Linnet pulling it open, eyes rounding with surprise and pleasure, himself pressing into her hand the beautiful present for which he was at this moment searching, saying how sorry he was for – well, for pushing his attentions upon her after their visit to the flicks that night . . . her warm smile, her open arms, her kisses . . .

It was a strange thing, Roddy thought broodingly, how a woman could look you in the eye and deny what was in her heart. Linnet loved him, she must do, because he loved her, didn't he? Had loved her from the first moment they'd met, when the little silly had got in the way of his toboggan – how like a girl! – and been knocked for six, and had been rather good about it. He'd liked her then because she was a spunky kid, never moaning about her scraped knees or her bruises but simply telling him off for muckin' up her messages. The Irish accent of her had fascinated him, too, though that had gradually faded and grown less over the years. But her satiny hair, the jut of her chin, the way her eyes smiled at you even when her mouth was serious, the sprinkling of golden freckles on her fair little face . . . God, she was his, she had to be, there could be no doubt of it! Why could she not see what was so patently obvious to him, that they were made for each other, could have no sort of life apart?

Still, it had not been wise to jump her in that doorway. Roddy touched his eye gingerly; she had a left hook which many a feller might have envied, you had to say that for her. A feller expects a female to kick and scratch so he bore no grudge for his bruised shins, but that left hook! She'd meant it, the little vixen, she'd packed all she had into that punch and taken his mind right off – well, off what it had been on. For a moment he had seen stars, and by the time his head had stopped whirling and his eye watering, she was marching off down the street, calling back some pretty unpleasant remarks from what he could recall. The one that stung had been *nasty, grubby little boy*, but she hadn't meant that, he was sure of it. And then, when he'd finally caught up with her and tried to apologise – without actually admitting he had been in the wrong, mind – she had said she looked on him as a brother. A bleedin' brother, when she'd never had even one of them and he'd had five! He had tried to tell her that a brother didn't behave towards a sister as he had always behaved towards her and she had said, frostily, 'I should think not!' and of course then he saw he'd put his foot in it again and had tried to make amends only she wouldn't listen. She had simply gone on walking, and walking fast, too. Roddy, with trampled feet and bruised legs, to say nothing of scratched hands and an incipient black eye, had not felt equal to arguing with her all the way from the Paramount Theatre on London Road to the Boulevard so had lapsed into sulky silence long before they reached the tram stop.

And a tram, even a Green Goddess, with its leather upholstery and wonderfully comfortable seats, is no place to make up a quarrel. Linnet flounced into the vehicle and sat down and Roddy, naturally, sat next to her and she kept shrinking away until she must have been pressed so hard up against the window that it hurt. Then Roddy tried to tell her how he felt about her and the man in the seat in front turned and, raising his voice to combat the noise, for even a Green Goddess wasn't exactly silent, told Linnet to save 'erself for 'er weddin' night an' be damned to the feller, and then laughed with great coarseness and advised Roddy to 'gerrin a cold bath' and do other things which would, he insinuated, resolve Roddy's state both of mind and body.

And Linnet had given Roddy one long, startlingly horrible glare and had turned to the window. For the rest of the ride and all the walk home she had been totally silent, never saying a word in reply to his lengthy and disjointed monologue. And when they got back to her place she had shut the door in his face, very nearly adding a swollen nose to the black eye she had inflicted earlier.

He had been cross – well, bloody annoyed, in fact. He had vowed he would never speak to her or ask her out again. But the annoyance hadn't lasted, not with him, because he was a magnanimous male and not a foolish and misguided female. Linnet, however, had borne a grudge, and borne it so effectively, what was more, that when he had gone round to Exchange Flags and hovered, she had simply pretended not to see him, had walked by him without a word or a look. Painful stuff, no matter how hard he tried to tell himself that she was misguided but would see the error of her ways very soon.

So when the *Mary Rose* had put into Southampton for repairs he had decided not to send her a telegram explaining that he would not be home for some time. Why should he? She had refused to accept his apologies, refused even to speak to him. If I play her game, ignore her, make her suffer, then she'll see reason and be nice to me again, his thoughts ran, incoherently it is true, but hopefully. And then, when she realises what she's lost, I'll return, laden with gifts, and it'll all be good again.

Only . . . only women were so *unreliable*, so confoundedly strange when it came to matters of the heart. Suppose she didn't repent of her nastiness to him? Suppose she kept it up, went on refusing to speak, or go out, or be good friends? Suppose, in short, he had sacrificed that good friendship, which was so valuable to him, for a quick fumble in a doorway after a romantic cinema show? Suppose he had lost her?

Roddy had been mooching along the street, hands in pockets, his mind a million miles away, but when that thought entered his head, so did an icy determination.

He could not lose her, she was the most precious thing in his life. He must make her listen to him, he must, he must!

He would get on the first available train home in the morning and would put his case before her just as soon as he could. Only first, of course, he must buy her a present so magnificent that the ice round her heart would melt and she would fall on his chest in gratitude.

Determinedly, he began to retrace his steps towards Edwin Jones' magnificent emporium.

After considerable thought, Linnet decided she would have to tell Rose where she was going, but most definitely not her landlady. She might have told Mrs Sullivan, who was very interested in the whole affair, but perhaps because of her quarrel with Roddy she had not been visiting the Sullivans as often as usual and suddenly it began to seem a rather odd sort of thing to do, to have a holiday looking after her boss's little girl. Mrs Sullivan was far too practical to assume that Linnet was fishing for a rich widower, but she might wonder what her young friend was playing at. Sometimes, indeed, Linnet wondered herself. She did not think of Mr Cowan as a gentleman friend, though he was both a friend and a gentleman, nor did she consider their friendship in any way romantic, though that was exactly how Rose saw it. Linnet liked the lifestyle Mr Cowan enjoyed and at times played with the idea of being the next Mrs Cowan, but she knew, really, that it was just a foolish daydream and nothing more. Mr Cowan was too old for her no matter what Rose might say, and he was too rich, as well. Men with houses in Sunnyside, with housekeepers, nannies, maids, gardeners, did not marry little secretaries. Besides, Linnet reminded herself, she did not want to marry anyone, not yet. Life was far too full and exciting.

But having a holiday in his house, acting as nanny to his little girl – that was different. And if she was right and Nanny Peters was the cause of Mollie's strange behaviour, then Mr Cowan would be grateful, Mollie would start to act like a normal child, and Linnet could crawl back under the wallpaper, she supposed a little sadly. She might enjoy her excursions into the good life, but she was, at heart, a realist. Once she had served her purpose and sorted Mollie out, then Mr Cowan's secretary would be just that once more.

So on the Saturday that her holiday job started Linnet told her landlady that she was going to the seaside with a friend from work. It said a lot for her dull reputation, she thought afterwards, that her landlady immediately assumed that the friend was a woman and the holiday resort New Brighton.

'Ave a good time, queen,' she called as Linnet, suitcase in hand, set out for the tram stop. 'Send us a card!'

Nodding and smiling, Linnet decided to persuade Mr Cowan to take her and Mollie to Llandudno next day; there she could buy a supply of cards which she could post, judiciously, over the coming fortnight. Few people, she guessed, would bother to look at the postmark and if they did would assume it had been marked twice, in error.

At work everyone apart from Rose – and Mr Cowan, of course – assumed she was going to stay with relatives who lived in North Wales. That was what they did so why should she be any different? What Nanny Peters thought Linnet had no way of knowing, but when she arrived at Sunnyside she learned from Mrs Eddis that Nanny Peters had gone off for her own holiday in no very good frame of mind.

'Said she didn't want no stranger lookin' after 'er little Mollie,' Mrs Eddis remarked, having forcibly removed

Linnet's case from her grasp in order to carry it up the stairs and casting a curious glance at the 'replacement nanny' as she did so. 'Said no one understood the kid like she did, that she'd ha' sooner chose someone to come in 'erself.' She reached the head of the stairs and stood for a moment to catch her breath. 'Made me wonder, that did.'

'What did you wonder, Mrs Eddis?' Linnet asked. 'Here, let me.' She reclaimed her suitcase firmly and this time Mrs Eddis let her do so. 'Did Mr Cowan not say that Mollie knew me?'

'No, Miss, nor he never said it were you,' Mrs Eddis assured her. 'Just kep' sayin' a friend were comin' in. And I wondered, 'cos we don't reckon, Ethel an' me, as 'ow Miss Peters were too good wi' Mollie.'

'You never said anything, Mrs Eddis,' Linnet said with a mildness she was far from feeling. Why on earth hadn't the woman told Mr Cowan of her suspicions? It would have confirmed his own fears and he would, presumably, have acted more speedily.

'Well, no, Miss. The nanny was chose by Dr Davies . . . it didn't seem right to question it,' Mrs Eddis said, going ponderously ahead of Linnet up the corridor and speaking over her shoulder. 'Still, all's well that ends well, they say.' She threw open a white-painted door. 'Your room, miss, wi' the connectin' door to the nursery.'

It was a pleasant room with a wide windowseat and a view over the park. Linnet put her case down on the chest of drawers and studied her surroundings with awe. There was a pink rug on the floor, pink curtains at the windows and a pink shade on the electric light overhead. The bed had a white lace counterpane flung carelessly across it, and there were two chairs, both basketwork, with fat embroidered cushions on the seats. It did not look as she had imagined a nanny's room should look to

Linnet, though she knew herself to be ignorant in such matters.

'Nice, ain't it?' Mrs Eddis said behind her. 'She did 'erself awright, did Nanny Peters. Kept bringin' stuff in ... most o' this stuff were in the spare room but it weren't used, so . . . but I mustn't stand 'ere chattin'. Make yourself at 'ome, miss, and ring if you want anything. Ethel will be up before the cat can scratch.'

'Where's Mollie?'

'Havin' a rest in 'er room. It's just through there, miss.' The housekeeper indicated a door to the right of the bed with a jerk of her chin. 'She'll sleep till she's roused, miss. Ever so good she is.'

But in fact, when Linnet looked into the nursery Mollie was lying in her bed, straight as a die, with her eyes wide open. She closed them as soon as she realised Linnet was there, though, so Linnet said cheerily, 'I've just popped in to see if you're awake yet, dear. It's time for some tea, but before we have it I thought we might have a play. But if you're still tired, of course . . .'

Mollie sat up. She had a small, triangular face, big, grey-green eyes and straight, very dark brown hair. 'Play?' she said looking round her carefully.

'Yes, play. Nanny Peters has gone away, she isn't coming back for a long time so we can play if we like. What would you like to do until teatime?'

Mollie slid carefully off the bed. 'Ring o' roses,' she said in her small, flat voice. 'Ring o' roses, please.'

Linnet went to take her hand and saw Mollie go rigid. Carefully and slowly, she said, therefore, 'I don't know your house very well yet, Mollie. I'm a bit afraid of getting lost. Will you take me down to the garden?'

Mollie looked at her. You could see all sorts of emotions warring on the small face. Then, wordlessly, she took Linnet's hand and led her, not out of the nursery door and onto the landing, but through the pink bedroom. She looked around carefully, then she peeped into the suitcase, unpacked but open now on the chest of drawers, then she looked up at Linnet. Linnet could read the unasked question.

'I'm sleeping here now, Mollie,' Linnet said reassuringly. 'Nanny Peters has gone away. She'll be sleeping somewhere else.'

Mollie didn't smile, but it was as though she relaxed all over. She even gave a tiny sigh. Then she pulled Linnet over towards the door. 'Ring o' roses now,' she said. 'Mollie *play*!'

The rest of the day passed in a flash. Mr Cowan, who had deemed it politic to keep out of the way for a bit, returned to his home to find his daughter and Miss Murphy playing games in the garden – very discreet, careful games for the most part – and then the three of them had tea on the terrace, the tea augmented by delicious cakes and tiny sandwiches. Then Mollie went with both of them to the park, fed the ducks and even ran on the grass. Mr Cowan marvelled at the change in his child and watched whilst Linnet made her a daisy chain and Mollie wore it proudly, keeping it on for the rest of the time they were in the park, during the walk home, and only shedding it, reluctantly, when Linnet promised to put it in water until the following morning.

'And now it's time for your bath and after that Daddy is going to read you a bedtime story,' Linnet said and Mr Cowan, primed, said that indeed he was and it would be a jolly good story, too. 'Do you want to come and watch me bath her?' Linnet asked, when she and Mollie were going upstairs. 'Mollie is going to swim and splash, you ought to see that!'

But Mr Cowan thought it might be wiser to let Mollie swim and splash alone for a day or so, and settled down with his *Evening Echo*. But he had scarcely done more than read the headlines when he heard a bell pealing vigorously and a couple of minutes later Ethel came hurriedly into the room.

'Oh sir, Miss says would you go up to Miss Mollie's bathroom, please. She really thinks you ought, sir.'

Mr Cowan immediately folded his paper and ran up the stairs two at a time. Miss Murphy was very inexperienced, suppose she had unknowingly done the child some harm? He burst into the bathroom to find Mollie sitting serenely in the tub surrounded by bakelite ducks. She jumped and gasped at his sudden entry but Linnet put a soothing hand on her shoulder and thereafter she ignored them both but continued to move the ducks around whilst her lips moved soundlessly and her eyes never left the toys.

'What is it, Miss Murphy?' Mr Cowan said quietly. 'The maid said . . . oh, my God!'

He had seen what Miss Murphy had brought him in to see – the child's upper arms and much of her torso were black with bruises.

'*That* is how Nanny Peters kept order,' Linnet said in a deceptively even voice. 'Nips, pinches, blows from a hairbrush – I daresay we shall never know the half of it. That is the reason Mollie always wore long-sleeved frocks – I did wonder why, but I never dreamed that woman would do anything so wicked. Sir, you'll surely dismiss her after this?'

'I shan't have to,' Mr Cowan said grimly. 'She must know she would be found out – she'll never dare show her face in these parts again. What an evil woman!'

'Yes. But at least Mollie's so young that the harm can be undone,' Linnet said. 'And I intend to spend the next fortnight doing just that!'

*

For the whole of the first week the sun shone every single day, and after a week of constant outdoor play, the company of other children in the park and the loving attention of Linnet and her father, Mollie positively blossomed. She began to chatter freely, she ran, she even shouted. At first she was delighted with any story her father told but she soon had the confidence to choose which story she preferred and very rapidly learned the words so that she could correct her father if he went wrong. As her confidence improved she actually seemed to grow prettier and everyone who came to the house remarked on the change in the child.

Linnet wondered if Mollie would begin to grow quiet again as time went on and once, when they were coming home from a day at the seaside, with Mollie leaning drowsily against her shoulder, Linnet said to the child, 'You'll never see Nanny Peters again, you know.'

'I know,' Mollie said. 'You're my nanny now, Linnet. I do love you.'

'Well, I don't . . .' Linnet began, but Mr Cowan turned towards her and put a finger to his lips.

'Hush,' he said. 'It's too soon. Later, Miss Murphy.'

When they got home and Mollie was safely bathed and bedded, Linnet went down to dinner with her employer and over steak and duchesse potatoes raised the question, once again, of a nanny.

'Because it won't do for her to grow too fond of me so that she resents the change,' she pointed out. 'She's had a bad time, sir, she deserves better than that.'

'She deserves to keep you,' Mr Cowan said calmly. 'And I hope she will. You are a delightful person, Miss Murphy, and I am beginning to think it isn't only Mollie who can't manage without you. You've made us both very happy – wouldn't you like to stay with us, Mollie and me?'

'I'm a secretary, Mr Cowan,' Linnet said uncomfortably. 'I'm not *really* a nanny, I'm not trained or anything. I love it here, and I love Mollie, but . . .'

'Well, you've another five days to go; let's see how you feel at the end of that time,' Mr Cowan said comfortably. 'In the meantime, I'm going to ask you to do another job for me – would you choose me a nice, sensible girl to act as nurserymaid? That woman said it wasn't necessary and to my shame it never occurred to me that it wasn't true, it was just because the fewer people who knew what went on in that nursery the better Miss Peters liked it. I simply accepted her at her own valuation, I'm afraid. But I'll never do so again, which is why I'd like you to find me a nurserymaid, Miss Murphy.'

'Oh . . . but I wouldn't know where to get a nurserymaid from,' Linnet said, worried at the thought of having to find a member of staff for her employer. 'I'd rather you or Mrs Eddis did it, sir.'

'Don't worry, I'll speak to the people at the employment exchange and get them to send half-a-dozen suitable young women up to the house. All you will have to do is talk to them informally and choose someone who will be kind and good to my little girl.'

'Oh, I can do *that*,' Linnet said, much relieved. 'I'd like to do that, sir.'

That conversation took place on a Tuesday. On the Thursday, seven nervous young women arrived at the kitchen door and were shown, one by one, into the small drawing-room where Linnet, at first extremely nervous too, soon settled into her stride and positively enjoyed interviewing.

'I advise you to employ Emma Alcott, Mr Cowan,' she said at dinner that night, having seen all seven of the applicants. 'She's bright and sweet-natured, very clean and intelligent and she really loves children. I don't think you could do better than Emma.'

'Good. Then would you ring the exchange in the morning and tell them your decision? The agency advised me on wages and on terms and conditions so you needn't bother about that. Just confirm that Miss Alcott has the job and ask her to start on Monday next.'

Oddly enough, it was that remark which made Linnet think. She agreed to ring the agency next day and went to bed, but not, alas, to sleep. Her mind was far too active for slumber. Next Monday the new nurserymaid, the sweet, pretty little Emma Alcott, chosen by Linnet, would start work. And on that same day, she, Linnet, would be back at her desk, taking dictation, typing up letters, filing, running errands, coming in early and leaving late. She would have butties for her lunch and not homemade soup, a crusty roll, a beautifully served salad with a lemon cream or a dish of strawberries to follow. She would drink tea and not coffee, would cook her own dinner and after she had eaten it would make do with her own company most of the time. Here, Mr Cowan shared her dinner, then they talked quietly in the twilight, or made plans for the next day. He told her amusing stories about the office and she told him how funny Mollie had been. They enjoyed each other's company until bedtime when Mrs Eddis came through with a tray on which rested two cups of hot chocolate and a tempting display of biscuits. Linnet checked that Mollie was sleeping soundly, undressed, got into her comfortable bed and slept soundly until morning.

Since Mollie's new-found confidence, the child padded into the room each morning and roused Linnet, who enjoyed being woken by a soft little hand on her face, a soft voice telling her that it was 'Morning time now, time to wake up, Linnet!' and always moved over to let Mollie come down the bed with her so that when Ethel came in with a tray of tea it was two faces she saw on the pillow, and two smiles which greeted her.

Back in the Boulevard you'll wake alone, make your own tea, get your own breakfast, come to that, Linnet reminded herself, turning her hot pillow over to get at the cool, uncrushed cotton. But that's freedom, isn't it? That's being a working girl, independent, a career woman in the making. That's what you want – isn't it? You'll be gossiping with Rose, smiling at the clerks and keeping the office boys in order, seeing Mr Cowan across his desk and nowhere else . . .

She turned over again and stuck her feet out of bed because it was a warm night and no doubt the reason she couldn't sleep was the heat and nothing else. But the moment she got comfortable her thoughts returned to her problem. What to do for the best? Having your own little room and being free between six in the evening and nine the next morning was important – wasn't it? Everyone knew that domestic service of any sort was low because you did not have the same amount of freedom and freedom was important – wasn't it? She turned over again and threw one of her pillows on the floor. She would sleep better flat, perhaps.

She had been surprised at the salary which Nanny Peters received, though. If you took into account the rent which Linnet paid for her room and the tram fares to and from work alone, then a children's nanny was laughing all the way to the bank. A nanny had uniform provided, the use of the whole of her employer's home plus, of course, the privacy of her own domain and her keep. A nanny's salary, then, was pocket money. Why, I could save just about all of it and after a few years I'd have enough to buy all sorts, Linnet thought, excited by the prospect of such riches. Rose won't earn money like that ever, probably, and she's really senior compared to me. If I ever *did* decide to get married then I'd have a real little nest-egg towards me own home, whereas even the best of secretaries found saving a tiny sum each week hard work.

She would miss Rose, though, and the companionship of the tall house on the Boulevard: scatty Margaret, prim Ellen, Mr and Mrs Prettywell and their horrid little sons, she would miss them all in different ways. And there was her room, which she had lovingly furnished, and her visits to the Sullivan family, still living in Peel Square. But nannies do get time off, she remembered, just in time to stop herself starting her arguments all over again. I can visit the Boulevard, Rose and the offices on Exchange Flags, and the Sullivans in Peel Square. If Roddy and I are friends again soon I can even take my days off when his ship docks so we can go out together.

Sleep came at last with the problem, Linnet would have said, unresolved. But when she was woken by Mollie climbing into bed with her next morning her mind must have made itself up whilst she slept for the first thing she said was, 'I'm staying here, Mollie, I *am* going to be your nanny!'

Mollie, enthroned upon her friend's stomach, simply leaned forward until their foreheads touched and gazed at Linnet out of eyes which looked, at such close quarters, as big as ponds. 'Buttie kiss!' she demanded. 'Give Mollie buttie kiss!'

'Butterfly, silly Mollie,' Linnet said, giggling. 'Put your cheek near my eye, then.'

Mollie complied and gurgled with delicious amusement as Linnet slowly batted her eyelashes up and down the child's soft cheek. 'More!' she said immediately Linnet stopped. 'More buttie*fly* kissings!'

'Not now, chick. I want to catch your daddy before he

goes off to work. We won't wait for our tea to arrive, we'll get ourselves dressed and go down to the breakfast room at once.'

'And that is a firm decision, Miss Murphy? You will stay with Mollie and me? I'm delighted, absolutely delighted – it is a great weight off my mind. And since you're sure you'll do the job, do you think it would be best to ring the agency and tell them that we no longer require Miss Alcott? She was, after all, only an insurance policy against a bad nanny or a period during which I might have had to manage without a nanny at all.' Mr Cowan smiled at Linnet. 'With you in charge of the nursery, Miss Murphy, I shall have no qualms,' he finished.

Linnet had sat down opposite her employer at the breakfast table without getting her breakfast, eager to tell him that she had decided to stay before she did anything else, but now she stood up and walked over to the sideboard. She lifted the lid from one of the silver tureens and helped herself to scrambled egg, then kidneys.

'Thank you, sir,' she said quietly. 'I'll ring the agency as soon as they open, and then I'll catch a tram into the city and do all that has to be done. What about giving in my notice at work, though?'

'I'll handle that,' Mr Cowan said at once. 'If you just write a little note I'll see to the rest.' He stood up as Linnet returned to the table and leaned across it, a hand outstretched. 'Welcome to my home, Miss Murphy,' he said, smiling broadly. 'I hope you'll be very happy in your new job and I know that Mollie and I are happy with your decision!'

Chapter Nine

Lucy was in the kitchen getting breakfast when the back door opened with caution and Caitlin came quietly into the room, her face anxious.

'How's Granny, Lu? I went down to the castle early, before the sun was up, but there was no sign of Finn and I just can't think of any more ways to get in touch wi' him. He won't be with the tinkers, he'll be at a farm somewhere, he could be ten miles up the road or a hundred!'

'Oh, well, you've done your best, Cait, which is all anyone can do. But she'd dearly like to speak to Finn one last time and well we both know it. She's goin' down quite fast, now. I wish I could think of something, but haven't I tried and tried until me brain nearly burst with it? As you say, he could be anywhere, curse the feller!'

'I told Arny Aniseed when he came by days and days ago to put the word around for Finn,' Caitlin said discontentedly. 'I made sure Arny, gossip that he is, would do the trick. It makes me wonder if Finn's further off than we think, alanna. I pray to God he's not hurt, lyin' in a hospital bed somewhere not knowin' his own name.'

'Now why on earth should you think that, you foolish girl?' Lucy asked irritably. The fact that the same fear occurred to her nightly did not make Caitlin's voicing of it any more acceptable. 'Will you not go putting daft ideas into me head – I've worries enough without that.'

'I know, and sorry I am that I said it,' Caitlin murmured, not sounding particularly sorry, however. 'But facts must be faced – is she in her right mind, still?'

Caitlin's own grandmother had gone senile towards the end but Granny Mogg, though failing fast, was still bright as a button mentally and, in fact, was quite an awkward patient. She had been living at the farm for six months now, ever since the girls had gone down to the castle with a basket of goodies for her – very like Red Riding Hood, as Lucy had remarked – and found her collapsed at the foot of the stone stairway. She had clearly fallen but how far or how badly she was hurt they could not say. They had hurried home, fetched the farmhands and a gate to carry her on, and brought the old lady back to Ivy Farm, where she had been, at first, put in bed upstairs in the best spare bedroom.

But it had been terribly hard work traipsing up all those stairs whenever Granny shouted – which was often – and besides, once she came to herself she announced that she'd acted like an owl and roosted in an old tower for years, but that she was a tinker and tinkers preferred to die at ground level.

'You aren't goin' to die, Granny Mogg,' Lucy had said comfortingly. 'The doctor says it's just a little concussion, so he does, with a poor old busted leg thrown in for good measure. You'll be right as rain when the bone mends.'

'No I shan't,' Granny Mogg said obstinately. 'I'm a tinker, amn't I? I telled fortunes round the fairs and the ceilidhs for years, d'you not t'ink I know me own fate? Anyhow, man born of woman is bound to die, same's pigs an' sheep an' all other earthly critturs. What makes you t'ink I's any different?'

Put like that it was a hard argument to beat so Lucy and her grandfather made up a bed in the small parlour and they carried Granny Mogg down and laid her tenderly between the sheets. And there, for six months, she had remained, frequently grumbling, occasionally escaping, to be found wandering the meadows with the enormous white nightgown they had found for her hiked up indecently high and someone else's gumboots on her skinny little legs.

She always came back willingly, however, having merely wanted, she said, to 'breathe real air an' feel the touch o' rain an' smell the sweetness o' the 'edgerows'. Lucy never pointed out that the window in the small parlour was open all day if the weather was clement enough and that she picked any wild flower she could find for the little green glass vase on Granny's bed-table. She knew that Granny, who had never lived under a roof until Finn ensconced her in the ruined castle, found having four stout walls around her irksome and secretly sympathised with her desire to simply escape from it all for a while.

Because a couple of years ago Maeve had finally come home with her friend Mr Caleb Zowkoughski, only to announce that she and Caleb were now man and wife. Lucy, cheated of a wedding, had probably looked sour, but Maeve had explained that she was not getting any younger, that she and Caleb were very much in love, and that they wanted a family.

'We felt we'd waited long enough,' Maeve had told her father and niece, sitting in the kitchen mending linen, for Lucy had saved her a pile of worn sheets and torn shirts. 'We knew we loved each other so we married. And as you know Caleb is an attorney and a very successful one, bless him, so when our little holiday here is over we're goin' to return to New York because that's where Caleb's business is.' She had looked lovingly at Lucy. 'My dear girl, in a year or two you'll be after meetin' a young man, after fallin' in love, after leavin' home. So I don't feel I'm lettin' you down, d'you see? You'd go from me soon anyway. But if you'd like to come home with us, to New York, and meet some young men . . .'

Home! She had used the word without a second thought and Lucy knew, then, that Maeve was lost to them. And as for leaving Ireland to go chasing across the Atlantic looking for romance, wasn't that just the sort of silly thing her mammy had done, and wasn't her main aim in life to prove that she was not at all like little Evie? Even her fleeting urge to be an actress had died a natural death now that she had to run Ivy Farm. So she kissed Maeve and shook Caleb's hand and wished them well, but refused to go back to the States with them.

'Sure an' aren't I just as happy as a bird here, in me own place?' she demanded. 'I've me friends, me work here on the farm, everything I could want. And I've mebbe met the man I'll wed one day already, so no point in searching further, Maeve. But I hope you'll come back and dance at me wedding and wish me well.'

Maeve hugged her and said she'd miss her, promised to come back for the wedding, hugged her father, hugged Caitlin, wept bitter tears . . . but went, left them to get on with it. Her letters came regularly, but it seemed to Lucy as though they said less and less. She had borne a son, they called him Padraig after her father, she hoped for a girl next so she could name the child Lucy, after her dearest. She had a nice house, she called it a 'brownstone', which seemed a strange thing to call a house, and a big yard, which apparently meant back garden. She held coffee mornings – Lucy and her grandfather exchanged puzzled glances – in aid of various charities and went to sewing bees and fourth-of-July parties. She lived, in short, a life which was so foreign to the Murphys that they simply stopped reading the letters properly and were just glad that their Maeve was so obviously, patently, happy.

Lucy wrote letters back, of course, but because she suspected that her news was not important to the new

Maeve, they were always a little stilted, a little artificial.

But right now, Caitlin had asked a question and Lucy, after a moment's thought, answered it. 'Granny Mogg's completely, totally, sane, if that's what you're meanin' when you say is she in her right mind. But she's livin' in the past today, and she wants Finn mortal bad. If only, if *only* we knew where he was and could get a message to him!'

'Why don't you get her to look in her seeing bowl?' Caitlin said suddenly. 'If she's in her right mind but livin' in the past she might pick him up easier.'

Lucy would have liked to scoff, but it was the first suggestion which, she thought, really might stand a chance. Of course she didn't believe in what Granny Mogg said she saw in the sweetie jar, but she had been right last time. Little Evie had died a violent death, Maeve had confirmed it, and though Maeve had looked and looked for Linnet, even going round to the address in Juvenal Street where her sister and the child had once lived, on her way back to Ireland, she had been unable to trace her niece.

'They did used to live 'ere,' the landlady had said, glowering sullenly at Maeve. 'But they left – went off to Americky. Never heard a word from either of 'em since, nor want to. They left owin' me money,' she added crossly.

So Maeve had admitted defeat, and had told Lucy that although she hoped the two sisters would meet up one day, it clearly wasn't going to be just yet. And Lucy had never mentioned that she was sure Linnet was in Liverpool and not the States because hadn't Maeve tried Liverpool and hadn't that sour old landlady told her the Murphys had gone to America? So she salved her conscience and put her sister right out of her mind once more.

'Well? What d'you think, Luceen?' Lucy broke a couple of eggs into the hissing fat and was about to answer when the back door rattled open and the men trooped in. Caitlin raised her voice. 'If you think the seeing bowl might have a chance we could do it after breakfast.'

'I'll take her through some tea and bread and butter in a minute and see what she says,' Lucy said, skilfully lading sausages, bacon, fried bread and two eggs onto a plate and handing it to her friend. 'It's a good idea, alanna, and it might just work. She's a clever old gal, our Granny Mogg. Give this plateful to your da' whilst I dish up for the rest, would you?'

And as soon as the men were sitting at the table, elbows squared, eating the food, she poured Granny Mogg a cup of tea, buttered a thinly sliced round of bread, and carried the tray through to the small parlour.

Granny Mogg was lying back against her pillows, her eyes closed. Her small, thin little face was pallid and there was an ominous shine on her brow and a blue line round her sunken lips. But she opened her eyes when she heard Lucy take the chair by the bed and gave both girls the ghost of her old, warming smile.

'Ah, tis good to see ye both together,' she said faintly. 'Was ye goin' to bring me me seein' bowl, then?'

In the astonished silence which followed you could have heard a pin drop. Lucy broke it. 'Yes, Gran,' she said baldly. 'How did you know? You couldn't have heard us talkin', surely?'

Granny's shoulders moved in the slightest of shrugs so Lucy held the cup of tea to her lips and jerked her head at Caitlin.

'Go and fetch it through,' she whispered. 'And try not to let me grandad see what you're doin'. Take a sip o' tay,' she urged Granny Mogg in her normal voice. 'Caitlin won't be long, alanna, she'll be back be the time you've drunk up.'

But Granny Mogg couldn't take more than a couple of tiny bird-sips. Then her head fell sideways on the pillow. 'Savin' me strength for the seein' bowl,' she whispered. 'Oh I does want Finn bad, alanna, I wants him wi' such a gnawin' hunger!'

'If you can tell us where he's at you shall have him,' Lucy promised. 'Ah, here comes Caitlin with your – your bowl.'

Caitlin had filled the sweetie jar with water and brought it in on a tray which she placed carefully across Granny Mogg's tiny, bony knees. 'There y'are,' she said bracingly. 'Want the curtains drawed across?'

The old head shook, then the old hands reached out and cupped the sweetie jar and through the almost transparent fingers the pale September sunshine seemed, suddenly, to fill the water with a thousand reflections, a thousand tiny pictures. The room, the girls' faces, the old woman's burning eyes . . . and something else, another scene, another face . . .

'Sure an' he's comin' this way,' Granny Mogg whispered slowly. 'Ye know the lakes? Where the old Quane stood wit' her ladies? He's passin' by there this minute . . .' she leaned forward, her eyes fixed, intent. 'Oh come to me, me lovely lad, me broth of a boyo, come to Granny Mogg for her eyes long to see ye!'

'Lady's View! But that's miles and miles away, up by Killarney,' Lucy said. 'It'll take him a month o' Sundays to get here, unless . . . is he on foot, Granny? Or is he after gettin' a lift?'

'He's on foot,' Granny said. 'You'll bring him to me, alanna? You'll not let me die wit'out seein' me boy?'

Lucy smiled at the old woman and took her hand. Useless to deny that she was dying when her face was like a fine, crumpled lawn handkerchief and her eyes already had that vague, other-worldly look. But Granny Mogg did not fear dying, she just dreaded going away without saying goodbye to her boy, Lucy knew that.

'I'll fetch him back, Granny,' she promised. 'Caitlin will give you your bread and butter, I'll leave right now. And I'll be back before the cat can spit; you know me, I get things done!'

'Aye, you'll be back,' the old woman said. 'He's doin' 'is best but foots is slow. You fetch 'im for old Granny.'

Lucy nodded again, smiled, and left the room, her mind whirling. She could fetch him back now they knew where he was but how? If she rode down to the lakes on either of the carthorses it would be quicker than walking, but not, surely, quick enough? Granny was mortally ill, she knew that, her life was moving rapidly towards it close. She must get Finn back, she must!

She went through into the kitchen and her grandfather raised his head.

'Has she gone?' he asked mildly. 'Poor old 'oman, has she taken her leave of us?'

'No, but it won't be long now. She told me where Finn could be found and she wants to see him,' Lucy said. No point in explanations. 'He's up at Lady's View, on the lakes. Grandad, how can I get there quickly?'

'In Tommy Muldoon's delivery van,' her grandfather said at once. 'It's new, but he'd drive you there as it's an emergency, I daresay. He goes up to Killarney now and then.'

'Oh bless you, Grandad! I'm off; I'll be back as soon as I can,' Lucy said. 'Pray God she lasts!'

Finn was walking at his best pace, arms swinging, legs going like clockwork. He calculated that if he continued at the same pace all through the day and night he might, just might, get to Ivy Farm in time. So when a brand-new delivery van, coming from the direction of his destination and heading for Killarney stopped beside him, his only thought was to wish it had been going the opposite way. He knew he would be hard pressed to arrive in time and a lift right now would have been a gift from the gods. When he looked up at the cab, however, expecting to be asked the way to Killarney or some outlying village, there, smiling down at him, was Lucy: guinea-gold hair gleaming in the sun, so many freckles that you couldn't put a pin between them, long grey-blue eyes narrowed into slits because she was so delighted to see him.

'Finn! Oh, thank God! This is Mr Muldoon, he's very kindly brought me to fetch you. Granny Mogg's . . . she's . . .'

'She's dyin',' Finn said, when Lucy's voice was unaccountably suspended. 'Poor old gal, but sure an' isn't she a good age.' He turned to the van driver, a well-set-up man in his thirties who was smiling down at him. 'Nice to meet ye, Mr Muldoon; you have my thanks for this day's work.'

'A pleasure, Finn Delaney. Hop aboard and we'll be off.'

'How did you know she was dyin'?' Lucy said. Tears stood now in her long blue-grey eyes. 'We couldn't find you, Finn, we were so worried.'

'I knew she'd not last much longer, so I set out as soon as I could. How did ye know where to find me, alanna?'

'I didn't; *she* found you in the . . . the seein' bowl,' Lucy said, leaning well out of the cab and whispering the information. 'Finn, do answer me – how did you know when the time had arrived to come to Ivy Farm?'

He grinned up at her, then set his foot on the step and swung himself into the van beside her. 'Move up, don't be hoggin' the seat,' he said briskly. 'Sure an' Granny

Mogg isn't the only one who can see further than most. And there'll be others comin' from the countryside around, later. Tinkers take care of their own.'

Lucy looked at him, her eyes rounding. 'But they don't know where she is,' she whispered. 'You've kept her safe all these years because they don't know where she is.'

'Some of 'em know,' Finn told her. 'Some of 'em, the old'uns, they know all right. How's she been?'

'Cheerful. But frail . . . very frail.' Lucy reached out a hand and took his fingers in hers. 'Oh, Finn, you've been gone a long time, we've missed you turble, Granny an' me.'

'I had money to earn,' Finn said shortly. 'I'm glad o' the lift, though. I wouldn't want to fail in me obligations. Whose idea was it to bring the van for me?'

The engine was noisy so speaking softly, almost into each other's ears, they could be sure of a private conversation, particularly as Mr Muldoon seemed to enjoy a tune and accompanied every mile of the way with loud and continual song.

'A bit of Caitlin and a bit of me grandad,' Lucy said at once. 'What were you doin' this summer, Finn, to stay away so long? Did you find a good-payin' job at once?'

'I've been drivin' a jauntin' car in Killarney and makin' the visitors laugh,' Finn said proudly. 'Me and Derry Crewe bought the jauntin' car between us, but I drive it mostly. A lot of Americans I do drive and they're generous to a poor Irish tinker so they are. I tell 'em stories, I sing 'em songs, I advise 'em where best to fish for trout an' salmon. Finn Delaney's a name to conjure wit' in Killarney, an' long may it stay so!'

'You're a divil of a feller, Finn Delaney,' Lucy said rather sourly. 'And were many of the Americans young and pretty – and female?'

'Divil a bit of it – ugly old maids every one,' Finn said,

untruthfully but with considerable tact. 'Not a sweet little colleen amongst 'em to rival the rose of Cahersiveen.'

As they drove along the pretty winding roads, the hedges heavy with wild roses and honeysuckle, Finn thought about the girl who sat beside him, with her burden of golden hair, the dusting of freckles across her little nose, the sweet, mischievous smile. And when he told her that there wasn't a girl to rival herself he saw that smile break out, saw how she cast her eyes down so that the expression in them was shielded from him by her long, curling lashes. And it made him smile, in his turn.

Women! They were all the same, and most of 'em were after Finn Delaney, with his strong, supple body and needle-quick mind! He was always willin' to oblige 'em, of course, particularly the lovely, wayward tinker girls with their long black hair and generous ways. But Lucy Murphy was safe from him; she was a young lady, a rich farmer's granddaughter and the apple of her grandad's eye. Finn Delaney had more sense than to meddle there, no matter how tempted. So he smiled at Lucy and squeezed her hand and then leaned across her and started to tell Mr Muldoon all about the summer he'd spent driving his jaunting car round the streets of Killarney, out under the strawberry trees to Lady's View, and further afield still. And Lucy listened and smiled peacefully now and then and it occurred to him that she was a very restful female, that she made no demands on anyone, that he could not have chosen a better person to care for Granny Mogg.

One day, he found himself thinking, one day, when I'm old and want to settle down . . . but he killed the thought, because he knew he would never be old, never want to settle down. He was a rover, an adventurer, and once Granny Mogg was gone he would go, too, and probably never come back to the flat watermeadows and the good fishing, to the old, ivy-clad farm in the hollow of the hills. Never again would he see the colleen with the long, blue-grey eyes and the sweet smile, because he could not take her from her rich farmlands and her loving family and give her nothing in return but a campfire, a ragged sacking tent, a jaunting car and the love of a feckless, faithless tinker.

They arrived in time. They entered the room, Lucy clutching Finn's sleeve, and Granny Mogg was sleeping, smiling in her sleep. But she woke at once when Finn spoke her name and began to talk to him, though in Gamon which was the tinkers' own tongue and not a language which Lucy understood. She spoke fiercely at first, then more mildly, and Finn knelt by the bed with her little, bent claw in his big, tanned hand and nodded, shook his head, answered in the same tongue.

'What does she say?' Lucy asked at one point, and saw that Finn's eyes, which were darker than the darkest peat-pool on the marsh, had filled with tears. But he answered her patiently and seemed to feel no shame to let the tears run down his lean cheeks since he did not bother to wipe them off.

'She's arrangin' her will,' he said quietly. 'She has property – oh, not the sort of property which you mean, but property, nonetheless. She has told me who is to have what and now she is content. Very soon she'll start on her long journey.'

Granny Mogg died that night, though Lucy was not present when the old woman breathed her last. Finn told her to go to bed, said he would watch with Granny Mogg all through the night, and next morning, very early, when Lucy peeped into the small parlour, Finn turned and smiled at her and came over to the doorway in which she hovered.

'She's gone, and gone whilst she slept with no pain or fuss,' he said simply. 'Just before midnight, it was. Don't fear that she died within doors, either, for that she would not have wanted. I carried her outside, for she weighed no more than a tiny child, down as far as the gate which leads to the watermeadows. And there she breathed two harsh, hard breaths and then no more. Peaceful, she went, which was as she would have wanted it.'

Lucy looked at the bed; very tiny and wizened did Granny Mogg look as she lay there, on top of the covers now with her limbs straight, her arms crossed on her breast, her eyes closed, her mouth, which had laughed so much, severe in death.

'She looks peaceful,' she breathed. 'Shall I fetch the midwife, to lay her out?'

Finn laughed. 'A midwife, for a tinker? No, there's no need. The others will be here by now, I'll go out and fetch a couple o' wise women in to her. They'll do what's necessary whilst you an' I make tea and take it out to the rest. The pyre will be the sod hut, of course, and as many branches as they've brought with them.'

'There's no one outside . . .' Lucy began, and stopped. She could hear small sounds now, which had not been there two minutes earlier. A mule shifted its feet and whickered and a donkey answered. A shod animal, a horse probably, clinked its hoof against the paving stones and a child called out in a shrill, carefree tone.

'That's the Tuam tribe; the others will follow before noon,' Finn said. 'They'll collect wood for the pyre, though the hut will catch easily; we've had no rain for ten days, a fortnight. And they'll have to set up camp, of course.'

'Right,' Lucy said. She bent over the bed and kissed

the still, small face. 'Goodbye, dear Granny Mogg; you'll be sadly missed.' She turned and went before Finn out of the room, along the passage and into the kitchen. To her surprise the fire was already blazing and as she and Finn entered Padraig Murphy turned to face them. He smiled.

'Sure an' isn't it a grand sight, all those people an' animals assemblin' in me haggard wit' the sun comin' over the top of the hills an' the mist risin' from the water?' he said, gesturing through the low kitchen window. 'And won't Granny Mogg have a send-off to be proud of indeed indeed, and her only a bit of a woman?'

'Thanks for putting the kettle on, Grandad,' Lucy said. 'Finn thinks we ought to make tea for them because he says they'll be busy now, finding wood for the pyre and setting up camp. And he's gone to fetch two of the women to – to lay Granny Mogg out.'

'Aye, aye. No confinin' coffin for a tinker, just a winding cloth,' her grandfather said absently. 'An' the warmth of the fire on your old bones to speed you on your journey. It's not such a bad way to go, alanna.'

'I know, but I'm going to miss her,' Lucy muttered. She was not ashamed of her tears, but she was afraid Finn would think less of her for them. Granny Mogg was out of pain and had passed over; there should be no need to cry for her now. 'I'll go and fetch more water.'

And for half an hour she and Finn carted water, made tea in the buckets which the tinkers brought to the back door, and kept themselves busy.

'I don't know that I want to see . . . the other business,' Lucy said, when Caitlin came over to help her to prepare breakfast for the farmhands. 'I think it will upset me . . . and they don't show much emotion, do they? Tinkers, I mean.'

'I'm going,' Caitlin said, surprising Lucy, for of the two of them Caitlin was usually the one to shrink back from unpleasantness of any sort. 'I want to say goodbye to her. It's – it's the last thing we can do, to give the old girl a send-off.'

'I wonder, will they have a ceilidh afterwards?' Lucy said. 'Folk do, though it's called a wake. And you're right, Caitlin; I'll come with you.'

So the two girls were present when the sod hut was pulled down, the fire lit, the delicate body consumed by the flames. And Lucy voiced what they both thought when they returned to Ivy Farm.

'It was beautiful,' she said wonderingly. 'I never thought it would be, but it was. I'm glad I went, and one day, when I'm really old, I shall ask if what's left of me can be turned to ash and spread on the waters of the lough whilst all around people mourn and tear their clothes and let their tears flow without shame.'

It was over and Finn knew that he should go. But before he could leave there was the bequest to Lucy, for she was to have Granny Mogg's ancient gold necklace, and that necklace could not be handed to a buffer woman, a woman who was not of the tribe whilst the women of the tribe could see or there would be trouble. The necklace had been passed down, from mother to daughter, for centuries, probably. But Granny Mogg had no daughter and her granddaughter-in-law had let her husband cast Granny out to die alone in a ditch, so she deserved – and would get – nothing.

The tribes did not have many laws, but the wildest and least law-abiding tribe would do its best to see that the wishes of the dead were honoured. Granny Mogg could leave her possessions to whom she pleased, there was nothing to say she could not leave her necklace to a buffer woman, but Finn was realist enough to know that there were women in the Tuam tribe, good enough women, who would do almost anything to get hold of that necklace. It was thought to have magical properties, it was revered and valued . . . but if Lucy kept it for special occasions and took care of it there was no reason why anyone should ever know she had it. They would think Granny Mogg had hidden it, or that it had been burned with her, on the funeral pyre. So Finn told himself that he could not leave until he had shown Lucy the necklace, handed it over and made her promise to keep it hidden whilst the tinkers were in the neighbourhood. Which meant remaining in the area for a few days, at least.

It was harvest time, so he had work in plenty. He worked for Padraig and Padraig said he had never had a better worker.

'Come back next year, boy, and you can sleep in the attic room and feed wit' the family,' he said heartily. 'Never did I know such a feller for work – ye can beat even Kellach who is at the height of his strength. Stay, if you will, for there's always work to be done on a thriving farm like this.'

Finn smiled and said he would think about it and wasn't Mr Murphy the best of men to make an offer so generous to a poor tinker? But he knew he must go, and soon.

'He won't stay; he's never stayed,' Lucy said in private to Caitlin. 'He's got to move on, it's in his blood. I pity the woman that falls in love with Finn Delaney, for he'll never stay in one place long enough to be caught.'

'He's grown awfu' handsome,' Caitlin murmured, with her rich, dark hair falling softly over her dark eyes and hiding the expression in them. Does she know I'm sweet on him Lucy wondered? Does she feel the same about him? Sad it is that we, who once shared everything, can grow secretive and solitary and keep the secrets of our souls from each other, just because a man has entered our lives.

'Yes, he's handsome,' Lucy agreed. 'But sure it's not looks that are important when you're after marryin' a feller.' Caitlin's eyebrows rose and no wonder; how my mouth gabs out the things I most want to keep to meself, Lucy mourned, and once more her mouth opened and words came out. 'Not that I'm thinkin' of marriage, me. Not for many a long day.'

She shot a quick look at Caitlin. Caitlin's cheeks were rosy and her eyes were very bright. 'Nor me,' she said quickly. 'Why, we're neither of us in our dotage yet; plenty of time for that kind o' thing.'

She is in love with him, Lucy thought, with a mixture of dismay and elation, because at least as things stood they'd both made fools of themselves. And fools was what they were since wasn't it as plain as it could be that Finn wasn't for the likes of them? Handsome, yes, charming, yes, but – but fickle as the west wind, and about as easy to grasp, Lucy reminded herself, and tried to work up a proper scorn for a man like that.

And then he came to her on a fine summer evening and said would she like to walk with him down to the lough now, and take a look at the castle and watch the sun setting over the mountains? And Lucy's mouth opened to say no she would not, she was far too busy and besides, what was the point? Only her heart got in before her head and her heart made her mouth say, 'That would be nice,' and then it made her body get up and walk beside him, out of the farmhouse, across the haggard, down the lane and into the sloping meadows, just as the sun was casting its last long, golden rays across the water.

'I've enjoyed bein' a part of your family so I have Lucy Murphy,' Finn said, as they walked.

He's going and he's going to tell me so, he's going to

say he'll never return, that we must say goodbye, Lucy's acute imagination observed dispassionately whilst her voice murmured politely that they had enjoyed his company and that Grandad thought him a marvellous hard worker.

'Ah, well, we can work, us tinkers,' Finn said. 'I didn't tell you before, alanna, but Granny Mogg wanted you to have something of hers to remember her by. It's in here.'

They had reached the castle and he gestured to the archway into the keep.

'I don't need anything to remember her by, I'll remember her all my life,' Lucy said with a rush of affection for the old woman. Whilst Granny Mogg lived, you came here twice, sometimes three times a year, her heart said soundlessly. I'll never forget her for that reason alone, though there are a thousand others.

'Well, maybe. But she wanted you to have it. It's in her old room. Will ye come up?'

'Of course I will,' Lucy said, momentarily affronted. 'It wasn't me that didn't like the stairs, Finn, it was Caitlin. I'll go first.' And she shot up the stairs so fast that Finn was left far behind laughing up at her as she pushed against the door and burst into the small, round room.

She had not been up here once since Granny Mogg had moved into the farm and she looked round, momentarily distracted. It had not changed at all, not one iota. The bracken bed was still piled up against the wall, the table was in the middle of the room, the chair pushed beneath it. Only the smell was different; now the little room smelt of mice and loneliness.

Finn came into the room and closed the door behind him. He went over to the bracken bed and shifted it from the wall and showed Lucy a small loose stone there. He pulled it out and pushed his hand into the hole, drawing it back with something wrapped in a piece of what looked like black velvet. He unwrapped the velvet and gold shone dully.

'Here,' he handed her the necklace and Lucy gasped, unable to believe that she was being offered something so heavily, richly glowing, but she took it and stood quite still, looking down at it.

It was very, very old, and every link was wrought in the shape of a bee, and each bee clung with its front or back legs to the bee before and behind it. It was the most beautiful thing she had ever seen, ever touched, and the gold was soft and richly coloured, but the necklace was heavy and cold in her hands and suddenly she was afraid. She shook her head and handed the heavy gold chain back to him.

'I don't want it; truly Finn, it frightens me. You must have it – I give it to you freely because . . . because I loved you, when I was a little girl. Take it and give it to – to your wife, when you marry. Please, Finn! I would rather you had it than anyone else in the world.'

He stood there, holding the necklace, his expression suddenly diffident. 'No, I can't take it, Luceen. It's the only truly valuable thing Granny Mogg possessed, it was her grandmother's, and her grandmother's grandmother's before that. It has come down in her family for generations but tinkers don't regard that, no one would blame Granny for not wanting her daughter-in-law to have it, not after what happened. She had no daughters of her own and she knew you loved her – she loved you. Please take it.'

Lucy put her hands behind her and shook her head. 'I can't. Besides, I've given it to you, as a present for your future wife. You can't refuse me that, Finn. Now can we go home?'

He looked at her for a long moment; his eyes seemed to burn into her very soul and she was sure he knew how she felt about him and despised her for it. But presently he reached out and took her hand and his fingers were warm and light, their grasp friendly.

'Thank you, alanna, for your gift. I'll wear the necklace round my own neck, for safe keeping, until the time comes to pass it on to another. And now I suspect you know what I'm going to say.'

'You're leaving,' Lucy said calmly.

'Yes. And I shan't . . .'

'You won't be coming back. It's all right, Finn, I understand. But – but you won't go for ever, will you?' Her composure slipped suddenly and she looked down, afraid he would read the naked love in her eyes. 'You'll come back one day, will you not, if only to dance at my wedding?'

He grinned then, a broad, natural grin, and transferred his hands to her shoulders, shaking her slightly.

'Little goose! I cannot for the life of me imagine you a sober wedded wife but no doubt it'll come to that one of these fine days. So if you want me at your wedding, you must send for me.' He stopped smiling suddenly and was serious. 'Alanna, I shan't come back because I turn my face forwards, always. Only Granny had the power to bring me back season after season, year after year. But now she's gone and I must go onward, I must see more of this land. If you ever need me come to Killarney and talk to the man who drives the yellow and green jaunting car; if it isn't meself then it'll be me good friend, Devvy. He'll tell you where I'm to be found, if I'm still on this earth.'

'Oh, Finn, don't say that,' Lucy quavered. 'You aren't going to die, are you?'

'Man born of woman is bound to die, Granny Mogg used to say. And remember, we're talkin' of the distant future, when you're going to invite me to your weddin'!

By then I'll be an old feller, if not a dead'un. Now come on, let's see you smile.'

She smiled though tears trembled in her eyes and Finn smiled too and then, very gently, he took her in his arms. He kissed her with tenderness, then with passion – and then he simply let her go and moved away from her.

'Enough of that, Luceen. Let me walk you home.'

Without another word they walked home; he saw her into the farmhouse, called out to her grandfather, said he needed to have a word with Kellach before he went to the barn to sleep. He walked away jauntily, without looking back, and Lucy went up to her room, undressed, washed, put on her nightgown, got into bed.

And once in bed she thumped her pillow and then turned over and sobbed into it, for she knew she would not see Finn when she awoke next morning. That kiss – those kisses – had been their farewell.

But he did the right thing, leaving, her mind said comfortingly just before she fell asleep. It isn't everyone who could live a tinker's life, and I don't even want to try. I love the farm, and Grandad, staying in one really beautiful place surrounded by people I love and respect. And some day soon I'll meet a man who matters to me more than anyone else on earth, and we'll marry and make beautiful love and settle down to raise a family.

But learning to live without even the hope of Finn was going to be awfully hard.

Maeve, in her neat brownstone house in New York, entertained Caleb's friends and made friends of her own. She soon had a thriving social life and worked for any charity which needed her, because Caleb was an increasingly popular and successful attorney and insisted that she employ staff to help in the house. Caleb wanted her to have a nanny for little Padraig, too, but Maeve drew the line at that. Could she not look after her own child as, once, she had looked after little Evie's? She pushed Padraig's pram in the park and although she did have a maid, a nice little girl who came from the old country, as Maeve did, as well as a cleaning woman who did the rough work, a gardener and a boot boy, she did most of the cooking and all of the food buying, trekking all over New York to get the proper ingredients for her soon famous dishes.

'Maeve's soda bread is out of this world, and her fruit puddings are better than mother made,' Caleb's business associates said. 'She's a fine woman, she worships Caleb and that li'l feller of theirs.' And they looked accusingly at their smart wives who never touched a mixing bowl and scarcely knew their own nanny-reared children.

So Maeve was happy and busy and though she often thought of home, of big Padraig and of Lucy, it was comfortably, fleetingly. They lived their own lives far away and their lives impinged upon Maeve's not at all.

But the little daughter she longed for did not put in an appearance, and for fear that little Padraig would grow up spoiled and selfish Maeve pushed him across to Central Park every afternoon, even when it rained or when snow piled up at the pavements edge, so that he might play with other kiddies on the grass, the swings, by the lake.

On a particularly pleasant October afternoon, when she was pushing the pram with Padraig just awoken and inclined to be grumpy, in it, she slowed by the lake to let him see the ducks, and what must the naughty boy do but heave off his brand new tweed hat with the velvet bow on top and throw it in the lake, where it bobbed amongst the interested and investigative ducks like a tiny curragh. And not only was the hat new, it went with his little tweed and velvet coat and had cost a great many dollars, so Maeve gave a cry of distress and looked round for a stick to prod it out before the ducks decided it was good to eat after all.

The only stick available, however, fell short by a good two feet of the object she was fishing for. With a sigh, Maeve began to unlace her sensible shoes; there was nothing else for it, she would have to wade in, and oh, though the sunshine was warm, she just knew the water would be cold! She gave her son, sitting up in the pram and beaming at the ducks, a black look, then rumpled his soft hair. He was only being a boy, bless him!

But as luck would have it, Maeve did not have to paddle. A young fellow in a seaman's jersey and rough navy trousers had seen her plight. He didn't even bother to remove his boots but simply walked a foot or so into the water, fished for the hat with the very stick Maeve had so unsuccessfully used, and returned the hat to her with a grin.

'Oh, that was so kind; thank you very much; I'm afraid me son's getting full of mischief and would rather walk than ride,' she explained, smiling at the young man. 'But he'll outgrow that, I hope.'

'Oh, all kids gerrin 'ot water when they're fed up of ridin' and would rather walk,' the young man said easily. He leaned over the pram. 'Oo's a bad feller, eh? But your mam's goin' to get you out o' there any minute, 'cos it ain't far to the playground.'

'You're right, I am. And what are you doing so far from home, may I ask?' Maeve said, as she began to push the pram towards the playground and the young man fell into step beside her. 'You're from Liverpool, England, or I'm much mistaken. I'm Irish, but I spent some time in your city a couple of years back and I could recognise that accent anywhere. What are you doing in New York?'

'I've got five days ashore so I come wi' me bezzie up

the river to tek a look around,' the young man said. 'How come you're here, missus?'

'It's a long story,' Maeve said, with no intention of telling it. 'What's a "bezzie"? That's a new one on me!'

'Best pal,' the seaman said. They reached the play area and Maeve unfastened her son from his prison and lifted him onto the ground, then sank down on the nearest seat. The seaman sat down too and held out a square, capable hand. 'Me name's Roddy Sullivan; nice to meet you . . . ?'

'I'm married to an American, I'm Mrs Caleb Zowkoughski,' Maeve said, shaking the hand vigorously.

'Nice to meet you, Mrs Zowkoughski,' the young man said. 'And what's the young feller-me-lad called?'

'Padraig, after me father back home in County Kerry, but we call him Paddy, usually. And when will you be back in Liverpool, Mr Sullivan?'

'In two weeks, if we're lucky,' the seaman said rather gloomily. 'We're runnin' timber from Canada to Liverpool this trip, wi' a two-day turnaround, but next time we'll be away very much longer – weeks an' weeks, because we'll be coastin' up and down America an' the West Indies, movin' timber. On our nex' trip we shan't make our 'ome port for a while, worst luck.'

'Why's that?' Maeve asked. 'I thought all young men wanted to see the world.'

'Oh aye, but I've 'ad a row wi' me young lady. It were all a mistake, she took wharr I said wrong, I never meant . . .' Mr Sullivan said, going a little red around the gills, Maeve noticed. 'You know 'ow women can be, Mrs Zowkoughski – bleedin' unreasonable, if you ask . . . oh, sorry, I meaned very unreasonable, o' course.'

'Tell me about it,' Maeve said tactfully, since it was all too clear that he had every intention of doing just that. 'Perhaps just telling someone will help.'

Roddy liked his companion; she seemed sensible and practical. Perhaps, he thought, hope rising, she really could advise him. She was a woman, after all, and would surely understand another woman's strange behaviour. So he outlined what had happened to cause the quarrel.

'She 'ad a good job in an insurance office, she were 'appy there. And when me back's turned for three lousy weeks, what does she do? She moves in wi' a rich old bloke from work, that's what.'

'Married him, do you mean?' Mrs Zowkoughski asked. 'In three weeks? That seems rather . . .'

'No, she din't marry 'im 'cos 'e's married already,' Roddy said unhappily. 'She just moved in, or that's wharr I were told.'

'Just moved . . . and he's already *married*? Oh, I suppose he's a widower, is he? But even so . . .'

'The old b . . . gent's very rich,' Roddy explained. 'He's gorra ruck o' servants, a motor, a big 'ouse . . .'

'Is she a gold-digger?' Mrs Zowkoughski asked. 'Well, I suppose she must be, if she was prepared to – to do that just because he was rich.'

Irrationally, Roddy immediately thought Mrs Zowkoughski prejudiced; it was not Linnet's fault, it was all down to the bleedin' millionaire she'd met up with, he'd taken advantage of her, that was clear once you'd thought about it.

He said so and Mrs Zowkoughski said judiciously that though it was wrong of the man to have offered a young girl everything but marriage at least she then had a straight choice, to behave well or badly. His young lady had chosen to behave badly in Mrs Zowkoughski's opinion, and Mr Sullivan had every right to be seriously annoyed with her.

'I advise you never to speak to her again, but to find yourself another young lady. After all, there are plenty about,' she said, smiling at him. 'I'm sure you can do better for yourself than yearning after a rich man's leavings, for that is what she'll become, unless he decides to offer her marriage after all, that is.'

'But she's only a kid, she's not seen much o' the world,' Roddy said rather wildly. He had thought he wanted the very advice he was being given but now he realised that what he truly wanted was someone to tell him to try again. 'She's got no mam to advise 'er, nor nothin'. She must ha' thought she were doin' the best for 'erself. It ain't as if I've ever asked 'er to marry me . . .'

Mrs Zowkoughski leaned across the bit of bench which separated them and took his hand. 'Go back home and tell her you love her,' she said warmly. 'Because it's plain that you do. Give her a chance to be sensible and she'll probably be happy to abandon her old man and his money for the chance of true love.'

'I will, then,' Roddy said, getting to his feet and giving Mrs Zowkoughski his most charming smile. 'I'll do just as you say, missus, an' thanks for listenin'. I'd best be on me way now, I'm meetin' some pals in a fish restaurant on 52nd Street an' that's a good walk from 'ere.' He waved to the little boy playing on the grass and strode away, his step lighter than it had been for a while. She was right! He would definitely give Linnet another chance, after all she didn't deserve to lose him because of one little mistake!

As he walked, though, he remembered that he had not told Mrs Zowkoughski Linnet's name – nor, indeed, nearly all the story; would her advice have been the same had she heard that the quarrel had not just been a quarrel but a fight as well? Because when he'd gone happily along to Exchange Flags to meet Linnet out of work and been told that she was living with some rich feller on a posh little street backing onto Prince's Park he'd seen red at once, and was still seeing it when he arrived outside the house and met Linnet, humming a tune beneath her breath, heading for the post box at the end of the drive to post a letter.

'Hello, Roddy!' she said, giving him a great big smile as though she expected to be greeted with equal enthusiasm. 'I didn't know you were ashore, how . . .'

She got no further. 'Don't flannel me, an' you'd best go back in there an' pack your bleedin' bags, queen,' he had hissed at her, grabbing her arm. 'Why, what a way to be'ave, an' you supposed to be such a little lady!'

She had got cross – how she dared, when you thought what she'd done! But she had, nevertheless.

'Let go my arm, Roddy,' she said, pulling against him. 'I'm not packing any bags, what on earth's got into you? I'm not just staying over, you know. I live here now, permanent.'

'With a feller old enough to be your father; I know,' he jeered. He had seen a middle-aged man edge a long-bonneted motor car cautiously out of the drive moments before Linnet had come singing into view. 'Well, I'm back now, and I won't stand for it, d'you hear? I won't let you lower yourself . . . many a man wouldn't want to 'ave nothin' to do wi' a girl what be'aved like you 'ave, but anyone can make a mistake and . . .'

'Roddy Sullivan, how dare you? I've not made a mistake, it's the best move I ever made! I get more money, I'll be able to save easier, and Mr Cowan's kind and generous. He'll take good care of me, he's already promised that as soon as I've settled in . . .'

'Not marriage? Don't say the old lecher's promised marriage, flower?' Roddy had gasped, suddenly truly afraid. It was hateful that his little Linnet – his, his! – had been tricked into moving in with an ugly old man, but suddenly he realised that her living with the feller, though it hurt like a knife through the heart, wasn't the end. But marriage! If she married him then that was it, he might as well leave right away. 'You wouldn't marry 'im, chuck? Marrying's for life, you know. You've made one bad mistake so don't make another what you can't alter.'

Linnet wrenched herself free of him and walked past him, nose in the air, cheeks scarlet with what he hoped was shame but suspected was rage.

'Bugger off, Roddy,' she hissed over her shoulder. 'I hate you! I thought you'd be pleased that I'd done well for meself. You call yourself me friend but instead you're just nasty, as usual. Well, if you think I've done the wrong thing then just bugger off, d'you hear me?'

He heard and was stunned. Linnet never swore, he didn't know where she had learned such language! Probably from her precious Mr Cowan, he thought bitterly, totally forgetting the many times he had sworn far more colourfully in front of her when they were kids. He tried to catch her arm again but she turned on him with such fury that he desisted, trailing behind her to the post box and back to the drive, telling her that she was going to regret what she'd done, but that he, Roddy, was prepared to be magnanimous about it. If she left right now he would see there was no talk, they could be married in a jiffy just in case . . . he paused delicately . . . in case her loaf had already been cut and there was a bun in the oven.

Afterwards, he was inclined to think that even such tortuous frankness had been a mistake. She turned and stared, a frownline appearing between her soft brows.

'Wha-at?' she said slowly. 'Why can't you say what you mean instead of talking in ri . . . oh! Oh, how *dare* you, Roddy Sullivan, how dare you even *think* such a . . . go on, I told you to bugger off, now bloody do it!'

And when poor Roddy tried to lay a hand on her arm and explain again that she had been taken in by an older man, that he, for one, did not blame her, she hacked him in the shins with a small but sturdy boot, at the same time swinging that wicked left hook – which, as a member of the weaker sex, she should never have possessed – and catching him right on the bridge of the nose. He staggered back – anyone would have – and cracked his head on the gatepost. And then, believe it or not, the wretched, unfeeling girl laughed. Laughed, as he clutched first his bleeding nose and then the great lump on his scalp and tried to see if his leg was broken!

'That's right, have a good cry,' she said tauntingly. 'And then go home to your mam and I hope I never see you again as long as I live.'

A good cry! His bleedin' eyes were waterin' from the unladylike punch and she accused him, Roddy Sullivan, of crying! All his love and concern for her vanished on the words.

'Bugger off yourself, you nasty little bitch,' he shouted. 'And you never will see me again, don't you fret – not as long as either of us shall live!'

And with that he had turned and left her, limping back to the tram stop and wishing Mr Cowan joy of her. Just let him cross her once, he told himself, and he'll feel that boot somewhere soft and see a fist atravellin' towards him, and serve him soddin' well right. A tram stopped alongside him and Roddy swung himself aboard. Oh, aye, Linnet's boot in his essentials would put a stop to his 'orrible ways, the dirty old man. But later, lying in his bed at home having refused to tell anyone why he had a swollen nose and a great lump on his head, to say nothing of a limp which Long John Silver might have envied, he did just what Linnet had accused him of.

He cried.

After the interlude in New York Roddy was desperate to

get back and the moment his ship tied up in Canning Dock he set out for home. He wanted his mother's advice.

'It's Linnet,' he told Mrs Sullivan once the preliminaries of greeting were over. 'She's not workin' in Exchange Flags any more, she's – oh, she's – she's –'

'She's nannyin',' Mrs Sullivan said placidly. 'She's gerrin' good money, our Roddy. An' Mollie, that's the feller's little girl, she's a good, pretty little kid. I reckon our Linnet's falled on 'er feet this time.'

Afterwards, Mrs Sullivan told her son that his jaw had dropped so low she feared he'd broke his foot but at the time she just went on ironing as though she had not shocked him into total, dazed silence. She finished a shirt and reached for another, got halfway through it and changed irons, since hers was cooling, for the one which was heating up beside the fire.

'Well, our Roddy? Goin' to see her, are you? She didn't say much when she come round – well, not about you, anyroad – but I suppose you 'ad another bleedin' quarrel?'

'I th-thought . . . I thought . . . I told 'er . . . oh, my Gawd!' Roddy slumped down onto the hard kitchen chair and buried his head in his hands. 'She'll kill me, she'll kill me stone dead our Linnet will! Oh, Mam, the things I said, the things I *thought*! She'll never look at me again, she'll . . .'

'I dunno why it didn't cross what passes for your mind that gels don't usually wear a uniform to live a life of sin,' his irrepressible mother said, ironing steadily. 'Or are you used to seein' our Linnie in a navy skirt an' jacket an' a white blouse wi' navy pipin'?'

'Oh, Holy Mother of God, I just thought she were lookin' even lovelier than usual,' the hapless Roddy groaned between his fingers. 'What'll I do, Mam? Will she see me, d'you think?'

'I dunno. You could try apologisin', I suppose, if you can bring yourself to admit you were wrong,' his mother said rather tartly. 'How you could ha' thought, for one minute, that our Linnie 'ud sell 'erself for a big 'ouse an' a motor . . .'

'But what was I to think?' Roddy groaned. He emerged from his hands and stared hopefully at his mother. 'They telled me she were livin' wi' a rich man on Sunnyside, no one said nothin' about bein' a nanny . . .'

'Take 'er a few flowers, a present,' his mother suggested, when he ran out of words and slumped back in his chair once more. 'Tell you what, son, drop 'er a line. Only this time *say sorry*, don't jig all round the point tryin' to justify what you've done.'

'I will,' Roddy said eagerly. 'I'll do it now.' He got up and was dragging his ditty bag across the floor when he turned back. 'You don't think 'e'll try it on wi' our Linnie, then? Or ask 'er to marry 'im?'

Mrs Sullivan shook her head sadly at him and carried a neatly ironed shirt over to the table to fold it. 'Don't you ever learn, son? Wharrever our Linnie does next depends on *you*. On *you*, you great lummock, understand? Now git an' write that note.'

In the room he shared with his brothers, Roddy got out pen and ink and the last sheet of his paper. He wrote the most abject of letters, apologising unreservedly for everything he had said and thought, assuring Linnet that he would always be her devoted friend, would do anything in his power to help her should she ever need it, would go to the ends of the earth and back to please her. Then he got out his savings and set off for Church Street. Once, when he and Linnet had been walking up Church Street, they had seen, in the window of one of the jewellers there, a slender gold bracelet with semi-precious jewels set between the links. Linnet had spent a long time with her nose pressed against the glass, admiring the bracelet. Well, now she should have it for her own and he prayed that it would melt the ice around her heart so that she would forgive him.

He longed to go to the house in Sunnyside himself and confront her, beg her forgiveness, but Roddy was learning at last. He was only here for one more day and if she didn't receive the letter first who knew what she might say – or do – to him? So he bought the bracelet, wrapped it in softest tissue paper, made it into a neat parcel, sealed it with red sealing wax and posted it and the letter to Linnet, at the Sunnyside house.

He hadn't said a word in either the letter or the note he sent with the parcel about not giving in if Mr Cowan tried anything on, because he knew she wouldn't, not really. He didn't even tell her that marriage to such an old man would be a miserable affair compared to marriage to him because that, too, would undoubtedly be seen as more nastiness. He just posted his parcel and his letter and walked back to the house in Peel Square with his fingers crossed.

And then, because he had no choice if he was to keep his job, he rejoined his ship and sailed away, without knowing whether his hot-tempered little love had accepted his apology or was even now burning his letter on a slow flame and stomping his bracelet underfoot.

He didn't really think she would do anything like that, though. Linnet had always been quick-tempered but she didn't have a mean bone in her body. She would read his letter, accept his grovelling apology, and wear the bracelet to show him, if he happened to pass by, that all was forgiven and they were friends again.

Or he hoped she would. But as his ship laboured through the heavy Atlantic swell there were times when he had his doubts; times when his eyes watered and he recollected the left hook and prayed fervently to God and the Mother of Jesus that he hadn't put his foot in it with Linnet for the last time.

'Holy Mother, keep her safe, make her love me,' he prayed. 'I'm a bit hot-tempered meself but I don't mean a word of it. I'm gentle as a lamb really, I swear to God I am. And may that old lecher Cowan burn in hell if he hurts one hair of her head!'

Chapter Ten

Linnet had got over most of her feelings of outrage that Roddy could have believed she was the sort of girl to take a lover – especially one as old as Mr Cowan – in the weeks which followed their quarrel. But she still felt quite cross with him, so when his letter arrived one Monday morning she didn't open the envelope at once. She put it in the little drawer of the bedside table in her room and left it, she told herself, to simmer.

And next morning, the package arrived. It was a pretty little parcel, with the scarlet sealing wax and the white outer paper, painstakingly addressed in Roddy's best hand – and he could write beautifully when he chose. But she didn't open it, she let it lie beside her breakfast plate where she could eye it broodingly from time to time.

What was in it? What could it possibly contain? In the end she carried it upstairs and dropped it into her bedside drawer and went down again to take Mollie out to the park since she knew her charge needed fresh air even on a rather chilly October day, when the wind was in the east and the sky threatened rain. So she and Mollie would go to the park where Mollie would play with any other children also there, and then they would come home again and Linnet would help Mollie with her big jigsaw puzzle, the one with pictures of animals, all with their names written on them. The jigsaw was an instructional one and was, Linnet hoped, helping Mollie to learn her letters.

Then they would go into the breakfast room where the

maid would serve them a light luncheon. After that they would go to the nursery and Annabel Withers, who lived up the road, would come to tea with Mollie and they would play together, sometimes pleasantly, sometimes not, depending on their mood.

Annabel's nanny, Edie Ryan, was only a year or two older than Linnet. She was a jolly, pink-cheeked girl who truly loved her charges – she had three, but two of them were in school, only Annabel being below school age. Linnet and Edie had speedily become friends and now they took it in turns to entertain each other's child to tea so that the one not on duty could have a bit of time to herself. Linnet, putting her charge's leggings on with minimal help from Mollie, found herself wishing that it had been Mollie's turn to visit this afternoon and not the other way round; then she could have opened her letter and her parcel at her leisure.

But the day passed. Mollie was fed, bathed, put to bed. Linnet went down to the dining room and had dinner with Mr Cowan, quieter than usual because of the letter and the parcel. In fact, as soon as the pudding was cleared away she excused herself; she would go to her room if Mr Cowan did not mind, she had some work to do.

'But I do mind,' Mr Cowan said, smiling sweetly at her. 'I enjoy our quiet evenings together, Miss Murphy. I like to hear what you and Mollie have been up to whilst I've been toiling away at Exchange Flags.'

It would have been rude to say that the enjoyment was all on his side as well as untrue – usually Linnet enjoyed their evenings, too. So she went with him into the white drawing-room and they talked for a little and Linnet kept forgetting what she was saying and staring into the fire until Mr Cowan gave her a searching look and asked, in a rather stiff voice, if she had a headache.

'Yes, I have,' Linnet said, trying to look pathetic. She

knew she could scarcely look pale, what with the warmth from the fire and the meal she had just eaten. 'If you don't mind, Mr Cowan, I think I'll go up early.'

He must have guessed she wanted to leave him but he just smiled and bade her goodnight. He is a nice man, Linnet thought, conscience-stricken. I really shouldn't lie to him – but what am I to do? If this was an ordinary job I'd walk away from it at six, but as it is I'm on duty twenty-four hours a day, or it feels like that. Nannies really do earn their salaries!

Up in her room, she closed the door firmly and went over to give the fire a poke. It was a tremendous luxury having a fire in her bedroom, a luxury which was all the sweeter because it was always lit, as if by magic, when she came up to bed. All she had to do was put a bit of coal on occasionally, or liven it up with the poker. Having dealt with the fire she went over to her bedside drawer and got out the letter and the packet. Then she drew her chair up close to the hearth, sat herself down, and decided to open the letter first.

It was a nice letter. He was truly sorry, he said, for everything he had said and thought about her living with Mr Cowan. He explained painstakingly that he had jumped to a wrong conclusion, told her how he had heard the news originally, explained that he was now bitterly ashamed of himself. He begged her forgiveness and said he would always be her friend. You could almost say he grovelled, Linnet mused, putting the closely written sheets back into the envelope and reaching for the packet. But Roddy need not worry because she had always known he was her friend and she would always forgive him as he, she knew, would always forgive her. That punch on the nose had been quite well received, all things considered. Linnet knew young men who would have punched her right back.

She undid the packet and the bracelet slithered out and fell into her lap, making her gasp. It was beautiful, really beautiful, easily the nicest thing anyone had ever given her – and it must have cost poor Roddy an awful lot of money, he must have spent every penny he'd saved, one way and another.

She slipped the bracelet round her wrist and fastened it and a tiny little note fell out and fluttered to the floor. Linnet bent and picked it up.

Hope you love it like I love you, it said simply. *Your Roddy.*

Over the weeks which followed, Linnet learned a thing or two about being a nanny which she had not even considered when she took the job.

The first surprise came when Mr Cowan asked her, quite mildly, if she would mind not wearing her new bracelet whilst she was on duty.

'It's very pretty, Miss Murphy, and I'm sure you enjoy possessing it,' he said. 'But it will give rise to talk – I'm sure I need not say more.'

Linnet murmured that she would take it off straight after breakfast and did so, but she could not imagine what sort of talk a bracelet could give rise to, and that night, at dinner, she taxed Mr Cowan with it.

'As you see, sir, I'm not wearing my bracelet since you desired me to take it off, but I have to admit I'm curious. How could it possibly give rise to talk? Surely no one thinks I would steal such an object?'

Mr Cowan shook his head chidingly at her. 'Come, Miss Murphy, I know you are very young, but what do you suppose my housekeeper thinks when she sees you for a month bare-wristed and then you turn up at breakfast one morning with a gold bracelet to which you seem so attached that you keep it on three days running?'

'It was sent to me, through the post,' Linnet said, her

cheeks hot. 'I expect Mrs Eddis wondered what was in my packet – well, now she knows. I don't see how anyone could think different, sir.'

'People sometimes believe what they want to believe,' Mr Cowan said. 'You are a young and lovely girl, living in a widower's house. Some people will say that I gave you the bracelet. Others will conjecture why I gave you the bracelet. Few indeed are those who will suppose it was sent you as a present through the post.'

If Mr Cowan had known about Roddy's black eye, Roddy's swollen nose, he might have been glad that a great stretch of highly polished walnut dining table separated him from his daughter's nanny. And Linnet managed to control an urge to fly across that same stretch of dining table and box his ears for him, because she realised he was only saying what he thought to be the truth. Poor man, as if she would have accepted a valuable present like a gold bracelet from an old widower and one, moreover, who was her employer!

'Well, if anyone has such evil thoughts, sir, I hope for their sake that they don't speak them aloud,' she said. Her voice was icy but her cheeks, she knew, flamed. 'The bracelet comes from a very old friend.'

Mr Cowan grinned then, and he looked younger and a good deal less censorious. 'A very old friend, Miss Murphy? As old as me?'

She had to smile, but did not answer him directly. 'I hope, if anyone ever says anything like that in front of you, sir, that you'll tell them roundly that I am not that sort of person, and that you are not either, Mr Cowan.'

'I'm very sure, Miss Murphy, that no one would dare to say anything of that nature to my face,' Mr Cowan said smoothly. 'However, I'll bear what you say in mind.' And then, whilst she was still thinking it a poor sort of reply, he changed the subject.

Another thing which Linnet learned about being a nanny was how very boring it could be. She loved Mollie and enjoyed her company, but she still got bored because there was simply not enough for her to do. Nanny Peters had prepared and cooked all Mollie's meals, but because Linnet had had no formal training Mr Cowan decreed that she and Mollie should be fed from the kitchen. The kitchen staff did not much like having to make a luncheon each day as well as doing a high tea for Mollie, but they had no choice but to obey and Linnet, too, could scarcely insist that she would enjoy cooking Mollie's luncheon, particularly when cook brought them such very delicious meals.

So Linnet, finding herself with leisure for the first time in her life, began to long for the office life she had so gladly shed, for a friend like Rose to giggle with, for the other lodgers back at the Boulevard – even the noisy little boys would have been a relief during the long, silent afternoons when Mollie was out to tea, or playing quietly with her toys.

It might have been better had the month been June instead of November, because it rained and rained, turning a visit to the park or the aviary to a purgatory of cold hands and wet feet, and although she could, in theory, have left Mr Cowan in charge of Mollie in the evening whilst she went to the cinema or even the theatre, she didn't much fancy trudging through the rain at either end of the journey.

The outings with her employer stopped because of the weather, too, though he told her he would take her and Mollie Christmas shopping in Chester as soon as the weather improved. Linnet thought Chester a delightful city – the rows intrigued her, and the old, Elizabethan shop-fronts – but would rather have spent a day going round Blacklers, Lewises and the Bon Marché on Church

Street. Christmas shopping would be fun, but it was too early yet, so she wrote letters to Roddy which she could not post, lacking an address, read books from Mr Cowan's library and moped.

And her days off, which had been promised, always seemed to disappear into thin air, because they were so difficult to arrange. She had not once visited Margaret or her other friends from the Boulevard, and had only managed to spend half a day with the Sullivans on one occasion. She was supposed to have a whole day off each week but who would look after Mollie whilst she went gadding? She asked Mr Cowan, timidly at first, and he said she had best speak to Mrs Eddis and Linnet wished very heartily that she had not agreed with her employer that she had no need of a nurserymaid once she took up the job. Nice, efficient little Emma Alcott was gracing someone else's nursery by now, allowing some other nanny to get away from her charge from time to time. But Mrs Eddis, though pleasant to Linnet, made it very clear that neither she nor the maids could take on the extra responsibility of Mollie.

'You could go out for an hour if you let one o' them other nannies take care of the kid, or you could go round to your friend's place and take the kid wi' you,' she suggested after Linnet had been living at the house for several weeks without a single afternoon off, let alone a whole day. 'The boss won't know – 'e probably wouldn't care if 'e did know, come to that.'

It sounded fair enough so after luncheon one day Linnet dressed Mollie in her scarlet coat and leggings and the little round scarlet hat like a pudding basin, put on her own navy overcoat and round velour hat and set off for the tram stop.

It was a very cold day; last night's rain had frozen to ice in the puddles and Mollie's little nose was as red as her coat and hat, but they hurried along, hand in hand, and hopped on the tram as soon as it arrived, both in the best of spirits at the thought of a break in their routine.

The nearest tram stop to Peel Square was Arden Street on Scotland Road but Linnet didn't get off there because she wanted to get some cakes at Ernest Beasley's. She and Mollie had fun choosing what Beasley's called 'pastries', and watched with watering mouths as the cakes were tenderly placed in a white card box with *Beasley's Bakery* on it.

'It's a nice present, isn't it, Linnet?' Mollie said, dancing along beside her nanny. 'Your friend will like the dear little cakes – and so will we, won't us?'

Linnet laughed and assured her charge that the cakes would give everyone pleasure and presently they turned in under the arch and entered Peel Square. It was, as usual, full of children playing a variety of games – hopscotch, jacks and ollies being the ones Linnet recognised – and Mollie hung back wistfully as they reached the front door. It was clear that to a child, Peel Square was a playground paradise and Mollie wished very much to stay out there whilst the adults talked.

Mrs Sullivan was delighted to see them, received the box of cakes with genuine pleasure, and made a great fuss of Mollie.

'Aren't you a big girl, young Mollie?' she said. 'Never did I see anything like it – you'll be as big as our Teddy at this rate!'

'I will,' Mollie squeaked. 'I do grow, don't I, Nanny Linnet?'

'She only calls me nanny when we're in company, it's plain Linnet most of the time,' Linnet said, giggling. 'Well, Auntie Sullivan, how are you – and the rest of the family, of course?'

'We're all well, even that stupid Roddy,' Mrs Sullivan said. 'Writ to you, did 'e?'

'Yes. We'd had a quarrel so he wrote to say sorry. He sent me the loveliest present . . .' Linnet shot out her wrist and the bracelet, donned for this special occasion, fell in a charming loop across her slim white hand. 'What d'you think, Mrs Sullivan? Isn't it the prettiest thing?'

'I think our Roddy's got good taste; and 'e's learnin' some sense an' all,' Mrs Sullivan said approvingly. 'You're fond of 'im in spite of everything, ain't you, queen?'

'Yes, he'll always be my good friend,' Linnet assured her. 'But he does lose his temper, and then I lose mine . . .'

'And my boy ends up wi' a black eye,' Mrs Sullivan murmured. Linnet shot her a conscience stricken look.

'Oh . . . oh, that! He – he walked into me . . . but it was a mistake, we made it up.'

'Glad to 'ear it,' Mrs Sullivan said. 'Now, young Mollie, why don't you run outside an' play wi' the other kids?' Mollie complied eagerly and Mrs Sullivan settled down in a shabby kitchen chair and smiled at her guest. 'Put the kettle on, chuck, an' you an' I will 'ave a cosy chat an' a nice cuppa,' she said comfortably. 'The littl'un can't come to no 'arm out there, the other kids'll see to that. Nor there ain't no traffic to worry about, norrin the square.'

At first Linnet kept popping out to make sure that Mollie was all right, but the child was obviously enjoying herself and soon she ceased to worry. Instead, she and Mrs Sullivan caught up on each other's news and presently, when Mr Sullivan came in, she was told all about his job as a nightwatchman and the dog which accompanied him on his rounds – it was a large alsatian called Grab and aptly named, apparently – as well as learning that Roddy was now on a bigger ship than the *Mary Rose*, carrying timber across the Atlantic. He could be away for as much as nine weeks at a time, but the money was good and he enjoyed the work.

'I b'lieve he popped to see you when 'e was last ashore,' Mrs Sullivan said tactfully, as they sipped their hot tea. 'We don't 'ave no address for 'im when 'e's on the timber run so we can't write back, an' 'e ain't ashore for long so 'e doesn't write to us much, either. Still, nine weeks will soon go.'

'In nine weeks' time Christmas will be over and there will be snowdrops in the churchyards,' Linnet said. 'What's the turn-round, Mr Sullivan?'

'After nine weeks 'e'll probably 'ave a week ashore,' Mr Sullivan said after some thought. 'You'll be able to see a bit of each other.'

'Yes. Only I think Roddy will have to come to me, because I'm having an awful job to get any time off.' And in a few swift sentences Linnet explained her position.

'Tell your boss 'e must gerra nurserymaid or you'll leave,' Mrs Sullivan said when Linnet finished speaking. 'Fair's fair, chuck. Everyone's entitled to some time off. I don't deny the child's a nice kid, but you need to gerraway from 'er for a few hours each week.'

'I know I do,' Linnet agreed gloomily. 'But it's not so easy. Mr Cowan's awful kind, but it's much harder to speak to him, somehow, when you're his nanny and not his secretary.'

'Hmm,' Mrs Sullivan said thoughtfully. 'Hmm.'

And then there was a shriek from outside which rivalled description. It had all the hair standing up straight on the back of Linnet's neck even as she scooted for the door. She wrenched it open and almost fell out into the square – and there was Mollie, engaged in a fierce battle with a small redhead over the piece of wood the kids used as a cricket bat. The redhead was the one emitting the terrible screams.

'Matty Stevens, shut your bleedin' gob or I'll shut it for you,' a slatternly looking woman screeched from her blotched and filthy doorstep. 'Come on you two, leggo that bat or I'll crucify the pair of ye!'

Mrs Sullivan peered out past Linnet, who was urging her charge to let go of the bat and come in this instant, not that Mollie was taking any more notice than the red-haired Matty. Both small girls continued to battle grimly whilst the other kids looked on, grinning.

'Break it up, you two,' Mrs Sullivan called. 'Mrs Stevens, we'll gerrours off if you'll do likewise wi' Matty.'

Mrs Stevens sighed and descended onto the battlefield, as did Linnet. Silently, both laid hands on her own child and tugged. Matty screamed once more and then turned and bit her mother's wrist. Mollie, meeker by nature, let go of the bat and said loudly, 'Bad girl, Matty, I'll crucify ye!'

Linnet gasped and shook Mollie's shoulder, whereupon Mollie looked up at her and grinned quite unrepentantly. Mrs Stevens laughed and dragged her small child towards her door. 'They ain't done no 'arm,' she said over her shoulder. 'Turble temper this 'un 'as – I guess it's the red 'air. Sorry, one an' all.'

'She's no worse than mine,' Linnet said grimly. She picked Mollie up and carried her into the Sullivans' kitchen. 'You're a bad girl, Mollie, what were you fighting over, anyway?'

'The bleedin' bat,' Mollie said primly. 'Freddy said I might have a go next.'

'It's norra bleedin' bat, chuck, it's a cricket bat,' Mrs Sullivan said, her voice shaking with laughter. 'Wharrever made you think it were a bleedin' bat?'

'Everyone else called it that,' Mollie said. 'Freddy said

it was my turn next wi' the bleedin' bat.' She allowed herself to be picked up and sat on a kitchen stool, then reached eagerly for the mug of milk Linnet was holding out. 'I'm thirsty, I am!'

'I just hope she forgets it by the time we get home,' Linnet said in a desperate under-whisper as she and Mrs Sullivan began to slice and butter bread and set out the cakes Linnet had brought. 'I don't think her father would be too pleased if she started cussing before her fourth birthday.'

'It ain't cussing, just sayin' bleedin',' Mrs Sullivan objected, cutting bread like a machine in thin, equally sized slices. 'It's just – just a way of describin' something, I guess.'

But Linnet, smiling noncommittally, knew that her employer was unlikely to agree with this cheerful sentiment.

When Linnet and Mollie got home, rather late, from Peel Square, they found that Mr Cowan was entertaining visitors. Fortunately, perhaps, it did not occur to him to ask Linnet where they had been, he merely came into the hall as they entered it and said in an undertone: 'Miss Murphy, my elder brother and his wife, Mr and Mrs Edgar Cowan, have arrived for a short stay. I'd be obliged if you would tidy Mollie up and bring her down to the white drawing-room before dinner. They've not seen her since she was a small baby and my sister-in-law is particularly keen to renew the acquaintance. Could you be ready in, say, twenty minutes?'

'I think so, sir,' Linnet said, remembering that Mollie would be showing traces of the jam she had eaten for tea to say nothing of chocolate cake. 'She's been playing out – should I, perhaps, bath her first?'

But Mr Cowan shook his head. 'No, no, that won't be

necessary, Mrs Edgar is very fond of children, she'll not be put off by a touch of dirt. Well, off with you both, I'll see you presently.'

Linnet and Mollie hurried up the stairs and along to Mollie's bedroom where Linnet stripped the child down to her liberty bodice and woolly knickers and then regarded her critically. Battling with Matty had scratched Mollie's left cheek and both her wrists, but other than that . . .

'Bathroom, for a quick wash, darling,' Linnet decided. 'Aren't you a lucky girl, you very own aunt and uncle are here to see you! You won't remember them, but they love you very much. They haven't been to see you since you were a tiny baby.'

She felt it politic to tell Mollie frequently that she was much loved, for Mr Cowan still found it difficult to show open affection towards his little girl.

'Don't 'member,' Mollie said now, as she was washed, brushed and dressed in a clean red woollen dress with patent leather strap shoes and long white socks. 'I'm hungry, Linnet.'

'Well, you had bread and jam and cake, but you didn't eat much at luncheon because you were so excited,' Linnet remembered. 'No time for a snack now, love, but we'll get you a buttie and a drink of milk before you go to bed. Am I tidy? You look very smart indeed.'

'So's you,' Mollie said, eyeing Linnet's navy suit and crisp white blouse. 'Can we go down, now? I'm very so hungry!'

'Ever so, not very so,' Linnet corrected automatically as they made for the stairs. 'Never mind, sweetheart, you'll soon be fed I promise you.'

They entered the white drawing-room rather tentatively, for Linnet had got it into her head than the older Cowans would be difficult and severe, but this proved anything but the case. Mrs Edgar was a plump, pretty woman in her early forties with her richly curling golden hair cut into a fashionable bob and a good deal of make-up on. She was wearing a tea-gown in tangerine silk with coffee-coloured fringes and shoes which exactly matched and when she saw Mollie she gave a crow of delight and held out her plump white arms.

'What a little treasure! Come to Auntie Bertha, Mollie darling, and tell me all about your day.'

Mollie was nothing loath. She settled herself on her aunt's lap and began to prattle happily, and presently she jumped down and ran out of the room to return with a new game which she very much wished to master. Auntie Bertha began to show the child how to flip one tiddlywink counter with another and Mollie was soon absorbed.

This left Linnet time in which to meet Mr Edgar and to tell him how bright Mollie was for her age, how intelligent. Mr Edgar proved to be a taller edition of his brother but, she thought, with more self-confidence yet a softer, less harsh attitude. It was hard to remember how gentle and shy Mr Cowan had been at work because in his own home he was rather dictatorial, but his brother, beaming at Mollie, demanding to be introduced to the new nanny, was clearly immediately at ease.

'So you're Nanny Murphy,' he said jovially, taking her hand and smiling into her eyes. 'You aren't very old and I always think young things get on best together, so you and Mollie should deal famously. I gather from my brother here that Mollie had a bad time with her previous nanny.'

'Yes, she did,' Linnet admitted. 'But that's all behind her now, sir. In a few months she's changed completely, and definitely for the better. Why, she's only just three but already she knows her letters and can count up to ten.'

'That's excellent; we'll have her addressing the House of Lords before she starts school at this rate,' Mr Edgar said jovially. 'Does she eat well? Sleep well?'

Linnet assured him that Mollie was a model child, enjoying her food and sleeping the clock round at nights, but after a few such remarks she heard the scuttle of Edith's feet in the hall and then a tentative *boiiing* as the gong was struck very gently. In the normal course of things Edith would have poked her head round the door and announced, 'Dinner's ready, sir,' for Mr Cowan did not allow the gong to sound for fear of waking Mollie. But since the child was still up and they had visitors to dine Edith clearly thought that a more formal approach was called for.

But it seemed as though Linnet was the only person who had heard the gong, or grasped its message, for the brothers continued to talk and Mrs Edgar went on playing with her little niece. I'd better say something or dinner will be spoiled, Linnet thought, so she went over to Mollie and took her hand.

'Come along, love; that was the gong for dinner, it's time you were in bed,' she remarked. 'You've not had your bath yet, either.'

Mollie slid reluctantly off her aunt's lap, tried to pick up the game board, and everything crashed to the floor, tiddlywinks bounding everywhere whilst the pot into which one was supposed to aim them fairly flew across the drawing-room parquet and disappeared under the chaise longue.

'Oh drat!' Mrs Edgar exclaimed. 'All my fault, I should have held onto it. We'll clear it up in a trice, but I'm afraid we may be a little late for dinner.'

Mollie, scrabbling on the floor with both fists full of tiddlywinks, looked up.

'Late for dinner? Mrs Eddis will crucify you,' she

remarked conversationally. 'I'm going to have a buttie though, aren't I, Nanny Linnet? Because I only had bleedin' bread and jam for my tea.'

Linnet knew there would be trouble, though at the time Mr Edgar had turned away to hide a twitching lip and Mrs Edgar had laughed without attempting to cover up her amusement. But Mr Cowan had looked mortified – and no wonder, Linnet thought crossly. Why on earth did Mollie have to repeat that particular phrase? But that was kids for you.

She didn't have dinner with Mr Cowan, of course, not when he had guests, so she and Mollie had a delicious high tea in the kitchen with the staff. Egg and cress butties were accompanied by tiny chicken pies, a speciality of which Cook was justly proud, and then they had a large helping of trifle, finishing off their meal with milk for Mollie and a large cup of tea for Linnet.

'Bedtime now, you little monkey,' Linnet said, carrying her sleepy charge up the stairs. 'Night night, sleep tight, please make sure the bugs don't bite.'

'What's bugs?' Mollie asked through a mouthful of thumb. Linnet sighed with exasperation at her own foolishness. Fancy using that particular little rhyme on such a delicate day for language!

'Nothing. It doesn't matter. Sleep well, Mollie, and don't wake me too early,' Linnet said, as she did every night. 'Do you want Mr Woggins?'

Mr Woggins was a pink plush rabbit with one eye and huge feet. Mollie nodded, her eyes already mere slits.

'Please, Linnet. On my tummy.'

Linnet placed the plush rabbit on Mollie's tummy and Mollie gave a deep sigh, curled her spare hand protectively round him, and slept.

I might as well go to bed, too, Linnet told herself. No point in going downstairs, Mr Cowan won't need my company tonight and it's awful snug in my room with the fire on and the lamp glowing. I'll read Roddy's last letter and write my diary and then I'll get into bed myself. I'm tired enough, heaven knows, what with one thing and another.

But life was not destined to be so simple. She had no sooner made up her fire and got out her diary than there was a knock on her door. Guessing that it was Edith with her hot drink, Linnet called out 'Come in!' and was astonished when the door opened and Mr Cowan slipped into the room.

'Miss Murphy, I have to speak to you! I couldn't very well send for you downstairs since my brother and his wife are there . . . please explain how Mollie came to use that – that very coarse expression.'

'She must have heard it,' poor Linnet said feebly. 'Other children in the park, or even an adult, shouting out when we're passing along the street. I'm afraid folk do occasionally use bad language, sir, even before children.'

'But she's never done such a thing before! Miss Murphy, where did you spend the afternoon?'

Trapped, Linnet decided she must answer honestly. 'I went to Peel Square, sir. Where I used to live before I got my room on the Boulevard. I – I visited my old nanny, the person who took care of me when my mother was busy.'

She had never told Mr Cowan that her mother had been on the stage, nor that her own upbringing had not been, perhaps, all that it might have been. She felt mean calling Mrs Sullivan her nanny, but it was the only sort of explanation, she felt, that Mr Cowan would understand. In the echelons of society in which he moved, a woman with six or so kids of her own would scarcely take on another one, though this was precisely what Mrs Sullivan – dear, generous Mrs Sullivan – had done.

'Peel Square; I don't think I know it. Is it a good area of the city?'

'It's between Cazneau Street and Grosvenor Street,' Linnet said evasively. 'It's just somewhere people live, that's all.'

'I see. And did you let Mollie out of your sight whilst you were there?'

'Yes, I did. She went out to play with the other kids whilst Mrs Sullivan and I had a cuppa and got the tea ready.'

'And did she, Miss Murphy, hear someone using foul language?'

Linnet sighed. 'She heard a boy call a cricket bat the bleedin' bat, if that's what you mean. Look, sir, if you're cross that I took Mollie with me to Peel Square, I'm sorry, but what choice did I have? I've not had a day off for weeks and weeks because Mrs Eddis won't take care of the child whilst I'm gone, and . . .'

'That, Miss Murphy, is just an excuse. And that reminds me; my sister-in-law remarked on your pretty gold bracelet – now did I, or did I not, tell you not to wear it whilst you were on duty?'

'You told me not to do so, but if you remember, sir, the moment I stepped through the door . . .'

'That's enough, Miss Murphy. I cannot allow you to take Mollie into a poor area of the city where she could easily pick up more than bad language. And I won't have my wishes flouted. If you can't oblige me on these scores then I think, perhaps, that we've come to a parting of the ways.'

'I see,' Linnet said quietly. 'Very well, sir. I'll pack my things and leave after breakfast tomorrow. I trust you'll pay me for the last three weeks?'

They were facing each other and Linnet saw the shock and uncertainty which flashed across his face, but she did not see what else she could have said. There was absolutely no way in which she could promise never to wear her bracelet again in his presence and neither could she guarantee that she would not take Mollie into a part of the city of which he disapproved. Not unless he employed a nurserymaid with whom Mollie could be left, and he had shown no inclination to do that.

'Now wait a minute! Do you mean to tell me you intend to deliberately flout my wishes? That you are going to insist on taking Mollie with you when you visit places like Peel Square?'

Linnet jumped to her feet, her cheeks hot. He was behaving with total inconsistency – ordering her to do something which she could not possibly help!

'Mr Cowan, I didn't intend to *flout your wishes* as you put it by wearing my bracelet! I was in a hurry to get Mollie ready to meet her relatives and I simply forgot I had it on! Is that clear?' She had shouted the words into his face and saw him blink and draw back without any sympathy. He had tried to take advantage of her dependency upon him and it hadn't worked – hard luck!

'Oh! Well, yes, I suppose . . . but Peel Square! You cannot pretend that was a suitable place to take a child, I suppose?'

'I was brought up there, which means it can't be all bad,' Linnet said hotly. 'And since you've refused to employ any help for me and your housekeeper resolutely insists that keeping an eye on Mollie isn't her job, again you leave me no alternative. It is take Mollie with me or don't go out, and if you expect me to work twenty-four hours a day, seven days a week, and never see my own dear nanny or my friends again . . . well, I'm not a black slave-girl sir and I don't intend to be treated like one. And now would you kindly get out of my room?'

She had told Roddy to bugger off, but Roddy was used

to being shouted at and Mr Cowan was not. He looked shocked; he went quite pale.

'Miss Murphy . . .'

'Out! This may be your house, but whilst I'm employed by you this is my room and I won't have you blustering and bullying me in here.' She marched past him, head held high, cheeks aflame, and opened the door. He hesitated, then walked towards it, hesitated again . . . left the room. He turned in the hallway, obviously about to utter some dignified last words, but Linnet, feeling joyfully free and wicked, didn't give him the chance. She slammed the door crisply and shot the bolt across. Then she sat down in her chair before the fire and let out her breath in a long, silent whistle.

Phew! Well, she had burned her boats and right now she didn't give a damn. She would not be treated like a slave, not for all the money in the world, not for the nice food, or the rides in the motor car . . . not even for Mollie, and she did love the kid.

It was a shame about Mollie, because God knew what the child would do when she left. But that was no longer her concern. She could not let herself be bullied and shouted at and never given a day off just for the child's sake. And anyway, Mrs Edgar – Aunt Bertha – seemed a very nice sort of person. She would probably stay for a bit and choose a good nanny for the little girl before she left.

Comforted, Linnet sat in front of the fire for a while, planning her next move. She would not get her old job at the insurance company back, that was too much to expect, nor would her landlady in the Boulevard let her have her old room again, and in any case she could not afford the rent, not until she found herself a decent job. But she would be free to walk the streets, to pop into a canny house for a cheap snack, to go to the flicks when she saw a film she wanted to see, to walk by the river, to sit on Mrs Sullivan's doorstep and chaff with the lads... free, free, *free*!

She sat dreaming in front of the fire for a long time. She thought about the companionship she had so missed and the warmth of the other girls at work and in her lodgings. She thought about Mrs Sullivan's untidy, crammed little house, the smell of ironing and cheap meat stewing over the fire, the row of patched boots by the back door. Mr Cowan had a beautiful home, a lovely way of life, a dear little daughter. But she, Linnet, knew now that the Sullivan kitchen with its smell of poverty and love was worth more to her than all the Cowan comforts.

I wouldn't swop a week in this house for an hour wandering the streets of Liverpool, free as a bird and with nothing in my pocket but a big hole, she thought wonderingly. I can't wait to shake the dust of Sunnyside off my feet, I honestly can't wait!

Next morning she was woken by Mollie as usual, then her tea-tray arrived. Linnet dressed herself and the child and went downstairs with a light and springing step. The quarrel was over and she felt peaceful and glad; she would go straight round to the Sullivans' house, dump her small suitcase (it wouldn't have much in it since during the months she had worked for Mr Cowan she had worn her uniform) and then start job-hunting. I'm an experienced office worker, and I'm well-fed and neat, I'll get a job, no problem, she told herself as she and Mollie walked into the breakfast room. She put Mollie into her chair, provided her with a lightly boiled egg, some bread and butter fingers and a mug of milk and helped herself to bacon and kidneys, then carried her plate to the table and sat down. Through the window she could see frost sparkling on the grass and the sun shining brightly; after days and days of rain, Linnet saw this as a good omen. Even the weather approved of her leaving this place!

But she had scarcely started her meal when the door opened and Mrs Edgar appeared. She smiled at Linnet, took a plate out of the hot trolley and began to fill it from the big silver salvers which stood on the sideboard. Then she brought her food over to the table and sat down opposite Linnet.

'Good morning, my dear. Good morning, Mollie. Mollie, darling, have you finished your nice egg? Then if I may I'll get you down and you can go and find your Uncle Edgar who will take you in the garden for half an hour whilst Miss Murphy and I have a chat.'

Mollie was happy enough to run off in search of her uncle, though Linnet thought rather apprehensively that the last thing she wanted was to be left alone with any member of the Cowan family right now. But there was little she could do about it so she continued to eat her breakfast, eyes on her plate, and only looked up when Mrs Edgar spoke directly to her.

'Now, Miss Murphy, what's this I hear? My brother-in-law is in great distress. He tells me you've given him notice and intend to leave today and he is upset that you should want to take such a step. Can you make things a little clearer for me?'

'Yes, indeed. Mr Cowan did not approve of my taking Mollie to Peel Square, in the city, where she played with other kids whilst I visited the woman who brought me up. He wanted my word that I would never do such a thing again. I told him that since he did not employ anyone but myself to look after Mollie, it was take her with me or remain a virtual prisoner in this house and that I could not agree to. So he suggested we should part company and I agreed. Far from handing in my notice, Mrs Edgar, I believe I was dismissed.'

'And you don't really want to leave? My dear, I'm so pleased, because you've done wonders not only with Mollie but with my brother-in-law, as well. He seems much more relaxed and in control and is certainly far happier with his daughter. So if I tell him it was just a misunderstanding . . . ?'

'It wasn't. I understood him perfectly and I believe he understood me. Furthermore, Mrs Edgar, last night I realised what a dreadfully boring life I was leading here. Oh, I don't deny my salary is good, my meals delicious, my work not over-demanding, but I'm never free for one moment to please myself. I never have an afternoon off, not an hour off, even. And that means I'm losing all my old friends and not making new ones. No, upon reflection I believe Mr Cowan was right. We should part company and go our separate ways. Mr Cowan will soon find a replacement for me, I'm sure.'

'But he's so pleased with the way you and Mollie get on, so delighted to find in you a bright, intelligent companion with whom he can discuss his problems. I assure you, Miss Murphy, that he will be deeply hurt and distressed if you insist on leaving.'

'It isn't up to me,' Linnet said, her voice rising a little. 'I was dismissed, Mrs Edgar, and so I'm going to leave. That's all there is to it. And anyway, kind though it is of you to intercede, I do think this is between Mr Cowan and myself.'

Mrs Edgar looked nearly as surprised as her brother-in-law had done when Linnet had shouted at him the previous evening. 'Well, you do speak your mind, Miss Murphy,' she said. 'I'll send Mr Cowan to you; he'll tell you you're mistaken.'

Linnet said nothing and Mrs Edgar got up and left the room. Linnet poured herself another cup of coffee and glanced once more through the window. The sun was fairly beaming in through the glass and she could see Mollie's small figure in the distance with her tall uncle beside her. There was such promise in the sparkling morning that she felt like leaving this moment.

The breakfast room door opened softly and someone cleared his throat uneasily. Linnet did not have to glance across the room to know who it was.

'Miss Murphy? May I . . . ?'

'It's your house, Mr Cowan,' Linnet said evenly. 'I'm just finishing my breakfast. Mollie had hers earlier and is walking in the garden with your brother.'

Mr Cowan came and stood opposite Linnet. He looked as though he had not slept well, if at all. Serve him right, Linnet thought cruelly. I might not have slept either if I'd not decided it was all for the best. Well, I'm leaving and he's going to have to learn to manage without me – let's see how he likes *that*!

'Yes, m-my sister-in-law told me. Miss Murphy, I spoke in the heat of the moment last night – won't you forgive me?'

For the life of her Linnet could not help smiling at him; he looked so stricken, so full of remorse! 'It doesn't matter,' she said. 'I'm sorry, too, probably Peel Square isn't what you want for Mollie – well, I don't suppose Mrs Sullivan wanted if for her boys, either, but it was all that was on offer. But I'll be out of your home soon, and you won't have to bother about me again.'

'But I want to bother about you! And I don't want you out of my home, I want you in it,' Mr Cowan almost shouted. 'I said stupid, selfish things . . . don't make Mollie suffer for my fault, Miss Murphy! Stay with us, please. You can have weekends off . . . I'll hire a nursery-maid, a companion for you . . . anything, if only you'll not go.'

It was awful, it cut the ground completely out from

under Linnet's feet. She stared at Mr Cowan, gaped at him almost, and prayed for the right words so that she might still escape.

'Miss Murphy? I'll ring the agency and get the girl, Emma, the one you recommended. I'll take time off from the office and keep an eye on Mollie myself until the nurserymaid starts. I'll increase your salary – you shall have a dress allowance, like my wife did – if only you'll stay with Mollie and me.'

Linnet wanted to say no, she couldn't stay, not now. She wanted to jump up from her chair and leave the room and pack her case and – and simply run and go on running until she got to Peel Square and the sensible, capable Mrs Sullivan. But she could not do it, could not hurt Mr Cowan so badly. So instead, she nodded reluctantly.

'All right, I'll stay for a while, at least. Until Mollie's at school perhaps. But I'm going to wear my bracelet every day, Mr Cowan, because it's – it's a pledge from my young man. We're going to marry one day, Roddy and me, and I won't hide his bracelet away as if it was some sort of guilty secret. Is that all right?'

She was looking into his eyes as she spoke and she saw the hurt, the deep, painful shrinking. And knew, as she had suspected when he came into the room and gazed so unhappily into her eyes, that Mr Cowan fancied himself in love with her. He hadn't realised it, not until she said she would go, and then he had thought of the long, lonely evenings, the solitary dinners, the responsibility of bringing Mollie up alone, and he just couldn't face it. He had told himself he was in love and had been willing to do almost anything to keep her here, in the house on Sunnyside. She had a horrid suspicion that, if she had not capitulated, he would have offered marriage next. And if he had, and she had turned him down, whatever would he have done then? But even now he had his pride. He would not willingly let her see that she had hurt him.

'Yes, that's fair enough, Miss Murphy, you wear your bracelet whenever you please.' He grinned then, the boyish grin which she liked because it made him look younger and more carefree. She had noticed that when he relaxed and forgot his responsibilities, he could be a pleasant companion who could talk and even joke without having to continually stress his seriousness and superiority. She much preferred that Mr Cowan to the reserved, uncompromising man who thought himself too important to mix with ordinary people and who tried to tell everyone, including Linnet, what they should and should not do. 'Now, Miss Murphy, can we forget our – our disagreement? It shan't occur again, for my sister-in-law has pointed out that you and I should work together to make this a happy home for Mollie, and I intend to do just that.'

'Certainly, Mr Cowan; I've forgotten it already,' Linnet said, pushing her plate away and standing up. 'And now I'd better go and fetch Mollie in. I'm going to take her on the tram down to the Pier Head so she can see the Mersey – she's Liverpool born and bred, sir, but she's never even seen our river. I was shocked, that I was!'

She said it to lighten the atmosphere, and it worked. He laughed. 'There, now you've proved I'm a bad father for I'd not thought to introduce her to the river. Incidentally, Mollie has a great-aunt in Birkenhead; you must take the child over on the ferry and visit her one day. She's a nice old girl, you and she would get on. Or perhaps I could take some time off and come over there with you. And next summer I thought we might go to a hotel in Llandudno for a couple of weeks; you would enjoy it as much as Mollie, I'm sure.'

'That would be nice,' Linnet said politely. She moved past him, opened the door, slid out into the hall. By next summer, she told herself, she would have seen Mollie settled with the new nurserymaid and would have no scruples about leaving. But Mr Cowan had followed her from the room, and as he closed the breakfast room door behind him she turned, smiled at him and spoke as easily and naturally as she could. 'I'll see you this evening then, sir.'

'Indeed. You'll dine with us tonight please, Miss Murphy. A foursome is easier and more comfortable than a threesome and I feel – I feel you are one of the family already. Mrs Edgar would like to know you better and so would my brother.'

'Very well,' Linnet said. She inclined her head and then opened the side door and ran down the garden to find Mollie, glad to end the conversation, which was bound to be rather stilted and awkward considering what had gone before.

Walking back down the garden with Mollie's small hand in hers and the child chattering away beside her, Linnet thought rather sadly that her courage had not been equal to escape when it came to the point. But she knew, really, that it had not been lack of courage which had stayed her hand. It had been a wry fondness for Mr Cowan, and a real love for Mollie. She could not leave them in the lurch, not once Mr Cowan had apologised. But because she had given in it did not mean she was happy with the situation. I can almost feel the prison bars closing round me, she told herself sadly. But it won't be for long, it can't be. Roddy will be home in a few weeks, he'll tell me what to do. He's sensible, is Roddy.

And for the first time it occurred to Linnet that to spend the rest of her life with Roddy, even if they did quarrel a great deal, wouldn't be a bad thing; not a bad thing at all.

Chapter Eleven

Spring had come suddenly, in the middle of April, bringing with it sunshine, wild, warm winds, sudden sparkling showers. And because everything always happens at the same time, Caitlin and Declan Franklin decided to get engaged the same month that the Stations came to Ivy Farm. And that meant, Lucy thought bitterly, that Caitlin, who was such a help, would be too busy with her own affairs to help with the Murphys' Stations. And with Grandad abed and her aunts busy with their own affairs, that left a great deal for Lucy to do. Because it was a big thing for a family, indeed for the whole neighbourhood, when the Stations came. The priest heard confessions and took communion in your home and all your friends and relatives came, so it was a great time for spring cleaning, and for sending letters to distant relations reminding them that the farmhouse had been singled out and that their presence was required.

In this particular part of Kerry the Stations, it was calculated, came round to each house no more than once in ten years, which gave you plenty of time to prepare, or so you would think. Only somehow things which should be done don't get done and the world doesn't come to an end just because you've not put a lick of paint on your doors for nine years. And then the tenth year comes along and you've got it all to do – every wall must be whitewashed, even walls which the priests and the congregation were highly unlikely to inspect, every floor stripped of old polish and then polished anew, every cushion cover, tablecloth and curtain must be taken down, tubbed, hung on the line, ironed, starched, put back in its place. In short, when a farm had the Stations everyone suffered.

It would, of course, be Lucy's first time, because ten years before Maeve had still been living at home, masterminding their every move, mothering them. And what was worse, Grandad was poorly. 'He'll be here for the Stations,' the doctor had said the previous week and Lucy, frightened, said, 'but surely it's not that serious, doctor? Surely Grandad will be here for years yet?'

Dr Leary had patted Lucy's shoulder, tried to smile. But it hadn't been much of a smile because he and Padraig Murphy had known each other all their lives, had drunk together, played tricks on each other . . . had attended each other's weddings and scoffed at each other's foolishness over this and that.

'He'll not last the summer, unless a miracle happens,' the doctor told her sadly. 'But he'll see the Stations out. Will you be wantin' to send for Maeve? I'll add a line to your letter if you like.'

But Maeve had just discovered that she was expecting again and was busy and happy. 'How can I write with bad news and get her tearin' back here, perhaps too late?' Lucy asked the doctor. 'It takes a long time to arrange a trip across half the world – is it fair, doctor?'

'No, it's not,' Dr Leary said, having given it some thought. 'Best say nothing, then. Maeve's not a young woman, to bear a child at her age is no light thing, best not add to her worries until we have to.'

'And Grandad's so happy,' Lucy said. 'He dearly loves the Stations.'

So she and Caitlin worked as hard as they could – despite her new preoccupation Caitlin did not let the Murphy family down – and the farmhands performed miracles on the outside of the house and in the farm buildings. The haggard was cleaner than it had ever been – save when Maeve had ruled when the Stations last came – and everything was planned down to the last detail. Friends and relatives, forewarned, would be arriving the day before if they came far and very early on the day itself if they were near. The old priest and his young curate would arrive early, too, the curate to hear confessions and the priest, of course, to say Mass. When the service was over breakfast would be served, if the day was fine in the yard, and when a long and leisurely meal had been eaten the priests, having done their duty by everyone, would leave, sped on their way by thanks and good wishes, carrying with them the dues they had collected before the service began. And then the real party would start. Huge meals would be set out on the white-clothed trestle tables and every scrap of food would be eaten, there would be singing, talking, dancing and story-telling, and guests who could do so would stay late into the night.

'If it rains it's the barn,' Lucy decided the day before, though the sky overhead had been clear for a couple of days. 'There's too many for the house, they'd be crammed in shoulder to shoulder. No, the barn's definitely best. What do you think, Caitlin? Shall we set up the trestles in the barn just in case the weather turns?'

Caitlin said leave it until the day, because surely the Holy Mother would look on an event like the Stations with approval, and see that the weather stayed good? And since Lucy agreed with her they put off making a decision, so when the day itself dawned bright and fair, without a cloud in the sky, the girls felt their faith had been justified and set about preparing breakfast with light hearts.

'They will all come and talk to me, alanna, so make sure I'm in me best,' old Padraig told Lucy as she brought hot water through so that he could shave. 'I'm wantin' to talk to me man of business when the priests leave, as well as me friends. He's comin', o' course?'

'Would Mr Eamonn miss the Stations at Ivy Farm? He'd sooner lose his right hand,' Lucy assured the old man. 'But if you're tired, Grandad, let business wait. Mr Eamonn can come to see you any time.'

Padraig grinned at her. He had all his teeth still and his grin was a pleasing sight. 'And I've got all the time in the world, so I have? Is that what you were goin' to say, alanna? Well, well, I've had a good life, better than most, and I'm an ole feller now. I don't grudge the leavin', but I want to settle things.'

'But you've made your will, Grandad,' Lucy said gently. 'That's all the settlin' that's needed, isn't it?'

He shook his head at her, smiling still. 'I do as I please, miss! Your aunts are comfortable, you've a good home here, but of late I've thought of your sister often and often. Who knows where she lays her head o' nights? Who knows if she's in desperate need? None of us, none of us. So I'm makin' provision for her, see? Poor child, poor little Linnet. Makin' sure she doesn't go short.'

'That's just like you, Grandad, but we still don't know where she is or how to get in touch with her,' Lucy pointed out. 'Maeve tried, years ago, without success. Why should you have better luck?'

He grinned again, a grin with a good deal of mischief in it. 'Oh, you'll try harder this time, alanna, and this time you'll succeed, mark my words. Because if you don't . . . but no matter, no matter. Hand me me razor and I'll get rid o' that white stubble – it makes me look like an old man so it does!'

By the time she climbed into bed that night Lucy was absolutely exhausted, but she was delighted with her first attempt at hosting the Stations. Everything had gone like a dream, exactly as she had planned it. Everyone had paid their dues, confessions had been cheerful and mercifully brief, relatives and friends had congratulated her and her workers on the state of the farm, the tidy house and the wonderful food.

Grandad had enjoyed himself, too. He had held court, seeming not to find so many visitors tiring, and had actually taken a little of the beautiful broth of beef bones and every vegetable she could lay her hands on, which Lucy had made for him.

'You've done well, Lucy,' her Aunt Clodagh had said as they met, briefly, in the dance. 'Maeve would be so proud if she could see you now! I used to think you were spoiled rotten, so I did, but you've turned out better than I ever thought. You've given us a wonderful day, my dear.'

It was high praise coming from the normally critical Clodagh, and Lucy swelled with pride. I'll remember today for ever, she thought, whirling up the line of dancers on Peder O'Rorke's arm. Peder was keen on her, he told her so often and she knew it was true. Caitlin and Declan, who worked in the grocery in Caher, couldn't wed until Declan had saved enough money to get them somewhere to live. Declan was an orphan so he had no family to help him and the Kellys lived in a small tied cottage, they didn't have room for another soul – and Declan was a good Catholic; the babies would come whether the young Franklins could afford them or no, so you didn't marry until you had at least a roof over your heads.

It was different for Peder and he often reminded her that she had only to say the word . . . he was a farmer's son from further up the valley, there would be no shortage of money to build a nice little house for two newlyweds and no need for anyone to scrimp and save.

'You'd be marryin' land,' Grandad said wistfully, whenever Peder's name was mentioned. 'A farmer's girl should always marry land.'

Sometimes Lucy was tempted, there was no doubt about that. She enjoyed the work on the farm and in the house well enough, but she often felt lonely and realised that, when Caitlin went, she would feel lonelier still. Besides, as Peder's wife she would have a position, a status, which she didn't have as Padraig's granddaughter, no matter how hard she worked. And with Padraig no longer able to tell them when to reap, sow, plant, plough, she had to ask the men or use her initiative.

I'm no good at the planning side of it, Lucy told herself, sitting by Grandad's bed and trying to learn all the things she had spent her childhood trying to avoid and ignore. Why didn't I listen when Grandad talked about sheep, cattle and crops?

But she hadn't and now she was having to ask questions, guess, take a chance. Mr Kelly had always worked hard but had no ideas other than to do as he was told and Tom Flanagan was ill and old. Kellach was a good worker but he had never taken a decision in his life and had no faith in his own judgement.

'Ask the ole feller,' he would say, looking worried. 'Mr Murphy will know, he knows all about it.'

So Lucy found herself alone, relying heavily on her workers to do the work whilst she tried to take decisions on matters of which she knew nothing. Padraig was a tower of strength, but she knew that he would not be here for her much longer and then what would she do? Marry Peder? Sell the farm and move away, to a town somewhere? There was no question of employing a manager, the farm could not, now, afford such a thing.

It'll be Peder, she told herself heavily the day after the Stations, as she made Grandad's early morning cup of tea. He loved the first cup of tea of the day and enjoyed it more than all the others, he said, because it had a special, first tea taste. So she made it carefully, carried it through, set the tray on the bedside table in the small parlour, went over to the window, drew back the curtains to let in the sunshine, the birdsong . . . stopped short . . .

He had not stirred. Very still he lay, propped up by the pillows, his expression serene, his hands with their knotted veins lightly clasped and lying outside the sheets. Lucy knew at once he was dead and pulled the sheet up over him. He died happy, Lucy told herself and she drew the curtains back across the window, shutting out the sunshine, the May blossom and the lilac and laburnum which he had loved to see. But she could not shut out the birdsong. As she went around seeing to all the things which a death makes necessary, she heard the birds singing their hearts out, as though they wanted to remind her that Padraig had loved them, would want the last sound he heard on this earth to be their songs.

And it comforted her.

Lucy and Mr Eamonn were in the solicitor's office, on opposite sides of the big desk, trying to solve the mystery of Linnet Murphy. It was more than a month since Padraig had died and there had been no answers to the many advertisements which Maeve had placed in the New York newspapers, nor had her other enquiries borne fruit. And now Mr Eamonn was explaining the importance of all this to Lucy herself.

'He's left the farm to the two of ye, jointly. You and your twin sister, Linnet Murphy.'

'Twin sister? Did you say *twin*, Mr Eamonn?' Lucy's voice came out high with astonishment.

'Did ye not know?' the solicitor looked at Lucy over the top of his glasses, then he nodded slowly to himself.

'No, I see ye did not; Maeve didn't like to mention it with the other one gone, I'd guess. But Linnet's your twin, so she is, and until we find her nothing can be done. Oh, you can work the farm, but there's money banked by your grandad which can't be released until the two of you can sign papers. You can neither buy nor sell, you must pay the wages from whatever you earn, but you can't pay into the bank or they'll hold the money for probate. And despite my begging Paddy not to tie your hands in this way, he went right ahead. The old divil had done it and died before it could be undone. So try to think where your sister could be, alanna!'

'I'm trying,' Lucy said slowly. She wondered why Maeve had never told her she had a twin, but then remembered her own attitude. She hadn't wanted to hear about Linnet, hadn't encouraged anyone, even Grandad, to talk about her. And Maeve, who loved little Evie, would have hated explaining to Lucy that her mother had taken one twin and left the other. To part sisters was bad, but to part twins . . . well, it would not be easy to explain away. Then she saw that Mr Eamonn was still staring at her, waiting for her to answer, so she rushed into speech. 'There must be something which would help, some clue Maeve hasn't thought of . . .'

And suddenly, she remembered the letters, her mother's letters to Maeve which she had found and read. She remembered, too, her own feeling that perhaps Linnet had never gone to New York in the first place. That she had stayed in Liverpool, left behind as once Lucy herself had been left.

If it was true, if her twin sister had never gone to New York, then there was little point in trying any harder to find her there. If she's in Liverpool I could catch a ship and search for her myself, Lucy thought, and suddenly she knew just what she was going to do.

There was nothing she could do on the farm that the men couldn't do every bit as well, and Caitlin could move in, for a wage, and look after the kitchen side of things whilst she was gone. And I can search for me sister me own self, and see a bit of the world at the same time, Lucy thought exultantly. But she was still in Mr Eamonnn's office and he was still regarding her curiously over the top of his spectacles. Lucy cleared her throat.

'Umm . . . you've made me think, Mr Eamonnn. I do believe I may have an idea where my sister could be. Is it possible to get sufficient money from the estate for me to go away for a week or two? Only I'd like to go myself, this time.'

'But Maeve's in New York, Lucy, she must know the place pretty well by now, and she's had no luck,' the solicitor objected. 'Surely to go all that way . . .'

'Oh, I'm sorry, I should have explained. Years ago, I read some letters my mammy had sent Maeve, and it occurred to me then that little Evie wrote as though she was alone in America. And I thought that probably Linnet had never gone to New York when my mother did, but had stayed behind, in Liverpool. But I said nothing to Maeve, because it didn't seem important. Only now . . . well, if I'm right she could be a lot easier to find!'

It proved easier to arrange than Lucy and Mr Eamonnn had anticipated, chiefly because when Maeve heard what her niece wanted to do she immediately sent a money order through the post which was sufficient to pay all Lucy's travel and would also cover her living costs for around two weeks.

'If you need more, telegraph,' the accompanying letter said. 'I'm so grateful to you, Luceen, for trying to find your sister. Losing her has been an ache in my conscience for many a long year.'

So Caitlin moved into the farmhouse and Lucy wrote

long lists of instructions, got Peder to advise her on what she should tell Kellach to do on the farm in her absence, packed a bag no less than three times – once with her best clothes, then with her oldest, then with her best again – and finally booked her tickets.

'I'm leaving on the first train tomorrow,' she told Caitlin importantly the night before she left when the two of them were in the kitchen making last minute arrangements for the weeks to come. 'I'm going to Dun Laoghaire to catch the ferry to Holyhead, then I'll get on another train for Liverpool. And when I get to Liverpool Mr Eamonnn says I should stay for the first night or so at the big hotel just outside the station. Until I get me bearings. Oh, Caitlin, I'm so excited!'

'Why, Luceen? Let's face facts, I've never t'ought you had much time for that sister of yours. You were always quite rude about her – "silly name" you used to say whenever she was mentioned.'

'Ye-es. I was a bit jealous, because Mammy took her and not me. It seemed like a slight, though I knew I was better off here with Maeve. And then when Maeve kept worrying about her – what she was doing, how she was managing – I felt jealous that she worried more about a girl she'd not seen since she was a tiny kid than she worried about me. I was just being selfish, really, but that's how it was. But once I knew that me and Linnet were twins, I felt as if I'd been cheated, as if I was only half a person and hadn't realised it till that minute.'

'I'd have loved a sister of me own . . . but I t'ink I know what you mean,' Caitlin said. She shot a sideways look at her friend. 'When I first brought Declan to meet everyone . . . well, I kept hopin' he didn't have a fancy for blondes, that he liked dark girls best. If I'd had a twin I'd ha' scratched her eyes out if she'd so much as glanced at him.'

'There you are, then, you do understand,' Lucy said triumphantly. 'But now I've got to find Linnet because without her I can't even begin to run Ivy Farm properly. Yet if I do find her, and bring her back . . . oh, I don't know. Sharing isn't – isn't something I've done much of and I don't know how I'll take to it and that's the truth. Why, the other day I found meself thinking I was glad Grandad wouldn't be here just in case he doted on her more than he used to dote on me! Would you believe a person could be so small-minded?'

'Marry Peder,' Caitlin advised. 'Then you can divide the farm. You can move in wit' him and this twin of yours can try her hand at farming here.'

'She won't know anything about farming,' Lucy objected. She went over to the pantry and took out a large tin with a picture of the English Houses of Parliament on the lid. Opening it to show the fine fruit cake within she added, 'Give this to the fellers for their elevenses tomorrow, would you? It should last a day or so, and then you could bake another. There's a tin of shortbread in there, though, so if you don't get time to bake . . .'

'Listen to the woman – as if I'd not spent the last few years in this kitchen alongside you, bakin' and roastin' and cleanin' wit' the best of 'em. Go and put the kettle on and we'll relax over a nice cup of tea. And, Lucy . . .'

'Yes?' Lucy said, as the silence stretched. 'Don't be embarrassed; say what you want to say.'

'We-ell, be nice to this girl Linnet, won't you? You've been awful lucky compared with her, you know. You've had Maeve, the farm, your grandad, and now you've got Peder if you want him. 'Tweren't her fault that your mammy took her away when she left and she didn't do all that well by her, seemingly. This sister of yours, she didn't even have her mammy for very long; from what you've told me, she's only had herself.'

'It's all right, I know,' Lucy said gruffly. 'I spent most of last night putting meself in her shoes and I'm going to be sweet as honey when we meet. But you can't make yourself like someone, you know, and I don't suppose I'm liable to like her after all these years. But I promise you, Cait, that she'll never know it. And now let's have that cup of tea, and we'll take a slice of me beautiful fruit cake, too!'

When Lucy got off the train at Lime Street Station in Liverpool she was tired, travel-stained and aching in every limb. The first train journey had been quite enjoyable – she had seen new sights, had admired, or deplored, the meadows and fields through which she travelled with a farmerly eye, had chatted to folk in the train and exchanged titbits of information about Cahersiveen and the people who lived there.

The ferry might have been fun, an adventure, had there been two of them, but when you were on your own new experiences, Lucy discovered, tended to be nerve-racking rather than amusing. She had never been on a ship before either nor gone further, at home, than the mouth of the lough in a neighbour's fishing boat. Now she was seeing waves of terrifying height and contrariness – she had imagined that out to sea waves behaved as they did nearer shore, but this proved to be anything but the case. The wind got up, the ship ploughed on, and the waves, instead of lining up neatly, seemed to attack the ship from every angle and to rear to impossible heights above the suddenly dangerous deck.

It was not long before Lucy, green of face and unsteady of foot, made her way below to cower in a corner, occasionally, alas, throwing up into a sturdy brown paper bag given to her by a sympathetic stewardess.

'Happens to us all it does, love,' the stewardess said in

a strange, sing-song accent. 'Better you will feel as soon as we dock. Now sit there and I'll bring you some seltzer. That sometimes helps.'

Lucy drank the seltzer, which was just very fizzy water, but it didn't help; well, it wasn't down there long enough, Lucy thought ruefully, reaching for a replacement bag. The only comfort was that all around her horrid noises proved she was not alone. Most of her fellow voyagers were casting up accounts simultaneously, it seemed.

The journey took about four hours and by the end of that time Lucy felt like a rag doll whose stuffing had been removed. When they docked she couldn't get off the wretched ship fast enough and onto dry land, but she felt too weak to make a break for the shore so simply allowed herself to be carried along by the crowds, and was soon standing apathetically in a line to climb aboard the train.

'Come along there, we're late,' the ticket collector said as he directed people to empty compartments. 'Ah, you gerrof at Crewe, queen. Tell someone in your carriage you want Crewe, you're awful green still.'

'Crewe? But I want to go to Liverpool,' Lucy said thinly. All her excitement, her spirit of happy independence, was at the bottom of the Irish sea in a brown paper bag. Never had she so longed for home and a bed which didn't move around! And her stomach ached with emptiness, yet she knew she would not be able to eat anything, probably for weeks. This is your fault, Linnet Murphy, she told her absent twin fiercely. If you'd not hidden away from us and then somehow got into Gramp's head when he was dying, none of this would have happened. I'd have inherited the farm and married Peder and never, never crossed the sea to get to this horrible old land – I wish I were back at Ivy Farm so I do!

'That's right, you want Liverpool so change at Crewe,'

the ticket collector said patiently. She was just thinking him rather a nice man when he turned to the man behind her and said bitterly: 'Bleedin' ignorant bogtrotter! These micks are all de same – never 'eard of Crewe station, an' it's only de biggest in de world, just about.'

Horrible ole divil, he's no right to be rude about the Irish, Lucy thought with unusual venom, sinking into a seat and leaning her weary head back against the plush upholstery. Bog-trotter indeed, just who did he think he was? I wish he might say that to a man – a man would have t'umped him for that!

But wishing wasn't much good; if wishes were horses then tinkers would ride, Lucy told herself, and got a stab of pain at the words. Oh, Finn, Finn! But you've forgotten him, she reminded herself fiercely, you've not so much as wasted a thought on him since Granny Mogg's death, and that was three years and more ago. Don't, for the love of God, start all that up again, don't start thinking of him now!

And for once, she obeyed her own injunction. She felt the train jolt and lurch, heard the whistle blow and various people call out, laugh, begin to push into the compartment. And then she was asleep and dreaming of green Cahersiveen meadows and the sea lough, blue beneath the sun.

'Wake up, luv! You're t'lass who wanted Crewe, aren't you? Well, we've arrived . . . come on, luv, do wake up!'

The voice was strange, the accent stranger, but the word 'Crewe' brought Lucy surging up from the depths of sleep. Groggily, she sat up; where was she? A bleary glance round confirmed that she was not at home but then she was pulled to her feet and her bag thrust into her arms.

'Move thysen', luv, or you'll be carried out of t'station!

You want to change 'ere for Liverpool. Hey don't forget thy coat!'

Half asleep still but rapidly coming round, Lucy scrabbled for her coat, her bag, her various possessions, and then stumbled out onto the platform. The train had been stuffily warm but the air on the platform was bracing, not to say cold, Lucy thought, trying to retract her head into the collar of her coat as a tortoise might when the chilly wind nipped at her sleep-crumpled cheeks.

'The train now standing at platform four is the twenty-one forty for . . .' a list of stations followed and just as Lucy was about to go in search of a porter the voice concluded, 'and Liverpool Lime Street.'

That was her train! But where was platform four? Lucy took a look around her and realised, for the first time, that this station was *huge,* absolutely massive. There were signs at various points, people scurrying about, a flight of stairs leading to an upper area, but she could not see a sign saying platform four nor another sign pointing to the Liverpool train. She was trailing miserably along the platform when an official-looking figure passed her. Quick as a flash, she grabbed the uniform-clad arm.

'Oh, excuse me, can you tell me where platform four is?'

The man looked down at her.

'Up the stairs, turn left, down the stairs, at the bottom of the second flight of stairs, turn left,' he said in a flat, uninterested tone. 'Better run, miss, if it's the twenty-one forty you're after. It's almost time 'e left.'

Lucy ran. She missed it.

Emerging onto Lime Street at eleven o'clock at night was quite an experience for a country-bred girl. Instead of being in darkness, as Lucy had assumed it would be, the street was brightly lit, and the gas lamps' flaring white light illuminated a number of smart and beautifully dressed ladies strolling idly along the pavements.

The theatre is near, I remember someone telling me so, it must have just opened its doors for the audience to leave, Lucy thought, staring with considerable admiration at the lovely ladies. It then occurred to her that it was not usual for a great many women to go to the theatre unaccompanied, yet there did not seem to be any gentlemen accompanying the ladies.

Then a gentleman came along. He was walking swiftly, not paying very much attention to his surroundings or not appearing to do so, anyway. And the ladies converged on him. They knew him, obviously. One asked him if he had found himself a bed for the night, another suggested that she was always willing to give any assistance she could to a kind gentleman like him, a third advised him not to consider Mimsie or Sal but to choose a decent girl like herself. Or that was what Lucy thought they said; their accents were by no means genteel and she had to listen carefully or she would have assumed they were speaking a foreign language.

But the gentleman understood them perfectly. 'Go away girls,' he said cheerfully and in plain English. 'Another time I'd be pleased to accommodate one or two of you, but tonight I've other fish to fry and a train to catch into the bargain.' And he hurried into the station which Lucy had just vacated, almost pushing her aside as he did so.

'Well I never did, those ladies aren't . . . aren't ladies,' Lucy said under her breath. 'I think I'd better find me hotel before I make any more mistakes.' And, bag in hand, she made her way quickly along the pavement to the grand foyer of the nearest hotel.

There was a smart young man on the desk. He looked

her over very carefully, but seemed to approve of what he saw for he gave her a smile and said, 'Was you wantin' a room, miss?' in a slow but pleasant voice.

'Yes, please. Just for the one night,' Lucy said and for the first time became conscious of her own brogue, because the young man said 'Pardon?' and she had to repeat the words, speaking this time as slowly and carefully as the reception clerk.

'Ah, I understand. Sorry, miss, a room for one night. If I might make so bold I suggest that you pay now, then if you have to leave early in the morning there will be no need to waste time settling your account.'

Wearily, Lucy found money, paid him, picked up her case. But the young man whistled and a boy appeared in a smart maroon uniform and enough gold braid to make him captain of a passenger liner at least. The boy took her case and her bag from her grasp and jerked his head at her.

'Folly me, queen,' he said briefly. 'Room 101.'

Dazed with tiredness and wide-eyed at the strangeness of the very first hotel she had ever visited, let alone stayed in, to say nothing of the sheer size of it, Lucy only realised he was expecting a tip when he opened the door of Room 101 and ushered her in. She turned to thank him and found an outstretched hand practically under her nose.

'Oh, sorry,' she said. She took out her purse again, selected a coin and put it on his palm. 'Thanks very much ... aha! Give me me bag, you young rascal.'

The boy handed over her bag, which he had slung across his shoulder to free his hands for tackling the door-key and her case. 'You're norras green as you're painted,' he said pleasantly. 'Sweet dreams, queen!'

Lucy tumbled into bed without so much as washing, though she did take a drink from the toothglass. But although she slept very deeply at first she was awoken in the early hours by strange noises from the room next door. Bed springs twanged, voices cooed and called and cursed, someone gave a couple of very loud shrieks, and then, abruptly, silence fell once more. Lucy, who had sat tremblingly upright in bed at the first sound, lay slowly down on her pillows once again. For the first time, she began to realise what life must have been like for Linnet once her mother had died. Of course it was possible that Linnet was in America, but Lucy did not think so. She knew almost nothing about her twin, had scarcely thought of her over the past twenty years, but now that she was actually in Liverpool she was getting a steadily increasing feeling that Linnet was near. That she had been in Liverpool all along – and that she, Lucy, was about to find the missing Murphy.

And alongside that feeling was this other, newer one. That far from being jealous of Linnet and envying her, she should pity her from the bottom of her heart. I had so much – Maeve, Grandad, Caitlin, Granny Mogg, she told herself. I've never in my life, until now, had to do anything by meself. Poor Linnet's been travelling alone, living alone, working alone. She's had to earn her own money, make it go round, find somewhere to live, even. And I've had my tickets paid for, my journey mapped out for me, and still I got lost, missed my train, arrived very late in the hotel, and I've absolutely hated it. Over the past day I've been frightened, sick, lost and lonely – so lonely! My sister Linnet's a brave girl to have faced a loneliness worse than any I've ever dreamed of – the loneliness of one small girl in this huge, frightening city!

Next day, Lucy left the hotel, bags in hand, and went in search of something cheaper and more suitable. Outside the hotel she hailed a taxicab and asked the driver to take her to a smaller, friendlier place than the big hotel in which she had spent the night.

'You want a boarding 'ouse, chuck,' the driver said, having given the matter some thought. 'Temp'rance, are you?'

'I'm from County Kerry,' Lucy assured him. 'A boarding house sounds nice. Will it be cheap?'

'Depends on the area. I think you'd best 'ead for a street what's quiet but central. Near the station, but not too near, 'cos o' the din. I should think Brownlow 'ill would suit, bein' as it's central but classy.' He glanced over his shoulder at her. 'An' you're young, you'll manage the climb,' he said encouragingly. 'From Ireland, are you?'

'Yes, from Kerry,' Lucy said again. She was gradually growing used to the Liverpool accent, having spent most of breakfast time simply listening to it as it surged around her, but she did realise that she would have to try to tame her own brogue a bit, if she was to be understood, that was. 'I'm searching for me sister – we're twins. I thought it would be easy to find her, but I'd not realised the city was so huge. Still, if she's in Liverpool, I'll find her – her name's Linnet Murphy.'

'Linnet. Unusual. Can't say I've 'eard of a Linnet afore,' the driver mused. 'You'll find 'er, though, if you keep askin'. Liverpool's norras big as you think, chuck.'

'It's bigger than Cahersiveen,' Lucy said and the driver chuckled, then drew in beside the kerb. 'There you are, Mrs Cordiner, The Lilacs, Brownlow 'ill. You'll be fine wi' Mrs Cordiner, she looks after 'er guests like a mother would.'

Lucy lugged her belongings out of the taxicab, paid the driver and knocked on the green front door. A large lady answered and said that she did have a room and that Miss was welcome to take a look before making up her mind.

Miss took a look and liked the place; it was clean, cheap and cheerful, what more could anyone ask? She explained her quest to Mrs Cordiner as she paid her first week's rent and Mrs Cordiner said she would put the word around for a Miss Linnet Murphy and would Miss Lucy Murphy like a cup of tea before she started out?

I'm going to be all right, Lucy told herself later, when the tea had been drunk, the house vacated, and she was on her way to the public library to see if they could help her. Mrs Cordiner's a nice woman, she'll do what she can to help and she won't cheat me. I'm going to find Linnet, I know it in me bones!

It was Linnet's day off and the day started bright and seemed likely to go on the same way. Linnet felt cheerful and happy from the moment she had jumped out of bed, not only because it was her day off but because it was sunny which must mean that summer was on its way at last.

Ever since the advent of Emma, the nurserymaid, Linnet had taken her time off without fail and since Mollie had started nursery school she did not even feel guilty at so doing. She usually went to the Sullivans' place and helped in the house, washing, ironing, cleaning, until it was time for the midday meal. Having worked hard all morning, the afternoon was usually given up to an outing of some description. Linnet treated Mrs Sullivan since she still spent very little of her salary and enjoyed giving pleasure. Besides, she was very conscious of the debt she owed the older woman. So Linnet and Mrs Sullivan took themselves off to a theatre or a cinema, or some other form of entertainment. Sometimes they took a tram ride or went on the overhead railway, at other times they treated themselves to tea and cream cakes at a posh café. In fine weather they set off as soon as Linnet arrived and went to Seaforth Sands, or New Brighton, or Woodside, anywhere within reach, in short. But today Linnet had a problem and needed Mrs Sullivan's advice, which meant, of course, that theatres and cinemas were out; she wanted quiet, a good tea, and plenty of time.

'We'll walk down the Scottie, takin' a look in the winders as we go, an' find ourselves a nice café for tea,' Mrs Sullivan said with relish. Now that her children were growing up and the older ones working, life was much easier. Roddy, Linnet knew, sent his mother home a generous allotment, as did the other boys with well-paid jobs. 'I only 'ope I can 'elp, Linnie. I don't need to tell you 'ow dear you are to me, chuck; you're the daughter I never did 'ave, that's what.'

'And you're more of a mam to me than my own ever was,' Linnet said ruefully. 'Come on then, let's window-shop!'

And for the first twenty minutes they enjoyed themselves thoroughly, just looking and dreaming. But then Linnet broached the subject which was bothering her.

'Mrs Sullivan, it's me and your Roddy. We've been going steady for ages, I'm ever so fond of him, but when he comes home however well we start off before long we're quarrelling. And I don't understand it, truly I don't, because I – well, I like him so much. He's funny and kind and very clever in his own way, and I long for his shore leave and then when it comes within two minutes we're starting to disagree, then to quarrel and then, sometimes, I give him a clack.'

'I know, queen,' Mrs Sullivan said ruefully. 'The 'ole Square knows, comes to that. But I do 'ave a thought on the marrer. When's the weddin', eh?'

Startled, Linnet gave a snort of laughter. 'We keep putting it off, because I promised Mr Cowan that I wouldn't leave him and Mollie in the lurch, and because now Roddy wants to leave the sea when we get married. I told him if he's going to come ashore then he's bound to get less money, so we'll have to save up harder and get a home of our own before we tie the knot. Well, it's all very well to say he wants to come ashore, but if he does I'm just scared we'd quarrel even worse than we do now. And I don't think I could stand it, quite honestly. I hate being cross all the time but it's beginning to be like that when Roddy's home. And I don't fancy constant bickering, because that's not good for a marriage, is it?'

'It wouldn't be, but you're wrong, chuck,' Mrs Sullivan said, stopping to peer at a display of silk blouses in a draper's window. 'I like that pink 'un, don't you? Pink used to suit me when I were young. Yes, you're wrong about quarrelling more if you were married than if you weren't. Waitin' for what they want ain't good for fellers, it's against their natural instincts to keep sayin' no to their – well, their desires, like.'

'I think I know what you mean,' Linnet agreed. Roddy's parting shot when last they quarrelled had been that if Linnet wouldn't, then he knew a girl who would. At the time she had been furious, jealous, distraught, but later, when she cooled down, she had also felt more than a twinge of guilt. She was very fond of Roddy and certainly wanted his lovemaking, could not prevent herself from responding hotly to his kisses and caresses. But then, when he tried to go further, she stopped him short. She did not want to make the mistake her mother had made, she wanted marriage and then babies, not babies first to complicate her life.

Now, she turned appealingly to her companion. 'But, Mrs Sullivan, you wouldn't want me to . . . you wouldn't expect me to let Roddy . . .'

'No, indeed,' Mrs Sullivan said hastily. 'But if you was

married, chuck, then it wouldn't arise. In a manner of speaking. I mean you wouldn't feel bound to push 'im back, would you?'

'No,' Linnet said rather doubtfully. There were definitely times when she wondered whether married life wasn't all a bit nasty, somehow, a bit crude. 'Only it – it worries me, rather. Roddy gets – gets quite rough.'

Mrs Sullivan laughed. 'Aye, men do,' she agreed. 'But it'll be all right, our Linnie, I promise you. Just marry the lad, an' let nature tek its course.'

'Right away? But we haven't got a place of our own yet and Mr Cowan needs me still, he says so every time . . .'

She broke the sentence off short. Mrs Sullivan raised quizzical brows. 'Every time you say you'd like to leave? That ain't fair, Linnet, an' well you know it. What's 'e playin' at, eh? You can't stay there for ever while poor Roddy goes wild for you, queen.'

'No, I know. But you see I'm not sure about – about Roddy and me and Mr Cowan's sensible and kind and – and what he's proposed . . .'

'Proposed? Linnet, you don't mean to tell me 'e's asked you to be 'is wife?'

'I didn't mean that, but . . . yes, he has,' Linnet said slowly. 'I like him very much but I don't love him at all, only . . . only when Roddy and I quarrel, and when Roddy says awful things and storms off, then Mr Cowan seems so quiet and sensible that I can't help thinking perhaps that's what I want and not – not all that love stuff.'

They were walking slowly along the crowded pavement, arm in arm, heads close. Mrs Sullivan gave Linnet's arm a squeeze.

'I dunno 'ow to say this, queen, but *all that love stuff*, it's what life's about, y'know. Love makes the world go round they say, and I tell you straight, wi'out love a marriage ain't worth tuppence. It wouldn't be fair to say as 'ow I think Roddy's the feller for you, bein' as 'e's me son, but I'm certain-sure that a bloke 'oo's quiet an' sensible ain't a bloke in love, whatever 'e may say. Love – love 'urts when things go wrong, it wrenches your guts, but when things go right . . . oh, then love's the crash o'drums an' trumpets, 'ot sunshine full in your face, the scent o' lilac when there's really only kippers. What are you laughin' at, young Linnet?'

'You were doing fine till you got to kippers,' Linnet wailed, mopping her streaming eyes. 'But I do understand what you mean, Mrs Sullivan. And I believe you're right. Roddy and I usually fight after we've been . . . well, you know.'

'I know,' Mrs Sullivan said. 'Here's Candwell's; time for a cuppa an' a pastry, eh?'

'Definitely,' Linnet said, following her friend into the refreshment rooms. 'I love Mrs Annie's sugar buns!'

They were shown to a window table and ordered a pot of tea for two and a selection of fancy pastries from the cheerful little waitress. Linnet began to chatter but she soon realised that Mrs Sullivan was not happy; the older woman kept starting sentences and then breaking off to stare broodingly at the pink and yellow rosebuds on the dainty china cups. Linnet leaned across the table and took Mrs Sullivan's work-worn hand in hers.

'What's the matter, Mrs S?' she said gently. 'You've gone very quiet on me!'

'I were just thinkin'. If you married that feller, that Cowan, I doubt I'd ever clap eyes on you again.'

'That's nonsense; of course you would, I'd come round just as often as I do now – more, probably,' Linnet said, but even as she spoke the words she knew she lied. Mr Cowan did not approve of what he called 'your past' and would make sure she had no time to keep popping round to Peel Square. And besides, it would be awkward, because although Mrs Sullivan was dear to Linnet she was dearer to Roddy, and Roddy and Linnet would avoid one another, it stood to reason. 'But anyway it doesn't matter, because I'm not going to marry Mr Cowan,' she added cheerfully. 'I'll promise not to, if you like. And now do choose another cake because all this talking has made me terribly hungry!'

'She's my twin,' Lucy said to everyone she came across. 'So she'll be very like me. Our mam was called little Evie and she was an actress at the theatre here.'

But although as a description it was good enough, no one seemed to know Linnet. And finally Lucy worked her way up to the theatre and asked the lady booking seats whether she knew a Miss Linnet Murphy, daughter of an actress called little Evie.

'You mean the exotic dancer,' the woman said. 'Oh aye, I remember little Evie. But she's not been here for years – went to the States wi' an American feller.'

'Yes, I know. But she left her daughter behind, didn't she?' Lucy said. 'So far as we know she's still in Liverpool somewhere – Linnet I mean – and I'm trying to find her. She's inherited some – some money from her grandfather so we have to find her.'

'Oh aye? Tell you who might know, Topsy Page. I 'member she lodged with Evie's daughter one time.'

'Oh, that's wonderful! Is she here? Can I see her?' Lucy said eagerly. It really seemed as though her quest was about to end at last.

'She's in tonight,' the woman said. 'Come round when the show's over, at about ten. Bring her a box of chocolates, she's mortal fond of sweets, and likely she'll ask you in. She's a nice enough girl.'

'Right,' Lucy said joyfully. 'A box of chocolates; I won't forget.'

Topsy Page remembered Linnet and was able to give Lucy the whereabouts of the rooms in Juvenal Street, but there, for the time at least, the trail ended. No one in Juvie, as it was called, could tell Lucy where the Murphy girl had gone though one young lad told her to try Peel Square.

'She were thick wi' a feller what lived there,' he said. 'I b'lieve, when 'er mam were out, she stayed wi' someone there. Or you could try the convent school. They'd know.'

Lucy tried to find Peel Square and when she did she was shocked; all those tiny, overcrowded houses built round a paved courtyard which never saw the sun, filled now with scruffy, down-at-heel kids. How could anyone live here? So she did not try very hard to run her sister to earth in this particular place.

'Lorra gairls around 'ere, chuck,' a fat woman in a droopy grey skirt and brown blouse told her at the first house she visited. 'Never know 'alf the names of 'em. Waste o' time anyroad, 'cos she ain't 'ere now. I'd know if she were.'

At the second house a man lurched out and tried to persuade her that he had Linnet tucked away in his kitchen. He caught hold of her arm and Lucy, really frightened, tore herself free and ran out of the court, telling herself that no sister of hers would have stayed in such a horrid place amongst such rough and dreadful people.

It had taken her most of the day to find Peel Square, so she went back to Brownlow Hill and ate a good dinner, determining to spend the next day at the convent school.

'The nuns'll know,' her landlady said comfortably, serving stewed apples and custard. 'They keep a track o' their pupils, the sisters do. You'll be lucky tomorrer, chuck.'

'A job in an insurance office on Exchange Flags,' Lucy murmured to herself as she left the convent the following afternoon. The sisters had been great, they remembered Linnet well enough though it had been years since they had taught her. But they couldn't tell Lucy which insurance company, so she would have to do some more foot-slogging.

It'll be tomorrow I find her, Lucy told herself, returning to her boarding house once more. 'Tomorrow will be my lucky day!'

There were a great many insurance offices on Exchange Flags and Lucy visited each one of them. And finally, at the Eagle and General, she struck gold.

'That's right, she worked here,' an elegant young lady said thoughtfully. 'She and Rose Beasley shared an office. Rose moved on six months ago – she and her feller got wed – but Miss Murphy went a while before that. Now, I wonder where she went? Not into another insurance office I don't think . . . want me to ask around?'

'Oh, please,' Lucy said gratefully. 'When shall I come back?'

The elegant one looked at her fob watch, then tapped her teeth with her pencil. 'Well, I'll put the word around – how about the day after tomorrow? Only it's a big firm, it may take me a while, and I do have a job to do as well!'

'That'll be fine,' Lucy said, though with sinking heart. She had been here nearly a week and if she didn't turn something up soon . . . and when I find her, I've got to persuade her to come back to Ireland with me, she remembered gloomily. If I were her I'd jump at the chance, but I'm not her. We've been brought up so differently that we probably don't even like the same things. She probably loves this city whereas to me its just miles of pavements and people who talk so fast I can't understand a word and live in terrible conditions. Oh, I do want Cahersiveen!

She trudged back through the streets to her boarding house but over dinner that night her thoughts took a different direction, thanks to Mr Harrigan.

Mr Harrigan was what Mrs Cordiner called 'a commercial', which was short, apparently, for commercial traveller. He proved to be a short, bald man in his fifties who travelled, he told Lucy, in patent medicines for a large pharmaceutical company. He was Irish, but no longer lived in that country since the market for his product was not so good 'over the water', but he was an enthusiast for the city of Liverpool.

'You don't like it, alanna?' he said incredulously when Lucy told him how homesick she was. 'You don't like this most beautiful of cities? Ah, but how much have ye seen of it? Have ye taken the ferry across the great River Mersey and seen it from the Woodside shore? Have you visited the art gallery, the museum, St George's Hall, the great lending library? And the theatres! Sure, the theatres of Liverpool are second only to the theatres of London – if they are second to them, which I doubt. My dear Miss Murphy, you must give the city a chance to prove itself!'

'I haven't had much time,' Lucy admitted. 'I've been trying to find my sister. But as it happens I am free tomorrow – how would you suggest I spend the day?'

'Take the ferry from the Pier Head to Woodside; once there, you'll see the most beautiful and impressive waterfront in the world, so you will. Then come back – you needn't go ashore, you can stay aboard – and get on the overhead railway and go along to Seaforth Sands. If you've missed your sea lough you ought to enjoy that. Then take a tram back to the city and get off at St George's

Hall. Take a good, long look at it – magnificent architecture! Then you can do the museum and the art gallery because they're only just across the road so they are. And if you've got any strength left, sit in St John's garden and contemplate life for half an hour, to recover yourself. Will ye do that for me, Miss Murphy? Your soul will be refreshed, I promise you.'

'Yes, I will,' Lucy said. She was sick and tired of city streets and city faces, she would enjoy a river trip. A thought struck her, however. 'The ferry – does it bounce around much? Sick as a dog I was on the ferry from Dun Laoghaire.'

Mr Harrigan laughed. 'Flat as a mill-pond it will be, and us with summer truly upon us. Have a good day, Miss Murphy.'

The following day started cloudy but by the time Lucy had eaten her breakfast and set out to walk to the Pier Head the sun was peeping from behind the clouds, and as she joined the crowd shuffling along the floating road to get aboard the ferry the sky was clearing fast.

I do believe I really shall enjoy today, Lucy told herself as she stood in line to buy her ticket. I don't intend to worry, or think about Linnet, or do anything other than relax today.

Having purchased a return she went and joined the other would-be passengers who stood in little groups, waiting whilst the ferry backed into its berth. She watched idly, but presently her attention was drawn to a young woman of about her own age, standing by the railings, with her back to Lucy, looking pensively out across the water. The young woman was thin, with straight, light-brown hair. She was wearing a navy blue jacket and skirt and sensible black shoes and she was clearly waiting for the ferry, as Lucy was. I wish I knew her, Lucy thought. She looks rather nice, though since I can't see her face I don't really see why I should think that. But some people you do like instinctively, and your instincts are usually right.

She was wondering whether she could go across and strike up an acquaintance when the ferry jostled itself into position, the gang-plank came down with a crash and people began to pour ashore. Lucy moved over against the railings herself so that she wouldn't get in the way, and by the time the crowds had passed and passengers for Woodside were being allowed aboard, she had forgotten all about the girl in the navy suit.

She remembered her again aboard the ferry, though, because she decided to take a quick look at the saloons and then return to the deck; even the slight movement of the deck beneath her feet reminded her all too sharply of her recent ghastly experience on the voyage from Ireland. As she came out of the saloon and regained the deck the girl in the navy suit came towards her, clearly about to go below. Lucy moved aside and then their eyes met and they exchanged smiles. The girl in the navy suit was slim and slightly built with fawny-brown hair which swung, rain-straight, down to her shoulders and her smile was friendly, forthcoming. Lucy spoke first.

'Hello! This is me first trip on the ferry, so I've been hopin' it wouldn't make me sick. Do you come over often?'

'I wouldn't say often, but this isn't my first trip,' the girl said readily. 'I've been over before, two or three times, and I always enjoy it. What makes you think you might be sick, though? It's a short crossing, you know.'

'I was terrible sick comin' from Ireland so I was,' Lucy admitted gloomily. 'I wanted to die so I did.'

The other girl laughed.

'Well, the Mersey isn't the Irish sea exactly,' she pointed out. 'But why don't you come below with me and then we can have a cup of coffee, or a lemonade? It might settle your stomach.'

'I think it might be safer not,' Lucy said cautiously. She looked over the rail at the gently moving water, at the gulls bobbing on the surface, then glanced back at her companion. 'I'd like a coffee so I would, but I durst not go below whilst the ship's moving.'

'Well, why don't you sit down by the rail and keep your eyes fixed on Woodside – that's the further shore – and think about the land, and I'll go below and fetch a drink for both of us,' the girl said in heartening tones. 'And when I come back we'll chat and that'll keep your mind off your stomach.'

'That's awful kind,' Lucy said. 'Let me give you the money, though. How much does a coffee cost aboard this ship?'

The brown-haired one shrugged. 'I haven't the foggiest idea. Tell you what, if you're going back on the same ferry as I am you can buy the coffee in the other direction. How does that seem?'

'Grand. And I can go back on any ferry, since I'm only going for to see the Liverpool shore from the other side,' Lucy admitted. 'There's a feller in me boarding house – shocked he was that I'd not seen the waterfront properly. So I said I'd spend an idle day, just lookin' around me.'

'And I'm only going on a message – when I get to Birkenhead I'm to buy some flowers and take them to an old lady who's been ill,' the brown-haired one said comfortably. 'So if you've nothing better to do, why not come with me? It's just a walk in the sunshine, you know, and then back to Woodside and the ferry again. Now you just wait here – I shan't be two ticks.'

Lucy sat in the sunshine and fixed her eyes on the further shore as her new friend had suggested, and sure enough she did not feel at all sick, not even when a tug steamed across the ferry's bows and the ship heaved on the swell. And presently, when the girl came back with the steaming coffee she took it, sipped, and then set the cup down on the slatted wooden seat beside her.

'Well now, how can I thank you when I don't even know your name?' she said brightly. 'I'm Lucy Murphy. How do you do . . . ?'

'That's odd,' the brown-haired one said cheerfully, setting her own coffee down between them. 'I'm a Murphy, too – Linnet Murphy.'

Lucy's mouth fell open. She gaped, there was no other word for it. And when she spoke her voice was thin and high. '*Linnet*? You're Linnet Murphy? Begod, but isn't that the strangest t'ing ever?' She grabbed the other girl's hand in hers and squeezed it hard. 'There can't be two . . . but Maeve said you were the very image of me as a child, yellow hair an' all!'

'Maeve?' The brown-haired girl was laughing; she thinks I'm an Irish madwoman, Lucy thought belatedly. 'Well, now, and isn't that odd? My mammy came from Ireland, way back, and there was a Maeve in her family – her eldest sister.' She gently drew her hand out of Lucy's grasp. 'But Murphy's a common enough name, I suppose.'

'Yes, but Linnet isn't,' Lucy said triumphantly. 'My mammy was on the stage at one time. They called her little Evie.' She watched as Linnet's thin face flushed to a delicate shade of rose, as her eyes rounded. 'You're me twin sister, the person I've come to Liverpool to find,' she said triumphantly. 'And now that I come to look at you, you've a great look of Maeve about you so you have.'

'And now that I come to look at you, you're rather like my mammy,' Linnet said with a distinct wobble in her voice. 'Oh Lucy, I can't believe it – a sister of me own!'

*

Linnet couldn't believe the extent of her own good fortune. Mammy had mumbled about relatives, but she had never even hinted that Linnet had a sister let alone a twin. And it seemed impossible that this golden-haired girl with the gentle, mischievous face had come miles and miles, just to find her, and had actually done so. The two girls sat on the sunny deck and at first could only stare at each other, now and again smiling with delight. My sister, Linnet kept thinking, my very own sister – a relative of my very own!

Presently, she put it into words. 'It's like Christmas and birthdays all rolled into one,' she said. 'To have someone of my own, I mean. I've got friends, of course, and a feller – do you have a feller, Lucy? – but no relatives, not that I'd met. I didn't even know how badly I wanted a sister of my own until you turned up. But I wonder why your Maeve thought we would be alike, because we aren't at all similar, really. You're terribly pretty.'

'You're not so bad yourself! And I think other people will say we're quite alike because we've both got the same sort of eyes and the same shaped face, only our hair's a different colour and I'm a few inches taller than you,' Lucy said. 'That's odd, that is, because Maeve always told me I was the small, sickly baby and you were big and bonny.'

'People change,' Linnet said ruefully. 'My hair was fair when I was young, but it got darker as I got older. I wonder why yours didn't?'

'Lots of Irish cream and butter, and lots of Irish honey; it keeps you blonde,' Lucy said with a giggle. 'But I've not told you why I've come to find you, Linnet. Do you mind if I start at the beginning? Only it's a long story and you'll want a bit of background.'

'I don't mind at all,' Linnet said, settling herself comfortably on the wooden slatted seat. She thought she would have been quite happy to have listened to this beautiful, golden-haired girl all day – this brand-new twin sister of her very own. 'Fire ahead.'

'Well, it was like this,' Lucy said after some thought. 'My grandad – and yours, Linnet – was an old man and he'd been very sick. But the Stations were coming to our home, we live near Cahersiveen, in County Kerry, so . . .'

'What are the Stations?'

'Dear God, you're a heathen,' Lucy said, smiling. 'Forget the Stations, 'tis just a Mass said in the home and attended by everyone all about. As I was saying, the Stations were coming to Ivy Farm so of course I was very busy, and Caitlin chose the same month . . .'

'Caitlin? Is she another sister? Another relative to me?'

'Caitlin's me best friend, she's the daughter of . . . look, just let me tell it, will you? Or I'll still not be finished be nightfall. Now, as I was saying, Caitlin chose the same month to announce that she and Declan were to wed, so . . .'

It would have been idle to pretend that Lucy was not a little disappointed to find Linnet was not a double of herself; the prospect of fooling people had been in its way rather fun. But to find Linnet had straight brown hair and was smaller than she and slightly built was, by and large, probably better for their eventual friendship.

She had not, at first, thought Linnet pretty, but as they grew easier together she revised her opinion. Linnet was fascinating; she would never lack admirers even without guinea-gold curls and a bee-stung lower lip. She had that quality of unselfconscious charm which soon had Lucy in its thrall, for all she had been determined merely to feel sorry for her sister. And Linnet was also a good listener. Having been told to keep her questions for after the story she sat there, hanging on Lucy's every word, her eyes gradually widening as the story progressed.

'And he's left the farm to the pair of us?' she gasped at the end, when Lucy produced her trump card. 'A farm? But Lucy, I don't even know how to keep a garden, let alone a farm. What good would I be to you if I did come back? And I've a well-paid job here, I'm a nanny so I get to save most of my salary and – and I'm thinking about getting married before the year's end.'

'I'm not saying stay for ever, Linnet,' Lucy reminded her. 'I'm just saying come over, see how you like it, and get things settled. Couldn't your – your feller come as well? For a week or two, maybe?'

'He's a seaman, on a timber haul at the moment,' Linnet said slowly. 'We've talked about getting married but we've not set a date, only now I want to make it definite. You see, the man I work for has asked me to marry him as well and when I say no, I'm afraid things could get difficult. He's a gentleman, he won't kick me out, but – well, you know how it is.'

'I can imagine,' Lucy agreed. 'So you'd better tell him no at once and come back to Ireland with me. Explain where you're going and why, that should make things easier, if anything.'

And after a thoughtful pause, Linnet reached across and grasped Lucy's hand tightly. 'I'll come!' she declared. 'My job will go down the pan but you said our grandad had left some money, too, didn't you? That will tide me over.' She beamed at her twin, her eyes brilliant with excitement. 'And it'll mean Roddy and I can get married just as soon as we can arrange it,' she added. 'Oh Lucy, I'm so glad we found each other! Will you dance at my wedding?'

'With all my heart. And perhaps, in a year or two, you'll dance at mine,' Lucy said, and told her sister about Peder and her grandfather's hopes that she would marry land and double the size of Ivy Farm. She tried to make it sound just what she wanted, and thought she had succeeded until Linnet reached out and squeezed her hand.

'It's not Peder you want, is it?' she said shrewdly. 'But there's someone just right for you around the corner, Lucy. Just you wait and see.'

Chapter Twelve

As it happened, it was a lot easier for Linnet to give in her notice than she had imagined it would be.

She arrived home with a sunburnt nose after spending most of the day talking to Lucy, full of trepidation over the task to come. She intended to tell Mr Cowan, as soon as she walked through the door, that she would be returning to Ireland at the end of the week because her grandfather had died. But she could well imagine the scene which could take place when she admitted – as she must – that she would not be coming back.

And then there was his proposal of marriage. She meant to tell Mr Cowan that she had considered very carefully, as carefully as he had implored her to, and was conscious of the great honour he had done her, but did not think she would make him a suitable wife.

It sounded easy when she rehearsed the words in her head; the snag came when she began to think of Mr Cowan's lines. She could imagine all too well what his reaction would be – she feared he would be angry as well as honestly distressed. She did not intend to give way, knew, after her talk to Mrs Sullivan, that it would be very wrong to marry him, but he was a good deal older than she and a wealthy man; to turn him down was going to take courage.

So it was a surprise when she walked into the house to find Mr Cowan with Mollie and Emma, the nursery-maid, all dressed in their coats and hats, waiting in the hallway.

He knows! she thought, and opened her mouth to start explaining but was forestalled by Mr Cowan.

'Ah, Miss Murphy, at last! I was in fear and trembling that you'd not come home before we had to leave – you're very late. I've news which I scarcely know how to impart! Do you remember Mr Aloysius Paulett, Miss Murphy?'

Linnet gaped at him. 'Aloysius who?'

He clucked impatiently. 'Mr Paulett, the Chairman of the Eagle and General; you can't have forgotten him!'

'I don't think we ever met,' Linnet said slowly. 'He was in the London office, wasn't he?'

'Yes, indeed. And two days ago the poor old fellow dropped dead in the middle of a board meeting. And today I hear that they've chosen me – me, Miss Murphy – to take his place! I am to go up to London immediately, the company will put us into a company house until such time as I purchase my own property, and I will be confirmed in the position within the next couple of days. In my wildest dreams I never thought . . . but there, I've always put the company before myself, always worked hard . . . and now, it seems, this is to be my reward.'

He sounded horribly complacent, Linnet thought. She frowned across at him, trying to take it all in. 'And Mollie? What about Mollie? She's happy at school, sir, she has friends in the neighbourhood . . .'

He laughed; behind his horn-rimmed glasses his eyes glittered. 'Mollie will want for nothing! Advancement such as this will ensure her future – and, indeed, mine. I thought that you, Miss Murphy, might hold the fort for me here until such time as . . . as you decide whether you wish to come to London with – with Mollie and myself. But now I must go, the Board are sending a chauffeur driven car for us . . . I'll ring up when I have time and you can tell me what . . . what you've decided to do.'

There was anxiety in the last words and Linnet responded to it at once.

'I won't be here,' she said quickly. 'Sir, I met a close relative in the city this morning who had come to tell me my grandfather had died recently and left me money and some property. I'm returning to Ireland at the end of the week to sort things out.'

Was it relief she saw behind those glasses? He tutted in vague disapproval, but . . . yes, it was definitely relief. The girl who was good enough for a provincial insurance executive would not, Linnet thought, be the right wife for the head of the company. He could not realise it, but she was every bit as relieved as he – more, probably.

'I see; well you must go, Miss Murphy, your duty is clear, you must not consider us, we shall do very well.' He could not hide his relief, his elation, almost. 'And since you've not yet taken your annual holiday this year you must take it now – I'll pay you for the full month.' He reached into his pocket and withdrew a cheque book. He scribbled for a moment and then handed Linnet the cheque which she put into her pocket without looking at it.

'Thank you, sir. May I wish you well in your new career? Will you be returning here in a week or so? To see to the house and so on?'

'I think not. In two or three months perhaps . . . but for the next few weeks we'll be busy people won't we, Mollie, my dear?'

Mollie nodded uneasily. She was too young for such an upheaval, Linnet thought, but she could not interfere, especially since she was about to abandon both father and child.

'I see. Then I'd better say my goodbyes before you go off on your adventure.' Linnet bent and kissed Mollie, shook hands with Emma, then held out a hand to Mr Cowan.

'Goodbye, sir, and good luck.'

Almost as she spoke the front doorbell pealed and Mr Cowan all but wrenched his hand out of hers and hurried to answer it. 'Come along, Mollie. Emma, it's our car,' he said importantly. 'Oh, Miss Murphy, you'd best tell Cook not to bother with dinner if you're leaving, too.'

When the front door had closed behind them Linnet sat down on the stairs and laughed until the tears ran down her cheeks. She had said that she was leaving, but not until the end of the week. Mr Cowan, however, clearly did not intend to pay for her keep a moment longer than was necessary. Well, that was all right by her; she wanted to get away, and away she had got. There was no point in feeling sorry for Mollie, no point in missing her, since she would under no circumstances have gone with the family to London. And what was more, it was plain as plain that Mr Cowan did not intend her to do so.

So Linnet went upstairs and packed all her things into a large gladstone bag which she found in the lumber room. She left her uniforms but took her shoes since she doubted that Mr Cowan would want to hand them on to his new nanny. She went down to the kitchen and explained the situation to Cook, Mrs Eddis and the maids and then she lugged her belongings down the stairs and used the telephone in the hall to ring for a taxi.

Her twin was staying in Brownlow Hill, at a boarding house run by a Mrs Cordiner. I'll go there, Linnet decided. If they haven't got a spare room then I'll find somewhere else, but it would be nice to be under the same roof as Lucy.

The taxicab drew up on the gravel sweep outside and whilst the driver carried her bag out to the car Linnet asked him if he knew a Mrs Cordiner on Brownlow Hill.

He said he did, promised to take her there and to wait until she was sure Mrs Cordiner had a room free, and handed her carefully into the back of his vehicle.

A short while later, Linnet was standing in the hallway of Mrs Cordiner's boarding house, paying off the cab and waiting for Mrs Cordiner to show her to her room.

'Life's full of coincidences, Miss Murphy, for I've another Miss Murphy stayin' wi' me this week,' Mrs Cordiner said as she ponderously ascended the stairs. 'She's in the room next door to you; and a very nice, well-brought-up young lady she is, too.'

'I'm glad to hear it, because she's my sister,' Linnet said with a twinkle. 'She came over from Ireland to find me, and find me she did.'

'Well, ain't that a thing?' Mrs Cordiner gasped. 'Said she were searchin' for a twin . . . you ain't very like each other, norrat first glance.'

'No-oo. But we've led very different lives,' Linnet said. 'Is she back yet? Only she won't be expecting me.'

As she spoke they reached the landing and a door flew open. Her twin stood there, beaming at her.

'Linnet! It *is* you! I got the oddest feeling that it was. What's happened? Was he very cross? As soon as you've seen your room come and tell me all about it!'

Naturally enough, Lucy's first thought was that now she could carry her sister back to Ireland with her without waiting until the end of the week, but Linnet speedily disabused her.

'I've got to see the Sullivans,' she said firmly. 'Mrs Sullivan is Roddy's mam and my greatest friend. They're not at all well-off, in fact I suppose at the time they took me in they were miserably poor because they had six sons and not much money coming in, but when I was in need

Mrs Sullivan rescued me and – and loved me. I couldn't go *anywhere* without letting her know, certainly not across the sea to Ireland.'

'Fair enough. Where do the Sullivans live?' Lucy enquired, and was rather shocked when Linnet said that it was indeed Peel Square.

'It is a poor neighbourhood, I know it,' Linnet admitted when her twin remarked timidly that the area seemed crowded and poverty-stricken. 'But everyone helps each other in Peel Square, not like in Sunnyside. Why, all Mr Cowan could think about this evening was his own advancement, he didn't really give a thought to Mollie being taken away from her kindergarten and her friends. And the neighbours in Sunnyside hardly know one another, though their servants are friendly enough. If I had to choose somewhere to live for ever and ever I reckon I'd take Peel Square sooner than the biggest, poshest house in Sunnyside. Now, do you want to come with me or shall I go alone?'

They had their first argument over the visit to Peel Square, but it wasn't a serious one. Over breakfast they discussed it and Lucy thought that Linnet ought to see Mrs Sullivan alone and not have someone she didn't know hovering at her shoulder all the while. Linnet agreed in one way, but she desperately wanted Mrs Sullivan to meet this brand-new sister of hers. So, in the end, they compromised. Linnet was to go in under the arch first, and Lucy would window-shop up and down Cazneau Street.

'The shops are bigger and better on the Scottie,' Linnet said, buttering toast. 'But there's a florist or two in Cazneau, ever such pretty windows they have, and there's Lewis Cann's tearooms and of course there's Laurence Meehan near the corner of St Anne's Street. You could pop in there and buy a book, then go to Cann's and have tea and buns. But if you want clothes, you'll have to go up to Great Homer, or the Scottie.'

'Cahersiveen's a grand little town so it is,' Lucy said loyally. She poured herself another cup of tea from the big metal teapot which their landlady had left on the table so that they could help themselves. 'But the shops here – Holy Mother, they're grand and big, even the small ones. Don't worry, Linnet, I'll be well-occupied for that half-hour. And I'm mortal fond of a good read – aren't we all, when we live in the country? So I'll be after taking a book or two back with me for Caitlin and me other friends. You'll be lucky if I'm not an hour behind you instead of just the half with so much to see and do.'

'Mrs Sullivan and me will settle down and gossip, or I'll give her a hand with the washing or the ironing,' Linnet said contentedly. 'Take your time, sister. We won't mind waiting on you.'

'I will. Now is breakfast over? Because if so, we really ought to get started.'

They walked to the tram stop and caught a Green Goddess which would take them to the Juvenal Street stop on Scotland Road. Linnet was happy to see her sister's eyes widen approvingly as they climbed into the tram.

'Grand, isn't it?' she said, taking her place beside Lucy on the brown leather seat. 'A few years back we only had ordinary trams with wooden slatted seats and slatted floors that the old fellers spat on, and the din they made had to be heard to be believed. But the Goddesses are wonderful, and so quiet!'

Lucy had not been on a tram before; she made enthusiastic noises but the tram's very quietness scared her and she was glad to get off when her sister jumped to her feet and made her way along the swaying aisle.

'Right you are. Now this is the Scottie – Scotland Road to you – and that there's Juvenal Street.' She pointed. 'We go through there to Cazneau and I'll show you the Peel Street entrance, then you can come back to it when you've had enough of window-shopping. Are you sure you'll be all right, chuck?'

'I'll be fine,' Lucy said at once. 'Don't worry about me. I may be a country girl but I've got a good head on me shoulders so I have. See you in an hour?'

'In an hour, then.'

And Linnet turned and dived under the arch into Peel Square, leaving Lucy in Cazneau Street.

Linnet didn't bother to knock, she simply burst into the tiny, square living room and ran through into the kitchen, where her friend was labouring over a pile of sheets with irons standing against the fire despite the heat of the day outside.

'Mrs Sullivan, you'll never guess what's happened to me!' Linnet, lit up with excitement, saw Mrs Sullivan's face grow anxious and pale. She shook her head at the older woman. 'It's all right, I've not done anything I'm going to regret for the rest of my life, I've left Sunnyside and Mr Cowan. Because my twin sister's turned up!'

'Your twin sister? Chuck, I couldn't be more pleased! Your mam were always a bit quiet, like, about your sister and there were times when I wondered . . . but you say you've met the girl, and she really is your twin? Like as two peas in a pod, are you?'

'No, not a bit,' Linnet confessed. 'She's taller than me and rounder, somehow, and she's got the most beautiful golden curls. She reminded me of my mam straight off, but she's not like her really. Too big and tall for a start, and too – well, she's not like little Evie, anyway. But she's nice, Mrs Sullivan, real nice, you'll like her, honest to God you will.'

'Any sister of yours is bound to be nice, queen,' Mrs

Sullivan said loyally, ironing away. 'So what's she doin' in the Pool, eh? Why's she 'ere?'

'Our grandfather died recently and he left the farm to the two of us, to be divided equally. And some money, as well. Apparently the family thought I'd gone to New York with Mammy, so first of all they advertised in the local newspapers over there and Maeve – she's Mammy's big sister – went over and looked for me. Only then Lucy said she got this feeling that I wasn't in New York at all. She found some old letters and read them and she said it seemed to her that little Evie didn't talk about me much because I wasn't with her, though folk had got the impression that Mammy had put me in lodgings in the country because New York wasn't a good place to bring up a child.'

'Aye, that's your mam all over,' Mrs Sullivan said frankly, switching irons and standing the old one back before the fire to reheat. 'She were good at givin' impressions, I noticed it meself. So why didn't this sister of yours come searchin' right away, after she'd read the letters? Why wait till now?'

'I don't know when she read the letters,' Linnet said. 'But she came now because she had this news for me, that I owned half of Ivy Farm. I suppose, before Grandad died, she was pretty busy herself, what with the farm and looking after him and everything. But she's here now, Mrs Sullivan, and she's coming round to meet you, only she said she'd let me get it all off my chest first – the inheritance and everything.'

'Right, go on then, tell me,' Mrs Sullivan commanded. 'An' while you talk fold this sheet wi' me, there's a good girl. It 'alves the work if there's two of us.'

'Course. Let me have a go with the iron whilst you sit and listen to me telling you,' Linnet said and as soon as the sheet was folded she seized the iron and began to pass it briskly across a white linen sheet. 'I don't mind ironing sheets, it's the shirts and frilly petticoats I find hard. Why don't you put the kettle on?'

Mrs Sullivan chuckled but complied. 'You're just like me, chuck, you do like your cuppa,' she said approvingly. 'Go on, then . . . your twin turned up. And what about old Cowan, eh?'

'It's a long story,' Linnet warned her, shaking out the sheet and sprinkling water from the jug over it to smooth the creases. 'But I'll start right at the beginning, when I got on the ferry to go over to visit Mollie's great-aunt, in Birkenhead. Mollie didn't come with me since it was my day off, but the old girl's been kind to me and she does like a bit of company, so I set off quite early . . .'

At the end of the story Mrs Sullivan's eyes were round. 'Wharra strange thing, you two meetin' up like that,' she declared. 'The Murphy girls' first meetin' was on the Mersey! Only wi' you marryin' so soon, queen, you won't be the Murphy girls for long.' She chuckled. 'We'll call you the Mersey girls instead. And wharra strange feller that Cowan chap o' yourn must be, to go off to London at the drop of an 'at. An' 'e didn't even arst you to go along o' the rest?'

'No, he didn't mention it. I knew at once that though I might have been all right as the wife of a regional manager, there was no way he thought I'd rise to being wife of the chairman of the board. Which was so much easier, Mrs Sullivan, than having to tell him I was turning down his proposal of marriage.'

'Ye-es, I see that,' Mrs Sullivan said doubtfully. 'But 'ow 'e could jest walk out on you, queen . . .'

'He's a strange feller, I'll grant you that,' Linnet admitted. 'But it was all for the best, so let's not talk about it. Let's talk about me going to Ireland with Lucy – what do you think of *that*, eh?'

'You're actually goin'? You're leavin' us? But not for good, queen? You'll come back in a couple o' months? Roddy'll be ashore again in a fortnight, you was goin' to tell 'im mebbe you ought to get wed, wasn't you?' She sighed deeply and then snatched the kettle off the fire as it began to splutter and hop its lid. 'I dunno, I shouldn't try to influence you, but I've always loved you, queen, an' I want what's best for you, an' Roddy's 'avin' an 'ard time . . .'

'I'll be back, but I don't know exactly when. Only, Mrs Sullivan, there's money due, Lucy swears it and she's not the sort of girl to – to muddle things. So with half a farm and some money of my own, maybe things will be easier for me and Roddy. Maybe we could work on the farm, d'you think?'

'Work on a farm? Eh, queen, our Roddy's not gorra clue about farmin', we don't even 'ave a patch to grow a spud or two, norrin the square. 'Sides, farmin's gorra be in your blood, they say. Mind, we was farmers ourselves way back, 'cos my fambly come over durin' the 'forties, when the tater famine came,' Mrs Sullivan said thoughtfully. 'But that's something you'd 'ave to talk to our Roddy about. An' when'll you see 'im, at this rate?'

'Well, I thought he could take a voyage out, people do, he's mentioned it before. Then he could come over to Ireland and have a look at things,' Linnet said eagerly. 'Oh, Mrs Sullivan, we'll work something out so we will.'

'So we will? Now that's Irish if you like – you're catchin' the brogue off your sister an' she's not been wit' you a week, yet,' Mrs Sullivan said, laughing. 'Leave Roddy a letter, chuck, I'll see 'e gets it, an' if 'e can, 'e'll come to you. 'Cos 'e do love you,' she added softly. 'We all loves you, our Linnie.'

'Yes, and because of that I'd never go off and leave

you,' Linnet promised. 'Not for good, I mean. Ah, I hear a knock – that'll be my sister.'

'Good Lord, gel, you never tole me 'er name,' Mrs Sullivan shouted as Linnet headed for the front door. 'She ain't Maeve, is she?'

'No, Maeve's our eldest aunt. My sister's Lucy, Mrs Sullivan, Lucy Murphy, and I love her already. And you're going to love her, too.'

After her sister had disappeared into Peel Square, Lucy wandered up the street, going from window to window, relaxing at last after the nerve-racking search for Linnet. She had found her sister and, contrary to her expectations, they had really liked each other almost on sight. Linnet, she thought, was grand, just the sort of sister she would have chosen had she had a choice in the matter. Sharing Ivy Farm with some people would have been next to impossible, but sharing with Linnet would be fun, she was sure of it.

Not that she believed Linnet would want to share the farm, because Linnet had already said, in the sweet, shy way which Lucy so admired, that farming was something which neither she nor her feller had ever considered.

'But there must be a way to divide it so we're all doing what we want,' Lucy had said reassuringly. 'There has to be a way!'

But it was not going to be easy. Before she even left Cahersiveen, Lucy had realised that this very question was likely to arise, so she had closeted herself with her grandfather's man of business and they had discussed it at length. Mr Eamonnn was a round and cheery little man with a great deal of common sense, and he had told her at once that the farm simply could not afford to pay out half its value to her sister.

'Farming's not what it was,' he said seriously. 'As ye know, m'dear, there's a depression on, and it affects farmers worse, in many ways, than other folks. The Murphys have been all right because you feed yourselves from what you produce and sell what's left over locally, in Caher. Dear old Padraig wasn't afraid to take a chance, either. You've good acreage put down to things not every other farmer produces – your grandaddy grew what would sell – and he wasn't scared to change things around, to have a go with sheep when everyone else was still fattening cattle. But bigger spreads are havin' troubles, so they are, because of the competition from the vast farmlands in the United States and the poor wages in other parts of the world. Grain prices have plummeted, but you've been growing corn to make your own bread, not trying to export it. Why, in England they can't sell farmland at any price, but even if you sold, which you'd not find easy, then where would your living come from? For the matter of that, where would you live? I've done me best to think of a solution, alanna, but I have to tell you selling up may be the only answer.'

'If I married Peder I could mebbe take half the land . . .' Lucy had said without much hope. But Mr Eamonnn was shaking his head.

'That wouldn't do, m'dear. Your sister, who knows nothing about farming, would be left with insufficient acreage to live on. She'd still have to employ workers, you see, and the land wouldn't support 'em. And no one in their right minds would buy half a farm for the same reason. No, you can't chop Ivy Farm in half wit'out it bleeds to death.'

Lucy had shuddered involuntarily. She could not bear that the place where she had been born and bred should bleed to death.

'It's like that Egyptian feller when the two women

both said the baby was hers, and he said the only way to settle it was to chop the little baby in half,' she said. 'Well, Mr Eamonnn, I'll prove meself the true mother of me land – I'll not divide it, I love it too well. I'd rather me sister had it all than let it come to ruin. Have you no suggestions for what the pair of us should do?'

'You could pay your sister a small yearly income, until the value of her half of the farm was paid off,' Mr Eamonn said. He sounded doubtful. 'It wouldn't be much, at first, because it will take you a while to recover from me old friend Padraig's death, but if prices pull up, who knows? You might be rid of the debt in twenty years or so.'

'Twenty years! Well, if that's the only way . . . thanks for your help, Mr Eamonnn, I'll bear in mind what you've said.'

So now, strolling down Cazneau Street in the bright May sunshine, Lucy had to face facts. She had meant to puzzle over the dividing of the property whilst searching for her sister, but instead she had simply put it right out of her mind. And even now, when she should have been racking her brains for a solution, all she kept thinking was, 'We'll get round it somehow,' and letting her mind go back to the cheerful fact that Linnet was coming to Ireland with her, would see the farm, meet her friends and relatives and would, surely, find a solution to their problem.

Presently, in her wanderings, she found the bookshop and browsed there for a little. She bought some books, tucked them into her string shopping bag, and then continued to walk along, staring in every window as she passed, keeping to the area but not minding which streets she visited. And presently she found a little sweet shop with the legend Kettles' Confectionery over the door, and hovered in the doorway. She had meant to buy buns but wouldn't it be a much nicer gesture now, and more appreciated by the young'uns, if she bought some sweeties for the Sullivan children?

The shop was small and dim and behind the counter, squatting on a very tiny stool, was an enormous woman with a pair of spectacles perched on her button nose and a tiny, hard bun of grey hair, lanced with many hairpins, on top of her head. She was reading a newspaper but put it down when Linnet entered and surged to her feet, leaning over the counter and beaming at her customer.

'Well now, missie, what can I get you? Is it for yourself or for a pal, eh? We've gorra good range o' fancy choc'lit all done up in boxes, but o' course I allus tell folk to buy 'omemade 'ere, to get the best value.' She waved an expansive hand at the tall jars on the shelves behind her. 'Lickrish, annyseed, taffy . . . we makes it all in our boilin' kitchen we does, an' you'd go far before you gorranything better.'

'I'd like two pounds of taffy, please,' Lucy said recklessly. 'And could you divide it into six bags?'

'Oh, aye, course I could.' The old woman lifted a huge jar of toffee off the shelf and banged it aggressively on the counter; the pieces, which had been firmly stuck together, began to jump apart. The old woman continued to thump the jar on the counter as she spoke until the pieces within were all separated. 'Aye, this is me best taffy, this. You'll not gerrany better in the 'ole of Liverpool. Oh aye, an' you won't spend a fortune, either, 'cos it's not 'spensive. Poor but honest, us Kettles, that's what I always say. Poor but honest.'

She tipped a rattling stream of toffee chunks into her scale pan, then put two one pound weights on the scale and adjusted the flow of toffee until the two hung equal. Then she turned to the shelf behind her, replaced the toffee-jar, and began to tip the pieces, a few at a time, into six conical brown bags.

'There y'are, queen,' she said at last. 'If you gi' me one and eight we'll part friends.' She chuckled again, beaming at Lucy. 'An' you won't get better,' she added. 'Poor but honest, us Kettles.'

'There's a piece of toffee still on the scale pan,' Linnet remarked, feeling guilty because the poor old girl plainly had not realised. 'If you could put it in the last bag . . .'

'Lor, 'ow could I 'ave missed it?' the old woman marvelled. She shook her head over her own stupidity and then looked past Lucy to the doorway. 'Ah, another customer!'

Linnet glanced round but the would-be customer must have walked past and by the time she looked back Mrs Kettle – if indeed the old woman was Mrs Kettle – was carefully placing all the small brown bags in a big brown bag and handing it across the counter. Linnet counted out one and eightpence, thanked the sweetmaker, and left the little shop. She did wonder about trying the toffee, but decided, instead, to make her way to the Lewis Cann tearooms and try their cream cakes.

The cream cakes – and the coffee which accompanied them – were delicious and when she left the tearooms, with a large bag of sugar buns for the Sullivan boys as well as the taffy, she went into Turner's the Florists and selected some purple, red and white lilac for Mrs Sullivan. The girl in the shop wrapped the stems in pretty paper and charged Lucy what she thought an exorbitant sum, but the scent alone, as the sun fell on the blossom, was worth it. Ivy Farm and the old barn against which the lilac trees bloomed came into her mind so strongly that it was like a visit home and she thought again that the farm was the most important thing in her life, that she could never leave it, not even for Linnet. But if there was no other choice, if they simply had to sell up in order to get a bit of money each, then she supposed that marrying

Peder and moving five miles further inland, to Culnagap Farm, would be a good deal better than starving at her own home, or moving far away.

She didn't remember Mr Sullivan until she happened to pass a tobacconist but then she went inside and bought an ounce of pipe tobacco. Laden, she turned at last towards Peel Square. Imagine living here, she thought as she walked along the crowded pavement of Cazneau Street. Imagine what my sister has had to put up with for all these years . . . it's lucky I am that I have a choice in the matter, that I can go home to Ireland . . . that a good man wants to marry me for that matter, and has offered me the shelter of his roof.

She dived under the archway into Peel Square. Children covered the paving stones, sat on doorsteps, ran and shouted. They were dirty, badly dressed, underfed, yet Lucy found herself smiling at them. Happiness shone out of their bright, hungry eyes and was clear from every movement as they shouted, chased, shrieked. My sister was right when she said this wasn't a bad place, Lucy thought as she approached the door of No 16. There's love here, and a sort of – togetherness. These kids would stick up for each other, fight for each other, if it came to the crunch. There are worse places than Peel Square, very much worse.

Mrs Sullivan was completely won over as soon as Lucy stepped through the doorway with her arms full of lilac, the scent preceding her, warm and strong and full of sunshine.

'Flowers, for me? Oh, bless me, the scent of 'em! Oh, miss, you don't know what it means to 'ave flowers, and such lovely colours, so many . . . the smell of 'em . . .' Mrs Sullivan's eyes were brimming, she clutched the flowers to her flat bosom, then buried her nose in them. 'I've not 'ad flowers since me weddin', an' that's a few months gone I tell you.' Still clutching the lilac she hurried over to the sink. 'They've gorra go in deep, cold water, then they'll keep longer,' she said over her shoulder. 'Oh, miss, what they must 'ave cost – you shouldn't 'ave! But I'm that grateful – ain't they beautiful?'

'Don't call her miss, Mrs Sullivan, she's Lucy,' Linnet said when she could get a word in edgeways. 'She's brought sweets for the boys, too, and some baccy for Mr Sullivan – isn't she kind?'

'No I'm not,' Lucy said at once. 'It's making sure of me welcome I am . . . you're me sister's favourite person, Mrs Sullivan, and that's good enough for me so it is.'

Mrs Sullivan turned from the sink. She had put one of the buckets of water on the draining board and had plunged the lilac into it. She smiled from one girl to the other, her cheeks very pink, her eyes bright now and no longer tear-filled.

'You're two of a kind, you Murphy gels,' she said. 'Or as I said to Linnet, you Mersey girls! Now, let's 'ave a cuppa whiles you tell me what you're plannin'. Because you ain't gettin' away from 'ere till I knows just when you're off to Ireland – and when you're a-comin' back!'

'You really did like Mrs Sullivan, didn't you?' Linnet said, when the two of them stood on the landing in their boarding house just before making their separate ways to bed. 'You weren't just saying it? She was so good to me when Mammy left me. If there is any money, I'm going to see she gets a share. Mr Sullivan's a nice enough feller, but he was hurt bad in an accident years ago and can't do much. She does it all, honest to God, she runs that family.'

'She's a dear, I really liked her enormously,' Lucy said reassuringly. 'I just hope you'll like our people as well when you meet them. So we'll buy you a ticket tomorrow, alanna, and we'll be back in Ireland the day after!'

'Back in Ireland . . . yes, I suppose it'll be going back for me, too,' Linnet mused. 'Though I wasn't very old when I left last time! I wish I could have met Grandad – you were very fond of him, weren't you. And Granny, of course.'

'I never knew Granny myself,' Lucy said, rather puzzled. 'She died before we were born . . . oh, you mean Granny Mogg!' she laughed. 'Aye, she was a grand old girl, you'd have liked her. But she wasn't a relative, alanna, just a tinker who was old and not strong enough to travel the roads any more. I told you about her dying, but I didn't say much about her living . . . well, she lived in an ancient, ruined castle about half, three-quarters of a mile from Ivy Farm, and Caitlin and I took care of her when – when no one else could. Tinkers don't like roofs, nor they don't like buffers – that's us, Linnet – but Granny Mogg grew fond of Cait and me. And a roof was a necessity, because she'd been terrible ill with a badness in her chest. But there, she lived to a good age and she died in her sleep.'

'Like our grandad,' Linnet said contentedly. 'I'm glad he didn't suffer, but I still wish I'd known him. Never mind, though, I know you, and I'm going to meet Caitlin, Clodagh, Kellach, Éanna . . . heaps of new people.'

'And Peder; I'm going to introduce you to Peder,' Lucy said with a touch of shyness in her voice. 'I will maybe marry him one of these days. He's a nice feller, Peder, we've known each other for always. It's may be not a bad thing to marry a feller who tipped tadpoles into your midday milk and tied a live mouse to your plait.'

'The horror! He sounds like Roddy, my feller, so I ought to be able to tell you if marrying him's the right thing for you to do. I'm going to write to Roddy when I get into bed and I'll post it in the morning. Mrs Sullivan thinks he'll take a voyage out and come over to Ireland, to Cahersiveen, and meet you. And then we'll talk over what we're going to do about the farm. But Lucy, dear Lucy, I won't have you selling up or doing anything like that because I don't think we need half the farm. Just a tiny bit of cash would be nice, especially if I don't get a job too quick when I come back here, but I don't need half the farm.'

'Who's been talking to you?' Lucy said suspiciously. 'You know nothing about it, not yet.'

Linnet laughed. 'Do I not? These walls are thin as paper, dear sister, and you talked in your sleep for hours last night! I don't want you worrying, because it isn't worth missing a night's sleep over. Half a farm sounds good, but it's much more than Roddy and I need, or expect, or deserve. You were the one who nursed Grandad, you worked on the farm, you managed it all for him. You should have the farm . . . and I mean that from the bottom of my heart.'

Lucy put her arms round her sister and gave her a hug. 'You're kind and generous, but we won't talk about it yet,' she said huskily. 'We'll go to bed and sleep well – both of us – and let decisions wait until we get home to Cahersiveen.'

When Linnet simply assumed that they would sail from Liverpool instead of catching the train to Holyhead, Lucy was dismayed.

'Tis a longer voyage,' she said apprehensively. 'I'm not sure it's a good idea at all at all.'

'Oh, you're a little longer on the sea, but it saves absolutely *hours* of messing about on trains and things,' Linnet assured her. 'I'll book us on an early morning departure though, so we won't arrive after dark.'

What could Lucy do but agree? The weather seemed set fair. So on their last morning she and her sister said their goodbyes and made their way to the docks.

'It'll be me first time on a big ship,' Linnet said excitedly as they made their way up the gang-plank. She squeezed Lucy's arm. 'Oh, isn't it thrilling? I'd be scared stiff if I was on me own, mind, but because you're with me it's just an adventure.'

'Hmm,' Lucy said doubtfully. The sea, even here in the dock, was *moving*. She did hope it did not intend to behave like that all the way from Liverpool to Ireland or Linnet might well end up wishing she was on her own!

It seemed strange to Linnet to be aboard the big Irish ferry instead of the very much smaller one which chugged several times a day across the Mersey between the Pier Head and Woodside. But that little ferry would always wear a special aura for her, because that was where she and her sister had first met. Mrs Sullivan had called them the Mersey girls – she wondered what name they would be given in Ireland.

But right now they were saying goodbye to Liverpool, watching the familiar, much loved skyline becoming smaller as they stood at the rail and waved to the tiny figure of Mrs Sullivan standing on the quayside surrounded by little Sullivans, all of them waving vigorously back.

'Look at Freddy, jumping up and down,' Lucy said in her ear. 'Or is it Toddy?'

'I don't know, they're too far away to say for sure,' Linnet said. To her horror her voice sounded shaky. 'Oh, isn't it awful, Lucy, I think I'm going to cry! And I'm only off on a lovely sort of holiday, but I never could bear saying goodbye.'

'Nor me,' Lucy said. Her voice, if anything, was shakier than her sister's. 'And I'm saying goodbye for much longer than you are, so I am. Your friend Mrs Sullivan's lovely so she is, and I don't like saying goodbye to her one little bit.'

'Let's go below and get a drink of coffee,' Linnet suggested. 'It will make us feel better. How stupid we are, standing here crying, when we're together! Come on . . . I could do with a bite, as well. They have doughnuts, I could smell 'em when we came aboard.'

'Oh, I think I'm best on deck,' Lucy said doubtfully. She remembered her last voyage on a ship and shuddered. 'We're coming out of the mouth of the Mersey now . . . here come the waves!'

'I can't see any,' Linnet said, leaning over the side and gazing down at the heaving, white flecked water below them. 'I've never been on a ship before, not at sea. Oh yes, that was a wave . . .' she turned to her sister. 'You're a bit pale, are you sure you wouldn't like to come below for a coffee and doughnut?'

'I'm going to sit down and look away from the sea,' Lucy said. She headed for a deckchair and subsided into it. 'You go if you want, I'll be all right up here.'

'I'll bring you something up,' Linnet offered. 'I shan't be long.'

Lucy closed her eyes. 'If you like,' she said wearily. 'Just a coffee, though, not a doughnut. I don't think a doughnut would be a good idea at all!'

Linnet enjoyed the voyage, though she felt terribly sorry for her sister. Lucy, pale green in the face, could neither eat her doughnut nor drink her coffee, so Linnet finished both off for her. And quite soon after Linnet had drunk the two cups of coffee and eaten the two doughnuts Lucy lost her breakfast, noisily, over the side.

'It's odd that one of us should feel splendid and the other so dreadful,' Linnet said at one point, holding her twin's head as Lucy tried in vain to turn her stomach inside out, or so at least it appeared. 'You're being iller than you need, though, queen. If you'd only eat something . . .'

A groan answered her. Lucy waved a pallid hand in the air and then subsided onto her deckchair once more, having for the moment, at least, given up the thought of being sick again.

'Yes, I know it sounds cruel, but if you'd just have a couple of plain biscuits or some seltzer . . .'

'They tried that on the way over,' Lucy quavered. 'Oh, if only the sea wasn't so rough! If only the weather would improve! Is it long before we dock?'

Linnet gazed out over a blue sea flecked with gentle white horses. Rough? This, rough? 'We dock in an hour,' she said, tactfully not mentioning the calmness of the sea or the blueness of the sky. 'Just you lie still, queen, with your eyes closed. That way you might drop asleep and sleeping helps to pass the time.'

'I'll never go aboard a ship again,' a sepulchral voice from the deckchair announced with bitterness. 'Tis clear I bring on hurricanes just by lookin' at a ship. If I'm spared I'll stay at home for the rest of me life so I will. I'm a home-girl, so I am, I don't travel well at all at all.'

Linnet made soothing noises and presently she realised that her sister had indeed fallen asleep so she sat quietly down beside her and despite her best intentions, dozed herself.

'Isn't it good to be on dry land? And isn't it strange that the moment there's firm ground beneath me feet I'm a different person?' Lucy demanded as the two of them stepped ashore at Dun Laoghaire. 'I'm starving hungry so I am – where's a café?'

'We've no time if we're to catch the train,' Linnet said doubtfully, but her sister was firm.

'I must eat or sure and I'll die,' she said simply. 'It's as empty as a drum I am and if I'm not fed I'll keel over. Come on!'

They found a down-at-heel little eating place where the food was cheap; they had floury potatoes boiled in their jackets and some sort of fish. They drank tea with it, and afterwards ate brack, which looked and tasted similar, Linnet thought, to what the Welsh call *bara brith*. Linnet, who had enjoyed the doughnuts on the ship, ate sparingly but the empty and drumlike Lucy squared her elbows and ate like – like a starving navvy, Linnet thought. She also drank huge quantities of tea . . . and then, of course, when they should have been catching the next train, having missed the one they should have caught, they needed to find a ladies' lavatory, so they missed the following train, too.

'It'll be midnight and gone before we catch a train at this rate,' Lucy moaned as they tumbled out of the lavatory and raced for the station. 'But at least no one's meeting us.'

'Then shall we get a bed for the night in Dublin and get a train in the morning?' Linnet said hopefully. She was worn out and wanted nothing more than to sleep. 'Come on, it won't cost the earth, and I've got some spare money.'

Mr Cowan's cheque, which was made out for a much larger sum of money than he had owed her, even for a month, had startled and amused Linnet. But she had cashed it quite merrily.

'He's paying me off, the old terror,' she said cheerfully, showing the cheque to Lucy. 'Just because he doesn't want to marry me any more! Well, since I was about to turn down his proposal he might just as well have saved his money, but he won't miss it and it'll come in handy for us.'

And now it really was coming in handy, for Lucy's money had run out. 'I feel awful mean, letting you pay,' she said now, following her sister across to the nearest bus stop. 'But it's worn out I am as well as penniless. We'll settle up when we're back in Caher, I promise you.'

They found a lodging house in Dominic Street and got themselves a bed for the night. It was a double bed in a tiny room, and they both fell into it in their underwear, having failed to find a lock on the rickety door.

'If anyone comes we'll crack him over the skull with our boot-heels and scream blue bloody murder,' Linnet said, shoving a chair up against the door and wedging the back of it under the handle. But Lucy was not impressed.

'This is Ireland, not Liverpool,' she mumbled, climbing into bed and heaving the covers up round her shoulders. 'Sure I am no one will come in here this night.'

'Ireland's not heaven; there are good and bad everywhere,' Linnet said rather reproachfully. 'We'd be safe enough in Liverpool from Liverpool fellers, I daresay, but there's all sorts roaming the docks.'

Both girls were proved right in a way since someone did try their door in the early hours; but what with the wedged chair and Linnet repeating some of the nastier threats she had heard Roddy using on his brothers, the door rattler decided to move on and troubled them no more that night.

The girls arrived back at Ivy Farm just as Caitlin was setting down the tea baskets on the verge of the hayfield. The men were carting hay today from the long, sloping meadows which led to the lough and Lucy stopped by the gate and set her suitcase down.

'They're our workers, and some neighbours who are

helping with the haymaking,' she told her sister. 'And that's Caitlin, the girl putting the baskets down in the shade. Haven't they a grand day for it? And we've arrived at the right moment – just in time to share their meal.'

The scene before them was enough to impress anyone, Lucy thought, with the sun beating down on the workers' heads, and everyone flushed from the heat and sweating from their toil, and the enamel buckets of tea and the loaves of buttered bread, the slices of fruit cake, the cold apple pie, spread out on the cloth in the shade of a great oak looking so appetising that she quite envied the haymakers.

The two girls leaned over the mossy five-barred gate.

'It's grand to be home so it is,' Lucy said quietly. 'It's your home too, Linnet. Do you like what you see?'

It was a fair scene indeed. The hayfield, pale gold beneath the sun, the workers sun-tanned and smiling, the trees in their summer finery casting a shade and the lough blue as the sky above and calm enough to reflect the towering hills and the little town nestling at their feet.

'I think it's beautiful,' Linnet said, her voice small and awed. 'Oh, this is a wonderful country, Lucy! I can't imagine why our mammy left, can you?'

Lucy shrugged. 'Fame and fortune, I suppose. Ah, Caitlin's turned... she's coming up to meet you, the word will soon go around that we're home!'

Caitlin arrived at the gate at a run. She beamed at both girls and hugged Lucy over the top of the gate. Then she stood back and held out a hand, her face wreathed in smiles. 'Welcome,' she said warmly, shaking Linnet's hand. 'You'll be Linnet – I'm glad to meet you at last. Welcome home to the both of you!' She turned to Lucy. 'Are you comin' in for a bite here, Luceen, or will you go back to the farm first? There's the kettle singin' on the hob in the kitchen and a fine cake waitin' for the first cut.'

'I think we'll go back to the farm, alanna,' Lucy said. 'Me sister's not seen it yet and we're hot and weary. But we'll come down to the meadow when we've rested up a bit.'

'Never worry,' Caitlin said. 'We'll be done here in good time, the men have worked like slaves to get the hay in before the weather breaks and we've only one more meadow to clear. Get off wit' you now then, and I'll start the tea.' She turned back to the meadow. 'Tea!' she hollered. 'Come an' dig in, fellers!'

They walked up the little, narrow lane, their feet scuffing tiredly in the white dust. Wild roses and honeysuckle sent their perfume into the warm air and birds sang and rustled in the hedgerows.

They rounded a bend in the lane and they were on the home straight, Linnet knew it without Lucy having to say a word. Here the lane wound between tall banks, mossy and cool, the trees arching over their heads to mingle branches, plunging the walkers into a sweet, dappled shade. They walked on, Linnet staring about her with wondering eyes. This was the lane down which her mammy had carried her years ago – she was about to set eyes on Ivy Farm for the first time . . . no, not the first time, for the baby she had once been must have known it.

Suddenly, unexpectedly, Lucy turned right, between two huge, mossy stone pillars, then stopped short. She turned to her sister, her face bright with excitement. 'Well? What d'you think of it?'

The house, the farmyard, the outbuildings, lay before them. Ivy Farm was built of grey stone and ivy massed along its walls, reached out curly tendrils as far as the slates of the roof. There were two doors, one with a porch, around which the ivy had been cleared to allow another creeper to take a hold, a creeper which was covered in pale purple blooms which hung like bunches of grapes amidst the light green, ferny foliage. The second door was ajar and within, Linnet glimpsed a wide room, the floor paved, the paving gilded with great slabs of sunshine. Outbuildings surrounded the yard on two sides and they were built of stone, too, but their slate roofs were much older, dipping and rising like the waves of the sea and covered with cushions of moss, yellow flowers, a white, waxy plant.

'It's . . . it's . . .' Linnet gasped. How could she tell her sister how she felt, how beautiful was the scene before her? But Lucy seemed to understand for she smiled and moved forward, into the yard.

'It's beautiful, isn't it? The creeper round the front door is a wistaria, I've always loved it, and the plants on the roofs of the buildings are house leeks and stone crop. Follow me!'

In a dream, Linnet followed, across the yard and in through the door, to a big, untidy kitchen. Lucy dumped her bag on the floor and turned to her sister.

'Farmers never use the front door save for weddings and funerals,' she said. 'We always come straight into the kitchen. Take your coat off and sit down – you look exhausted.'

'I am,' Linnet said. She was looking round the kitchen. It was big, with windows on either side of the back door and there was an odd sort of squeaky, twittering noise . . . it seemed to be coming from a cardboard box set down close to the big black cooking range. She peered into the box and saw it was heaving with fluffy yellow chicks. She had seen day-old chicks for sale in the city so she knew what they were but had never got so close to a group of them before. She looked across at her sister, heaving the kettle off the top of the range. 'There are chicks in that box – can I touch them?'

'Course,' Lucy said, tipping the contents of the kettle into a battered old teapot. 'There's kittens, too, see the hatbox? Spit must have had them whilst I was away.'

Linnet went over to the hatbox, which was on the other side of the range. The kittens were, if it was possible, prettier than the chicks. Linnet hung over both boxes in turn, cooing incoherently. This was a farm, there would be baby cows, baby horses . . . she was so happy she almost forgot that she was on strange ground and when Lucy thrust a cup of tea into her hand she very nearly forgot to thank her.

'Lucy, do you have baby cows and baby horses as well? Oh . . . thanks for the tea, I'm dry as dust! Only I've never seen a baby cow . . .'

Lucy laughed and came and pushed her sister gently into one of the shabby, comfortable chairs, then bent over and plucked a kitten out of its nest. She plonked it on Linnet's lap and then balanced a large slice of fruit cake on the arm of the chair.

'Here, you can hold a kitten if you like – I remember when I dearly loved baby things! Then, when you've drunk your tea and eaten your cake we'll have a tour of the house. Later we'll go round outside, but I think for this afternoon the house will be quite enough for you to take in.'

'I can't believe it,' Linnet kept saying as she ate the cake and stroked the kitten and sipped at her tea. 'I just can't believe I'm here, where Mammy . . . our Mammy . . .'

Her voice broke and she ducked her head but Lucy saw the tears and knew that no matter how badly little Evie had behaved towards her, Linnet had loved her mammy. Lucy went over and sat on the arm of her sister's chair.

'It was all a long time ago, alanna,' she said gently. 'Our mammy's long gone, long gone. Now we must make our own future, but we'll never be alone again, because you've got me and I've got you. And whatever we do, wherever we roam, we'll hold each other dear in our hearts. Now, are you going to come over the house with me, or must I go by meself?'

Linnet gave a sigh, pulled a hanky from her sleeve and blew her nose, then stood up. She put the kitten back in its nest and ate the last of her cake. Then she smiled across at Lucy. 'I'm ready,' she said. 'Will I bring my bag up so you can show me where I'm to sleep tonight?'

The neighbours were delighted with Linnet.

'The image of Maeve, the little darlin',' Mrs Kelly said, sighing sentimentally. 'But Maeve was plain, useless to deny it, and she's a pretty t'ing, that sister of yours. So I don't know why they look alike, I just know they do.'

'I noticed it meself, first go off,' Lucy confessed. 'And you know what, Linnet's like Maeve in other ways, too. She catches on so quick over farming matters you'd think she'd been reared here. I show her how to do a thing once and it's there in her head for ever, I'm sure. And though she never got much chance of cooking while she was a nanny, she picks up my recipes in a moment so she does.'

'Aye. But it's because she wants to understand, to be a part of it,' Mrs Kelly said shrewdly. 'I explained about broody hens and d'you know, she's writ it down? So she won't never forget, she said.'

'I'm so glad,' Lucy said. 'I wanted her to take to it, but I never dreamed she would – not so fast, anyway. But as it is, I do think that we might make a go of it between us. You see, once Caitlin and Declan marry there will be a big gap here, and you only come in a couple of mornings a week now. So if Linnet did decide to stay there would be work for her.'

'Aye, there would. And what about her young man? She says he'll be coming on the train in a few days.'

'That's right. They're hoping to marry so Linnet wants to talk to him about it. Mrs Kelly, he's from a – a very poor area of Liverpool, he knows nothing about farming . . .'

'But he comes from farming stock, Linnet told me so.'

'Yes, but I think that was so far back – they left in the 'forties, because of the potato famine – that I doubt he's got any interest in the land at all at all.'

'Well, if he's not goin' to be a farmer, then mebbe the feller could get a job in Cahersiveen,' Mrs Kelly said with unimpaired cheerfulness. 'Or mebbe he could go to sea and come back to Ivy Farm and his wife when he was ashore. They'll be an asset to Cahersiveen, the young folk.'

'We've not met Mr Sullivan yet; he may not be nice at all,' Lucy said, but Mrs Kelly just laughed and shook her head reprovingly at the younger woman.

'Not nice, when Linnet loves him? He's a dote, I'm sure of it!'

Chapter Thirteen

Roddy got off the train at Cahersiveen station and it was raining: gentle, soft rain, the sort that gardeners love, but the sort that penetrates clothing, soaks hair, even infiltrates footwear. The sort of rain, Roddy thought ruefully as his stout seamen's boots thudded onto the platform, which meant you turned up at your destination looking like a drowned rat and squelching. Which didn't matter on some occasions and mattered very much on others. It mattered today.

A week ago he had arrived home after an exhausting voyage to find his mother in a state of high excitement.

'It's Linnet,' she had gasped almost before he was through the doorway. 'She's gone off to Ireland wit 'er sister, Lucy! The gel came for 'er, Roddy, after all these years, an' a lovely gel she is, too. Their old grandad died an' left 'em the farm between 'em so they 'ad to go back an' see to things – lawyer's things, you know. Linnet left a letter – she wants you to tek a voyage out, son, an' go over there. You'll go, won't you? Now don't gerrall obstinate an' pig-'eaded this time, just give it a bit o' thought, don't start . . .'

'I'll go.' He didn't have to think. Where Linnet was concerned there could be no thought, no reasoned judgement. He loved her, wanted her – damn it, he *needed* her, as she needed him, though whether she knew it yet was another matter. They quarrelled and fought, hurt each other, made it up, quarrelled again. But that did not mean that they weren't deeply in love, though sometimes he got so exasperated with her . . .

'You'll go, son? You'll tek a voyage out an' go over to Ireland? Well, an' I thought I'd 'ave to argufy an' explain . . . Here, read the letter, though I've telled you most, I reckon.'

She hurried across to the mantelpiece and took down a brown envelope wedged behind the clock. It had his name sprawled across it in a rather wild hand, very different from Linnet's usual neat script. He commented on it as he slung his ditty bag on the table and began to slit the envelope open.

'She were in an 'urry, judgin' by the writin'.'

'That's right, she were,' his mother agreed. She was peeling apples and the kitchen smelled sweetly of the fruit. 'It all 'appened so quick, son, you'd scarcely credit. You see, what 'appened . . . but I'd best let you read the letter.'

Roddy, reading, grunted. But the letter was a good deal clearer than his mother's garbled explanation for all that.

Dear Roddy,
My twin sister has come for me because we've inherited the farm where Mammy was born and bred. I left the Cowans because they went to London. My sister's name is Lucy and she's very, very nice. The address is Ivy Farm, Cahersiveen, County Kerry. I don't know how long I'll be here, but it would help me a lot if you would come over for a week or so. Lucy would love to meet you. Could you come? It would help me a lot. Please come.
Your Linnet.

Below was a small pencilled sketch map of the area with arrows leading from the main street, across the bridge and out to a small square labelled Ivy Farm.

Roddy read every word through twice and studied the map; then he put the letter down on his knee. He whistled thoughtfully beneath his breath, then glanced at his mother through his eyelashes. What exactly did she know? He had had his suspicions about that Cowan feller, always so quick to take Linnet out in his car, to pay her a bit extra, to dance attendance on her. But he'd not said anything to Linnet because she would have been offended and said Mr Cowan was a gentleman, as if that made any difference! Gentlemen, Roddy was sure, had exactly the same feelings, urges and the like, as fellers. Besides, Linnet wouldn't let any bloke go too far, Roddy knew that. None better. His own hopeful advances were always slapped down and briskly, too.

Mrs Sullivan looked up from her work. 'Did she tell you the Cowans 'ad moved to London? Oh, she were treated shabby there, but she just laughed – you know Linnet – and said she were glad to be out of it. So off she went to Ireland wit' a month's money in 'er pocket in lieu o' notice, 'appy as Larry.'

'Oh,' Roddy said rather feebly. 'There weren't no – no trouble, then?'

'Norra bit of it,' his mother said cheerfully. 'They parted fr . . . well, I were goin' to say they parted friends, but that ain't true. They parted as nanny an' guv'nor, I'd say.'

'Oh. Well, that's awright, I suppose,' Roddy said, having given the matter some thought. ''Cos once or twice it seemed to me . . . but there, I were wrong. There weren't nothin' . . .'

'No, nothin',' Mrs Sullivan said. 'When'll you leave, eh? End o' the week?'

'In a day or so,' Roddy said easily. 'Gorra get tickets an' that. She's give me the address so I'll tell 'er when to expect me.'

It had not taken long to arrange to miss a voyage. He said he would probably be signing on for the following one and the shipping clerk just nodded. An experienced seaman could usually get a berth, they guessed he would probably be back.

Then there was his ticket for the ferry and his train ticket, too. He packed a few things in his ditty bag, kissed his mam, bought sweets for the kids, shook hands with his dad, and left. He marched down to the dock with a silly grin on his face because not only was he going to Linnet but she had said she needed him, had almost begged him to join her in Ireland.

He had rather enjoyed being a passenger instead of a deckhand, what was more. He prowled all over the ship, talked to the seamen, got taken on the bridge. He drank a couple of pints in the bar, refused to play cards with a group of sharp-looking characters in one of the lounges, leaned over the bows and watched the mysterious land grow bigger and clearer.

The train journey across Ireland was enjoyable, too, though overlong for an impatient swain going to see his lady-love. But sailors are used to seemingly endless journeyings so Roddy took this one in his stride and passed the time by examining the scenery – lakes, bogs, rolling meadowland and wooded hillsides – as the train chugged along.

It hadn't started to rain until well past Killarney but now it seemed to have got into its stride. Because it had been so fine when he set out Roddy had not bothered to wear his seaman's cap and now it was probably right at the bottom of his ditty bag so he just shrugged his shoulders up to protect his ears and headed for the roadway which he could just see past the station's ticket office.

He did wonder about a taxi, but although he had had plenty of time on his hands both on the ferry and in the train, he found that he still needed to think. So he strode out along the street, scarcely glancing at anything or anyone, just savouring the fact that Linnet needed him, had sent for him, had signed herself 'Your Linnet' for the first time for months.

He knew that to reach the farm he must go down towards the sea lough and find Barry's Bridge. He found it easily, first passing the ruined barracks on his right just as Linnet had said, and strode across its length, once again never glancing down at the water beneath but keeping his eyes fixed on the gently rising hills ahead. She was near, now! He could feel frissons of excitement chasing up and down his spine and his face wore a broad smile despite the falling rain, the weight of his ditty bag, and a secret worry that this twin of hers, this Lucy, might resent him, be jealous of his closeness to her recently discovered sister.

The road wound on and Roddy followed it until he came to the lane leading off on his left. There was no sign to say 'Ivy Farm this way', but Roddy knew that it was because of Linnet's squiggly pencil-map, so he turned left.

He reached the mossy stone posts and turned in through them. He saw, spread out before him, the farm, the outbuildings, the yard where hens pecked and purred over their finds. He saw lilac and laburnum trees laden with blossom and a well with a slate roof and buckets standing beside it. The trees were diamonded with rain-drops and the buckets, as he approached, were half full of water so that the drops rocked the surface and tinkled against the sides.

The farm was bigger, older, more impressive than he had expected. A thin, orange-striped cat came round the corner of the house at a trot, with something gripped in its mouth. It saw Roddy and in one swift, sinuous movement it turned and retreated the way it had come. I hope everyone's not goin' to be like that, Roddy thought apprehensively. I hope they won't all turn and run when they clap eyes on me! But he approached the nearest door, a plain wooden one, ignoring the more elaborate one with the porch around it. He knocked. Waited.

Linnet knew he would be arriving some time today, but not when. For once she could not bring herself to leave the house, so she told Lucy that she would do the housework and make the midday dinner and she was busy now doing just that. She scrubbed a large quantity of potatoes, threw them in a saucepan with stock made out of beef and mutton bones, added some carrots and onions, and put it to simmer on the side of the stove. Then she made an apple pie, climbing up to the apple loft and carefully picking out the best fruit because she wanted her twin to know she really could cook and – and she wanted Roddy to enjoy the pie.

And all the time she was bustling round making beds and sweeping floors and cooking, she told herself that she was not excited, that she was looking forward to seeing an old friend, showing him round, but that was all. But she knew it was not all, of course. She knew that having Roddy here would complete the scene, that once he was here she would know what she should do. It was not so much a matter of asking his opinion, it was more seeing how they got on together in this place.

If they quarrelled here, she did not know what she would do, but they would not stay. Life without Roddy wasn't bearable, but then life with him had not been any great treat, so somewhere along the line they had gone wrong. This was their chance to put things right, to make it work, and if they made a mess of it, then . . .

Then we don't deserve each other, or happiness, or any

other good thing, Linnet decided, wielding the rolling pin with a fierceness not at all in keeping with her usual cooking methods. She had some paste left over and was rolling it out, sprinkling it with sugar and currants, folding it over several times and making shortcakes. Then she brushed the cakes with the top of the milk so that they would shine and popped them in the oven. And all the time her mind was miles away, with Roddy. She wondered what train he would catch and whether he was already on his way or still wandering around Dublin. She wondered what he would think of it all when he finally arrived in Cahersiveen. She wished that it hadn't decided to rain because it would mean he would arrive soaked and cross and that would make Linnet cross and before they knew it, they would be quarrelling again.

Outside, in the quiet farmyard, a hen croodled away to herself, the rain pattered on the slates overhead, someone crossed the yard. Immediately Linnet was alert. She ran over to the window but as she was trying to press her nose to the rain-spattered pane there was a knock and she flew across to the back door and tugged it open.

He stood there, grinning at her. His hair was sleeked to his head, his face was wet . . . she flung her arms round him, hugging him breathlessly. She had not known she had felt alone here but she had, she had!

'Linnet! Oh, Linnet!'

She dragged him into the kitchen whilst his wet mouth was still searching for hers, and then they kissed, whilst the rain on his duffle coat was absorbed by her thin cotton dress and they clung closer and closer, murmuring love-words.

'Oh, Roddy, I didn't know how badly I've missed you till this moment,' Linnet said at last, standing back from him. 'Take off your wet coat at once before you catch your death!'

'Take off your wet frock before you catch yours,' Roddy said, grinning, but he struggled out of his coat as he spoke and handed it to Linnet, who hung it on the back door. 'I'm a thoughtless feller – you'd best go upstairs, get changed.'

Linnet looked down at her pink gingham dress and laughed.

'You're right, I'm as wet as you, pretty near. Oh, Roddy, I'm that glad you've come – what d'you think?'

'Of what? The countryside's rare pretty, and the house – what I've seen of it – seems a good solid buildin'.'

Linnet shook his arm. 'You know what I mean! Bring your bag and I'll show you round and later I'll take you to the Kellys', where you'll be lodging. Then whilst you unpack I'll go and put a dry frock on. And after that we can talk.'

Downstairs again, clean and dry, Linnet bustled round making tea and talking whilst Roddy sat in one of the easy chairs and watched her with such contentment glowing from his eyes that Linnet felt tears come to her own. What had been the matter with her these past months? She had found fault with Roddy, criticised, slapped him down, when in truth all she wanted was his love. But now, with the new serenity she had found at Ivy Farm, she could see all too clearly the tensions and stresses, the uncertainties, which had made her so unfair to her love.

A part of me was proud of living in a big, posh house and having Mr Cowan wanting to marry me, she thought with deep shame. I kept seeing these little pictures of me as his wife, driving around in the car, going to all the big shops, all my old friends so envious. But I never thought about the other side of it – him as my husband. And as soon as I did, as soon as Roddy's mam made me look, then I knew I couldn't go through with it.

She poured the tea and carried the two cups over to where Roddy sat, but when she would have handed him his cup and gone over to the other chair he shook his head reprovingly at her.

'What's wrong wi' this chair?' he asked, catching hold of her and pulling her onto his lap. 'What's wrong wi' a bit o' cuddlin', eh, queen?'

'You'll spill my tea,' Linnet squeaked as the cup rocked perilously. 'This is my second clean frock today, don't go spilling my tea, Roddy!'

He took the cup from her and set it down on the floor, beside his own. 'Shan't spill a drop. Oh, Linnet, isn't this lovely? A big, clean kitchen, the stove mutterin' away, the rain patterin' on the winder pane, and – and just you an' me.'

'Yes, it is lovely,' Linnet said. She buried her face in the side of his neck. 'The whole house is lovely, isn't it?'

'Yeah. But it's only lovely because you're in it,' Roddy said frankly.

'Could you live here, with me, Roddy?' Linnet said dreamily. 'Oh, and I didn't mean to say that until you'd seen the farm and met my sister Lucy . . . oh what a fool I am!'

'I could live anywhere if you was there, queen,' Roddy said, stroking her arm. 'I could live in Africa or – or the Arctic, if you was there.'

'Silly! I'm serious, I mean could you learn to farm and live out here a long way from – well, from Liverpool and Peel Square and so on?'

'I don't know whether I'd be any use at it, but I'd 'ave a go,' Roddy said. 'I ain't afraid o' work, no seaman is. But someone 'ud 'ave to tell me what needed doin'.'

'Ye-es, but if they told you. . . ?'

'Wait an' see 'ow I shapes up,' Roddy advised her. 'Now 'ad you better introduce me to this sister o' yours?'

'They'll be coming in for tea in a few minutes, you'll meet Lucy and the others then. Tell you what, I'm learning to milk a cow, d'you want to come and watch me have a go?'

He laughed but stood up, tipping her off his lap. Then he put his arm round her waist and gave her a quick squeeze and a kiss on the soft side of her face. 'You're on! Where's this 'ere cow what's goin' to let you 'ave a go at 'er?'

'She's waiting at the gate by now, to be let through. She's a dear little thing . . . come on, then, no point in putting coats on, it's a short run to the cowshed. Follow me!'

Together they dashed out into the rainy yard, across it and into the cowshed. Linnet caught Roddy's arm.

'I'll bring her in, you wait here.'

Roddy waited and in rather less than a minute Linnet reappeared, leading a small red and white cow on a rope halter.

'She's the easiest to milk,' she said as she was tying the cow in her stall. 'She's quite happy to chew the cud whilst I try to bring the milk down. Now you watch, Roddy – it's harder than it looks.'

She fetched a milking stool and a bucket, squatted down, leaned her head against the little cow's red and white side and began to tug the long teats firmly through her fingers. The milk squirted into the bucket and Linnet turned her head and grinned lopsidedly at him.

'What d'you think of that? Good, aren't I?'

'You are,' Roddy said, very impressed. 'Can I have a go?'

'In a minute, when I've got an inch or two in the bucket,' Linnet said. 'Oh, Roddy, it's so nice to see you again – you don't know how horribly I've missed you!'

'What I don't understand, chuck, is why you should miss me worse 'ere than you did in Liverpool,' Roddy said practically. 'You never saw me for weeks at a time when I were at sea and when we did meet we quarrelled.'

'Yes, and it was mostly my fault,' Linnet said. 'And before I left I knew it was you I wanted, that if I had you . . . if we were really married, I mean . . . then we'd probably never quarrel again. So leaving the city felt like leaving you, and it was horrid, and I missed you all the time.'

Roddy crouched down beside the cow and kissed the side of Linnet's face again. The cow rolled her eyes and shifted uneasily; it was clear she did not approve of people canoodling whilst she was giving milk.

'Oh, Linnet, you don't know 'ow I've longed to 'ear you say that! And you mean it this time, d'you? Rain or shine, wet or fine, you'll marry me?'

'Course I will,' Linnet assured him. She squirted a final squirt into the bucket and turned towards him. 'If you want me to I'll come back to Liverpool with you, but if you felt you could stay here it would make me – and Lucy – ever so happy.'

'If there's work for me, and a place for us . . .' Roddy began, then pulled Linnet roughly into his arms. The stool tipped against the bucket, the bucket rolled noisily onto its side, the cow mooed and kicked out at the bucket . . . but Linnet and Roddy were oblivious. Tightly clasped in each other's arms they were kissing with total concentration. In fact they did not notice the figure in the doorway until Lucy took a step forward and cleared her throat.

'Hmm-mm! Excuse me, Linnet, but do I take it Roddy's arrived? Because if the feller who's trying to gobble you up isn't Roddy Sullivan then I've a word or two to say to the pair of ye!'

Things moved at an amazing speed once they got started. After Lucy had been introduced to Roddy the three of them had gone all round the entire farm. They had to walk a good distance since they owned the land from the lough's edge to the mountain top and Roddy wanted to see everything. And then Lucy had to explain to him how the farm had been run when her grandfather had been alive, how it had been run since, and how – she hoped – it would be run in the future, by herself, Linnet and Roddy plus the farmhands.

'And what will 'appen when you're wed?' Roddy asked at one point. 'Because you will be wed, an' sooner rather than later, I'd bet.'

Lucy smiled at Roddy. He was a nice young man, as nice as Mrs Kelly had expected him to be, but that did not give him the right to pry into her private life. Linnet, she supposed, must have told him about the ardent Peder and everyone's freely expressed expectations that the two of them would marry.

'I'm not thinking of marrying just yet,' she assured him. 'I guess you've heard I've a young man, but I'm not sure . . . But if I married and moved away then you and Linnet would have Kellach and the Kellys, though not Caitlin, of course. But as I said I'm not thinking of marrying yet.'

'Well, look, Lucy,' Roddy said, having apparently thought this over. 'We'll strike a bargain, the three of us. Linnet and I will work 'ere, doin' our very best to learn farmin' ways, for six months. We'll 'ave to marry, because . . .' Roddy blushed, to Lucy's considerable amusement. 'Well, because it's only right, see? And if we don't get wed, we'd mebbe quarrel like we did at 'ome. But we won't mess you about, we'll work as 'ard as we know, won't we, Linnie? And at the end of six months we'll see 'ow we've gorron. If we're no good to you, we'll slope off back to the Pool, but if we've managed to be useful, we'll stay wi' you and wi' Ivy Farm. Is it a bargain?'

And Lucy, agreeing, felt lighter of heart than she had done since her grandfather's death. Ivy Farm had a chance, and so did she – so did they, come to that.

'But Linnet's already very useful,' she told Roddy. 'And I've a feeling that you'll have the will to learn and the strength to stick it. So I'm thinking we'll be all right, the three of us.'

Caitlin married Declan and became Mrs Franklin the September after Roddy had taken up residence with the Kellys. She was blissfully happy in her rooms above the grocer's shop in Cahersiveen and sang the praises of married life loudly and meaningfully to the Murphy girls when she visited the farm.

Despite Roddy's words, he and Linnet had not been able to marry as quickly as they would have liked for two reasons; one was that from the moment they woke until they fell into bed each night, every day was as full as an egg. Because they were new to the work they found themselves aching in every limb as muscles they had never known they possessed came into play, and their brains ached, too, from taking in all the information which Lucy, Kellach and the Kellys bombarded them with. Another, more important reason was that Mr Sullivan had a stroke about a month after Roddy arrived at the farm and though he lingered for five or six weeks, he had then died.

Roddy and Linnet had returned to Liverpool for the funeral and had been astonished at Mrs Sullivan's well of grief and at how she seemed to have grown small and old in their absence.

'Some folk might 'ave thought 'e weren't much good,' Mrs Sullivan said sadly, as they returned home after the funeral to have a bit of a wake in the tiny house in Peel Square. 'But 'e were kind to me an' the kids, which is more'n you can say for all the old fellers. An' 'e gave me what 'e could – never spent it on 'isself whiles we went wit'out. So give 'im a chance to settle in 'is grave afore you wed, our Roddy. Let your marriage wait on 'im, until I'm over it all a bit an' can come over to Ireland an' do me part in the ceremony. Don't be rushin' into things with your mam not there to shed a tear an' wish you luck.'

And somehow, it wasn't so hard to comply with her wishes when they were so very happy, and so hearteningly busy, too.

'I never thought we could go on so well without being married,' Linnet told Roddy as the weeks slid into months. 'Besides, I wouldn't want to upset your mam, Roddy. She was more than a mother to me, she was a friend as well, and I want her at my wedding. Only – only I hope we won't have to wait *too* long.'

Winter came and Christmas was celebrated, the twins' first Christmas together. It was a quiet time for farming and Linnet and Roddy were by now, Lucy told them, indispensable to the welfare of Ivy Farm.

'But you've waited and worked hard and thought of others, and now you really should get married yourselves,' she said firmly one evening as the three of them sat round the fire doing the bookwork. Or rather Linnet was writing the figures down, Roddy was dictating them and Lucy was toasting bread in front of the flames. 'I don't see why you should have to wait until the spring, write to your mam, Roddy, and tell her that you're getting married in February. Send her money for her tickets and say we expect her a week before the wedding and afterwards, for another week at least. Will she bring the small children with her?'

'They ain't so small, now,' Roddy said. 'But me Auntie Bertha's moved in – didn't we tell you? – so she'll give an eye to our kids. Oh aye, February sounds grand, eh, Linnie?'

'It sounds lovely,' Linnet said wistfully. She was finding it increasingly hard to see Roddy go off to the Kelly cottage each night, though Roddy had not once hinted that she could be a little more generous if she chose. It was as though being happily together all the time had made it easier for Roddy to wait whilst it became daily more difficult for Linnet.

'Good. And Caitlin's going to have her wedding dress altered to fit you, so that's one expense you're spared, Linnet.' Lucy turned a scorched face away from the flames and handed her twin a slice of lightly burned toast. 'Here, you have this bit, and pass me another. Then Roddy had better drive into Caher tomorrow and see the priest. And you must write to Mrs Sullivan immediately, of course. And I shall start planning the wedding feast.'

Later that evening, Roddy and Linnet slipped into the moonlit yard and went for a bit of a walk, as they did every night. It stretched their legs, got them ready for bed, and allowed them some privacy for a last goodnight kiss.

'I wish your Lucy would tell Peder yes and gerron with it,' Roddy grumbled as they walked, arms round each other, down the lane towards the lough. 'He's good lookin', good company, he's gorra nice bit o' money tucked away . . . an' the honest truth is that you an' I and the fellers could make a go of this place. If your Lucy weds and moves away then there's no end to the things we could do 'ere, you an' me. Why, I've gor ideas for changin' things which would suit the land, I reckon.'

'But Lucy doesn't love Peder,' Linnet said sadly. 'It doesn't work unless you love someone, Roddy, so your plans will have to wait. She likes him all right – he's a nice person – but she doesn't love him. I mean how could you go into a bedroom and close the door and – and take your clothes off with someone you didn't love? I mean no one could, could they?'

'We-el, if she were pretty . . .' Roddy began and got thumped for his pains by a giggling Linnet.

'Roddy, how like a feller! A woman couldn't, she – she just couldn't. So don't you try and persuade her, there's a good feller. Because I'm ever so fond of Lucy and I wouldn't want her to feel we wouldn't mind if she moved on.'

'I couldn't persuade no one to do nothin',' Roddy said. 'But if she won't take the plunge with Peder, queen, there's another what will. Did you see young Bridget O'Reilly makin' eyes at Peder an' teasin' 'im to dance with 'er at the Christmas ceilidh at the O'Rorkes'? I tell you, if Lu doesn't mek 'er mind up quick she won't 'ave a choice in the matter.'

'If Lu doesn't want him then it's only fair that someone else should get him,' Linnet said at once. 'But I'll have a word with her, love.' She pulled him round the corner into the warmth of the stackyard and cuddled against him. 'Kiss me, then we'd better go in before we freeze to icicles,' she whispered. 'Oh Roddy, I can't wait until February!'

They waited, in fact, until March. And then, on a wild, sweet day, with a boisterous wind tossing Linnet's veil and sunshine gilding the churchyard one minute whilst raindrops sparkled down the next, they were married at last.

Linnet looked beautiful and no one knew – or cared – that she was wearing Caitlin Franklin's altered gown. She carried a bunch of early primroses and had a wreath of snowdrops in her shining, fawn-coloured hair and Lucy, in deep blue silk, was her bridesmaid.

Mrs Sullivan cried, everyone threw confetti, and then they went back to Ivy Farm for the wedding feast which had kept both girls cooking for days. The neighbours brought gifts, a fiddler played for the dancing and Peder O'Rorke kept trying to get the bridesmaid into a corner . . . and Bridget kept trying to do the same to him.

'We're pulling Ivy Farm back into profit and we're learning, all of us, how to live and work together,' Lucy told Mrs Sullivan, after the bridal pair had departed, in the late afternoon, for a very short honeymoon – they were staying one night – in Killarney. 'I honestly think that Roddy is a natural farmer and as for Linnet, it's in her blood from not too far back at all. They're going to make a go of it and I couldn't be happier for them.'

'You're right there,' Mrs Sullivan said. 'Well, well, we can't call you the Murphy girls any longer, Lucy. Though you'll always be the Mersey girls, to me.'

Lucy chuckled. 'I like both names,' she said. 'But I'm still the Murphy girl, and likely to be.'

'And why is that?' Mrs Sullivan asked. The guests had all departed and the two women were sitting in the kitchen with the fire banked down for the night, having a cup of cocoa before wending their way to bed. 'You could marry that feller tomorrer, if you chose. Why doncher?'

'Because I don't love him and I think it's important to love the man you marry,' Lucy said baldly. 'Respect is all very well, but I don't think it's enough, not in the long run.'

'Sometimes love comes after the weddin',' Mrs Sullivan said presently. She sipped her cocoa. 'I've known gels what goes to their weddin' bed cryin' for their mammy an' spends the next forty years wit' a smile from ear to ear.'

'But not girls who were already . . .' Lucy broke off. 'Anyway, they must have been . . .'

'Not girls who were already in love wi' someone else?' Mrs Sullivan said softly. 'Are you in love, already, queen? Well, don't the feller 'ave eyes in 'is 'ead? You're as sweet as you're pretty, so is the feller blind an' deaf not to snatch you up?'

'No. No, he isn't blind or deaf, and I think he likes me a little. But he likes his freedom more,' Lucy said rather bitterly. 'He didn't want to settle down, stay in one spot. So he left me, and he's never come back, or at least if he has he's never let me catch more than a glimpse of him. I tell meself that one day I'll get him out o' my system, out o' my mind and my heart. But that day hasn't come yet . . . sometimes I think it never will.'

The two women sat there in silence for a short while, and then Mrs Sullivan leaned over and patted Lucy's knee. 'You'll find your path,' she said. 'Dunno where it'll lead, or who'll be there to 'old your 'and, but you'll find it, one o' these days.' She stood up. 'Bless me, I'm fair wore out – it's been a long day. I'm for bed.'

'I think I'll just get a breath of air before I come up,' Lucy said. 'I shan't set my alarm tonight, I think we deserve a lie-in tomorrow. And Kellach's going to do the milking, so there's no need for us to stir ourselves.'

'Put a coat on; don't go catchin' cold,' Mrs Sullivan said. 'Eh, that pretty dress . . . it'll get mired, tharrit will.'

Lucy was still in her blue silk frock but she laughed and shook her head at the older woman. 'Oh, a bit of farmyard muck won't hurt it and it's a mild night. See you in the morning, Mrs Sullivan.'

As the moon rose in the sky Linnet and Roddy lay, for the first time in their lives together, in each other's arms. The bed was big and soft, a feather bed into which they had sunk gratefully, and now Linnet put her hot face against Roddy's cool, muscular shoulder and tried to relax and be natural with him, for they had known each other all their lives, so why should she feel so – so odd?

She hadn't understood a good deal of the rich Kerry brogue being talked around them in the hotel dining room and had gradually become convinced that every eye in the place was upon her, guessing, speculating, and that every guest in the hotel was waiting for the moment when she and Roddy disappeared into the same room and closed the door behind them.

She had blushed and mumbled and hung her head and wished herself anywhere but in the smart dining room of the best hotel in Killarney, and now, in their bed, she clung to Roddy and admitted that she was afraid, that she did not know what to do next, was not at all sure she wanted to know.

'It don't matter, queen,' Roddy said gently, when her painful whispers died away. 'A weddin's a weddin', we're man and wife. What follers is up to us, between us two, what no man may put asunder. Not now.'

'And – and must we . . . ? I'm – I'm ever so tired,' Linnet faltered. 'I love you so much, Roddy, but I'm not at all sure . . .'

'And I love you so much that if you're tired we'll go to sleep,' Roddy said comfortingly. 'We'll 'ave a bit of a cuddle an' then we'll snore so loud they'll think we've been wed for an 'undred years!'

'Oh, Roddy, I always knew you were the nicest feller

in the world,' Linnet said with an involuntary giggle. She relaxed against him, then leaned up on her elbow to kiss his cheek. 'You understand me so well and you're so kind to me!'

'I know I am,' Roddy said nobly. 'There, sweet'eart, you go to sleep if you want to, but there's no 'arm in a bit of a cuddle, first.'

Linnet agreed that there could be no harm in it at all, and so tenderly did Roddy cuddle, and so gently persuade, that long before the moon had begun to fade in the sky they were truly man and wife.

The moon was still climbing the sky when Lucy went out into the farmyard. It was very beautiful out here with a full moon shining down from the dark sky and the stars twinkling frostily. It made her think of another night . . . but she ignored the twinge of sadness and walked across the yard and out between the stone pillars, turning to her left along the lane.

It was, as she had said, a mild night, with a boisterous March wind blowing. Lucy walked steadily on, her eyes fixed ahead, her thoughts far from here. She thought about Linnet and Roddy, in their hotel in Killarney, savouring their love, their nearness. She thought about Peder, in his warm farm kitchen, stockinged feet stretched out towards the fire, hair rumpled, thoughts turning to the next day's work, to his beasts, his fields. Perhaps to her in her blue dress, saying no she didn't want to walk in the woods with him, no she couldn't see him next day, and thank you but she was fond of her own company so she was and there was no point in him sitting here trying to talk to her when she had other guests . . .

Cruel, cruel to treat Peder so, but sometimes she was so lonely she actually ached with loneliness. Sometimes she longed for a hand in hers, a man of her own, someone who would be, to her, what Roddy was to Linnet. Longed, in other words, for Finn Delaney with his dark eyes and his black hair, with his charm and his iron will, even for his indifference.

She had walked further than she realised because she was at Barry's Bridge. Too far; she should turn now, make her way back. Only she had such a longing to cross the bridge all of a sudden, to go at least to the middle, to look into the limpid dark waters and to see, at last, that little mermaid, combing her long, golden hair.

He came along the road in his jaunting car as he had come along half-a-dozen times a year ever since he'd left her, all those years ago. He had followed her in crowds, almost close enough to touch yet never touching. He had haunted the farm, watching from a safe distance as she went about her work. He had seen, with real dismay, the appearance of another man and had been prepared, almost, to throw off his disguise and step forward, challenge, declare himself.

But the feller wasn't interested in Lucy but in the other girl, the one they said was her twin sister. Twin sister! She was nothing like his Lucy, nothing like at all at all. No, his golden girl had no match, no equal, and she would wait for him until he was tired of wandering, until he was old and grey and wanted to settle down.

But sometimes he almost couldn't stand it, he wanted her so bad, so cruel bad! The touch, feel, sound, smell of her haunted him, her remembered face smiled at him, for him, with all its old sweetness and spirit. If only he could conquer the desire to move on, but he doubted he ever could and it wouldn't be fair to a farmer's girl to find herself with a feller who had no easement in him.

And besides, he mustn't be tied down. He was Finn Delaney, the best driver of a jaunting car ever seen in

Killarney, the only feller who could thatch a stack, plough a straight furrow, tickle a trout out of the brown pools and into his fry-pan, stand up in the jaunting car as it tore over ground so uneven and rough that others clutched at the seat in terror, or fell out onto the hard old earth below.

Oh aye, there was only one Finn Delaney. But – but he had to see her now and then, to calm his mind and ease, for a short time, the ache of longing for her.

So he came into Cahersiveen in his jaunting car and drove quietly through the moonlit streets and out to Barry's Bridge. He planned how he would tie the horse up in the long meadow which led down to the lough and prowl around the farmhouse and hide up in the big old barn where once he had slept after Granny Mogg's funeral. If he waited long enough she would come out, feed the hens, milk one or two of the cows to help out the farmhand, potter around and then go in to cook breakfast. He would see her, hear her – he would not touch her.

He turned the jaunting car onto the bridge and slowed the horse to a walk. The horse was not sorry; it was a good long run from Killarney to Cahersiveen and the horse would have much preferred its stable and a meal of hay, the harness hung up, a good stiff brush taking off the dirt of the day.

The moon was high in the sky, spreading its silver over the whole black landscape. The lough below him was as bright as a mirror, the moon swam on its surface and sent arrows and spears of white light dancing over the water.

He reined in and leaned over to look deep into the water, then looked away – and there was her face, not a foot from his, staring at him as though she could not believe her eyes. He stared back, taking in every detail of her from the dark, flowing dress to the smooth oval of her face, the lovely line of her throat.

'Finn?' It was scarcely more than a whisper but it thrilled through him like a lightning strike. 'Finn, is it really you?'

'Aye, my sweetheart, my dearest, it's really me. Is it really you, little Lucy?'

She nodded, her eyes still fixed on his face. They were dark as pits, shaded by moon-shadow, and he saw, suddenly, that her face was sad where it had once been merry, that the line of her lips drooped, that beneath the dark silk of her dress her figure was less rounded than he remembered it.

'Finn, why didn't you come back?'

'I did . . . but I kept hidden from you. I had to see you, ástor, but I dared not let you see me; it wouldn't have been right, see, when I knew we couldn't – couldn't be together.'

She lifted her chin, then put a hand on the side of the jaunting car. 'Why not? Why could we not be together?'

'Because I'm a tinker, always on the move, and you're the girl who owns all this . . .' he spread his hands, indicating the size of her acres. 'Your grandad died and you inherited; they talk, townsfolk.'

'And that is enough to stop you taking what's yours? A farm, a bit of talk?' She sounded not sad now but angry, scornful almost. He watched her small white hand on the edge of the jaunting car, saw her fingers tighten, the knuckles whiten. He looped the reins and leaned nearer her whilst the horse stood still, glad not to be galloping, to have a bit of a rest in the quiet, windy moonlight.

'Taking what's mine? Ah, Luceen . . . you don't know how I've wanted you.'

She shrugged. 'Talk, Finn, just talk. If you knew how I'd wanted you, now – that would be a very different story. Because I didn't know where you were or what you were doing, and a woman can't just go chasing after a feller, she has to wait. But you . . . you can't have wanted me at all at all.'

Her voice was light now, amused! Anger filled him, that the hugeness of his love, which had begun to take over his life, to hurt him with her absence day and night, should be reduced, by her, to mere talk. He leaned closer still, until his lips all but brushed her brow.

'Lucy Murphy, I t'ought I could live wit'out ye, I t'ought I would be better wit'out ye, but I was wrong. I need you as a bird needs the air under its wings . . . will ye come with me?'

She did not answer, but he could tell by the way she stood, by the set of her head on her slim, strong shoulders, by the look on her face, that her decision was taken, had been taken long ago.

He leaned out of the jaunting car and took her under the arms and lifted. She came easily up into the jaunting car and he stood her on the board floor and then reeled back as she threw her arms round his neck, hugging him hard, hard!

'Oh dear God, Finn, I thought I'd lost you, so I did! There's no one for me but you and I've always known it. There's no shame in me any more, I can tell you I love you, have always loved you, and if I'm makin' a fool of meself, I don't care!'

Finn gave a subdued whoop and put his hands to the back of his neck. He unhooked the bee-chain and put it, warm from his skin, round Lucy's white neck. Then he unlooped the reins and put a hard, strong arm about her waist and clicked to the horse.

'Now you're mine, alanna, for you wear Granny Mogg's gift, to be given only to my woman,' he said, and skilfully turned the jaunting car so that it faced towards the town. 'If you come wit' me now, it's an end to your settled, farming life. As Finn Delaney's wife all I can offer you is the road, Lucy Murphy!'

They clattered off the bridge and Finn turned the horse's head towards Killarney, towards the grey road which wound on and on and would take them, eventually, anywhere in Ireland that they wished to go. Lucy stood beside him, slim and strong in her beautiful silk dress with her pale hair tossed by the breeze of their going and her pale face set steady as she looked at the road ahead. Finn felt a stab of guilt and slowed the horse, to give her a last chance to change her mind, get down, and she gave an impatient little yelp and snatched the reins from his hands, bringing them down sharply on the bay mare's neck.

'Giddup, horse,' Lucy Murphy said fiercely. 'Finn Delaney, are you never goin' to tell me you love me?'

Finn threw back his head and laughed and then he let her keep the reins and put both arms round her and turned her to face him and began to kiss her.

The horse, finding the reins suddenly loose on its neck, cantered on for a bit and then slowed first to a trot, then a walk, then to stillness whilst it ate the rich grass at the roadside. And in the back of the jaunting car two young people who had loved and hungered for each other for many a long year, loved, and hungered no more.

Strawberry Fields

For Sally Mimnagh,

who gives more than she takes . . .

and for the famous Mimnagh cats!

Acknowledgements

My thanks go first to Mrs Violet McKay for telling me about her childhood spent around Stanley Road and Snowdrop Street, and then to Ruth Baker, whose family were brought up in the Walton Road area and who, as a Salvationist, was able to set my feet firmly on the right path when it came to writing about the Army.

Still in Liverpool, I am very grateful to Captain Ray Collings of the Salvation Army for all the help unstintingly given, and in particular for taking me and my husband to meet Colonel Martha Osborne, who not only has an incredibly detailed and accurate memory, invaluable to anyone writing about the past, but whose sense of fun and wonderful narrative style have given me enough material for the next book as well as this one – many, many thanks, Martha! Thanks, also, to Tom Officer for lending me books on Ireland, and to Chris Billing for the loan of computer parts when I was desperate.

And moving over to Ireland, thanks to the staff of the Gilbert Library, who took endless trouble to find the books and information I needed. Then there was Billy Doren, whose knowledge of Dublin – and the books written about it – was second to none, and last but not least, my thanks to Sally Mimnagh, who told me more about the Irish in one evening than I could have learned from books in a dozen years.

Chapter One

December 1924

It was Christmas Day, 1924, and it was snowing. What was more, the snow was lying. Sefton Park was a wonderland, the grass smoothly blanketed, the trees outlined in white. All the way down Aigburth Road Sara Cordwainer, who was twelve years old, admired the magical scene. She sat between her mother and father in their big Rolls-Royce motor car, with the chauffeur, Robson, cut off from them by a glass panel, and stared with all her might, convinced that the snow had come because she had been good – and because it was Christmas, naturally.

Already, her day was planned. Church first, which was much more exciting on Christmas Day than on any other day of the year, then round to Snowdrop Street to pick up her old nanny, and home for all the wonders of Christmas dinner – roast turkey, crackers, a plum pudding to which Cook would set light just before she brought it into the room – and at tea time, presents round the Christmas tree in the white drawing room.

There would be a present at church today, too. The Reverend Atwell had started giving the young members of his congregation a present at the Christmas morning service six years earlier, and now it was expected. They were religious presents, of course, but nonetheless welcome, because they heralded the start of Christmas proper, Sara thought. She had kept everything the Reverend Atwell had given her, had them still. The first one had been quite simple; a beautiful picture of Jesus in his long white robe with a number of small children clustered at his knee. *Suffer the little children* . . . the text beneath the picture read.

Ever since then the small, gaily wrapped parcels had been handed out at the church door as the congregation were leaving. Nanny, who had retired when Sara started school, didn't approve. 'You get enough presents without the church handin' you more stuff,' Nanny had said, that first time. 'There's kids down Kirkdale and Bootle who don't get one present come Christmas, let alone half a dozen. Why don't the Reverend Atwell think of them, eh, stead of givin' hand-outs to folk what've got more than they know what to do with?'

'I don't know,' Sara said, puzzled. Surely there was no such thing as a child without presents on Christmas Day? Parents, uncles, cousins, friends, they all gave Christmas presents, so surely, unless a child was positively steeped in sin, it would find something in its stocking on Christmas Day? 'If they came to our church they'd get a present though, Nanny. Why don't they come to our church?'

'Because they go to their own churches, that's what,' Nanny said with a snap in her voice. 'I'd like to see the reverend gentleman's face if the Carberys or the Sullivans turned up at 'is church!'

'Oh, well, if they go to their own churches, they'll get their presents there,' Sara said, very relieved. 'And if they don't go to church . . . but I expect they do, even the poor ones. Church is free, isn't it, Nanny? No one pays to go to church, it isn't like the tram.'

Nanny had explained to her that the small boys who hung on to the back of the trams did so because they had no pennies for a fare. 'They'd sooner ride inside, specially when it's cold an' snowy,' she said. 'But they need any pennies they get for other things . . . food, coal . . .'

But now, sitting snugly between her parents as the big car sailed smoothly churchwards, Sara was thinking more about the joys of Christmas than about Nanny's disapproval of the Reverend Atwell. At Christmas there was lovely food, nuts and chocolates on the sideboard, a big bowl of fruit which anyone could eat. Children were not usually encouraged to eat rich food, but Christmas was different. Why, this very morning schoolroom breakfast had included bacon and egg as well as the more usual groats and bread and butter. Sara was not particularly interested in food, but she was very conscious of atmosphere, and she loved the sparkle and excitement of Christmas, the fact that Nanny came to stay for two whole days, the festive air, even the groups of ragged children singing carols. The servants usually gave such singers mince pies and sometimes pennies, though Sara's parents did not approve.

'It encourages them to beg for money instead of working for it,' Sara's mother had said, and her father, equally against the practice, said that children were the responsibility of their own parents, not the parents of others.

But even so, Sara felt unusually content. She did not always enjoy school holidays, but this year she had spent a lot of time with Jane Carew, one of the maids. She and Jane had spent a happy afternoon threading peanuts on strings which they then hung outside the schoolroom window. Watching the blue tits, chaffinches and other little birds pecking contentedly at the nuts was a winter pleasure which never palled.

The car began to slow as it reached the street upon which the church was situated. There were people outside already, talking and laughing, and as the Cordwainers got out of the motor snow began to fall once more.

'More snow! I'll make a snowman in the park after luncheon,' Sara said, scarcely realising she had spoken aloud until her mother rounded on her.

'In the park, on Christmas Day? I don't think so, Sara, that wouldn't be at all suitable. Besides, you'll be busy entertaining Nanny.'

'Well, the garden, then,' Sara said equably. 'Nanny can watch; I'll make one in the garden.'

Her father turned and looked down at her. It struck Sara suddenly that he looked at her as though he didn't like her very much. So she smiled at him questioningly, though she had to tilt her head back to do so, for he was a tall, thin man. Disappointingly however, he did not smile back: he frowned. 'Not the garden,' he said sharply. 'Snow is only beautiful when it's untrodden. I won't have you churning up the snow in the garden. Get Nanny to show you a card game . . . or you could read to her.'

The chauffeur, about to close the car door behind them, gave Sara a most peculiar look. What a day it was turning out to be for looks, Sara thought, astonished. If she had not known what a very fortunate child she was she would have thought that Robson's was a pitying look. He cleared his throat and touched his cap deferentially, then spoke.

'If Miss would like to construct a snowman in the back yard, sir, I'd be happy to clear up after her. I meant to brush it clear of snow this afternoon, in any case.'

'Very well, Robson,' Mr Cordwainer said wearily.

'Sara, you may play in the back yard if you wish, after luncheon.'

'But only for half an hour,' Mrs Cordwainer broke in petulantly. 'Nanny has a snooze after luncheon, but I don't intend to find myself entertaining her when she awakes. Sara really must be indoors again by then.'

'All right, Mother, I'll come in as soon as Nanny wakes,' Sara said soothingly. 'There's Mrs Buckman, she's beckoning you.'

Mrs Cordwainer, who had seemed in a poor sort of mood for Christmas Day, brightened.

'Adolphus, I *must* have a word with Beatrice,' she purred, her voice, which had been lemony in the car when the subject of snow was raised, suddenly turning creamy. 'Wait, Sara.'

Sara waited. Her father moved off to talk to a couple of dark-coated, solemn-looking men, the car moved away with Robson at the wheel, and though she glanced round hopefully, no one she knew came into sight. Most of the congregation were already in the church, she supposed, and she edged nearer the grown-ups.

Then she saw the girl, standing against the church wall with a baby on her hip. She must have been thirteen or fourteen, older than Sara anyway, and she couldn't guess at the baby's age, not being knowledgeable about such things, but the girl didn't look old enough to be the child's mother. She's probably minding her, Sara thought, moving a little closer. Martha, in my class at school, minds her little sister sometimes.

It was then that she noticed the baby's feet. They were bare, and a horrid purplish blue colour. And when Sara looked down, the big girl didn't have proper shoes either, only a pair of cracked and gaping boots, many sizes too large. And neither was warmly clad, though the baby did have a thin blanket half-wrapped round her, from which the blue, bruised-looking feet protruded.

The big girl saw her staring and moved closer herself. She smiled. She didn't have very many front teeth and those that she did have were broken and grey-looking. But there was something in her smile . . . it made Sara want to cry and also to hit something or someone very hard, though she could not have said why she felt either emotion.

'Hello, chuck,' the girl said. 'You goin' into church?'

'That's right. In a minute, when my mother's stopped talking to her friends.'

The girl smiled more broadly. 'Oh aye, I've gorra mam like that an' all. Talk the 'ind leg off of a donkey, mine.' She turned the baby so that it faced her. 'You know what I mean, don't you, our Moll? Our mam clacks from mornin' till night, don't she, queen?'

The baby gurgled and a thin little hand appeared above the blanket. The hand patted the girl's cheek, then withdrew quickly back into whatever warmth the blanket offered.

'Well, ain't you a one?' the girl marvelled. She turned back to Sara. 'Understands every word, she does . . . clever little bugger!'

'She's very pretty,' Sara said, more from politeness than anything, but when she looked into the baby's face, she saw she had spoken no more than the truth. The baby had skin like milk, big, blue eyes and soft little tendrils of red-gold hair which curled all over her small head. 'How old is she?'

'She'll be a year old in February,' the girl said, then added, in a very much quieter voice, 'If she lives, acourse.'

'If she . . . is she ill, then?' Sara asked, appalled by

the matter-of-factness of the remark. 'She's awfully cold, her feet are quite blue.'

'Nah, she's not ill; but she only 'as buttermilk, an' the clinic nurse says it ain't enough,' the girl explained. 'Me mam won't feed 'em for long, says it drags 'er down, and me da's out o' work, see – an' when 'e's workin' chances are 'e won't bring nothin' 'ome, 'cos 'e likes 'is bevvy, does our da, and that costs.' She sighed. 'You don't know what to want for the best, eh? If 'e's sober 'e beats us up, if 'e's drunk there's nothin' to eat. Why, me sister Grace – she's goin' on four – got a bang across the 'ead last night what knocked 'er cold, just about. Still, the ould feller went off drinkin' this mornin', so I left Grace lie. Me da won't go 'ome till the boozers close, now.' She jiggled the baby on her hip. 'We's glad of it, ain't we, our Moll? In fact it would be a good Christmas if we 'ad something other than buttermilk for the littl'un 'ere.'

'Doesn't the baby drink tea? Or orange juice?' Sara asked. Now that she was so close she could smell a rather nasty, sour sort of smell hovering round the couple. She had never heard of buttermilk, but it sounded all right. 'What does she eat? Bread and butter? Oh, but today it'll be roast turkey, I suppose, and plum pudding. Do babies eat things like that?'

The girl shrugged. 'I dunno. She ain't never 'ad the chanst. Nor me, neither.' She gestured towards the church porch, towards which the congregation were now drifting. 'You'd best gerrof, your mam'll give you stick, she's hollered you twice ... you are Sara, I s'pose?'

'Oh goodness ... thanks,' Sara said, turning away. As she turned the girl put a hand out, then hastily withdrew it and tucked it into the cloaklike garment which she wore round her shoulders. It was a man's jacket with the sleeves cut off and the armholes roughly stitched closed, Sara realised. But the movement, suddenly, said all the things that the girl had never put into words. *I'm hungry,* it said. *I don't know where my next meal's coming from, nor the baby's, neither. And you're so warm in your pretty red coat and hat, your nice woolly gloves . . . don't go just yet, don't leave me out here in the cold!*

'Sara! Come here at once, please, your father and I are about to take our places.' Mrs Cordwainer's voice was that of someone used to being obeyed, which was probably why she turned straight round and went into the church, her hand tucked into her husband's elbow, enabling Sara to turn quickly to her new friend, stripping off her white woollen gloves as she did so. She thrust them at the older girl.

'Here, take these, put them on the baby's feet, they're ever so nice and warm. And . . .' her hand plunged into her pocket and came out again with a bright, shiny shilling. ' . . . Here's something for Christmas, just a little present. Buy some milk!'

The girl took the gloves wonderingly, turning them over and over, then she smiled brilliantly at Sara and took the shilling as well. This time, the smile turned her small, pale face into a thing of such beauty that Sara didn't even notice the state of her teeth.

'Thanks . . . you are good, I 'opes you don't gerrin trouble for 'elpin' me like this. Are you sure . . . But I sees you are . . . I'll get some milk right away, Moll shall 'ave a Christmas treat, a bottle of it, warmed all nice. Me an' 'er's ever so grateful, Sara.'

'What's your name?' Sara asked shyly, preparing to depart. 'I know the baby's Moll, but what are you called?'

'She's Mollie Carbery and I'm Jess,' the girl said.

'We're from Kirkdale, we ain't from these parts, we've walked a good ways to get 'ere, Moll an' me. Kept our minds off of our bellies, see? Now we'll walk 'ome, and we'll 'ave somethin' to look forward to, eh, Moll? Some milk for you, an' mebbe a loaf or a cake for me. Ta, Sara.'

'Bye,' Sara called softly. She ran into the church porch, then slowed to a decorous walk, glancing over her shoulder as she did so. The girl, with the baby hitched up on her hip once more, was making her way along the road, walking fast considering her burden.

Sara slid into the pew beside her mother and dropped to her knees. Her mother cast her an angry look but said nothing; there were people too close who might overhear. And presently the service began, with pomp and ceremony and some of the nicer carols. And during the third carol the sidesmen took the collection and Sara suddenly remembered where the shilling had come from. It had been her collection, and now it was being handed over a counter somewhere, in exchange for milk and food.

She watched the plate approaching. It was a huge affair and today it was well laden with money, notes even. I'll pretend to put something in, Sara thought, delving into her pocket. I'll have to, because church isn't a good place to explain something to a grown-up.

But she was saved by the collection itself as it turned out. Mrs Cordwainer saw the plate, heavily laden, making its way towards her, and obviously realised that her daughter's shilling would stand out as being the smallest contribution so far. She nudged her husband and said something to him in a low voice, there was a moment's scuffling, and then Sara felt something large and round being pressed into her palm.

'Put it in the plate, dear,' her mother hissed. 'I believe I gave you the wrong coin this morning.'

Sara did not argue. She put the heavy silver coin into the plate and passed it along to her mother, then her father, watching them contributing generously with a feeling of puzzlement. It was all wrong! They had ignored the shabby little girl with the baby in her arms even when they had seen their daughter talking to her. They refused to give money to carol singers, saying the children were begging, and even grudged them the mince pies and hot cocoa which the staff handed out. Yet they put generous amounts of money into the collection plate at church and saw to it that she, too, gave sufficient.

My parents are definitely Christians and therefore good people, Sara told herself. They go to church every Sunday, and Mother goes to sewing circle and makes clothes for the heathen in Africa. When the Liverpool Goodfellows came round collecting for Christmas parcels for the very poor, her parents always put money into the box. Yet they had not even seemed to notice Jess and the baby.

I'll ask Nanny why they don't give to Liverpool children, Sara decided as the congregation got to its collective feet to sing the last hymn. She'll know, and she'll explain it to me. Only I do wish that someone, either my parents or someone else's, had seen Jess and baby Mollie and given them some money, too. Perhaps as much as a whole half-crown . . . imagine what they could have bought with that!

And when the service finished the Cordwainer family made their way out of the church, pausing in the porch to wish everyone the compliments of the season, whilst Reverend Atwell handed Sara a small flat parcel, gaily wrapped, and told her to be good and to enjoy her Christmas.

I never thought, I ought to have told Jess to come in and bring Mollie; probably the reverend would have given them both presents, Sara thought, assuring the clergyman that she would be good and would try to enjoy her Christmas. 'But there were two little girls outside . . .' she was beginning when the reverend switched away from her to the next child, behaving as though she had not spoken at all. More puzzled than ever, Sara turned away. How very odd grown-ups were, to be sure. They preached goodness, kindness, but they didn't appear to practise what they preached, not even clergymen.

Outside, the snow was still falling, but more gently now. Robson wasn't in the car but he came hurrying over to it when he saw them.

'Sorry, sir,' he said to Sara's father, opening the back door with a flourish. 'I never went out of sight of the car, but I had to keep movin', else I'd have frozen stiff in me seat.'

'You could have exercised in your seat, I suppose,' Mr Cordwainer said irritably. 'I do trust you've not been drinking?'

'No, indeed, sir, I never touch a drop,' Robson said and Sara, whose eyes seemed to have been opened today by her encounter with Jess, realised that Robson, a grown-up, was actually frightened of her father. Why? What could her father do to Robson, who seemed a sturdy, independent type of man? Nothing, surely! Except dismiss him.

Jess had said her father was out of work and had implied that this meant there was no money for milk. Sara frowned. Robson had no babies who needed milk, but if he lost his job he would also lose his room over the garage and the meals he ate in the kitchen with the rest of the domestic staff.

'I'm glad to hear it,' Mr Cordwainer said, but he said it as if he did not believe a word and Sara saw the chauffeur's unease deepen. Quickly, without stopping to think, she burst into speech.

'Wasn't it a lovely service, Mother? I liked the last hymn . . . I wonder what my present is, this year?' She turned to the chauffeur. 'What did the other drivers do, Robson, whilst we were in church? What did Mr Hartley's chauffeur do?'

Robson turned to her eagerly. 'They walked, same as I did, Miss Sara. We must ha' covered a couple of miles, I'd say. Mr Hartley's man suggested the walk, an' he said we looked like a brigade of guards, so smart in our uniforms, all marchin' along the pavements swingin' our arms to keep warm.'

Mr Hartley was very rich; he had a house in the South of France and his wife wore mink, wonderful sables and Paris dresses. Their daughter was being educated in Switzerland and their son was at Eton. None of this meant much to Sara, but she knew her mother always talked about the Hartleys with a sort of awe, as though they were special people, like the King and Queen, or the handsome young Prince of Wales. So she imagined that her parents would be pleased that Robson had followed the Hartley chauffeur's lead.

Mr Cordwainer helped his wife into the vehicle, then pushed Sara in ahead of him. He said, through the glass panel once Robson had run round and jumped behind the wheel, 'Oh well, if Hartley's man went walking I suppose there can be no harm in it. Home, Robson.'

'No, Robson, *not* home,' Mrs Cordwainer interrupted pettishly. 'Dear me, Adolphus, it's Christmas Day!

Drive to number three Snowdrop Street, Robson. We are to pick up Mrs Prescott at that address.'

The chauffeur touched his peaked cap and put the car into gear. He had started it as soon as they appeared so that the engine was purring softly when they reached the vehicle and now it moved slowly away from the kerb as Mrs Cordwainer leaned back against the dark leather upholstery and heaved a sigh.

'I shall be glad when Christmas is over,' she said crossly. 'Well, Sara, aren't you going to open your parcel?'

'Yes, Mother, if I may,' Sara said. She was still feeling annoyed with Reverend Atwell but that was no reason for not opening a present. She untied the scarlet ribbon and unwrapped the paper, to reveal a cheaply bound copy of a book entitled *Bible Stories for the Little Ones*.

'Very nice,' Mrs Cordwainer said in a bored voice. 'How good of the Reverend Atwell.'

'I've already got a copy,' Sara said mutinously. 'Can I give it to someone else, Mother?'

'Certainly not. What would people think?' Mrs Cordwainer said at once. 'How very ungrateful you are, Sara.'

'I don't mean to be. But what good are two copies of the same book to me?' Sara said rather plaintively. Inside her head she added, *and it's a rotten book, too,* but she knew better than to say it aloud. 'I daresay there are lots of children who would love a copy of their own.' Her opinion of the Reverend Atwell had not been high since he had ignored her in the porch, but any lingering liking had just nose-dived. He had given her the same book two years running, which must mean that he didn't put any thought at all into those carefully wrapped little presents. 'It's greedy to have more than one needs of anything,' she added craftily. 'You've often said so, Mother.'

'Oh, very well, but don't say anything to Nanny,' her mother instructed. 'Goodness, it's started to snow again – I do trust we'll get Nanny home again when her stay is over without too much trouble.'

I wish she could stay for ever, Sara thought wistfully, but once again, knew better than to say it out loud. Mrs Prescott was a duty to her parents, not a pleasure.

The car was driving very slowly now through the whirling snow and Sara's attention left the passengers and went to the scene outside. Normally she would have been watching out for familiar landmarks but now, because of the snow, she scarcely recognised anything. But she knew where they were when they came on to Stanley Road, with the beautiful smell of railways and docks getting stronger the nearer they got to their destination.

Sara had asked Nanny once why all the streets in her area had such pretty names. Snowdrop, Crocus, Pansy, Daisy, Woodbine, Harebell and many more.

'It's much prettier than Aigburth Road, or the Boulevard,' she complained. 'I'd rather live somewhere called after a flower any day, Nanny.'

'Aye, the names are pretty enough, but that's about all you can say,' Nanny assured her. 'They're mean streets, narrow and noisy, and the folk what live on 'em don't have much. Still, what they have they share, and they stand by each other in times of trouble. You can't say fairer than that.'

The car crawled carefully down Stanley Street as far as the corner of Snowdrop. Robson slowed, peered into the side street, then stopped the car. You could see at a glance that there had been no attempt, here, to clear the snow and down the middle of the road was what looked suspiciously like a slide; at least four or five rough-looking boys were sailing along it with shouts of pleasure.

Robson turned and slid back the glass panel. 'I dussen't go no further, sir,' he announced. 'If I stop down there I doubt I'd get 'er goin' again. You stay here and I'll go and fetch Mrs Prescott out.'

'I'll go,' Sara said eagerly. She adored Nanny and didn't want to waste a moment of her company and also the thought of running down the street and past the sliding boys was fun, an adventure. But Mr Cordwainer nipped that in the bud at once.

'No you don't,' he said grimly. 'Young ladies don't go gadding about in this type of area without an escort. Besides, you'll get soaked and I don't want the upholstery to get wet.' He turned back to the chauffeur. 'Very well, Robson, go and get Mrs Prescott. We'll wait here.'

Robson cast a quick glance in the back of the car. 'What number did you say, sir? Not all the houses have their numbers displayed . . .'

'I know the house,' Sara said eagerly, recognising a cue when she heard one. 'I'll go with you, Robson, and show you the house.'

She was out of the car and walking along the pavement beside the chauffeur before either of her parents had opened their mouths to argue and indeed, as she closed the door behind her, her mother was talking to her father about Mrs Aubain, whose new hair-style had caused much comment in church that morning.

'Thanks, Robson,' Sara said, glancing up at the chauffeur as they walked.

'Thank *you*, Miss,' Robson said. He grinned at her and Sara grinned back, both entirely understanding the meaning behind the words. 'Mr Hartley was the magic word, eh? I must remember that. Your Gran's house is the last but one, isn't it?'

'My Nanny's house ... yes, it's the one with the brass knocker,' Sara admitted. Her grandmother, a very fierce, correct old lady, lived in a large house in Crosby and enjoyed ill-health; it would have been lovely had Mrs Prescott been her grandmother, but you couldn't have everything, Sara reasoned. Grandmother could have been worse – she could have lived nearer, for instance. 'And it's the loveliest brass knocker, too, a dolphin it is. When I was little, I had to jump to reach it, but now, of course, I just go on tiptoe.'

The sliding boys stopped sliding to stare as they passed and one of them shouted, 'It's Mrs Prescott's Sara – wotcher, Sara! Ain't it great to 'ave snow, eh?'

'Hello, Jackie,' Sara said, delighted to recognise the speaker. He was a Callogan, his mother and father and a great many children lived just up the road from Nanny. 'Yes, the snow's good, isn't it? And how are you? How's Bet and Bert and the others? And your mam and da, of course.'

'We're awright, ta,' Jackie said. 'You awright, Sara?'

'Very well, thanks,' Sara said. 'It's Christmas, so Mrs Prescott's coming to stay. I love it when she comes.'

'When is you goin' to come to Snowdrop Street, then?' Jackie said at once, leaving the slide and his companions and falling into step beside Sara and Robson. 'You ain't been 'ere for a 'undred *years* just about. I 'pose your mam don't want you playin' wi' the likes of us.'

Sara felt her cheeks burn; once, she had come to Snowdrop Street whenever her parents felt like going away for a few days, and she had been in seventh heaven, but ever since discovering that Nanny let her play out her parents had refused all her desperate requests to stay with Nanny Prescott.

But it could have been worse. At least Nanny Prescott still visited them in Aigburth Road, so Sara had a good deal to be thankful for. Being denied even the solace of Nanny's down-to-earth, outspoken company would have been unbearable.

Now, she turned to Jackie. 'They say I'm too old to play out, it's for kids,' she said apologetically. 'But Mrs Prescott doesn't think that. Tell Bet I'm asking for her, and perhaps, one day, I'll come and stay again.'

Jackie dropped back as they drew level with number three. 'I'll tell 'er,' he said resignedly. 'Ta-ra, queen.'

'Ta-ra, Jackie,' Sara echoed, and saw the chauffeur's lips twitch, but then she was standing on tiptoe and reaching for the knocker, excitement flooding through her. She seized the brass dolphin and brought him down in a quick rat-tat, then stood back, but Mrs Prescott had obviously been watching for them for the door shot open to reveal her standing in the doorway, her round and rosy face breaking into a beaming smile.

'Sara, love! Give your old Nanny a big hug, then!'

'Oh, Nanny,' Sara gasped, hurling herself into the older woman's arms. 'Oh, Nanny, I do love you! Isn't it grand that it's snowing? Oh, Nanny, I wish you could stay for ever . . . where's your baggage? I'll carry it.'

'Baggage, child? But I'm only comin' to Aigburth Road for the day,' Mrs Prescott said. 'Your mam invited me; she said *for the day* when she wrote.'

Sara stared. 'But Nanny, you always come for Christmas, that's today and Boxing Day, sometimes the day after that, too. Oh, Mother was saying earlier that . . ' She remembered just what it was her mother had said and hesitated before completing the sentence. ' . . That

I was to be sure to keep you entertained,' she said rather lamely.

Mrs Prescott was already in her brown coat with boots on her feet, furry mittens on her hands and a felt hat pulled down firmly over her greying hair. Now she put Sara gently to one side and walked through the doorway, then turned and carefully locked the front door behind her.

'We'll talk about it,' she said diplomatically. 'Mebbe there's a mistake. Now are you going to carry my handbag, dearie? Because there's a little present for you in there.'

'I will carry it, gladly, but the best present's you, Nanny,' Sara said rapturously. 'Oh, just knowing you were coming to stay makes it a good Christmas, and now the snow's just making it perfect! Say you'll stay the night, though, Nanny! I couldn't bear it if you were to go home and leave me all alone again.'

'Alone? And you with two good parents and a house full of servants?' Mrs Prescott said, but she looked pleased, nevertheless. 'Good morning, Mr Robson; nice to see you again.'

'Good morning, Mrs Prescott,' the chauffeur said politely, touching his peaked cap. 'No bag, today?'

'Not today. I'll have a word with Mrs Cordwainer when we reach the car but I'm certain her letter specified Christmas Day itself. Take my arm, Sara, it's really slippery and I don't fancy fallin' on me bum before all them boys.'

Sara, laughing, took the older woman's arm on one side and the chauffeur, after the slightest of hesitations, took her other arm. Walking carefully, for the icy pavement was treacherous, the three of them made their way back to the car.

'Madam,' Robson said, throwing open the passenger door. 'If you'll just climb inside . . .'

Mrs Prescott got in nimbly and settled back in her seat, then turned to address the Cordwainers, shooting back the glass panel in order to do so.

'A merry Christmas to you both! I've not packed a bag since your letter just said Christmas Day, Mrs Cordwainer.'

Mrs Cordwainer leaned forward. Sara, watching her, saw the colour rise beneath the powder on her mother's cheeks. 'Surely I said *for Christmas*, Nanny? In our book, that means for the Christmas holiday, which is both days. But since you've not packed a bag . . .'

Sara opened her mouth to protest but her father spoke before she could do so. 'Letty, my dear . . . it won't take Mrs Prescott a moment to pack a bag. Indeed, the child can help her.' He leaned forward. 'If Robson takes my wife and myself home now, and returns for you and Sara in an hour . . . would that be sufficient time for you to pack a bag?'

Sara could have jumped for joy but she knew better than to do such a thing. Instead, she smiled demurely at Nanny, though with pleading in her eyes. Oh, let Nanny say yes! She could go back into number three Snowdrop Street when Nanny did and check that her own little room upstairs, where she had stayed as a child, was still just as it ought to be! She could open the window and lean out and see that much-loved, much-remembered view of the railway, then the docks, then the gleam of the Mersey! Sometimes, on a clear day, the blue line of the Welsh hills could be seen against the sky . . . sometimes she was sure she could see New Brighton, almost hear the funfair!

'Nanny?' Sara's hand was on the door.

Nanny had been looking militant but suddenly she relented. She smiled and put her own hand on the doorhandle. 'An hour will be adequate,' she said firmly. 'Thank you, Mr Cordwainer, I'd be happy to stay for Boxing Day.'

It seemed odd to enter the well-loved little house to find the kettle not singing on the hearth and no fire in the grate, though it was neatly laid with sheets of the *Echo* scrumpled up and kindling sticks and small pieces of coal on top of them. Nanny had clearly not lit the fire that morning for the room struck chill and Sara shivered even as Nanny began to strip off her gloves, take off her coat, and carefully remove her black felt hat.

'Nanny, I know the fire's out, but . . . well, if you really thought you were coming back tonight, wouldn't you just have damped it down? And it's cold in here, you couldn't have had a nice breakfast or a cup of tea or anything! Did you really mean to come home here tonight?'

Nanny shook her head and tutted reproachfully, but Sara saw she was smiling. 'You're a knowing one, queen! Your mam invited me for Christmas Day, but I thought she'd probably stretch it to Boxing Day too, if I played me cards right. It's just that I don't like to be took for granted, chuck. Oh, I don't kid meself, I know I'm not exactly as welcome as the flowers in May, but I don't see much of you, nor you of me, eh? So I thought I'd call your mam's bluff.'

'She can be funny, sometimes,' Sara admitted. 'Where's your bag, then?'

'Behind the sofa,' Mrs Prescott said. 'Eh, now what's me pride done for us this time, Sara? We've gorran hour to kill in this freezin' cold house . . . what say we pop next door, have a warm by the Rushtons' fire? It's Christmas Day, we shan't get turned away.'

'We wouldn't on any day,' Sara said. 'I daresay we could go anywhere here and be made welcome, eh, Nanny?'

'Oh aye, what we have we share,' Mrs Prescott said. She headed for the front door. 'But I'd not trouble some of 'em . . . the Carberys, for one. Eh, wharra life they lead, them! A baby every year, himself out o' work this past six months, and scarce a mouthful of bread in the house most days, no matter how they try to mek ends meet.'

'I met someone called Carbery,' Sara said. 'It can't be the same family, though. They were outside church this morning.'

'No, it wouldn't be them; too far to walk on empty stomachs,' Mrs Prescott said. 'This is a poor neighbourhood, but the Carbs have touched bottom, I reckon. Still, maybe Stan'll get some work in the new year. And maybe he'll not drink all his money away this time, if he gets a job.' She glanced sharply down at Sara's hands. 'Where's your gloves, Miss?'

'I gave them to the girl I was telling you about outside the church,' Sara said rather diffidently. 'She had a baby in her arms, Nanny, and the baby's feet were *blue*. She was so pretty, but so very cold . . . I gave her my collection, too,' she added rather guiltily.

'You did? Good for you, chuck,' Mrs Prescott said decidedly. She opened the front door and ushered Sara out. 'Give a knock next door, and I'll explain what's happened. What did your mam say?'

'Oh, she'd given me a shilling, but when she saw the plate I think she realised that everyone else had given more, so she slipped me a whole half-crown. I put that in and she probably didn't realise I hadn't added the shilling as well,' Sara said. 'She's not noticed the gloves yet, though. I was lucky, because she hates it when I lose gloves.'

'You can say you left 'em at my house, and by the time Christmas is over she'll likely have forgot all about them,' Mrs Prescott said comfortably. 'Which gloves were they?'

'Oh, Nanny, I'm sorry, they were the pretty white angora ones you knitted me at the start of the autumn term,' Sara said guiltily. 'But the baby's feet were so cold . . .'

'You did right,' Mrs Prescott assured her. 'Them as have should give freely to them as haven't. I spent years tryin' to din that into my employers and their children, but it passed over most of their heads like water off a duck's arse. Seems you're kindly by nature, Sara.'

'Some people don't seem to care much about the people near them, Nanny . . .' Sara began, but at that point the door of number five flew open and a thin, angular woman with a huge smile and very few teeth shouted, 'Eh, if it ain't Annie Prescott and the little gal!' and pulled them both into the warm, overcrowded little room.

'Eh, Marj, we're frozen stiff an' we'd kill for a nice cuppa,' Mrs Prescott said, holding out her hands towards the blazing fire. 'I'm off to the Cordwainers' for a couple of days so me fire's out, no chance of anything 'ot. Believe it or not I'd forgot to pack me bag, so they've gone off 'ome whiles me and Sara here gets a few things together.'

'Kate, gi's a couple o' cups,' Mrs Rushton shouted and an indistinct voice replied that she'd not be a minute, she'd just gorra gerra brew on the go. 'Now,

Annie, what've you been up to, eh? You was sayin' only yesterday that you was packed an' ready.'

'Aye, well . . .' Mrs Prescott broke off as a spindly girl in her mid-teens came into the room, carefully holding two chipped white cups which steamed invitingly. 'Oh, Kate, luv, you're worth your weight in gold! We're that thirsty, Sara an' me, that our tongues are hanging down to our knees. And on Christmas Day, an' all!'

'Auntie Annie, you're always up to somethin',' the girl said jokingly, handing both females a cup. 'Sit yourselves down . . . I'll bring you t'rough a mince pie presently, or a piece of apple pasty if you'd rather.'

'Thanks, queen, but it 'ud only spoil our dinners, and the tea's a treat, jest what the doctor ordered,' Mrs Prescott said, sipping the scalding liquid. 'Eh, isn't a decent cuppa a treat, our Sara? Bet you never get better'n this at 'ome?'

'No, I never do,' Sara said, not quite truthfully, for she did not enjoy strong tea, much preferring milk or the delicious lemonade that Cook made for the schoolroom. 'It warms me up right down to my toes, Nanny.'

'Aye, that's right, a nice cuppa's a real winter warmer,' Mrs Prescott agreed. 'Eh, there's good smells comin' from your kitchen, Marj – can I smell a roast?'

'You can. With three of me boys in work, Kate here bringin' home an apron full of goodies from the Bellmans, and Alf workin' regular on the railway, we can afford a decent Christmas. I cooked the goose up at Sample's yesterday, now it's heatin' through whiles the spuds an' the cabbage boils. Aye, life's not so bad, this year.' She beamed at Mrs Prescott and Sara. 'I could give up the pub cleanin' tomorrer, if I'd a mind – we'd scarce miss the money.'

'Aye. But there's others not so lucky,' Mrs Prescott

said soberly. 'Them next door to you; things ain't so good when you've a dozen kids, none of 'em workin' yet, and your old man's not done a hand's turn for six months.'

'A dozen kids? In a house the same size as yours, Nanny?' Sara started to say, then stopped short. There were quite a lot of kids in this house and they all had to sleep somewhere. Either in the decent front, or the small back, or in the slip of a room which Sara thought of as her own. But . . . twelve kids and two grownups? How on earth did they manage? She looked interrogatively at her nanny, who was placidly drinking her tea from the cracked and handleless cup.

'I know, poor souls,' Mrs Rushton said. 'But there ain't many of us what haven't known the pain of an empty belly, so you do your best. Alf took 'em round a leg o' mutton yesterday and some veggies; they'll not sup on blind scouse this Christmas at any rate.'

'It won't go far between fourteen of 'em,' Kate said. She was a plain, cheerful girl with straggly hair and ears which stuck out, Sara thought, like a car with both doors open.

Mrs Prescott was about to reply when the door burst open and a crowd of kids surged into the room. They were all thin, with untidy hair, and they were all grinning from ear to ear.

'Is the dinner cooked?' shouted an urchin of about Sara's age. 'The smell's that good, Mam, I dunno as I can wait another second!'

'Well, try,' Mrs Rushton said grimly, 'because norra mouthful will any of yez get until your da's home. But if you're real starvin', there's a new loaf on the kitchen table and a packet o' margarine . . . there might be some jam an' all if you look behind the meat safe.'

The kids surged out of the room, shouting and laughing, and Kate turned to her visitor.

'Our Seth works at the jam factory; that's where I'll work when I leave school,' she said, sitting down beside Sara on the lumpy sofa. 'They give you jam cheap, sometimes, so we're better off'n some. Not bad, eh? Where'll you work when you're growed?'

'I'm only twelve,' Sara said. 'I haven't thought, not yet. I don't have any brothers or sisters, you see, so I can't work with them.'

'Only twelve? I'd ha' put you at thirteen, mebbe fourteen,' Kate said flatteringly. 'They grows 'em big up your way, queen. Have a mince pie!'

The pies looked good, but Sara was still uneasily conscious of what Jess had told her. Not everyone could eat, even when they were hungry. These people seemed happy and successful and talked cheerfully, but the mother hadn't offered the kids pies, it had been bread and margarine. She was being offered a pie because she was a visitor – but she would go home presently and have a very large luncheon, with plum pudding and fruit to follow. And there would be boxes of chocolates and heaps and heaps of nuts and at teatime more food, more treats.

'No, thanks, Kate,' she said, therefore, 'I don't want to spoil my lunch.'

And when they'd finished their tea Nanny said they'd best be getting back because she didn't want anyone thinking she'd not had a bag to pack . . . more laughter . . . and they had said their farewells and left, with Christmas wishes ringing in their ears.

One thing struck Sara as odd, though. As they were about to open Mrs Prescott's front door Mrs Rushton stuck her head out into the cold and shouted after them, a halo of steam rising from her open mouth.

'Ask your Letty if she ever thinks about the Sunday school treat, the year we was twelve,' she shouted. 'We 'ad some fun on New Brighton funfair! Our Sid remembers it an' all, he often asks after Letty.'

Sara, who knew that Nanny Prescott had once been her own mother's nanny, pricked up her ears. If Mrs Rushton was referring to her mother, she would have liked to hear a bit more! She glanced enquiringly at Nanny, but the older woman was inserting her key in the front door, turning it . . .

'That's nice. I'll tell her,' Mrs Prescott said vaguely, and then she had unlocked the door and they were inside the chilly little room once more, and Mrs Prescott sat at a chair in the window to watch for the chauffeur whilst Sara ran upstairs to take a look at the front bedroom.

It was lovely, running up the narrow, creaking stairs, turning on the tiny landing and going into the slip of a front room. Sara felt a warm glow envelope her; she had been so happy here! She had sometimes felt that the only times she was really alive were when she was with Mrs Prescott, sleeping in the little front room, kneeling on the floor on a summer's evening with her nose pressed to the glass, staring out at the railway, the docks, the river.

She had stared out at life, too, passing constantly in the street below. Kids at play, adults on their way to and from the public houses on Stanley Street, the occasional drunk lurching along, taking a short-cut from Commercial Road through into Stanley, a dog, sauntering along behind its owner, sniffing at walls and lamp posts, lifting a leg, breaking into a trot.

There wasn't a lot of life on Aigburth Road, or if there was she was unaware of it, because the grounds of her home protected her from such doses of reality. And the nursery with its barred window was high up, and lonely, too, very different from the little bedroom on Snowdrop Street. So now Sara knelt on the floor and pressed her nose to the glass as, outside, the flakes of snow continued to fall.

It wasn't easy, on such a day, to see her favourite view, but it was just possible. There it was, outside the window, her own particular, beloved slice of life. But today there was little or no movement from the railway – presumably no trains, or very few, ran on Christmas Day – and even the Mersey, steel-grey against the downward-swirling flakes, was quiet.

Still. Despite it being Christmas Day there was some movement in the street. The sliding boys had scattered and gone as the snowstorm increased but someone was even now making her way along the pavement, head shrugged down into shoulders, bundles firmly grasped in skinny arms. It was a girl, skinny and underfed, with something wrapped in a blanket on one arm and a soggy paper bag from which large objects – they looked like loaves – protruded. Sara had been breathing on the glass and fogging it up; now she rubbed frantically, trying to make herself a proper peephole. Yes, there was the figure, passing closer now, almost directly beneath the window . . . frantically, Sara tried to get the window open, she leapt to her feet and wrestled with the little round latch that locked the top half of the sash in place, got it back, shoved and pushed at the bottom half . . . it was opening, icy air – and a great deal of snow – was rushing into the room, Sara was leaning out, head and shoulders into the storm, her voice rising.

'Jess! Jess, it's me, Sara . . . oh, Jess, do look up!'

But Jess, if it was Jess, continued to slog along

through the snow, head down, her shopping clutched fiercely to her skinny breast. And the child, if it was the child, was now completely immersed in the thin blanket.

Reluctantly, Sara withdrew into the room once more. It couldn't have been Jess, it would have been too much of a coincidence and anyway, if it had been, she would surely have recognised her own name and looked up?

Struggling to pull the window down again, rather conscience-stricken by the great wet patches of melting snow on the linoleum, Sara glanced once more at the fast disappearing figure – and promptly tried to push the window up once more. But by the time she had got it a couple of inches from the sill, it was too late. Girl and burden had disappeared.

'But it *was* Jess,' Sara told herself miserably, making her way downstairs in answer to Mrs Prescott's shout. 'It was Jess, because the baby's feet were sticking out under the blanket – and I could see my white angora gloves!'

Chapter Two

Jess was as near freezing as a human being could be, she decided as she walked as fast as she could along Snowdrop Street. But beneath all the cold there was a warm little glow. That girl, Sara, had been a nice kid, and the money she'd handed over had bought not only some loaves of bread but two currant buns, a large piece of cheese and a bully beef tin full of milk.

She had been heading home, but now she paused in her onward rush. The trouble was, it was Grace and the baby who needed the food most and if the others saw it, it wouldn't last long. Wouldn't go round all that far, either. Mam always fed Da and herself first, then the boys, then the girls. Yesterday there had been a proper stew, made especially for Christmas – a neighbour had donated the meat. But somehow, it had all got ate, and neither Grace nor Mollie had had a sniff of it. Grace had been poorly, so hot you could have fried an egg on her, and Mollie was too little to fight her corner. Jess herself had only had a boiled potato and a smear of gravy and that hadn't gone far between her and Mollie.

Jess sighed and stood still for a moment, doubly burdened by the sleeping child and the food. What should she do for the best? Grace was a dear little soul but she'd never manage bread and cheese, not with the fever she'd had. Jess had given her the buttermilk, warmed, with bread crumbled into it and the kid had scarcely managed two mouthfuls before she fell asleep again. But Mollie must be very hungry, and Jess herself was empty as a drum. If I don't get something inside me soon I'll be no good to the others, Jess thought, immediately practical. I'll go somewhere quiet, eat some bread and cheese and a bun, feed Mollie the milk with some bread in it, and then go home later with what's left.

But where to go? Jess looked around her. The snow was falling thickly but surely there must be a suitable place where she could make up some food for the baby and feed her, undisturbed? Snowdrop Street was no good, someone might spot her and take the food off her, or her da might stagger down the road and try to bash her brains out just because she was the eldest. But there was always the marshalling yard.

Jess looked across Commercial Road, towards the railway lines. There were a great many buildings there, all different. Many a time, when she'd been younger, she'd played around in the sheds which the workmen used as shelters from the weather, somewhere to eat their carry-out. Surely she could find somewhere where she would be sufficiently sheltered to feed the child? Once Mollie's small belly was full and she'd had a bite herself she would take the rest of the food home, no problem. Grace might be persuaded to eat a currant bun soaked in milk, that was soft and easy enough. And I might have the second bun meself, Jess thought with watering mouth. Eldest children, she knew from bitter experience, make do with the leftovers, they don't often feast on currant buns. Accordingly, Jess hurried across Commercial Road, heading for the tiny cabins where the men working on the lines congregated at dinner-times. Someone would be about, but she might find one of the cabins empty.

In her arms, Mollie wriggled. She was such a pretty

baby, but she was usually hungry, same as all the kids were. Jess sighed and speeded up a bit.

'Not long now, Mollie-o,' she said comfortingly, giving the warm bundle which was her baby sister a hug. 'Jess's goin' to give you bread 'n' milk – what about that, eh?'

Mollie gurgled. 'Jess, Jess, Jess,' she chanted beneath the blanket. 'Milla-milla, Jess milla-milla.'

'That's it,' Jess said stoutly. She wriggled through a hole in the fence and began to cross the great swathe of wet and shining lines. 'Bread an' milk for you, my little love, bread and milk for Jess's best girl.'

The first hut she approached was full of men; she would have backed away but one of them hailed her.

'What are you doin' round here, alanna?' one of the navvies asked curiously, in a strong Irish accent. 'If you're after nickin' coal you're in the wrong place. What's that under your shawl, child?'

'It's not a shawl, it's a cut-down jacket, and it's me sister under it,' Jess said, her teeth chattering. 'I'm not tryin' to nick anything either, honest to God, I just want somewhere to feed the littl'un – I got food . . . see?'

She held up the soggy paper bag which contained the loaves, and lifted the bully beef tin to show that, too. Drawing closer to the cabin she saw that it was lit by a coke burner and that, Christmas Day or no Christmas Day, the men were all in their working clothes.

'Sure and she's speakin' no more than the trut',' another man put in. He gestured to an empty drum standing near the stove. 'Siddown, lass. You're welcome to a warm by the fire, you an' the babby.'

By now, Jess was so cold that warming up would be painful, she knew, yet she could not resist the lure of the coke stove. She crept nearer . . . oh, the warmth was bliss, sheer bliss. And it was so nice to see friendly faces around her, too!

'Thanks very much,' she muttered. 'I'll just break up some o' this bread into the milk . . . is it awright to put the littl'un down?'

'She's a real little beauty; a dote,' one of the men declared. 'Reminds me of my little Eilis, back home in County Cork.' He held out a huge, calloused hand to the baby. 'What do they call you, alanna?'

'She's Mollie,' Jess said. Her fingers were still so cold that she could not feel them and this was not helping her to break into the loaf of bread. The man who had spoken gave an exclamation and took the loaf from her. He produced a clasp knife from his pocket and began, very handily Jess thought, to carve into the bread. As he cut he dropped the pieces into the milk, then stood the tin down by the stove.

'There! Leave it a minute to warm, then Mollie can have a good meal so she can.' He turned to Jess, giving her a rueful smile. 'You look as though you could do with a bite yourself, alanna. What's your name and where do you live? You should be in wit' your mammy and daddy on a day like this, what with the snow and the cold.'

'I'm Jess,' Jess admitted rather cautiously. These men – there were four of them – seemed well-intentioned enough but you could never tell. They might tell the scuffers that she was on railway property, send them round to the house, and then Mam would screech at her and Da would thump . . . no, you never told adults the whole truth, not if you were wise.

'And where do you live?' the questioner this time was younger than the rest, a young man with bright, dark eyes and soft dark hair under the navy cap which he pushed to the back of his head. 'We're from God's own country, which, mebbe, you've guessed.'

All the men laughed and Jess, encouraged, smiled too.

'Oh, I'm from nowhere in partic'lar,' she said, picking a sop out of the bully beef tin and popping it into the baby's eager mouth. 'We're keepin' out o' the way, baby an' me. Our da's 'ad no work for weeks, but when he's gorra bit o' money he'll be down the boozer, an' 'e were give five shillin' by a pal. Off 'e went, merry as Larry, but when 'e comes back 'e's likelier to kick than kiss.'

'Aye, I've known fellers like that,' the boy said. 'Best stay here for a while, then. No harm, not today.' He asked no more questions, to Jess's relief. These men were so kind, it would seem unfriendly to continue to deny them her name and address.

'We're none of us ourselves when we've drink aboard,' the first speaker said. He looked shamefacedly at Jess. 'But I've never hit woman nor child, no matter how much of the hard stuff has passed me lips.' He grinned round at his companions. 'Me old woman would kill me if I tried such a t'ing,' he added innocently. 'And she'd make two of me, would Deirdre.'

'Oh, Peader, your woman's soft as a lamb and you know it,' a big, ginger-haired man said, grinning. 'Sure an' she's built like a fairy so she is!'

The first speaker, who must be Peader, turned back to Jess, his eyes soft, sorry. 'So your old fella's fierce in drink, is 'e? Well, you give the littl'un a drap o' this, my treasure, that'll warm the cockles of her heart, and be the same token, have a drap yourself.'

He held out a bottle; it was black and smelt horrible. Jess put a hand out, touched it, then withdrew quickly, shaking her head.

'No thanks,' she said frankly. 'We don't like the smell, baby an' me.'

'It's good porter,' the dark-haired Peader said. 'Just a wee drop in the milk, alanna, and the baby'll smile for us. It isn't after gettin' you tiddly I am, but warmin' the pair of you.'

Warming! All of a sudden Jess wanted desperately to be warm, and to know that Mollie was warm, too. She let the man tip a small quantity of the rich, strong-smelling stuff into the milk and she continued to feed the baby, now and then taking a piece of the soaked bread for herself.

And he was right, it was warming! What with that, and the fire, and the good company, she had seldom felt better. The boy, who told her his name was Brogan, picked the baby up and began to play games with her, but presently Mollie, sated with bread and milk and soothed by the fire's warmth, simply lolled against his chest, eyelids drowsily closing.

'She's sound off,' Brogan said in a whisper to Jess. 'Do you want to take her from me now, get her home while she sleeps?'

Jess was warm herself now, and weary – so weary! 'I don't think I could walk home,' she murmured, for several of the men were snoozing, their faces ruddy from the fire's glow and the porter. 'Can I sleep here for a little while?'

'Course you can,' Brogan said. 'Course you can, girl. Sleep sound, sleep sound. And when you wake you can share my can o' tea, and have a bite o' bread an' cold mutton.'

Jess murmured her thanks and tried to raise her heavy eyelids, but the combination of a full stomach and warmth and the porter was too much for her. Very soon, she slept.

*

Brogan waited until both their visitors were fast asleep and then he, too, curled up on the floor. A couple of little girls had made his Christmas, for until they had walked into the cabin he had been suffering from such terrible homesickness that he had been afraid of breaking down in tears. Especially when Paddy began to sing in that light tenor voice of his. All the old songs, the ones Brogan's mammy had sung to him and his brothers when they were small.

He'd sat there in the faint firelight and remembered all the other Christmases. Never a penny piece to spare, never a great deal of food – but oh, the wonderful warmth of togetherness they had shared! A fire of turf or some hoarded coal, meat if they were lucky, but fish and potatoes almost always, little presents for the kids – a peg-man for Bevin, who was the youngest, a cracked pair of secondhand boots for another brother, a much-darned and patched jumper for a third, bought off the tuggers' carts as they made their way back to the Jewman who employed them in the heart of Dublin.

It wasn't a rich Christmas, Brogan knew that all right. But it was a good one. They went to mass, naturally, and somehow they always managed candle-money, and a bit over for to put in the box for the poor and needy.

'We're the poor and needy really, amn't we, Brogan?' the brother next to him in age, Martin, had said wistfully, once. 'When our daddy's out of work we don't have much.'

But it wasn't true, for didn't they have two whole rooms in their tenement block, the front first-floor pair as they called it? A whole room for sleeping in wasn't common by any means, no indeed, and they divided it, mornings, with hung sheets so that each could have his moment of privacy to wash and dress himself. And wasn't their living room neat as a new pin, and always clean water in the bucket by the fire and the Sacred Heart on the mantel kept dust-free, with a glass vase always sparkling before it, even if they could only rarely afford a flower or two to stand in it? So, 'There's many worse off than us, Mart,' he had told his brother. 'Oh, aye, many a one would envy us. But we aren't rich, nor even well-to-do, I grant you that.'

And when he and his daddy had realised that they would have to go over to England to work, how the family had wept and cried! Mammy tried hard to be brave, but she clung to Peader and to her son at the last moment.

'We've always managed,' she had said, her voice trembling and thick with unshed tears. 'Sure and we'll manage again. Don't go, don't leave us!'

But there was so little work in Dublin, that was the trouble! Peader had been a docker, but he'd rarely succeeded in catching the stevedore's eye and without doing that you'd scarce make enough money to buy bread let alone pay rent or keep the kids halfway decent. Brogan could still remember those awful mornings when his father had returned, silent, from the quays. Often he could not look at them, shamed by his inability to provide.

'I couldn't catch his eye,' he would mumble guiltily. 'Sure an' didn't I run like a greyhound along to the next read, and no more luck, me, that time? But there's other work beside labouring on the ships. I'll find something, sweet Deirdre, I'll not let you down.'

It wasn't really a matter of letting down, Brogan understood that. His mammy worked hard in her own right, trekking out into the countryside around Dublin, picking potatoes, then selling them in Moore Street,

Francis Street or anywhere else where she could find a pitch.

Brogan had worked too, of course. Selling the *Herald* and the *Mail* to the citizens of Dublin from the time he was ten, barefoot in the snow in winter or under the pitiless sun of high summer. He had jumped on and off trams to sell to folk on the top deck, hurled himself in front of jarveys crying his wares as they tried to start their handsome horses off at a fast trot, and finally taken home the unsold papers in wintertime to wedge against the old window frames in an attempt to keep out the wicked winds.

But even so, the money didn't keep them. Not quite. Always nearly, never completely. They would be doing well, eating regular, making ends meet as Mammy said, and then suddenly disaster would strike. Once, they put up the rent. Once, they increased the cost of the newsboy's licence, and you couldn't sell without a licence. Who 'they' were Brogan was never sure, just a part of that vast, throbbing over-class which seemed to spend all its time making sure that the poor remained poor.

Those small disasters had almost done for them. They'd had to go, cap in hand, to the St Vincent de Paul Society, who had sent round a tall, thin man with a long, cadaverous face and squinty little eyes. He had sat in their fine parlour and cross-questioned mammy until she had shed bitter, helpless tears. Why did they need the relief? What had changed? Could they not manage with one room less if the rent was too much for them? Others did it – if they could just cut their coat according to their cloth. . .

'I sold me winter coat, sir,' Mammy had said, not understanding. ''Twas that we ate last week, but now 'tis gone . . .'

The Vincents man pulled down his mouth and asked more questions. Who was in work? Why did not her husband find some other employment if he could not catch the stevedore's eye at the docks? There *was* other work, he had it on good authority that they were taking on labourers at such and such a place . . .

But now he and Peader, his father, were in decent work, and able to send almost all of their wages home. Rent in Liverpool was their biggest expense but they had found a lodging house which was cheap and relatively bug-free, and Peader said they must eat well – the work was too hard to stint themselves in that direction. Brogan knew that they were luckier than some, that they must put up with being far away in return for the benefits of regular work. And besides, his mammy was frugal and would save all she could and perhaps one day, perhaps when summer came, they could catch the ship home again and stand in the bows and watch as Ireland came into view through the land-haze. And until then at least they were earning, knowing that despite their homesickness, and the rough voices about them, they were taking some of the burden off Deirdre O'Brady.

Brogan sighed and felt the baby's warm weight in his lap with satisfaction. He had missed the kids, working with men all day and lodging with an old couple who cared nothing for the men in their home save to see that they didn't come indoors the worse for drink. So it was nice to have a baby in his arms again.

And presently, tired and satisfyingly full, with a mug of unaccustomed porter inside him, Brogan, too, slept.

He woke because the baby was wriggling against him, patting his face with one warm, starfished hand. He struggled into a sitting position – he had fallen over whilst he slept, to sag against the wall – and looked around him. The men had all gone, back to their work he supposed. The railway gangs did all sorts; some of them walked a stretch of line, they loaded and unloaded coal or great sides of meat for the cold storage depots, they cleared landslides and created cuttings. Sometimes they manhandled trucks on to whichever stretch of line needed extra freight, or replaced damaged sleepers with new ones . . . oh, they had a thousand and one jobs. But today being Christmas Day they could take it easy – or easier, at any rate. They had volunteered to come in today because they were far from home and could do with the money. And because of the dreadful weather and the sudden snowstorms, they could well find themselves desperately needed. Repairs had to be carried out at once when something went wrong in order that the engines could be ready and in the right place when they were needed next day.

So now, Brogan sat up and looked around him. The coke stove still burned brightly and there were signs that the men had left hurriedly – the tin mugs they drank from were laid on their sides, the newspaper-wrapped bread, cheese and cold mutton had been abandoned, but other than that he was alone with the sleeping girl and the baby.

The snow must have caused a problem, Brogan thought, getting to his feet, the baby still tucked in his arm. I'd best get out there now, or there'll be trouble – why did Peader leave me to sleep, I wonder? He sat the baby on the ground near the girl, who was slumbering still, well away.

'Stay there, Moll,' Brogan whispered to her. It would be a cryin' shame to wake the girl Jess so it would and her such a poor, skinny young thing! 'Wait wit' your sister until she wakes.'

The baby looked up at him, beaming, showing a tooth in her bottom jaw. Then she began to crawl towards the source of the warmth and light – the coke burner. Hastily Brogan turned her with his boot, edging her in the opposite direction, but it didn't last. The baby gurgled and set off once more for the stove, chuckling. Brogan, already turning towards the doorway, paused, uncertain. He could wake the girl, but it seemed awful hard – why should he not simply tuck the baby inside his donkey jacket and take her with him? It wasn't as though he would be outside for long, he would only go and find Peader, see if he was needed. If he was, he'd run back, wake the girl, leave the baby in her care, but if he wasn't, he would go back to the cabin and play with the baby himself, keep her occupied, until the girl woke naturally.

The thin blanket lay under the girl's head, but his coat was warm. He tucked the baby under his coat, buttoned it up, and set off into the early winter dusk. The baby was so light it made him want to cry all of a sudden, but he scolded himself. You're a man, Brogan O'Brady, he reminded himself, you work as a navvy, you can't shed tears because a baby's half-starved. And anyway, I'll tell the girl to bring her down again in our dinner-break. There's always something from me carry-out which she could have and welcome. We won't desert her, now we've found her.

When Jess awoke it was full dark and for several moments she had no idea where she was. She lay on a hard floor – well, there was nothing strange in *that* – but instead of darkness, with a lighter patch where the window should have been, there was a comforting red glow – and she was warm.

Luxuriating in this unusual awakening, she simply lay there for a moment, gazing round her. Warmth in winter! It so seldom happened to her, but it was true that right now she was warm and cosy from the top of her head to the tips of her toes. So Mollie must be warm too, and . . .

Mollie! In a flash, she remembered everything, the girl called Sara in the beautiful red coat and hat who had given her money and a pair of white woolly gloves, the baker's shop where they had let her have three fine loaves of bread and two currant buns, the dairy where she'd bought the cheese and they had poured a generous measure of milk into the old bully beef tin. Then there was the long walk through the freezing snow and wind . . . and the discovery of the cabin and the friendly Irish navvies.

But . . . where were they? She was alone, the baby had gone . . . had Mollie crawled out into the darkness? Jess scrambled to her feet and ran to the doorway. To eyes which had been gazing dreamily at the coke burner, the early evening outside seemed black indeed, but no baby cried against the shrilling of the wind. She could see no small, crawling figure amidst the gleaming rails.

But she could not see the men, either. Quickly, because she could not bear to lose her few possessions, Jess returned to the cabin and picked up what was left of the loaves, the little white gloves which must have fallen from the baby's feet, and the thin blanket. All the milk had gone, gobbled up as sops by herself and the child. It did not cross her mind that the men might have taken Mollie for her own protection, she simply knew that she must find her little sister. Mollie was an innocent child, Jess her only protector. She simply must find her!

Alone, with the blanket around her shoulders giving her what little protection it could, Jess set out into the storm.

Brogan slogged across the rails to where, dimly, he could see a lantern's light, and speedily found himself reunited with his father and the other men. They were standing by the side of the track, looking anxiously towards the engine sheds. Peader greeted him with relief.

'Ah, there you are, me boy! I was wonderin' whether I ought to run and get you, though you were sleepin' so sound, you and the little girls . . .'

'What's happened, Daddy?' Brogan asked. 'I woke and found you all gone so I guessed you'd been called away.'

'Landslide,' his father said briefly. 'Further up the line. They're sendin' us up on an engine to see if we can clear it. We could do wi' your muscle, Brog.'

'Right; but I'd best run back to the cabin . . .' Brogan was beginning, when he heard the thump and rattle of an approaching train.

'Too late, boyo,' Declan said. 'She's comin', and she won't wait for no man, let alone a bit of a boy.'

The engine drew up beside them. The driver, a Liverpudlian, leaned out, blinking against the falling flakes.

'Let's be 'avin' you, fellers,' he said cheerfully. 'No need to watch for signals today, we're the only train on this line. Gerrin the guard's van, then we can gerrup steam. It's ten mile out, by whar' I've been told; a tree's acrost the line an' the snow's caused a landslip. But you're big fellers, it won't take you a month of Sundays to clear it.'

'True,' Peader said. They waited until the guard's van was level with them, then they clambered aboard. Peader turned to heave his son up by one elbow, then stared at him. 'What's that you've got under your jacket, son?' he began to say, when the train started to move . . . with the men and the hidden child firmly ensconced in the guard's van.

Panic hit Jess as soon as she was out in the middle of the rails, trying to get across them to a light she could see burning, vaguely, through the fast-falling snow. Her bare feet, in their holey, battered boots, were constantly stubbed against a rail or a sleeper she could no longer see for the blanket of snow, and the lantern light seemed to move as she ran, and always further away.

But she knew she must keep going, must find Mollie. Her little sister was only a tender baby, and would not last long alone and blanketless under such conditions.

She heard a noise coming from the direction of the engine sheds but ignored it. She had lived near the railway long enough to know the sound of an engine being coaled up, getting up steam, but she knew it took a long time, too. Probably someone was preparing the engines for work the following day. So she simply hurried on, climbing on to a sleeper, then hurrying between the lines, sure that if she did not move fast when she did find Mollie, the child would be a tiny, frozen corpse.

She was actually standing on a rail when she felt it begin to vibrate. That's odd, Jess thought vaguely, and jumped down on to the hardcore between the rails, wincing as it penetrated the cardboard soles of her boots. There aren't any trains today, the fellers said so – wonder what that is, then?

She glanced to her right as she stepped on to the

next rail, which was vibrating worse than ever . . . and opened her mouth to scream.

But she never made a sound. The train struck her, carried her along, dropped her . . . devoured her into its great, clanking steel maw.

She never heard the squeal of the train's brakes nor the engine note change as the driver decided he had hit a slight obstruction on the line and speeded up once more. Like a rag doll she lay where she had been thrown, oblivious, at last, to rain, hail or snow, to wind and weather.

As soon as he could, Brogan showed Peader the child's small face beneath his coat and told him what had happened, but what with the rocking of the train and the warmth, Mollie was fast asleep again and Peader shrugged, chuckled, and said not to worry.

'The girl was sleepin' when you left her. Likely she'll sleep sound until we get back,' he said comfortably. 'She'd drunk porter, she was warm, she felt safe. Sure she'll sleep until the job's done.'

The other men grinned when they saw the baby, but agreed with Peader that no harm would be done by taking her with them.

'I never seen a child sleep sounder than young Jess,' Declan said. 'She'll not worry about the babe, not yet awhile.'

And then they arrived at the scene of the landslide and Brogan left the child wrapped warmly in his jacket in a corner of the guard's van whilst he and the other men struggled to clear the line. The tree, a huge one, had crashed down, bringing what looked like a mountain of earth with it. The men looked at the great tree, measured it with their eyes, spat on their hands and waded in. They got the tree off the line by sheer brute force, three a side, with Brogan doing his best and the fireman and the driver, who were 'big-wigs' and shouldn't have had to labour, willingly giving a hand. After all, it was Christmas Day!

Then the driver and the fireman climbed back into the cab and the labourers got out the huge, oddly shaped shovels which Brogan had found so hard to handle at first, and began to dig.

'Sure and I never t'ought I'd be movin' mountains almost on me own when I crossed the water,' Paddy panted, but the big shovel swung rhythmically as he spoke and he never missed a load. 'A good job they offered double pay today, for I'm sure as a man can be that this is double work.'

'You want to do it wit'out your donkey jacket,' Peader joked. 'Look at me son, now, an' him as skinny as a tinker's ass, but he's swingin' wit' the best of us, so he is.'

It took longer than they had guessed, however, and it was full dark before they climbed back into the guard's van, dog-weary.

'The girl's bound to have woke be now,' Brogan worried. 'Sure an' she'll want me guts for garters so she will when she sees I've got the baby.'

'She won't wake yet; she'll be deep in her first sleep,' Paddy protested. 'That wee girl hadn't had a warm sleep or a dacent meal for months be the look of her. Just you sit down an' rest, Brog. 'Twon't harm.'

So Brogan sat down in the draughty guard's van, and he was so tired, so muscle-weary, that soon he slept.

Brogan dreamed. He dreamed he was in a huge meadow, gay with flowers, and a soft breeze blew the scented air to him and the sun shone gold out of a clear blue sky overhead. The hedgerows were full of wild roses and honeysuckle, with the verge pink with foxgloves.

Brogan wandered in the meadow for a while, drowsily content, whilst the bees hummed and the birds sang and called and the sweet scents of summer charmed him. And then, coming across the grass, he saw a girl, and as she got closer, he saw that it was Jess, and he knew she had come for the baby.

He looked round wildly; there was no railway line, no embankment, no engine or train or anything of that nature anywhere near. And the girl was smiling at him, holding out her hands to him.

He turned away; how could he tell her he had taken the baby, and now he had lost her? But he could not run from her, so he stood his ground and presently he turned reluctantly towards her and he saw that she was very clean, and that her tangled hair had been washed and brushed. She looked pretty, he thought wonderingly, she was a really pretty girl, no longer a forlorn and ragged waif.

She smiled sweetly at him, then she spoke. 'Brogan? Where's me baby sister?'

He began to say he'd lost the child, and then something made him remember putting her inside his donkey jacket. He shoved a hand into the breast of it and there was the baby, cuddled up against his chest, warm and softly sleeping. He grinned at Jess and drew back the coat to show her the child nestling within.

'There she is, alanna,' he said softly, relief washing over him in waves. 'There she is, safe as houses and pretty as a picture. Will you be takin' her now, then?'

He went to hand the baby over, but Jess shook her head. To his horror, he realised that even as he watched she was growing fainter, until she was no more than a mist of a girl against the flower-filled meadow.

'No, I can't take 'er; it wouldn't be right. And I've gorra go. But you'll tek care of 'er for me, won't you, Brogan? You'll take care of me baby sister, me heart's darlin'? You wouldn't throw 'er on the world's mercy, Brogan, when it don't 'ave none?'

'Oh, but I'm a feller, fellers don't look after babies . . .' Brogan began, but it was too late. The girl Jess had faded like a wraith of mist in the morning sun, and even as he drew the baby out of his coat and held her imploringly towards her sister, the dream faded and he found himself awake and cold, whilst the guard's van continued to clatter along the tracks towards the city.

And presently, when the train came to a halt in the station yard and the men tumbled out, the dream had vanished and Brogan headed for the cabin with no premonition of what he was to find.

Brogan stared around the little cabin, scarcely able to believe his eyes. The girl Jess had gone! She was not curled up on the floor in front of the still-glowing coke burner, she was not sitting on the oil drum, nor taking the opportunity to have a bite from the food they had left for her. She was nowhere to be seen. Brogan stared around unbelievingly for a moment, then turned to his father, who had followed him in. The other men had taken the shovels and equipment back to the store.

'Daddy, she's gone! There's neither hide nor hair of her – she's even taken the little bit o' blanket so she has!'

'She'll have woken up and taken a little walk, perhaps,' Peader said doubtfully. 'Only . . . 'tis mortal cold out there for a skinny lass wit' nobbut rags to her back.'

'But she knew I had the baby,' Brogan said. 'When she fell asleep I was still playin' wit' the little one. Surely she'd have searched for us, not just – just gone?'

'She mebbe only woke up minutes ago,' Peader said reassuringly. 'She'll be out there now.' He turned back towards the doorway. 'Come on, wit' the pair of us callin', 'twill take us but a moment to find the lass.'

'I only took the baby out because she would crawl towards the stove,' Brogan muttered, turning up his coat collar and plunging into the darkness close on his father's heels. 'No baby-stealer, me, though she's a good little one, this one. Oh, Daddy, will she hear us against this storm?'

For now the wind was stronger, if anything, the flakes thicker.

'Never a peep will she hear if we don't shout,' his father called back, crossly. 'Let's be hearin' you, lad – Hey, Jess, JESS! Where are you hidin', alanna?'

But no sound came back to them out of the silent, snow-covered yard. In fact after covering most of the ground between the cabin and the engine sheds, Peader turned to his son and shook his head.

'She's took shelter somewhere, to wait out the storm,' he shouted. 'No use to search further, lad. We'd best get back to the cabin ourselves, see what . . .'

'There's someone over there, Daddy,' Brogan shouted back, gesturing to what looked like a thickening of the snow ahead of them. 'It's the fellers – have they found her?'

They hurried eagerly towards the other men; Declan walked along with a shovel over his shoulder but Paddy had taken off his working coat and was carrying something wrapped in it. The cold was so bitter that with one accord all the men turned back to the cabin; it was no weather for explanations. But once inside

Paddy laid his coat tenderly on the floor and opened it out so that a face just showed between the rough lapels. No one looking at that pale, still face could have thought her still alive.

Brogan gasped. 'Dear God, it's the girl Jess! Is she froze, Paddy? What in the name of all that's dreadful happened to her?'

'The train must ha' caught her crossin' the lines,' Paddy said heavily. 'Hours since, probably . . . eh, it must have been our engine, on the way to move that bloody tree. She must ha' died at once, Brogan, lad, she'd not have known a t'ing, I promise you that.'

'The train hit her? But what was she doin', Paddy, wanderin' around the yard in such weather? When I left her she was sleepin' sound, I swear it.'

Paddy shrugged and went to cover the face again, but Peader stayed his hand.

'No, Paddy, don't! Are you sure she's gone?'

'Aye. We found her across the lines, man – what was left of her.' Paddy drew the coat almost reverently across the ash-pale face. 'On Christmas Day! But He's taken her to be with His angels, no man can doubt that. I'll go for a priest.'

'And the police,' Declan said wearily. 'They'll have to stick their long noses in, no doubt.'

'Aye, no doubt.' Peader looked across at his son. ''Tis a sad and cruel way to go, son,' he said carefully. 'And we'd all have give our right hands to save the child's life, but it's happened. We've all seen death before, the death of an innocent. You must never blame yourself, for I know you, Brog. You'll start thinkin' that if you'd not taken the baby, if you'd left her here, the girl might be alive now. Well, I'm tellin' you, son, that first it was the will o' God and second that if you'd left the baby it might have been that little one who died. She could have pulled the coke burner over . . .'

Brogan was staring at the dark bundle, which had once been a loving, caring girl. Now he leaned forward and pulled back the coat. He gazed at the girl's face and suddenly his dream came back to him in every detail, he could hear her voice, low, pleading, speaking to him from the heart.

You'll tek care of 'er for me, Brogan? You'll take care of me heart's darling? You won't throw her on the world's mercy, when it don't 'ave none?

'Brogan? She was a good girl she was, she'll not bear you any grudge, nor haunt you in any way.'

His father's voice was fairly throbbing with the intensity of his feelings, and he put a hand out to draw the coat back over the dead face, but Brogan stopped him.

'In a moment, Daddy,' he said gently. 'But Mollie must look her last on her sister.' He drew the baby, rosy and only just stirring, out of the breast of his coat. 'See, Mollie? That's your sister who loved you, who died for you. She wanted me to take care of you for her, and I'll not disappoint her.'

'Take care of her? But she's got parents . . . brothers and sisters . . .' Peader said doubtfully, only to have his son round on him.

'To be sure she has; a drunken father who beats his kids and a mother who has no time for them. Daddy, I should have known Jess was dead, because I dreamed of her, when we were coming home in the guard's van. She begged me to take care of the baby . . . she said Mollie was her heart's darling and she didn't want her thrown on the world's mercy, for it has none. What can I do but try to take care of Mollie for her?'

'But the parents will want her back; the police will be round here . . .'

Brogan knelt on the floor and put the baby down beside the dead girl and Mollie touched the cold, white face, then turned back to him. She scrambled back on to his knees and pushed her thumb into her mouth, then turned her face into him. Brogan tucked her back inside his coat and looked squarely at the ring of faces surrounding him. 'Well, fellers? What would you do?'

There was a long, long pause whilst each man consulted his own thoughts, his own conscience. Then Paddy spoke for them all.

'If I had a dream like that, sure an' I'd keep the littl'un as long as I was able. But it'll be a hard road for you, Brogan me boy. I must say, I don't hold wit' fathers who rule their kids wit' their belts nor mothers who give birth and then hand their babbies over to the older kids to bring up, but there's laws in England same as there are back home. It won't be easy.'

Peader looked thoughtfully around the cabin, at the faces in the glow from the coke burner, all serious, concerned.

'You must go home, boy,' he said after a moment. 'Right away, you must go home. We'll tell the authorities we found the lass on the line, it'll be a while before they know who she is or where she hails from, and we'll say nothing about the baby.' He smiled at his son. 'Ah, your mammy's wanted a girl all her life, aren't you the lucky fella to be bringin' her a little daughter!'

'Home!' Brogan could feel a smile starting. To go home – and with such a gift for his beloved mammy! 'Oh, but someone's bound to notice the baby on the ship, there'll be talk . . .'

'Go on the next boat out, and keep the babby quiet until then,' Paddy said. 'If you feed her well and keep her warm she'll not bawl out. Do as your daddy says, boy. Take her to your mammy.'

'More sprouts, Sara? How about you, Nanny? We've left most of the tureen untouched, don't distress Cook by sending such a quantity of vegetables back to the kitchens, I beg of you!'

Mr Cordwainer was trying to be jovial, to instil some Christmas spirit into the proceedings, but his best efforts were being thwarted by his wife, who was plainly sulking, and slightly by Sara, who had not got over the disappointment of losing Jess. This is turning out to be the oddest Christmas ever, Sara decided, as she allowed her father to spoon a few more sprouts on to her plate. Why on earth had Nanny passed on Mrs Rushton's message? It had only made mother angry.

But that had been no excuse for Mrs Cordwainer's behaviour ever since. She had criticised every single course, found fault with Sara's table manners and told her husband that he had chosen the wrong wine.

Sara realised that her mother's anger was partly directed against herself; she had undoubtedly invited Nanny for Christmas Day without realising that the older woman would assume she was not welcome for Boxing Day. This had made her look grudging in her husband's eyes. But to continue to make everyone feel uncomfortable seemed so unnecessary that Sara could not begin to account for it. Grown-ups, Sara decided – not for the first time – simply went their own way regardless and expected children to make the best of it.

And Nanny was too quiet; it worried Sara, who knew that Mrs Prescott liked to talk and laugh. In fact her Christmas Day was already in grave danger of being spoiled.

'Well, Sara? Have you quite finished? Sure? Then

since you're the last I'll tell Cook to bring in the pudding.'

Mr Cordwainer tinkled a little bell by his right hand and after a pause, the long door at the end of the dining room was flung open and Cook appeared, extremely red in the face, bearing the flaming pudding before her. Mr Cordwainer clapped rather self-consciously and Mrs Prescott followed suit so Sara, trying hard as well now, said, 'Hooray!' in a rather squeaky little voice and then clapped too.

'Really, Adolphus,' Mrs Cordwainer said as soon as the cook had left the room, 'you've not even tasted the pudding yet; the time for congratulating Cook is when we've tried the pudding, not before we've even cut into it. I daresay it will be nasty and we'll have to send it back untouched.'

Mr Cordwainer turned to his wife but before he could say a word Nanny was before him, and she was clearly furious – even more furious than either Cordwainer, Sara could see.

'Letty, you should be ashamed of yourself! I hope never to see a nastier exhibition of unrestrained temper . . . and from a child I brought up to the best of my ability, too! Now are you going to apologise and begin to behave prettily or shall I order the car to come round and take me straight home?'

There was an appalled silence. Sara, looking from face to face, thought she had never seen her parents so dumbstruck. And what on earth did it mean? Surely not that her beloved nanny was going to turn round and leave, after they had persuaded her to stay, too? She knew Mrs Prescott had been Mother's nanny, too, but she had never heard Mrs Prescott speak to her mother in any but the mildest terms, she had certainly never heard her so angry. But her father was nodding his head slowly, as though he agreed – oh, what on earth was going to happen?

And it had all started, she was sure, because Nanny had mentioned Mrs Rushton and Sid and a Sunday school outing, long ago. Sara supposed that there must have been a Sunday school trip both from the Snowdrop Street area and from wherever her mother had been brought up. But why Mrs Cordwainer should so dislike it being mentioned . . . and then Mrs Rushton had seemed to know Mrs Cordwainer quite well, she'd said 'when we were twelve'. Actually, that gave Sara her first moment of doubt. Mrs Rushton was *old*, her hair was grey and her figure sagging. Oh, she was nice all right, but definitely old.

But a moment's thought cancelled that one out, too. Mrs Cordwainer had one child, not six or seven, and she had servants and a big house, a car, a chauffeur . . . naturally she looked less strained than a woman who did all her own work, and cleaned public houses, as well. And Mother dyes her hair, too, Sara remembered. Its bright colour sometimes faded and then became bright once more, so Sara knew she dyed it. It was probably true, then, that Mrs Rushton and Sara's own mother were the same age and had gone on the same Sunday school trip. But that didn't explain Mrs Cordwainer's crossness, nor the martial sparkle in Nanny's eyes.

'Well, Letty?' That was Mrs Prescott. She's really brave, Sara thought, seeing the scarlet flame in her mother's cheeks. Suppose she's too brave – suppose Mother just tells her to go? But it was Christmas and Nanny, in some mysterious way, seemed to have the upper hand. Even as Sara stared, round-eyed, her mother heaved a sigh, glanced up towards the ceiling with an expression of pained long-suffering, and spoke.

'I'm sorry I've offended you, Nanny,' she muttered. 'Let's all have a helping of this delicious pudding . . . Adolphus, will you serve?'

Nanny, passing her plate, gave Sara a small, secret smile, but Sara saw her mother watching her and did not add fuel to the fire by returning it. Instead, as she passed the plate, she gave Nanny's hand a discreet squeeze. And Nanny squeezed back, before turning the conversation neatly into safer, less inflammable subjects.

It's going to be all right, Sara thought thankfully, as conversation became general once more. And after we've had our meal, I'm going to show Nanny how to make a really huge snowman in the back yard!

Chapter Three

On the day after Boxing Day, Sara awoke to find that the snowstorm which had battered the city for two whole days and nights had ceased. Outside her window frail sunshine shone on trees and hedges heaped with snow, on a garden which might just as well have been a meadow so totally snow-blanketed was it, and on the hushed and wonderful world of deep winter.

'Miss Sara, it's time you were gettin' up. I'm now goin' down to fetch your breakfast.' Jane popped her head round the edge of Sara's door and beamed at her. 'The bloomin' snow's stopped, which is one blessing, an' the sun's shinin'. Your pa said we was to go to the park today, so that's just what we'll do, soon's I've finished me work.'

Sara sat up in bed and smiled back at Jane. 'Oh, lovely, I love the park,' she said enthusiastically. 'Poor Nanny, she loves it too, but we didn't get much chance to do anything, not with the storm. Just my luck, that it stops the very moment she goes home. But still, it'll be fun to go out of doors. You could help me make a snowman, Jane.'

'I could an' all,' Jane agreed. Jane was a nice girl, only six years Sara's senior, but she had a good many jobs around the house which she had to see to before she could think of amusing her young charge and Sara got thoroughly sick of hanging around whilst the maid helped with the laundry, ran errands or toiled around the place with a brush and dustpan. But today, Sara thought happily, standing before the schoolroom fire and buttoning her woollen stockings on to her liberty bodice, they were to spend at least some time out of doors. Mr Cordwainer, seeing her disconsolately hanging about the hall when he left the house the previous day, had announced that she looked pale and that it would do her good to visit the park daily, until school started once more in ten days' time.

'Your life in the school holidays lacks purpose, Sara,' he said severely, which Sara thought supremely unfair, since any purpose she had in mind was immediately squashed by either one or other of her parents. 'You need employment – the devil finds mischief for idle hands, you know.'

But though it was a shame that he had managed to turn a treat – which was visiting the park – into a duty, Sara was still grateful to him. He took very little notice of her as a rule, now he had twice done something which had, in its way, made things easier for her. She still remembered his approval of Nanny, his making it plain that he thought she was in the right rather than his wife.

And today is sunny; we'll have a really good time and Mother won't be able to stop us by saying Jane has work to do, because Father's orders are paramount, Sara thought gleefully, quoting, in her mind, the very words her mother used when it suited her to blame her husband for some irksome order or other. She fastened her back suspenders, not without difficulty, for they were small, fiddly things, straightened her skirt and was standing with one foot in a pom-pommed slipper and the other still clad only in a black woollen stocking, when the door opened and Jane came into the room. She was carrying a tray with Sara's breakfast egg, a plateful of bread and butter and a mug of milk on it, and whilst she transferred the contents of the tray to the schoolroom table, she announced in a mournful voice that she would have to go downstairs at once, to see the missus.

'Why, Jane?' Sara asked idly, picking up her teaspoon and tapping the brown egg thoughtfully upon its bald cranium. 'Does she want us to go shopping with her? Oh, don't let's! Father said I might play in the park, or – or go for walk by ourselves.'

'It ain't that, Miss Sara,' Jane said unhappily. 'My little brother Freddy just come to the back door. Mam's been took bad, she's in the Stanley 'ospital, they say it could be 'pendicitis. And if it is, someone's gorra look after the littl'uns.'

'Oh, I see,' Sara said rather blankly. She had been really looking forward to getting out of the house for a while, but now she felt ashamed that she had never thought to ask Jane about her family, but the girl had only recently been promoted to take care of her, Phyllis having left for a livelier household with more children – and more money, she had told her charge. 'Well, I'm awfully sorry your mother's ill, Jane, but of course your first duty is to her. You'd best go off, then.'

And Jane, having set Sara's breakfast down upon the table, promptly went, to return presently saying in a tone of hushed excitement: 'Madam says I may go home and see how things are. I'll not pack, since it may be a false alarm, but Madam says as how she'll see to you this morning, Miss.'

'That's kind of her,' Sara said glumly. She could imagine few worse fates than being 'seen to' by her mother on a snowy morning. 'I hope you find your mother much better, Jane.'

'Thank you, Miss,' Jane said buoyantly. 'Mind, a few

days at home's a bit of a treat . . . in a way, acourse,' she added hastily, plainly feeling that she was being tactless in making such an admission. 'It's always nice to see me brothers and sisters.'

As she spoke she was taking her navy-blue coat and her matching hat with the pale green ribbon off the hook behind the nursery door and slipping them on. Sara could see that the maid was enjoying even the thought of going back to her home, and envied her. If only I had brothers and sisters, how pleasant being without Jane could be, she thought wistfully. There would be more than one, then, to plead with Mother and Father, or even to defy them! Perhaps a brother would always be able to get round Mother, like Christine Andrews says her brother can, or a sister could actually *enjoy* shopping, and do it instead of me. And then all the brothers and sisters could go to the park together, skate on the lake, make snowmen, have snow fights . . . we could do lots and lots of things. None of us would have to depend on a servant, because we'd have each other for company, and for taking care.

But it was not to be. I'm sure there are advantages in being an only child, Sara thought, picking up her spoon as Jane left the room. She eyed the egg broodingly for a moment, and then decapitated it with unnecessary violence. Off with your head, off with your head! But it was no use railing against fate; she was an only child, and a terribly lucky one, who ate three good meals a day, wore warm clothing and never had to dread the snow and frost.

Because Sara knew she would never forget Jess and the baby and the way Jess's hand had stretched out and then tucked itself back into her jacket again. Mother said the poor begged for money instead of working for it. Sara knew, now, that in many cases that simply was not true. The poor would, for the most part, far rather work, but they didn't have the chance. And dimly, somewhere in her mind, she knew that there was another unfairness; that many of the women living in Snowdrop Street, even those who loved their families, did not actually want fourteen or fifteen children. It was yet another of the strange penalties of being poor, she supposed.

But it was not something she could ask about, of course. Jane would blush and giggle and say she didn't know she was sure, Nanny would tell her she'd understand when she was older, and Mother . . . well, she had no idea what Mother would say because Sara could never question her mother. Mother has no patience with children and precious little with grown-ups, Sara found herself thinking, and blushed. What a bad girl she was, to feel like that about her mother! I love her, of course I do, she told herself, sipping milk from her blue china mug. Only . . . she doesn't like me very much at all, she's never hugged me or given me a kiss and a cuddle in her life, which is why I'm more at home with Nanny than with her.

But being discontented with one's lot was a sin, so being discontented with one's mother must be even worse. When she comes up presently and tells me to put my nice coat and my best hat on, and my shiny black boots, so that she can take me off to Lewises and Blacklers and all the other big stores, I'll try to look pleasant, Sara planned. And once we're there we'll go round and round the millinery departments and the fashion departments and look at dresses and hats and hats and dresses . . . and she'll be horrified if I suggest that it might be fun to play in the snow for a little.

Sara finished her egg and had some marmalade on the bread and butter. Then she piled her dishes on the tray and set off for the kitchens, three floors below. Normally, Jane would have taken the tray down but since she was away, Sara reasoned, there would be a good deal of disorganisation downstairs. The Cordwainers did not believe in employing more servants than were absolutely necessary, which meant that when a maid was sick or absent or even on a day off, everyone else in the servants' quarters had to work twice as hard.

She was on the ground floor and heading for the green baize door which led to the kitchens when her mother came out of the breakfast parlour, looking abstracted. 'Ah, Sara,' she said, peering at her daughter. 'What on earth are you doing?'

She rarely wore her spectacles but was extremely shortsighted, Sara knew.

'I'm taking my dishes down to the kitchen, Mother,' Sara said dutifully, however. 'Jane's mother is ill – didn't she tell you?'

'Oh . . . yes, of course, I was forgetting. And what are you going to do with yourself this morning?'

Sara's heart lifted. So it wasn't to be a dreaded shopping expedition, then!

'Well, Father said I was to go out, so I could go to the park with one of the maids, if one can be spared,' she said, therefore. 'Perhaps Ruby might enjoy a walk?'

But even the suggestion was enough to bring her mother's thin brows together in an impatient frown.

'Oh no, Sara. We pay the maids to work, not to enjoy walks,' she said tartly. 'Read a book, or – or do some sums.'

'But that isn't going out of doors, and Father said . . .' Sara began, indignation taking the place of caution. Her mother, who had begun to move on towards the stairs, stopped short.

'Oh, your father said so, did he? Well, I really can't spare a maid and the snow's far too thick anyway. You'll simply have to content yourself with the schoolroom.'

Her foot was on the bottom stair. Sara raised her voice in a last desperate plea for understanding, perhaps even sympathy.

'I *must* go out, Father said so! Oh, I wish Nanny was still here, she loves to walk in the park!'

Sara expected her mother to continue to climb the stairs, perhaps not even to answer her, so she was astonished when her mother whipped round, looking extremely cross.

'Well, she isn't. But if you're so keen to see her I'll get Robson to take you round there this afternoon. No, you can go this morning – why not? And I'll tell Adolphus that you can stay there until Jane comes back. And no playing out in the street, do you understand me?'

Sara would have promised anything, done anything, but she knew the value of a bombardment of words. If she played her cards right she need not actually make any specific promises at all.

'Oh, Mother, thank you,' she said fervently. 'I'll do everything Nanny tells me and I'll help her in the house, go shopping with her . . . I'll be very, very good.'

'I'll order the car for eleven o'clock,' her mother said, not bothering to reply. 'And I'll send for you as soon as Jane's back. And if it isn't convenient for Mrs Prescott she'll have to bring you home herself,' she added spitefully. 'And pay for a taxi – unless she brings you on the tram, of course.'

'Thank you, Mother,' Sara said again. She did not add that she knew Nanny would have walked home with her if necessary, nor that Nanny would be delighted to have her as a guest. Her mother, she knew, was quite capable of suddenly deciding that it had not been a good idea after all, and sharply retracting her promise.

But nothing of the sort happened. Her mother climbed the stairs and vanished around the corner and Sara continued on down to the basement.

In the kitchen, her news was greeted with some relief.

'It ain't that we don't want you, Miss Sara, but it's awkward, wi' Jane away,' Bessie explained. 'There's so much work, see, and cartin' your trays upstairs of a mornin', lightin' the schoolroom fire, makin' you a luncheon . . . well, it's all extra, when Jane's off.'

'I don't mind at all, because I like being at Nanny's so much,' Sara said. 'We have a lovely time, Nanny and me. Can I give you a hand with the washing-up, Bessie?'

'It's good of you, Miss, but I'll do it in no time. You go up and pack yourself a bag,' Bessie said diplomatically, clattering dishes. 'And don't forget to wear your wellington boots, acos the snow's that thick you'll be soaked, else.'

Sara agreed to do so and hurried back up the three flights of stairs once more, to the schoolroom high up under the eaves. She had never packed for herself before but could see no difficulty; she would just pack her nicest things and some play-clothes and then go and wait for Robson to bring the car round.

'Where's all your knickers, queen? And I can only find odd stockings.'

Nanny had been absolutely delighted to find her charge on her doorstep, beaming and rosy, with the news that she was to stay with Mrs Prescott until the girl Jane returned to her duties. She had hugged Sara, and kissed her many times, thanked Robson for his care of her and carried her off to the neat front parlour, where she put a match to the fire and then brought in some ginger biscuits and a cup of hot milk.

Explanations had taken up the next twenty minutes, and Nanny had said she was sorry to hear about Jane's mother and would visit her at the Stanley, which was only just up the road. Then they had talked of all they could do over the next few days, and then they had examined Nanny's bowl of bulbs, which Sara had given her for Christmas and which they had examined only a couple of days before. There were four snub green noses showing above the soil; Sara was anxious about the fifth, for she had planted the bowl herself, with the assistance of Rogers, her father's gardener, and did not like to think that one of the bulbs might have been bad.

But now, unpacking in the chilly little front bedroom, for Nanny would not have dreamed of lighting a fire upstairs unless someone was sick, Nanny was showing some dismay over Sara's choice of clothing.

Sara looked at the garments spread out over the single bed. 'What's wrong, Nanny? I put in some knickers, didn't I? And some stockings. Only I wanted to bring my tartan kilt and my nice green cardigan . . . and then there were boots, and extra socks, and my pom-pom slippers – oh dear, and if I go back Mother will probably change her mind and make me stay.'

'Well, we won't risk that, but you need more than one spare pair of knickers, love,' Nanny said. 'And I can't find a single pair of stockings, they're all odd.'

'How can they be odd? They're all black, and woolly, aren't they all alike?' Sara asked. 'I can't see any difference. Besides, it doesn't matter, does it? Stockings are stockings.'

'And pairs are pairs. But I suppose we can manage with the stockings. And I'll take you on the tram to Paddy's market and we'll buy some knickers.' Mrs Prescott smiled grimly. 'That'll teach your mother to send you to me without the proper clothes!'

'Why? What's wrong with Paddy's market?' Sara asked, ferreting through the clothes in her bag. 'I've got my coral beads in here somewhere . . . oh yes, they're in my black strap shoes, I knew I'd put them somewhere safe.'

'There's nothing wrong with it, but your mother don't like it because Paddy's market sells secondhand clothing. Do you mind secondhand clothing, queen?'

'No, not at all,' Sara said unhesitatingly. 'So long as it's fairly clean, of course.'

Mrs Prescott laughed. 'Only fairly clean? You're a one and a half, young Sara! Come on then, I've done up here, we'll get ourselves a bite to eat and then we'll walk down the road, do some shopping. What do you fancy for your tea tonight?'

They were in Samples, choosing a cake, when a woman standing at the counter, a woman who Sara half-recognised as living in Snowdrop Street, spotted them. She was talking to the baker and jabbing a finger at a big yellow bowl covered with a washed-out piece of linen but as soon as she saw Sara's companion she turned to greet her.

'Afternoon, Annie. What're you givin' for the wake, tomorrer? I'm tekin' fruit buns – that's the mix, there. Mr S is goin' to cook it up for me. Our Ruth's gorra nice piece o' boilin' bacon an' Mrs Lamb's givin' a couple o' dozen eggs. You can't expect the Carbs to mek a contribution, with 'im bein' out o' work an' 'er 'avin' the young 'uns to see to.'

'Afternoon, Hannah. I'm doing sandwiches,' Mrs Prescott said. 'I saw your Ruth, so I'm doin' fish paste and cheese. It's a terrible thing . . . the poor feller who was drivin' the engine must be half out of his mind!'

'You're right there,' the other woman agreed. 'Eh, I've allus worried about the rails bein' so near, but who'd ha' thought it could come to this?'

Sara pricked up her ears. What had happened? Had there been a train crash? She loved to look across at the big engines getting up steam, and at the lines and lines of goods trucks, but she knew there were accidents; trains collided, or left the rails, or crashed too hard into the buffers.

'Tragic,' Mrs Prescott said. 'Though that poor kid had a mis'rable life if you ask me. Stan hit the kids more'n he praised 'em . . . and there was never enough to eat. Nesta isn't so bad, though she's no patience with kids, but her old fella . . . well, you know how it is.'

'Aye; none better. My Ben drank once, but 'e's give it up now, thank the good Lord. Now tell me, Annie, 'ave they 'eard owt of the baby?' Hannah Evans was small and round with brown, birdlike eyes and a set of very white false teeth which looked as though they had been made for someone a good deal larger. Now she looked hungrily at her companion, as though gossip was edible, Sara thought, vaguely disturbed by the idea.

'Baby? What's this all about, Hannah?'

'Well, it seems young Jess took the baby out walkin' with her, an' when they found her, they didn't find no baby.' Hannah Evans paused discreetly, glancing down at Sara and then, quickly, away. 'Only from wharr I've been told the train went right over 'er . . . I thought mebbe there weren't no way to tell . . .'

'I've not heard any more than you have,' Mrs Prescott said quickly. 'I'll see you tomorrow, then, Hannah.'

'Right, Annie. I'll be off then. If you hear anything more, let me know.'

Mrs Prescott agreed and presently she and Sara left the shop with a large fruit cake in the wickerwork basket Sara carried.

'Nanny, what happened to Jess? I met a girl called Jess outside the church, on Christmas Day. I told you.'

'Yes, so you did, queen, but there's a mortal lot o' gels called Jess, and I doubt Jess Carbery would walk all the way to . . .' Sara's exclamation cut her off short. She looked down at the child. 'Oh, love, don't say it were *that* Jess?'

'Yes, it was, Nanny! What happened to her?' Sara asked, in anguish. It was something bad, she just knew it was, as much by the older women's tone as by their actual words.

'She – she was killed, love. By a train. Hit by a train. They say she died instantly, there weren't no sufferin'.'

Sara stared down at her boots and saw them wobble as tears brimmed in her eyes. Poor, poor Jess! She'd had so very little, now she had lost even that. But what about the baby? Jess had adored that baby – how would it manage, without her?

'And Mollie? The baby? I told you, Nanny, I gave Jess my angora gloves to keep the baby's toes warm. Did she have Mollie with her?'

There was another pause before Mrs Prescott answered her, and then Sara could tell that she was thinking hard.

'Yes, her mam says she had the baby with her, but folk are that ungenerous . . . they wonder, you see, if

Nesta . . . well, if she got rid of the baby, somehow. There are women what want babies . . . or she might've handed the child over to an orphan-home, once she knew about Jess. Jess took care o' the baby, see? But no one knows, rightly. Mollie's disappeared.'

'You told Mrs Evans you didn't know what had happened to the baby,' Sara said, fighting to keep her voice steady for her eyes were still brimming. She remembered them so well, it seemed impossible, and impossibly cruel, that Jess was dead and Mollie bereft of her only friend and protector. She remembered Jess saying *if she lives,* remembered her own shock at the words. Now it was Jess who had died and from the sound of it, Mollie had either died too or simply disappeared. She turned her face up to her nanny's, the tears still unshed. 'You did say you didn't know, Nanny.'

'Well, Mrs Evans is a good woman but a rare one to gossip,' Nanny explained. 'I didn't want to see bad made worse, queen. There's plenty what think wherever the baby is, she's better off than wi' the Carbs, which makes you wonder. A sweet, pretty thing she was, Mollie Carbery, but there's no doubtin' it, livin' wi' that family she couldn't be neither sweet nor pretty long. Not without Jess, that is,' she added.

'And when did it happen?' Sara said as soon as she had command of her voice again. 'I saw her at noon on Christmas Day I suppose, or thereabouts.'

'It was later on that same day,' Mrs Prescott said. 'Jess had bought bread and some milk and when she left the baker thought she meant to go straight home, but my guess is that she realised her father would take the food off her – or her mother, for that matter – and went into the goods yard. She'd lived near the lines for long enough to know that they only run a Sunday service on Christmas Day, but there had been a landslip because of all the snow, I suppose, and a train was taking a gang of men to the spot to clear the line for traffic next day. Neither the driver nor the fireman saw Jess, and probably, what with the driving snow and the wind and the darkness, she didn't see them, either.' Mrs Prescott touched Sara's cheek with a gentle hand, smoothing her bright hair back from her face. 'She didn't feel a thing, queen; it were too sudden, too quick.'

'She said she'd buy bread and milk with the money I gave her,' Sara said in a small, choked voice. 'She must have done just that. Oh, Nanny, Mother would say I should never have given her the money . . . and how I wish I hadn't! You could say the money was stolen, only it was me who stole it, not Jess. Could God have got muddled and punished her because the money should have been in the collection?'

Mrs Prescott stopped short and caught Sara's shoulder, turning her so that they faced one another across the snowy pavement.

'Don't you dare even think such a thing, queen,' she said fiercely. 'Remember the picture in your room? Suffer the little children to come unto Me, He said, and that's just what He meant. Our Lord would never punish a child in such a way, why you'll be up there with a gold crown on your 'ead and a pair o' wings on your shoulders 'cos you give that poor little kid a bit of 'ope. No one, not even your mam, would criticise you for givin' to the poor, at Christmas or any other time.'

'Oh. Good,' Sara said faintly. 'Will they find the baby, Nanny? Will they find little Mollie?'

'Oh, bound to,' Mrs Prescott said comfortably, turning her face towards home once more. 'And if they don't it'll be because someone took pity on 'er, and took 'er away from them Carbs. Now best foot forward, queen, or I won't have a potato peeled by teatime!'

Brogan got off the ferry when she berthed and stood for a moment on the quay, fighting the tears that brimmed his eyes. He had wept, and others with him, as the ship drew near to the land and they knew they were almost home at last. But now they were ashore the air was thick with fog, the streetlights could barely be seen through it. Smells which he associated with his home and nowhere else assailed his nostrils; fish, seaweed, mud, and the scent of boiled potatoes coming from the tenements behind the docks where the women were cooking the evening meal.

It was cold, but nowhere near as cold as Liverpool; a mildness in the air, which he thought was reflected in the manners of the people, was as much a part of Dublin as the Liffey, flowing brown to the left of him, or the domed Custom House, or Ha'penny Bridge, which he would presently cross in order to reach the maze of little streets known as the Liberties, where the O'Bradys had lived as long as any of them could remember. And God knew why those streets should be called the Liberties, Brogan thought bitterly now, glancing down the front of his coat at the slumbering child which he held to his breast. Liberty wasn't something which came naturally to those who struggled to survive there: he only hoped he was doing the right thing for this defenceless scrap.

In fact Brogan knew very well how the Liberties had been given their name. All Dublin children were taught in school that, long ago, the Liberties had been a straggle of mean huts and the people there had not been taxed, because they were outside the city walls and had none of the good things which the citizens of Dublin had. So they nicknamed the area 'the liberties' because of not paying tax and there you were, a misnomer if ever he heard one.

But now, all he could think of was his own place, his mammy cooking a meal for the family, his brothers clustering round, one boy telling about his day, another interrupting, all laughing, getting as near the fire as they could, happy to have exchanged the chilly, fog-bound streets for the little oasis of comfort and warmth that was the O'Brady living parlour. Brogan, striding on, smiled to himself. He would get such a welcome! His mammy would undoubtedly weep all over him . . . oh, but when she saw the baby! He'd had seven brothers, four of whom survived, but there had never been a girl, never a sister for them. It had grieved his mammy, who had always dreamed of a girl-child, but she'd made the best of it.

'Sure and aren't I the lucky one, with fellas all around me?' she teased them. 'Oh, who wants old girls when they can have fine, strong sons?'

When he had first come ashore he had thought it milder than Liverpool but as he walked through the quiet quays the wind began to creep inside his collar, up his sleeves, and it was cold. He turned his coat-collar up and peered down at the baby once more. She was rosy-cheeked, sleeping soundly. Eh, but she'd been good! Not a peep out of her had there been, neither on the journey across the Irish Sea – Brogan had clutched her fiercely as the small ship crashed into the trough of a wave and staggered up to the crest – and everyone had thought he was fighting seasickness. Good job I wasn't, he told himself now with grim humour. How would I have managed if I'd wanted to lean over the side? I'd have lost Moll for sure!

But he hadn't, so all was well. And very soon now she could come out from her hiding place and reap the admiration which, Brogan thought, was her due. Besides, she was soaking wet. The men had clubbed together and bought a pile of towelling for him to use but he had no means of washing it aboard so had simply jettisoned each piece and moved on to the next – and the last had been the last, so he should hurry himself, get back to his mammy, who was someone who understood a good deal more than he did about babies.

He crossed O'Connell Street, admired the brightly lit shop windows, the figures of one or two smart couples strolling along it. He reached the Ha'penny Bridge, and climbed the steps, then set off across it. It was really called the Metal Bridge or the Wellington Bridge, but everyone knew it as the Ha'penny Bridge, from the days when they'd charged you a halfpenny toll to cross. It was a beautiful bridge and even with the fog swirling and hiding the waters of the Liffey, dazzling in haloes round the gas-lights, it was a lovely sight with its delicate wrought-iron railings and the arches which spanned the walkers beneath.

He could have taken several ways from here to get home and the fog seemed thicker by the river but nevertheless he decided to stick to the Quays. He walked swiftly, his scarf up round his mouth now in the fog and deepening dusk. Where Merchants Quay met Low Bridge Street he turned left, then began to weave his way up towards Thomas Street. He turned right into Cornmarket and then he was on Thomas Street, crossing it, diving down Francis Street and then into Swift's Alley, his breathing quickening, a smile tilting his mouth. Home! Swift's Alley might not be everyone's idea of gracious living, but . . . it was home!

He dived into the narrow entry, turned right, and there it was. A tall tenement block with the washing lines which looped the house-fronts hung with limp, unmoving linen, the lines themselves beaded with moisture. He guessed that the womenfolk would have left their sheets and towels hanging out rather than bring them into the rooms still soaked through. He hurried in through the doorway, feeling the child stir sleepily against him. The lobby was damp with all the footsteps of folk passing through but it was clean; a good deal cleaner, he thought protectively, than some of the big public buildings he had known. It smelt of carbolic soap, fish and potatoes, with the faint rivery smell which seemed to hang over the whole city – and of course the smell of the fog. A smell of coal fires, and salt-sea, and wet wood and stone.

He climbed the stairs quite slowly, able to wait now that he was so close. The baby woke properly; it was time for her to be fed, he supposed. She began to struggle but he soothed her, cooed to her, kept his coat round her. She was his reason for coming home, his special surprise, she must not put in an appearance too soon!

The door to the O'Brady room was closed. He turned the handle carefully, then pushed the door open cautiously, bit by bit, so that he could see inside without being seen. The door opened straight into their main room, naturally, with the second room leading off from the first, with no door on to the communal landing.

'It's a fire hazard, that inner room,' a priest had said once, when he was visiting them. 'How would you get the children out safe, Mrs O'Brady, if there was a fire ragin' in your nice parlour?'

'Sure an' I'd t'row 'em t'rough the window,' his

mother had said, smiling. 'My kids are full o' spirit, Father – they'd bounce, every last one of 'em.'

The priest had smiled, too.

'But best keep a bucket of water in the bedroom, even so,' he had advised mildly. 'Bouncin' fireballs is no joke, Mrs O'Brady.'

But now, Brogan looked into the room, and it was as if he had the second sight; everything was just as he'd imagined it. Mammy, stirring a pot, the steam making the little black curls round her face curlier than ever. The boys with their tin plates at the ready, watching for the moment when Mammy said it was done and dipped into the stew with her big ladle. The firelight turning the faces to rose and gold, the lantern on the table casting a cool primrose light, hissing softly away to itself.

Someone gasped; Mammy turned. She stared for a moment, then the ladle flew into the fire and Mammy flew across the room seizing Brogan so hard, squeezing him so fiercely, that he feared for the baby.

'Mammy! Ah, Mammy, I've missed you sore! But don't squeeze me to death, I've a present for you under me coat!'

They were all round him, hugging, exclaiming, asking where Peader was, why Brogan had come home alone – and after Christmas too, when all the fun and frolic was over and done for another year!

'Did you have a good Christmas, my dearest?' his mother asked, still hanging on to his coat sleeve as though she dared not let him go in case he disappeared. 'We had a good time, or as good a time as we could have, wit'out you and me darlin' Peader. I sold oranges on O'Connell Street on Christmas Eve, and I had a line waitin', honest to God I did!'

His mother was delighted with her fruit-selling, she

wanted everyone to know that it wasn't only potatoes she could sell, no indeed, selling was something at which she excelled, her shining eyes said. And wasn't she the prettiest woman ever, Brogan thought fondly. Her eyes were blue as summer skies, her hair black as a raven's wing, and she had dimples and the sweetest smile. No wonder Dubliners had queued up to buy her oranges on Christmas Eve!

'I made five bob in an hour,' his mother was saying. 'Where's me present then, Brogan? Did your daddy send it? Oh, why didn't he come home wit' you, son? He's sadly missed; isn't it dull and flat without your daddy, then?'

The boys agreed that it was and stared at Brogan's coat, which was now heaving gently as the baby tried to escape from its folds.

'It's a puppy!' yelled Martin. He had always wanted a puppy but Mammy said it wasn't fair with them living on the first floor and no way a puppy could run out to do his business.

'A puppy!' Donal echoed. He was a sturdy six-year-old and toothless until the second ones came through. He grinned gummily at his eldest brother. 'Jeez, Brog, you've brought our mammy a puppy!'

Hastily, before hearts were broken – and Mollie was seen as second-best – Brogan undid his coat and lifted the baby from her warm little nest. Peader had formed a sling from an old scarf which had held her secure all through their journey but now she stared at the faces around her as though she could not believe her eyes.

'It's a girl,' Brogan said, but he felt there could be no doubt. Mollie was so pink-cheeked, so bright-eyed, the picture of feminine charm and innocence from the top of her curly head to the tip of her rosy toes, and Brogan heard the admiring gasps, the cries of 'Oh, Brog, what a little dote! Where did you get her, the darlin'? Is she yours, boyo?' with real pleasure. They liked her – and Mammy was gazing at Mollie as though... oh, as though all her dearest wishes had come true!

'Brogan? Where... How... Who...?'

''Tis a long story,' Brogan said, taking off his coat and hanging it on the hook behind the door. 'Serve up the meal, Mammy, whiles I tell you how I come by her.'

'You're a good, kind fella, and 'twas no fault of yours that the child's sister was killed,' Deirdre said when his story – and the plate of stew and potatoes – was finished. 'Sure and I'll look after her as though she were me own flesh and blood, and won't I love her as I love me own, too?'

'I never doubted it,' Brogan assured her. 'Daddy's the same, he didn't want her to go back to a man who beats his kids. She's no trouble,' he added hastily. 'And I'll send all me wages home, same as before. I'll work harder, Mammy, so you aren't burdened by the kid.'

'She's no burden,' his mammy insisted. She had taken Mollie on her knee and had spooned bread and milk into her eager mouth. 'But, Brog, I've just had a t'ought. What'll we tell the neighbours?'

'Tell 'em she's an orphan from the country, left wit' us by a cousin,' Niall said after a moment's silence. 'Do you remember your cousin Fidelma? Doesn't she seem a likely one to do somethin' strange, now?'

Everyone laughed except for Bevin, who was too little to remember the strange cousin who had come a-visiting two years since, and driven them all mad with her odd ways and her demands to be taken here and there, to see the sights of the city.

'Ye-es, but not concernin' a baby,' Mammy said at

length. 'It 'ud be better if we picked a cousin called Mairenn, who did wrong and dared not take her child home to the farm with her. Can you remember that? You're the baby, Bevin, you tell me the story.'

'I'm not the baby now, am I though?' Bevin said proudly, pointing at the child on his mother's lap. 'She's the baby – Mollie's the baby. Oh, isn't she a pretty one, Mammy? Isn't she tarrible sweet now?'

'She is. Now tell me where she come from, me little jewel.'

Bevin frowned.

'From – from heaven, Mammy? From God, to us, for bein' good?'

The bigger boys began to laugh and jeer, but Mammy stopped them short with a frown and a shake of the head.

'That's very true, Bevin, and aren't you a broth of a boy now, for knowin' it? But what'll we tell folk who ask how we come to have such a lovely wee girl, now?'

Bevin had been scowling angrily at his brothers but now his brow cleared. 'Oh, that's aisy, so it is,' he said scornfully. 'Mairenn from the farm done wrong, and dussen't take the baby back with her, so we took her, the darlin'.'

Mammy clapped, Brogan cheered, the boys all laughed and followed suit. Even the baby, enthroned upon Mammy's lap, smiled and gurgled.

'There we are, then,' Mammy said triumphantly. 'She'll be Polly O'Brady from now on . . . my dear little Irish Liverpool baby!' She turned to Brogan. 'You'll be stayin' now, won't you?' she coaxed. 'You wouldn't want to go back to that old Liverpool, they'll mebbe ask you questions you can't answer, son.'

The child recently re-christened Polly had finished her bread and milk so Brogan took the dish and carried it over to the basin standing on the table against the wall. He put it in the basin and then refilled the kettle from the bucket and stood it on the metal trivet which poked it into the red heart of the fire.

'Mammy, I wish I could stay,' he said from the heart. 'But there's no job in Dublin that 'ud pay me like the navvyin' job in Liverpool. And though Mollie – I mean Polly – is small now, she'll eat her share, need clothin', go to school when she's big enough. It all costs, Mammy.'

'We'll manage, but I daresay you're right and you should be with your daddy,' his mother said contentedly. 'Can she crawl, the little cherub?'

'Put her down on the rag rug and you'll see for yourself,' Brogan said, smiling. His mother, who had borne so many children, was like a child with a lovely new dolly. She could scarcely wait to take it out, show it to the neighbours. 'Where'll she sleep, Mammy?'

'Where but in me bed, the dote,' Deirdre said fondly. 'And later, in a nice orange box. For I have to work, no matter what. But the rest of you came on the streets with me when you were small, well-wrapped up in a nice fruit box, she'll be no different.'

'She's too big for a fruit box, Mammy,' Brogan said anxiously. 'She'd be out of it and crawlin' amongst the traffic in no time. See?'

And sure enough, Polly was off, crawling briskly across the linoleum, heading for the fire's glow. But she was re-directed by several small, grubby hands, and when she reached a chair she tried to pull herself into a standing position by it and was much praised by the onlookers.

And presently, Brogan went into the second room with his brothers whilst his mammy pulled out her bed, which was a good straw mattress, a pillow and a couple of blankets. She cuddled Polly, already sleeping soundly, down, and then bade her sons goodnight.

'I'll not wake Brogan, he deserves a lie-in, but the rest of you had best be up betimes,' she said as she stood in the doorway between the two rooms with her hair brushed out so that it was like a dark halo around her head. 'There'll be oatmeal for breakfast and some bread and jam. We've still got some left over from me Christmas store.'

'I'll get up when me brothers do,' Brogan said. 'I don't mind, Mammy, honest. I'd as soon be up, because tomorrow I must get me a ticket for the return trip on the ferry boat. Daddy and the other fellers are covering for me – they've told the boss that I was called back to Ireland on Christmas Day to see a sick relative. But I don't want to lose me job, and Daddy's hopin' for advancement quite soon. He's steady, is our daddy, and the bosses know it. Sure and it wouldn't do him a good turn if I stayed away any longer than I need, so I'll be off when I can.'

His mother sighed but she knew better than to argue. Brogan knew that the harder his daddy worked and the more money he earned, the sooner he would be able to come home here for a good holiday if not for ever, and his mammy realised it too.

'Right, Brog,' she said. 'See you in the mornin', then, me laddo. And it's sleep you're in there for, boys, d'you hear me? No chatterin' half the night and keepin' your brother from the rest he needs.'

But nothing could have prevented Brogan from sleeping that night, not the narrowness of the straw mattress he shared with Martin and Donal, not the whisperings of the older boys, not even the terrible throttling snores of Niall, who suffered with catarrh. And once he was asleep he did not stir until morning, though he dreamed, and twitched, and cried out a couple of times.

He longed to dream of Jess again so that he could ask her forgiveness, but all he dreamed of was that the baby ran away from him on the ferry, and climbed the rail and fell over the side, and when he dived in after her it was straight into thick yellow fog, in which not even the brown waters of the Liffey could be seen or felt.

Chapter Four

When Brogan got back to Liverpool it was to find the snow melting in a fierce, almost springlike wind, and the whole city in an uproar over the missing baby.

'There's been a piece in the paper,' Peader hissed to him when they were in bed that night in their lodgings. 'Mollie's mammy says as how she's been stolen away by gypsies . . . but one of the fellers says she's tryin' to make capital out of it so she is . . . hopin' someone will pay her money for her loss. Sure and would you believe a woman could be so wicked?'

'Jeez, I hope they never find out where the littl'un's gone; and we've decided to call her Polly, by the way, for safety's sake,' Brogan whispered. 'Because if they try to take Polly away me mammy will kill me and anyway, that woman, that Mrs Carbery, she never had no time for the kid, Jess said so. Oh, Daddy, I don't want to be throwed in gaol – specially not an English gaol.'

'Devil a bit will they throw you in gaol; for what can they prove, eh?' his father whispered back. 'A nine-days' wonder, so it is, and that's the end of it. Give it another week at the most and no one will know who you mean if you say "Mollie Carbery".'

'I hope you're right,' Brogan said devoutly. 'Best say nothing then, eh, Daddy?'

'Far best,' his father said shortly. 'I'm goin' before a board to see whether they think I could do safety man;

there's a dacent pay rise goes wit' the position. We don't want to risk losin' that, do we?'

So Brogan decided to pretend that he, too, had never heard the name Mollie Carbery. He would think of the child always, now, as Polly O'Brady. And on that comforting thought he slept at last.

Sara thoroughly enjoyed her stay with Mrs Prescott, though she was sorry when the snow began to melt so that Snowdrop Street no longer looked white and enticing but grey and drab and wet, instead.

Despite Mrs Prescott making sandwiches for the wake, neither she nor her young charge attended Jess's funeral.

'They're an unpleasant family, or the parents are,' Nanny told Sara. 'Neither her nor him would raise a finger to do anything for the child whiles she was alive, and they'll do precious little now she's dead. Nesta – that's the mother – talked to the *Echo* because she hoped to make capital out of her loss, but whatever money they paid her for her story went on drink.'

'But Nanny, women don't drink, do they?' Sara said doubtfully. 'I know men drink, but I thought women stayed at home.'

'Well, you were wrong. Nesta Carbery drinks whenever she's got the means to go down to the Jug and Bottle and buy the stuff,' Nanny said distastefully. 'It'll not be long before they're turned out, anyway. People like them never pay the rent.'

Sara would have liked to have paid her respects to Jess, particularly as she still felt deeply guilty over having given Jess stolen money. Despite her Nanny's comforting words she still felt uneasily that the money might have been unlucky in some way. But the days passed, and once or twice she saw members of the family passing by, grey-skinned, apathetic, miserable, and had to echo Mrs Prescott's words – that perhaps poor Jess was the lucky one.

And the neighbours didn't like them, didn't extend to them the same tolerance they extended to others, though they were quick to offer food, clothing, even odds and ends of bedding, to help the family after their loss. She saw that good women, like her nanny and her neighbours, would exchange a word or two with Stan or Nesta Carbery and then quickly move away, as though they did not want to remain in their company. It seemed strange to Sara.

Finally, however, she managed to put her finger on what was wrong. The neighbours felt let down that such a family could exist in their very street, and that they could do nothing about it. A good many people in the street had large families and struggled to keep their kids and themselves fed and clothed, but no one simply gave up on the kids and concentrated solely on themselves. No one but the Carbs, that was. He bragged and bullied, she whined and whinged, but it was easy to see that anything which went into their home would end up on the backs or in the bellies of Nesta and Stan. The kids, from the moment they were born if Mollie was anything to go by, would have to fight their own battles, make their own way in life.

'Sara, my dear, Jess and Mollie were very unfortunate little girls, but they've gone to a better place,' Mrs Prescott said to her the day after the funeral, when she saw Sara moping around the house. 'Have you seen Grace Carbery? She's like a little ghost, wanting something that those wretched parents of hers can't, or won't, give. As for Mollie, I don't, myself, believe she's dead. I think someone saw her and pitied her and took her away to another, better home. But in any event, you must stop blaming yourself or even thinking about them now. It's downright morbid and unhealthy, and if you continue to do it, then I'll have no choice but to send you back to Aigburth Road and your mother and father.'

'Nanny, you wouldn't,' Sara gasped, unable to believe that her nanny could possibly sink so low, but Mrs Prescott nodded firmly.

'I would, queen. Once you were home you'd stop thinking about them, so if you can't do it here, you'd best go home.'

'I'll stop blaming myself if I possibly can,' Sara promised unhappily. 'I know it's silly, or a part of me does, but there's another part which says I took money which didn't belong to me, and I know that's bad. The Reverend Atwell is awfully strong against theft, I'm sure he'd say at once that money intended for the church must go there, no matter what.'

There was a short silence, and then Mrs Prescott went out of the room – the two of them had been sitting by the fire in her parlour – and rummaged around in the back kitchen, to return presently with something in her hand. She held it out.

'There you are; a shilling. It's for your collection next Sunday,' she said briskly. 'You are to put it in the plate together with whatever money your parents may give you. So that's easily settled.'

And oddly enough, it was. A great wave of relief washed over Sara as she took the money and put it into the pocket of her best coat.

'Oh, Nanny, thank you,' she breathed, reaching up and kissing Mrs Prescott's soft cheek. 'You don't know how much better I feel!'

And it was true. Knowing that she would presently be paying the money back to the church from which she felt she had taken it removed the burden of guilt from Sara and made her feel very much better.

And the very next day she met the boy.

'Oh, Sara, me head's splittin',' Mrs Prescott said next day, when she and Sara met over breakfast. 'I don't even fancy the porridge, and it's usually me favourite way to start the day. Can you be a good girl, queen, and amuse yourself today? You'll have to do some shopping for me – can you go along to the chemist, and ask Mr Hanson for some of his headache cure? It's better than aspirin, most of us swear by it. And then I need some scrag end to make a stew – I'll have about a pound in weight – and tell Mr Lowey I'll have a nice lean piece of pork for the weekend; I'll call in Saturday. Oh, and can you get me half a dozen eggs, and then you can play out, if you like. Only don't stray too far, and if you can bear it, come in around noon and see how I feel. If this headache keeps on, though, all I'll want will be a cuppa and some more aspirin tablets. Now can you manage all that or shall I get Mrs Rushton or Kate to give a hand?'

'Of course I can manage, Nanny,' Sara said rather hotly. 'I love shopping, and I won't let anyone cheat me. Not that they'll try, because they know I'm staying with you.'

'Right. You could call round for young Cammy – you and she get on well, I've noticed that.'

'We do,' Sara owned. 'She's taught me ever so many games, Nanny. Some of them are real good ones. But she's the best skipper in the world, I should think – she can do all the fancy steps and when we race I keep missing jumps but she turns the rope as smooth and even as – as a wheel. Yes, I'll give her a call when I go past.'

But when she got round to number five Snowdrop Street, she was in for a disappointment. Cammy had really bad toothache. She came to the door, her face swollen and lopsided, with a hot rag held against the offending cheek, to tell Sara that she was being dragged off to the dental hospital in Pembroke Place.

'I don't want to go,' she confided in a breathy whisper. 'But me mam'll 'ave me guts for garters if I don't gerron on the tram with 'er and go up there. And right now I woun't care if they pulled me bleeding 'ead off, so long as the pain stopped an' all.'

'You would; it would hurt like fun I bet,' Sara said. 'I am sorry. though, Cammy. I'd come with you, but Nanny's not well and I'm going to do her marketing and take care of her. She's got one of her heads.'

'You mek it sound as though she keeps spare 'eads in a cupboard,' Cammy said, then winced and put a hand to her cheek. 'Oh, gawd, don't mek me laugh, it's too bleedin' painful! See you later, then, queen. Be good.'

It was easy enough to be good when you were doing the shopping, though Sara still found it exciting to go by herself along Stanley Road. She didn't hurry, either, in fact you could have said that she dawdled. Past the tobacconist with its little tins of pipe tobacco, boxes of rich-looking cigars and packets of cigarettes with a handsome, if elderly, sailor on the packet, and on to the Misses Irving's confectionery shop. A lovely window this, you could almost smell the sweets, though the toffees, liquorice walking sticks and sherbert dips looked rather dusty and neglected. But through the door you could see the big jars of sweeties, and the smell which came out was enough to set a child's mouth watering.

King's grocery shop came next. Quite interesting,

with lots of advertisements stuck to the window glass so you could hardly see inside, and sacks of flour, oatmeal, haricot beans and lentils piled up against the wooden counter. Nanny shopped at King's, so in Sara popped and bought six fine-looking eggs.

After that there was only the chemist, Mr Hanson, on the corner of Fountains Road, and because she needed to go in she scarcely glanced in his window, though the big jars of coloured water caught the light as she passed them and looked, for a moment, like enormous rubies and emeralds. Inside the shop she explained about Mrs Prescott's headache and was given a tiny pink bag with some tablets in.

'Two, three times a day, with a nice hot cup of tea,' Mr Hanson said. 'She'll be right as a trivet by tomorrow morning.'

And once over the road, which she crossed cautiously, conscious that she was unaccompanied by an adult, there was a good walk past the Stanley Hospital – she ran most of it – to cross Easby Road and reach her favourite shop.

It was a pawnshop – Williams was the name above the door – and his window was a delight. Clothes, curtains, shoes, ornaments, bits of furniture, toys. It was a treat just to look, though Nanny would never even pause a moment by the window of the pawn.

'Why not, Nanny? There's some very pretty things,' Sara had said, tugging at Mrs Prescott's sleeve. 'Do come and look!'

But Mrs Prescott had been firm. 'They're unredeemed stock,' she said. 'That means the folk put 'em in pawn and then couldn't find the five bob or whatever to get 'em out again. It's a sad window if you ask me.'

But Sara, though she acknowledged that it was sad

when people didn't have the money to buy their things back – she was hazy as to the actual business conducted by pawn-brokers – still enjoyed looking in the window and was able, this morning, to have an uninterrupted stare, though she was jostled somewhat by passers-by, for the street was busy with people shopping after the holiday.

Despite the fact that she knew herself to possess many more of the world's goods than most people, Sara still yearned after one or two things in the window. A pair of china kittens with blue eyes and grey fur, their little heads tilted to one side, for instance. They would look lovely on the schoolroom mantel, or even in her bedroom. And then there were the ice skates. Fancy, a pair of ice skates in Stanley Road! Whoever had put them in pawn must have either nicked 'em or been rich, she and Cammy had decided when they discussed it, because ordinary folk did not own ice skates.

But wouldn't I love a pair, Sara thought now, nose pressed to the glass like any other wistful but penniless urchin. I bet I could skate ever so well, if only I had some skates to put on. But then it'll be spring soon, and the ice will all go away, so there's not much point in wanting *them*. How about a nice tennis racquet? Only I've no one to play with. Well then, how about a skipping rope?

But gazing into the pawn was not what Mrs Prescott had meant by 'amuse yourself', so Sara gave the objects of her desire one last, long look and then trotted past Miss Gourley's hairdressing establishment and Mrs Lang's florist shop with scarcely more than a glance. The florist was exhibiting a display of rather weary-looking holly today and the stiff wax heads wearing unattractive and over-curled wigs in Miss Gourley's window were too like dead people to Sara's way of thinking. So she hurried along until she reached the butcher's for which she was bound.

Mr Lowey's shop was not full, but there were women waiting to be served so Sara took her place at the end of the line, scuffing her feet in the sawdust and trying to breathe shallow because the smell of blood and bones was not pleasant. However, the line moved quickly and presently she was standing at the top of the long wooden counter, with Mr Lowey's boy, a spotty-faced individual called Bert, facing her.

'Yes, Miss? Can I get you somethin'?'

'Mrs Prescott said to ask you for some scrag end for a stew and a nice lean piece of pork for roasting, she'll pick the pork up Saturday,' Sara recited. 'About a pound of scrag, she said.'

'And how is Mrs Prescott?' Mr Lowey called from further down the counter. 'Not poorly, I 'ope?'

'She's got a headache,' Sara admitted. 'It's really bad, that's why I'm doing her shopping. But after I've done I can play out.'

'Well, at least the sun's shining,' Mr Lowey observed. 'You'll 'ave to run about to keep warm though, chuck. It don't do to 'ang about when the wind's cutting like this one is.'

Sara hadn't noticed that the wind was particularly cold but walking home with her now laden shopping basket she did think that perhaps, since Cammy was busy at the clinic, wherever that might be, she might stay indoors, do a jigsaw, or write another story in her homework book. She had begun one only the previous day in which a brigand with a big black beard, a heroine who looked very similar to Sara and a friendly orange cat figured large. It might be fun to go on with it . . . at least until Cammy returned from the clinic, hopefully minus both the toothache and the tooth.

Accordingly she returned to number three and made a cup of tea, then carried it carefully up the stairs, for Mrs Prescott had succumbed and gone back to bed.

'Oh, bless you, queen . . . you've got the pills an' all,' Mrs Prescott said huskily, as soon as Sara appeared round the bedroom door. 'Once they're down the little red lane I'll feel heaps better. And nice hot tea – oh, I am being spoiled today.'

'What about some bread and butter, or a piece of the fruit cake you got back from Samples yesterday?' Sara said softly. She felt like a nurse, and very virtuous into the bargain.

'No thanks, queen, nothing to eat. But you make yourself something before you go out to play,' Mrs Prescott said. She had taken the little pink pills and now she lay back on her pillows, smiling faintly. 'When you come in for tea, I'll probably be up and scrubbin' the kitchen floor for something to do!'

'I don't think you should, Nanny; I'll come in before it gets dark and see how you are again,' Sara said. She guessed that Mrs Prescott would feel a good deal more comfortable if she knew her charge was safely playing out and not fiddling around in the kitchen below, where there were so many things which could do her harm. Sharp knives, hot fire, even an attempt at cooking could be dangerous if you spilled boiling water over yourself. 'Well, if you're sure you're all right I'll be off, Nanny. I'll buy myself a pastie from the shop for my lunch. I've got some change.'

'That's grand, queen,' the woman in the bed said feebly. 'I don't fancy you tryin' to cook and that's a fact, though I know you've a sensible head on your shoulders. And now I think I'll have a bit of a nap.'

She lay down on the pillow again and, Sara suspected, was asleep before her guest had left the room.

True to her word, Sara walked down to the nearest canny house and went in. It was only someone's front room on Stanley Street, but the lady of the house, Bessie Arthurs, stood behind the counter which her sons had made for her, dispensing soup for 2d, stew for 4d – more if you wanted bread and butter with it – and a meat and potato pastie for 6d. Sara, whose mouth had watered at the sight of those hot meat and potato pasties, produced her money, seized her pastie, thanked Mrs Arthurs for her kindness and made for the door once more. It was a *huge* pastie, it could have fed three or four . . . but she would manage most of it without too much trouble. She would just take it home and . .

Her thoughts stopped short. If she went home Mrs Prescott would worry, she just knew it. No, she would take the pastie somewhere quiet . . .

Somewhere quiet? On Stanley Road? In the school holidays nowhere was quiet, even down the jiggers you'd find kids playing. I'd best go over to Kirkdale recreation ground, Sara thought rather desperately. It's too snowy for the kids to bother to go there, and the Free Library is only a stone's throw away; when I've finished my food I can nip over to the library and take a look at the books.

It was a cause of some grievance that Mrs Prescott didn't like her to borrow books from the Free Library.

'You could catch anything, queen,' she said disapprovingly. 'There's all sorts handle them books, you could get scarlet fever, brain disease . . . oh aye, you may widen your eyes at me, but books carry disease, I'm tellin' you.'

But Cammy borrowed books from there, and most

of the women in Snowdrop Street, and they didn't drop dead from brain disease. I'll risk it, Sara decided as she plodded up towards Orwell Road. It's a shame though, the pastie will be cold long before I get to the reccy.

However, she tucked it inside her warm coat and ran quite a lot of the way and turned into Sessions Road rather hot and breathless but still with the pastie nicely warm against her chest.

Down past the side of the Free Library she went and into the recreation ground. The bowling green was still snow-covered, but most of the flower-beds and lawns were clear, now, and Sara quickly found a seat which was quite dry. There were no kids about, either, which was nice; usually the place swarmed with boys illegally playing football and girls skipping, but it was dinner-time. No doubt the kids were all indoors, having their meal.

Sara unwrapped the pastie; the smell curled up, delicious, warming, promising. She took a big bite and chewed vigorously. It was absolutely prime, as good as any food she had ever eaten, and she was really hungry, it was ages since breakfast.

Then she saw the girl. She was a tiny creature of about four or five, skinny and big-eyed, and dressed in a ragged cardigan over a patched dress. The dress was too short, so that it did not hide her bare legs, blue with cold. She was staring at Sara's pastie and as she turned her head she reminded Sara sharply of someone.

''Ello, Miss,' the little girl said. 'Vat smells good!'

Sara smiled at the child's wistful expression. 'Hello! Yes, it does smell nice, but it's far too big for one person. Are you hungry? I can break it in half easily, then we can both enjoy it.'

'I'm turble 'ungry, I am that,' the girl said. 'The fing

is, I 'aven't 'ad no time for no dinner. I'm huntin' for me baby sister.'

Sara stared at the little girl and suddenly she remembered Jess saying that she had another sister, a sister who had been poorly on Christmas Day. Could this be that sister? She did look rather like Jess with her pale, draggly hair, and thin white face.

Sara stood up. 'What's your name?' she said, carefully. She did not want to frighten the child off. 'I wonder if – if I might have known your sister, you see.'

The child stared at her briefly, then her eyes returned to the pastie in Sara's hand. 'I do 'ave a sister; she's called Addy,' she said. 'Who's you?'

'I'm Sara. Just let me divide the pastie and then perhaps we can have a proper talk.' Sara smiled at the little girl, divided the pastie into two pieces, and then held one piece out enticingly. 'You said you were hunting for your baby sister; would that be . . .'

One minute the child was taking the pastie, the next she had glanced over her shoulder, eyes widening. Sara followed her gaze but all she could see was a man in a navy cap and jacket walking unconcernedly across the grass, so she turned her attention back to the child once more, only to find that the little girl had vanished.

Startled, Sara glanced around her. There was no one nearby but, over to her right, she saw a small, shabby figure, running as hard as it could along the gravelled path. She reached the end of the path and swerved to her right, disappearing into a bed of snow-laden shrubs.

Sara jumped to her feet and set off in pursuit. It was, in a way, my fault that Jess got killed, and I still don't know what happened to baby Mollie, she told herself as she ran. But if I go straight across the grass I won't be far behind the kid and perhaps if I reached her we could talk, I could explain . . . help her. That might make up for what happened to Jess. And the kid did say she was searching for her baby sister – oh I do want to catch her and tell her it's all right, I'm her friend!

But the skinny little scrap could really run and Sara was still a long way behind when she herself ran full tilt into someone. A sturdy someone, who caught hold of her shoulders and said, in a rich Irish accent, 'And where d'you t'ink you're goin', alanna? Dear God in heaven, you nearly had me flat on me back and me twice your size and weight!'

'Nowhere . . . anywhere . . . I'm trying to catch up with a – a friend,' Sara panted, trying to wrench herself out of the man's grip without any success at all. 'I don't know why she ran away, unless she thought I was going to ask for the piece of pastie back! Do let me go, sir, because I did an awful thing . . . someone was killed . . . and that little girl . . . oh, now she really *has* disappeared – might have been the sister . . . Jess and Mollie's sister, the one who got left behind on Christmas Day! If I could find her, talk to her, then between us we might find Mollie!'

'If the kid's disappeared . . . *Jess,* did you say?' The man held her away from him, holding her by the shoulders now. 'And *Mollie*? Not – not Jess and Mollie Carbery?'

'Yes, that's right,' Sara said. She realised that her eyes were tear-filled and scrubbed crossly at them with both fists. 'It was a Carbery, I'm sure it was. She – she told me she was looking for her baby sister, she said she was hungry but she hadn't time . . .'

'Look, alanna, I knew Jess too, and the baby as well . . . but there's no point in standing out in this cold. Come over to the shelter. At least we'll be out of the rain.'

Sara had not even noticed that it had started raining but now she looked about her and saw the raindrops pitting the remaining snow, falling quite hard on the gravel paths and the empty, winter flower-beds.

'Are you comin'? Devil a bit do you know me, but take a good look; I'm sixteen, me name's Brogan O'Brady, and I've never harmed chick nor child in me life, I promise you that.'

Sara stared. He looked dependable, she thought, and nice. He had very dark hair beneath a navy cap, eyes so dark a brown that they were almost black, and a square chin. He was wearing a navy jacket and trousers and big boots and despite the cold, or perhaps because of it, his face was flushed. But Nanny had said not to talk to strange men ever, under any circumstances. Did he count as a man, though, at sixteen? It was a knotty problem. Surely it would be all right – she would be sixteen herself in four more years! She stared very hard at him and decided to trust him.

'Yes, all right, I'll come with you,' Sara said, making up her mind. Nanny also said you had to judge people as you found them, and she found this young man worthy of her confidence. 'My name's Sara – Sara Cordwainer. What did you say you were called?'

'Brogan. 'Tis Irish,' her companion said. 'This way; we aren't supposed to cross the grass but I daresay there's no one to notice, and it's the quickest way to the shelter.' He pointed as he spoke and Sara saw, on the opposite side of the grass, a rustic shelter with a seat in it.

In rather less than a minute the two of them reached it and sat down, turning to face one another as they did so. Then they both smiled, Sara rather diffidently.

She had made a fool of herself, talking about Jess and Mollie like that: what must he have thought? But she found out soon enough.

'Now, Sara. When did you meet Jess, or have you known her a while, maybe?'

'No, I met her the day she died, on Christmas Day. They were outside our church when we went for morning service. Jess had Mollie in her arms, you see. I feel awfully bad about them both, because . . . but tell me how you knew her.'

'I met her on Christmas Day too, but late on, in the afternoon.' Brogan paused, frowned, then continued. But he looked down at his hands now as he spoke and did not meet Sara's eyes. 'Oh Jeez, now I come to think I reckon I was mebbe the last person to see her alive. You say you saw her outside your church?'

'I did. She was outside my church with the baby,' Sara said. 'They were dressed in – well, in rags and they were cold and hungry so – so I gave Jess my collection and my white angora gloves. She put them on the baby's feet. Then they went, and I read in the paper that she bought bread and some milk and wanted somewhere to go and eat and must have wandered on to the rails . . .'

She stopped short, giving an involuntary shudder as she did so. 'I thought it was my fault that she died – she bought the food with my shilling, you see. If I hadn't given it to her she could have been alive today. So I'd love to find Mollie, or the other sister, to – well, to try to make up, I suppose.'

Brogan patted her arm. 'Aye, I can see that you would think that. But Sara, if it hadn't been for me Jess maybe really might have been alive. I'll tell you about it.'

*

Brogan was careful what he said, of course, because the secret concerning the baby was no longer his to reveal. But he liked this serious young girl with the deep blue eyes and the gentle, sensitive countenance; her guilt was absurd, but he could understand it. He, too, had suffered from guilt over Jess's death until his parents had convinced him that the poor little girls were both of them better off, now.

So he told Sara how he and the rest of his gang of navvies had met the young girl carrying the baby, how they had fed her, taken her in, warmed her . . . and left her sleeping when the landslip occurred.

'And when we came back, they'd gone,' he said heavily, at last. 'We looked for 'em all over, without any luck. Until we met one of the other men, carrying Jess's body wrapped in his coat. Now you thought yourself guilty, alanna, but as you can see, my guilt was the greater. If I'd woken her, instead of leavin' her sleepin' . . . well, who can say what might have happened?'

'And Mollie? The baby?'

'We looked all over the marshalling yards but we saw no child,' Brogan said truthfully. 'She couldn't have been wit' her sister, that's for sure, and she was too little to get very far on her own. 'Tis my honest belief that some good person must have found her, and taken her away to be loved and cherished, as babies should be. And from what poor Jess told us, it was the best thing to do so it was, for her father was an awful feller by what she said, and her mammy little better.'

'So there really was no blame on you,' Sara said thoughtfully. She looked up at him and smiled, a very sweet smile. ''Twasn't your fault, Brogan.'

'No? When if I'd woke her, instead of leavin' her there, sleepin', her life might have been saved? What worries me most is that Mollie was crawling, you know, and she might easily have crawled out of the cabin. Then Jess would have woken up and gone in search of her sister, and got killed.'

'It could have happened, of course,' Sara said after a moment's thought. 'But you can't ever know, Brogan. If things had been different, if you'd woken Jess, she might have picked up Mollie and gone out with her and they might both have been killed instead of only one. Don't you think that's even likelier?'

'I think you're right,' Brogan said. 'The hand of God is over us all, alanna, and we should neither of us take on guilt. Shall we have a bargain? We'll stop blaming ourselves for what we couldn't help. How about that, eh? Will you shake hands on it?'

'Yes, of course,' Sara said. She put her small paw into Brogan's large one and they shook hands solemnly. 'Oh . . . that little girl! I'd forgotten her. Do you think she might have been a Carbery, Brogan?'

'Nothing likelier,' Brogan said. 'But she'll turn up again, Sara, and when she does, either you or meself will try to give her a bit of somethin' to eat and a few coppers.' He smiled down into the small face lifted to his. 'But this city's full of kids in rags wit' no food in their bellies. Times are hard . . . Dublin's the same.'

'Do you mean that we should help anyone we can help?' Sara asked. 'I will then . . . and when I do, I'll think of Jess. And I'll say my prayers for Mollie, and hope that wherever she is, she's well and happy.'

'That's the ticket,' Brogan said. He sighed and stood up, stretching. 'Now no more blamin' yourself for what you can't help, eh, young wan? I'm on a night-shift this week; better get back to me lodgings or I'll be good for nothin' be eight in the mornin'.' He paused, looking down at Sara. 'I'll let you into a secret, Sara. I've lived in England for a whole twelve months now, but sadly do I miss my mammy, my brothers and my little sister. There's fine men work on the railways, but very few young ladies, such as yourself. I'd like to meet you again, have a bit of a crack. I'd like to tell you all about us O'Bradys, from mammy right down to Polly, who's the youngest of the family so far.'

'I'd like that ever so much,' Sara said eagerly. She stood up too, and dusted down the front of the little red coat she wore. 'I don't have a lot of friends of my own, apart from school chums, when I'm in Aigburth Road. Where do you live though, Brogan?'

'We lodge in Beckett Street, me daddy an' meself. It's not too far from here.'

'Well, I'm staying in Snowdrop Street; that's off Stanley Road,' Sara told her new friend. 'I've a friend called Cammy who lives a bit further along the road but I would like to see you again.'

'Snowdrop runs between Commercial Road and Stanley, doesn't it? We walk through there, sometimes, when we're comin' home after a day's work. Will you an' me be meetin' somewhere round there, now and then, to have a bit of a talk?' Brogan turned up his coat collar and stepped out of the shelter into the rain. 'Best get goin', young Sara!'

'That would be very nice,' Sara said. 'Only . . . where could we meet? Once I'm at home I only get to go to school and back, but when I'm with Nanny it's easier.'

'Then you must visit Nanny more often,' Brogan said. 'I miss the young chisellers more than you'd imagine. There's no kids workin' on the railways.'

He laughed and Sara laughed too.

'No, I suppose not, but I'm not a kid, you know. I'm twelve. What's a chiseller, though? If you don't go too fast I'll walk along with you – you can tell me what it's like, working on the railways.'

Companionably, they fell into step and began to cross the park. The rain was light but Sara was glad of her thick coat and pulled out the scarf she wore round her neck, tying it over her head.

'A chiseller's just a way of sayin' a young boy, a young blood. As for working on the railways, 'tis hard work, but not unpleasant most of the time. We're out of doors in all weathers, of course, and soaked to the skin or froze now an' then. Me daddy's up for the job of safety man and a grand job that is, so I'm hopin' he'll get it. But I've other ideas so I have. I go to the Gordon Institute 'cos in March I'm hopin' to start work as a fireman, which is the first step to bein' an engine driver meself so it is.'

'I know the Institute; it's opposite Crocus Street, isn't it?' Sara said. She giggled. 'I've seen young men going in and out so I thought it was a public house.'

Brogan laughed with her. She's a dote, he found himself thinking. A pretty, lively young wan who's kept too close, from the sound of it. 'No, 'tis for the learnin' and betterin' of the working man,' he told her. 'Sure an' they treat you like a school kid, but 'tis worth it to get the learnin'.'

They were on Orwell Road now, Sara having to walk fast to keep up with his longer strides, though Brogan conscientiously kept slowing down. And on the corner of Rickman Street, alongside the fried fish shop, Brogan drew his companion to a halt. He pointed.

'I'm after gettin' some fish an' chips for me dinner, before I go indoors. Want some?'

'Oh, Brogan, I bought a pastie for my dinner and I never ate it . . . but whatever did I do with it? I halved it with the little girl who ran away . . .'

'Sure, you left it on the seat, where you'd been sittin' when the child approached you,' he assured her. 'It'll be in some creature's stomach be now . . . I'll get you some fish and chips; wait here.'

'I'm glad someone's got it, then, but I've got some money . . .' Sara began, but he shook his head at her.

'No, no, I'm buyin', don't shame me by refusin'. And since you know the Gordon Institute, I'm after goin' there three evenin's a week, save when I'm on a shift which stops me, so you can find me there, five to seven or five past nine. You'll come? You won't forget?'

'I'll come whenever I'm staying with Nanny,' Sara promised. 'And I'm going to be staying with Nanny regularly, from now on. Otherwise there'll be trouble!'

'I can tell you've a sharp tongue and a determined nature,' Brogan said solemnly, making her laugh again. 'But I can't tell whether you prefer cod or haddock – you'll have to let me know which to buy!'

'I like both, and besides, I don't know which is which,' Sara assured him. 'Are you sure you've got time though, Brogan? You said you wanted to get some sleep before your night-shift.'

Brogan assured her he had plenty of time and went into the fried fish shop. She was a good kid. Talking to her had cheered him up, made his day. It would have been lovely to tell her that the baby was safe with his mother in Dublin, but sure and such knowledge would be far too heavy a burden for a child of twelve to bear. He'd keep in touch with her, however, talk about his family to her, and maybe one day, when Polly was a woman grown, he would be able to share the secret with young Sara Cordwainer.

Little Grace Carbery had hoped the girl would share the big pastie with her; she looked a friendly sort of girl, but just as Grace had taken the proffered piece she had seen the park keeper coming and had made herself scarce. She had been in bad odour with him ever since she and Jess had sat themselves down on the bowling green to eat a melon they'd prigged from a nearby greengrocer's shop.

'We don't want your sort here,' the park keeper had shouted, and he had hit at their bare legs with the long twig broom with which he'd been sweeping the gravel paths. 'Gerrout, you iggerant slummies.'

So naturally, when she saw the man approaching, she had run as fast as she could to the other side of the park and then made her way back through the bushes, quick and skinny as a snake, until she was behind the seat which backed on to the bowling green. With Jess beside her she might have faced the man out, she thought wistfully, together they might even have cheeked him, but by herself all she could do was run and hide.

But after a few frightening moments she had peered through the prickly, evergreen hedge, and seen that the park keeper wasn't a park keeper at all, but simply a feller in a navy donkey coat – and he and the pretty girl seemed to know one another, since she had run slap bang into his arms and there they were, chattering away, heading for the opposite side of the rec.

Grace looked carefully round her; no one was near. She squatted on the ground and took the first bite from her half of the pastie, closing her eyes the better to savour it. It was delicious, one of the nicest things she had ever tasted! I'll save it, she thought, eat it slowly . . . just one more bite . . .

The half pastie disappeared into Grace's tummy and she stood up and went hesitantly towards the seat. She had noticed something lying on the wet wood . . .

The rest of the meat pastie was there! There was one bite taken out of it but it wasn't even a particularly big piece . . . oh, had the girl left it for her? If so . . .

Grace sat down timidly on the extreme end of the seat, looking nervously around her like an animal which fears a trap. Was it a trick? Would the girl come back presently and pick up the pastie and walk off with it? But nothing happened. When she looked across the couple had disappeared into the falling rain and the pastie was getting soaked. If she didn't do something it would be ruined, worthless.

Hesitantly, Grace reached out both hands and picked the half-pastie up. Seconds later, she was savouring, for the second time that morning, the most delicious meat and potato pie she had ever tasted. Oh, the flavour of it, the richness of the gravy, the warm and lovely taste of the onions! I really oughter save a bit, she told herself, but somehow it all got eaten up there and then, on the seat, in the rain.

And presently, when she got up and made her way back to the road once more, she felt full and comfortable for the first time for ages. And very grateful to the pretty girl who had given her half the pastie and then left the rest of it too, sitting on that wet wooden bench.

But she did wonder why she had told the girl she was searching for her sister, when she knew very well, really, that wherever Mollie was, she was better off, because she wasn't with the Carberys. Without Jess, Mollie's life wouldn't have been much, Grace thought now, heading for home. She was soaked and needed to get out of the weather before her father came back from wherever it was he went during the afternoons. Pubs, clubs, she had no idea, she just knew he was usually out of the house until very much later in the evening.

She had been heartbroken by Jess's death, because Jess had been the only member of the family who cared about her. When she, Grace, had been the baby of the family Jess had carted her around on her hip until she got too heavy, as Jess had been carting Mollie right up to her death. And though the new baby was, naturally, her first responsibility, she still cherished Grace as much as she could.

But you can't be a baby once you're four years old; you're a proper, big girl, once you're four, Jess said so. And poor Grace, trying to be a proper, big girl, had still envied Mollie because she had Jess, and had envied Jess because she had Mollie. Indeed, her first thought, after the appalling shock of Jess's horrible death, had been that now Mollie could sleep beside *her*, keep *her* warm of a night. But even if Mollie hadn't disappeared it wouldn't have worked because Grace knew she didn't have Jess's strength. She was only four, going on five. It took her all her time and energy to keep herself alive, she could never have taken on the responsibility for another soul, not even that of a baby like Mollie.

Chapter Five

Summer 1931

'Polly O'Brady, will you put that kitten down this minute and do as I tell ye! Your big brother and your daddy are comin' home tomorrow and no end to arrange. I'm after wantin' a heap o' things and you've done nothin' today but play.'

Polly was sitting on the living-room windowsill with a book beside her and the ginger kitten in her lap. She could scarcely remember the time when the O'Bradys had lived in two rooms, for now they had four, all on the first floor which meant having it to themselves, apart from the stairs, which were common property.

With the money she made from street selling plus what Peader and Brogan sent home, Deirdre had gradually taken on two more rooms, so the old bedroom was now a proper kitchen and the two back rooms were bedrooms, one for the big boys and one for the small boys, Polly and her mammy.

Now, however, Polly glanced across the room at the kitchen door; me mammy's got eyes that see round corners so she has, she thought, awed, for there was no way that she could be seen from the kitchen sink so far as she could make out and she'd only picked the kitten up minutes ago.

'I'm not playin' now, Mammy, I'm doin' my eckers,' she said untruthfully, picking up the blue exercise book and waving it vaguely in the direction of the kitchen door. Her homework had been done a week or more ago since this was summertime and schools were out, but she had been looking it over just now, which was the same as doing it, more or less. 'You know you said to do it now, so's it wasn't a bother to me later, when Brogan and Daddy come home.'

'Sure and I know you're bound to do your eckers, but you've got all the holidays to tackle it, alanna, so don't give me that! Brogan's more important to all of us than any old schoolwork, so leave the kitten, come away from them books, and get after those messages.'

Polly pouted and gave the ginger kitten a cuddle. She had named it Lionel and stuck to the name though her brothers codded her about it and told her that it was no name for a kitten, particularly a ginger one.

'It's no dafter than her calling the dog Delilah,' Niall had pointed out. He was a man grown, and very rarely teased. 'Particularly since Delilah's a girl's name and the dog's a feller. Samson, now, that's a good name for a dog. You could have called him Samson, alanna.'

But Polly had preferred Delilah, so the dog, a large, odd-looking creature of indeterminate parentage, was known as Delly by everyone except her and did not seem to mind what he was called so long as he was with the O'Bradys most of the time, particularly Polly.

'Polly, do as I tell you now; I'm warnin' ye!'

Polly knew when her mother was serious. She set the kitten down on the floor, jumped off the windowsill and dusted the fur off her short pleated skirt.

'All right, Mammy, I'm goin',' she said placatingly. 'I'll just give a bit of a wash to me hands and brush me hair, then I'll be off. Is it a list you've been writin' in there?'

'Yes, I've written a list,' her mother called back. 'You'll want to go to the market on Francis Street because you'll get good stuff there. Or Iveagh market, of course. And Tad will go wit' you, if you ask him nicely. There's a lot to carry for a little girl.'

'Tad's a monster, so he is, and he won't go anywhere wit' me, not if I know it,' Polly said indignantly. Last week Tad had been her best friend, but he had codded her once too often. 'Worse than a brother he is to me . . . much worse. I'll never speak to him again . . . not politely I won't.'

The door between the living room and the kitchen was open and now Deirdre poked her head round it. She was smiling.

'Oh, you, Polly O'Brady, you're always full of what you'll do to poor Tad every time you argue, but you're rare fond of the lad, are you not? Who gave you your very first kitten? And that wretched mongrel dog of yours? And the mice?'

'It was Tad, though the cat ate the mice,' Polly admitted. 'But Mammy, last week Tad took me all the way over to O'Connell Street to see the fine shops and then he wouldn't let me ride home on the tram, he said weren't me legs made for walkin' like the legs on him were. And yesterday I wanted to swim in the Basin and he said it was for boys, not girls. He said to swim in the bleedin' canal if I wanted . . . he said bleedin', so don't shout, I'm only repeatin' what he said! So you see he's mean to me, Mammy.'

'You're spoilt, that's the trouble. We all give you your own way too much,' Deirdre said with mock severity. 'Will you take Ivan with you, in the pram, then you won't need help wit' the carryin'?'

Ivan was the youngest O'Brady now. Polly had somehow assumed that she herself would always be the youngest and had been astonished and hurt when Mammy had told her that she was going to have a little brother or sister. She had chosen a sister and had been offended as well as surprised when the baby turned out to be a brother after all, but she had grown quite fond of Ivan in her way, though she kept a close watch on Mammy and the brothers to make sure they didn't favour the baby above her.

'Oh, Mammy, I can't take Ivan, he keeps wantin' to walk so he does, and doesn't that hold me up more'n anythin' else?' Polly asked. 'I'll ask Tad if he'll come, then, if there's more than I can carry alone. Honest to God I'll ask him, Mammy.'

'I believe you; t'ousands wouldn't,' Deirdre said, handing over a long list written on the margin of the *Herald* newspaper. 'Just think, Polly, tomorrow and the day after and the day after that Brogan and Daddy will be here, takin' us out for a day, jokin' you, playin' wit' Ivan . . . it'll be the first time Daddy's set eyes on Ivan, d'you realise that?'

Since Ivan, who had been napping in the kitchen, curled up on the old wooden rocker, chose that moment to wake with a roar of 'Mammy! Ivy wanna d'ink so he do!', Polly could only envy her father his happy ignorance. Ivan had not been a placid baby and he was not a placid toddler and since it is the fate of the older children in a family to keep an eye on the younger ones, Polly knew better than most what a trial Ivan could be.

'When I was a baby I was put to the Poor Crèche, on Meath Street, I wasn't landed on me brothers day and night,' Polly scolded Ivan when he whined for something. 'The ould wans there didn't give me no peggy's leg to keep me quiet, nor take me for walks through the markets to keep me amused. They smacked us if we cried and gave us yesterday's bread and watered buttermilk so they did. And that's what'll happen to you, me fine feller, if you don't do as I say.'

But of course Ivan was unimpressed. 'Wan' kitty,' he whined. 'Wanna cuggle kitty.'

So now, faced with taking Ivan or approaching Tad Donoghue, it was no contest. Polly and Tad had parted on bad terms, but she would have to go round to his room and speak softly to him, or suffer the various outrages which a healthy, spoilt two-year-old can put on an elder sister.

'Here's the money, then,' Deirdre said, handing Polly the worn little red purse which Peader had sent for a Christmas gift several years since. 'And there's a few pence extra – you can treat yourself and Tad, or you can pay him for carryin', see which he'd rather.'

'If I could take the pram without Ivan . . .' Polly ventured, but Deirdre shook her head.

'Oh no, you bold madam, I've heard tales like that before so I have! Just you run off now, and don't be all day about it, either. I've got the sheets on the line but I'll want a hand to fold 'em, later.'

With four whole windows to call their own, sheets were not the insurmountable problem they had once been, but even so, sunny days were a blessing to thank the good God for, Mammy often said. She hauled in her rope, hung out her wet linen, then prayed, and with a bit of luck, with wind and sun, they would be dry before darkness fell. Little clothes could be hung on the wooden clothes horse before the fire, but in winter sheets were more of a curse than a blessing. Living in Swift's Alley, you had to keep washing all the time, and sweeping, cleaning, burning. The women did their best but there were four families in each of the four rooms on the next storey up and they suffered from fleas, bed-bugs, all sorts. It wasn't their fault,

Mammy said. They had so little money coming in they couldn't afford the carbolic, the Keatings powder, the time to scrub, even. But the O'Bradys were lucky because they'd got Niall, who was working as a clerk in an office and bringing almost all his wages home, and Martin, who was working hard at senior school and helping his Aunt Bridie to sell fish, door to door, at weekends and Donal, who sold the *Mail* and the *Herald* after school and all day during the holidays, the way Brogan, Niall and even Martin had once done. And best of all so far as wages went, they had Daddy and Brogan, working across the sea in Liverpool and earning better money than they could ever have brought home for labouring jobs in Dublin.

Not that Brogan was a labourer; not any more. He was fireman on an engine, and working like a black slave, he told them, at evening classes, for to better himself.

'What could be better than a fireman? Or an engine driver?' his younger brothers wondered aloud, but Mammy said engine driving was cold, dirty work.

'One day, all my sons will wear smart suits and white shirts and work in offices, and we'll have a nice little house on Dominick Place, right near the park, or we could move out of the city, go down to Booterstown, or Black Rock,' Mammy would say dreamily. 'Fancy, livin' at the seaside, with the sands to play on whenever you wanted.'

So because they had earners, now, and not so many babies – it never crossed Polly's mind to wonder why their mammy no longer produced a baby each year, as she apparently had before their daddy went off over the water to Liverpool – Mammy no longer had to drag herself and her wicker cart out of the city before day broke, to pick potatoes when they were ready, nor did she squat on the pavement all the rest of the day, selling those same potatoes to anyone who would buy.

'I'm a lady now,' she would tease, as she got them ready for school or cooked hot porridge for the workers and made a huge pot of tea. 'I work a little, now and then, for extrys, but I'm not a wage slave, thanks to me boys and me dear Peader.'

Things were different in the Donoghue household. There were a grush of kids, as the boys said, ranging from Tad, who was nine, to the newest baby, a girl named Aileen, and though the boys tried, and Mr Donoghue was a docker and often in work, he never took a penny of his money home for his family, regarding it as his own property.

'If me ould feller dropped dead tomorrer we'd be no worse off,' Tad often said. 'We'd be *better* off, because we wouldn't get bate till we was black an' blue, and nor would me mammy.'

Polly hated Mr Donoghue and was afraid of him, too. He would swagger out of the tenement building, having eaten the lion's share of any food that was going, with his tall ash stick, the mark of his trade, and his wide leather belt with the brass buckle. Down to the nearest pub he would go and when he wasn't drinking he was out at the brickfields, playing pitch and toss with the school which the men had formed there. If he won, he drank heavier than ever. If he lost he came home and belted his wife or beat his kids.

So in a way you could understand why Tad could be tricky, at times. Which made it easier to bear. And though he didn't have anything to speak of, he was generous. Polly guessed that the kitten he'd given her had been stolen from a litter, that he'd found the dog Delilah wandering the street and nicked the mice and the smart cage from one of the expensive shops on

O'Connell or Parnell Streets. But he'd given them to her freely, when he could easily have sold them – you couldn't say fairer than that, could you?

So having made up her mind that Tad was at least the lesser of two evils, Polly left her own block and headed for Gardiners Lane and the Donoghues'. They lived on the top floor, in an attic room with a sloping ceiling – a dozen of them, more or less. Mrs Donoghue was a nice woman, but her ould feller blacked her eye most days and sometimes she walked funny, sort of bent up, and other times her face was swollen out to the side, or one arm she kept clutched to her body.

'The ould feller found a clock in 'is carry-out,' Tad had said on one occasion when she'd mentioned Mrs Donoghue's swollen face. 'So he belted her. God love her, she doesn't deserve it. When I'm a man I'll kill that bugger stone dead so I will.'

'What's a clock?' Polly had asked Niall that night. 'Not the sort that you hang on the wall, the sort you find in your carry-out.'

Niall looked puzzled but Martin gave a roar of laughter.

'It's a cockroach, Poll,' he said at once. 'Who found one in their carry-out? Not your friend Tad?'

'No. He doesn't get a carry-out. It was his daddy, and his daddy belted his mammy and Tad said one day he'll kill the bugger stone dead so he will.'

'So he ought,' Mammy's voice said from the fireside where she was mending socks. 'So he bloody ought. That feller's bad or mad or a bit of both. I thank God fasting that Peader's not that kind o' man.'

But now, hovering by Tad's tenement, Polly wondered whether to go straight up and knock, or whether to hang about hopefully. But it was past ten in the morning, surely Tad's ould feller would be down at the docks, or at the pub, or even out at the Brick-fields, by this time? There was one good thing about tenement life, though; everyone knew everyone else's business. So Polly hadn't been hovering more than a few seconds when a woman came out. She had an armful of wet linen and a fancy peg-bag. It was Mrs Wilson, a hard ticket as the boys called her. Mammy called her a stuffy-nose, but Polly quite liked her. Mrs Wilson might look down on her neighbours and talk of her days as the priest's housekeeper before she'd caught Mr Wilson, and him only a tram-driver when all was said and done, but she approved of the O'Bradys.

'You keep the children nice,' she had said to Polly's mother once. 'I've only the one, but it's hard enough keepin' him decent, let alone half a dozen of 'em.'

Mrs Wilson was beginning to peg her clothes on the line, but she turned and smiled down at Polly as she did so.

'Mornin', Polly – is it the eldest Donoghue chiseller you're after wantin', then? He passed me on the stairs just now so he can't be far away.'

'Thanks, Mrs Wilson. I'll go and take a look in Thomas Street, see if he's out there.'

She hurried out into the road, well aware that Tad could be miles away by now, and probably was. What a nuisance, and she'd got a list a mile long, she could have done with Tad's muscles for to carry her messages home!

She found him eventually on Thomas Street staring into the window of Byrne's the poulterer. Polly knew from past experience that there would be a nasty smell from the chickens, ducks and pigeons hanging on either side of the doorway so although, like Tad, she coveted the feathers, she rarely lingered outside Byrne's. She hurried over to Tad though and reached him just as he bent forward, grabbed a handful of particularly fine feathers from a cock's tail, and pulled.

The whole string veered sideways alarmingly of course, and Mr Byrne, from behind his counter, roared a threat, but Tad, with a handful of feathers, was away, running down the street at a pace which had Polly panting in seconds. But she caught him up at last and gave him a thump with her shopping basket.

'Tad! What did you want to do that for, and me wit' me mouth open, about to ask if you'd help wit' me messages? I had to run like the wind to catch you,' she added aggrievedly. 'And me basket's heavy even wit' nothing inside!'

Tad was small for his age but very strong – he needed to be as Polly well knew. He had dark hair which curled when it was given the chance – but Mrs Donoghue made the barber shave her boys' heads so they didn't need a haircut more than once in a couple of months – and blue eyes fringed with thick, black lashes. He had a nice grin, a soft voice, and a fund of hair-raising and probably untrue stories which made him popular in the lobbies and stairways when the kids congregated to scare themselves with talk of ghosts, banshees and other such things.

'I thought you wasn't never goin' to speak to me again, because of not takin' you swimmin' in the Liffey,' Tad said, but he grinned as he said it. 'I thought you hoped you'd never see me again in this life – wasn't that what you shouted?'

Polly dismissed this with a wave of the hand not engaged with the basket. 'I may have said a thing or two, in me temper,' she admitted airily. 'But well you know, Tad Donoghue, that I was never after meanin' any of 'em. You busy?'

'Busy doin' nothin', yes sure I am,' said the irrepressible Tad. 'But I don't mind doin' nothin' with you, if you're in a better mood than you were yesterday. Where's Delly?'

'Donal's took him on the fish round,' Polly said. 'I said he could; if there's one thing Delilah does love, 'tis a nice piece of fish. Or even quite a nasty, smelly one,' she added conscientiously, remembering Delilah's unfortunate predilection for ancient herrings. 'I was nursin' dear Lionel, sittin' in the window mindin' me own business and thinkin' about the summer, and then Mammy said she wanted messages doing and here I am. Only I've got a list as long as the bloody Liffey,' she added pathetically. 'And how I'm to carry me basket back once 'tis loaded wit' stuff God above knows.'

'Oh, give it here,' Tad said with all his usual good nature. 'I'll lend you a hand. Where's first?'

'Thanks, Tad,' Polly said, handing over her basket. 'Me mammy said I could treat you if you give a hand. What 'ud you rather, ice cream, cake or tuppence?'

Tad shrugged. 'Dunno as I mind, Poll. Let's get the messages done, then we'll t'ink about it. Where's we to go first?'

Polly consulted her list and sighed. It was indeed long and would mean quite a lot of walking.

'Mammy wants us to go to the Iveagh market, and then to Moore Street because she says they've the freshest fruit in Dublin. She's sent the big boys for the spuds, thanks be to God,' she added piously. 'Spuds weigh heavy so they do.'

'There's no need to traipse to Moore Street wit' everything half the price on the Francis Street stalls,' Tad said firmly. 'Or did she want to send you over the Liffey for a reason, d'you think? If your daddy's comin' home today was she after sendin' you for something he really likes?'

Polly consulted her list again, then shook her head. 'No, it can't be that, for there's not even tobacco on me list – I don't know that me daddy smokes, come to that. We'll start in Francis Street then, Tad.'

'Sure,' Tad said, hefting the basket. 'Will we be buyin' ribs, from Durney's?'

'That's right,' Polly said. 'Why?'

'We might ask Mr D for some bones for your Delly,' Tad said. 'Then I could take 'em home for me mammy to make us a broth. Pork bones make good broth, wit' an onion or two and mebbe a carrot.'

'All right, we'll do that,' Polly told him. 'I'm wantin' a good shirt to fit our Donal from the Iveagh, too. Mammy says he's growed out of his old one and she won't have me daddy shamed on Sunday, at Mass.'

'Oh, the old priests don't notice, 'tis the other old women who point, if you're raggedy,' Tad said knowingly. He was usually raggedy. 'Mind, me daddy's always smart. Mammy puts his suit, shirt and shoes in the pawn on Monday morning, early, an' takes it out again on Saturday, late. Wish I had a dacent suit to pawn,' he added wistfully. 'I could do wit' the money.'

'Well, mebbe,' Polly said vaguely. As they talked they had made their way through the crowds of shoppers on Thomas Street and turned right, into Francis Street. 'What'll we do when we've got our messages, Tad? It's a beautiful day, wouldn't you say? Too nice for hangin' round the alley.'

'We could do all sorts if we had pennies for the tram,' Tad said. 'We could go all over.'

Polly smiled. 'Right you are, let's go to Phoenix Park, shall us? It's nice there, Niall said so.'

Tad pulled a face. 'It's real hot today; I'd sooner go

to the canal, then we could swim,' he said longingly. 'I can swim – almost. We can go to a quiet bit, where the fellers don't go. Would you like that?'

It was definitely an olive branch but even so, Polly looked doubtful. 'Last time we was there we saw that dead dog, remember? The poor feller, wit' his legs in the air and his poor eyes clamped shut. I don't want to swim wit' no dead dog.'

'Aw, janey, that won't happen again,' Tad protested at once. 'Anyway, I'll look after you, alanna. You'll be safe wit' me.'

Brogan couldn't stop smiling. Making his way across Liverpool, down Beckett Street, along Fountains Road, he smiled like an idiot whether anyone was looking at him or not. And when he and Peader got on the tram just outside the Stanley Hospital, even the conductor, taking their fares, noticed it.

'Where's you off to, then?' he enquired blandly. ''Cos you've gorra grin on your gob like a bleedin' Cheshire cat.'

'I'm goin' home,' Brogan said simply. 'First time for five years. I've been livin' in Crewe for eighteen months because the work took me there, so I've been away from all me family, even me daddy here. It's good to be seein' them all again.'

The conductor whistled sympathetically. 'No wonder you're grinnin', pal! And don't tell me, you're from God's own country – right?'

'That's right. Dublin. Swift's Lane, off Francis Street.'

The conductor heaved a sigh. 'I come from there meself, or rather me mam did,' he said reminiscently. 'She were just a child when her mam and da crossed the water – her family live there still, in Enniskerry. O'Mara, the name is. We've never been back, ourselves, but me mam talks about Enniskerry as though it were paradise – always 'as.'

'Dublin isn't paradise, and Swift's Alley's a bit rough, mebbe,' Brogan said. 'But there's something about it . . . I dunno.' He turned to his father. 'What do you say, Daddy?'

Peader shrugged. He had told Brogan that life in Liverpool wasn't the same without him, that he was seriously considering trying to get a bit of a decent job in Dublin when they got home, but Brogan doubted if he would really do such a thing. He was the safety man for a large gang now, on good money with a lot of responsibility. Of course he missed his family, anyone would, but his conscience would not let him take the easy way out. Returning to Dublin and no job, letting his wife and kids keep him, was not Peader's style. He had always looked down on the men of the tenements who took it for granted that their wives would support them and the large families they gave them. He'd disapproved of a baby every year, too, and told his sons frankly that they should learn self-discipline before they married. Brogan had not been at all sure what his father meant at the time, though he knew now. A woman should be loved, honoured and cherished, his father had told him when Brogan took his first young lady to the cinema. You young fellers think women are only good for one thing – taking to bed. Well, that's selfish, wicked and wrong. If you give a girl a baby then you have to support the pair of 'em, and if you want your wife to stay healthy and sweet then you must deny yourself from time to time.

Brogan had said he understood and promised to be careful; it hadn't been difficult. The girls he took out were nice girls, but they hadn't lit any particular flame within him. It had been easy simply to say goodnight to them after a few kisses, easy to part. But now there was a girl he thought he cared about, only she'd been sent away. And anyway, he was a man and Sara Cordwainer was a child – but bidding fair to become a very lovely young woman.

But now Peader, who had been looking out of the tram window, turned to face the conductor.

'Sure and isn't everyone's home special?' he said. 'The air's softer, over there,' I guess, and the water's sweeter. The girls are prettier, the people kinder. Otherwise perhaps we'd not want to go back so bad.'

The conductor laughed and patted his shoulder.

'Aye, the Irish are a lovely people and there's Irish in most of us scousers,' he said in his heavy Liverpool accent. 'Good luck to you, fellers, and good sailing.'

When they reached the dock the sky overhead was blue, the sun shining.

'We're goin' to have a good voyage, Daddy,' Brogan remarked as they hefted their bags up the gangplank, jostled by a great many other would-be travellers. 'Not like the last time – janey, how the waves heaved! Still, even that weren't as bad as when I took the wee one over under me jacket.'

He had lowered his voice but even so Peader glanced anxiously about him.

'Don't speak too loud, lad,' he muttered. 'I'm always careful. Your mammy would kill the pair of us if we had to take Polly from her. Deirdre's a kind and lovin' woman, but who'd have thought she'd take to the child the way she has? She dotes on her, dotes.'

'So do we all,' Brogan said. He had last seen Polly when she was only two years old, but under his mother's care she had grown prettier and more self-confident than ever. She was talking well, walking, playing nursery games . . . he had been as proud of her as though she had been his own get. But now she was a really big girl, seven years old, and doing well at school. Mammy wrote regularly and Polly often added a little letter of her own and Brogan was always astonished at her cleverness. He couldn't wait to see her now, the child that he had stolen, or rescued, depending on your viewpoint, he supposed.

'The nuns all t'ink she's a little wonder, so they do,' Peader said now, as they settled themselves in the bows, eyes front. Everyone wanted to be the first to spot Ireland through the heat-haze which hung over the land, and here in the bows they would be shouting 'land ho!' long before the rest of the passengers. 'She's always bringin' home holy pictures and medals for good work.'

'I know,' Brogan said. 'I often wonder about the other kids, you know, the other Carberys. I used to catch a glimpse of one or two of them, but I suppose they changed as they grew up. Anyway, I've not seen one for ages.'

'Do you still see that girl you telled me about?' Peader asked presently. 'What was her name, now? I disremember it.'

'You mean Sara. Sara Cordwainer. No, we've not met for years, Sara and meself. There was trouble more than a year before I left the Pool – did I not tell you? Her father discovered that she and I had met once or twice whilst she was staying with her old nurse. There was nothin' in it bar friendship, she was only fifteen or so, but he's an awful toffee-nosed feller, real high in the instep. She wrote to me once and told me they were sendin' her away to school and she didn't know the address, so I couldn't write back. She said they'd stopped her visitin' in Snowdrop Street. I went and visited her gran, but she said there was nothin' she could do.' Brogan sighed. 'Poor kid, and we was only good friends when all's said an' done. Still, there you are. It's all over, not that there was anything . . . but she's a young lady now, not a child, I doubt I'd recognise her if we met face to face in the street.'

He knew he would know her again, though, thought he'd know her anywhere. He'd felt awful sorry for her the last time he'd seen her, being treated like a criminal just for walkin' alongside a feller in workin' clothes. He had spotted her walking along Stanley Road with a basket swinging from one hand and when he'd called she had rushed across the pavement and hugged him, clearly very pleased to see him once more.

Brogan was equally pleased to see young Sara. They had met several times over the years and had enjoyed one another's company on each occasion, the age-gap becoming less and less important as she grew up. She was bright, intelligent, understood the work he did in evening classes, discussed it with him, encouraged him. On previous occasions they had been to the Walker Art Gallery together, and to the Museum, too. Once, they'd gone to a cinema show – Brogan had given her a cuddle when the film was frightening – and once to the pantomime. He had enjoyed her enjoyment of the show more, by and large, than the show itself. But it had been twelve months since they had met, for it was only possible to do so when Sara was staying with her grandmother in Snowdrop Street. So of course he'd been delighted to see her again, delighted at her unselfconscious dart into his arms, as well.

'Brogan!' she had said, her eyes shining, her mouth curving into a smile. 'Oh, how nice it is to see you! It must be almost a year since we met – my mother's been poorly so it hasn't been possible for me to stay in Snowdrop Street. But you're on your way home, you don't want to stand gossiping here. Can we meet later?'

'Sure we can,' he had said, delighted. She was turning into a beautiful young creature, with rich dark curls tumbling on to her shoulders and a perfect, heart-shaped face lit by big, dark-blue eyes. 'I've so many t'ings to tell you – I've passed all me exams so far and me family are well – I've a letter from me mammy tellin' me all Polly's latest tricks. Shall we walk along the road now and have a cuppa, and you can read me letter? Then we might go along to the Commodore, there's a cowboy film on, you've always liked a good cowboy film.'

He knew she loved the cinema and was fascinated by his family, particularly Polly. She often gave him small presents to pass on to the child, which he faithfully did – a length of velvet ribbon, a silver locket, a tiny enamelled box for trinkets, a warm woollen scarf. Now he beamed down at her, reflecting that she must have cheered other passersby too, with her bright, animated little face and the way she swung her basket.

'Look, I'll walk you back to Snowdrop Street so you can explain to your gran that you're with me,' Brogan said. 'Then we can go to Cunningham's Dining Rooms so that we can have tay and a fancy cake while we talk.'

'That would be lovely,' Sara said. 'Oh, Brogan, you look so happy and well! Come on then, you'll have to lead the way. Nanny and I don't go to posh places like Dining Rooms!'

He had laughed, taken her arm to swing her round . . . and the car had drawn up beside them. A man got out. He was tall and cruel-looking with slicked-back black hair and a thin, high-bridged nose.

He looked at Brogan as though he were a dog-turd he'd just trodden in, then he turned to Sara.

'Get in the car,' he said, and his voice was like a whiplash. 'How dare you walk the streets like a common tart and consort with filth from the gutters?'

Brogan stared, almost unable to believe his ears, but Sara turned to him at once, tears brimming in her big eyes.

'Brogan, I'm sorry! It's my father . . . I have to go.'

The last words were cried rather than spoken as the tall man jerked her across the pavement and almost threw her into the car. He tapped on the glass panel which divided them from the driver, and the car shot off. The last Brogan saw of Sara was her tearful young face turned beseechingly towards him, a hand raised in farewell.

He'd taken his courage in both hands after that and gone round to number three, Snowdrop Street. The lady who answered the door said that she was Mrs Prescott and listened when he tried to explain what had happened, how mistaken Mr Cordwainer had been. Then she had smiled at him and held out a plump, work-roughened hand.

'You'll be Brogan; Sara often spoke of you,' she said. 'I'm Mrs Prescott, I was once Sara's nanny, and her mother's, too. But I don't think I can help you, because I know Sara's father to be an arrogant and unbending man. He's said he won't allow his daughter to stay in my house again and I'm afraid he means it. But one of these days, when she's older, she'll come back to me. I can do nothing until then.'

'What if I write?' Brogan said desperately. 'I'd like to write to her fine, so I would. There can be no harm in a letter, surely?'

'She'll never receive it,' Mrs Prescott assured him.

'They're sending her away, to a school somewhere, and all her letters will be opened. Mr Cordwainer told me to my face that he'll tell the school authorities she's not to receive any letters, including mine. Oh, she'll write to me, I've no doubt of that, and perhaps we'll manage to arrange something, but for now there's nothing I can do.'

And she had been right. Not a word had he heard from Sara from that day to this, though he thought of her often. She was already special to him. He had hoped they would meet again, one day, but he supposed, now, that it might never happen. He was a fireman, soon, he believed, to be an engine driver, but to go higher he might have to leave the LMS, maybe even leave the English railway systems. And he intended to go higher. One day he would have a wife and family to keep and he did not want to do it by taking a job in a foreign land and scarcely ever setting eyes on his dear ones. He admired his father for doing what he did, but it was not for him. When he married – if he married – he would not want to leave his wife for years at a time. And the only way to be sure of being able to support a family was through a well-paid job.

'Well, a shame it is that your friendship with the little girl was cut short. But you're goin' back to the land of beautiful colleens, so you'd best forget your Sara and whatever trouble there was,' his father said comfortably, now. 'Besides, there's no reason for you to marry just yet. Marriage changes a feller – and a woman, for the matter of that. Too many youngsters jump into marriage and into bed and discover their mistake too late, that's what I always say.'

'But you and Mammy are well-suited, wouldn't you say?' Brogan said slyly. He knew how desperately his daddy loved his mammy – and missed her, too. 'Why shouldn't we think of that, us O'Bradys?'

'Ah, well now, your mammy's one in a thousand,' Peader said. 'And I'll be settin' eyes on her in a few hours . . . ah, glory be to God, I'm a lucky feller!'

'Is that it, Daddy? Or is it a cloud?' Brogan's knuckles were white from gripping the rail, his eyes stung from the strain of peering ahead. On the horizon he could see a line, darker than the line of the ocean, with a faint haze hovering over it.

His father slung an arm about his shoulders. That's it, son,' he said softly. 'That's Ireland – God's own country. Oh, God love you, we'll be ashore in no time . . . see the lighthouse? We'll be seein' Dun Laoghaire plain as plain in a moment. And then Dublin, son – home!'

Side by side they stood by the rail, eyes straining ahead, taking note of every landmark on the coastline of Ireland, in imagination already disembarking, making their way through the familiar streets, turning into the Alley, mounting the stairs . . .

'See it? See it? That's Ireland so it is! We're comin' home!'

Brogan saw the land shimmer and twist and saw his father duck his head, cross himself, begin to thank God for the smooth crossing, for the coming landfall. Heard the murmur around him . . . *We're home; that's Ireland that is . . . and we'll be dockin' in the heart of Dublin within the hour.*

He turned away from the rail for a moment to look at the people straining towards the land. Mostly men, who had been away for years, working to feed their families. Good men, reliable men. Loving men. Men not ashamed of the tears in their eyes. Like his father; like Peader.

Sara stepped down off the train at Lime Street station and looked curiously about her. Someone would be meeting her, that was for sure, but she had no idea who it would be. Father? Mother? Possibly even the chauffeur, though whether the family still employed Robson she had no means of knowing.

She had been away from home for three whole years now, and she was a young lady of eighteen, not a girl any more. And she had not missed either her parents or her home one bit. But she had missed her nanny and Snowdrop Street and had been absolutely furious when she had discovered her father's ban – as though she had been some flighty little piece intent on an assignation, instead of merely loving her old nanny and wanting to meet a friend who happened to be a young man.

'A labourer,' her father had sneered as he bundled her into the car. 'Have you no pride in yourself Sara? No pride in your family, your station? Even if you had merely been passing the time of day, as you say, you don't behave like that! Smiling, letting the creature take your arm . . .'

'He didn't take my arm,' Sara had shouted, embarrassed and angry all at once. 'He turned me round – I was going in the wrong direction, only I didn't know it. Father, I've met Brogan perhaps a dozen times over the past three years, we talk about a friend from Snowdrop Street, someone we both knew, who died – '

She got no further. She had no *friends* in Snowdrop Street but only acquaintances, and she could not possibly share a *friend* with someone who looked like a – a dirty chimney sweep anyhow.

Sara had said no more. Her father ranted and she sat silent. But at home, her mother had started as well and between them, they had made her life so miserable that when the day of departure dawned, it seemed that she was not heading for a punishment, but an escape.

And so, in a way, it proved. The school was in Switzerland, on the edge of Lake Como. There were mountains, the lake itself, wonderful countryside where grapes ripened on the hillsides in autumn and the meadows were ablaze with wild flowers in summer. She found she could learn languages with ease and could soon make herself understood in French, German and Italian. What was more, she made many friends, for the girls at the school were intelligent and interesting.

They thought it a little strange that she did not go home at holiday times, but not very strange. England was a long way off. There were seven other girls from England out of a total of a hundred and fifty pupils and only one of them went home as a matter of course for the long summer vacation.

Sara had realised long ago that she was an unloved child and it had made her very unhappy, since it seemed obvious that a child who cannot arouse affection in her own parents must be repulsive indeed. But school put things in perspective. Mother love did not come naturally to all parents, she learned, and English parents, apparently, particularly upper-class English parents, were often deficient in maternal and paternal love. As she got to know the other girls she realised that they, too, suffered, particularly her friend Anita, whose parents also treated their offspring with hurtful indifference.

'But I started at boarding school in Bournemouth when I was seven, and I soon realised that lots and lots of parents don't really care for their children,' she assured Sara. 'Some of them were really cruel and the children were awfully unhappy, but I had a wonderful nanny who took great care of me, and a big sister who is just perfect... so I stopped worrying that Mummy and Daddy scarcely ever visited the nursery when I was home in the holidays. I mean they didn't seem to think much of Veronica, either, and there isn't a nicer person in the world, truly there isn't.'

So Sara took comfort from this and wrote dutiful letters home and tried not to care that her parents' rare replies were always more like lectures than letters. And in due course she sat the necessary examinations and passed them, and prepared to rejoin the real world, which meant to leave school, and Switzerland, behind her.

Thanks to the school she now spoke French, German and Italian fluently, and Madame Audierne, who was headmistress of the school, had made sure she was taught a good many social graces and a good deal of commonsense. Sara understood a great deal about fashion, about the importance of always looking one's best, and about being a gracious hostess. Mme Audierne boasted that her girls left school able, if necessary, to entertain and amuse the highest in the land, and though Sara acknowledged that this was a flight of fancy, she still realised that she was now the possessor of considerable poise and self-possession.

Standing on Lime Street station however, watching the hustle and bustle of passersby, it did occur to her that she was also singularly ill-equipped to reach her home on foot. Despite the heat she was wearing a fashionable Robin Hood hat, an equally fashionable dark-green suit with curved white lapels, silk stockings and high-heeled strap shoes. Not the sort of clothes in which one set out on a long walk. Coming up in the train she had been studying a copy of *Woman* magazine, and thought wistfully that life would have been pleasanter had she been clad in a pair of the extremely fashionable beach pyjamas and a huge straw hat – and think of her father's rage should he see her in such an outfit!

There was a taxi-cab, of course. She could go outside, hail a cab, and then demand that either her parents or a servant pay him when they reached Aigburth Road. But before she could do anything so desperate, a voice hailed her.

'Sara? Sara! Over here!'

It was Mother, exquisitely turned out as usual and with a hat very similar to the one Sara wore perched rakishly on her tinted head. Sara found herself smiling, glad to see her mother, though she reminded herself sharply not to get carried away. She had managed very well without parents for three years and they had clearly managed very well without her. She must never become dependent upon them again, either for love or for any sort of moral guidance. So long as she remembered that, she thought, they might rub along quite comfortably.

So she went forward and laid her cheek carefully against her mother's powder and paint, and then pointed out her trunks and got a porter to carry them out to the car, which was waiting, her mother assured her, outside.

'Father couldn't come, he's at the office, of course, but I thought I'd better meet you myself in case Robson didn't recognise you. It's been a long time,' Mrs Cordwainer said coolly and Sara said sharply, 'I'm surprised you recognised me yourself, Mother, for I'm sure you saw very little more of me than Robson did, one way and another.'

For a moment she wondered if she had gone too far, but she need not have worried. Her mother was looking thoughtfully at Sara's outfit, and nodding approvingly. She had probably not even heard Sara's words.

'That is a very pretty hat,' Mrs Cordwainer said. 'Pearls would look well in the neck of that coat – do you have some pearls?'

'Not so far as I know,' Sara said. 'And I don't know that I want any, thank you. I think that pearls would look dull against the white of the lapels.'

This time her mother really did look surprised, then she shrugged and took Sara's arm.

'You're quite the fashionable young lady,' she said lightly. 'I shall enjoy having you at home now you're grown up. Come along, I want to see what other clothes you're hiding in your trunks. And in a few days we must talk about having a coming-out party for you. You are eighteen, after all.'

Sara said nothing, but she smiled to herself as she followed her mother's elegant back out of the station. If she really thinks that I'm going to turn into a paper pattern of herself she's got another think coming, Sara told herself grimly. Wait till she hears I want a job! Wait till I say I'm off to see Nanny for a weekend – and just let them try to stop me now!

Brogan and Peader had a marvellous welcome when they reached the house in Swift's Alley. Mammy wept and hugged them, the boys cheered and shouted and asked if there were presents in the bags, and Polly beamed and jumped up and down until her curls danced and kept gabbling away in her sweet, breathless voice until Mammy laughed and told her to stop or she'd be sent off to bed so she would!

'But there's roast ribs and a huge pan of new spuds and butter for our tea – I got the butter from the dairy on Francis Street, Mammy sent me there wit' me friend Tad from the next block,' Polly informed Brogan. She could not remember him too clearly – she had been two when he'd last been home – but Peader had been back more recently and she almost throttled him with hugs.

'Colleen, colleen, don't strangle me dead before I've so much as walked in the door,' he begged, and then his wife cast herself on his chest and he hugged her close whilst tears ran down his cheeks and dripped on to her black curls. 'Ah, Deirdre, Deirdre, me darlin' girl, never has a feller missed a woman more, I've been heartsick for you every day these t'ree years.'

Brogan turned away, catching hold of Polly's small hand. They deserved a moment to themselves, those two, who had worked so hard and longed for each other so much and who were reunited at last.

'Come on, Polly, you show me the new rooms, and then you can take me a walk around the city,' he said encouragingly. 'Donal, Bevin, you come too . . . now where's that fine boy I've heard so much about – me baby brother, Ivan?'

'He's there, the bad spalpeen,' Polly grumbled, hooking the baby out of the corner where he was beating a pile of building blocks with a small wooden hammer. 'Aw, come on, you tarble boy, Brogan's goin' to take us a walk.'

'Where would you like to go?' Brogan said when they had descended the stairs and were crossing the courtyard. 'Go on, you choose.'

There was a babble of suggestions. Donal pulled at

his sleeve, Polly clung to his hand, Bevin, who was twelve now, nudging thirteen, ran ahead, shouting the news to the neighbourhood that 'Me brother's come home so he has!'

This was home, Brogan thought contentedly, suggesting that they should do one thing at a time now, and not to forget he was home for a whole two weeks. Home was kids bawling at you, the pram which Polly and he were pushing between them bouncing over the cobbles, the sky soft and blue overhead.

'I don't care where we go, then,' Polly said, capitulating as suddenly as she had begun the argument. 'Go on, Donal, you choose.'

'Sure an' anywhere'll be fun,' Donal said, promptly following suit. 'We could go to the Basin, Brog. That's what Bevin 'ud like.'

'Then the Basin it is,' Brogan said. 'I'll just pop into John's Lane on me way past, though. Light a candle that I'm home safe.'

'Mammy'll do that an' all,' Polly observed, whilst Donal, who was fourteen and a practical person, remarked that most of the men he knew would have wanted to pop into Deegan's pub on their way past rather than the church.

'I'll do that later,' Brogan said, not wanting to appear a cissy in his brother's eyes. 'Come on, 'tis a long walk to the Basin from Swift's Alley!

Chapter Six

Brogan and his father had returned home on a Saturday. In true Irish fashion there was a downpour of rain on the Sunday, wetting the faithful, Mammy said gloomily, as they made their way both to and from Mass. Monday, too, dawned overcast – not that the O'Bradys cared! You could sell newspapers in any weather bar rain, the boys always said, and it was the same with fish, which never sold well on a Monday anyway. Folk wanted fish for Wednesdays and Fridays, that was obvious, so unless they fancied it specially, they would not buy the rest of the week.

So when Tuesday proved to be a brilliant day, the family decided that everyone would take the day off. The boys deputed others, cousins, friends, to do their jobs and everyone put on their oldest, most practical clothing, for today they were going to Booterstown on the train, to pick cockles on the long, sandy strand.

It was the height of a child's ambition, Brogan thought, as he watched his mammy cutting a carry-out for each of them. His mother's famous soda bread, a lump of real butter which Polly had run down and bought from the shop on Francis Street earlier, wrapped in cabbage leaves to keep it cool, and a screw of salt in a piece of blue paper. They would pick enough cockles for to make a meal, and lastly Mammy had got a big, scarlet tomato each from one of the market stalls. Riches! And Peader carried a covered bucket with tea in it – they would make a fire of sticks to heat it up, if they could find enough dry ones, that was. If not they'd drink it cold. 'And why not? Sure and I have me bottle of cold tay every day of me workin' life,' Peader reminded them.

They walked to the Tara Street station in a noisy, laughing crowd, Mammy and Daddy arm in arm, Mammy holding Ivan on her hip. Only he was a heavy, wriggling burden and since they couldn't get the pram on the train Brogan took charge of him, letting him walk a wee way, then picking him up and running with him to catch up with the others.

'I'm your horsie, amn't I, big feller?' Brogan said when Ivan screamed to get down again. 'Give your horsie a cut – a little one, mind – and he'll gallop right round the corner wit' you.'

Ivan liked that. He liked sitting on Brogan's shoulders, too, and hanging on to Brogan's ears and yelling to every passerby to 'Look at me! I'm onna norsie, so I am!'

The family piled into a carriage as soon as the train drew in, only Mammy and Peader managing to get a seat. But no one minded. Brogan piled their carry-outs and their jackets on the long string hammock of a rack which hung above the seated passengers' heads whilst his father sat himself carefully down next to his wife, the bucket of tea stood on the floor between his boots.

The train started with a jerk and Peader steadied the bucket whilst Donal hung out of the window despite many warnings from Mammy that it was dangerous and he'd get a blast from the engine in his eye and then he'd be sorry. He was still shouting against the wind that he wasn't the sort of donkey to go gettin' things in his eyes when he squawked and withdrew his head, one hand to his face.

'Oh, 'tis the size of a housebrick, I'll die for sure,'

Donal roared, and Niall told him he was a donkey indeed whilst Mammy scolded and Daddy said he'd done the same himself, many a time, and advice came both from family and other passengers. Pull your eyelid down over your eye now, feller. Blow your nose real hard, that'll do it. Screw up your eyes to make the water come, then blow your nose. But Bevin, probably imagining a trip to the hospital instead of a day at the seaside, turned and gave his brother a hearty clout. The blow made Donal shout again but his eye watered so much that the blast ran out with the tears and he was cured, though he glared at his brother resentfully.

When the fuss was over Brogan hung on to the luggage rack and gazed at the gardens and houses rushing past the window and Polly and Bevin hung on to him. Polly kept talking, though he could not hear much above the racket of the train. She kept pointing to the pictures which hung below the luggage rack and eventually Brogan realised she was asking which of them was Booterstown.

He examined the brown photographs, then leaned forward and ran his finger along the titles beneath each.

'None of 'em's where we's going,' he told Polly. 'Well, not today. Booterstown's a good place, you'll like it right well. But we'll go to those other places one day, alanna . . . we'll go to Killarney, and the beautiful Wicklow Mountains, and to Ballybunion. When you're a bit older.'

Polly just nodded. She did not even look surprised at such optimism and Brogan realised that to Polly all things were still possible. She had been in Dublin most of her short life and this would be her first visit to Booterstown, but she didn't waste time wondering why they'd not been before or when they'd go again, she just enjoyed the present . . . or would, once they got there.

Presently, Polly stood on tiptoe and shouted something else at him.

'What was that?' Brogan bawled, but at that moment the train slowed and stopped and there was a stampede for the platform. Brogan picked the baby off his mammy's lap and slung him round his neck, the child's fat little legs on either side of his face. Then he jumped down, turned and lifted the little ones down, finally offering his hand first to his mammy and then to an old lady who thanked him in a very regal manner, though she then wiped her nose on her sleeve, which didn't look quite so good.

Mammy came down on to the platform like a queen, with only the lightest touch of her fingers in his . . . she was a wonderful woman, Brogan thought with delight. How many women did he know who'd borne nine children, raised six of them, and taken on another child, yet still managed to smile and laugh more than she sighed, to seem carefree when burdened with a thousand worries – and had skin like new milk still, and hair without one strand of white? Not many, that was for sure. Not any, now he came to think.

'Mammy, you're a wonderful woman so you are,' he said to her, bowing and making Mammy laugh and flick his nose with her finger and the baby scream with pretended fear and cling like a limpet to Brogan's long-suffering ears. 'I hope I may meet a woman like you one of these days, else I'll not marry, I promise you. You leave every other woman I've met in the ha'penny place, so you do.'

'Your mammy's one in a t'ousand; when the good Lord made her he threw away the mould,' Peader said, jumping down and then reaching back for the bucket.

'Praise be to God, we'll get there wit' our tea-bucket unspilt at this rate!'

Polly waited patiently until they reached the beach, and then, sitting on the sand beside Brogan and taking off her plimsolls, she asked the question that she'd been trying to get out for ages, only the train clattered so, and the boys kept talking.

'Brogan, I wish we could have brought me friend Tad wit' us, so I do. Tad's never seen the sea, it's too far to walk to Booterstown and the Donoghues don't have pennies for the tram or the train.'

Brogan had undone his boots and was pulling off a pair of wonderful thick socks. Polly thought his feet must be stinkin' hot and said so, but Brogan said the woollen socks kept his feet cool because they sucked up the sweat and stopped his feet from scraping on the boot-leather.

'And as for your friend Tad, why didn't you call for him? Mammy and Daddy would have brought him, sure they would,' he added, wriggling his freed toes which were white as Polly's own. 'We wouldn't have grudged the lad a train ticket.'

'I didn't think,' Polly said sadly. 'It's selfish I am, Brogan, for he's a good friend to me. But he doesn't live in Swift's Alley now.'

Brogan raised a brow, then stood up, bent down and pulled her to her feet. 'Why not? Tell me whilst we paddle.'

They ran over the sand and down to the water, which creamed soft and easy against the shore. They both paused at the edge, then went in solemnly, slowly, and Polly's feet felt the salt sea water for the first time and she squeaked, and kicked foam, and decided that it was the best thing in the world so it was, and she'd come here again so she would. Kids could earn money, she and Tad would earn money for the train ticket and come here and spend days and days on the beautiful golden beach!

But Brogan wanted to hear about Tad, so she marshalled her thoughts, took his hand, and spoke as they waded deeper.

'Well, the Donoghues aren't a very nice family – that is, the mammy and daddy aren't very nice. Well, that isn't right either, Brogan, because the mammy's nice, all right, but she can't stop the daddy taking all the food and beating the kids up and blacking her eye every Sat'day night, just about. He's a wicked great man, Mr Donoghue, he beats Tad's ould wan wit' his fists an' the kids wit' his big ash stick . . . he's a docker . . . and he drinks all the money away, even the money Mrs Donoghue makes from her work. Well, it's not so bad when he is working, but when he doesn't get a job then he goes home and searches for the money . . . she hides it, of course. And when he finds it he takes it though she cries and cries. So that was what happened to the rent money, it was so. He took it, an' when Mrs Donoghue couldn't pay sure an' the landlord turned 'em out. So now they live in Gardiners Lane, and it's all the fault of Tad's ould feller.'

'The wicked bugger,' Brogan said between his teeth. He said it low, and vicious, but Polly heard it clear as clear. He had sworn, this wonderful big brother of hers, who was a fireman on a real train like the one she'd just travelled on, and who was studying each night at a big school for fellers, to better himself! But she did not say she'd heard; she guessed she'd not been meant to do so. 'But, Polly, why do you call Mrs Donoghue "the ould wan"? You don't speak so about your own mammy.'

'It's what Tad calls her,' Polly said, unrepentant. 'So anyway, last Christmas Tad's ould feller drank the rent money for three whole weeks, and they couldn't stop him. And the landlord turned them out – God love them, they all stood around crying, with their things at their feet, whiles Mr Donoghue tried to kill the landlord's men and got locked up by the polis and bound over to keep the peace.'

'And what happened to the rest of 'em?' Brogan asked. 'Ah, see that swirl in the sand there, alanna, by your right foot? That's a cockle, diggin' himself down deeper.' He rolled up his sleeve and plunged a hand into the water, producing a round, fat cockle shell. 'Now I'll put it in me pocket . . . go on wit' the story.'

'I will, so,' Polly said. 'So everyone was sorry for them, and then someone told Mrs Donoghue there was a house wit' rooms going begging in Gardiners Lane. It's a good place to play, because of the ruins, but the house there is awful. The walls run wit' wet and the windows don't fit properly and there's cracked glass in 'em anyway. They can get water from a tap at the bottom of the road but it's a long way to lug it, and though Tad's awright, the younger kids always have coughs and colds, boils on their necks, flea bites and bug bites . . . it's an awful place, honest to God it is.'

'Well, next time we go out we'll take your friend,' Brogan said soothingly. 'And all the cockles you pick you can take round to him. And a nice loaf, to eat wit' the cockles . . . mebbe even a lump of butter, eh?'

'Oh, yes *please*, Brogan,' Polly said eagerly. 'You are kind; Mammy's kind, too. When I was cross with Tad a few days ago she told me to go and make up wit' him, she even gave me some money for to treat him wit'. Only . . . Mammy said we would pick cockles for our carry-out; will there be enough for Tad's whole family? There are a real lot of them.'

'You and me'll pick like machinery,' Brogan said promptly. 'I'll show you where the cockles hide, how they look when they're buryin' themselves, and you'll soon get the knack. Come on, we'll have a contest, you and me.'

It's quite definitely been the best day of me life so far, Polly thought dreamily, as, sandy, damp and satisfied, they made their way to the station to catch the train back into Dublin. She had burned the tops of her feet because they'd caught the sun even through the water, but hadn't she picked a grand bag of cockles, indeed? Brogan had helped and had explained to Mammy and Daddy that he and Polly wanted to take them home for the Donoghues, and the family had done so well at the picking that there was plenty for everyone at dinner-time.

'You break 'em open by putting the lip of one cockle between the shell of another and twisting,' Daddy told them. 'At home, we'd boil 'em and they'd open themselves, but here on the beach it's open the shells the hard way and suck 'em out one at a time. Aren't they the best t'ing out, now? Fresh and sweet – Molly Malone herself didn't sell better!'

The train was late, but that didn't matter, not to Polly, at any rate. Daddy, Brogan and Niall were going down to Deegan's pub when they got home again, and they would bring a jug of porter back to drink with the rest of the cockles and lemonade or ginger beer for the kids.

'It's been a real holiday, hasn't it, Bev?' Polly said when at last the train chugged in and they scrambled for seats. She sank back on to the hard wood, glad that the train was almost empty going this way, feeling sleepy, sun-kissed, satisfied ... and knowing that the blue cloth bag of cockles would be divided fairly and half of it given to the Donoghues. 'Oh, Brogan, will you come wit' me when I take the cockles round? Only I'm that scared of Tad's ould feller, and you're big, he won't want to knock you about.'

'He'd better not try,' Mammy said, overhearing. 'Or I'll go round there meself and knock his ugly head off his ugly shoulders, so I will. And you'll come wit' me, won't you?' she added, nudging Peader, who was half-asleep already.

Peader sat up and gave her a mock salute. 'Certainly, certainly,' he said groggily. 'What was it you said, me little flower?'

Laughter, codding, full stomachs, damp feet in hot plimsolls, sand between the toes ... what's best, Polly thought dreamily, sagging against Brogan. Oh, but the memories I'll keep in me head for the rest of me life, that's the best. I'll see it in me head whenever anyone says 'cockles' or 'Booterstown'. What could be better than that?

Tad lay on his back on the straw mattress which he shared with his two younger brothers and his sister Meg, who was eighteen months old. The other boys were already snoring, replete after the best meal they'd had for weeks – cockles, three whole loaves of fresh bread and sufficient butter for all to have a share.

Polly and that Brogan feller had brought the food round. Tad hadn't met Brogan before, or not that he could recall, but he had liked him. Not just because of the food, either, but because Brogan had been real nice to Mrs Donoghue, and had told Tad they were real sorry they'd not thought to invite him to go along, but that next time they wouldn't make the same mistake.

So Brogan was all *right*. And Polly was a fine lass, though there was times when he wondered about her. She said some strange things, so she did. She said she could remember being *born*, of all things – said she'd been pulled out of warm darkness, which must be the doctor's bag, into a room full of dancing firelight and friendly faces. And she said Brogan had pulled her out, and sat her on her mammy's knee, and her mammy had hugged her and cried.

Only it couldn't be so, because Tad didn't know anyone who remembered being born.

Then there was her name. All the other kids in her family had decent Irish names; Polly was an English name. And all the O'Brady chisellers were dark-haired, but Polly had lovely red-gold curls.

She's a changeling; the fairies brought her and swopped a little O'Brady child for her, and one of these days she'll simply disappear, Tad told himself. But he didn't believe it, because sure and didn't everyone know that changelings were spiteful creatures, who'd trick you soon as look at you? Polly wasn't like that at all at all, she was gentle and kind – though she could take your feet off at the ankles so she could when she played hurley with a bundle of rags and a piece of plank.

She was only a kid, though. And a girl – girls weren't supposed to want to play with boys at all, let alone play hurley. But Polly would do anything. She might have curls and big blue eyes, but she could take the football off a bigger and better player, tricksy as a cat on her small feet, and she could run like the wind, hang on to a moving tram by the post on the rear, climb a wall like that same cat, though God knew where she found the footholds . . . she was all right, was Polly O'Brady.

Tad sighed and opened his eyes. They had a nice home, did the O'Bradys. And they talked nice to their mammy, and hardly anyone hit anyone else. All kids fight, everyone knows that, but apart from giving one another a smack from time to time, the O'Bradys never seemed to want to scrap. And Mrs O'Brady was pretty, like a young girl, and she never had black eyes, or too many babies, or a swollen cheek, such as his own mammy tried to hide from time to time.

But there were several earners in the O'Brady family, and he, at ten, was the eldest Donoghue. He did his best to make a living, carrying all the money straight home to his mammy, but it was hard because he was small for his age and there were days when the Donoghues didn't eat and then he wasn't much good at any work he happened to pick up.

But Polly liked him. He knew she did.

Above Tad's head there was a huge yellow-brown fungus growing out of the blackened wall; he quite liked that fungus. It came and went according to the season but right now it was in full fig, with a wavy edge and an odd, rather exciting sort of smell. He lay in the darkness gazing up at it and thinking about Polly, and about the cockles, and the seaside she had talked about with such enthusiasm.

There were scutterings in the dark corners. Black clocks, with their many legs going and their hard-shelled bodies clattering. It took a blow with a hammer to kill them, they were so big and strong. Or you could tread on them with a booted foot, only Tad didn't have boots – wouldn't have, until he started work. Unless a miracle happened, of course. Unless his daddy dropped dead and stopped stealing his mammy's small savings whenever he was out of work.

Tad had rather liked living in Swift's Alley, and in a way he liked living in Gardiners Lane, too. There weren't many houses in Gardiners Lane, but there were lots of ruins. The ruins had been houses and shops once, he knew, but they'd simply crumbled away and fallen down, and now they made good play places, if you were careful. And in summer, the wild flowers grew here, the tall pink spires of flowers which Polly said were called rosebay willowherb, the yellow piss-the-beds, the bright, golden-eyed daisies. A lot of kids played in Gardiners Lane but not a lot lived there. The tall, skinny house, leaning sideways, in which the Donoghues lived had been condemned years ago, but that only meant the landlord charged less rent. And filled the house to overflowing when he could.

Still. We've got two rooms here, Tad told himself drowsily, as sleep at last began to steal over him. We'd never have run to two rooms in Swift's Alley, but here there was no one to stop us taking over this room . . . and not many fellers in Dublin can say they've got big yellow funguses and trees growing in their bedrooms!

The tree had seeded in the fireplace and sprung up, growing amazingly strongly all things considered. It reached for the sky, ignoring the narrow little window which, in any case, had no glass in it, and Tad knew, because he'd gone out and stood well back and looked as hard as he could, that already a bunch of hopeful leaves had appeared out of the chimney top.

The only time Tad could remember the landlord coming round Mammy had been warned by little Liam. Liam had rushed into the room and grabbed her skirt.

There's a man, Mammy, lookin' in the downstairs

front,' he had gabbled. 'Mrs Donovan said to tell you he'll be up in five minutes.'

Mammy had said not a word. She had gathered the bigger children round her with a gesture and they had stormed into the second room. It was tiny, cold, damp, and it had not taken them more than two minutes to clear all signs of occupation. They had piled the mattresses up, higgledy piggledy, in the living room, then assembled rather self-consciously, round the fire. Mammy had started to cut the loaf, Biddy had hauled the baby on to her lap and begun to sing to him, and the other boys had bustled round getting dishes out and pretending to lay the table for a meal.

The landlord knocked, but came straight in after, never giving them a chance to go to the door.

'I've come to have a look at me property,' the man said gruffly. 'You've just the two rooms?'

'Just the one,' Mammy said. 'As you very well know.'

He stared very hard at her, then gestured around him at the children clustered near the small, sullenly burning fire.

'And where do all them children sleep? Answer me that!'

'Here,' Mammy said. 'Where else?'

He said nothing but stalked over to the door and flung it wide, then went across the narrow hallway and flung open the door opposite, too.

He looked around the damp little room with the tree growing up in the grate and the big, wavy fungus on the wall. He looked at the pigeon droppings on the floor – pigeons roosted on the roof and the broken tiles let their droppings in – and at the boards to the right of the door which had rotted clear away from the weather in the winter. Then he turned and stared at his audience of Donoghues.

'You could have this room as well for another bob a week,' he said in quite a different tone. 'Not big enough for another family, you see . . . if you don't take it, I can't let it.'

Mammy said nothing. She just stared at him, then let her eyes slide past him. To the damp, the rotted boards, the tree, the pigeon droppings, the glassless window.

'Should we say sixpence?' The landlord was almost whining now, almost appealing to their better natures! 'I'm not a rich man, I can't afford to have a room stand empty.'

'Mend the roof, and put glass in the window.' Tad was astonished at the sound of his own voice, he almost looked round to see who had spoken. 'It might be worth sixpence a week then.'

The landlord stared at him. A long, thin face, set with mean little eyes, a thin nose, a thin, tight mouth turned down at the corners. 'But you don't spend money on a house that's been condemned!'

'Sure and a decent body wouldn't ask rent for it, either,' Tad pointed out. His mammy smiled, but to herself, as though at her own thoughts. 'Two bob a week me mammy pays for our room, and the kids is always sick 'cos it's so damp. It even smells of damp.'

The landlord stared, then turned to Mammy.

'You'll have trouble with that chiseller one o' these days so you will,' he said angrily. 'Fellers like that get carried home on a door.'

'For speakin' the truth?' Mammy said, suddenly making up her mind to be equally bold. 'For tellin' you what you should have knowed – that the place isn't fit for anyone to live in as it stands?'

The landlord frowned, then turned away. He began to descend the stairs, calling back to them over his shoulder. 'Very well, I take it that you don't want the second room. And I like the rent on time, don't forget that, either.'

'You'll get it,' Tad called after him. 'For the one room.'

So now Tad lay in the darkness in the miserable, smelly, damp little room with his brothers and sisters sleeping all around him and mused on his lot. Why did his mammy let his daddy hit her? Why did she let Daddy hit his kids? Why didn't she make him give her money, if only a little, towards the rent, the food? Why did Daddy get the lion's share at mealtimes? And above all, why, in God's name, did Mammy keep on having babies, year after year after year, when she couldn't feed them, when for three years now, the babies had died?

Polly's mammy didn't keep having babies. Sure, she'd had Ivan, but she hadn't had any since. Women who kept having babies weren't all that strong, and they had to pay money to the women who brought the babies, or to the doctor who brought them. Then they were very weak for a while after, and they had to feed the baby which sometimes meant they couldn't work.

I'll ask at school, Tad decided finally. And I'll ask the father why are people made so different and why do men hit their ould wans? Or perhaps not the father; I'll ask Mr Roberts, at school. He's a grand man so he is, he'll tell me if he knows.

Beside him, Dougal kicked out, then turned over, making their straw pallet rustle and squeak. Meg was lying on her back and snoring fit to bust, her arm flung out, her fingers curled as though in her dreams she grasped at something. Tad sat up on his elbow and very gently turned Meg over so that she was lying on her side. He couldn't bear the thought that a clock might crawl across her face and fall into the open cavern of her mouth. She might be choked to death and she was only little. Also, it stopped her snoring.

He glanced around the room. All the others appeared to be asleep and Liam was whimpering; full stomachs could give you nightmares when you weren't used to it, or keep you awake half the night. Because it was summer the air coming through the window was flower-scented, almost pleasant. It made Tad think of the Brickfields, and the canal bank, and the green countryside which he had never yet set eyes on. It sounded nice, did the countryside. Polly had told him that when times had been hard her mammy had gone out into the countryside and picked spuds to sell in the Moore Street market. And even now, if they needed something extra, she would go and pick gooseberries or black currants and sell them, too. Polly had gone picking gooseberries with her mammy earlier in the year; she said it was lovely, really lovely, away from the city.

Tad had thought himself well on the way to dreamland, but suddenly he sat up. A thought was coming clear in his head and it was a good one, he didn't want it to escape him, he wanted to remember it, to bring it out and look at it lovingly in the days to come.

Everyone starts somewhere, that was the thought. All men, his own daddy, Polly's daddy, had once been a boy, as he was. And not only them but Mr Roberts the schoolteacher and the landlord, the lamplighter who walked up and down the street with his long pole and made the gaslights flare, the fishmonger in his striped apron and straw hat, the tram conductor who took pennies from the grown-ups and shouted at the chiselers who stole free rides and jumped off his vehicle before he could demand payment.

The Lord Mayor of Dublin, even, with his gold chain and his fancy medals, he had been just a boy once. And the film stars at the picture palaces, and the soldiers who stamped up and down the streets in their smart uniforms . . . they had all been just boys, once.

So it stood to reason, Tad told himself, that a boy could be anything. He didn't have to be like his daddy, whether that daddy was a cruel, drunken docker, or – or the Lord Mayor of Dublin himself. He could put his mind to it, and he could be anything! Tad looked around him, at the dirty little room, the crowded mattresses, the moonlight streaming in through the window and falling, silver-striped with the black of shadows, across the beds. I'll be Somebody, he told himself, slowly lying down again. I'll work and scheme and try my hardest, and I'll be Somebody, so I will. I'll go down to that place Polly went and I'll pick cockles and sell 'em, or I'll dip a big net in the sea and find fishes and sell them, too. Or I'll pick potatoes and knock the dirt off and stand in Moore Street market and sell them. But whatever happens, I'm not going to end up beating some poor woman in a crowded, dirty little tenement room in Gardiners Lane.

And on that thought, Tad fell happily asleep.

They hated leaving, hated going back.

'But sure and I'd hate bein' home and out of work,' Peader said resignedly as he and Brogan stood at the rail and watched Ireland getting smaller and smaller behind them. 'And wasn't it a grand holiday, Brogan? Ah, we couldn't have had a better time if we'd been millionaires.'

'That's true so it is,' Brogan agreed. 'And it won't be too long, Daddy, before you're home for good. After all, Mammy's got a good deal of money put by and now Niall's got a good job and Martin's looking for one . . . well, you'll be able to go home to stay. Then you'll find a job, even if it doesn't pay like being the safety man for the gang does.'

'I've thought of applyin' for a job with the Irish railways,' Peader admitted. 'But we're doing well so we are. I'm half afraid to make changes, in case it turns out they're for the worse. But I do hate to leave, indeed I do.'

'True. But I don't know that I'd want to go on living in Swift's Alley,' Brogan said, surprising himself. Wasn't it home to him and hadn't he been brought up there when all was said and done? But back in Crewe he lodged with an elderly couple and they had a fine, clean little house and a wonderful garden. The front was a picture, all flowering trees, shrubs and flower borders with a circular lawn and an ornamental pond, but the back garden, which was very long and large, was laid down to vegetables and when they found out that Brogan was fascinated by the thought of growing things the Simpsons gave him a sizeable plot for himself.

'Grow what you like, lad,' Mr Simpson said. 'If you do the work I'll buy the seed and Mrs Simpson will cook what you produce for our meals. Anything that's over you can sell, because I'm too old to tackle a great garden like this alone. What d'you think?'

'I think it would be grand,' Brogan said honestly. 'Sure and there's nothin' I'd like better than to try me hand at growin' things.'

He had worked hard in the garden and it had taught him a lot. When he came home after a day of heaving coal in the heat of a small cab he simply wanted to rest, but very soon he found that digging, planting and weeding in the open air was a most relaxing and rewarding pastime.

'You've got green fingers,' Mrs Simpson said when she came down the garden and saw his rows of peas, broad beans, summer cabbage and carrots all coming on apace. 'Not everyone can grow things, you know.'

'They look more like black to me,' Brogan said ruefully, examining his hands, but Mrs Simpson just laughed and said it was a way of saying he'd the magic touch, that he could grow things where others failed.

'When winter comes, get Mr Simpson to show you how to enrich the land with manure from the farms,' she advised. 'We all need food to make us grow and the good earth is no exception.'

They were not Catholics, yet they seemed to be good people. They attended church every Sunday and gave to various good causes and had decided to take in a lodger not simply for the extra money to augment the pension, but because both Mr and Mrs Simpson liked young people about the place.

'We were never blessed with children,' Mr Simpson told him one evening as they worked in the garden, for they shared the work now since Brogan wanted to try his hand with flowers as well as vegetables. 'And since neither the wife nor myself have brothers or sisters we have only remote relatives left now, no close family. But we've a great many friends, a nice home . . . and now you, Brogan, to bring a bit of life into the place!'

'What's wrong with Swift's Alley?' Peader said now, dragging Brogan back to the present, to the ship's rail, the heaving sea beneath the ship, the sight of their homeland vanishing into the mist. 'You never found fault wit' it before, lad.'

'Oh, Daddy, it's not finding fault that I am, it's just

that I'd like to see Mammy and the kids in the country, with a bit of space round them. You've not seen the Simpsons' place, not far from Crewe, but it's made me realise that there are other ways of life which are . . . kind of slower, softer, I suppose.'

'I thought the same meself, in fact,' Peader said slowly. 'I asked your mammy if she'd like to live somewhere else, somewhere wit' a garden, perhaps, and she said she would indeed, but not yet. Not until we're safe, whatever that may mean.'

Brogan nodded slowly. He knew what his mother meant and so did his father, but the truth was they scarcely knew what it was to be safe, with landlords always liable to put up the rent, the council to increase the fees you paid at school, or an employer deciding to give you the boot. Safety, if it meant security, he concluded, was not for the likes of them.

But that didn't mean that they could never be safe. I'm still working at me books, he reminded himself fiercely, and soon now I'll be driving an engine, or perhaps I'll learn about motor-car engines so I can put them right when they go wrong, for it's a practical turn of mind I have, or so my teachers at the Gordon Institute told me. And once I've got a good enough job, then I can make Mammy safe, see that she's secure, so that she isn't worried where the money's coming from.

Peader, standing beside him, sighed. 'Women! But one of these days we'll whisk her away to live somewhere decent, eh, Brog? Ah, Ireland's gone into the mist now; let's go below and have a glass of porter!'

Sara didn't wake on Sunday morning until the maid swished her curtains back and let the mild September sunshine flood into the room. Then she sat up in bed, stretched, yawned, and blinked across at the maid.

'Morning, Bessy! It looks a nice day.'

'Morning, Miss Sara. Did you enjoy yourself, last night?'

'It was very nice, thanks,' Sara said politely. 'I danced every dance and had supper with Captain Franklyn. He'd be a lot nicer if he didn't keep feeling his moustache in that horrid, sly sort of way, as if it was a false one and he was afraid it had fallen off.'

Bessy snorted, then tried to turn it into a cough. She came over to the bed and took the cosy off a small teapot. 'Tea, Miss Sara?'

'Oh, please, Bessy. I want to go round to Mrs Prescott's this morning. After all, I've been back in Liverpool three whole weeks, it's about time I went to Kirkdale, whatever anyone thinks. And it's the harvest supper at church this evening; I wonder what I should wear? I do have rather a lot of new clothes . . . Mother and I seem to spend all our time shopping.' She did not add, *It's the only thing we have in common*, because that would have been unkind, but she knew it was true, nevertheless. In the three weeks since she returned her mother had taken her out every morning, sometimes to meet friends, sometimes to go round the picture gallery or the museum, but mostly to visit the shops, particularly the big stores.

Sara sat up on her elbow and sipped her tea. 'Now the harvest supper – that takes some thinking about because not only will the Reverend Atwell be there, Mr Alan Hepworth will attend, too. So that means best bib and tucker, eh, Bessy?'

'You shouldn't joke about Mr Hepworth, Miss Sara He's always calling round, asking after you,' Bessy said, her hand on the door knob. 'Besides, Mrs Cordwainer approves, so I suppose that means he's gorra bob or two,' she finished, dropping her 'smart' accent and grinning at her employer.

Sara grinned back. 'You're right there, except that he's gorra bob or *three*,' she said. 'Actually, he really is rather nice and all the girls are after him, so reeling him in would be quite a catch.'

'Then do it,' Bessy advised. 'Has he asked you yet, Miss?'

'Twice. But he expects to have to dance to my tune for a bit longer, he's made that clear,' Sara said cheerfully. 'Oh, I shouldn't tease him, but I'm not at all sure I want to marry anyone, yet.'

'Don't blame you,' Bessy said. 'I ain't goin' to marry anyone till I'm good and ready, and when I do I'm goin' to make the feller sign a contract to say he'll hand over his pay packet without openin' it first, that he'll give me everything I want that he can afford, and that I can go dancin' twice a week without him.'

'Bessy, you are truly disgraceful, you shame womanhood,' Sara said, giggling. 'I'll remember that the next time Mr Hepworth proposes; I'll say would he like to glance at the contract I've got in mind and see whether he approves and would like to sign on the dotted line.'

Both girls laughed, then Bessy sobered, and opened the door.

'If you want anything, Miss, just ring the bell,' she said, and let herself out on to the landing.

Sara finished her cup of tea, then she swung her legs out and stood up. My life is hollow and full of vanity, she told herself. When I was a child I wanted desperately to help girls like Jess Carbery, but there was so little I could do. But now I ought to be able to do my bit. Yet when I talked about getting a job Mother and Father said I should wait until I'd settled down in Liverpool again and when I wanted to offer my services to one of the charitable institutes I was told I would be doing someone else out of a job. And at the back of my mind there's this skinny young girl who didn't have enough to eat, who spent all her time and energy trying to keep her little sisters alive – and whose life was brought to a terrible close because no one cared enough. I'm sure if she could do so Jess would say to me now, 'Find Mollie! Look after Grace! And all I do is what everyone else does – I go to parties, attend church services, and tell myself that one day I'll find out what had happened to the Carbery family and perhaps do my bit towards helping them. But life's never that simple – I'm still a child so far as my parents, and authority, are concerned.

But before she considered her future, she would go and see Mrs Prescott. She had announced her intention of going over to Snowdrop Street as soon as she reached home, but somehow it had never been convenient for her to go visiting, and because she wanted her homecoming to be as trouble-free as possible, she had postponed undertaking the journey. She could not believe that her mother and father would continue to disapprove of her visiting her old nurse but in any event, she did not intend to put it to the test. She would go first and talk about it later, she decided.

Accordingly she got up, dressed in a bronze blouse, grey suit and black court shoes, then went down to the breakfast parlour.

Mrs Cordwainer was sitting at the table, nibbling toast. She looked up and smiled as her daughter entered the room.

'Ah, Sara dear – good morning! I thought we'd go out to Crosby later to visit my friend Fanny.'

Sara smiled and took her seat at the table. She reached across for the toast, then changed her mind; it would be cold by now, she was late. Instead, she poured herself a cup of coffee from the tall silver pot.

'Good morning, Mother, isn't it a lovely day? But I'm afraid I can't come out to Crosby with you, I've a previous engagement.'

'Oh? With whom, dear?'

'I'm going to see an old friend, someone I've known for years,' Sara said truthfully. 'But I've not seen her since I left the city, though we did write from time to time.'

'Ah, a school friend. And will you be back for luncheon? You won't forget the harvest supper tonight, dear? It helps to raise funds for the poor of the Indian subcontinent, I believe. I've bought half a dozen tickets, several of our friends and relatives will be coming.'

'How nice,' Sara said vaguely. 'I'll be back in good time, Mother.'

'Good. You're calling a cab, I presume?'

It was a discreet way of finding out just where she was going, Sara guessed. She smiled, looking down at her plate. 'No, indeed. It's not far at all, only a few steps in fact.'

Her mother relaxed. She really doesn't want me to see Nanny, Sara realised. It's absolutely ridiculous, but I'm going to have to be very careful. If Mother was jealous of my affection for Nanny I could understand it, but she doesn't love me herself, I've always known that. She *likes* me now I'm a grown-up, a young woman, and she is beginning to enjoy my company, but loving . . . well, that's a very different kettle of fish.

'Oh, then if you really can't come with me, my dear, I'll get a cab to Crosby as soon as I'm properly dressed. Your father has the car. I wonder if Mrs Spry would care to accompany me? She's thinking of buying a little property outside the city. I believe I'll send Fletcher round to ask if she'd like to come with me.'

How extraordinary! She doesn't like to be alone, that's why she's been clinging to me, Sara thought, astonished. Well, I never would have thought it – and when I was a child she was always so eager to get rid of me!

Presently she went up to her room and got her handbag, settled her new hat at a becoming angle on her dark curls, and set off. She found herself more excited than she had been since her homecoming, for once in the streets, by herself and on foot, a good deal of her past came flooding back. Going off to school in the city with her satchel on her back and her hockey stick in one hand and one of the maids, impatient to return to her work, hurrying her along. The tram ride with other girls also wearing the navy and scarlet school uniform, everyone chattering, exchanging gossip, writing in each other's autograph books. A craze for fortune-telling, another craze for cigarette cards, a time, earlier, when she never trod on a crack in the paving stones for fear that it would open up and swallow her. Then there had been the piano lessons, to which Jane had accompanied her whilst Robson drove them to the teacher's home and came back for them an hour later. That had meant going through the city at night, with the lamps lit, the gas flaring softly, white, primrose, deep yellow. And the great buildings towering above the small girl and her companion – St George's Hall, the Picton Library, the Walker Art Gallery – as much a part of her past as were the stairs which led up to the nursery, the long, echoing corridors of her school and the smell of cabbage and boiled socks which heralded a school dinner.

But nostalgia attacked her hardest on the tram, when

she climbed aboard it on Croxteth Road and it began to rattle along towards the city centre. They passed her old school and she saw that it wasn't a huge or imposing place but quite small compared with the Swiss school, and they passed a friend's house and she craned her neck, hoping to see Eliza, but all she saw was a black cat, sunning itself in the front garden.

She had to change trams on Old Haymarket and stood for a moment, tapping her foot impatiently on the big, fudge-coloured paving stones. But then her tram came along with 'Stanley Road' written on its board and she hopped aboard and went and sat on one of the hard slatted wooden seats. Well she remembered *them;* her bottom had been striped by them many a time!

And presently, the excitement began to build as the tram rattled along, sounding its bell warningly as the crowds on the streets, trying to dodge amongst the traffic, grew thicker and less willing to give way. The tram roared along the Vauxhall Road and Sara saw familiar, much-loved sights and the smells which went with them; the great bulk of Tate & Lyle's sugar refinery, scenting the air with sweetness, further along the smells from the distillery, further yet the scent of freshly cut wood from the saw mills . . . and a glimpse, always longed-for when she was on the tram with her nanny, of the Leeds & Liverpool canal, the water gleaming dully, like unpolished pewter, under a cloudy sky.

And then they were on Stanley Road and she was so excited that she could not stop smiling. When she was first in Switzerland she had thought about Brogan a lot, remembering him with great affection, but gradually, as the years passed, she began to see that they had scarcely known one another, really. But she had liked him so much, even being on Stanley Road again made her see a picture of him in her head. His dark hair and eyes, the height of him, the easy strength . . . her tummy gave a most peculiar lurch when she remembered him hugging her in the cinema once, when she'd been scared by the film. She must find him again, tell him she was back, renew their friendship.

Through the window she saw the long procession of milliners and hairdressing establishments, picture palaces and pawn-shops, passing in front of her eyes. And then she saw her stop approaching and she jumped to her feet and the conductor tinged his bell, the tram driver applied his brakes . . . and she was getting down . . . she was there!

Chapter Seven

In three years, very little had changed. There were still a great many people thronging the pavement, many carrying small attaché bags or worn suitcases. They were women, Sara knew, going to the pawn to collect their decent stuff for Sunday. Soon they would be reclaiming blankets as the weather grew colder but for now it was mainly Sunday suits, the respectable shoes, the ornaments for the mantel if you were having a bit of a hooley round your place, Saturday night.

Several people glanced at her, then looked away again. The differences between a child not yet fifteen and a young woman of eighteen are considerable, Sara realised, and besides, though she had been respectably dressed as a child, she had not been smart or fashionable. Now she was both, and suddenly she began to feel a little uncomfortable, even a little ashamed.

Who was she to walk down this busy, happy road in a suit and hat which had cost more than a good many of these people earned in a year? She had done nothing for it, after all. She despised her parents for being greedy and uncaring, but what had she actually done for those less fortunate? Once, long ago, she had given a child a pair of gloves and a shilling and because of it, the child had died. Oh, she knew it hadn't been her fault, she could not possibly have known that a spontaneous, generous act would have such terrible consequences. But what had she done since?

Sara sighed and turned the corner into Snowdrop

Street. It was no use feeling sorry for herself, because that was just what she was doing, really. A child has very little real power; she had done what she could without arousing adult wrath and if it hadn't been enough she was sorry, but the past is the past. Now, however, she was eighteen years old and had real earning power, if only she could find someone to employ her. And then she would use her money properly and wisely, and she would make those enquiries about the Carbery girls which she had always intended to make once she grew up. Or she hoped she would. Human nature being what it is, she reflected gloomily, she would probably marry some suitable young man, leave her job, and start a family. That was what most girls did and Sara knew it was what her parents expected her to do. Whether she would or not remained to be seen, for though she thought Mr Hepworth very pleasant, she was not at all sure that she actually wanted to marry him.

She reached number three and took the brass dolphin in her hand. She no longer had to stand on the step to reach it. She lifted the knocker, let it fall, then stood back and waited.

She heard the footsteps at once and smiled to herself. Good old Nanny, the years hadn't changed her light step! In fact she sounded younger than ever, as though not seeing Sara for three whole years had brought about a magical shedding of the burden of age. But before Sara had done more than think this the door opened and a woman appeared in the doorway. She was probably in her middle thirties, Sara thought, with a plain but kindly face, dark hair pulled back into a bun and very bright dark eyes.

'Good mornin', queen,' she said cheerfully. 'And what can I do for you this fine mornin'?'

'Oh!' Sara stammered, totally taken aback. 'I've come to see my nanny . . . Mrs Prescott, I mean. Don't say she's ill!'

'Oh no, she's not really ill, but she's not been too good . . .' The woman peered at her, then light seemed to dawn for she smiled suddenly. 'You wouldn't be young Sara, would you? Sara Cordwainer?'

'That's right,' Sara said. 'What's been the matter with Nanny? I've been away from home for three years, you see, so I've not seen her all that time, but we've been exchanging letters and she never said anything about her health failing. Only she's not one to grumble about herself, so I suppose she wouldn't have said? Er . . . are you a neighbour? A friend?' Another thought struck her. 'Mrs Prescott is here, isn't she? She's not in hospital or anything?'

'No, she's here,' the woman said. 'I'm sorry, chuck, wharrever am I thinkin' of?' she stood aside, gesturing Sara to enter the narrow hallway. 'I'm Mrs Prescott's lodger, my name's Boote – Clarrie Boote.' She held out a square, capable hand. 'How d'you do, Miss Cordwainer! Your gran's much better now, out of hospital, on her feet, but she's having a sit down and a cuppa, wi' a biscuit or two to dunk in it.'

'How do you do, Miss Boote,' Sara said, feeling quite weak with relief. Thank goodness Nanny was all right now – but what had ailed her?

She put the question to Miss Boote, who sighed.

'Well, I could say anno domini, Miss Cordwainer, but I suppose it's a combination of things, really. She got a nasty old infection which swelled all her joints and gave her a high fever so they whipped her into the Stanley. They did a good job, cured the fever, but ever since she's found it hard to move about much. It's chronic rheumatism, if you ask me, brought about by the 'flu, or whatever it was.'

'How awful,' Sara breathed. She could not imagine her nanny ill. But Miss Boote said she was better, which was something to hold on to. If Nanny wasn't here I don't know what I'd do, she thought. She's like a rock, always steady, always understanding – always there.

'Yes, Mrs Prescott has a good deal to contend with,' Miss Boote agreed. 'But I give a hand when I can.'

'I'm glad you're here,' Sara said, though she wondered why Nanny had suddenly decided to let one of her rooms. 'She isn't getting any younger and the company will do her good.'

'And me rent helps,' Miss Boote said frankly. 'I gather there was a rift in the family and she don't get much help from *that* quarter.'

'I don't think she's got any family, or not anyone really close,' Sara said cautiously. 'But Nanny's always been very independent.'

Miss Boote, who had been about to open the parlour door, turned and stared at her.

'No family?' she said slowly. 'Then what do you call yourself?'

'Mrs Prescott was my old nanny,' Sara explained. 'She is no relation. I call her nanny because . . . well, because she was my nanny until I started school.'

Miss Boote snorted. 'Your nanny? She's your grandmother, child – didn't you know? Oh aye, her daughter Letty married your dad and she's had no time for her mam since the day she was wed. She let your gran move into the house and take care of you when you was small . . d'you mean to say she never let on that you was all related?'

Sara leaned against the wall, with its pattern of brown roses on a cream ground. 'Related?' she said faintly. 'My grandmother? But she can't be – Mother's mother lives in Devonshire, she's an eccentric and doesn't care for children. And I know Father's mother quite well, though to be honest, we don't like each other much.'

'Devonshire! When your gran telled me she'd let her daughter tell you fairytales rather than lose you altogether I couldn't believe me ears,' Miss Boote said scornfully. 'Didn't anyone ever let on? They must ha' known, surely?'

'If they did they never said,' Sara assured her. 'I must see Nanny – I must ask her why she didn't tell me herself.'

'Well, go slowly, like,' Miss Boote advised. She put her hand across the door, preventing Sara from simply rushing in. 'Remember she's been poorly, so just take it slow, don't get her all excited and aerated.'

'I won't,' Sara said at once. 'But I have to ask! It isn't that I disbelieve you, in fact I'm certain you're speaking the truth, but – well, you know how it is.'

'Aye, I do. You must be fair astonished,' Miss Boote agreed. 'Just remember to go gently, though, queen. I don't suppose it's been easy for your gran all these years. There must have been times when she longed to tell you, and I aren't sure what stopped her, either . . . some threat, I daresay, knowin' your mam as I do. Or did, rather,' she added conscientiously. 'Because we've not set eyes on each other since her marriage. We don't move in the same circles, like,' she finished.

'Wait a moment, Miss Boote,' Sara said urgently, as Miss Boote went to open the door. Another question had come to the forefront of her mind. 'You say you knew my mother – did you know her from when she lived with her mother?'

'Aye, though she were a good bit older than me. My

mam and your gran was neighbours, chuck. We lived quite near here in them days, just round the corner in Commercial Road. Me dad were landlord of the Great Mersey public house for a while, then the drink made him bad so he took a job as a warehouseman and we moved into a little house in Commercial Road. We stayed on until Dad retired . . . in fact we didn't move out till they found a house in Formby, ten year back. So you see, I knew Letty quite well, she used to take me to school if me mam was busy. She were a right tartar,' she added reminiscently. 'Very sure of herself, and very pretty. You have a look of her, only you've a sweeter expression.'

Sara was about to ask the next question when a voice came faintly through the heavy wooden door.

'Clarrie? Who is it? It sounds . . . it sounds . . .'

Sara waited no longer. She flung open the door and ran across the room to where Mrs Prescott sat in a chair by the fire. She looked a little greyer, and possibly a trifle more frail, but otherwise she was just Sara's dear nanny, the person she loved most in the world.

'Oh, Nanny, it's me, I'm home! Switzerland was wonderful, but it wasn't home and I'm just so glad to be back at last. But how are you? Miss Boote said you'd been poorly, but were better now.' She kissed the older woman lovingly, then stood back. 'You look very well,' she said bracingly. 'But you've not much colour in your cheeks – what a pity it's autumn . . . but the weather's fine enough for some outings to bring back your rosy glow, Nanny! I'll tell Mother I want the car in a day or so, when we have another sunny morning, and we'll go out on the spree. Oh Nanny, it's so *very* good to see you again after all this time!'

Mrs Prescott was smiling, her cheeks pink, her eyes very bright. 'Oh Sara, my dear girl, I was beginnin' to wonder whether they'd ever let you come back!' She heaved a huge sigh. 'There's somethin' I've got to tell you, and I aren't lookin' forward to it one bit for I can't help feelin' I'm breakin' my word. But . . .'

'You don't have to tell me a thing, *Gran*,' Sara said, emphasising the word. 'Because I know, and I couldn't be more delighted than if I'd been told my gran was Queen of England. It's the best news in the world, it's made me so happy I want to sing, and if you don't want to go into details I'll quite understand.'

'Clarrie, you're a very dear girl,' Mrs Prescott called, but all she got from Miss Boote, halfway up the stairs, was a chuckle, so she turned back to Sara. 'Well, I can't pretend I'm sorry that all the lies and evasions are over, Sara my dear, but when you were born Letty made me swear on the Bible that I'd never breathe a word of our relationship and I were so besotted with you, queen – you were the loveliest baby – that I'd ha' done anything, promised anything, just to be allowed to help bring you up. For it were clear from the first that your mam wasn't goin' to take an interest, and intended to turn you over to servants,' she finished.

'Why wouldn't my mother admit you were her mother, though?' Sara said thoughtfully. I don't mean to upset you, Gran, but it seems very odd. Father must have known, for instance.'

But Mrs Prescott was shaking her head.

'No, he didn't know the whole truth, because Letty told him a fairytale, too. She said she was adopted, that I'd always wanted a child of me own so I'd adopted her from a respectable couple when the father died.' Mrs Prescott sighed. 'Eh, havin' Letty was me one mistake, and didn't I pay dear for it! You see, queen, I never had a husband. The truth is my mam put me in service with a rich family out at Bootle, but

I was a flighty piece and I got into trouble. The baby's da was me employer, and he was married, of course, so when they realised what had happened I was sacked, in disgrace. I had a hard time of it because me own parents cast me off – they were strict chapel – so I had to earn enough money to rear me child and keep meself, but somehow, I did it. Yet Letty despised me from the moment she discovered that her father had been a married man, and rich. She despised me first because I were weak enough to get in the family way and then because I'd not made use of her father. As soon as she could she left home, and invented a past for herself that satisfied her. When I said it were lies she got very angry, and said if I wanted to see her ever again I'd go along with it.

'Well, for a long time I let her go her own way. She married, but she didn't invite me to the wedding, and I understood when she told me the story she'd told Adolphus. A rich, reclusive mother living in Devonshire was all right for outsiders, but Adolphus had to know a bit more than that, so she became an adopted child.

'But that, of course, gave me certain rights and to do your father justice, queen, he insisted that I be treated as part of the family, even though his wife refused to acknowledge me even as an adoptive parent. So he invited me to stay when Letty's time was near, and when you were born the nurse brought you through . . . and I knew I'd do just about anything, queen, to be near you.' She patted her granddaughter's hand. 'The rest you know, just about.'

'Yes, thanks to Miss Boote,' Sara said. 'I'll go and put the kettle on, Gran. Well, what a story! And you kept it to yourself all those years!'

'Aye, because Letty said so long as I kept me mouth

shut and never telled you I were your grandmother she'd see I saw you regular. Which she did, until she shipped you off to Switzerland.' She paused, to turn in her chair as Sara walked behind her, heading for the kitchen. 'She said she'd not broken her side of the bargain because no one could see you whilst you were abroad, but I didn't see it like that. Other kids come home, holiday time, I telled her. Why not our Sara? But she wouldn't give in, said it was fair enough, so I talked it over with meself and decided when you came home, I'd tell you everything. And now I'm going to close my eyes for ten minutes whilst you mash the tea; I'm wore out . . . isn't that odd?'

Sara said that it wasn't odd at all, then went into the kitchen and began to prepare a tray. No wonder I never liked my mother; she's a liar and a cheat, she thought. She cheated Father by making him believe she was adopted, not illegitimate, and she lied to me and forced Nanny – I mean my grandmother – to lie to me, too.

Presently she carried the tray, laden with teapot, cups, milk and sugar as well as a prettily painted plate piled with crumpets, through into the living room and put it down on the low table in front of the fire. Her grandmother, who had been lying back in the chair with her eyes closed, looking very weary, opened her eyes and smiled.

'Sara, that does look nice! Now I've told you the truth, and I want you to promise me something. Don't hold it against your mam, queen! She lied herself into a position where she simply had to tell more lies, you see. If your father had been a gentler, more understanding feller, she could have owned up, told him – and you – the truth, but he's a cold fish, is Adolphus. I used to comfort meself with the thought that they were well suited, and I reckon you're a throw-back, queen, because you aren't at all like either of them. But having it out with Letty wouldn't do anyone any good, so . . . will you promise me?'

And oddly enough, it was easy to make the promise, knowing very well that Gran was right. What is done cannot be undone and nothing would change even if she did confront her mother with her past misdeeds. Forcing Mrs Cordwainer to face up to what she had done would help no one, least of all Gran.

'Old history, old history,' Gran said, when Sara tried to put her thoughts into words. 'You're right, queen. It's best buried and forgot.'

Sara speared a crumpet and sat forward in her chair, holding the fork out to the fire and toasting both her face and fingers as well as the crumpets. And looking round the firelit room, and hearing the clock in the corner strike four, Sara thought she had seldom been happier.

'Are you ready, Sara?' Mrs Cordwainer was standing in the circular hallway of the big house on Aigburth Road, pulling on her pale leather gloves. She was wearing a cream and gold dress with a mink jacket over it and her hair had been curled and piled up on top of her head. Mrs Cordwainer noticed Sara and posed for a moment in front of the big cheval glass to the right of the front door, then turned to her daughter. 'I don't like to be late, even for a harvest supper, which is scarcely the same thing as a service. But the Reverend Atwell will want to say a few words, and your father has been told he may be asked to say grace, so it wouldn't do to be late.'

'I'm ready,' Sara said coolly. 'You look very smart, Mother.'

'Thank you, Sara. You do me credit – that silk coat

is very pretty and goes well with your dress. Green suits you, and the shoes are delightful . . . yes, really elegant. I always wore very high heels when I was younger but now I find them difficult to walk in. Ah well, there are compensations in growing a little older . . . we mature ladies can wear fur with aplomb; fur tends to make young girls look older than their years, I always think. Your father's gone to bring the car round; he isn't finding it easy to cope with so we'd best go outside and wait for him there.'

'Where's Robson? Or is it his day off?' Sara asked idly as the two of them left the house and stood outside on the gravel sweep waiting for the car to come round. 'I haven't seen him since I've been back. I know Father does drive himself quite often now, but not to social events, does he?'

'Oh, Robson left last week,' Mrs Cordwainer said coolly. 'I'm not sure of the details, but the government took us off the Gold Standard, whatever that may mean, and the pound slumped, or your father's shares fell – something of that nature, anyway. So your father decided he would have to make some economies.'

'But Robson's been with us since I was a kid; what'll he do? Where will he go?' Sara asked. 'What about his flat? Surely Father won't need it? Can't Robson stay there?'

'No, indeed. We could let that flat for a nice little sum, if the need ever arose. As for where he is now, I'm sure I can't say.'

'But what will Robson *do*?' Sara repeated helplessly. 'Without a roof over his head, even? What will happen to his wife?'

'She'll go wherever he goes, of course,' Mrs Cordwainer said impatiently. 'No doubt he'll get another job somewhere and move into whatever accommodation the new job offers. It's not as if they had children.'

'They did have a child,' Sara said in a low voice. 'They had a little boy, but he died when he was three. Don't say you didn't know, Mother, you must have!'

'I most certainly did not; I know nothing about any of the staff, other than that which it was my duty to know,' her mother replied immediately. 'Robson's private life was none of my business – nor yours, I might add. Ah, here comes Adolphus.'

There was a note of relief in her voice. Her mother did not like being cross-questioned about the sudden disappearance of Robson; she obviously considered it a matter of such little importance that discussing it seemed absurd.

She is the most selfish woman alive, Sara told herself as she and her mother waited on the drive for the Rolls. I'll have to go down to the kitchen tomorrow, see if I can find out what's happened to the poor chap.

Despite her father's many driving lessons with Robson, it seemed that he was not a natural behind the wheel. The car, when it finally came round the corner, was spitting and coughing, with a red-faced Adolphus behind the wheel. He stopped to let them get aboard but would not switch off the engine or linger a moment longer than necessary.

The bloody thing is as temperamental as a woman,' Sara heard him say furiously as he wrestled with the gear lever. 'I'm not at all sure getting rid of Robson was a good thing; I'm of the opinion that two of the maids, or the cook, could have been dispensed with more easily.'

'Nonsense, Adolphus,' her mother said immediately. 'You're an intelligent man, it's only an *engine*, for goodness' sake, you'll soon learn to master it. And do go a little faster or we'll be last, and I hate arriving anywhere last.'

But when they reached the big marquee set out in the square in front of the church it was already full and the Reverend Atwell was impatiently consulting his watch. When he saw the Cordwainers his brow cleared, and he waved to them and hurried over.

'Ah, my dear Mr Cordwainer . . . Mrs Cordwainer, Miss . . . I was almost giving you up,' he said with somewhat strained joviality. 'You have been deputed to say grace, Mr Cordwainer, I was beginning to become a little anxious.'

'Well, we're here now,' Mr Cordwainer said shortly. Sara saw that he had oil on his hands and a smear of it across his forehead. 'It's that cursed motor car – I don't seem to be able to handle it like Robson could.'

Mr Atwell clicked his tongue, whether in sympathy or in reproof for the swear word Sara could not say, then he took her mother by the elbow and began to lead them into the marquee.

This way, Mrs Cordwainer . . . I've written out a grace for you to say, Mr Cordwainer, I hope you can read my writing . . . if you could walk this way . . .'

He was ushering the family into the marquee when there was a concerted gasp from behind them. Sara glanced back. A trio of small and dirty boys were hovering just outside, peering within, and for a moment Sara saw the scene through their eyes and was impressed.

The long tables were covered with stiff white damask cloths and were laden with food and fruit of every conceivable sort. The cutlery shone silver by the light of hissing oil lamps, and waiters in black and white hovered solicitously behind the guests. There were flowers, too – pink, crimson and yellow roses, long-stemmed carnations, and the blue and silver-grey cultivated thistles so beloved of flower-arrangers. The scene, glowing with colour, must seem like another world to the urchins who were gazing, wide-eyed and open-mouthed, at the scene.

The Reverend Atwell glanced back too, gave an exclamation of annoyance, then smiled sweetly at the Cordwainers and pointed to three chairs just inside the entrance, at the very end of the long table.

'There you are, I hope you won't find the seating draughty but of course those who arrived early took the better places . . . do sit yourselves down . . . the grace is written out on that sheet of cream vellum, if you'd be so good as to run through it in your head, Mr Cordwainer, whilst I deal . . . excuse me a moment.'

He had spoken in his usual hushed, rather syrupy tones, but as he turned away from them and hurried back to the marquee entrance his voice changed completely, becoming sharp and shrewish, with overtones of bullying.

'You! You boys! What d'you think you're doing, eh?'

'We're jest lookin', your rev'rince,' a boy replied in a clear, piping treble. 'It's so grand, your rev'rince, so we was jest tekin' a look.'

'Well, you can clear off,' the Reverend Atwell said menacingly. 'Go on, clear off, we don't want your sort here!'

'Very true,' muttered Mr Cordwainer, on Sara's right. 'Abominable urchins; they'll probably chatter whilst I'm trying to read this confounded piece of paper and that would finish me – finish me!'

'They're only kids,' Sara began, and then heard the boy's treble raised once more.

'Oh, but your rev'rince, there's a deal o' grub there –

you can't eat all that grub, surely? There might be some of them bread rolls over, per'aps . . . or an apple?'

'This food isn't for the likes of you, it's for the ladies and gentlemen who come to my church,' the Reverend Atwell said furiously. 'Go on, get out! You'll get nothing but a thick ear if you remain anywhere near this marquee.'

Sara turned in her seat. She could feel her face growing hot but she had to speak, she could not let such remarks go unchallenged. She cleared her throat and spoke. 'Mr Atwell, the children are doing no harm – surely if you were to give them some fruit . . .'

Her voice was lost in the huge marquee, but her father heard. 'That's enough, Sara,' he said crossly. 'Just let me concentrate on this abominable writing, for God's sake, or I'll muff it, I know I will.'

'But, Father, to deny those little boys even a piece of fruit . . .'

A gentleman sitting opposite her, wearing a dark suit and pince-nez, nodded approvingly, but before either of them could speak the Reverend Atwell was again in full flood.

'Did you hear what I said? You're upsetting my parishioners with your begging,' he hissed. 'Out, out, OUT!'

Afterwards, Sara supposed that it had happened so quickly that only one or two people were aware of it. A subdued voice said, 'Shame!' – it came from the gentleman opposite – but elsewhere, the subdued hum of private conversation continued. Beside her, Mr Cordwainer muttered over the grace and her mother murmured gossip to the lady on her further side. Reverend Atwell beckoned to a waiter and several of them approached the marquee entrance whereupon the boys fled precipitately into the darkness.

Sara sat very still, shame and self-disgust flooding over her. Why had she not stood up to Reverend Atwell properly, refused to be hushed? Because she was a coward, that was why – because she didn't want to make a fool of herself in public.

The vicar returned to the table and took his place. The waiters began to hand bread rolls, to pour wine, to bring out from some hidden kitchen heated plates. Sara took a deep breath. She could at least do something to show how she felt!

The waiter leaned over her shoulder with a round basket full of small bread rolls, a saucer of butter in the middle. 'A bread roll, Miss? And some butter?'

'Thank you,' Sara said. She took the basket firmly out of his surprised hand, then stood up, pushing back her chair as she did so. 'I shan't be a moment.'

She carried the bread rolls and the butter out of the marquee and into the darkness of the city square. The boys had not gone far; she could see them sitting in a row along someone's low house-wall, every face turned towards her, like hungry sparrows watching for a householder to throw them crumbs.

'Boys, there's some bread and butter here,' Sara called, her voice much stronger out here than it had been in the marquee. 'Would you like some?'

Would they! There was a stampede! The bread was taken, divided, rubbed in the little curls of butter, devoured before her eyes. And they'd not begged, and they did thank, Sara thought triumphantly, as the basket was returned, empty, in an incredibly short space of time, to a chorus of 'Fanks, Miss, that were great . . . you are good.'

'Glad you enjoyed it,' Sara said. 'Don't go away.'

She returned to the marquee, and her place at the long table.

*

'I was never so ashamed in my life! Taking great platefuls of food out to those . . . those slum kids, simply marching out with it as though you had a right to it! The Reverend Atwell didn't know where to look . . . his wife was hissing to her neighbours . . . I'll never be able to hold my head up again.'

Sara's mother's voice was shaking with rage and embarrassment and what was worse, the car wouldn't start so here they sat for all to see whilst Mr Cordwainer, hot, grease-smeared, cross, tried again and again to turn the engine over with the starting handle – and failed.

'I simply gave some boys some food,' Sara said patiently, for the umpteenth time. 'They weren't begging, they asked very politely if there might be some over, and Reverend Atwell was abominably rude to them. So I took them a few bits and pieces.'

'A few bits and pieces! You were offered potatoes and you took the entire tureen – the same with the green peas and the baby carrots! The waiters were sniggering, everyone was staring . . . and then you took them out a whole strawberry flan – do you know what Scottish strawberries cost, Sara?'

'No, and I don't suppose you do, either,' Sara said. 'Do stop nagging, Mother. We have so much, who are we to deny others a share?'

'You're nothing but a prig, a nasty little prig,' her mother said suddenly. 'If this is your nanny's influence . . .'

'Nanny Prescott has scarcely seen me for the past three years, so I don't really see how she can be blamed,' Sara said quietly. 'But you are right over one thing; Nanny always tried to teach me to be generous to those less fortunate than myself.' She paused, but reflected that so far as she could see, her mother couldn't be angrier, so she might as well get it out of her system all at once. 'You talk a lot about heathen in Africa and being generous to others, Mother, but neither you nor my father have ever raised a finger to help those who need help most. You give money sometimes, you sew cotton vests and gossip with your friends, but you don't attempt to do anything to alleviate the terrible poverty on our own doorstep. Why, it wouldn't have hurt you to keep Robson on and cut down on the money you spent on clothes and shoes, but it never crossed your mind, did it? It would have been too great a sacrifice.'

There was a moment of shocked silence and then Mrs Cordwainer began to cry. Between wails, she asked God what she had done to deserve such a child, one who actually dared to criticise her own mother, one who made trouble for her parents, made them look ridiculous, wore on her back sufficient clothes to pay a chauffeur for six months, yet blamed an entire congregation for not letting slum children take the food they had paid for from the harvest supper . . .

'Letty, if you don't stop I'll go mad,' Mr Cordwainer said. He pulled open the door of the car, walked round to the passenger side, and almost dragged his wife on to the pavement. 'It won't start and I, for one, have had enough. I'm getting a taxi. Are you coming, or do you prefer to walk?'

'Adolphus, speak to Sara! She's done our reputation more harm in the last hour than I would ever have believed possible! We shall be laughing stocks . . . and what is more, I'll never dare show my face in church again, not until she's apologised to Reverend Atwell and promised on her word of honour never to do such a thing again.'

Mr Cordwainer turned wearily to Sara. For the first

time it struck Sara that he looked rather ill as well as bad-tempered.

'Well? Are you going to do as your mother says?'

'No,' Sara said firmly, though with fast-beating heart. 'I don't think I did wrong to give the children some of the food, so I can't say I'll never do such a thing again. And I thought Mr Atwell behaved extremely badly – he made a laughing stock of himself, I didn't have to do a thing.'

A taxicab, cruising past, was hailed and came over to the kerb. The driver leaned out.

'Yessir?'

'The Towers, Aigburth Road, my man,' Mr Cordwainer said briskly. 'Come along, Letty, in you get. We'll sort it all out under our own roof.'

Mrs Cordwainer, still protesting but with increasing feebleness, got into the taxi but when Sara would have followed her, her father held out a restraining hand.

'No, Sara. Will you apologise to Reverend Atwell and promise never to behave in so common and blatant a way again?'

'No, I won't,' Sara said immediately. 'I told you, Father, that I thought . . .'

But she was talking to thin air. Her father jumped into the cab and banged on the glass and the cab drove off, leaving Sara standing on the kerb staring foolishly after it. The last she saw was her mother's face, spiteful, triumphant, as the vehicle rounded the corner of the square and disappeared into the night.

It was late, and because the car had been so difficult the Cordwainers had been the last to leave – or to attempt to do so, at any rate. The Reverend Atwell had taken himself off very much earlier, without so much as a glance in Sara's direction, and the rest of the congregation, though they had called goodnight and appeared at least not hostile, had gone long since. Now, Sara stood hugging herself in her thin silk coat and wondering what on earth she should do. It was miles to walk home and besides, she guessed by her father's attitude and that last glimpse of her mother that if she did walk home she would find the house barred against her. But what to do? She had no money, of course, so she could not hail a taxi even if there was one passing, nor could she catch a tram. Her beautiful black patent leather shoes with the thin little ankle straps were not practical for walking anyway and . . . she glanced upwards . . . it was going to be a very cold night. The sky was clear, the stars twinkled and a moon lurked behind a chimney pot. She would have to keep moving or she'd freeze.

Accordingly, she took a few steps along the pavement, and stopped again. The paving stones were very uneven; perhaps she had better walk in the road? But cobblestones, she soon discovered, were worse to walk on than the most uneven paving, so she returned to the side walk and then went over and sat on the wall where the children had sat earlier in the evening. She had best orientate herself. She would go to Kirkdale, of course, and knock her grandmother up, but previously she had always either caught the tram or been taken to Snowdrop Street by car. Which way should she begin to walk?

After some thought she turned her steps towards the direction in which she seemed to remember St George's Hall lay. If she could find that, she could make her way home quite easily.

She had been walking for no more than ten minutes when she realised that she had thought of Snowdrop Street quite naturally as her home. Well, so it is, she thought defiantly, plodding along with increasing difficulty and clutching the silk coat close to her throat. It was more like home than the house on Aigburth Road, even though she had been brought up there. Number three Snowdrop Street was home to her because her grandmother loved her, had looked after her with tender care. Under no circumstances could she imagine Gran simply deserting her in the street at dead of night!

However, she had been deserted, which meant, so far as Sara could see, that she need never go back to the Aigburth Road house again. I'll live with Gran for ever now, and make something of my life, she told herself. I don't want Father's money or Mother's lifestyle, I just want to live with Gran and lead a useful sort of life. I'll get a job, and catch a tram to work each day and Gran and I will have holidays by the seaside sometimes, and sit and talk by the fire . . .

But she had forgotten; Gran had Miss Boote, now. For a second she just stood stock still whilst dismay and misery washed over her. Gran had a lodger! Miss Boote was very nice, a sensible, down-to-earth sort of woman, Gran was very fond of her, but it had not hitherto struck Sara that Miss Boote must be sleeping in the little front room, the room that Sara had, quite unconsciously, always considered her very own!

So what to do? For tonight, in an emergency, she could sleep on the sofa, she supposed. And perhaps there was some way . . . she could not share Gran's bed, that would not be fair, but there must be someone, somewhere, who wanted a lodger, as Gran had? Someone who would give her a room?

She had no money, of course. This would mean she could not afford to become a lodger until she got work of some sort, and she doubted she would get work without an address. But this was no time for such sombre thoughts, such foolish apprehension. She would make her way to Snowdrop Street and ask Gran to let her sleep on the sofa just for a night or two, and then, together, they would work out some plan for Sara's future which did not include a return to Aigburth Road.

Satisfied that she was doing the best thing, Sara began doggedly to walk once more.

Peader had been on a late shift. He trudged home rather than walked, because he was tired and because he no longer lived right on top of his work.

When he was given the job of safety man and began to earn better money he decided to change his lodgings and now he had a slip of a room all to himself in the home of an elderly couple in Salop Street, just off the Walton Road.

Peader liked it very much. Walton Road was lively; a positive hive of activity in fact, so that he felt he was at the centre of things once more as he had been in Dublin. And he liked the situation of his new home, too. Behind the jigger which ran along the back of all the small houses in Salop Street was the Co-op bakery and the smell of fresh bread which permeated the area was a lot nicer, to Peader's way of thinking, than the smell of railway engines, oil and soot, which he lived with all day long. Then there was the Queen's Arms public house on the very corner of Salop Street. It was lively, too, but in a good-natured sort of way and Peader, who had never been a heavy drinker, soon took to going there for half an hour of an evening. Sometimes he played dominoes, or pitch and toss, but usually he just sat in a corner and yarned with one or two other quiet men, like himself.

After the pub came a building contractor's yard,

then a couple of houses, and then the Salvation Army Barracks, which amused Peader because next to that was the Queen's Cinema . . . everything you wanted, he told Deirdre in his letters home. Mammon, which was the pub, God, which was the Barracks, and entertainment, which was the cinema. Of course for him, God wasn't really represented by the Barracks; his faith needed the warmth of the Catholic Church, but he knew Deirdre would appreciate the joke.

And after Mass on a Sunday, Peader had taken to cinema-going, joining the long queue which stretched right across the front of the Barracks sometimes, and was glad that the government had not yet succeeded in stopping 'Sunday flicks'.

He missed Brogan, though, and had been very pleased when, shortly after their return from their Irish holiday, Brogan wrote to say he was coming to Liverpool to sit an examination and could his daddy possibly let him share his room for a couple of nights? Naturally Peader wrote back at once saying 'yes', so Brogan would be along in a day or two, to sit this exam at the Gordon Institute, where he had studied when he first came to England.

Now, Peader was crossing Stanley Street though, still a long way from home, and it was midnight and past and a frosty one, at that. Still, it was better than fog – anything was better than fog.

As a safety man he dreaded fog because his gangs couldn't work – it was far too dangerous – and without the safety man the trains couldn't run, either. And Liverpool is a foggy city, what with the Mersey, and the coal fires and the industry. So when it was foggy Peader was sent off up the line with a supply of detonators, to warn approaching trains that they were near a station and must begin to apply their brakes.

'What's a safety man, Daddy?' Polly had asked when he had last been home, sitting on his knee and stroking what she called his 'rustly' chin, because he'd not shaved for a day or so. 'What does a safety man do?'

She was delighted when he told her that he watched out for his gang, warning them of approaching trains and thus preventing accidents, and mystified her when he said that when it was foggy he did it by putting detonators on the lines, because detonators were explosives, and she thought that it was very wrong to lay explosives on a railway line, someone had said it was wrong . . . people did it in the Troubles, and it was a naughty thing so it was.

But Peader had explained; the detonators were put on the rails and when the train ran over them they exploded, making a lot of noise and creating quite a display of sparks but doing no damage whatsoever.

'Then what's the use of them?' Polly the practical asked. 'I thought you meant they stopped the train dead, blew it up, *pow, pow,* like that!'

'You're a horror so you are,' Peader told her, laughing. 'The bangs tell the engine driver that he's getting near a station and must begin to apply his brakes, for it takes a big engine quite a distance to get to stopping.'

'Oh, I see,' Polly had said, scrambling off his knee. 'I'll be a safety man when I grow up – I like bangs so I do.'

But tonight Peader and his gang had just been doing their usual job, checking that their length of line was safe, that the points were in the right position for the next train, that there were no little landslips, that the troughs were full of water so the moving train could extend its scoop and replenish its water tank as it passed . . . and having done their duty, they had dispersed to their several homes where they would stay until their next shift in two days' time.

What made Peader pause when he saw the girl he could not imagine, except that it was so very late, so very cold, and she looked so very forlorn. But she didn't look like a street girl. Peader steered clear of the Liverpool street girls. They weren't like the unfortunates of the Dublin slums, they were pert, sleazy, foul-mouthed girls, who swore and shrieked and laughed and sold their favours to anyone who could pay their price. And they didn't just hang about the streets looking pathetic, either. They accosted, teased, accused. No, Peader would not have paused had he thought the girl a Liverpool whore.

The girl didn't see him. She was wearing a thin, shiny-looking coat which she hugged about herself, and a long skirt which swished against the paving stones as she walked . . . and she wasn't walking either, not really, she was more stumbling along, as though every step was a pain to her.

Peader turned towards her, uncertain. Suppose he scared her? But she had stopped and was leaning against a shop-front, her hand to her heart. She looked pale and sickly, but that was probably the gaslight.

Making up his mind, he walked over to her, stopping when he was well short of her. It would be too bad if she shrieked out when all he intended was to ask her if she was all right, needed help.

'Are you all right, ma'am?' he said, therefore. 'It's awful cold and late for a young lady like yourself to be on the street. And not too safe, either,' he added, remembering tales he had heard of men taking to burglary, robbery, all sorts, when they were out of work and down on their luck.

'Oh . . . hello. Thank you for asking . . . it's these

shoes,' the girl said. 'They're no good for walking, I can assure you. But I've not got far to go, now, – I'm heading for Snowdrop Street.'

'Oh aye? I know it; I used to lodge near there. But I'm on Walton Road now so I've quite a step still.' He looked at her thoughtfully. 'Will you reach Snowdrop Street though, ma'am? You look wore out. I could give you me arm for the rest of the way if it 'ud help. It's no distance, really.'

'Well, I am tired . . . and I'm cold, too,' the girl admitted. 'But it's not fair to take you out of your way. I'll manage, but thanks, anyway.'

Peader looked at her more closely still. She was even younger than he had thought, probably in her mid to late teens, and very much a little lady. And now that he was so close he could see she was wearing evening dress, and the thinnest coat imaginable, as well as downright silly shoes. One heel was already turning over – they weren't up to walking, that was plain.

'It's no bother,' he said, therefore. 'I'll walk you to Snowdrop Street, for I've a daughter of me own and I'd not like her to be out on the street so late at night and in such flimsy clothing. Take my arm.'

After a moment's hesitation the girl sighed, pulled herself away from the wall and took his proffered arm.

'Well, I will, and thank you very much indeed,' she said. 'It's really awfully good of you, because I've been very frightened as well as very tired, and I'm so cold I can't even feel my hands or feet. And now I'm beginning to wonder what on earth I'll do if I can't make my granny hear when I knock the door. She isn't expecting me, you see, and she sleeps in the back, not the front.'

'She isn't expecting you?' Peader said gently. 'You've not run away from home, alanna? Because if so, perhaps you should t'ink again. Your mammy is probably half mad wit' worry.'

The girl laughed rather bitterly. 'Half mad with worry? I think not. And anyway, I haven't run away from home, I've been turned out. Or rather, I've been abandoned, left.'

'In that dress?' Peader said. 'You'd best tell me the whole tale – my name's Peader O'Brady, by the way. I'm safety man for a gang of navvies on the railway there.' Her jerked his head, indicating the distant yards. 'What's your name, alanna, or would you rather not say?'

He half expected this pretty girl to deny him her name but the girl stopped walking for a moment to stare at him incredulously and then she began to laugh, softly but with real mirth.

'My goodness, this is so incredible, Mr O'Brady, that it's almost like a theatrical farce. My name is Sara Cordwainer, and I believe I know your son, Brogan.'

After that, of course, he had to hear the whole story. Sara poured it out, keeping nothing back. The harvest supper, the rage of her parents, the abandoning of her in the dark square. She told Peader how she had discovered that the woman she had been told was her old nanny was really her grandmother, how her parents had tried to keep her from that same grandmother, and how desperate she had felt when she had recently realised that there was now no spare room at number three Snowdrop Street.

'But your ould one has a whole house to herself, bar one room for the lodger,' Peader pointed out. 'Sure and she'll find a spot for a granddaughter, so she will. Can you doubt it, alanna, if she loves you?'

'Oh, you're right, she'll try to fit me in, but it won't

be fair to disturb her and upset Miss Boote,' Sara said, distressed at the mere thought of causing more trouble, more unhappiness. She acknowledged to herself that her parents would be unhappy, if only because they felt she had made fools of them. 'It's a tiny house, truly, Mr O'Brady.'

'Well, I don't think you should worry, because I'm sure you'll be all right,' Peader said. 'As for your gran not hearing you knock – have you ever heard an Irishman shout?'

It made Sara laugh, and that was good for her. She was even beginning to feel warmer, with Peader at her side. And presently, when they reached Snowdrop Street, he proved his point. When polite knocking with the dolphin knocker produced no response he took her elbow and steered her to the jigger.

'The back way's often the best,' he whispered. 'Come on, I can unlock the gate – if it's locked, which I doubt.'

There were no street lamps in the jigger but the moon was still bright enough to guide them to the right back yard. Peader stood under Mrs Prescott's bedroom window and threw a handful of gravel at it. It sounded like pistol shots in the dark of the night, but when Sara called 'Gran? Are you there? It's me, Sara!' it was only a moment before the curtains were drawn back, the window slid up, and Gran's face appeared in the gap.

'Sara? My dear child, what on earth . . . wait, I'll come down.'

'I'll leave you now,' Peader said diplomatically. 'You'll have a lot to tell your gran so you will and I've a way to walk.' He took her hand and shook it. 'When me boy comes over here to take his exams in a day or so, maybe we'll walk round, pay you a visit.'

'Oh, I *wish* you would,' Sara said eagerly. 'I've not seen or spoken to Brogan for three years. And in a way it was his fault that I was shipped off to Switzerland . . . oh, I can hear Gran at the door, do come in for a moment, you've been so kind!'

But this Peader refused to do and in fact by the time Mrs Prescott had unlocked and unbolted her back door and creaked it open, he was probably already on Stanley Road and heading, fast, for home.

'What's happened, love?' Mrs Prescott said as soon as she got Sara indoors and in front of the dead but still warm parlour fire. 'That evening gown will never be the same again and as for your shoes . . . well, girls will be girls, I suppose.'

'We went to the harvest supper and I disagreed with the Reverend Atwell's attitude and said so. Afterwards my father said if I wouldn't apologise he wouldn't take me home and I was in the middle of explaining why I wouldn't apologise when he told the taxi driver to drive on and they left me,' she said briefly. 'Gran, I forgot about Miss Boote, but can I sleep on your sofa tonight? I'm just absolutely exhausted and so cold that if I don't cuddle down soon I'll probably fall over.'

'The sofa? No, indeed, we'll share my nice double bed,' Mrs Prescott said decidedly. 'Come along, I've a hot-water bottle in already and plenty of blankets. Remember when you were small and used to stay with me? I'd put you to bed in the little front room and by midnight you'd be in bed with me, cuddled up all warm and close, because you said you were frightened, alone in the other room.' She chuckled. 'Not that you were frightened, you little monkey, you just liked to share my bed, and wake me up at the crack of dawn in the morning, and play old harry with my lie-ins.'

'Yes, I remember. Oh, Gran, I was awful then and I'm awful now,' Sara said. 'I'll try not to put my cold feet on you, and I'll try not to wake you too early, as well. Not that I will, I'm far too tired myself.'

And presently she climbed between the sheets, clad in a vast cotton nightdress belonging to her grandmother, and cuddled down blissfully into the warm bed.

'I'll bring you a cup of hot milk with a drop of rum in it,' Mrs Prescott promised, but by the time she came up the stairs again, with the hot milk and a plate of marie biscuits, Sara was fast asleep.

Grace came out of the front door at the fastest pace she could manage and shot across the pavement, turning right around the side of the house and making for the roadway beyond the court. Her father had recently come home from the pub, and he was in a wicked rage. He had smashed in through the door, she had heard his onslaught, heard the door slam back into the wall, and he had started to scream and curse, shouting that his wife was a slut, his home a filthy hole fit only for rats, his kids bastards who wouldn't piss on a man if he was afire.

Grace had been asleep in the bundle of rags which was the best they could manage for a bed, with assorted young Carberys beside her, but she woke pretty fast when her father began to shout. She sat up, every nerve quivering, her heart thumping so hard it could actually be seen when she glanced down at her thin chest. Bang, bang, BANG it went . . . he's coming, he's coming, HE'S COMING!

The Carberys had long since been turned out of Snowdrop Street for non-payment of rent and now had the basement flat in this tall, ugly block. The kids slept in the back room and the family lived in the front, which meant that if you wanted to leave the back room you had to go through the front. And that meant risking a confrontation with Stan Carbery, and a drunken Stan Carbery was terrifying. But if he came through . . . Grace wondered whether she might burrow so deep into the rags that he would not find her, then abandoned even the thought. She dared not risk it. She simply had to escape . . . she would make a run for it the moment he wasn't looking.

She slid out of the rags and padded over to the door which separated the two rooms. It wasn't closed – well, it wouldn't close, her da had broken the hinges years back – so she was able to see through the crack into the dim, candlelit room beyond. Her mother was backed into a corner, swinging what looked like a black bottle full of something, and she was shouting almost as loudly, now, as her husband.

'Gerrout of 'ere, you swine,' she screamed. 'I'll break this bottle over your bleedin' 'ead if you comes one step closer!'

Mam must be very drunk, Grace reflected. Usually she fled the moment her husband entered the house if he was in a violent mood. She never even woke her kids, so that they could defend themselves, but let them bear the brunt of her husband's wrath. But tonight she was fighting back, it seemed.

'The wicked bugger ma' me leave 'is bloody rotten pub,' Stan Carbery roared. Grace caught a glimpse of his face – scarlet, bug-eyed – as he lunged at his wife, but she waved the bottle and he pretended to change his mind, beginning to shout again. 'He shaid I were the worshe for booze, the wicked bugger!'

'So you bloody are,' his wife shrieked. 'Gerrout, go on, gerrout of me 'ouse this instant, Stan Carb!'

'Whose bloody 'ouse? *Whose* bloody 'ouse?'

The trouble was, the door opened the wrong way.

Grace would have to run round it once it was open in order to get out of the outer door, and then she would have to climb the area steps . . . she shuddered at the thought of her father clawing her back down again by the legs, falling on her, crashing his fist into her skinny, vulnerable frame. He'd near killed her a couple of times . . . oh, if only Jess were still alive, Grace thought, whilst the sweat of terror beaded her brow and made her breathe short. If Jess were still alive she'd think of something, do something!

But in the further room, her father had suddenly begun to see things. Grace knew the signs and thanked her stars. He was hitting out at nothing now, wiping the air with both fists in a desperate, ugly paroxism of fear. Whatever he imagined was attacking him was doing a good job, Grace surmised, as he suddenly dodged and began to retreat, shouting all the while.

'No . . . no, you don't, you buggers . . . gerroff, will you? Leave me be, I ain't done nothin' . . . leave me be!'

It was the moment. Grace slid round the door and set off at a fast pace across the room. She was out of the living-room door and tugging at the outer one when her mother said: 'Wharra you doin', you little bitch? Don't you run off an' leave me to tackle this bastard by meself! Stan, she's . . .'

It acted like a spur. Grace tore the door open, shot through it and ascended the area steps so fast that she could not afterwards remember her feet so much as touching them. And at the top, she simply ran, though she had no stamina and knew she would speedily have to stop to regain her breath.

But there was no pursuit. Panting, sobbing, she made for the one place where her father would not pursue her – the graveyard of the nearest church. And once there, safely ensconced in the shed where the sexton kept his gardening tools, she had leisure to think.

Why had Mam given her away to her da like that, knowing him to be capable of killing when the drink was on him? And why was it always her who was the object of his greatest fury, his most violent wrath? Addy, her only remaining sister, who had run away eight months before, said it was because Grace had been Jess's favourite, and their father had always hated Jess.

'Why, Addy?' Grace had asked helplessly. 'Why did he hate Jess? She was good, was Jess, real kind an' all.'

'She weren't 'is get,' Addy had explained kindly. 'Our da always said our mam played 'im false when she got our Jess.'

'I don't understand,' Grace had said. 'What d'you mean?'

Addy had sighed and cast her eyes at the sky, but at least she had answered.

'Mam was 'avin' a baby, see? She weren't wed, not then. She telled our da it were 'is baby, that 'e was the dad, see? So then they got wed. Only our da reckoned she'd gone wi' another feller, an' the baby – Jess – were the other feller's. See?'

'I think I do,' Grace had said. 'I wish . . . I wish our da di'n't 'ate me so much, Addy.'

Addy had shrugged. 'Our da 'ates the 'ole lot of us,' she said cynically. ''E 'ates me 'cos I'm the eldest gal, an' you 'cos you're the next, an' Reggie 'cos 'e's a little lad, an' . . .'

Grace had got the message though and from that moment on had accepted, albeit sadly, that her father hated her. She had not known, until this minute, that her mother hated her too.

But at least I'm safe now, for a bit, she told herself,

curling up on a pile of old newspapers. She checked the pocket of her ragged cardigan and the possession she most prized was still there, so that was all right. And the sexton didn't hate her. He left the door of his shed unlocked and the newspapers handy . . . she thought he must pity her and pity was better than either hatred or indifference.

But she still wished Jess was alive, wished she'd been able to find baby Mollie and take care of her as, once, Jess had taken care of the young Grace.

In her worn-out, confused mind, she told herself that the next best thing to being loved was loving.

And then she slept.

Chapter Eight

Sara slept like a log and didn't even stir when Mrs Prescott got out of bed next morning and crept down the stairs to get breakfast for Miss Boote – not that this was in any way necessary, for she and her lodger had long ago come to an understanding. Miss Boote made the breakfast if she was downstairs first, cooking a pan of porridge and cutting bread, making a pot of tea and so on. But if Mrs Prescott was about early they sometimes had an egg, or even fried bread and a piece of bacon, for Miss Boote was secretary to the manager of the County Bank on Walton Road and bicycled to work which meant, Mrs Prescott insisted, that she needed a good breakfast to keep her strength up.

But when Mrs Prescott came quietly into the bedroom, having waved Miss Boote off on her trusty steed, Sara was sitting up in bed and stretching and declaring that she hadn't had such a good night's sleep for ages and ages, and did Gran think that they might find her a job today?

'Goodness, Sara, whatever next?' Her grandmother said, thoroughly startled, for though Sara had mentioned getting a job before she had not taken her seriously. 'I can't imagine your father lettin' you work for your living – not if he didn't like it when he saw you speakin' to a young railway worker, and objected because you gave children some spare food. He would undoubtedly think you were letting him down.'

She was half-joking, but soon realised that her granddaughter had thought the whole thing through very thoroughly.

'Yes, Gran, I know what you mean, but they've washed their hands of me, you see. They simply drove away from me – I could have been robbed or murdered or anything. You'll say they'll guess that I've come to you, but if so, why haven't they been in touch, to find out? They haven't, have they?' she added with a transparent hopefulness which went to the older woman's heart.

'No, they haven't,' Mrs Prescott admitted. 'But I'm sure they would have been terribly worried if they'd realised you had no money, no means of gettin' either here or back to your home . . .'

She was interrupted. 'I have no home,' Sara said firmly. 'Apart from here, I mean, and I can't stay with you, Gran. It wouldn't be fair.'

'It would be the best thing that ever happened to me,' her grandmother told her. 'Miss Boote and I are very good friends, but it's through circumstance, you see. You are my flesh and blood, chuck, and I've loved you from the day you were born. Don't go off and leave me alone again!'

'Oh, Gran . . . but you'll want your bed to yourself . . . and you need Miss Boote's money, I know you do . . . and I can't pay you anything until I get a job,' Sara said, her brow creasing with worry. 'If I could have a little bed in the parlour . . .'

'You shall have a little bed in my room; we'll sell the double bed and buy two singles at Paddy's market,' Mrs Prescott said. 'I saw respectable, clean secondhand beds for sale the last time I was there. How snug we'll be, queen! I like to read before I nod off – how about you, eh? I 'member you always used to read in bed as a child.'

'I still like to read, but Gran . . .'

'No nonsense, no argufying,' Mrs Prescott said briskly. 'It's agreed, then. I'll sell my double bed and buy two singles this very day – you can come with me if you don't mind walkin' slow – and then you may take a look around for likely employment. We might do worse than ask Miss Boote, in fact, now I come to think, because she works in a big bank, they might easily need another young lady to do whatever it is they do in banks.'

Two days after Sara arrived at her grandmother's house, Brogan came knocking on the door. Sara, delighted to see him and wanting to know what had been happening to him in the three years since they last met, asked him in, but the visit was not a success.

Brogan, who had seemed self-confident, breezy, amusing, when they'd met before was not at all at ease in Mrs Prescott's neat front parlour, or with the young lady Sara had become, she could not tell which it was, she could just sense the unease. And he seemed shy of talking about his family, which had previously been a favourite topic of conversation. In fact he sat on the small sofa, dwarfing it with his size, and played with his cap on his knee and avoided her eyes. So in the end Sara asked him what on earth was the matter.

'Nothin',' Brogan growled, staring at his cap. 'Nothin' at all at all.'

'Then why won't you look at me when we're talking?' Sara asked, frustrated and disappointed that this meeting, which had meant so much to her, was going so badly. 'Your cap can't be that much nicer to look at than my face!'

He laughed, but reluctantly. 'If there's somethin' the matter, then that's it,' he muttered. 'You're a young lady now, and a smart one. You don't want nothin' to do wit' the likes of me. I was a fireman on an engine, now I'm drivin' goods trains on branch lines; if I'm lucky I'll move to passenger trains next. If I spend the rest of me life workin', then I'll mebbe end up ownin' a little house, ridin' a decent bike, respected by me workmates. Nothin' in this world could mek me gentry.'

'Who cares?' Sara said scornfully. 'I like you as you are, Brogan. Now do stop being so silly and tell me all about Crewe, and your lodgings.'

He tried, that was the worst part. She could see him trying. He looked steadily at her as he spoke and he described his lodgings, his garden, even his work on the great engines chuffing all over the country, taking the LMS passengers to their various destinations. But Sara saw his eyes were full of misery and in the end she just couldn't stand it. She interrupted a laborious description of one of the stations he visited as seen by a railwayman needing a bite to eat by jumping to her feet.

'Brogan, I'm sorry, but you know I'm job-hunting – I told you, didn't I? I've an interview with a Mr Esmond at the Ocean Accident Insurance this afternoon and it's in Exchange Buildings, wherever that may be. So I'll want to be getting something to eat before I leave and . . .'

Brogan got to his feet, too.

'It's all right, it's all right,' he said quickly. 'Just goin' I was . . . I want to do some revisin' for this examination. It's mathematics – you need to know mathematics if you're goin' to get on. Say goodbye to your gran for me, and t'anks for the cup of tea.'

And whilst Sara, appalled at herself, was beginning

to stammer that she hadn't meant . . . there was still time . . . he had left the room.

'Brogan, don't . . .' she began, running after him, but he was halfway down the road, cap pulled low, coat collar pulled up, before she had got further than the step.

It put a damper on the rest of the day, of course. Sara changed into the grey flannel suit she and Gran had bought from a dealer in the market – it was a bit on the large side, but a piece taken out of the waistband soon cured that – and cleaned the shoes she had picked up at the same time. It was the first time Sara had ever worn a garment which had first been worn by someone else and she hated it, but needs must, she told herself resolutely. It had been washed and ironed, what more did she want? One thing was certain, she did not intend to go, cap in hand, back to Aigburth Road for the rest of her clothes – not after the things that had been said.

For the day after she moved in with Mrs Prescott, the Cordwainers had come visiting. They had sat side by side on the small sofa and tried to lay down rules for Sara's return and future conduct. And when Sara and Mrs Prescott had made it clear they were not interested, both parties had lost their tempers.

'If you don't come with us right now, today, you'll never darken my doors again,' Mr Cordwainer had shouted, just like the papa in a Victorian melodrama. 'You're spoiled and selfish, you never gave a thought to your mother and myself when you stormed off after the harvest supper.'

'Stormed off? Father, how can you say such a thing? I was still speaking when you just jumped into the taxi cab and told the driver to take you home! You left me, without a penny piece, to make my own way home!

And what's more I was in evening dress, with an icy wind blowing . . .'

'Rubbish,' her father blustered, his cheeks reddening slightly. 'We implored you to accompany us, your mother and I, and you refused to do so. What choice had we?'

'You're a liar, like Mother,' Sara shouted, shaking with fury. She had always thought herself a meek soul but now she discovered that this was not so. 'She lied to me and to you too, for all I know. Mrs Prescott's my grandmother, Father – did you know that? Yes, and that means she's your wife's mother . . . and look how your wife treats her! Believe me, I'm happier here than I could possibly be living in Aigburth Road surrounded by lies and evasions. You can tell your smart friends any story you like, maybe they'll even believe you, but here people are judged on what they do, not what they say. And I'm staying here!'

'Then we've much to be grateful for,' Mrs Cordwainer shrieked, her voice rising to unladylike heights. 'How dare you call your own mother a liar – your own mother, Sara! As for lying to you, I did no such thing! I simply kept the truth from you because . . . oh, because it didn't suit me to have people, my sort of people, knowing about my background. I'd risen above it and I didn't intend to be haunted by the – the spectre of Snowdrop Street! It was for your sake I did it, you detestable little prig – for your sake! Oh, what a serpent we've nourished in our bosoms, your father and I! You've had the best of everything, a marvellous education, beautiful clothes . . .'

'But no love,' Sara said softly, almost to herself. 'Never, never that.'

It hadn't ended there, of course, there had been more. But they'd left at last, handing out another ultimatum on the doorstep. Either Sara repented, apologised and came home at once . . .

'Goodbye Mother, Father,' Sara said politely at the end of the tirade. 'I shan't be seeing you for a while I don't suppose, so take care of each other.'

It took the wind out of their sails. They stared at her, then her father gave a strangled snort and marched round to the driver's side of the car, leaving her mother to fumble with the handle of the passenger door and sob into her handkerchief.

But at least I know where I stand, now, Sara said to herself as she walked to the tram stop in the grey flannel suit and the sensible black walking shoes with a small cream-coloured felt hat pulled down over her hair. I've got to earn my living, so I'll accept the first job I'm offered, and I'll give Gran most of my salary and keep myself decent with the rest. I've had eighteen years of being given whatever I wanted in the way of material things, now I'll try to see how I manage on my own.

Two hours later however, sitting disconsolately on the tram as it roared and rattled up Vauxhall Road, it wasn't nearly so easy to be optimistic. Mr Esmond was very kind, he said her languages were undoubtedly useful and she certainly seemed fluent – not that he could tell, since he knew only a modicum of schoolboy French – but the fact was, it was necessary to use a typewriter, and he could not afford to pay her a wage whilst she learned something which every other young lady he was interviewing had been doing for a number of years.

'But they don't all speak French, German and Italian, do they?' Sara had said hopefully, giving him her very best smile. He had smiled too, but wearily, even as his eyes had flickered approvingly over the grey suit, the flat shoes. I believe Gran really was right; I'll stand a better chance of a job in respectable, rather worn clothing than I would in something smart and new, Sara realised.

'No, you're the only one with any sort of command of foreign languages,' Mr Esmond admitted. 'But there's a lady who runs a small translations bureau a few streets away from here. We use her if we have an emergency. And she can type.'

'I see. Well, it's been nice meeting you,' Sara said, getting to her feet and holding out a hand. Mr Esmond shook it, looking stunned. How odd – did he expect me to snarl at him, or burst into tears? Sara wondered. But apparently it was the right thing to do because having shaken her hand he went over to the door and held it open for her, speaking as he did so.

'I'm sorry to have to disappoint you, Miss Cordwainer, because I know jobs are difficult to find these days. But will you take a bit of advice? There are a number of establishments in the city which teach young girls all the essentials of office work, including typing. Or there are evening classes at which the same skills can be acquired. I believe it would be sensible to acquire such skills before applying for other jobs.'

'But some people don't want typing, do they?' Sara asked hopefully. 'Employers must know not everyone can type.'

'That's true, but most girls who are trying to find a job straight from school are fourteen or fifteen, considerably younger than yourself. I doubt you would be taken on as an office girl, not at eighteen years of age.' His eyes flickered over her again, assessingly. 'Look, your parents chose to continue your schooling so surely they wouldn't balk at a secretarial course? It's not costly and you'd find it easy work after all those foreign languages!'

'And without secretarial skills you don't think I'll get work?' Sara said slowly.

'Oh yes, you might get shop work. But an employer is going to expect an eighteen-year-old to have had experience, you see.' He gave her an encouraging smile. 'It's a bitter pill, more schooling, but it's for the best. Good luck, Miss Cordwainer.'

It was not until she was actually on the tram that Sara began to feel, for the first time in her life, that she was a failure. She had been rejected because her skills were inadequate, because every other girl Mr Esmond interviewed could, at a pinch, have done the job.

So as the tram rattled down Vauxhall Road Sara scanned the copy of the *Echo* which she had bought from a street vendor, replayed Mr Esmond's advice over in her head, and faced facts. She spoke several languages and she had passed several examinations, but she could not type, nor could she keep books. The paper did not have thousands of job advertisements, but every single one for office staff specified either book-keeping or typing. There were one or two office juniors wanted but she was sure that Mr Esmond had hit the nail on the head; she would not get offered such a job because she was too old, and anyway, the salary for such a position was so tiny that it would scarcely do more than pay her tram fare from Kirkdale to the city centre each morning.

Still, it was no use sitting here fighting silly tears and letting despair drown her. She must be practical. As soon as Miss Boote arrived home this evening, she would take her to one side and explain her predicament. She had seen very little of the lodger apart from their first meeting and Gran said that Miss Boote did good works, evenings and weekends. Perhaps I could help her, Sara thought hopefully. Then, if I had to get just a little, tiny, badly paid job, at least I'd be doing some good, somewhere – and I wouldn't feel so guilty, either.

When her stop came she got off the tram and headed for Snowdrop Street and as luck would have it just as she reached the front door and was about to tap and open it, Miss Boote came cycling down the road. She usually came straight past the front door, on to Commercial Road, and down the jigger on Pansy Street, because she left her bicycle in the back yard overnight, but today, seeing Sara, she dismounted and wheeled her bike on to the pavement.

'Hello, Miss Cordwainer,' she said. 'Any luck with the interview? Mrs Preston told me you were seeing an insurance company this afternoon.'

Sara shook her head. 'No, they needed a typist,' she said rather bitterly. 'It didn't say that in the advertisement or I wouldn't have bothered to apply. Still, the man was very nice. He gave me some good advice, or I imagine it was good advice. Miss Boote, I wonder whether I might beg a few moments of your time when you've had your evening meal? Only I do need to talk to someone about jobs!'

'Certainly,' Miss Boote said cheerfully. 'Tell you what, I'm working in the soup kitchen on Westminster Road tonight; care to come along, give a hand? We can talk as we work, and no one will interfere with us.'

'I'd like that very much,' Sara said promptly. 'But . . . won't they expect me to – to bring something with me, like bread, or vegetables? Only I don't have any money at all, apart from what Gran gives me for the tram.'

Miss Boote laughed. 'No one will want anything but your labour, Miss Cordwainer,' she said cheerfully. 'But you'll see, this evening. Can you be ready by seven? Only we serve from seven to ten, and after that it's just preparing for the next day, so I get there around seven if I possibly can.'

'Yes, of course. Only I don't have a bicycle and I don't know where Westminster Road is,' Sara told her new friend. 'And I can't ask Gran for any more tram fares.'

'A tram fare wouldn't do you much good, anyway,' Miss Boote assured her. 'Trams don't go across the city, through the small streets, you'd have to go into the centre and out again, which would make you later than if you'd *crawled*, I daresay. What about a seater?'

'A seater?' Sara stared. 'What's that?'

'You sit on the bike seat and I stand up and pedal like fun,' Miss Boote explained. 'Or you could sit on the carrier,' she slapped it, 'which might be a bit safer, come to think. Only I daresay you wouldn't want to be seen two to a bike, eh?'

'I don't mind at all,' Sara said stoutly, though inwardly her heart failed her a little. If anyone she knew saw her they'd think she'd run mad or returned to her second childhood. Kids rode two to a bike, not adult ladies! But still, she didn't have a tram fare, she didn't fancy walking . . . 'It will be fun,' she added defiantly. 'Seven o'clock it is, then. Shall I wear my grey suit?'

Miss Boote laughed heartily and ran her bicycle down the pavement again and on to the road. 'To serve soup? No, no, Miss Cordwainer, you should wear your oldest rags – everyone else will!'

'Ready, Miss Cordwainer? Hop aboard, then.'

Feeling really silly, Sara sat herself astride the narrow little carrier which was just above the rear mudguard.

She clutched the bicycle seat and smiled a wobbly smile at Gran, who was watching them and laughing – it was enough to make a cat laugh, Sara thought ruefully as Miss Boote shouted to her to hold tight and launched herself, and the bicycle, into a wobble away from the kerb.

'We're off!' Miss Boote called back over her shoulder. 'Not much traffic about, fortunately, but we'll push across Stanley Road, I think. You slide off when I stop, Miss Cordwainer.'

Presently, Sara 'slid off' and they pushed the bicycle across the busy road, then remounted to turn into Fountains Road, which was wide and, to Sara's relief, relatively traffic-free.

'I try not to breathe along this stretch, 'cos of the Stanley Mortuary,' Miss Boote announced breathlessly over her shoulder. 'Been down here before, have you, Miss Cordwainer?'

'No, I don't think so,' Sara said. 'Are you sure you wouldn't rather I walked, Miss Boote?'

But Miss Boote assured her passenger that it was 'a piece of cake, honest', and continued to pedal on and to shout over her shoulder as she did so.

'We're just passin' St Athanasius' Church,' she announced presently. 'Big, ain't it? And St John's Presbytery's there . . .' the bike wobbled perilously as she pointed. 'And a bit further along yet, between the Saddle Inn – that's a nice pub, very quiet – and the Kendal Castle – that's a bit livelier – there's the Jewish synagogue. If it were Saturday you'd see 'em all comin' out wi' their little caps on and their long beards. All we need is a mosque, I tell them at the Barracks, and everyone's represented round here.' She laughed heartily at her own joke.

How odd, she seems to know the public houses as

well as she knows the churches, and she obviously takes a great interest in both, Sara thought. Now I wonder why that is?

She was soon to know. They turned into Westminster Road, wobbled along for a few hundred yards, and stopped beside a hall with big doors which opened out on to the pavement. Several shabby-looking men were making their way towards it and Miss Boote hailed them as she passed.

'Evenin', Mr O'Hare! How's your rheumatiz? Evenin', Mr Ross, come to give us a hand gerrin' rid o' that broth you like? Evenin', Mr Fellowes, I've brung you me copy of yesterday's *Echo*, I know you like a read before bed.'

The man thus addressed turned and laughed. 'I thought that 'ud be you – you're a caution you are, Miss! 'Alf the time that newspaper *is* me bed! Still an' all, I'm grateful for it.'

Miss Boote brought the bicycle to a halt outside the hall and waited whilst Sara disentangled herself from the carrier, then stood the machine in the small wooden porch.

'Come along in, Miss Cordwainer, and I'll introduce you,' she said. 'When we've finished wi' the soup though, I'll have to leave you for a few minutes. I'm goin' round the pubs tonight, so I'll need me uniform or God above knows what the customers will think.'

'Uniform?' Sara said, thoroughly bewildered. 'What uniform?' It was news to her that it was necessary to wear a uniform to go into a public house, but then so far as she knew women never went past the doors of the pubs. Oh, round the back, perhaps, to get a jug of ale which they would drink at home, but never up to the bar!

Miss Boote took her elbow. 'Ah, there's Mrs Puddifoot – you'll like her, she's a good sort. And Miss Edrich, and Mrs Callowe . . . they'll show you what to do, but by the time I leave – and I won't be long away, not above an hour – you'll have picked it up.'

'But the uniform,' Sara persisted. 'Why the uniform, Miss Boote?'

'Because if you go into a pub without the uniform they might think . . .' Miss Boote broke off, staring incredulously at Sara. 'Don't tell me your gran hasn't said anything to you? I'm a Salvationist, Miss Cordwainer, a member of God's Army!'

At first, Sara worked in a daze, scarcely able to believe what she was doing. Her parents had despised the Salvation Army and had brought her up, she now realised, to do the same. She had put money in their collecting tins behind her mother's back from time to time, and once or twice she had listened, with tapping foot, as they sang carols in the streets at Christmas, but other than that she had seldom thought about them, save as people in rather old-fashioned clothing who appeared in the city centre, armed with shiny brass instruments, and played bouncy hymns and the better known carols.

'They sing in the streets; for *money*,' her mother had said, as though it was a crime so dastardly that she hardly dare put it into words. 'They wear *uniform*, the women as well. The bonnets are all right, but those heavy coats and skirts!' She had shuddered expressively. I wouldn't been seen dead in them, and the shoes are really frumpy – dreadful things.'

'I'm told they do a lot of good,' her father had said. 'For the lower classes, of course. But then so do the Goodfellows.'

Damning by faint praise, Sara had thought it, and

now, as she worked beside Miss Boote, Miss Callowe, Mrs Puddifoot and Miss Edrich, she realised that her father had been way, way out. The Goodfellows collected money for the poor, they didn't work for them. They didn't put huge aprons round their middles and clean and prepare great mountains of vegetables, chop bones with a hatchet to make stock, beg butcher's scraps to enrich their soup. They didn't serve the soup, either, unlike her fellow workers, none of whom was too proud to take it over to an old woman who sat dribbling down her stained coat, only just able to lift the bowl to her lips.

'Where do you get the vegetables?' she asked Miss Boote at one stage, when a skinny boy came in, staggering under the weight of a sack of cabbages. 'They can't all be presents!'

'Yes, they are, the shopkeepers are always generous,' Miss Boote told her. 'The joke of it is, we have a lot of kiddies and women during the daytime, though it's mainly men at night. And if we have to buy anything – crockery, utensils – it is paid for by the ould fellers of the wives and kids we feed!'

'Then they contribute willingly? But why don't they give their wives the money, then their wives could make soup for them,' Sara, ever practical, said. Miss Boote laughed and ladled more soup into more tin pannikins.

'It don't occur to them that they're contributin', for the most part,' she admitted. 'We go into the pubs with the *War Cry* and tell them we need the money desperately, for to feed the poor. They've had a few, they're merry, very likely, so they put their hands into their pockets – it's only a few pence, and they think it'll keep us quiet, off their backs. Yet that money goes to help to feed their wives and children, more often than not.'

'You mean they'll give you a few pence, but they won't give it to their wives?' Sara asked, shocked. 'That doesn't make sense.'

'It makes very good sense. You see, we're in the pubs and the fellers what drink their money away love the pubs. They're amongst their mates, it's warm and cheerful in there with no crying kids, no hungry, weeping wife. So they'll put on a bit of a show, boast a bit, chuck their money about. Sometimes they offer to buy us a bevvy, as they call it, and we smile ever so sweetly and tell them to pop the money into the collectin' tin, we'll have our bevvies later.'

'Well, I don't understand it, but it's good,' Sara said after a moment's thought. 'What else do you do for the poor, Miss Boote?'

'We run hostels for the homeless, places where wives can stay when their husbands beat them up, soup kitchens – this is one – and cheap canny houses where those with a few pence can get a good, hot meal. And we try, very gently, to show them that God cares. That's if they want to come to the citadel, that is.'

'I see. And – and could I come to the citadel? I don't mean to be one of you, exactly, I just mean to see what happens there.'

''Course you could,' Miss Boote said briskly. 'Well, I'm off to do me stint in the pubs down the Walton Road. God knows, there are plenty of pubs there, yet it's a poor area. The women have large families and a lot of the men are unemployed.'

'Don't they get this assistance they talk about?' Sara asked cautiously. She had heard others besides her father being contemptuous of anyone who could not manage, saying that the person should ask for public assistance.

'It's means tested,' Miss Boote said briefly. 'Can't stop now, queen, got to be off. But I'll be back in an hour and we'll tootle off home on me old bike, eh?'

She disappeared into the night and Miss Callowe, who had been standing beside Sara cutting the long brown loaves and handing over a slice as each diner approached, poked her in the ribs. She was a girl of about Sara's own age, with lovely smooth, light-brown hair, but she had gaps in her teeth and those that remained were grey and unhealthy-looking.

'Hey, Miss Cordwainer... Lord love you, what a mouthful! D'you have another name?'

'Yes, I'm Sara,' Sara said happily. 'What's your first name, Miss Callowe?'

'Margaret, but everyone calls me Maggie,' the girl said. 'Are you goin' to join us? The uniform's lovely, honest. I got a new one a few months ago 'cos my old 'un was too tight and very worn, so Captain Edwards helped to pay for it, because I work in Sykes the baker on Walton Road, and it ain't a job what pays much.'

'The uniform is pretty, but I don't know about joining you,' Sara said guardedly. 'Actually, I haven't got a job at all at present so I can't afford so much as a new hanky.'

Maggie laughed. 'You'll gerra job, you're ever so pretty and your teef's good.' She indicated her own mouth. 'Mine are awful poor – the dentist up at the centre says it's 'cos I weren't fed right, as a child.'

'Goodness – what did your mother say when he said that?'

There was a pause before Maggie spoke.

'I ain't got no mother, nor no father, norrany more,' she said quietly. 'They dumped me in a children's 'ome when I were five. I 'spec' they're dead, now. So you see, the Army's more'n just a friend, it's me family an' all.'

'I see,' Sara said inadequately. 'I'm sorry, Maggie.'

'Don't be sorry; likely it were the best thing that could 'ave 'appened to me,' Maggie said, suddenly cheerful. 'I gorra lorra friends, the Army 'ostel's a nice place, an' one day I'll marry some feller an' gerra place o' me own.'

'I'm sure you will,' Sara said gently. 'Oh, the soup's running low; what happens now?'

'You shout someone . . . Mrs Puddifoot will do . . . an' they'll bring a fresh pan through,' Maggie told her. 'What's left's a bit thin an' all . . . ask Mrs P for more veggies in the next lot.'

On her way home that night, sitting on the back of Miss Boote's bicycle, Sara thought about her evening. She had enjoyed it tremendously, even though what she had secretly hoped for had not come to pass. She had not found herself serving either the missing Carbery or the other one, Grace, the older girl that Jess had mentioned. Well, if she had served them they had both changed, which, Sara thought ruefully, would not be out of the question – she herself had changed.

But she had looked very hard at every child aged around seven or around eleven; that was how old Mollie and Grace would be, by now, she had calculated, and none of them had had either Mollie's wonderful red-gold curls or Grace's extraordinary likeness to her elder sister.

But even if I've not actually helped either of those children, I've helped others whose plight may be similar, Sara told herself robustly, as Miss Boote dismounted from the bicycle and she slid off the back. It would have been an *unbelievable* coincidence had I met either of them on my very first foray into trying to help the poor.

And presently, over a hot cup of cocoa, she told Miss Boote that she had been looking for the Carbery children, just in case her friend knew of them.

'I've not heard of 'em,' Miss Boote said when Sara finished the story. 'But has it occurred to you, queen, that they might have bettered theirselves by now? They might be doin' all right, Mr Carbery could've finished wi' the booze and the kids might be properly fed an' that. You never know. It does happen, with God's help.'

It was a cheering thought to go to bed on, and Sara fell asleep happily, hoping against hope that Miss Boote was right. But though the dream hadn't troubled her for years, that night she dreamed of Jess, and the tragedy, and it seemed to her that Jess was trying to tell her something, trying to tell her that she must keep on looking, because there was something she could do for Jess's little sister. And in the dream Jess came right up to Sara and whispered in her ear and Sara suddenly knew what it was Jess wanted and what she herself must do.

But when she woke in the early hours she could remember only the unhappiness on Jess's small, pale face, and a sense of loss.

Next morning Sara was late up, but despite this she was extremely cheerful. She sang as she washed and dressed and, in the kitchen, ate a hearty breakfast of porridge and toast.

'Who's left you a hundred quid?' her grandmother asked, cocking her head on one side. 'You sound happy this mornin', our Sara!'

'I am. Until last night, Gran, I felt so sorry for myself

you wouldn't believe. I told myself I was an unloved child, that my parents hadn't prepared me for real life, that I was a failure. I – I don't mind telling *you*, Gran, but I've set my heart on finding that Carbery baby and making sure she's all right, so the soup kitchen seemed a good place to start. I didn't see any sign of her, but somehow I'm sure I will, one of these days. And last night I met someone much worse off than myself, and she was cheerful, sensible . . . she counted blessings she didn't have, and was happy. So who am I to moan and grumble just because my parents didn't care for me much, and I don't have a job or any visible means of support?'

'I'm glad you feel like that, queen,' Mrs Prescott said rather drily, 'because I had bad news this mornin'. Your mother wrote. To be blunt, she's stopped my allowance.'

'Allowance? I didn't know she made you one, Gran. But why on earth has she stopped it? Not because I'm here, surely?'

'Oh no, she doesn't mention you. She says that Adolphus has lost a good deal of money from this coming off the Gold Standard, whatever that may mean, and can no longer afford some of his charities.'

Sara, who had been cutting herself another slice of bread, stopped short, the knife halfway through the loaf. 'She said *what*?'

'She said your father can no longer afford . . .'

'I heard what you said, I just couldn't believe . . . Gran, how dared she say such a thing! You, a charity, indeed! Oh, I'd like to make her eat her words!'

'Aye. A cold thing, charity can be, when what's given is given grudgingly. But after a few minutes' thought I realised your mam didn't mean nothing by it. She was simply saying to me what she had been saying to a good few others, I'd guess. I remember you said they'd dismissed the chauffeur . . .'

'Yes. Without a thought for him or his wife,' Sara said, bitterness returning at the thought of poor Robson on the street. 'The flat went with the job of course, but they wouldn't let them stay even though it's empty, now.'

'Well then, losing the little pension your father paid me won't put us on the streets, because so long as I can pay the rent we've a roof over our heads, and Miss Boote's money means we can pay that without too much effort,' Gran said reassuringly. 'But I won't lie to you, queen. We'll be in Queer Street if you don't get work quite soon. I'm very thankful you're here with me, though, for I doubt I could manage without some help.'

'Oh, Gran! Do you mind telling me what Father paid you?'

'Well, he used to pay me ten shillings, the same as my other pension, but he put it up to a guinea a week about four years ago. I was having a bit of a struggle so one day I put on me best things and got on a tram and visited your father in his offices. I said I didn't want to upset his apple cart, but me rent had gone up and I wasn't findin' it easy to manage. He doubled the money he gave me immediately and I thought he was very generous, but afterwards, I wondered if he thought I was about to blackmail him! Because I'd never called at his office before, and he seemed very anxious to get me out in good order, so to speak.'

'Oh, Gran, as if he could have thought such a thing! Then for the past four years you've had a total of thirty-one shillings; and you've been paying all your bills, your rent, your food, with that?' Sara said wonderingly. 'How on earth do you manage?'

'Very nicely, queen, up to now. The rent's eighteen and six a week, Miss Boote pays me eighteen shillings, I put a bit aside for Christmas, birthdays and so on, and that left me with well over a pound a week for food, coal, lamp oil, and all the other small household expenses. Oh, I managed very well, in fact. But losing a whole guinea . . . well, it's going to make things hard, very hard.'

'I don't think you can manage,' Sara said after some thought. 'Thanks to Miss Boote the rent's paid, but you have to feed her, and yourself, on rather less than ten bob a week. And what with coal, and lamp oil, and tram fares, you'll never do it. Oh, if only I'd got that job with the Ocean Accident! The money was very good – twenty-two bob a week, and luncheon vouchers!'

'Oh, I'll learn to manage on less, once I get used to it,' Gran said bracingly. 'After all, before Miss Boote came along I managed. Only I have to feed me lodger decent, and that *is* goin' to present a problem.'

'I'll get a job,' Sara said between gritted teeth. 'I'll get a job if it kills me, Gran!'

'Sshh! If you bounce about an' keep gigglin' we'll never see her.' Tad grabbed Polly's hand and squeezed it warningly. 'And I'm tellin' you, if she looks in our direction, just you duck down, Poll, or run like the divil . . . 'cos if it comes to gettin' out of here fast I'll leave you in the ha'penny place so I will!'

It was Christmas Eve and Tad and Polly were ghost-hunting in the ruins in Gardiners Lane.

No one went there, not after dark. Not even lovers, Tad had said authoritatively, and he should know, living next door to it as he did.

'In ten years' time our tenement will be a ruin just

like next door,' Tad was apt to boast. 'Sure and aren't the walls fallin' down already, and there's a tree growin' up through me bedroom, leaves an' all in summer, an' if you don't believe me I can show you so I can.'

Polly believed him. She had seen the tree, and the fungus, and admired both, but when she went back to her neat home and sat down to her tea – pink shrimps and bread and butter with apple pancakes for afters – she had burst inexplicably into tears.

'What's the matter, alanna?' Mammy had asked, concern in every line of her body as she bent over her daughter. 'Don't you like the nice pink shrimps? And there was me, thinkin' they were your favourites!'

'They are, they are,' Polly had wailed between sobs. 'And I don't have a tree growin' in me bedroom, nor a fungus the size of a nellyphant above me bed! Nor I don't go to bed hungry five nights out of six!'

And her mammy had crooned and cuddled her – and marched out of the house and round to Gardiners Lane and when she marched back she had Tad with her. Polly had got the impression that she had Tad by the metaphorical ear, and had probably fought a battle to get him at all.

'Here's Tad come to have tea wit' you, Polly me love,' she had said cheerfully, pushing Tad into a chair. 'He's never tasted pink shrimps you say, so I thought it would be nice if you shared 'em.'

But that had been ages ago; last summer. Now it was Christmas Eve and Polly and Tad were out to find the banshee.

Mrs Crumplin had heard the banshee time out of mind, she had told the children a couple of days before. She had heard her a-wailin' and a-shriekin' in the ruined houses and she'd told the father so she had and what had he done? Nothin', nothin' whatsoever, because he knew full well that if he came and sprinkled the holy water and exorcised her – if you could exorcise a banshee – then six months later, sure as sure, down he'd drop, stone dead!

'I don't believe in the banshee,' Polly had said stoutly, clutching Tad's hand. 'She's not a ghost, not really. My brother Niall says she's just superstitious nonsense.'

'Oh, aye? And since when's your brother Niall an expert?' Tad had said hotly. Polly suspected that he was quite proud of the banshee in the ruins next door and did not want cold water poured on the story. 'And if it wasn't the banshee we heard as I were walkin' you home last night, Polly O'Brady, what was it?'

'It was a cat,' Polly said accusingly. 'You *know* it was a cat, Tad, you *said* it was a cat. Or a dog, you said.'

'I didn't want to scare you,' Tad said rather unconvincingly. 'I didn't want you clutchin' me and squawkin' before me pals.'

So of course she had called him a big liar – and wasn't it God's truth? – and he'd denied it and told her that if she really didn't believe in the banshee, then how about a hunt through the ruins on Christmas Eve?

'It's one of the best nights in the year for ghosts,' he had said. 'So if you really don't fear such t'ings . . .'

And now here they were, on Christmas Eve, within a foot of the ruins, with a clear sky above them and a big moon shining and a frost making Polly's toes tingle.

'We'd best hide in where the front room was,' Tad said, taking her hand firmly in his. He pulled her in under the wobbly wooden door arch and ducked sideways. 'Here, crouch down, where the fireplace was, and wait . . . and don't you dare giggle!'

'I won't,' Polly assured him in a low voice. Truth to

tell, she had no desire to giggle. It was spooky in here, pitch dark but for the silver wash of the moonlight coming through the empty doorway. Indeed, when she glanced up at the house wall, which ended a dozen feet in the air, she half-expected to see the banshee, outlined against the moon, sitting on the wall and combing her long, draggly grey hair. But all she saw was the moon, the jagged outline of the wall, and a thin, bare tree-branch held supplicatingly out towards the moon's disc.

'You'd better not giggle, I'm tellin' ye,' Tod said. 'Are you scared?'

It would have been nice to have said that of course she was not scared since she knew the banshee didn't exist, but Polly felt she was in the wrong place for a whopping lie like that. Even if the banshee didn't exist the devil did, the father said so in church on a Sunday, and she had no desire for a creature such as that to suddenly manifest itself beside her and drag her off to hell for telling big lies.

'I am, so,' she admitted therefore. 'It's dark as the divil in here, Tad . . . will we go out again? We'll see the banshee just as well outside.'

Tad put an arm round her and hugged her to him. He smelt faintly of dirt, of boiled potatoes and of young boy, but his hug was comforting. Polly, cuddling gratefully close, decided it was a nice smell so it was. It made her feel brave.

'There; is that better? Are you still afraid?'

'It's better, but I'm a bit afraid still,' Polly admitted. She did not want Tad to take his arm away and leave her cold and alone again. 'How long'll we have to wait before . . .'

Even as she spoke they heard it. An unearthly moan, rising, rising, until it was a full and terrible caterwaul of grief and woe, uttered, Polly was sure, by no mortal mouth.

'Oh, God have mercy on us,' she squeaked, clutching Tad and trying to burrow into his ragged jacket. 'I want to go home, I want me mammy!'

'In a minute,' Tad hissed. 'We don't want to walk right into her, that's for sure. I don't want her throwin' her comb at me so's I die inside six months, indeed I don't.'

'Where is she, then?' Polly quavered. 'Oh, Tad, it's gettin' closer so it is – let's run home to your house!'

The wailing was indeed getting closer. Tad was beginning to answer her, to tell her that she was safe with him and they'd hang on where they were until the banshee had given up for the night and gone elsewhere, when there was the lightest of light thumps on the wall above them. Looking up, Polly very nearly screamed aloud, for she saw a pair of burning lights, an outline . . . and then she realised what it was. It was a big old cat, that was all – he must have been as scared by the banshee as Polly herself had been and was looking for human comfort.

'Oh, Tad, the poor cat . . . pussy, pussy, come here,' Polly coaxed, almost forgetting her own fright at the cat's abrupt arrival. 'Does the banshee like cats? Only if not, we'd better . . .'

The cat was outlined against the moon now, so that Polly saw the subsequent events quite clearly. The cat threw back its head and opened its mouth, and from its throat came the long, wailing note, the sobbing crescendo, the final, awful, yowl which Tad had so convincingly blamed on the banshee!

He must have known she'd guessed, though, for his embrace became imprisoning and Polly could feel him laughing right down through both the arms that held her. Furious, she bit and thumped until he let her go, then jumped to her feet.

'Tad Donoghue, you're a liar and a cheat! You *knew* that cat came here to make that noise, I bet you've watched it many a time from your bedroom, haven't you? Oh, you just wanted to scare me . . . I hate you, you're wicked, I – I hope you have a rotten Christmas, so I do, and a thin old New Year!'

She would have run out, left him, but he jumped to his feet and grabbed her arm, though he was still shaking with laughter.

'Polly, Polly, Polly! Sure an' I was only jokin' wit' you! I did know the cat yowled on the wall there, but we could've seen the old banshee, because Mrs Crumplin's heard her many a time, she says, an' there's no sayin' that she wouldn't have come anyway, tonight bein' Christmas Eve and all.'

Polly paused. He did have a point, she supposed. 'But you knew about the cat, you just wanted to scare me,' she said accusingly. 'That was a mean trick, Tad Donoghue.'

'It was,' Tad said, pretending to hang his head. 'And it's sorry I am, alanna, but I couldn't resist. Aw, come on, let's wait a bit longer.'

But Polly wouldn't. She was cold and though the terror had warmed her through very nicely, she could still hardly feel her feet.

'No, I'm headin' for home,' she said firmly, turning towards the gaping doorway.

'You're scared,' Tad said. 'You know she could be in one of the other ruins so you do, but you won't look, not little Miss Polly!'

'I will so,' Polly said at once. 'But I don't believe a word of it – remember that, Tad Donoghue!'

'Right, right. Let's have a look at the rest of the ruins,

then, and go home after that,' Tad said. 'Take my hand, then if either of us sees anything, we can drag the other one away.'

'If we see anything, we shan't need dragging,' Polly observed as they set off along Gardiners Lane, heading for the next ruined building. 'We'd be off like shot from a cannon. Though ghosts don't hurt you, do they – apart from the banshee, I mean?'

'Dunno. There's one down your way chucks things about,' Tad said. 'Polter-something. They move furniture and throw vases. And the banshee doesn't hurt you, exactly. It's only if she t'rows her comb at you . . .'

'You'll die within six months; I know,' Polly sighed. 'And why the old terror's got a comb, when everyone goes on about her draggly grey hair, all knots, is more than I can make out.'

'She's a woman, that's why. Women like to think they're beautiful even when they're not,' Tad said. 'I 'spec' the old banshee thinks all the fellers admire her, draggly hair an' all.'

They were laughing and kidding now, quite loudly, all thoughts of banshees and ghosts forgotten for the moment, at least. The second house was, furthermore, even more a ruin than the first. It was little more than half-walls, and in summer the grass and wild flowers ran riot over its fallen bricks. Now, the two children went over to it, climbed the lowest of the walls, and stared critically around them.

'Nothin' here. Nor anyone, either,' Tad said after a brief inspection. 'Oh, I've had enough of this, Poll. Let's go to your place. Your mammy might be roastin' chestnuts.'

'All right,' Polly agreed. She, too, was tired of the tricky moonlight and the cold. 'Which way'll we go?'

It was possible for two agile – and wicked – children

intent on taking a short cut between Gardiners Lane and Swift's Alley to scramble their way over walls and between tenement blocks, but tonight Polly decided she would rather go the long way round. Climbing a wall silvered by moonlight and jumping into the thick ink-black dark the other side meant one could end up with broken knees or worse.

'Let's go along Francis Street,' she said therefore. 'The stalls will be open till midnight – we might get a bargain.'

'With what?' Tad asked. 'Have you got any money, then?'

'Not a farden,' Polly assured him. 'I forgot. But someone might *give* us something they didn't want or couldn't sell. You never know. Besides, it'll be nice to have the gaslights; sort of warming.'

Tad agreed, so the two of them set off along the dark, deserted length of Gardiners Lane and presently emerged into the hustle and bustle of Francis Street, with the gaslights hissing and dispensing their strong white light on the vivid scene and the stallholders shouting their wares, wishing customers a merry Christmas and heckling passersby to buy their holly, mistletoe, oranges, wooden engines, rosy apples.

But the two children weren't on Francis Street long for they took the first left turn they reached and were soon in the lobby of the O'Bradys' tenement block.

'Come on up,' Polly urged Tad, groping across to the stairs, for the place was unlit and windowless, save for a tiny cracked glass pane in the door. 'If Mammy isn't roastin' nuts I'll get some pennies and we'll go and buy some.'

'Oh well, awright then,' Tad said with a reluctance which Polly knew very well was assumed. Poor Tad seldom had luxuries such as roasted chestnuts! 'Only I'd best not be long – me mammy may need me.'

Up the stairs they went but halfway up them someone opened a door on the landing above and light flooded out, golden lamplight, looking warm and inviting.

Polly paused, for someone was coming down the stairs towards them. She was a young girl of thirteen or fourteen with light-coloured hair, and she was smiling at them. It was a rather sweet smile, Polly thought, returning it.

'Your mammy must have heard us comin' up,' Tad said in Polly's ear. He passed her, then turned to grab her hand. 'Come on – you're tired, I'll give you a heave.'

'Mammy didn't hear us comin',' Polly observed scornfully. 'Don't you use your intelligence, Tad Donoghue? 'Tis the lady here . . . Mammy opened up to let her out.'

Tad looked up the stairs, then down them. 'Which lady?'

'Why, the one . . .' Polly stopped short. 'Sure and she passed us, Tad, and went on down. Don't say you didn't see her?'

'I did not. And nor did you, Polly O'Brady,' Tad said roundly. 'Because there was no lady, that's why, and we'd best hurry or your mammy will close the door and we'll be in the dark again.'

'But I *did* see her, truly I did, Tad,' Polly panted, hurrying up the stairs in her friend's wake. 'She was lookin' right at us. She had light-brown hair an' a raggedy shawl thing, and bare feet . . . and a lovely, friendly sort of smile.'

They reached the landing and Tad pushed Polly ahead of him into the O'Brady living room.

'Hello, Mrs O'Brady,' he said. 'It's a cold evening, out . . . you've had a visitor, have you?'

Mrs O'Brady had a big shovel in her hand; she had just withdrawn it from under the hot coals and the nuts smoked black and sweet on it. She turned to smile at the two of them, but shook her head in answer to Tad's question.

'Visitor? No, we've had no visitor. I heard you two talkin' as you came into the lobby, so I opened the door to give you some light on the stairs.' She turned to her sons, squatting on the hearthrug with hopeful eyes fixed on the chestnuts. 'Go and get some salt, Bevin,' she ordered. 'Salt is great wit' hot chestnuts.'

'Told you so,' Tad said triumphantly. 'There wasn't no woman, Polly, you imagined it.'

'Oh! Well, perhaps she came from one of the upper floors,' Polly suggested. 'She was only a girl, Mammy, thirteen or fourteen I suppose, and she had a raggedy shawl on, and bare feet. Or it may not have been a shawl.'

'Was it one of the poor unfortunates?' Mammy said, lifting nuts off the shovel and gasping as they burned her finger-ends. She handed them round to the boys, then loaded the shovel afresh and pushed it back into the coals. The girls she alluded to were country girls who had come to Dublin to work in the houses of the rich and become pregnant, usually by the master of the house. When they were turned out they had to sell their favours or starve, for they had no means of returning from whence they came and in any event, knew their parents would not have them back in such a condition. The people of the Dublin tenements felt great pity for such unfortunates, and helped them when they could and never blamed them for plying the only trade they knew. 'If one of those girls . . .' she paused delicately. 'If one of them had business in the block they might come in for a while, I suppose. It might have been one of them.'

'No, it wasn't an unfortunate,' Polly said at once. 'Sure an' don't I know most of 'em by sight? But this girl wasn't like that. I could tell. She wasn't old enough, I don't think.' Polly paused, uncertain how to convince. Could she say that the unfortunate girls were rarely that shabby, that dirty? And they didn't have calm, serene smiles. 'She was more like a sort of angel,' she said apologeticaliy. 'I know she wasn't an angel of course, but she had that sort of look.'

Tad guffawed, but Polly's mammy gave her a curious glance. 'And you say she was thin and dirty, with a shawl round her shoulders and bare feet? Yet she had the face of an angel?'

Tad guffawed again and Polly's mammy gave him a handful of nuts so hot that he spilt them and had to scrabble about on the rug to pick them up. Polly gave the nuts a kick, scattering them still further. 'Hold your noise, you!' she said rudely. 'He telled me the banshee was shoutin', Mammy, and it was just on old tom-cat.'

Her mother smiled. 'Want some nuts, alanna? Well, I can't answer your question because I don't know who the girl was, the poor darlin'. Eh, bare feet on such a night – Christmas Eve, too!'

'She wasn't cold,' Polly said, then looked surprised. Why was she so certain? No one person could ever judge the coldness or misery of another, surely she must know that?

'She was a ghost!' Tad shouted suddenly, then crackled the burnt shell off a nut and pushed it into Polly's indignantly opening mouth. 'G'wan, Poll, you wanted to see a ghost an' now you've seen one!'

Polly started to shake her head, quite prepared to

give Tad a thump for his mockery, but her mother put a hand on her, quieting her.

'Not a ghost; an angel,' she said quietly. 'A Christmas angel, who can't be seen the rest of the year, but becomes visible for a few moments on the eve of the Christ child's birth.' She dropped a kiss on her daughter's smooth brow. 'You're a very lucky girl, alanna,' she said lightly, but with an underlying seriousness which Polly could hear even if Tad could not. 'To see such a one. Good will come of it.'

'I've seen me guardian angel,' Polly said, awed. She knew it was true, too, truer than Tad's old banshee. 'She had a sweet face, Mammy.'

'Well, there you are then,' Mammy said, jiffling the shovel to make the nuts turn themselves over. 'More nuts, boys.'

And then, before Tad could scoff or Polly question, she turned the conversation to Christmas presents, to the goose which the baker on Francis Street was cooking for them, to the Mass which they would attend next morning. And she gave each child hot milk with a drop of spirit in it and told Tad he could sleep on the sofa if he wanted to stay the night. But he said he'd best be getting back since his mammy might need him, and made his escape.

Polly went off to bed glowing with expectation and happiness. She had seen her guardian angel, not many people could say that, and it was nearly Christmas Day!

Chapter Nine

The first Christmas that Sara spent at Snowdrop Street was like no other Christmas she had ever known. Despite her efforts she was not in a permanent job – not a proper one, that was. But at least she was earning money.

She had talked to Miss Boote as soon as she could about her chances of getting a job – any sort of job, because once the tiny allowance from the Cordwainers had been cut off, it was pointless trying to take Mr Esmond's advice about training. There was simply no money available for such a thing.

'I could pawn something, I suppose,' her grandmother had said, looking undecidedly around her neat living room. 'I've never done it before, but then I've never been desperate. Oh, queen, I feel so helpless! I'm too old to earn and that's a fact, and yet for you to take some dreadful little job with no prospects seems so wrong! There must be some way of getting enough money to see you through secretarial school – I wonder whether I might sell some bits and bobs?'

'You're pawning nothing and you're selling nothing,' Sara assured her grandmother firmly. 'There must be a way round it; I'm going to talk to Miss Boote as soon as she comes in tonight.'

Miss Boote, practical as ever, had a solution, of sorts.

'Evening classes,' she said firmly. 'Anyone can better theirselves at evening classes. And in the meantime, what's wrong wi' shop work?'

'It doesn't pay as well, does it?' Sara asked rather cautiously. She did not fancy standing behind a counter all day, but told herself that needs must. If it was all she could get then she would have to try shop work.

'It doesn't pay badly, not if you go for a saleslady in one of the big stores,' Miss Boote had assured her. 'And you've got the right accent, the right looks . . . and they'll give you a sort of uniform – black dress and shoes, that sort of thing. I'm not sayin' it's ideal, but I am sayin' it's worth considering.'

She was right and Sara knew it, so she set about lowering her sights a little and six weeks before Christmas was taken on by Barringtons department store, in their glove and accessory department.

'It's sixteen shillings, which is very good for a beginner,' Sara told her grandmother excitedly as she came into the living room and stripped off her washleather gloves. 'I'll be handling some awfully pretty stuff, too . . . and the other girl, Miss Warrender, seems really nice.'

Miss Warrender was nice, and so was the floor walker, Mr Bratby. He took Sara to lunch one day and told her she had the makings of a first-rate saleslady, and Miss Warrender and she giggled all afternoon about it.

'He'll be sneakin' up to you in the staff room and pinchin' your bum next,' Miss Warrender said. 'He's sweet on you, I can tell.'

'Oh, Miss Warrender, you're crazy. He's forty if he's a day and married with three kids,' Sara said. She felt so *young*, chattering to Miss Warrender, running to and fro at the customers' behest, being sent on errands by the senior staff. It was like being back at school again, with prefects and teachers telling you what to do and your friends to giggle with.

But it was too good to last. She had been minding her own business one icy morning in early December, cleaning the glass top and sides of the big display case, when she heard a young man addressing her fellow assistant. Men didn't frequent the glove department as a rule, so being only human, Sara turned round and looked.

Miss Warrender was serving a tall young man with dark hair, wearing a light-brown mackintosh and a darker brown trilby hat. From where she was standing it was difficult to see his face so Sara moved round as unobtrusively as she could and got behind the main counter once more. She was beginning to polish the glove-drawers whilst still concentrating on the customer, when a voice said, 'It's a pair of dark-brown gloves I'm searching for, Miss. Size . . . oh, I'm not too sure about size. My mama's hands are very slender, similar to . . .'

He glanced at Miss Warrender's hands, which could have been described as chunky, and then, helplessly, across at Sara, polishing away. He brightened. 'Similar to that young lady's, I suppose.'

It was Alan Hepworth – and he was looking at her hands, completely ignoring the rest of her. Sara bridled, then sighed and returned to her work. She should have expected it – she was a shop assistant, not a woman at all, now. But Mr Hepworth was talking.

' . . . If she wouldn't mind trying them on,' he was saying. 'Only my mama will be so disappointed if I get the wrong size – normally, she would come in herself but she's got a slight cold in the head . . .'

Later, Miss Warrender would say to Sara: 'Cold in the bleedin' 'ead my foot; 'e were buyin' them for 'is fancy woman!', but that was just her way. You had to have a laugh, she would have said, or you might as well cock your toes up.

Now, however, she was on duty. She turned to Sara. 'Miss Cordwainer, there's a gentleman here . . .'

Sara moved forward even as Mr Hepworth raised startled eyes to her face; the name had done it, of course.

'Sara? I can't believe it! Your mother told me you'd returned to Switzerland . . . oh, I suppose you're home for the holiday, but what on earth are you doing behind that counter?'

'Selling gloves,' Sara said rather tartly. Trust her mother to think up some fairy story that couldn't possibly hold water for long! She turned to her colleague. 'Yes, I'll try the gloves on for the gentleman, Miss Warrender.'

'Thanks, Miss Cordwainer.' Another customer loomed, a fat, peroxided lady with long scarlet nails and a discontented expression. 'I'd best attend to this lady, then, if you'll take over here.'

With no real choice, Sara picked up the dark-brown gloves lying in a welter of others on the counter.

'Are these the ones, sir? The colour is called dark chocolate . . . they're top of our range, very superior, soft leather.'

'Yes, I daresay,' Mr Hepworth said distractedly. He lowered his voice. 'What's going on, Sara?'

'I don't live at home any more,' Sara said patiently. 'I'm working for my living, as you can see, Mr Hepworth.' She slid the gloves on to her hands; they fitted beautifully and felt wonderfully warm and comfortable, too. She held out her gloved hands. 'See?'

'No, I don't,' Mr Hepworth said. 'Your parents must be distraught! You can't like being a shop girl for goodness' sake!'

'It's rather nice, actually,' Sara said, taking the gloves off with great care – she remembered the times at home that she had peeled her gloves off inside out and cast them on the nearest chair; but she hadn't known then that they cost a week's wages and more, and could split if handled roughly. 'It's a living, anyway. Shall I try these ones on now, sir?'

'Yes, yes, why not? Well, I don't understand it. Your mother definitely gave me to understand that you were in Switzerland. I asked when you'd be coming home and she said she didn't know. My mama said . . .' he paused and looked cautiously at Sara and it occurred to her that she didn't know Alan Hepworth at all, nor he her, despite the fact that they had kissed in the comfortable darkness of a taxi, and she had once spent a couple of hours in the cinema, fighting off his rather tentative advances.

'What did she say?' Sara said, however, suddenly curious. It might be interesting to find out whether her mother managed to fool women of her own age and station in life.

'Well, I don't know whether I ought to say this . . .'

'If you don't get on with it, I'll have to serve someone else,' Sara said impatiently, seeing a skinny, fashionable young woman approaching the counter. 'I can't turn down sales, Mr Hepworth, because I'm paid on a bonus system.'

'Oh! Look, I'll have the dark-brown ones, and would you try the lighter ones again, please?'

Sara pulled them on and Mr Hepworth leaned a little closer. 'My mama said that your mama was unnatural, and had no affection for you. She said it stuck out a mile, though I can't say I'd ever noticed.'

'Your mother was right,' Sara said. 'My mother doesn't like me very much. The chocolate-coloured gloves are thirty shillings, sir, and the lighter ones twenty-eight and eleven.'

'I'll have both,' Mr Hepworth said recklessly, pulling out a fat wallet. 'Wait till my mother hears that I've found you – and where!'

Sara sold him the gloves, sending his bill and his bank note off in the little jar thing which whizzed it along to the cash desk where Miss Addington abstracted it and sent back his change and the receipted bill. Then she turned to the next customer and began serving her, for the department was getting busy.

Two days later, her mother turned up. She said nothing to Sara, she just went to the counter and began to try on gloves, ordering Miss Warrender to fetch the appropriate scarves and handbags to match her choice in an impatient, unpleasant way. She's heard I'm here and she's come to make sure, Sara thought. Good! Now she can see I'm not afraid of hard work and I'm coping without them!

An hour later, when her mother had placed an enormous order and gone on to gowns, the floor walker came over, rather diffidently, and told Sara she was wanted in the office.

'Wharrever for?' Miss Warrender asked. 'Lord, when we're so busy, too!'

Sara, whose feet were aching, thought that a trip to the office would be quite restful compared to running backwards and forwards, fetching gloves, scarves and leather handbags for impatient ladies who no sooner set eyes on them than they wanted something different. So she went at a walking pace through her own department, across lingerie, through gowns and up the stairs which led to Ye Olde Oake Restaurant and the offices.

The girl behind the big desk looked up at her, brows arching.

'Yes? Can I help you?'

'I'm Miss Cordwainer, from gloves,' Sara said. 'I've been told to come up to the offices.'

An expression of pity crossed the girl's face, but she said, 'Oh yes, Miss Cordwainer, it was Miss Whyte wanted to see you. Go straight through.'

Sara went to Miss Whyte's door, knocked and entered. Miss Whyte was a fat, elderly lady with grey hair piled up on her head and an anxious expression. She looked up when Sara entered the room but did not smile. She indicated a chair, however, then began rearranging some artificial red roses in a green glass vase, fiddling with them as though she did not want to meet her employee's eyes.

'Sit down, Miss Cordwainer. I'm afraid we've had a complaint.'

'A complaint?' Sara was completely bewildered. 'I'm sorry, Miss Whyte, I don't understand. We're awfully busy but I don't think I've left anyone waiting and I didn't take my lunch-hour today because of Miss Elgar from gowns being off . . .'

'It isn't that. Well, not precisely, anyway.' Miss Whyte cleared her throat uncomfortably. 'A – a customer said you'd been pert, Miss Cordwainer. She – she said that she wasn't prepared to shop at a place which employed pert young girls. And she's a very good customer.'

Sara sighed. Suddenly, she understood.

'It was my mother, wasn't it, Miss Whyte? Mrs Cordwainer. I imagine she told you she wouldn't shop here whilst you continued to employ me. Is that a good guess?'

Miss Whyte was as red as the artificial roses. Sara could see her trying to make sense of what had happened and failing; only seeing a good customer whistled down the wind because of some young girl she scarcely knew.

'No, it's not that at all . . . a customer said you'd been pert and we really can't have that sort of thing, as you realise. I'm sorry you take the attitude that the store is somehow to blame . . .'

'I don't!' Sara said, shocked at such a blatant twisting of the facts. 'I never said that, I just said that it was my mother who had complained. And it was, wasn't it, Miss Whyte?'

There was a moment's silence whilst Miss Whyte struggled with her conscience, and then she heaved a deep sigh.

'It was Mrs Cordwainer, yes. She told me she wanted you to return home, said you'd left after a quarrel . . .'

'It wasn't true, Miss Whyte. My mother turned me out.'

'Yes. I did wonder . . . but there's no doubt that your mother won't shop here whilst we employ you.'

'It's probably just an idle threat, Miss Whyte,' Sara said, even as her heart descended into her neat black court shoes. 'She's shopped here all her life, I can't see her changing to another store just because I work here.'

'Miss Cordwainer, have you any idea how much money your mother spends in this store each year?'

'A – a hundred pounds? Fifty?' Sara was guessing, but she had to say something. 'But no matter what she spends . . .'

'Last year she spent three hundred and fifty pounds fifteen shillings and sixpence. This year she has already spent four hundred and seventy-two pounds, nine shillings and elevenpence. These are vast sums, Miss Cordwainer, so it means that at a time when by and large customers are spending less and less, your mother is not someone we can afford to lose.'

'I see that,' Sara said, with increasing despair. 'But I have no money except for what I earn, I can't afford to lose my job!'

'Mrs Cordwainer spends many times your annual salary in our store, Miss Cordwainer,' Miss Whyte said gently. 'I'm sure, if you will just go home and tell her you're sorry for whatever took place, you will have no need either of your salary or your job with us. I shall be sorry to lose you – and so will gloves – but your mother's ultimatum has left us no choice.' She held out the pieces of paper she had been fiddling with. 'Your cards, Miss Cordwainer.'

Sara could not believe this was happening, yet she knew it was, knew that what her mother had done she had done quite deliberately, after some considerable thought. She had – she thought – cut the ground from under Sara's feet; now Sara would have to go home!

Sara turned towards the door; at least she now had some experience to talk about when applying for another job. Provided her mother could not run her to earth she might be safe at some other store. She had got the door half open when something occurred to her. She turned.

'One of these days, Miss Whyte, I shall probably be a married woman with a reasonable income at my command. If you think that I shall shop at the store which turned me away at a customer's spiteful whim, then you are very much mistaken.'

Miss Whyte sighed too; she looked very sorry, but Sara could tell that the older woman's resolve had not been shaken.

'I've no doubt you're right, my dear, but that, as you say, is in the future. The present is hard and getting harder. No one ever thought the Wall Street slump would continue to affect trade the way it has, and going off the Gold Standard does not seem to have helped at all. In fact, unless business looks up, there may not *be* a Barringtons of Liverpool by the time you're a married woman.'

'Well, I tried,' Sara said ruefully. 'Is it any use asking you if you'll give me a reference? Only I've worked hard for you, and I've learned a lot. It may be possible, if I have a good reference, to get another position.'

'Certainly. I'll write one myself and give it to you before you leave tonight,' Miss Whyte said. 'But for your own sake, Miss Cordwainer, I think you'd be well-advised to look for work outside the centre of the city.'

'You're probably right,' Sara said, not pretending to misunderstand the warning. 'I'm sorry about the threat, but I had to try. It's not only me, it's my grandmother I have to think about. I'm living with her and she only has a tiny pension.'

Miss Whyte stood up and came round the desk. She patted Sara's shoulder, then shook her hand.

'I feel very bad, very bad,' she said heavily. 'It would not be true to say I had no choice, but your mother does have influence, Miss Cordwainer. She told me so. She said she would put it about that I'd encouraged you to flee from home, she'd see that I lost customers from all walks of life, but particularly those in more affluent circumstances. And she could do it, you know. Would do it, if I . . .'

'It's all right,' Sara said. 'You'll pay my wages at the end of the week, when I leave, I hope?'

'I'll see you're paid the full week, but you must leave tonight,' Miss Whyte said. 'Come to accounts with me and I'll see to it right away. No need to go back to gloves, except for your coat and bag, of course.'

When Sara got home and told her grandmother and

Miss Boote there had been a good deal of recrimination, but then Sara said that she would not be beaten, Miss Boote gave her three cheers, and Mrs Prescott went out to the kitchen and came back into the living room carrying a bottle of sherry.

'It's for medicinal purposes, usually, but I think we need cheering up before we begin to plan our campaign,' she announced. 'Miss Boote, you've been a good friend to my girl; what do you suggest?'

Miss Boote looked embarrassed.

'Well, there is one thing . . .' she began. 'But I scarcely like to suggest it.'

'Fire ahead,' Sara told her. 'Any idea has to be better than mine, because my head is quite empty.'

'All right, I will. You know I work in a bank on Walton Road, quite near the Salvation Army Barracks?'

'Yes, I know. Not that you talk about it much,' Sara said. 'Oh, Miss Boote, don't say there's a vacancy in your bank?'

'No; wish there were,' Miss Boote said gruffly. They were sitting round the fire and she stared steadfastly into the flames. Oh Lord, her idea must be so dreadful that she dare not face us whilst she talks about it, Sara told herself. Never mind, any job is a job, with Christmas coming up.

'The Co-op have got a big bakery just past the Barracks,' Miss Boote said at last. 'They're gettin' ready for the Christmas rush and lookin' for temporary staff. It pays well, because it's temporary,' she added. 'You'd get eighteen bob a week, mebbe more.'

'But I don't know anything about baking,' Sara said doubtfully. 'What good would I be to them?'

'Go along and find out,' her grandmother said decisively. 'Sara, my dear, if you can just get work for a few weeks it will tide you over until something more suitable comes up. I'm afraid you won't get anything but temporary work this near Christmas; for the most part firms are suited.'

So Sara went along to the Co-op bakery and got a job, though not the one she had imagined at all. She rushed into the house at six that evening, with her hat on the back of her head and one shoelace undone, to announce the moment she got through the doorway, 'I got it!'

'Wonderful,' her grandmother said, giving her a hug. 'What're you doin', flower?'

'You'll never guess! I'm delivering, on a big old bicycle with a huge metal carrier at the back and another at the front. Each carrier has a big basket on it . . . they asked if I could ride a bicycle so I said I could . . .'

'But you can't,' her grandmother observed, aghast. 'Oh, queen, you'll get killed! The roads are so dangerous, all that traffic, horses, cabs, motor cars, trams . . .'

'I shan't get killed because I'll be careful, and the job starts on Monday, so I've time to learn on Miss Boote's machine,' Sara said. 'And you'll never guess – it's twenty-two and sixpence a week and they'll want me until mid-January – a whole lovely month!'

And then Christmas arrived, and when Miss Boote announced that she would be serving Christmas dinner to the poor, and Sara said she would like to go along, Mrs Prescott said that she might as well go too.

'I'm not a Salvationist, but I believe in giving practical help where it's possible,' she said. 'And what's more practical than serving a Christmas dinner? Besides, it would be no pleasure for me, to eat alone.'

'We wouldn't let you do that, Gran,' Sara said at once. 'We'll be back mid-afternoon, won't we, Clarrie? We thought we'd eat our main meal in the evening.'

'Nevertheless, that would mean I'd be alone all day and I'm not standing for it,' Mrs Prescott said firmly. 'How I'm to get there I don't know, since the trams run a Sunday service on Christmas Day and I'm afraid me walkin' days are over, but I'll get there somehow. I might get a taxi; I don't think I could walk.'

'I'll give you a seater on my delivery bike, Gran,' Sara teased. She had learned to ride the machine just in time to start the job, and though she admitted privately to Gran that she and her loaves, cakes and puddings had several times met the hard ground, she had managed to dust both herself and her bakery goods off so that no one knew what had happened.

'And since they're going to sack me halfway through January I don't suppose it matters whether someone tells on me or not,' she had told her grandmother when describing her experiences on the bike. 'Besides, I haven't fallen off nearly so often lately. I'm getting quite good at it.'

The problem of getting about was becoming a very real worry for Mrs Prescott however, and though of course Sara knew a taxi was possible, fares would be a problem.

'It won't be long before she can't manage to step up to the tram,' Sara told Clarrie Boote, when her grandmother had gone early to bed one night. 'I suppose we could run to a taxi on Christmas Day, but what about other events?'

Miss Boote said little, but that evening she turned up with a wheelchair. It wasn't new and it wasn't smart, but it worked.

'There you are, Mrs P, your chariot,' Clarrie said proudly, bringing it round to the front door. 'All you need is someone to push you, and you're away!'

'Where did you get it?' Sara marvelled. 'You are so clever, Clarrie!'

'I asked Major Brett what happened to his old mother's chair, and he said we could have it. She died twelve months back,' Clarrie explained. 'They're ever so handy if your legs aren't so good.'

So Christmas Day dawned and the three women set off. Clarrie and Sara took it in turns to push the wheelchair, not bothering to bring the bicycle because Clarrie was in uniform and Sara wore her only decent garment, the grey flannel suit.

They had left early. Sara woke before seven and went downstairs to make tea for them all. After that she helped her grandmother to dress and then made breakfast. It was still only seven-thirty in the morning as they wended their way through the empty, echoing streets, talking softly so that they woke no one who still slumbered. The air was crisp, with a nip in it, the pavements and hedges rimed with frost, and as the darkness gradually gave way to dawn they drew gradually nearer their destination.

'Well, I never thought I'd be goin' off to work on Christmas Day,' Mrs Prescott said over her shoulder as her two companions swung along the pavements in the first pale dawn light. 'Apart from the years when your parents asked me over, Sara, I've had quiet Christmas Days, by and large. And aren't I looking forward to this one, with lots of people to talk to and lots of laughter!'

'You can be sure of that,' Clarrie said. 'We laugh a lot, in the Army.'

'It's funny,' Sara said, jumping the cracks in the paving stones as she walked along as though she was still eight years old and not eighteen. 'I seem to laugh much more now than I ever did at home – or at school, either, for that matter. I go to back doors and bakeries and retail outlets as they call them, and everyone's jolly, they all have a laugh with me, tease me about the bike, the way I ride it, even the way I talk. All sorts of things make them laugh – the way I pull my skirt over my knees, how I wobble all over the road when I glance over my shoulder, how I look in the rain when I'm as wet as a herring . . . It's amazing, really it is. Why, even when I worked in Barringtons, Miss Warrender and I would have a good old giggle.'

'Aye. They say religion's the opiate of the poor, but I think laughter is, meself,' Clarrie said. 'Belief in God is good, it gives you a glow and satisfaction, too. But laughter takes you right out of yourself, like.'

'In that case, I'm surprised the rich haven't taken out a patent on it and refused to allow others to indulge,' Gran said from her wheelchair. 'Still, let's be thankful that we can still laugh all we like. I'm sure I still do . . . especially now I've got you two young'uns using your legs for me!'

'They don't think much o' laughter, the rich,' Clarrie observed. 'Nor the powerful, for that matter. When did a teacher ever encourage her class to laugh? When a maid giggles, chances are she'll get give the order of the boot. And do you know why? Laughter puts folk down, that's why. It makes the pompous look foolish and the proud trip and fall.' She grinned at them. 'That's why I'm in favour of it,' she declared, 'and why you'll always hear laughter in the Army ranks. How are you feelin', Mrs Prescott? I never realised before how bumpy the pavements are!'

'It's the kerbs that are worst, I think, and cobbles, of course,' Sara said. 'Never mind, Gran, you're nearly there – just think of the Christmas dinner we're going to be preparing, and serving . . .'

'And eating,' Clarrie put in. 'There'll be plenty, there always is.'

'All right then, and eating. Just put up with the bumps for another few hundred yards and you'll be in sight of the Barracks!'

Grace and the black and white kitten had found each other on Christmas Eve, when the pubs were spilling their customers out on to the pavement with shouts of 'A merry Christmas!' and much laughter.

Grace had been hanging about outside the Mile End pub on Scotland Road, partly because she knew from experience that landlords – and customers – would sometimes feed starvelings such as herself and also because when the bakers in Scott's, which was next door to the pub, finished their night-shift they were generous with left-overs – buns that hadn't risen right, the 'corners' of the big, square fruit cakes they made and sold by the piece, farl which had gone stale and so on.

She was managing quite well, was Grace, mainly because she did her best, now, to keep away from her home. Nights were dangerous there, unless you worked it so Da was asleep before you went in, so Grace usually slept rough except when it was so bitterly cold that she was afraid to be out. But though her father was bad tempered in the morning quite often, he was rarely violent. Violence went with the drink, or with the frustration of having no money and therefore being unable to drink.

So there was Grace, bundled up in any number of old, torn rags, sitting in the corner of the pub doorway waiting for closing time. And here by the pub she stood a good chance of food. Men with a bellyful of beer would hand over the remains of their carry-out, or a few coppers, to a child such as herself provided she was around at the right time.

And the kitten, tiny, milky-eyed, clearly must have got the message, for it came round the corner, huge ears pricked, tiny, thin body poised for flight . . . and walked almost into Grace's arms.

'Hey, little feller,' Grace said. He was so soft and fluffy, so wide-eyed and wondering! 'Come an' see what I've got!'

He came. He purred astonishingly loudly, his whole body vibrating with the sound. He rubbed against her skinny ankles, then jumped on to her knee. He accepted a share of a nice, soft currant bun, then he stood on his hind legs, reached up . . . and licked her chin.

Grace had forgotten what it was like to know a flood of total, complete love. She kissed the kitten between its ears, on the end of its tiny pink nose, and then she tucked it up warm, against her body, protected from the wintry chill.

'You an' me, we's both strays, kitty,' she told it as it settled, purring, close to her heart. 'We'll be give some nice food presently, an' then we'll find somewhere snug to sleep, jest you an' me. An' tomorrer's Christmas Day – we'll go to the soup kitchen down the Scottie an' 'ave somethin' to eat . . . we'll 'ave a real good Christmas will us two.'

The kitten purred on and when the pubs were empty and Grace had pennies in her pocket and her collecting bag full of bits and bobs of food, the landlady, cleaning through, put her head out of the door.

'Here, chuck – you goin' home, now?'

Grace, wordless, shook her head, ready to run. But there was no need, on this occasion, at least.

'You're one of the Carbery kids, ain't you?' the landlady said. 'Eh, we've 'ad your ould feller in 'ere once or twice. Well, tomorrer's Christmas . . . no, by 'eck, it's today already! Come on, then, you can sleep in the bar. Just this once, mind.'

Grace needed no second invitation. She was over the threshold and curling up on one of the brass-studded leather benches before you could have said 'knife'.

'Thanks, missus,' she said, as the landlady closed the outer door and went through the room to return to her own quarters. 'We're ever so grateful.'

'We?' the landlady said, raising her brows. ''Oo's we when you're at 'ome?'

'Me an' me kitten; he's asleep in me jacket,' Grace said.

The landlady laughed.

'You're both welcome,' she said. 'I'll get you a breakfast tomorrer, set you up for the day, like.'

Grace thanked her again as the older woman left the room, closing the door gently behind her. Then she snuggled down. What a Christmas this would be – breakfast, a kitten . . . what more could she ask?

Brogan arrived in Liverpool from Crewe on just about the last train to run on Christmas Eve and went out for a drink with his father before settling down for the night. They went to the Queen's Arms on the corner of Salop Street and Walton Road and had an enjoyable time, for Brogan knew a number of the regulars there and they all wanted to know how he was going on.

He enjoyed telling his former workmates that he was now an engine driver, and he enjoyed the conviviality, the bright bunches of red-berried holly, the mistletoe bough nailed to the central beam, but all the while he talked, sang, listened to singing, his mind was elsewhere.

If Sara's still in Liverpool with her gran I'm going to

go round, tell her how I feel about her, ask if we can exchange letters, be friends again, he kept telling himself. This time I'll not sit like a tongue-tied fool in her gran's front parlour whilst she wonders what on earth's wrong with me. Tomorrow I'll go round there and give her the present I've bought and ask her to come for a bit of a walk with me.

And once we're out of the house and by ourselves, without her gran a-listening from the kitchen, I'll tell her about Polly, because when you love someone you don't have no secrets from each other, and I'll ask her to be . . . well, I'll ask her if she'll be my girl.

'Brogan, you aren't singin', kiddo,' one of his erst-while workmates said to him as the pub rocked to a spirited rendering of *Hark the Herald Angels*. 'What's up, then? Are ye too 'igh-nosed for the likes of us, now?'

'Cat's gorris tongue,' someone called out. 'Or 'e's in love; tek your pick.'

Brogan just smiled his slow, good-natured smile and sat back in his seat and thought of Sara. She was so pretty, so lively . . . so very, very special! Of course she was a lady, but then wasn't his mammy a lady, too? Not rich nor important, but a lady, nevertheless. So there was no harm in him at least asking Sara . . .

'Come on, son, you must be wore out,' his father said at length, getting to his feet. 'Ah, here come them Army lasses . . . let's be on our way.'

'What Army lasses?' Brogan said as he and his father pushed their way through the crowds of revellers towards the open door. 'Do you not like them, Daddy?'

'They're harmless enough; they take their magazine, the *War Cry*, round the pubs and use the money for the poor,' Peader shouted above the confused babble of sounds around them. 'See them, shaking their tins?

They'll be making a Christmas dinner for them as wouldn't get one otherwise, so I'll pay me whack as we pass. Come on, lad, you're asleep on your feet and we must be up for early Mass tomorrow.'

Brogan looked at the bonnets bobbing along through the crowd of drinkers and grinned. 'Oh, *that* army! I'll put a copper or two in the tin as well if I can get near enough.'

But he couldn't reach the tin so he handed his loose change to the nearest drinker and had the satisfaction of hearing it going from hand to hand, hearing a soft, sweet voice raised in thanks as the money clattered into her tin.

'We don't want the paper, Miss,' Peader roared above the din. 'It's a contribution, that's all.'

'God bless you, friend,' came back the answer, and then they were out of the pub, the doors swinging to behind them, and under the frosty stars.

'We'll not be up too early tomorrow,' Peader remarked as he unlocked the front door and swung it wide. 'Eight o'clock Mass is early enough, I fancy. We'll go to St Mary's; it's not far.'

Brogan agreed; he would have agreed to anything which meant that he could get to Snowdrop Street sooner.

'You'll forgive me, Daddy, if I leave you, in the morning?' he said as they climbed into their beds, for Peader had borrowed a folding bed for his son's brief stay. 'Only I'd like to go round and see a friend for an hour or two. I'll be back for me dinner.'

'Fine,' Peader said. 'I'll have a crack wit' me pal Barney up the road. Or I might give a hand wit' the dinner.'

His landlady, Mrs Burt, was a friendly soul who encouraged her lodger to come into the kitchen and 'potter about', as she put it. Peader, a domestically minded man, enjoyed this very much better than a more formal lodger-landlady relationship and agreed with his son that good lodgings could make all the difference.

So, satisfied that his father would be happily occupied whilst he himself went on his visit, Brogan very soon settled down to sleep.

Next morning he awoke with a glow of anticipation such as he had not experienced since he was a child. He was going to see Sara, and this time he would tell her what was on his mind and not sit with his mouth open and no words coming out.

He went to Mass with his father and afterwards they exchanged small gifts and ate a hearty breakfast – bacon and egg, fried bread and a good deal of toast and marmalade. Mrs Burt then set Peader to cleaning sprouts, sitting on a stool in the doorway and chatting to his friend Barney, who had popped in, he said, to wish everyone the compliments of the season.

'Dinner's at one o'clock, no later,' Mrs Burt called jovially after Brogan's disappearing back, and Brogan shouted that he'd not be late and continued to stride purposefully down the road.

It was a sharp morning but the sun was out. Brogan whistled as he walked. He'd enjoyed his breakfast and he was looking forward to his dinner, but the best part of the day was almost upon him.

Sara!

He reached Snowdrop Street and felt his heartbeat increase. What would she be doing? Cooking dinner, with a smut of flour on one cheek and her hair curling in damp tendrils on her cheeks because of the heat from the fire? Or sitting before the fire with her gran, opening a present, or . . . or . . .

He had reached number three. He hesitated for a delicious second, then knocked.

A moment later he knocked again, fear replacing the anticipation in his heart. Where on earth was she? She would have gone to church by now, surely, and come back to prepare the dinner? But there was no sound in the house and when he peered through the front window the fire was either damped down or out, he could not tell which.

He was about to knock again when the front door of the next house opened and a young woman in her early twenties appeared on the doorstep.

'Mornin',' Brogan said politely, touching his cap. 'Can you be tellin' me what's happened to the ladies of this house? I've come round to wish them the compliments of the season but I've had no answer.'

'I 'eard you knock, so I thought I'd best come an' tell you they've gone out,' the girl said. 'Went off ever so early, all three of them.'

'Three?' Brogan said questioningly, his heart doing a nose-dive down into his boots. 'But I thought . . .'

'Oh, aye, but there's three of 'em livin' there now, you know. There's Mrs Prescott, Sara, who's Mrs P's granddaughter, and this Boote person.'

'Boote? Who's he?'

'Boote is Army – cor, I made a joke – an army boot,' the girl said, grinning to herself. 'Me mam said that's where they've gone, to the Barracks or whatever they calls it. I ask you, on Christmas Day – what a place to go for your dinner! Oh, that Boote . . . the two of you ain't met, then?'

'No,' Brogan muttered. 'No, we've not met.'

'Oh. Well, Sara's very thick wi' the Boote, I don't

mind tellin' you. Off they go, the two of 'em, on bikes during the week and on foot at weekends, 'eads together, laughin', talkin' all sorts. Me mam says it's nice, but I ain't so sure. We're all good Catholics in this street, we've none of us 'ad no time for the Army. Still, there you are, it's young Sara's choice, ain't it?'

'Y-yes, I suppose . . .' Brogan stammered. 'Sara's really fond of this Boote, then?'

'Oh, aye, rare fond,' the girl confirmed. 'They'll be back teatime, though, if you'd like to come round later. All three of 'em, mind.'

'Thanks,' Brogan said. He turned away. 'Thanks very much. I'll come back later, then.'

But as he made his lonely way back across the streets to Walton Road, he knew he would not be back later. There was no point. He would not go back again.

By the time mid-January arrived Sara was convinced she would never get another job which was as much fun as that of a bread-delivery girl. But she knew she must work at something, so when Miss Boote told her that there was a vacancy in the laundry, she applied.

The laundry was not a particularly pleasant place. When she went for the interview Sara had to cross the main washing room where row upon row of immense earthenware sinks were filled with steaming hot water. Women, in suds to their elbows, stood in front of the sinks, beating the washing with dolly-pegs. When they thought the sheets were clean they would hook them out of the hot water with wooden tongs, dump them on the slimy wooden draining boards whilst they drained off a bit, and then carry them over to the opposite side of the room, where the rinsing was done in different sinks.

The women in this room were mostly in their middle

years so far as Sara could judge; the younger girls were employed in the ironing room and in the packing department, where the job vacancy was. The clerk who had brought Sara across for her interview explained that here you had to be very smart because every garment, particularly the shirts, had to be folded in a special way and pinned, too, so that even the sometimes rough handling of the delivery staff would not unfold them.

'What matters is that when the customer unfolds the shirt, the collar and the dickie part are uncreased, and the cuffs, too,' the clerk said. 'Remember that when you do the test.'

'I will; did you say delivery staff?' Sara said, immediately interested. 'I've been doing delivery for the Co-op bakery. Only over Christmas, of course,' she added truthfully.

'We use vans, and boys,' the clerk said. 'But our packers is all women. He smiled at Sara. 'Packing ain't so bad, the gals seem to like it awright.'

The supervisor who conducted Sara's interview was a sour-looking spinster with sharp eyes behind tiny gold spectacles. She knew Sara wasn't like most of the girls who worked in the laundry, Sara guessed, but could not quite decide precisely why that was. So she sent her down to the packing room for a test to see whether she was what she termed 'neat-fingered' and, forewarned by the clerk, Sara made a good attempt at the folding of two shirts, two enormous sheets and a pile of handkerchiefs.

'You'll do; start Monday,' the supervisor said almost grudgingly. 'Be here by eight o'clock sharp.'

'I will,' Sara said. 'You didn't mention the salary . . .'

'The wage,' the supervisor corrected. 'It's paid weekly, on a Saturday night, and it's ten shillin' a week for the first three month, risin' to fourteen shillin' and sixpence if you give satisfaction an' remain with us.'

'I see. Thank you very much,' Sara said, thinking that whilst ten shillings a week was dreadful, fourteen and six was not to be sneezed at. She turned to leave the office, hoping against hope that she would be able to find her way back to the main gate, for the laundry was immense. It included a huge courtyard criss-crossed with rope clothes lines, for in the bad old days the clothes had been hung outside, and a modern drying room where blasts of hot air from the furnace which heated the water dried the clothes in a surprisingly short space of time.

'You'll get your uniform on Monday . . . best be here by seven-thirty, so's you're ready for work by eight,' the supervisor said, stopping her in her tracks just as she reached the door. 'Did you see the uniform?'

It was the ugliest uniform imaginable, Sara thought sadly, but there you were. What was that quotation? *Better a dinner of herbs where love is* . . . Well, in her case it was better an ugly uniform and hard work where love was than coldness and a beautiful home.

Not that she expected to find much love in the laundry! The supervisor did not look the sort of woman who enjoyed much – probably her chief enjoyment, in fact, would come from bawling out those under her. No, the love would be provided by Gran, and for friendship and a sense of purpose, there was Clarrie Boote and the Army.

'I'll send for a clerk to show you out,' the supervisor said sourly as Sara's hand began to turn the door-knob. She walked over to the door, pushed past Sara and called out to the young man who had accompanied Sara across to the offices earlier. 'Mr Brown, take this person to the main gate.'

'No *please* from the old bat, you notice,' Mr Brown said ruefully as he accompanied her. He was a young man of about Sara's own age with red hair, freckles and a decided squint for which he wore large tortoiseshell-framed glasses. 'Did she introduce herself? Thought not, that's like the old bat. She's Miss Bateman, actually . . . the old bat to you and me now, Miss. And I'm Peter Brown – Pete to me pals.'

'I'm Sara,' Sara said rather shyly. She doubted that she would have much to do with someone as important as a clerk, though. Miss Bateman had made it pretty plain that packers were the lowest of the low. 'Will I work directly under Miss Bateman, Mr Brown?'

'You'll see 'er from time to time, but she ain't in the packin' room,' Mr Brown said reassuringly. 'Miss Todd is over you . . . she's awright is Miss Todd.'

Sara worked hard at the laundry for three months, from mid-January to mid-April. She found the work tiring and exacting – at least on her delivery bicycle she had been able to sit down on the saddle as she made her way from one part of the city to another – but she soon discovered that whilst her hands were busy her mind could be anywhere. Dreaming, in fact, made the job bearable. And also the fact that, after three months, her wages would considerably increase. Sara wasn't greedy by any means, but she found it very hard to manage on what the laundry paid her.

'It's not wharr I wanted for you, queen,' her grandmother had said when she returned on Saturday night after her first week, 'but I can't deny the money's a help. What are you doin' this evenin'?'

'I'm going along to the Barracks, with Clarrie. I'm joining the Songster Brigade and we're having a rehearsal. Remember Clarrie saying that Miss Gotts was in hospital and too ill to take part in fund raising and so on any more? She's been most awfully kind to me, Gran. Clarrie and I visited her in the Stanley last night and she's given me her uniform. We're roughly the same size and she said, if I could make use of it . . .'

'Oh, flower, does that mean you're a Salvationist, now?' Mrs Prescott said, looking distressed. 'But you've always gone to church!'

'I went to church because my parents took me, and when I moved in with you I went to chapel, because that was where you went. But I'm going to the Barracks for myself,' Sara said gently. 'I've never seen the point in a religion which simply paid lip-service to fairness and goodness. The Army don't do that, Gran. They work very hard for what they believe, and they sing hard too, and laugh hard!'

'Yes, I remember. I enjoyed my Christmas Day more than I've done for years,' Mrs Prescott admitted, a smile curling her lips. 'That Major . . . he'd ha' made a cat laugh!'

'I know. I love going to the services as well as to the singing,' Sara said. 'Why don't you come along sometimes, Gran?'

'Do you know, I believe I will?' Mrs Prescott said slowly. 'What was it somebody said? *Why should the devil have all the good tunes*?' She chuckled. 'And why should the stuffy, self-satisfied upper classes, who put money into a collecting tin and think that's sufficient, get all the best congregations? Yes, I'll come along to the Barracks with you on Sunday, see what I think of a proper service.'

That had been in January. Now it was April, and Sara, who was now an extremely quick packer, had been told to call at the office on her way home, to see Miss Bateman.

'My three months is up, so I should get a pay-rise,' she said excitedly to Liz, the girl who worked next to her on the packing bench. 'I could do with a few bob more. Gran and Clarrie and I manage all right, but it's by the skin of our teeth sometimes.'

'You *should* gerrit,' Liz said rather cautiously. 'But the old bat's mean as 'ell's 'ot, chuck. If she can see a way to get out of payin' you she'll grab it, I tell you straight.'

'I'm fast, I'm tidy and I've never arrived late or left early; let her find fault if she dare,' Sara said at once. 'What's more, I've gone to marking without a single moan when we're ahead with our work in here. And no one in their senses can stand marking.'

Marking was done in a small, hot room by a team of girls with special indelible pencils and reels of tape. On sheets and towels the customers' surnames and their laundry number were marked on the actual article, but on clothing a tape would be made and then stitched in where it would not be noticed. On the tail of a shirt, the hem of a nightgown, the waistband of pyjama trousers. Sara was no seamstress and very much disliked the pernickety, fiddly business of sewing on the tapes, though she thought the writing part was rather fun.

But it was the position of the marking room which made it so unpopular. It was right up against the offices, and Miss Bateman was forever popping in and criticising one's work, one's handwriting, the positioning of the tapes . . . Sara shuddered at the thought of being within reach of Miss Bateman whenever she was sent through there.

'You shouldn't write so nice and neat. You should cultivate sweaty 'ands, like I done. She never axed me to mark but once,' Liz said, her hands continuing to smooth and fold as she talked. 'Still, it's better than bein' sent to iron shirts what've been starched, I can tell you.'

When they were short in ironing Liz was often called for and though she grumbled, she took a pride in her work. Sara laughed at her.

'Oh, you! You shouldn't iron so beautifully, then. If you'd got any sense you'd rest the iron on a shirt-tail a moment too long, or turn cuffs under instead of over.'

'Yes, well. The money's not bad,' Liz said. 'Eh, look at the clock – we'll be 'eadin' 'ome in twenty minutes.'

'Via the offices,' Sara said. 'Come with me, Liz! I'll be really upset if the old bat tries to deny me that pay-rise.'

And half an hour later, when she came out of the supervisor's office, she was as upset as she had anticipated.

'The rise? Oh yes, I can have the rise. If I move to marking full-time,' she said furiously, her eyes big and shiny with unshed tears. 'So I said I'd rather stay in packing if she pleased and she said very well, but I'd have to work another three months on my present wages. Oh, Liz, and Gran and I have talked about what we'd do with the extra money . . . I thought I'd do an evening class, learn shorthand and typing.'

'Never mind; I dunno a single gal as gorra rise after three months,' Liz said consolingly as they walked down to the gate. 'She never lets anyone gerraway wi' that three months business, it's always six.'

'Hmm. Well, one of these days I'll find something else, something which pays more money for shorter hours,' Sara said darkly. 'And then won't I just tell her what to do with her job!'

Chapter Ten

June 1932

'Are you excited? I'm the most excited I ever was,' Polly said, stroking her mammy's dark curls. It was a fine June evening and having put young Ivan, protesting vigorously, to bed, the two females of the family were wedged into the windowseat of their living room, chatting quietly and occasionally turning to stare down at the other members of the family, indulging in a game of hurley in the street below.

'I believe you've mentioned that you're excited over the "do", if you can call a celebration of Mass at the Eucharistic Congress a "do", a grush o' times already today,' Mammy said drily. 'You've even worked Ivan up, and he a babe of three! He shouted at me when I put him into his bed that it weren't fair; he was too young for to join in the game of hurley and nor he couldn't go to the Mass tomorrow, and wasn't Phoenix Park his favourite place, now?'

'I'd have been down there too, so I would, playin' hurley wit' the fellers, only I'm to stay pure for the Mass tomorrow,' Polly observed, turning to look out of the window and bringing a snort of amusement from her mammy's lips. 'What's so funny, Mammy? You can't stay pure *and* play hurley with the boys, can you?'

'I don't think your purity would be affected by a game of hurley,' Mammy said. 'But never mind, I won't have you out there now, tirin' yourself out and your big day tomorrow. Come on now, tell me the rest.'

'Well, Sister says if we've not got white veils sure and wouldn't a piece of butter muslin do the trick fine? And we're to assemble by the Wellington monument at an ungodly hour . . . only she didn't say that, Tad said that . . . and we'll all be marched to our places and all the children in the whole of Ireland will be there, you betcha!'

'Don't talk American slang,' Mammy said disapprovingly. 'Or I'll stop you going to the tuppenny rush so I will. There's a lot of rubbish shown to kids these days, I know it.'

'You don't, because you never come to the fillums,' Polly said, rubbing her head against her mother's neck like a small, affectionate cat. 'I'm quite tired; am I all ready for tomorrow, Mammy? For the biggest day so far in me whole life?'

'You've got your veil, and your white dress, white shoes, white ribbon,' Mammy said, counting the items off on her fingers. 'Did the sister say to take your dinner or a drink? If all the children in Ireland are crammed into Phoenix Park won't you need a bite and a sup?'

'Sister said not to drink too much or we'd want to go, and sure no one would think of such a thing wit' all the holy fathers around,' Polly observed. 'But we can take a little bottle if we like.'

'To go into?' Mammy said, then laughed apologetically; her daughter's outraged glance told her she had overstepped the mark. 'No, of course not, how foolish I'm bein'. The sister means you to wet your whistle with cold tea when the Mass is over.'

'That's right,' Polly said sleepily. 'Will I go to bed

now, Mammy? Only I'm after callin' for Aideen before 'tis light, tomorrow mornin'.'

'Poor babe! Yes, all right. I'll come and tuck you up.'

'I'm not a babe, I'm eight,' Polly said, climbing down from the windowseat and knuckling her eyes with both fists. 'If tomorrow's me big day, and Aideen's big day, and Tad's big day, is it the biggest day in the whole world for children everywhere?'

'Well, no, because they aren't all going to a children's Mass in Phoenix Park, to see all the papal dignitaries,' Mammy said. 'Now come along, into bed wit' you and I'll bring you a hot drink. You'll sleep better and you won't need too much drink in the mornin'.'

'All right. Mammy, I wish I could stand near Tad tomorrow. But they're puttin' the boys one side an' the girls the other, Sister says it's only right. And besides, Tad's at the National School now and I'm at the Convent, and the nuns don't think we should mix even wit' the girls at the National,' Polly said drowsily. 'I'd sooner stand wit' Tad, Mammy.'

'What about Aideen? You wouldn't let Aideen stand all alone, would you, alanna?'

'No-oo, she could stand on me other side,' Polly observed. 'I'm so excited, Mammy, that I'll never sleep a wink all night; you do know that? Everyone in my class is so excited they won't sleep a wink, not a wink!'

'Sure, you won't sleep a wink,' Mammy said soothingly. And when she came back and Polly was sound asleep she only smiled, and drank the hot drink herself. But she did wonder, as she got ready for bed, whether it was right of her to pay out money to have Polly convent-educated, when the boys all went to the National School.

But a wee girl's different, she told herself resolutely as she climbed into bed beside her sleeping daughter.

Sure and haven't I always known she was a special child, God-given, so should have extra special care taken over her? Besides, ever since Polly began to talk about her guardian angel I've known that her sister, the one Brogan told me about, was still watching over her precious one. I wouldn't like to let that little girl down. And it's fine teachin' they get at the Convent, a grand education. Polly will turn out a real little lady so she will and that's what we all want.

Dawn breaks early in June and Polly was up in time to see the first light greying the sky. Mammy woke her, speaking low, stroking her face.

'Polly, me love, you'd best get up now. Aideen's mammy will be wakin' her, and Tad'll be stirrin', and you don't want to be last, do you?'

Polly came wide awake on the instant, eyes round, feet feeling for the rug.

'Has mornin' come, then? Oh, where's me white dress? I mustn't be late, I'd never forgive meself . . . hold on . . . is me bottle of cold tea ready? Sister says cold tea is good for us. Where's me veil? I need pins . . . oh, I haven't washed . . . I haven't brushed me hair . . . me teeth . . . oh janey, I'm in a state so I am!'

'Calm down, alanna,' Mammy said, laughing. 'Just do things one at a time, like you usually do – I've called you before the boys because you've got more to do. They're wearin' their best things, sure they are, but that doesn't mean white veils an' that. Now first, wash. The fire's lit and the water's warmin' in the kettle. Then clean your teeth, then brush your hair. I'll fix the veil and put a ribbon in presently. Now stop *worryin'*, for you're in good time, you won't be late. I'm sure Aideen isn't even up yet, and as for Tad, he'll be like

Bevin and Donal, he'll leave everything to the last moment. He'll still be snorin', I daresay.'

'Oh, but it's different for boys; boys don't care,' Polly said, flapping barefoot through into the kitchen and hopping with impatience whilst her mother took the kettle off the fire, poured hot water into a bowl and stood the bowl on the side table. 'And anyway, you know what Tad's mam and dad are like.'

'I do,' her mother said, fetching a clean piece of towel from the slatted shelf beside the fire. 'He'll get himself up and no fuss, either.'

'If he comes,' Polly said rather bitterly. 'He was sayin', after school yesterday, that wit' a million children there no one 'ud notice one feller less. I told him I'd kill him and never, never marry him if he missed a chance to clear out his immortal soul, but you know Tad.'

'I daresay his immortal soul will survive uncleared,' Mammy said, smiling and bending down to give the fire a poke. 'You're a bit young to be considerin' marriage, though, alanna.' She straightened, a hand to the small of her back, then took a piece of soap off the mantel and handed it to Polly . . . 'Wash well now, behind the ears an' all remember, for wouldn't you feel bad if the holy father thought to himself, *there's spuds that child could grow behind her little lug-holes*?'

Polly, washing, giggled. 'If he wants to see where spuds could grow he'd do better on the other side of the Park, where the boys are. There!'

'What d'you mean, *there*? If you think you're clean, Polly O'Brady . . .'

'Well, you do me nails, then,' Polly said grandly, holding out a small white hand whose black-rimmed nails made her mother moan beneath her breath. 'Sure an' I don't know how me nails do it when I keep the rest of me hands spicky-clean. Mammy, I am goin' to marry Tad, one day. We've agreed.'

'Oh well, if you've agreed, there isn't a thing I can say,' her mother said placidly. She began work on Polly's nails, using a sharpened matchstick. 'You could grow spuds in the stuff I'm gettin' out from here, young lady, I tell you! What on earth have you been doin wit' yourself?'

'Playin', mostly,' Polly said. 'Hurry, Mammy, hurry, I've not got me white dress on yet nor I haven't brushed out me hair nor put me veil on . . . I'll be late, I know I will!'

Polly trailed home from Phoenix Park later that day, head in the clouds, one hand firmly grasped by Mammy, the other by Bevin, for the whole of Ireland, it seemed, had congregated in the park that day and it would have been all too easy to get separated.

The older boys had made their own way home and because of the vast numbers Polly had been unable to find Tad, but Mammy, with Ivan in her arms, had stayed as close to the crowd of children as she could get and had pounced on Polly and Bevin the moment the service was over. Now they were making their way out of the park as fast as they could, the children, at any rate, eager to get fed and watered, for a hard biscuit and a sip of cold tea had been no substitute for a proper meal.

'Did ye see God, Polly? I saw 'm,' Ivan remarked as they made their slow way across the seemingly endless grass. 'Big an' white he was, wit' gold hair like yours, Poll. He was floatin' on a cloud smilin' an' beamin' down on all the pretty lickle girls an' the smart chisellers.'

Polly sighed impatiently. 'What an eejit you are, Ivan

O'Brady! You only see God when you die an' go to heaven. If you saw somethin' now 'twas an angel so it was.'

'Oh,' said Ivan, considering this. 'Well, I seed an angel, then. Did you see 'um, Polly?'

'I seen me own guardian angel,' Polly said loftily. She did not intend to be bettered in holiness by a child of three! 'More than once I've seen her. She takes good care of me, so she does.'

'A girl angel? There ain't no such thing as a girl angel,' Bevin put in loftily. 'Angels are big, hefty fellers wit' t'umpin' great wings. You wouldn't catch a puny weak girl carryin' wings like that – she'd founder at the first flap.'

'My guardian angel doesn't have wings,' Polly said at once, ruffling up like an angry turkey cock. 'My guardian angel doesn't need wings, she's got a shawl thing . . . she spreads it out like this . . .' she held out the skirts of her white confirmation dress, ' . . . and she can go anywhere in no time at all at all. She's me friend, my angel.'

'Oh, yeah? She sounds a quare ould wan to me,' Bevin said nastily. Holiness in such enormous quantities, Polly concluded, had been a bit much for her older brother. 'What's her name, then, Poll, if you're such pals?'

'Jess,' Polly said without a second's hesitation. Her mother stopped short so suddenly that Polly, lagging behind, bumped into the backs of her legs. 'That's her name, Jess.'

'Angels aren't called Jess,' the irrepressible Bevin said jeeringly. 'Are they, Mammy? Angels are called Gabriel, or – or Saint Something, not just Jess.'

'Don't argue about such things, Bev,' Mammy said, beginning to walk forward again. 'Anyone want to pop in to the chipper on our way home? I'll stand you all one and ones, for a treat.'

And with the happy prospect of a fish and chip supper, angels were forgotten, for the moment at least.

Sara did not have the pleasure of telling Miss Bateman what to do with her job quite as soon as she would have liked, but the opportunity came at last, though not before Sara had received the promised pay-rise.

As Miss Bateman had grudgingly promised, in July Sara's money was increased to fourteen and sixpence and things became a little easier.

'We're fine now, for the summer, but when winter comes we'll be scrapin' the bottom of the barrel again,' Gran said. 'Still, you've done awful well, Sara love. There's not many as bring in fourteen and six every Friday.'

Sara agreed that she was lucky, but she didn't feel it. She felt ill-used. She had tried and tried to get another job with absolutely no success. She had started evening classes but no employer wanted a young woman of nineteen who had only experienced evening classes and shop work. They could not offer her the sort of money they would offer a beginner, kind employer after kind employer told her. When you've got some office experience under your belt . . .

Yet when her chance came she did not, at first, recognise it.

She was at the Barracks, taking a Sunday school class because Miss Boote was otherwise engaged. It was a large class and the children were on their school holidays so they were bored, weary of the bad weather – it had rained all week – and consequently difficult to handle. They were poor children from the many slums in the area, but they were by no means lacking in spirit, or indeed, in inventive devilry, and Sara had already been sworn at and had a small offender standing in the corner from whence, whenever he thought her attention was elsewhere, he would turn round for a second, tongue hanging out like a Dix's carpet, and then turn back to face the wall once more, shaking with laughter.

'Have you finished your silent reading? Good, then we'll play a game,' Sara said presently, struck by a brainwave. 'It's a sort of hide and seek, only you won't have to leave this room. I used to play it when I was your age.' She took a piece of chalk and went over to the small blackboard, then after some thought, wrote the word 'Barracks' on the board.

'See that word? Well, it says "Barracks", doesn't it? But hiding inside that eight-letter word there are others, and you must find them and tell me how many words you think there are. The winner gets to choose the next long word. Do you understand?'

They understood and looked bored. They don't want to stretch their brains, Sara thought despairingly, they want to stretch their legs and their arms – they want a *real* game. But it's raining cats and dogs out there, I can't possibly let them play real hide and seek – this will have to do.

'Good. Then everyone who wins a round gets to write the next word on the board, and gets some dolly mixtures. I'll have to buy them on my way home, but . . . no, I've a better idea. The first one of you to get five points can run a message for me, down to Demarco's, and buy me the sweeties. Now come on, how many little words can you see in "Barracks"?'

A hand went up; slowly.

'Yes, Mark?'

'I see two, Miss.'

Another hand promptly began to wave.

'Three Miss, three if you count the "s" as one!'

'All right, Albert, give us your three.'

'Bar, Miss, like they 'ave in pubs, an' rack, like a clo'es rack, an' racks, more'n one rack.'

The kids laughed. They sat up straighter, their interest caught.

'What's the longest word you know, Albert? Because you have to write a good, long word on the board now.'

'Salvation, Miss . . . I can spell it, an' all.'

'Oy, Albert, wharrabout Colonel? Can you spell that, eh?'

'He's doing Salvation . . . come along, Albert, here's the chalk.'

Albert speedily got the necessary points and was despatched for dolly mixtures, these being the smallest sweets Sara could think of and thus the easiest to divide, and the game changed, at the suggestion of the small boy who had been in the corner for telling Miss Cordwainer that he would listen if he bleedin' well felt like it and not 'cos she told him to.

'If you lerrus use the letters in a different order, we could make an awful lorra words,' he said excitedly. 'Like "Carpet", what we only got three out of, like . . . if we'd changed the *order* o' the letters we could of made tea, pea, cat, crap . . . all sorts.'

Sara looked at him suspiciously; was he being rude again? But he was beaming at her, and she saw that he had a cheeky, intelligent little face and also that he was enjoying the challenge of using his mind, of sorting out the letters in a given word to form others.

'Well done, Andrew. Anyone else want to have a go?'

They were cautious about it, but after half an hour

the room rang with shouts as the children outdid each other, even the duller children being able to offer one or two suggestions once they understood the game.

And in the middle of this, a woman whom Sara had seen in church but never spoken to walked into the room.

'Miss Boote . . . oh, I beg your pardon, Miss Cordwainer, I didn't realise you were taking this class. Is everything all right?' She lowered her voice, moving nearer to Sara as she did so. 'It was the noise . . . I know what these children can be like, they aren't an easy class, and I thought poor Miss Boote might be glad of a third party, so in I came . . . but you all look very happy, I must say.'

'I'm sorry, Lieutenant,' Sara said, feeling her cheeks warming. 'But it isn't a game you can play quietly . . . we're word-making.'

The lieutenant turned and looked at the blackboard with its scribbled words, the main one above, the smaller ones below. She looked back at Sara, brows rising.

'These children are playing at word-making? Or are you doing the work for them?'

'No, indeed,' Sara said immediately. 'Every one of the small words has been suggested and written in by a pupil. And the latest main word, 'Songster', was Biddy Callan's.'

'*Biddy*? But I didn't think she could read or write,' the lieutenant hissed. 'She's the youngest of twelve, you know, and . . .'

'She may not be able to read or write, but she knew the word "Songster" and she can make little words from big ones by the sounds,' Sara explained. 'The girl sitting next to her, Annie, she helps, but Biddy does most of the work, really she does. Why don't you stay and watch for a moment?'

Lieutenant Marks stayed and the children, as children will, played up to this unexpected audience by giving of their best. One or two of the suggestions were a little near the knuckle but Sara passed over them and to her relief, though the lieutenant's eyes twinkled, she, too, pretended to notice nothing.

When another officer came in to say that Sunday school was over for the day and would the children like milk and biscuits before they left, he found the children in great form, sharing out a bag of dolly mixtures whilst Sara and the lieutenant chatted.

'I'm impressed, Miss Cordwainer,' the officer told her. 'These are difficult children, and you've kept their attention and kept them happily employed for two whole hours on a wet Sunday afternoon.'

'I've just said the same,' the lieutenant said, smiling. 'In fact I've just asked Miss Cordwainer if she would consider working with children. In a paid position, I mean.'

'And the upshot of it is,' Sara told her grandmother jubilantly when she got home that night, 'that Miss Marks has offered me a job, teaching! She runs a small school in the Walton Road area – it is fee-paying, but the Army sponsors most of the children – and she needs someone to teach the little ones, the children of five to around seven. She and her sister teach the older kids,' she added. 'Oh, Gran, what do you think?'

'It sounds very nice indeed, queen, far better than that laundry. But what 'ud they pay you, each week? I wish it didn't matter, but it does.'

'The salary is thirty-eight shillings a week,' Sara said, wide-eyed. 'It sounds too good to be true, doesn't it? But it isn't, it's what teachers are paid. And if I work hard and become qualified, I'll get more!'

'Aye, but you aren't qualified,' her grandmother

pointed out. 'What are the chances of gettin' qualifications, queen?'

'Well, I don't know. But I got my higher school certificate, or the equivalent, in Switzerland so Miss Marks is going to see what she can do. I believe there are teaching courses; if I could save up enough and go to college and pass the exams then I should be able to teach anywhere.'

Mrs Prescott had been sitting in the chair by the fire, shelling peas into an enamel colander, now she put the peas on the hearthrug and the colander on the nearest chair and held out her arms.

'Come and give your gran a big kiss,' she said. 'Oh, I'm so pleased for you, love! To leave that miserable laundry, and to gerra job where you'll be usin' your intelligence . . . it's what I've always wanted for you.'

'It's a dream come true,' Sara admitted. 'And tomorrow I'm going over to the offices to have a word with Miss Bateman!'

Time passes, time passes, Brogan told himself, sitting like a gentleman in a third-class carriage, bound for Liverpool. It's gettin' on for a year since I was last in the city and it's taken that long for me to want to go back. But it was true; time does not only pass, it heals, too. By March, Brogan had been able to admit that Sara had a perfect right to fall in love with a soldier if she so wished. By June, when his mammy's letters were full of this Eucharistic Congress and how beautiful Polly had looked in her communion veil, he had also been able to see that since he had never given Sara the faintest inkling of his own feelings, she could not possibly be expected to take him into account at all, far less consult him before getting herself a feller.

By the end of October, when the hunger marchers

were fighting the London bobbies and Ramsay MacDonald was 'urgently reviewing' the government's policies on unemployment, he was able to tell himself frankly that he simply could not be in love with a girl he'd met, at most, half-a-dozen times, most of the meetings being between himself, a young man, and the child she had been then.

And if, by some freak chance, he had been in love, then he had better pick himself up by the scruff of the neck and chuck himself out of love, give other girls a glance now and then.

So when Peader had said he was going back to Ireland for Christmas this year and invited Brogan to join him, Brogan decided he would, and that he'd go up to Liverpool a couple of days early. He hardly ever used the holiday to which he was entitled, why not ask for some time off now?

He did, and it was granted. Brogan's employers admired his dogged hard work, his handling of the enormous engines he drove, his even temper and the fact that, like his father, he rarely drank.

'Most railmen drink; 'tis the only relief from the tarble thirst you get from workin' in the engine cabs, and it eases the strain on your muscles when you've been luggin' great bundles an' boxes o' goods off the trucks,' one of the other men said to Brogan. 'Why not you, Brog?'

'Sure, I do drink,' Brogan had protested. 'But not the hard stuff. I'll have a glass of porter now and then . . . but I'm not wedded to the drink, like some of youse.'

And this time, maybe I'll go round to Snowdrop Street and get her out of me system once and for all, Brogan told himself as the train chugged nearer and nearer to its destination. Maybe I'll greet her as a friend, meet her young man, and get her off me mind and out of me heart, for until I do, I won't look at anyone else and that's God's truth.

Because Brogan was lonely. He could understand, now, his father's quiet longing to be back in Dublin, to hold his children on his knee, to share the fireside with his wife. Me daddy's a grand man, one of the best, he told himself now. To stay away, earnin' money, when he's all that love an' affection waitin' at home! Where does he find the strength?

But Peader was strong; Brogan had always known it. Peader knew he could go home, take up his life again, maybe even get a job, though that was uncertain. But once he was home the babies would start coming again, one a year, and Deirdre would start looking like all the other tenement wives – worn out, weary, weighed under by kids they could barely support, let alone bring up the way they wanted to.

'Sure an' I love your mammy and I'd do anythin' to stop that happenin', so I would,' Peader had said heavily, when they had been discussing going home again. 'But I'm a good Catholic an' she's a good Catholic . . . if you're together the babies just come. And how many fellers have jobs, in Swift's Alley? Half a dozen? And what do they earn? Nothing, compared to us, Brog. But bringin' me family over here, now . . . well, I'd do it like a shot – will do it, once I've put enough by to get a nice little home.'

'How much more do you need, Daddy?' Brogan asked. He had been contributing, lately, to that nice little home, because he was earning good money and scarcely spending any. Of course he had always sent money home, but even so his savings were mounting.

'I reckon another two years will see me sendin' for them,' Peader said contentedly. 'Eh, but I can't wait to see their faces when we've got a good little house with a bit of garden, near to the railway but not too near, and we're all settled down in it, snug as bugs in rugs.'

Brogan worried a bit because he knew his father had never mentioned such a move to Deirdre, and guessed that his mother would take some shifting, so she would. Niall and Martin were in good jobs now, Donal was bidding fair to be the first member of the O'Brady family to go on to further education – they talked about a degree – and even Polly was shining brightly in school and had her own circle of friends.

How would they transplant? And – the big worry – what if someone recognised Polly and wanted to take her away from the O'Bradys? It would break Mammy's heart, and Daddy's . . . and mine, for that matter, because I'm desperate proud of Polly so I am, desperate proud.

She was a lovely kid. Pretty, intelligent, lively. If anyone tried to take her away from us I'd kill 'em, Brogan thought with unaccustomed violence. So what'll happen if Daddy brings the family back to Liverpool?

He remembered the other child, the little girl who had told Sara she was searching for her baby sister. What had happened to her? Brogan knew the family had been thrown out of Snowdrop Street long ago for non-payment of rent. He had heard about it from a fellow railman, how Stan Carbery had blustered and hit the kids, shouted and yelled at everyone, whilst his wife had wept and begged him not to take it out on them for indeed it was no one's fault.

And from that day to this, there had been no word of them. Had they moved to cheaper housing somewhere, had Stan got a job, become respectable? If I tell Daddy we might lose Polly if he brings them across the water, will he change his mind? Sure and that would be a terrible thing to do, with him so desperate hungry for his Deirdre and their children. Could the Carberys all be dead, wiped out in some epidemic or other? He remembered them as a large family of hungry, impoverished children. Surely such a family would make some sort of mark on the community in which it lived?

Brogan sighed and decided he would ask around. And when they were in Dublin, over Christmas, he and Daddy would sound out the family on how each member felt about crossing the water. Niall wouldn't come, nor Martin. You didn't get a job in a bank, or a good position in the offices of Guinness, and then whistle them down the wind for a parental whim. Besides, Niall had a young lady, they were saving up to get married. No, Niall and Martin wouldn't come over, under any circumstances.

The train was slowing down now, though. Familiar sights began to pass slowly by outside the window; Lime Street station loomed, with the platform crowded with people either meeting this train or waiting for the next.

Brogan stood up and reached for his bag, then, because he always believed in helping those less fortunate – which, in this case, meant every other person in the carriage – he reached the rest of the luggage down.

'Journey's end, ladies,' he said pleasantly to the two dried-up little spinsters who had sat opposite him since Crewe, eating mints – in a very ladylike way though – and discussing, in faint, mouselike tones, what they would do for Christmas. 'Are you goin' on from here, or is Liverpool your destination?'

'We're continuing on to Crosby, by bus,' one of the ladies said. 'If you could see a porter, young man, we would be most grateful . . . our cases are heavy.'

'Sure, I'll give someone a shout,' Brogan said easily. 'And I'll put your cases on the platform meself.' He turned to the rest of the carriage. 'Anyone else need a hand, now?'

Sara had enjoyed her first term as a teacher mightily, but she had found it tiring, though why she should do so after her months in the laundry she could not understand.

'Leaving, Cordwainer?' Miss Bateman had said unbelievingly when she had gone into the offices to give a week's notice. 'Are you not satisfied with the wages we pay you? Packing is a simple job which any neat-fingered girl could undertake. You are well-rewarded by any standard.'

'Money isn't in question, Miss Bateman,' Sara said. She was tempted to drop the title, since Miss Bateman had done so from the moment Sara's job had started, but she thought she might need a reference one day – or a handkerchief laundered, she thought wickedly. Miss Bateman would launder a handkerchief nicely, but writing a letter of reference would probably be beyond her! 'I've obtained other employment.'

Miss Bateman's mousy eyebrows rose into her hairline.

'Really? Where, may I ask? Which of our competitors would be foolish enough to take on a girl as high and mighty and discontented as yourself?'

'Of course you may ask, Miss Bateman,' Sara said gently. 'But I'm afraid I shan't be answering. You phrased your question so rudely, you see.'

Miss Bateman goggled. There was no other word for it. Her tiny eyes seemed to start from their tiny sockets and her mouth formed a large, horrified 'O' of sheer disbelief. No one, Sara was sure, had ever answered her back before, let alone accused her of rudeness.

'Good afternoon, Miss Bateman,' Sara said, seeing that the older woman was, temporarily at least, bereft of words. 'I shall leave next Friday.'

She was halfway down the corridor and heading towards the big laundry room when the office door shot open behind her.

'Miss Cordwainer!'

So my title has been reinstated, seeing as how I'm leaving and joining the world outside the laundry again, Sara thought, amused. But she turned gracefully towards the office doorway, in which Miss Bateman was now framed.

'Yes, Miss Bateman? Did you call me?'

'You'll work until Saturday noon,' Miss Bateman said crisply. 'A full week is specified.'

Sara had said nothing. There was no point. She would wait until Friday, check her wage-packet, and then decide what to do. And anyway, working another five hours wouldn't hurt her.

But now, with Christmas fast approaching and the holidays soon to start, she found that she was exhausted. She had spent the last couple of weeks making Christmas decorations with her class, buying simple ingredients and showing them how to turn peppermint oil, icing sugar and cochineal into pink sugar pigs, cutting newspaper into strips, painting them and gluing them together to make paper chains. She had even taken four members of her class out to Fazackerley on the number twenty-two tram and from thence to Simonwood, where the five of them spent a wonderful day cutting holly and mistletoe from the woods and hedgerows to decorate the classroom.

And Gran was not well at all. Her rheumatism had

got worse and worse and now her joints were so painful that she could sometimes scarcely move. So when Clarrie made her suggestion Sara seized on it with delight.

'I'm goin' home for Christmas, to me folk in the country,' she told Sara one evening when they were up at the Barracks, cutting vegetables into cubes for soup. 'Well, I say country – it's Formby, in fact, which is more seaside, I suppose. I were wonderin' . . . would you and Mrs Prescott like to come home wi' me? Mam and Da would be tickled pink, they've heard so much about you both, and provided you don't expect nothin' grand, I think you'd enjoy it. Me mam's a great cook an' she loves entertainin'. They're Army, of course,' she added. There's a Hall not too far from my parents' place, so we can go there for the Christmas services and so on.'

'Oh, Clarrie, it sounds wonderful,' Sara said eagerly. 'I'm awfully worried about Gran, you know. Her rheumatism seems to be getting worse so rapidly. Dr Mac says he'll take her into hospital for a few days, try to get a better idea of why this stiffness has come on so suddenly, but Gran says she won't go. She says there's nothing they can do so why don't they just let her struggle on. And aspirin helps, apparently. And she's got some awful smelly stuff she says the cab drivers used to use on their horses . . . that helps, too.'

So on Christmas Eve they set out for Formby, not on the tram but on a crowded service bus.

'It's better for all this luggage,' Clarrie said, eyeing the boxes and bundles her guests had brought with them and shoved under the seats and piled in the aisle with some dismay. 'Wharron earth have you gorrin there, the pair of you?'

'Christmas cakes, Christmas puddings, a box of fruit,

two steak and kidney pies . . .' Sara began, counting them off on her fingers and only laughing when Clarrie said mockingly: 'Coldhamcoldbeefpickledgherkins-salad . . .'

'No quotin' *The Wind in the Willows*, 'cos it were my copy you read, cleverclogs. As for the grub, we wanted to make a contribution,' Mrs Prescott said. 'God above knows how long my fingers will flex enough to make pastry and cakes, so I'm usin' me gift whiles I can.'

'Oh, keep your fingers active at all costs,' Sara begged, twinkling at her grandmother. 'If you stop cooking we'll go and live somewhere else, won't we, Clarrie? Because you're the best cook in the whole world, Gran.'

'Oh, you're safe for a bit,' Mrs Prescott assured her. 'So far it's just me knees, me shoulders and me back . . . what's left is workin' fine.'

'Then sit back and enjoy the scenery,' Sara said. 'Oh, isn't it wonderful to be going away for a holiday? Especially into the country and beside the seaside, all at the same time – I feel really adventurous!'

'Don't give us none of that – you've lived in Switzerland, you know about travel, Miss Boote remarked. 'I wonder what me mam's got for us teas?'

'Gran, are you awake?'

Sara and her grandmother were sharing a bed in the Bootes' back room, which had been converted into a bedroom because Gran couldn't manage the extraordinarily steep and narrow stairs. They had eaten a grand tea with potted shrimps and boiled ham, potatoes from Mr Boote's own allotment and milk from the farm down the road.

'Lovely to have it fresh, instead o' tinned,' Clarrie

said. 'Though it's easier to use tinned at the Barracks; it don't go off as fast.'

'Well, the apple pie's prime,' Mr Boote observed. 'You're a genius with pastry, Mrs Prescott, and I'm a good one to judge, for until I tasted your apple pie I'd ha' said Mrs Boote had no equal; now I'm not so sure.'

Great hilarity all round, especially from Mrs Boote, who was very like her daughter to look at, small and plump with kindly eyes.

And the evening had continued in the same vein. They had played cards, betting with matchsticks because, Mrs Boote said, the Army had seen too much of the seamy side of betting to agree with it. Then they had tea and mince pies, and Mrs Prescott assured Mrs Boote that she hadn't met her match for marvellous, light pastry.

'I'm not denyin' I'm good,' she said solemnly, 'But you're better, Mrs Boote, and I never thought I'd say that to a livin' soul.'

So now, lying in the strange bed, Sara kept her voice low.

'Gran, are you awake?'

'Just,' came the muffled reply from under the sheets. 'But 'twon't last, queen, for I'm very tired.'

'Aren't they nice, the Bootes?'

'They're grand people. She's been a good friend to us, has Clarrie. I won't feel so bad, leavin' you, with them to give an eye.'

'Leaving me?' Sara sat up in bed, cold dread flooding over her. 'What do you mean, Gran?'

'Well, queen, I'm no chicken. One of these days I'll leave you – you must have known that!'

'Oh . . . one of these days, yes, I suppose . . . but the way you said it, it sounded close, somehow,' Sara said uneasily. 'Don't scare me, Gran, by talking like that. I don't know what I'd do if you weren't waiting for me when I come home.'

'Well, I'll be around for a while yet, no doubt,' her grandmother said comfortably. 'Unless you kill me off by keepin' me awake all night, that is!'

She laughed and after a second's hesitation Sara joined in. But the seed had been sown, and Sara knew her grandmother was right. Mrs Prescott was seventy-three and no longer as strong as she had been and she had to warn her granddaughter not to expect her to live for ever.

So she's just being practical, Sara told herself, heaving the sheet up over her shoulders, and I must be practical, too. Gran's old; I mustn't set so much store by her company that I go to pieces when she dies. I've got to learn self-sufficiency, as Gran once did – as Clarrie has.

But she knew, as she felt sleep overtaking her, that it would not be easy.

She wasn't there again, of course. Brogan went round and knocked on the door as soon as he and his father had finished their supper on Christmas Eve and no one answered, though the neighbour poked her head round the door. It wasn't the same girl as last time but a younger, prettier one. She smiled at Brogan.

'Hello – they're away. Gone for Christmas. They'll be back day after Boxing Day.'

Brogan groaned. 'Oh lor, and I'm off meself in the morning, to Dublin on the boat. Isn't that just me luck, now?'

'Well, when will you be comin' back?' the girl asked curiously. 'Can you not pop round then?'

'I might,' Brogan said cautiously. 'Only . . . is things

the same? Have Sara and her gran gone away wit' her army friend?'

'That's it,' the girl said. 'Gone to stay wi' the parents, Mr and Mrs Boote, as 'ouse guests.' She sighed enviously. 'They'll 'ave a gay old time, I reckon.'

'I'll try an' come round again when I'm passin' through on me way back to Crewe,' Brogan said, trying to sound firm and resolute but merely succeeding, he thought, in sounding offended by Sara's absence. He had taken off his cap when the girl had first spoken, now he replaced it on his head. 'Season's greetings to you, Miss,' he finished.

Walking down the road, hands in pockets, head down, Brogan tried to tell himself that he should take this as a warning. Sara was obviously living in the pocket of this Boote person, he couldn't blame her, but he had best forget her.

After all, I didn't do a thing to keep meself in her mind; I didn't even write, he reminded himself. Only letters were so hard, you had to put on paper things you wouldn't mind saying, but didn't fancy seeing in black and white.

He was home at his father's lodgings before the dark depression hit him, mocking him with his total inadequacy, his stupidity, the sheer absurdity of expecting a girl like Sara to take a feller like him seriously. He sat glowering in the chair by the fire and Peader, assuming that his son, like himself, was suffering all the awful pangs of extreme homesickness and was unable to bear the thought of waking, tomorrow morning, with only the voyage on the ferry ahead of him instead of the usual jollities of Christmas Day, said they'd best be off to bed, for they'd a long day ahead of them tomorrow.

'I've a long life ahead of me, and I don't know what

I'm goin' to do wit' it,' Brogan said morosely. 'I'm sick an' tired of bein' alone, Daddy, sick an' tired.'

'Never mind, boy,' Peader said bracingly. 'By this time tomorrow we'll be in the bosom of our family – for a whole week!'

And if Brogan's smile was not as wide as it could have been, Peader was too absorbed in his own happy anticipation to notice.

Christmas in Dublin would have gone well but for the vexed question of the family crossing the water. Deirdre, when it was put to her, did not show any of the enthusiasm at the thought of being with her man again, living as a proper family once more, which Peader had confidently expected. Instead she pulled a doubtful face; sure and wasn't she Dublin born and bred? She'd never considered leaving the area, she was happy here, knew everyone, was known by everyone. She didn't want to end up living in a foreign country, not understanding the people, not knowing the customs, longing all the time for Dublin, the Liberties, even for Swift's Alley and the neighbours she had known all her life.

And Peader, who never grumbled, who had lived alone in England now for twelve years, suddenly saw red – he, who had never shouted, never thrown his weight about, actually shouted, went red in the face so that veins stood out on his forehead!

'*You* don't want to live in a foreign country? *You* won't understand the people, or know the customs? What about me, you selfish bitch? Haven't I lived there for a dozen years, sent all me money home, been heartsick for Dublin, for you, for me kids . . . and haven't I stayed there, regardless, so's you could be happy, have a decent life? Yet when I ask if you could come over the water to be with me, what do you say?' Peader put on a squeaky voice: '*Oh, Peader, but amn't I Dublin born and bred? What would I do in a foreign country, knowin' no one? How would I live, not understandin' their ways?*' He reverted to his own voice. 'In twelve years, Deirdre, I've never laid an eye or a hand on another woman, I've t'ought of you every night, every mornin'. But by God, if you won't come back wit' me, then that's goin' to change so it is!'

Polly, who had been curled up on the hearthrug, leaning against Delilah, with Lionel purring on her lap, stared with big eyes at this sudden and unexpected parental storm. Her father had used a bad word – worse, he had used it to describe her mother who was the best person in the whole world! And what had happened to their lovely Christmas contentment? It had vanished the moment Daddy started talking about them living in Liverpool so they could all be together. But now Mammy was crying and Daddy was quiet, his big hands resting on his knees, his eyes cast down.

'Mammy,' Polly ventured. 'What's Liverpool like?'

'I don't know, alanna, and I don't want to know . . .' Mammy began but this, it appeared, was too much for Daddy. He crashed out an oath and jumped to his feet.

'I'm not stayin' where I'm not wanted,' he said thickly. 'I'm for the pub – are you comin', Brogan?'

Brogan never argued with anyone and now Polly saw that he looked acutely unhappy. But then he seemed to remember something, and he stood up.

'I'll come wit' you, Daddy,' he said. 'Mammy needs time to think – and to remember, perhaps.'

It sounded threatening. Mammy thought so too, for she gave another strangled sob and held out her hands to Brogan, but he turned and left the room in his father's wake, only casting one quick, comforting glance at Polly. *It's nothin', really,* the look seemed to say. *They'll be over it in a trice, alanna, and kissin' an' huggin' by bedtime.*

It would have been nice had she believed it, but the minute the door closed behind them Mammy ran over to her, picked her off the hearthrug and gave her a fierce, rib-cracking hug.

'Sure an' you wouldn't want to go over the water to Liverpool, would you, my darlin' girl?' she said coaxingly. 'It's a cold, dark country, England, full of cold, dark people. They don't sing, nor worship, nor even speak as we do. Ah, you'd be unhappy far from your school, from Aideen . . . from Tad, for that matter. Say you'd rather stay here, wit' your mammy.'

'I'd rather stay wit' you, Mammy,' Polly whispered, but she felt a traitor even saying it. Brogan and Daddy were so good, they worked so hard, Mammy was always saying she wanted them back in Dublin again. Well, they couldn't come back, Daddy had explained it so that even Polly understood. But they could go to him. He had said a house in the country, a bit of a garden . . . a good life. Was that so terrible? Was it so bad to live in another country, when you were living with someone you loved?

But Mammy was crying again, great big tears were coursing down her cheeks and plopping on to poor Delilah, who looked up, eyes heavy with reproach. He wanted his warm and cuddly Polly back on the rug, and Lionel, stalking indignantly towards him having been tipped unceremoniously off Polly's small lap, was making him nervous. Delilah's large, tent-like ears quivered apprehensively upright as he wondered what the ginger cat might do to him, when Lionel got close enough.

'Your mammy's not a selfish . . . a selfish person, is she, Polly?' Mammy was saying between sobs. ''Tis your daddy's who's the selfish one, threatenin to take me across the water – me, a Dublin rose, to be torn up by me roots and planted in cold Liverpool soil . . . oh, I cannot, cannot bear it!'

'Daddy won't make you go, Mammy,' Polly said. She found she was crying herself – oh, Mother of God, what a great baby she was, thank heaven Tad wasn't here, for devil a bit of sympathy would she get from him, for blubbin' like a baby just because her mammy was doing the same. 'Daddy's good an' kind, you've always said so. He sends all his money home, the dote, an' he's not a drinkin' man, either, thanks to all the saints.'

Hearing her own words quoted back at her stopped Mammy in her tracks. She sniffed, wiped her nose on the back of her hand, then began dabbing at her eyes with the linen runner which stopped the Brylcreem from the boys' heads getting on the nice chairs.

'He *is* good and kind, alanna. So why does he want to make me so unhappy?'

It was unanswerable, of course. But even as she spoke, Mammy loosened her grip slightly and Polly slid through her hands like a trout through water and landed back on the hearthrug where she immediately flung her own arms round Delilah and gave him a kiss right on the end of his wet, black nose.

'Dear Delly,' she said against his soft face. 'Shall we go a walk? It's Christmas night, we might see Santy Claus – or the banshee!'

'Oh, bugger the banshee,' Mammy shouted suddenly, as Polly got to her feet. 'You're not goin' out there alone and leavin' me here, so miserable? Ivan's been asleep this past hour and the boys aren't home yet . . . I don't want to be here alone!'

'But Delilah's got to go out for his last visit,' Polly

pointed out primly, conveniently forgetting the many times she had whined to Donal or Martin to take the dog out for her because it was cold outside and she was terribly tired. 'When he was a little puppy you said to me, you said, "Who's goin' to take him out at dead o' night for his last visit?" and I telled you then I would, so I have to, of course.'

'Oh, all right, leave me then,' Mammy said wearily. 'I'm goin' to bed.'

And for the first time ever that she could remember, Polly came back to the house, fresh and tingling after a brisk run through the streets with one hand on Delilah's shaggy head, to find her mother actually in bed and to all intents and purposes, asleep.

I wonder should I jump in beside her? Polly asked herself as she changed out of her clothes into the shift she wore in bed. Only she did say I was to have the mattress in the livin' room, and I could lie it on the sofa if I'd a mind.

When she was in her shift Polly went and poured herself a drink of water and then pulled out the mattress. Her bedding was folded up on top of it and she shook it out, hoping that Daddy and Brogan would come back in before she was asleep so that one or other of them could sit by the fire and read her a story. She was perfectly capable of reading herself a story, of course, but Mammy had formed the habit of story-reading when Polly had been small and somehow the habit had continued – and Ivan loved the stories too, which was nice. The two of them sat on either side of Mammy, thumbs in mouths, and listened in perfect amity for once. And then sleep came so much quicker and easier, with lovely story-thoughts churning gently round in your brain and all your worries banished.

But the clock on the mantel ticked and tocked and

the pendulum swung hypnotically and Lionel, curled up in the crook of Polly's knees, purred so deeply and vibrantly that soon keeping awake was more than Polly could cope with. Her eyelids drooped, firelight dazzled on the lids, thoughts slowed . . . and she slept.

She was woken by soft voices; men's voices. Brogan and Daddy. She did not want them to know she was awake so she opened a crack of her eye and peered at the clock on the mantel first. It said three o'clock in the morning – she had scarcely known there was such a time! And Daddy and Brogan were sitting on either side of the fire, in the good chairs, talking.

'Daddy, I know how you miss her, I know, none better.' Brogan was saying. 'I don't know the hunger, because I'm a single feller, but I know the missin'. In me own way I miss the kids, too, specially Polly. But Daddy, would it be fair to take the littl'un back to Liverpool? There's that to consider when you're thinkin' it out, too.'

'No need.' That was Daddy's voice, dark and flat with despair, but with a slur to it that Polly had never heard before. 'Deirdre won't cross the water; mebbe I shouldn't have asked her.'

'You had every right,' Brogan said, his gentle voice almost angry. 'Every right in the world, Daddy. Mammy cannot realise, she cannot have thought, of what you've done for our family. Why, you've been after givin' them the best years of your life, and when Mammy thinks on, she'll be shamed by what she's said tonight.'

'I called her a selfish bitch,' Daddy said dully. 'When I know in me heart she's the most generous woman who ever walked this earth. Why did I do it, Brogan? Why did I set my tongue to words I'm ashamed of? It wasn't the drink for I'd not touched a drop, as you well know.'

'Well, you've touched a drop now, so don't go maudlin on me,' Brogan said, with humour in his voice. 'You've a hard head on you, Daddy, for you drank enough porter to drown a better man – I never seen anything like it in all me puff. Now shall I be helpin' you into bed? Or will you jump in as you are?'

'I'll wake Deirdre,' his father said crossly. ''Tis a wife's duty to help her man to bed when he's had a few. If I'd been like other men she'd have been helpin' me to bed these many nights . . . and suitin' me when I got there, too.'

'Daddy, hold your tongue or you'll be sorry in the mornin'.' Brogan was laughing, Polly could tell. 'Suitin' you, indeed – you sound like Father O'Leary when he's got one of his hell-fire preachin' moods on him. Go on, I'll give you a hand out o' them trousers.'

'You will not!' Daddy sounded as though he'd suddenly come wide awake. 'What if the child woke? I'll go to me bed now, Brog, and 'tis time you went to yours. You'll be sharin' wit' Donal an' Ivan. Don't squash 'em in the night; I was always afeared to squash 'em when they were babbies an' slept in our bed.'

'I won't squash anyone, Daddy.' Brogan was laughing again. 'By the waters of Liffey, you'll have a head on you in the mornin', no error. Night, now.'

'Night, son,' Daddy said, and Polly heard him fumbling his way out of the room. Then she heard voices murmur for a few minutes, then silence.

After a few moments she opened her eye another crack and risked a peep. Brogan was damping down the fire. He was still grinning to himself. Perhaps it won't be so bad as it seemed, earlier, Polly thought hopefully. Grown-ups is so strange, perhaps by morning they'll have forgot they quarrelled.

Presently, the rosy glow of the fire damped, Brogan took the candle, which had guttered low in any case, and left the room. Polly could hear him moving around for a while, then she heard the bed creak, and then there was silence.

What a day this has been, Polly thought suddenly. Mammy and Daddy had a fight with words, the first ever, and Daddy had too much porter and talked in a funny way, the first ever for that, too. Then they said more about Liverpool than they ever had before . . . and we might go and live there, when Daddy's saved up enough money to buy a little house with a garden.

But that would mean leaving Tad, her thoughts continued. Sure an' I can't do that, not wit' Tad and me marryin', the way we said when we're old enough. But then she wouldn't marry until she was old . . . twenty, maybe . . . so she might as well live in England as here, until then.

But three in the morning, after all the excitements of Christmas Day, is not a good time for lying wakeful. Before she had done more than remind herself what an odd day it had been, Polly was asleep once more.

'Peader, me dear love?'

'Sorry, I was tryin' not to wake you,' Peader mumbled, dealing with his own trousers, darkness and all, for despite his brave words to his son he did not fancy his chances of getting Deirdre out of bed to undress him just because he was a mite the worse for drink. 'Go back to sleep now, I'll manage.'

'Peader, I've been lyin' here thinkin'. Never was there a better man alive than yourself, nor a more selfish, cowardly ould wan than me.'

Even with his head thick from too much porter and his soul aching from too much plain speaking, Peader chuckled. His young and pretty wife, who so deeply resented the Dublin habit of referring to the woman of the house as 'the ould wan' that she had forbidden her sons to use it, could not prevent her tongue turning traitor on her when she was deeply moved.

'Well, alanna, and I'm sorry I said what I did so I am, for I know well that it was the shock made you speak as you did. If I could come home to stay . . . but my darlin' girl, my little colleen, I'd not turn you into the chief wage-earner again, whiles I ran from ship to ship searching for work, or sweated my guts out on the railways, earnin' less in a month than I do in a week across the water.'

'No, I know you wouldn't.'

Peader, his outer clothing removed, climbed carefully into bed beside his wife. He lay down, then turned and took her in his arms, half-afraid she might pull away.

But she did not. She lay, almost purring, in his embrace and then began to say again that she was sorry, that she had not meant . . . that she would go with him to the ends of the earth if that was what he wanted.

'And sure no one'll know our Polly for any but our child,' she said breathlessly, arching her body against his. 'Ah, Peader, say you forgive me!'

'Forgive? We both spoke hastily, out of turn,' Peader said. It was all he could do to keep his hands still on her, he longed for her with such violence, such heat! 'Now we'd best sleep, alanna, for I'm goin' to have a thick head in the mornin', me son says.'

'Are you not goin' to love me?' Deirdre said in a small, coaxing voice. 'Ah, love me, Peader, show you forgive me for the wicked t'ings I said!'

Peader hesitated – and was lost.

'I forgive you, my own, my sweetheart,' he told her. He let his hands run gently over her sweet, smooth body, anticipating what was to come. 'Oh, Deirdre, I've wanted you so, longed for you so!'

'Do you think I've not spent nights cryin' because you're far away, not able to comfort me?' his wife said softly. 'Ah, Peader, 'tis no life for either the one nor the other, kept apart. You are right and I was wrong. When you're ready for me, I'll cross the water for you.'

He sighed deeply and then squeezed her hard, not heeding her laughing, breathless protest.

'You're the only woman I'll ever want, ever look twice at,' he whispered. 'Kiss me, Mrs O'Brady!'

Chapter Eleven

September 1933

Sara woke early, which was unusual because it was Saturday and Saturday, so far as she was concerned, was a real day of rest. On Sundays she went to church at the Barracks, taught Sunday school and helped with the dinner which was served to those who would otherwise not receive one. She loved Sundays because she was with her friends and doing work which she enjoyed and knew to be useful, but Saturday was the day she indulged herself. A lie-in, a trundle round the shops pushing Gran in her wheelchair, a cold meal at midday, a trip to the cinema to see the latest Hollywood epic, a good high tea with a couple of boiled eggs, or potted shrimps, or a piece of smoked haddock . . . yes, Saturdays were good days.

Sara lay where she was for a moment; what had woken her? Then she remembered. Of course! Today was moving day.

Ever since the previous Christmas, Gran had been finding it more and more difficult to manage for herself. Finally, at Easter, the doctor had told Sara that she would do well to try to move her grandmother into a small flat or a bungalow.

'Your grandmother has rheumatoid arthritis; her joints are almost immovable already, though her mind is both lively and active. She's managing quite well now, but if she could cut out the stairs her life would be far more comfortable. You've only the parlour and the kitchen downstairs in Snowdrop Street, and there is a step to negotiate to get out of the front door, so converting would be difficult, if not impossible. But get her on one floor, in a property where the wheelchair can be used indoors, and I believe she'll flourish for many years to come.'

Sara nodded. She had noticed how hard it was now for Gran to heave herself up the stairs and how exhausted she was after each fresh attempt.

'You rent the house in Snowdrop Street? Then it should be possible for you to make a move. If you could get something near the school where you teach, then you would find things easier all round.'

'I'll have a try,' Sara had promised. 'I'll ask the Army whether they know anywhere suitable.'

The Army ran what they called eventide homes for old people, but she knew without even asking that Gran would not be happy in such a place. The trouble was, the disease had attacked her whilst she was still a busy and bustling housewife. She would not be content to sit all day with other old people, who were just waiting for the next meal. And anyway, Sara did not want her grandmother to become bedbound a moment before she was forced into it.

That night, as the two of them were serving in the soup kitchen, Sara had told Clarrie what the doctor had said.

'So I'll be looking round for somewhere nearer the school,' she explained. 'Will you come with us, Clarrie? It'll be nearer for you as well, since school and your bank are quite close.'

'I'll go wherever you an' Mrs Prescott go,' Clarrie said at once. 'You oughter get somewhere without too much trouble, things being the way they are.' She jerked her head at the line of people waiting to be served. 'There's more of 'em every night,' she said quietly. There's more people out of work every day, folk goin' broke, wages being cut. Look at that queue.'

Sara nodded. She had noticed that all the Army's soup kitchens were now being attended by large numbers of people who would once have scorned to accept a bowl of free soup and a hunk of bread. The Depression was biting deep in Liverpool and many were out of work or existing on tiny wages. Sara's own salary had been cut because numbers of children attending the school had dropped sharply. Parents who could scarcely feed their families had to put their children into the state schools rather than use their pitifully small resources on even the cheapest of private education.

Clarrie, however, asked to take a cut in her salary, had faced the bank manager out and refused point-blank.

'I'm cheap any'ow,' she said firmly. 'I do the work of a feller but you don't think to pay me a feller's salary, even though I'm not livin' wi' me parents so I 'ave the same expenses as a feller. If you cut me money then I won't be able to live in lodgings, see? And me parents live too far out; it wouldn't make economic sense for me to come all the way here to work.'

The bank manager had, as Clarrie put it, 'huffed and puffed a bit', but he had not tried to reduce her salary again.

So Sara and Clarrie had set out to find a more convenient house which they could afford, and ended up well-satisfied. An Army family, living in Florence Street, found themselves in financial difficulties after the husband lost his job. He was a builder by trade however, and instead of haunting the labour exchange he set to and converted his small home into two flats.

So, hearing, on the Army grapevine, of Sara's plight, Mrs Flaherty offered to let them rent the ground-floor flat which, she assured them, would be plenty big enough and would be ready for them to move in shortly.

'Me an' Bernie will manage fine wi' the top flat,' she said eagerly. 'Oh, Miss Cordwainer, you don't know what a weight off me mind it would be to 'ave at least some money comin' in regular.'

'Well, it doesn't seem much,' Sara said doubtfully, but she, her grandmother and Clarrie felt that, if they all contributed, they would be able to manage.

'It would be a life-saver,' Mrs Flaherty said. 'And seeing as you're Army we'd be on the same footin', in a way. But come round an' tek a look, Miss Cordwainer, see what you think.'

Sara and Clarrie had gone round the same evening, and were delighted with the flat. It was well-planned and would allow them a bedroom each, and a small living kitchen. Best of all, though, when Sara explained to Mr Flaherty that her grandmother was in a wheelchair and finding walking very difficult, he immediately said he could build a water closet on the kitchen, so that Mrs Prescott would not have to go out in the cold to spend a penny.

In due course they had taken Mrs Prescott to view the accommodation and, as Sara had anticipated, she was charmed with the flat.

'I don't want to use me wheelchair more than I need,' she said, eyes shining as she looked round the tiny kitchen. 'But I can gerrit in here, if I've a mind. I'll be able to whizz out to the shops if I want . . . no difficulty manoeuvring me wheelchair through that nice wide doorway! And the kitchen's so neat – everything to hand – that I'll be able to do me cooking, I'm sure I shall!'

'And if you don't feel up to it, Mrs Flaherty will give you a hand,' Sara said tactfully. 'It couldn't be better, really, because though I *could* come home at lunchtime, it would put Miss Marks out.'

'And there's the Victory Picture Palace, only a couple o' doors away,' Mrs Prescott said, pursuing her own train of thought. 'I could go there every afternoon, if I had a mind.'

'And if I'm needed, the school's no distance,' Sara agreed. 'Clarrie's bank is no distance, either. And the Barracks is handy, too.'

'And the Flahertys are my type of people,' Mrs Prescott added. 'We'll do all right here, chuck.'

So now it was moving-in day. Sara got out of bed and looked around her, at the room she had shared with Gran for months now, but found she had few regrets over moving to Florence Street. She had grown fond of Walton, and agreed with her grandmother that it would be good to live in such a lively part of the city.

She washed quickly at the washstand, trying not to splash, then dressed, but by the time she finished her grandmother had woken up. In fact she had swung her legs out of the bed and was trying to get her slippers on.

'Don't bother, Gran,' Sara said, kneeling down beside her. 'I like to help you to dress, you know I do, and besides, it's far too early for you to be up!'

'Oh well, if you insist,' Mrs Prescott said, letting Sara help her back into bed. I tell you, growin' old tries a body's patience, queen. Are you goin' to get me a nice cuppa?'

'I am. And then I'll give you a hand with dressing, your shoes are difficult I know, and then we'll start getting ourselves organised. Thank goodness the stuff's all in boxes and tea-chests, all we've really got to do today is to see that old Mitchell doesn't break half the china and glass whilst he's loading it on to his cart and count the tea-chests in and out. And once Mitch is away Clarrie and I will give the place a brush through and then we'll all get a taxi round to Florence Street.'

If it weren't for me you could have managed on the tram,' Mrs Prescott observed as Sara crossed the living room and headed for the back kitchen. 'Eh, it'll be strange not living in Snowdrop Street – I've been here almost fifty years, you know. Still, I'm not far from me old pals, they can come visiting if they've a mind. And it's not often I ride in a taxi . . . I'll feel like royalty!'

The move, contrary to Sara's expectations, went like clockwork and by three that afternoon they were in their new home, and very tidy it looked, with the furniture in place, the curtains up, and the brand-new linoleum laid. Sara had suggested taking the Snowdrop Street linoleum with them but Mrs Prescott had been firm.

'It's been on the floors fifty years, queen, it won't move. We'll leave it for the new people,' she said. 'We'll go down the Scottie; a couple of rolls of linoleum won't break us and it's nice to have a clean floor to start out.'

But they took the living-room carpet, old though it was, and it came up clean, without any fuss or bother.

'Buy the best and you'll not regret it,' Mrs Prescott said now, surveying the old carpet and her decent sofa and chairs. 'Looks right homely, don't it?'

The girls agreed that it did and bustled about lighting a fire, getting the tea and generally making themselves at home.

'I'm taking the *War Cry* round tonight, though,' Sara said quietly to Clarrie as they worked. 'Can you stay with Gran, Clarrie? Only I don't want to leave her alone on her first evening in a new place.'

Clarrie agreed that she would stay in, so at seven o'clock Sara put on her uniform and set off for the Barracks.

The place was bustling, as usual. Adjutant Edcott, a middle-aged lady with rather unlikely black hair, came over as soon as she saw Sara.

'Ah, Miss Cordwainer,' she said heartily. 'You and I are doing the local public houses this evening and it's your first time, isn't it? Mostly the men are pleasant to us, but one or two can use language . . . do you blush easily?'

Sara nodded, feeling her face grow hot, but Adjutant Edcott only laughed.

'I see you do,' she said, still chuckling. 'Well, well, it's a very pretty blush. My own attitude to bad language overheard in public houses is that I'm not on my own turf, so I can't object. As you know, dear, nice women don't frequent such places so the men feel they can blaspheme freely. Will that worry you?'

'I hope not,' Sara said. 'But Adjutant, you should hear some of the children at school when they don't know there's a teacher about. Their language would make your hair curl, honestly it would.'

'Well, there you are, then. You won't mind the odd naughty word. And the men are generous, particularly those who are . . . well, a little merry, should we say? Yes, it's amazing what they'll put into the collecting tin. And a good job too, because we need every penny we can get in these hard times. Shall we set out?'

'I'm ready,' Sara said, checking the seams of her

stockings by twisting round and staring down at them. 'I like to look neat when I'm out and about, don't you?'

'I do. We owe it to the Army, I always think. Very well, Cordwainer; best foot foremost now!'

Together, the two women marched along the pavement and into the first public house they reached.

'We're doing very well,' the adjutant said after an hour or so had passed. 'My dear, you're becomingly flushed, I'm sure that's why your tin is so heavy. A critic once said to me that it was immoral, taking young girls into public houses to persuade drunken sots to part with their cash, but that's not how I see it. It makes the men feel good to see a pretty girl, they find it easier to pay up, and giving to charity is good for one's immortal soul. See?'

'Considering how many people are out of work I think we've done well to get as much as we have,' Sara said later, as they crossed the road, heading for another public house. 'And people have been quite polite, too. It hasn't been too bad at all.'

She did not add that she had enjoyed herself, because it would not have been strictly true. She had not enjoyed many of the fulsome compliments she had received, nor the hot hands on hers, nor the leers, winks and muttered comments which the speakers might have assumed – wrongly – that she did not understand. And the smell of alcohol, cheap cigarettes, sweat and dirt was not too pleasant, either. But she had enjoyed the singing in one pub, the good-natured chaff in a second, the simple friendship the men showed to one another. And the fact that some of the men, particularly the older ones, showed a great respect for the Army.

'Your lot saved me grandad's life, just about,' one man said. 'He's in one of your eventide homes – happy as Larry, he is, now. Got other old'uns round him, see – and he ain't in the workhouse, which he were tarble scared of.'

He put a handful of small coins in her tin and Sara, smiling, thanked him. 'God bless you,' she said. 'That goes a long way towards helping others, like your grandad.'

But now, crossing the street, walking briskly with the heavy tin held protectively inside the shelter of her coat, Sara felt the glow of success. She had done well! This was her first try at taking round the *War Cry* and it had not been as bad as she had expected. I'll do it again, she told herself, breathing in the clean night air. It's worth a bit of hassle and embarrassment to know you've done so well.

'Queen's Arms next . . . and that's the last,' the adjutant said briskly, as they approached the big public house on the corner of Salop Street. 'They're a nice crowd in here – mostly Irish. A lot of 'em are navvies, working on the Mersey tunnel, and the rest are railmen, mostly. You want to hear 'em sing . . . eh, it can tear the heart from your breast, but don't you tell them that – they're all Catholics, and they don't sing a good, rousing hymn tune, they go more for ballads, laments, that sort o' stuff.'

'Not *Nellie Dean*?' Sara said mischievously. They had heard the song rendered in almost every pub they visited and were both heartily sick of it by now. 'I'd be grateful for anything that wasn't *Nellie Dean*, I believe.'

Adjutant Edcott was saved the necessity of replying because they reached the Queen's Arms at that point and plunged in through the open doorway.

Immediately, Sara sensed a different atmosphere to that of the Pacific Hotel, which had been their last stop. The pub was less crowded, for a start, and the atmosphere a good deal purer, for few of the assembled men were smoking. And though most men had a pint before them they were talking quietly, playing cards, laughing . . . and singing.

'It's enough to tear your heartstrings,' the adjutant beside her murmured. 'They're far from home and their songs say what they cannot. Still, we've work to do,' and she stepped forward with her sheaf of newspapers and her collecting tin. 'Evening, gentlemen, would any of you like a copy of the *War Cry*? We don't charge, but if you would like to put a contribution into the tin . . .'

Sara moved forward, smiling, thanking, and would not have noticed the large, quiet man in the corner if he had not spoken to her as his money tinkled into her tin.

'I hope you do some good wit' me money, Miss, for I'm putting most of me pennies away so I am . . . I'm hopin' to bring me family over come springtime, if I've managed to rent a decent little place by then.'

Sara glanced at him and was beginning to say she hoped he would soon find somewhere nice when she took a closer look. He was smiling up at her, an innocent, friendly smile. He had not recognised her – but why should he? She was disguised by her bonnet, but he looked no different from the way he had looked on that long-ago night when he had walked her home after her parents had abandoned her outside the church.

'Mr O'Brady? It *is* you! Don't you remember me? I'm Sara Cordwainer, you walked me home when I was out rather late one night. Your son Brogan was a friend of mine, but I've not seen him for years. Has he gone home to Ireland?'

Peader O'Brady looked at her properly for the first

time, looked at the person beneath the bonnet, not just the uniform. Then he grinned delightedly, revealing big, white teeth.

'Miss Cordwainer! Well I'm blessed! I didn't know you belonged to the Army.'

'I didn't, not when we met. But I joined up quite soon afterwards and I've never regretted it. How – how is Brogan? And yourself, of course.'

'Brogan's fine, and so am I. He's a train-driver now, for LMSR, working out of Crewe. He's done well. And what are you doing, Miss, apart from collecting money for the Army?'

'I'm a teacher in a small school,' Sara said. 'Brogan always said he'd drive the train one day – I'm very glad for him. Is he happy? Married? I suppose he could easily have children, for he must be . . . twenty-three or so by now. I'm twenty-one.'

'Sure an' Brogan's twenty-five, and devil a bit is he married.' Peader looked at her, his cheekbones reddening. 'He went round to your place last Christmas, and the Christmas before. He – he wanted a word.'

'I don't think he ever arrived,' Sara said. She frowned. 'Now wait a minute . . . last Christmas Gran and I – and Clarrie, of course – went to stay with Clarrie's parents, in Formby. But the Christmas before that – that would be 1931 – was my first Christmas with the Army. We were out all day, serving Christmas dinner to those who needed it. Oh dear, I am sorry I missed him.'

'Aye. He got real down,' Peader said. 'He did want a word.'

'I'm sorry. And now he's in Crewe, you say?'

'Aye, that's it; Crewe. But he visits me from time to time.'

'Well, next time he's in Liverpool you must tell him

to come and see me,' Sara said, suddenly gay. It would be lovely to see Brogan again, to watch the slow smile dawn in his eyes, the slow smile curve his lips. 'The only thing is –'

'Come along, Cordwainer, don't stand gossiping there,' Adjutant Edcott said bracingly. 'I've sold out – how have you done?'

'Oh, I've two left . . .' Sara smiled at the square-faced man sitting next to Peader. 'Would you like a copy of the *War Cry*, sir? We don't charge, but if you feel you can afford a contribution . . .'

The man grinned at her and stood up the better to get at his pockets.

'Sure an' you're welcome to a copper or two just for de sake of your lovely smile,' he said gallantly. 'And Seamus here will have one too, eh Seamus?'

''Tis lucky to take the last,' Seamus said, dipping into his own pocket. 'Though we'll be askin' for soup from your kitchen, Miss, when de tunnel's dug and finished.'

'Won't be long now,' someone else volunteered. 'Eh, it's been a wicked ole job – wicked. What wit' the water running down the walls an' the great rocks to be blasted out . . . eh, it's been wicked.'

'Last one gone, Adjutant,' Sara said, smiling at the men. She leaned down and spoke directly to Peader.

'Don't forget, next time Brogan comes, tell him to be sure to call.'

'I will, but Brogan said somethin' . . . is there a feller named Boote . . .?' Peader said, reddening still more. 'I wouldn't want to be after raising false hopes . . .'

'Our lodger's name is Boote – Miss Clarrie Boote,' Sara said. 'Oh, I must go, but don't forget – tell Brogan to call.'

And then they were outside the pub once more, and above them the sky fairly hummed with stars.

*

Grace saw the two Salvationists come out of the pub; she was lurking in the shadows of the Queen's Arms on Walton Road, waiting for closing time. She didn't spend as much time as she once had outside the Mile End pub, even though Kitty now lived there. The kitten had grown into a handsome cat and after a terrible scene at home, in the course of which Kitty had been lucky to escape with his life, Grace had taken him round to the Mile End pub and asked the landlady if she would keep him.

'Me da tried to kill 'im,' she explained, her voice breaking. 'They need me at 'ome, now, but me da will use Kitty to keep me in line. 'E says 'e'll strangle Kitty if I doesn't do what 'e says.'

The landlady's eyes were soft and sorry; she took the cat and told Grace she could come round whenever she liked to see Kitty, and Grace availed herself of the offer whenever she could. But because she was now big enough to be useful at home, she had begun to roam more widely, trying to keep well away from the neighbourhood of their court. And since the Mile End was a pub occasionally favoured by her father, Grace tended to hang around mostly on the Walton Road. She missed Kitty and the friendly landlady, but she liked the neighbourhood – there was a prime soup kitchen quite near, she'd had many a meal from the Army people who manned it, to say nothing of free boots, the loan of an Army blanket, and once, a lovely thick jersey to see her through a patch of bad weather.

She liked the Sally Army, but she never hung around near the Barracks or the soup kitchen for too long; she didn't want anyone to put her into the workhouse or any other institution, so she never let them know she slept rough six days out of seven. And at this time of night, she kept well out of sight. But she sighed to herself as the two women came out of the pub, smiling, talking. It would have been nice to have called out, had a word. Nice, but dangerous. But very soon now the pubs would want to close and the men would come out and she might get all manner of bits and pieces, to say nothing of coppers. She watched the bonnets bob off down the road, then went back to lean against the pub door.

And wait.

The news of her evening was too good to keep to herself. The minute Sara arrived home she told Gran that she'd met Brogan's father.

'And he said Brogan had been in Liverpool two Christmases ago and last Christmas, and he'd called in Snowdrop Street, but we were out,' she told Mrs Prescott. 'Imagine – he did call! I thought he'd forgotten all about me, or moved away, or both. Mind, he could have written, but men don't like writing much, do they?'

'Not labourers,' Mrs Prescott said, a trifle sharply, Sara thought. 'But no doubt he's a nice enough young man, in his way. Did you give the father our new address?'

'Oh goodness, I quite forgot,' Sara said, hands flying to her cheeks. 'Oh, how stupid I am, the poor fellow will go round to Snowdrop Street and think I'm deliberately keeping out of his way! Oh, Gran, what a fool I am! But I know where Mr O'Brady goes of an evening, and it's not too far from here, so I can always pop in and tell him we've moved.'

'Well, that's all right, then,' Mrs Prescott said. 'It's time you met young men other than Army ones.'

Sara bristled. 'What's wrong with Army ones?' she said. 'They're very nice.'

But inside herself, she was saying softly, *But they aren't as nice as Brogan O'Brady, that's for sure.*

It was a real pea-souper, Brogan thought, examining the range of instruments sparkling before him on the footplate of the engine and wishing that one of them was a magic eye which could see through fog. Weather like this was the very devil, because you simply could not tell where you were. Time stopped mattering, you had to slow down so much, and though you should be warned of a station's approach by the detonators on the track, you would not have been human had you not worried. Men did forget . . . and then you would go right past a station and there would be trouble from indignant passengers, hours late already, wanting their homes and their beds.

'Hold hard now, Harry.' Brogan leaned out of the cab and peered through the swirling fog. Harry Brett, his fireman, stopped shovelling coal for a moment and they both listened. Somewhere a cow lowed, the sound as mournful and pessimistic as a foghorn at sea. 'We're in flat country because we've not been through a cutting for a powerful while, and we're a way from a town, because of the cow. But that doesn't mean there isn't a station coming up. Oh well, we should know quite soon now.'

Presently they got steam up again and began to move rather faster. And of course the minute they did that the detonators went off, sending Brogan reaching for the brakes.

'Dear God in heaven, those bloody things will have me heart stopped yet,' he said, whilst Harry stopped shovelling coal for a moment to wipe his face with the rag which hung at his belt. 'This'll be Stafford, then. Thank God, we're makin' progress.'

'Home by midnight at this rate,' Harry said. He hated getting in late because it meant he would have to walk home – the buses would have stopped running and Harry lived some way from the station. 'And we're on earlies tomorrow.'

Brogan sighed. 'Aye, and I was goin' to write to me family tonight – we're scattered all over, now. There's most of 'em in Ireland, but Niall has recently gone to America, then my father's in Liverpool, there's me in Crewe . . . if we didn't write we'd lose touch.'

They crept into the station, slowed even more, stopped. The guard shouted and Brogan leaned out of his cab once more. All down the train doors were opening, people were jumping down, porters rushed about . . . they didn't look too pleased with life, Brogan noticed. Ah well, everyone hates late trains. And the newspapers would be late, too . . . they were beginning to load them, and the big brown post bags, into the luggage van. The guard came along the platform towards him, looking tired and cross.

'I'm goin' to get a butty from the refreshment room seein' as we're runnin' late,' he began. 'Do you want somethin', fellers?'

'A cup of tea and a currant bun or a cheese sandwich . . . lemonade will do if they don't have tea,' Brogan said. 'Same for you, Harry?'

'Aye, something to eat and anything to wet my throat,' Harry decided. 'I'm easy.'

'Good,' the guard said. 'If one more bugger asks me why the train's runnin' so late I swear to God I'll swing for 'im. Right. We've got six minutes here, 'cos o' the post; train won't pick up many passengers tonight, though. Folk don't wait when we're this late.'

'If they cut down any more on the number of trains folk will have to walk,' Harry observed. 'Wish we had a New Deal, like the Yanks. They know how to deal with a Depression, they're making new jobs, you know, puttin' bread into the mouths of those who lost their jobs through no fault of their own. Not like here, where it's every man for himself.'

'We don't have a Roosevelt,' the guard reminded him. 'We've only got old Ramsey Mac.'

'True. And I think the fog's thinnin' out a bit – the wind's gettin' up, that's why. Go on, Fred, or we won't have time to drink the tea before the refreshment room is shoutin' for their mugs back!'

It had been a long, hot summer without a drop of rain to green the grass or grow the potatoes. Forest fires had raged at the height of the drought and folk living in the tenement housing had longed desperately for a cool breeze, and for rain. But the kids were delighted when the weather only broke a couple of days after they returned to school.

'Sure an' it can rain all it likes now,' Tad said generously, sitting cross-legged on the O'Bradys' window-seat and watching the rain pelting down outside. 'Because it's only school it's ruinin', and I've no time for school. In another couple o' years . . .'

'You'll be out and workin', Polly chorused with him. She knew the remark off by heart and sometimes she wondered whether Tad said it so often because he was afraid. There weren't many good jobs around and Tad, with his threadbare clothes and his bedraggled person, seemed less likely than most to find one of them.

But work or no work, Tad and Polly had enjoyed the summer holidays, that was for sure. They'd fished for pinkeens in the Grand Canal, netting them out of the greenish, turgid water and into glass jam-jars which they would later use as their admission to the tuppenny rush on Saturdays. Tad was a good swimmer and showed off by diving into the water under Griffith Bridge; Polly preferred the other side, known as the Shallow, where she could dabble and paddle and dream, and sometimes practise the three strokes which was the most she could manage before her feet sunk to the muddy bottom. And since Tad still sold newspapers Polly had taken to helping him, getting almost as good at leaping aboard a traffic-stranded train and off again before it moved as her brother Brogan had once been.

Tad didn't make much money, but at least he made some, and as he assured his small helper, anything was better than going back to Mammy empty-handed.

'Because the ould feller's into everythin',' he assured her. ''Tis not his money alone that gets spent in Deegan's, but every penny he can find, these days. Mammy's earnings, mine, young Dougal's even. So I never take money home, not even a kid's eye. I take bread, sausage, spuds . . . things to eat. An' if me ould feller's on the warpath, sure an' I keep out o' the way till he's cooled down.'

So when the weather broke in the first week of the new term, Polly shrugged her shoulders, thanked the good God for a fine summer, and continued to help Tad with his various tasks.

Weekends were different, though. At weekends, after you'd sold your papers or carried sacks of spuds around or run messages for anyone who asked, your time was your own.

'We'll go after blackers,' Tad said the first Saturday as the two of them sat in the windowseat glumly watching the rain. 'Sure an' if it goes on rainin' we'll be the only ones, so we'll get a grush o' berries. The jam factory buys 'em if you get nice ones, or your mammy could make blackberry an' apple pie.'

'Where'd she get the apples, though?' Polly asked. 'Unless you buy her some.'

Tad snorted. 'Buy her some? When we can box the fox? 'Tis early days, the fellers won't be after apples yet awhile, but you an' me, we could go round to the house by the park. Sure an' the orchard there's too big for one family so it is.'

'Mammy says boxing the fox is thievery,' Polly pointed out self-righteously. 'And I don't want to do thievery.' She thought it over. 'Well, I don't want to get caught,' she amended.

'Polly, when did I ever lead you into trouble and get you caught? We'll be in and out before the folk at the big house know there's a Christian soul in the place beside themselves. Trust me!'

It was true that though Tad had led her into several hair-raising adventures, he usually managed to extract her from the same without damage, but Polly was still doubtful. And picking apples and blackberries in the rain would be nasty, chilly work.

She said as much to Tad, who looked offended at this criticism of his fine, money-making idea.

'Sure an' it'll stop rainin' any minute, alanna. Trust me!'

'Why should I? You aren't a weather prophet. And besides, even if it stops the trees will be powerful wet an' so will the blackers.'

Tad heaved a sigh and slid off the windowseat. Ivan, building bricks on the rug, turned to stare at them. 'Has it stopped?' he asked. He had been asking the same question ever since breakfast, and Polly sighed.

'No, it hasn't,' she said. 'But we're goin' out anyway, Tad and me.'

'You're takin' me!' Ivan shrieked, jumping to his feet so hastily that he spilt building bricks everywhere. 'I'm goin' out if you're goin' out!'

But at that point Polly's mother appeared, a pair of spectacles perched on the end of her nose, a letter in her hand.

'No, you aren't goin' anywhere, Ivan,' she said briskly. 'Polly an' Tad's goin' to post me letter, that's all.'

She held out the letter and Polly took it. 'Who's it to?' she asked automatically, and then, glancing at the writing on the front of the envelope: 'Oh, it's to my daddy. Did you give him a kiss from me, Mammy?'

'Probably,' Mammy said absently. 'But I had a lot to say to him; mebbe I didn't remember to send your kiss. Why don't you write one on the back of the envelope, Polleen? Then he'll be sure to see it first off.'

'I will,' Polly said joyfully. 'Where's your pen, Mammy?'

'In the kitchen; I went there for some peace and quiet, away from the young gentleman there,' Mammy said, jerking her head at Ivan, sitting amidst the ruins of his brick castle and glaring tearfully up at them. 'Now no nonsense, Ivan, your sister has a message to run and you'd only slow her down.' She winked at Polly. 'Sure an' she won't be long.'

'Watch Lionel; by the time he's washed himself from heel to toe we'll be back,' Polly said, smiling at her little brother. 'Be a good boy for Mammy now.'

Deirdre watched as Polly drew crosses on the back of the envelope and added the words *kisses from your loving Polly,* and then she watched as the two youngsters went out of the room. She listened as they clattered down the stairs, then watched again as they emerged in the street below. The letter was still firmly grasped in Polly's small and probably grubby hand.

I've done a wrong thing, a wicked thing, Deirdre thought suddenly. I ought to run down the stairs, and across the yard and into the alley. I ought to stop Polly, say there's somethin' in the letter I forgot, get it back . . . throw it into the heart of the fire. That would be the right, the kind thing to do.

But it had taken her months to screw up her courage after Peader's last visit, and actually write the letter that had been forming in her head ever since last Christmas. And this morning, when she looked out of the window and saw the rain coming down like stair rods, sure and hadn't it seemed the right moment, the best opportunity she was likely to get? The kids were home to give an eye to Ivan and she could sit quietly at the kitchen table and compose the letter.

Why hadn't she written it before? Why hadn't she told him that she'd thought it over and she couldn't leave Dublin? Not wouldn't, just couldn't. Because hadn't he been away a dozen years or more and hadn't she grown used to being a woman alone? But with money coming in, a little voice reminded her mockingly. Her life was easy compared to most, she didn't even have to work, scarcely remembered the bad old days when Peader had been here, getting one day's work a fortnight perhaps, whilst she tramped out to the farmlands, dug potatoes, paid the farmer for them and wheeled them home again in her wooden box on wheels which had once belonged to a rich man's perambulator. She had wheeled them to the markets, Moore Street, Francis Street, anywhere, and sold them, with Brogan in an orange box beside her, then Niall, then Martin.

Peader had been good to her, even then. Helped all

he could, raced desperately along the docks from read to read, imploring work, putting himself out for the other men, even going out to the tips when things got desperate, to pick over the rubbish. Rooney men they called them, tip pickers, ragged and hopeless, they were down there all hours, turning over the rubbish for something they could sell. Old metal, decent rags, glass bottles – anything.

And then he had come to her and said there was work over the water. Well-paid work, too.

'They'll be diggin' a tunnel under the Mersey in a year or so,' he had said, eyes shining. 'And there's men wanted on the railways . . . me pal Johnny's goin'. He says it's his last chance to get out o' debt. Well, we're not in debt, alanna, but at the rate we're goin' God alone knows how long it'll be before we have no choice. Pawning's all right, but borrowin' money . . . well, that's the way to trouble.'

She had begged him not to go, not to leave her, but they'd both known that it was go or starve. She was expecting her fourth child and it had been a bad pregnancy. She'd not been able to get out to the fields for the spuds and buying in and then selling didn't make the money. Brogan was eight, he'd started in selling newspapers and Deirdre had always vowed to give her boys their childhood. No work until they were twelve, she and Peader had said. But it all went by the board when the kids were crying for food, their cheeks hollowing . . .

Peader had left for England and the money had started coming immediately. Good money. He'd worked on the London Underground, tunnelling through the cold clay and never a word of complaint out of him, though he told her afterwards that there were times he was so tired and so sick from the foul air that he'd been tempted to miss a day or two, get himself right.

But he'd never done it. He'd worked grimly on until he heard of vacancies for linesmen and labourers on the railway in Liverpool, then he'd applied and got it. When Brogan was fourteen he'd sent for Brogan, too. There was work for a strong lad and since Brogan could share his lodgings a roof over his head was no difficulty.

So why can't I go to him, run his home for him and bring up his children in Liverpool, just as if it were Dublin? Deirdre asked herself. And didn't rightly know the answer. She liked her home, her neighbours, her life . . . but what was any of that compared to Peader? She loved him, always had, always would . . . but crossing the water? Living there, with the English, a people she hated and feared? Sure, Peader did it, but she wasn't a man, she was a weak woman, and she could not face it. Better that she should tell Peader now than later, when he'd got a place for them and was expecting her to arrive with all her goods and chattels.

So why did she hang out of the window, in the rain, and try to see whether she could still catch a glimpse of Polly and Tad? Why did she suddenly snatch Ivan up in her arms, fling her old waterproof round the pair of 'em, and go chasing down the stairs like a girl again? If she knew she was right, had made up her mind . . .

She knew where Polly would take the letter, because Polly was good about things like that. She'd go to the Post Office on James Street because she'd not trust a precious letter to her daddy to an ordinary post box. So if I hurry I can still catch her before she pops it into the letter box, Deirdre told herself. Kids always dawdle when they're sent on messages, it's grown-ups who are always in a hurry.

She ran, breathless, and told Ivan he was a great lump so he was and in the end had to put him on the pavement, seize his hand, and run with him through the rain, splashing in and out of puddles, avoiding the piles of rotting vegetables, old rags and other debris which littered the pavements.

'Shall we have a pie?' Ivan said breathlessly as they passed a bakery. 'I'd like a pie, so I would.'

'Not now, me darlin' boy, later, when I've caught your sister,' Deirdre panted. 'Later, I promise.'

Ivan was a good boy, though spoilt. His mammy was in a hurry, he would just have to hurry too, was his attitude. Once he complained of a pain in his side, once he fell down and was heaved summarily to his feet again. On and on they ran, mother and son, and they reached the Post Office just in time to see Polly and Tad turning away from the letter box.

'Mammy!' Polly cried. 'We've done it, we've posted your letter to Daddy!'

And she had to say, good, thank you, alanna, because she had asked the child to post it. But she must have looked desperate worried, for Tad put a hand on her arm.

'What's the matter, Mrs O'Brady?' he asked kindly. 'Did you leave somethin' out, then?'

'I did . . . and put somethin' in that I never should have,' Deirdre said distractedly. 'Oh, Tad, I never should have . . . but there, I suppose I can go home, write again.'

'We can't get it out of the box,' Polly said, looking worried. 'Oh, Mammy, you did say to post it – and it's got me kisses on the envelope so it has!'

'Never mind, it's me own fault,' Deirdre said turning away from the box. 'I'll go straight home this minute and write another letter . . . just a note, you know, wit' the things I missed out of the first letter all put in.'

Ivan was snivelling, clutching his side, so she swung him into her arms. 'Ah, come on, don't let me down now, you've been such a good boy,' she said coaxingly. 'I'll buy you a pie so I will, and we'll make our way home and have a good cup of tea.'

But when she reached home the fire had gone out and it took a while to relight. And then Ivan was cross and kept complaining that his breath hurt in his chest so it did, from hurrying. Deirdre ministered to him, relit the fire, made some tea and then sat herself down to write a second letter.

In many ways it was easier than the first, yet still she toiled over it, anxious to get it right. She'd realised how selfish her first letter had been, she'd forgotten all he'd suffered over the years, she *would* come over the water to him when he'd found them somewhere to live.

Having written the letter she put it in an envelope and looked around for a stamp. No stamps. She must have used the last one on the previous letter. Sighing, she went to her drawer and got out some pennies, then placed them, and the letter, on the small table by the door. When Polly came home, worn out, God love her, she would ask the child as a special favour to take the second letter to the post, and she'd give her and Tad a kid's eye each – a threepenny bit – for the message.

There was a piece of bacon to boil for their dinner and a great many spuds to peel, for though Niall was in America – doing very well, his letters said – the rest of the family was still at home so there were many mouths to feed. I'll make a duff for after the bacon, Deirdre told herself. A nice duff with a bit of sugar and plenty of suet . . . that will line their stomachs.

Humming to herself now the letter was written, working away at the meal, occasionally breaking off to make sure Ivan was all right, Deirdre found all her old calmness and pleasure in small things return. Idly, she wondered why she had written the damned old letter in the first place. She'd been feeling out of sorts for a month, two months, perhaps that was it? She was no longer young . . . Brogan was twenty-five so she'd been married twenty-six years, and she'd been twenty-two on her wedding day.

I'm forty-eight, an ould one indeed, Deirdre thought, chopping onions and wiping the resultant tears away with the back of her hand. Forty-eight years old and as frightened of change as a four-year-old! Worse, because a four-year-old would relish change, not understanding the complications.

But it was no use repining; the first letter was on its way, the second about to join it. Sure and with my luck he'll open the first and be terrible upset, Deirdre told herself. But then he'll open the second . . . and the sun will come out and the rain will stop and he'll be his old self again.

After some time it occurred to her that the kids should have been home by now. But kids being kids, they could have gone off on any wild goose chase. They'd be home for their tea – she knew them!

It wasn't a long walk to the big house, but you had to go down a country lane, which meant that Polly dawdled, because she did love country lanes so she did! There were the verges, with grass up to your knees, and the hedges, rich with different varieties of trees, and there was the white dust of the road which, when it rained, turned into the smoothest, richest mud in the world. It had rained a lot today, had only stopped within the last half-hour. The kids loved to make mud balls at the canal when the dredger barge had done its work, sludging up the rich, oozy mud from the bottom of the canal and dumping it on the bank. But this mud, in Polly's expert opinion, was even better. It was white, for a start, or perhaps not quite white, but more cream. This splodge is clotted cream from the dairy and that splodge, sure it's only buttermilk, Polly dreamed, pushing the mud ahead of her with a plimsolled foot. The mud would go through the hole in the toe of the plimsoll, but who cared, especially since it would probably rain again before nightfall. Now the sky was clear, the sun had only just set, the whole world seemed to sparkle at them, but later, on their way home, Polly laid a bet with herself that it would rain again, washing the mud from her plimsolls – and feet – as well as a bath would.

'C'*mon*, Poll, get movin', girl,' Tad called impatiently from ahead. 'If you don't hurry we'll be boxin' the fox in the dark, an' you won't like that!'

'I thought we were goin' to collect blackers,' Polly said, breaking into a reluctant trot. 'You said blackers first, then apples. And it's gettin' awful late.'

'But blackers are free, we can get 'em any time. Apples is more harder. If we get the apples this afternoon, then we can get blackers tomorrer, easy.'

Polly saw the logic of this. 'All right, then,' she said uneasily. 'Only I don't want to find meself in the police station so I don't.'

'For boxing the fox? 'Course you won't. Come *on*, Polly!'

The two of them accordingly hurried along, hand in hand, with Tad instructing Polly how she was to make a bag out of her skirt, into which he could drop the fruit.

'What's wrong wit' your pockets?' Polly asked indignantly. Why should she do all the work, take all the blame? 'You've got pockets; girls only have knickers.'

'A skirt carries more,' Tad said. 'Besides, it means you needn't climb the trees. If you come to the foot of the wall and stand against it, I'll drop the apples down to you.'

It sounded all right, so Polly trudged on, but in fact she had been right when she said it was getting late, though it looked as though the rain had gone for the duration. By the time they reached the russet-bricked wall which encircled the big orchard, it was already dusk. Stars were pricking out in the deep-blue sky overhead and on the horizon a faint, greenish line heralded the last of the sunset.

'Give me a back,' Tad commanded as soon as they reached the wall. ''Tis too late for goin' down on the grass, I'll have to pick what I can from the nearest trees and t'row them down to you. Come *on*, Poll.'

Polly hunched down and felt Tad's feet thump her momentarily in the small of her back as he bounded up on to the high wall. She straightened, a hand in the small of her back and peered into the shadows cast by the overhanging tree branches.

'You all right, Tad?' she whispered. 'Hurry, it's gettin' darker by the minute so it is.'

'Hold out your skirt, woman,' was the only reply she got, but she could see that Tad was feverishly picking . . . and they were big apples, the size of a baby's head. Cookers, then . . . they'd make a wonderful pie. Polly's mouth watered at the prospect.

Presently the first apple descended. Polly caught it and shoved it up her knicker-leg where it felt very large and very obvious. If someone came along, whatever would she say?

She put the point to Tad, who said, 'They're windfalls, stupid. Anyone can pick windfalls. Here's another for you.'

He threw it gently and Polly fielded it, beginning to feel more confident now as the darkness grew steadily deeper. But she wished she'd thought to bring a bag . . . she had already exhausted the holding power of her knickers. Four large apples were the limit there, so it really would have to be the skirt.

Then she heard the noise. Footsteps, not quiet ones either, solid, tramping sort of footsteps. Someone was coming along the dusty lane!

'Tad – ' Polly began, turning towards the sound – and was hit fair and square in the middle of the forehead by apple number five.

Tad, having started to throw the apple, saw Polly turn away, tried to grab the apple back, and fell heavily off the wall as Polly went down like a ninepin, flat on her back in the long, rain-wet grass. Tad was starting to scramble to his feet, when he, too, heard the footsteps. He froze, then his hand snaked out and caught Polly's wrist, warning her not to move. The grass was long and very wet, no one would voluntarily walk in it when they could walk along the roadway. If they kept very quiet . . .

'What about here, Mick?'

A hissing, sibilant whisper and the footsteps stopped. Whisperers are usually up to no good. Thank God, Tad thought fervently, they'll be no keener to tell on us than we would be to tell on them. But they sound old . . . twenty, maybe thirty. Men, not boys. Oh, Mary, Mother of Jesus, pray for my sins . . . make them fellers go away and I'll sell some of me apples an' buy you a big candle, I promise you that so I do!

'Well . . .' the answering whisper was loaded with doubt. 'We'll not get the dogs over wit'out a struggle. Dere's a little gate furder along . . . 'twould be best to try dere.'

Dogs! Oh, my God, Tad thought, and began to pray in earnest.

'How much furder, Mick? Only we want to be able to see somethin'; how can we set traps if it's pitch-dark?'

'I've a 'lectric torch, you fool. Aw, c'mon, me man, 'tis not much furder.'

Tad waited for an agonising moment until the footsteps started up again, then he lifted his head. He had time to see that the whisperers were two tallish men with lurchers held on short lengths of rope, when there was a deep and ghastly groan right by his ear. Polly was going to give the game away!

The shadows turned; Tad could see them even through the dusk, and the dogs turned too, ears pricked, muzzles scenting the air.

'What was dat?'

Desperately, Tad put his hand over Polly's mouth. She groaned again, a sort of bubbling moan and then said loudly, through his desperate fingers, 'What did you do that for, you spalpeen? Me head's split in two so it is!'

It sounded awful, even Tad realised that; hollow, spooky. And the men clutched each other and then set off at a gallop up the lane, knocking into each other and cursing volubly until they were out of sight.

Tad sat up and then scrambled to his feet. He reached for Polly and dragged her, like a rag doll, to her feet, too. 'What the hell were you doin', shoutin' out like that?' he demanded wrathfully, giving her a good shake, but the minute he let go of her shoulders she fell straight down again, frightening him considerably. He knelt beside her.

'Polly? We've got to get out of dis, girl, or we're dead men!'

Polly did not move. She muttered something, but she did not move at all. In the dusk he could just make out the pale oval of her face; her eyes were closed and her mouth drooped pathetically. Oh, dear God, I've kilt her stone dead, Tad thought frantically. What the devil do I do now?

When the duff was made and simmering on the fire, Deirdre took Ivan some bread and margarine with good strawberry jam on it, a big mug of milk and a few broken biscuits. He was mollified to be given a meal in his bed and graciously ate everything that was offered, including the broken biscuits which were a big treat. He counted the pieces, then tried to fit them together, then ate them anyway, crowing with delight when he found one of his pieces was the sort with hard pink icing on it . . . everyone wanted those particular biscuits, he assured his mammy, because they were lucky, so they were. And he hadn't even picked the pink 'un out himself which must make it luckier than ever. And then, to his mother's astonishment, he never even suggested getting up and having dinner when the rest of the family got home, he just snuggled down and was asleep within minutes.

Poor wee feller, he was cold after runnin' through the wet streets after his sister, Deirdre thought remorsefully. All my fault . . . but now he's settled early, so I might as well make the best of it. I'll get the spuds on to boil, then the meal will be ready when Polly and the boys arrive. I'll ask Tad in for a bite, since he's been runnin' my messages today.

Deirdre pulled the pan of spuds over the fire, then got out her mending. She lit the lamp and, presently, Martin came in, kicked off his lace-up shoes, undid his tie and his stiff shirt, and threw himself down in an easy chair.

'Mammy, I'm wore out,' he said. 'Am I first in, tonight?'

'Not for long by the sound of it,' Deirdre said as footsteps hurried up the stairs. 'This'll be Polly and Tad, I daresay.'

But when the door burst open it was Donal and Bevin, talking nineteen to the dozen. Both boys did jobs after school, Donal sold turf from door to door and Bevin delivered newspapers. He didn't sell them, as Tad and Polly did, he just delivered them, but he earned enough for picture-money, with some left over for extras. He was saving up for a bicycle, not a new one, a secondhand model, and thought he would have sufficient money by Christmas. Both boys greeted their mother with absent-minded affection.

Mammy, that's a good smell so it is and we're starvin', amn't we? Is it nearly ready?'

'It is ready. We're just waitin' on Polly and Tad.'

'I'll wash first,' Bevin said. He grabbed the kettle off the fire, spilled some water on the hearth and got shouted at for his pains.

'Cold water if you please, Bev! Don't play around, the pair of ye! Come and set the table as soon as you're clean, Donal.'

'That's Polly's job,' Donal grumbled, but it was automatic rather than meant. The boys knew Polly always pulled her weight and so they didn't mind doing the odd feminine task if she was late, or busy.

When the boys had washed and the table was laid, Deirdre began to get really worried. 'I sent them on a message . . . little devils, they must have gone straight out to play when they'd done it,' she said, trying to peer down into the street. 'Martin, go to the corner and see if you can see them. Tell them dinner's on the table.'

Martin went down the stairs and across the courtyard, then Deirdre lost sight of him. He was gone ten minutes, during which time she dished up, then Martin came clumping up the stairs once more.

'They aren't in the alley, or not that I could see,' he said positively. 'I yelled blue murder, Mammy, but there wasn't a sign of 'em. Can I have me dinner now?'

By eight o'clock Deirdre was frantic.

'Go to the police, Martin, and tell 'em we've two kids, one of them a young girl, missin' from home,' she said. 'The rest of you, search the streets. Bevin, you go round to Gardiners Lane an' see if the Donoghues know anything. I'll have to stay here with Ivan . . . hurry, boys!'

Tad got Polly, still semi-conscious, across his shoulders, staggered perhaps a hundred yards along the verge to where some thick bushes grew against the wall, and let her down with a bump. 'Now will you wake up?' he said crossly, sitting down beside her. 'Sure an' aren't girls a terrible trouble to a feller?' He bent over Polly and stared hard at her small, pale face. 'Are you sleepin', Poll?' he asked, his voice suddenly laden with uncertainty. She looked so very small and remote, lying there. 'Oh, say you aren't dead!'

Polly opened her eyes. Large and dark and bewildered, they gazed around her, then lighted on Tad's face. A small smile tilted her mouth.

'Tad! Where am I?'

'Lyin' on your bloody back in the grass whiles

I almost die of fright; we were near trod on by two fellers, near kilt and ate by their two dogs, near took up by the polis,' Tad said wildly, in a hissing whisper. 'So keep your voice down an' lets get out of here!'

'Where's here?'

'We were boxing the fox, and you got hit on the head by an apple . . .' Tad began and was interrupted.

'Did it fall off the tree?'

It was tempting to say it had, but Tad did not trust Polly's innocent, almost dreamy tone.

'No, it didn't. But it knocked you out cold. Now can you get to your feet, girl?'

'I'll try,' Polly said feebly. 'Where's the men, Tad? An' the polis?'

'Gone,' Tad said tersely. 'Upsadaisy!'

'It must be midnight . . . it must be later,' Polly said in an aggrieved tone as they rounded the corner into Swift's Alley at last. 'What's all the people doin' up at this hour?'

'It isn't that late,' Tad said reassuringly. 'Probably no more'n ten o'clock. Anyhow, we'll be home in two ticks.' They reached Polly's block and Tad peered into the dark interior, then turned away. 'See you in the mornin', Poll.'

'Oh no you don't, you aren't runnin' out on me,' Polly hissed, grabbing his arm. 'I'll be kilt, so I will, but you're goin' to be kilt as well.'

'Oh, but not twice! Me own mam an' dad . . .'

'They won't touch a hair of your head for bein' late,' Polly said scornfully, with unconscious cruelty. 'They prob'ly won't even notice. It's me that'll get the legs slapped off me. Only if you tell 'em how I were hit on the head and made unconscious . . .'

'If I tell 'em that it's me that'll get kilt, good an'

proper,' Tad said, horrified at the mere suggestion. 'The bloody apple done it, but who'll get the blame? Who always gets the blame when you're in trouble, St Polly!'

'I gets into trouble on me own account so I do,' Polly said stoutly. 'Aw, c'mon, Tad, else I'm goin' to sleep on the stairs. I dussen't go up alone.'

'Oh, all right then,' Tad growled. 'It's dark an' all . . . give me your hand.'

Clutching each other, the two of them climbed the stairs. Slow and soft, because neither wanted a scene in the open. They fumbled noiselessly across the landing and opened the door into the living room. Tad would have done it cautiously, to hear what the first words were to be in order to have a head start if tempers were roused, but Polly simply opened it and marched into the room.

Her mammy had been sitting by the window, staring out into the dark. She turned as the door opened . . . and flew across the linoleum, arms held out.

Tad would have dodged and probably ducked as well, then run for it. Polly ran, too, he had to give her that. But towards, not away. And was folded in a warm embrace whilst Mrs O'Brady, with tears pouring down her cheeks, hugged and hugged and said: 'Oh, me darlin', we've been desp'rit worried, we've been round to the polis, we've had the whole family out huntin' . . . indeed, they're all out there still, combin' the streets.'

'Shall I go an' tell 'em she's all right?' Tad said faintly. He could imagine what Martin would do to him if he did not spread the good news, and Martin and Donal always stuck together so he'd get whipped by the pair of 'em, not just by one. 'I'll not explain, I'll just say she's home an' safe.'

Tad had always liked Mrs O'Brady. Now he liked her more than ever, for she gave Polly one last hug, then came over – he tried not to wince away – and hugged him, too.

'You're a terrible pair but I knew you'd stick by me daughter, Tad,' Mrs O'Brady said, letting go of him and tousling his already tousled head. 'It halves the worry when I know you're together. Now, Tad, come back as soon as you've found the boys; I've got a hot meal waiting.'

'Sure, Mrs O'Brady,' Tad said. She was a lovely woman so she was! 'I'll be back before you know it.'

And he most certainly was, since he met the boys as soon as he emerged into the alley. Martin looked a little anxious but Donal and Bev were taking it pretty well, considering. Bev was eating a toffee apple on a stick and Donal was kicking a smooth, round pebble in front of him, giving it most of his attention. But they all three grinned at him as he began to speak.

'She's awright, fellers. I'm awfu' sorry, your mammy said you were worried, but we got back as soon as we could . . .'

He was poised for flight despite what Mrs O'Brady had said but it seemed he was not to be thumped, on this occasion at least.

'We knew you'd be all right. Picking blackers, were you? Polly said you might. Only we knew if Mammy thought her ewe lamb was roamin' country roads in the dark she'd do worse than just worry.'

That was Martin, shoving his hands into his trouser pockets and heading for home at a good pace.

'What about the polis?' Tad said nervously. The very mention of the name made his stomach turn over. The police only had to set an eye on a chiseller to read his mind, Tad knew, and his mind didn't always want a readin' by the law. 'Your mammy said she'd told the polis.'

'Never a word did we breathe to 'em,' Donal said. 'Sure an' we *knew* you'd be safe as houses, but no use tellin' Mammy. 'Search, tell the polis, get the neighbours out,' she shouted, so we made ourselves scarce.'

'I'm glad,' Tad said in heartfelt tones. 'But s'pose we had been in trouble, Don? S'pose Polly had needed help?'

'Sure and hasn't our Poll got her own guardian angel?' Bev piped up. 'She's always tellin' us about the young girl in the ragged shawl who looks after her. Who are we to stop a guardian angel doin' her work?'

'True,' Martin said. 'I don't want no guardian angel comin' at me for tryin' to take over the job! 'Sides, Tad, you're by way of bein' a bit of a guardian angel yourself. If she were in trouble, I guess you'd get her out, eh?'

'If I could,' Tad admitted, remembering the weight of Polly across his shoulders as he'd carried her inanimate form to deeper cover. 'Oh, fellers, your mammy asked me back for a meal . . . is it all right if I come?'

'Sure that's fine,' Martin said, speaking for them all. 'I wouldn't mind somethin' meself. What *were* the pair of yous up to, Tad?'

'We was boxin' the fox,' Tad admitted, getting poised to run all over again. But the boys just nodded; they'd all done it in their time. 'Then some men came along with those thin, long-nosed dogs . . . can't think o' the name . . . and we had to hide till they'd gone past.' He heaved a sigh. Truth would always out. 'Polly were at the foot o' the wall and I were on top, throwin' the apples down. Only she heard the fellers and turned her head away just as I chucked an apple, and it got her right on the noddle.'

It was a relief to hear them laugh loud enough to

drown the sound of their footsteps. Bev folded up, holding his stomach.

'You hit Polly on the head wit' an apple, and you're still standin'?' he asked incredulously. 'I wonder she didn't marmelise you!'

'She – she couldn't. She dropped like a stone, I'm tellin' ye,' Tad admitted. 'Down she went, *bam*, and down she stayed whiles the fellers went past.'

The three boys laughed again; if anything, louder.

'Sure an' we love our little sister,' Martin said at length, wiping tears of amusement from his eyes. 'But Mammy spoils her rotten; 'twon't do her any harm to be took down a peg . . . she's all right now, I guess?' he added without much anxiety.

'Right as a trivet,' Tad assured him. ''Cept for a bump on her forehead.'

'Perhaps she'll have a black eye in the mornin',' Bev said hopefully. 'What'll she tell the nuns, fellers?'

But they had reached the tenement block and Martin frowned at them, stifling their mirth.

'Quiet now; Mammy will be puttin' the food on the table and if you want to eat tonight, fellers – I'm not countin' you, Bev, fillin' your face wit' toffee apples an' your sister lost – then you won't let Mammy catch you sniggerin'!'

Going up the stairs behind the older boys, Tad digested the conversation. Polly's brothers loved her, he knew that all right. They were proud of her, though they liked to cod her, make her mad with them. But they thought she was spoiled, needed taking down a peg, and they hadn't torn Tad limb from limb for clonking her on the nut with an apple. Far from it, they thought it a huge joke. Behind the broad O'Brady backs, Tad gave a little grin. Sure an' didn't he love Polly himself, and didn't he like to cod her along sometimes, too? And she was spoiled – how many kids would have run at their mammy the way she had, when she was four hours late for her tea?

But Tad didn't mind. Mrs O'Brady trusted him with Polly, and so did her brothers. And so, of course, did Polly. She followed where he led, did as he did, and let him deal with the consequences. Why, she had been frightened to go up to the O'Brady rooms without him, yet she must have known, in her heart, that her mammy would simply be glad to see her safe!

Women is definitely funny, Tad concluded as the living-room door opened and a most delicious smell wafted out. Definitely funny – but wonderful cooks!

The apples were divided – three for the Donoghues and two for the O'Bradys – and apple dumplings were made by Mrs O'Brady, lacking blackers for the time being. In fact the apples were a thing of the past when three days later, Polly, in the living room, called through to her mother working in the kitchen.

'Mammy, what's the money doing on the mantelpiece?'

'Which money?' Deirdre said, coming into the room wiping her hands on a piece of towel, for she had just finished preparing vegetables for soup. 'I don't remember putting any money on the mantel.'

'It's pennies,' Polly said. She was running her hand along the back of the mantel shelf and she held out two large coins . . . 'They were on top of . . .'

'Me letter! Oh, God love him, it's the letter I meant to send to your daddy the day you boxed the fox and come in late! Oh, alanna, that letter should have gone days ago!' Deirdre dropped the towel and ran across the room, seizing the letter and holding it, for a second, against her breast. 'What'll I do, what'll I do?'

'I'll post it for you now,' Polly said. ''Twon't take but a minute. I'll get stamps from the post office . . . I'll fetch Tad at the same time.'

'But it's days . . . oh well, let's hope your daddy understands.' Deirdre put the letter and the pennies into her daughter's hand. 'Off wit' you, then. And this time, don't be late!'

Chapter Twelve

Peader read the letter slowly, over breakfast. Then he read it again. Then he put it down by his plate and stared at it. What in God's good name was the matter with his own Deirdre? Blowing hot and cold, yes one minute, no the next. She *knew* he had started saving for somewhere nice in the neighbourhood. He'd even spoken to the boss at work, saying that grand though it was being safety man for an area like his, he wasn't getting any younger and had thought that, if a country station wanted either a safety man or a simple linesman, he might think about changing jobs.

The boss knew Peader's worth, and agreed that in the fullness of time such a change might be arranged. So whilst a move might not come for a while, come it would, and a quieter area would be better for Deirdre and the children. Not that they'd ever known a quiet area, but he felt instinctively that his wife would find it easier to transplant herself and her family if he could offer her the enticement of a village, a proper garden, birds and flowers and fresh vegetables instead of shops, stink, crowds.

But before he could even do so, she had thrown his offer back in his face. Polly, bless her, had put kisses on the envelope, but there were precious few kisses inside it! Just that she wanted to please him but couldn't, wouldn't, contemplate a move such as he had suggested.

'Bad news, Mr O'Brady?' Mrs Burt said sympathetically. 'It's a long way from home you feel at such times.'

'Yes,' Peader said. 'Well, not good news. But it's all right, I'll get me mind round to it in time.'

And then it was time to go to work, to take his carry-out and his bottle of cold tea and go and join his gang.

He thought of little else though, all through that long day. And when, in mid-afternoon, the fog began to swirl in from the Mersey, creeping up to hide first the horizon, then the water, then the docks, the rails, everything, he scarcely took it in at first.

'Paddy, you're doing the charges on the Southport line,' his boss said at three in the afternoon. Unless it clears, that is. Be back here by seven. I want them set in time for the 8.03.'

'Right,' Peader said. He was used to being addressed as Paddy by the ignorant non-Irish. 'I'll be back.'

He trudged to the bicycle shed, loosed the padlock and rode off. Somehow the ride seemed twice as long as usual due to the heaviness in his heart. Not coming! There had been no kindly 'maybe', or indulgent 'perhaps'. Just 'not coming', and he had to come to terms with it. And the fog was, if anything, thicker. He got off his bike in the end after he'd hit the kerb twice and nearly come a cropper, and pushed it, sticking close to the pavement, keeping right in the gutter . . . and even so he found himself on Tetlow Street and had to cut down Heather Street to reach his lodgings.

Mrs Burt made him a good tea but was cross when he said he had to go out again. 'Sure an' they work you like a black,' she grumbled, making him up a fresh carry-out despite his protestations. 'I know how it will be, Mr O'Brady, you'll find yourself trudging that line until all hours. Fog isn't only the seamen's curse, it's the railwaymen's, too.'

Peader laughed. 'You should hear the passengers,' he said. 'The trams stop runnin', and the buses. Taxi drivers are so busy peerin' out t'rough the windscreens or out o' the side winders that they miss your street . . . Fog's the curse of the English nation so it is.'

'Don't you get fogs in Dublin?' Mrs Burt asked curiously, handing him his hat. 'If that's true, I'll be movin' over there meself.'

Peader tried to laugh again, but the remark hurt as much as a punch in the gut. Movin' there herself, indeed! Oh God, if only Deirdre's letter had said that she'd come to him! Once, she would have, he knew it. But over the years of managing alone she had somehow grown hard, less loving. With independence, it seemed, had come indifference. His happiness, which had once been their happiness, had been paramount. Not any more.

'Are you takin' the bike, Mr O'Brady?'

'More trouble than it's worth,' Peader decided. 'I'll walk. See you later, Mrs Burt.'

He set off through the fog. He would stick to the kerb, count the turnings, and not get lost. He ought to know the way blindfold after all these years.

He arrived in good time, picked up his detonators already packed into the old haversack, and set off. As soon as he was clear of the yard itself the fog smelled different; of coal-dust of course, of damp and mildew, but also of loneliness. You're all alone out here, Peader me boy, the fog declared, clinging as diamonding dewdrops to his donkey jacket, his serge trousers, even his big heavy boots. And you'll stay that way because they don't have the gangs out in this, too dangerous, and the next train's not due till eight and it'll be late. Bound to be.

There was no way of telling where you were, of course, you simply had to count your paces. The trouble was, Peader was so full of unhappiness that he could not concentrate. Twice he had to go back, all the way back, to the road bridge, which was a point that not even the fog could hide, and retrace his steps.

But he decided on the third attempt that he was probably more or less in the right spot. He would count the rails, put his detonators in position, and walk back. Then he'd have his cold tea and his bread and Maggie Ryan – not that Mrs Burt would have heard of him having only Maggie on his bread; there was cold mutton in some of the sarnies and good red cheese in others – and set off again to reset the line if the fog hadn't lifted in time for the ten fifty-eight.

He fumbled the detonators out of his haversack because his hands were cold and his mind elsewhere . . . why, why, WHY? . . . and then began to walk back towards where he knew the station to be. He hadn't gone ten yards, though, when he saw a shape ahead of him in the fog. Another safety man? Had someone ordered two of them to protect the same length of line? It did happen.

'Hello,' Peader said loudly. 'Who's dat?'

There was a pause, then the figure, which had been turned away from him, turned towards him.

'Hello? It's awright, I'm not doin' no 'arm, I'm just a-goin'.'

A girl's voice. Quite a young girl. Peader continued to walk towards her. He said in as kindly a voice as he could manage, 'You're trespassin', chuck . . . are ye lost? This is a dangerous place to be on such a night.'

'It is a bad fog,' she agreed. She coughed, a small,

tearing cough. 'It 'urts me chest . . . which way is home?'

He was close enough to see her properly now. She was small, and very pale, she looked to be nine or ten but her eyes were old, anxious. Twelve, maybe? Or perhaps thirteen?

'Come along, mavoureen, let's both of us get . . .'

He was walking towards her across the rails when he felt, against the sole of his boot, the rail vibrate. Just a gentle tickle of vibration at first but getting stronger and more definite by the minute.

'Train!' Peader shouted. 'Get off the rails, alanna . . . to your right now!'

She hesitated, staring blankly at the fog bank behind him, her eyes big and black in her small face.

'Which way's right? I can't hear no train . . . I'm searchin' for me baby sister, you see . . .'

Peader broke into a run. He ran along the track, shouting at her, and she took fright and turned from him, running along the track too, but not swerving off to right or left, simply continuing to run between the vibrating rails.

'Gorl, you'll be kilt! Off dese rails . . . don't matter which way!' Peader's voice came out as a bull's roar and the girl hesitated for just long enough. Peader's stride lengthened. He reached her, seized her small, skinny body by her little, sharp-boned shoulders, and threw her to one side, not heeding her startled cry which rose to a scream, a shriek, higher and higher . . .

Or was it the engine's scream? Or Peader's? For Peader was still not clear of the rails as the 7.03 from Southport, running late because of the fog, smote him, throwing him out of its path to crash like a rag doll on to the sleepers several feet away.

*

She ran through the night, through the fog, scarcely noticing as it parted to let her by and closed in behind her. She must get help, she must, she must! That nice man had been trying to help her, he'd thrown her clear but hadn't managed to jump clear himself. And it was just what had happened to Jess, she could remember the talk, the sighs, the short-lived intentions.

Her mam had been upset, of course, but all she'd wanted really was to show everyone they weren't as black as they'd been painted. She bent everyone's ear about her lost baby, her dead daughter, but folk round their way were judged on their actions, not on what they said. And Mam was too fond of letting the kids go their own way whilst she and her husband tore each other apart.

Grace had never known any security, not once Jess had died. And she'd been envious of the baby right from the start, because Grace had been Jess's little sister, the one Jess looked out for, until the new baby had come along.

Even now, when Grace lay down somewhere to sleep, she could lull herself off by reliving the first three or four years of her life, when Jess had loved her best. Her sister's wiry, half-starved body had given all its warmth and comfort to the little sister sharing her blanket, her scrap of bread, her cup of weak tea.

Then Moll had come along and for a while things continued as before, Jess looking out for Grace, Mam for Moll. But then Moll became a nuisance to their mam and got passed on to Jess – and Grace was out in the cold.

She had wished Jess no harm, but the same could not be said for the baby. She had longed for the baby to be dispossessed so that she could creep back into that thin blanket, lie down in Jess's arms, have at least a crumb of that concern for herself. And then Jess had been killed and the baby had vanished and she had known what true loss was. But she had loved Jess with all her heart, so she had known that somewhere, Jess would be worrying over her baby sister. And it occurred to Grace, for the first time, that if she could find Mollie then she could hug, nurture, cuddle the baby. She had lost Jess, but she might still salvage some love for herself.

So she had searched and searched. She had crept round to big, smart houses and begged from back doors and asked about babies . . . and got sent off with a flea in her ear more likely than not. She had fed her hunger on promises of Mollie's rosy-cheeked warmth, on the love the little sister would feel for the big one, once she was restored to the bosom of her family.

But Grace knew she herself was thirteen or possibly fourteen, and in the ten years which had elapsed since Jess died she had never seen hide nor hair of her little sister. She thought the baby must be dead, and she hadn't been hunting for her tonight, either, it was just an excuse for being on railway property. In fact she had been hunting for the men's carry-out. Grace knew that railway workers quite often didn't eat all their food, that sometimes they scattered it for the birds, or left it where hungry urchins might find it. Some of them fed stray dogs, some stray kids, she had heard one of the men remark, and she knew it was true.

So Grace had been scavenging in the foggy marshalling yard earlier, when the man had spied her and called out. She had let him get very near her, fascinated by the rich Irish brogue, the kindness in the dark eyes. And then the train had come, and he had been hit . . . and she must, she must get help!

She could see a light shining ahead of her, just visible

through the fog. She had a stitch now but she ran still, and came panting up to the light. It was streaming out of a small hut and when she poked her head round the open door she saw five large men, a coke-burning stove and a dog.

'Someone's been hit by the train!' Grace shouted, her voice very thin and small suddenly. 'He's up the line . . . he's hurt bad!'

The men surged to their feet. The oldest, who had a beard, said: 'Can you show us where, chuck? Can you find 'im again in the fog? Is it a railwayman, or someone else? A kid, perhaps?'

'It's a railwayman,' Grace said breathlessly. 'Folly me!'

With the men hard on her heels and the fog swirling around them, thick and yellow as phlegm, the little group set off. Don't let 'im be dead, God, Grace prayed as she did her best to retrace her steps. Oh God, don't let 'im be dead!

When the train had passed, silence crept back. The fog seemed to sigh and settle, thicker than ever, densest, perhaps, around the man's body, lying motionless beside the tracks.

The only sound was the *drip, drip* of water, falling from the overhead wires. And another sound . . . was it the patter of feet, running, running, away from the terrible figure across the sleepers? Or was it the patter of the blood which ran from the man's terrible open mouth?

Brogan knew within the hour.

'There's been an accident, Mr O'Brady,' the policeman said, standing on the doorstep, his helmet in his hand. 'You've got to get to Liverpool, pronto. It's your dad; a train hit him.'

Brogan didn't wait to ask questions, there was, in any event, no time. He went with the policeman to the station where he boarded the train and reached Liverpool an hour later. He went straight to the hospital where they had taken his father's broken body.

'You could telegraph your mother,' the nurse said kindly. 'She's not on the telephone, I suppose? Or you could telephone the nearest police station, they'd gerrin touch for you.'

'I'll telegraph,' Brogan said tightly. He straightened. 'I'd best send a telegram.'

He had been given his father's clothing and had checked through as the staff had requested, to make sure that nothing had been taken. There was a large blue and white checked handkerchief, his father's old hunter watch, stopped now, and some loose change. And the letter.

He had read the letter because he'd not understood how his father could possibly have got in the way of the 7.03 when he knew, none better, that it was expected. Like all the men who walk the lines, Peader could have got careless, but – in fog? At night? When every bone in your body, every solitary muscle and nerve, is on the look-out for that tell-tale vibration in the rails?

After he'd read the letter he'd understood and for thirty minutes a great longing to feel his mother's slender throat between his hands had consumed him. But . . . she was only a woman, she could not help her feelings, her desperate desire for her own home, her own place. Besides, to be angry, wanting revenge, was no way to help any of them. His mother would be no better a person if she carried a load of guilt to the grave. Better that she never knew his daddy had received the bloody letter, that she was simply told he'd been struck by the train whilst fixing detonators to the line, in fog.

So he went and sent his telegram – *Peader hit by train stop Please come stop Brogan* – and then returned to the hospital.

They were having their tea when the knock came at the door. Mammy was presiding over the pot with Polly beside her and the boys in their appointed places. Polly jumped up and opened the door; the boy handed over the small yellow envelope and Mammy looked up, saw him – knew. Her face whitened as though the blood had been dragged away from it and her eyes darkened. A hand flew to her throat. Whilst the boys were clamouring, Mammy snatched the envelope from Polly's fingers and tore it open. She read it at a glance, then tottered over to her chair and collapsed into it.

'Is it me daddy? What's happened, Mammy?'

Deirdre said nothing; she simply sat, staring at the telegram, until Polly took it from her and read it aloud.

'*Peader hit by train stop Please come stop Brogan.*' Polly frowned. 'Daddy's been hit . . . oh, Mammy, Mammy, is me daddy . . .'

There was silence. You could have heard a pin drop. Then Donal took the telegram from his sister's fingers and knelt down by his mother's side.

'Mammy? Does it mean Daddy's gone? And Brog doesn't say where we're to go, nor anything! I'll go down to the post office, telephone to England, see what I can find out. You wait here now – understand?'

Deirdre nodded, closed her eyes. Donal ran from the

room; they heard him clattering down the stairs, then they heard the outer door slam.

'I wish Martin was home,' Polly whispered. She sat down on the floor, close to her mother's chair, clinging to Deirdre's skirt, and after a moment her mother sat up a little straighter and took her daughter's hand in hers.

'Martin won't be long, alanna. And Donal will be back soon enough, you see.'

But it seemed a long time before the door opened again and when it did, Donal slipped back into the living room.

'Did you get t'rough to Brogan?'

'Is he . . . is he . . .'

'What happened, son?'

The questions came all at once and from more than one throat. Donal went straight to Deirdre and knelt down before her. He took her hands and spoke directly to her.

'Mammy, I got t'rough to the polis, an' they put me t'rough to someplace called the Stanley Hospital. Daddy's awful bad, but there's hope. They want you to get the next boat. Will you pack a few t'ings now, then we'll take you down to the docks for your ticket.'

Deirdre got up. Moving like a sleepwalker, she crossed the room and went out, leaving the door ajar. Polly, white as a sheet, glanced at her brothers, then followed her mother out of the room. Within seconds of them leaving there were footsteps on the stairs and Martin came into the room. He looked round.

'Where's Mammy? I was workin' late . . . what's up?'

'Daddy's hurt bad. Hit by a train,' Donal said. 'I telled Mammy to pack a bag; Brogan sent a telegram, saying Mammy must go across the water.'

Martin hissed in his breath. 'What happened, for the Lord's sake? Daddy's a careful man . . .'

'It was foggy, so Daddy was laying the detonators,' Donal explained quietly. 'He couldn't have heard the train, because he stepped into its path.'

Unnoticed by any of them, their mother had come back into the room. At Donal's words she threw back her head and gave a keening wail. 'Ah, Peader, Peeeaaddder . . .'

It was uncanny, horrible, coming from their happy, humorous mother. Martin stepped forward, raised a hand and slapped his mother sharply across the cheek. The keening wail stopped as suddenly as it had begun. Deirdre put her hand to her face, incredulously, as though she expected to find blood running. Then she shook her head in a dazed fashion and took a deep, gulping breath.

'Martin, your daddy's dyin' and it's all . . .'

'He's not dead yet, Mammy,' Donal said. 'Martin and me'll take you down for to catch the boat. You've packed a bit of a bag, now?'

'I have. But . . . but I can't be goin' alone, I can't, I can't!'

'I'll go wit' you, Mammy,' Martin said. 'But I can't stay, I'd lose me job for sure. Still, once you're wit' Brogan you'll be all right, hey?'

'Aren't we all goin', then?' That was Bev, staring from face to face.

'No, indeed,' Martin said. 'Too many people are worse than too few. Donal, can you give an eye to 'em for a day or so? Make sure no one steps out of line?'

'Yes, sure I will,' Donal muttered. 'Is there nothin' else I can do indeed, Mart? Poor Daddy! What a turble t'ing.'

'Aye. No, there's nothing else, save keep 'em safe

until . . . until I can come home.' He turned as Polly came back into the room. 'Got Mammy's bag packed? Good girl.'

'Mammy's puttin' her coat on, then she'll be ready,' Polly said. 'Will I come wit' you, Martin? To take care of me mammy? She's not well, poor soul.'

'I'll take care of her,' Martin said. 'You do as Donal tells you, alanna, and keep house for Mammy. I'll be home in a day or so and Mammy'll come back as soon as she can.'

'Right,' Polly said. She was still pale. 'Martin, will ye give me daddy a kiss from me? To make it better?'

Bev started to speak, then stopped. He turned from them, his shoulders shaking. Donal got up from the table and put his arm round his brother and Martin, too, stood up.

Bev . . . come on, man, don't give way. We'll all do what we can . . . We all love, Daddy . . . come on, we'll all have a bit of a cry, then it won't seem so hard and cold.'

Deirdre came back into the room. She was wearing her black winter coat, a rather pretty rose-coloured felt hat and her black court shoes. She carried a shabby black hold-all and her cracked, black leather handbag.

'Ready, Mammy? Kisses all round, then.' The children crowded round, hugging her, kissing. 'Now you'll be prayin' for Daddy, each day, all of you?'

'Sure we will,' Polly said through her tears. 'Though if Daddy goes to Jesus he won't stay in Purgatory a moment, once Jesus knows who it is waitin' to come into Heaven. He'll have our daddy out o' there quick as you can.'

Martin caught hold of her and hugged her very tightly for a moment, then he spoke over the top of her red-gold curls.

'Sure and Daddy's mortal bad, alanna, I'd be the last to deny it, but he's not knockin' at the pearly gates yet awhile. 'Tis prayers for the livin' you must be makin', not prayers for the dead!'

'But Mammy said our daddy was dyin'.'

Deirdre's eyes filled with tears and colour flooded her cheeks. She picked Polly up and hugged her hard, then kissed the child's smooth, tear-wet cheek. ''Tis wrong I was to say such a t'ing, alanna. If we all pray very hard every day, your daddy will come home to us so he will.'

That night, after they had waved the ship off on its way to Liverpool, the boys and Polly walked back to the Liberties and when they reached Thomas Street, without a word said, they turned automatically into John's Lane Church.

It seemed odd to go into the church when there was no service on, Polly thought, but the red lamp burned on the High Altar and the blue one in the Lady Chapel and somehow the church no longer seemed strange but calm, serene. When Donal beckoned she followed him and the other boys into the Lady Chapel and Donal went and bought them a candle each. Polly knew which one was hers, it was thinner than the others and a tiny bit smaller but it was, she decided, the nicest. Donal lit the taper which was laid by the big candle and then brought the light over and the children lit their own candles, and Polly went on her knees and stared at her candle flame very hard and then began to pray.

The O'Bradys were not an exceptionally religious family. They went to Mass on a Sunday, paid their dues, bought candles, kept a shrine on the mantelpiece, holy water in a stoup by the door. But they did not ask the father before taking decisions, never visited the church mid-week, did not expect or ask for any particular favours from God.

Peader was less religious even than that. When he was home in Dublin he usually went to Mass on Sunday, but Polly guessed that he seldom attended church in Liverpool. Deirdre had once asked him about his church over there in her presence and, taken by surprise, his replies had lacked conviction.

'Sure an' you're a heathen, Peader O'Brady,' Deirdre had teased. 'Don't tell me; I know it all. A little drink here, a little drink there, and sure Sunday's over before you know it's begun, so it is.'

But now, praying as she had never prayed in her life before, staring at her candle flame, something happened which gave Polly comfort as well as conviction. Beside the candle flame and just behind it, she could just make out a vague figure, a shape. It was the girl Polly had first glimpsed on the stairs and now, when Polly looked straight at her she wasn't there, but when Polly stared at the candle and concentrated, she came, smiling, back.

She's me guardian angel, and she'll look after me daddy for me, because I know well how horrible it would be wit'out me daddy, Polly decided. And presently, when the boys scrambled to their feet, she got up and took Donal's hand and hugged it tight. Donal was sixteen, as good as a man, and he had snail trails down his face where the tears had been shed; poor Donal, he had neither her faith nor her guardian angel.

'Don, it'll be all right,' Polly whispered as they made their way home. 'Me guardian angel was in church so she was, and she smiled at me, gentle and beautiful. She's goin' to take care of our daddy, I know she is.'

And Donal, who had laughed before today and

codded her about her guardian angel, looked down at her and smiled and squeezed her hand.

'I'm sure she will,' he said, keeping his voice low as Polly had done. 'I'm sure she will, alanna. For a train's a turble big t'ing to be hit by. Our daddy will want all the help he can get to make him better so he will.'

Deirdre sat by the bed. Peader had tubes leading out of here and into there. He had so many cuts and abrasions on his face that she'd not recognised him at first . . . ah dear, and he so beautiful! But the spark of life still flickered, though he lay, eyes closed, face stern, far from them.

The nurse who was looking after him told Deirdre that he was a very strong man, strong as an ox, with a strong heart and good lungs.

'He'll need that strength in the weeks to come,' she had said, and Deirdre had smiled like an idiot. 'Weeks to come' meant he wasn't going to die in five minutes, which was how he looked with his grey skin and his mouth half open and his eyes sunk back into his head. 'You pray for him, Mrs O'Brady, and spend as much time as you can with him whilst his wounds heal. Who knows? He may walk out of here yet.'

That plunged Deirdre into depression again, because that made it sound as though it would need a miracle to get Peader on his feet again. But all you could do was pray and stay, pray and stay, and perhaps one day Peader would open an eye, smile, speak.

'His injuries are terrible,' the doctor had said when Deirdre had first arrived. 'It's a miracle he's here at all, Mrs O'Brady. But with every day that passes wounds heal a little bit and blood strengthens, bone knits. If we can just keep him alive . . .'

'Home each night at six, Mammy,' Brogan told her,

and though she had tried to insist that she must stay with Peader, she saw the sense of it in the end. Besides, the nurses made it plain they didn't want her all night as well as all day.

'We can do wit'out you as a patient, too, Mrs O'Brady,' Sister Lucy Flanaghan told her roundly. Lucy, being a Dublin girl herself, spoke out as one Irishwoman to another. ''Tis ill you'll make yourself, my dear.'

So Deirdre took herself off home each night to the small house in Salop Street, and slept in the bed where her Peader had slumbered for the past dozen or so years. And if his pillow was wet with her tears by midnight, sure and didn't she keep her unhappiness to herself when she went on to the ward? Cheerful she was then and optimistic, holding his poor hand, with the stitches marching across it like a railway line and stroking his cheek and telling him to get well soon, please, for hadn't she come a hell of a long way to see him, and wasn't it a poor thing that she was forced to sit by his bed and talk to herself, now?

But Peader never stirred, never moved a muscle or made so much as the tiniest sound. Nurses came in and made his poor, stiff limbs exercise, they wagged his arms and legs and turned him over, and Deirdre winced at the great, livid scars all over him and wondered, sometimes, whether he would ever be well. But then she would chide herself for her lack of faith and thank God he was still alive and on her way home would rush into the nearest church, which happened to be St Athanasius', on Chancel Street. There she would light a candle, genuflect, and then pray hard until her knees ached and her chaotic and painful thoughts gradually eased and smoothed out. Only then would she make her way back to Mrs Burt and the meal which awaited her.

'How shall I pay her?' she had asked Brogan just before he left for Crewe. A good job had to be nurtured at a time of high unemployment and Brogan dared stay away no longer. Martin, having delivered her and seen his father, had caught the next boat back to Ireland and the rest of the family. 'I've no money, son.'

'I'm paying; don't worry about it,' Brogan muttered. 'I'll leave you some money, Mammy, and send you more each week.'

Standing on the station platform, they had looked at each other, each knowing the worry that nagged them.

How long? How long would Peader lie there and how long could Deirdre stay? It was all very well to say she'd stay for ever, but the only money coming in back in Dublin was Martin's with Donal's part-time work and any pennies Polly could earn. Soon rent would be due, food would run short, school fees would be demanded for the coming term. Brogan sent what he could but he was supporting Deirdre and himself as well as the family, now. He could do no more.

'We'll manage, Mammy,' Brogan said quietly at last. 'If the worst comes to the worst sure an' aren't there the St Vincent de Paul men, or the Assistance? The kids will not starve.'

'They'd starve sooner than call in the Vincent's men,' Deirdre said. 'They humiliate you, Brogan, tell you that others manage on less. Your daddy saved us from all that. Oh, dear God, let him get well!'

'The Ward Sister's hopeful,' Brogan said. 'Mammy, here's me train, I can't stop. But I'll be back to see the pair of youse as soon as I've a day or so off. Ring the booking office at Crewe station if there's any change. They'll see I get the message.'

'I will,' Deirdre promised. 'And I'll write you each week, son, when I write to Polly and the boys.'

She waved the train off, and then returned to the Stanley, and her man.

'It's goin' to be a funny old Christmas so it is,' Polly grumbled to Tad as the two of them made their way through the Francis Street market one Saturday afternoon in early December. 'No daddy, no mammy, and no presents, either. And precious little dinner, Martin says.'

'I'll give you half what I make if you help me wit' the papers,' Tad said, but without much enthusiasm. 'We can't pick spuds because the ground's froze hard, but I suppose we could go for cabbage. They cut cabbage, don't they? You don't have to dig or nothin'.'

'Tell you what; we could get holly and mistletoe and hawk it round the big houses, the rich houses,' Polly said suddenly. 'I know most of 'em have it growin' in their gardens, but they buy it usually. Why don't we do that?'

She was sick and tired of keeping house, to tell the truth. Sick and tired! She had never realised how hard mammies worked, and finding out had put her right off marriage, and that was the truth so it was.

She just never stopped and the boys, who had been good with Mammy, weren't good with her at all. They would peel spuds at a pinch, and they brought water up and emptied the slop buckets and that was it. Everything else was Polly's job, Polly's responsibility, and she was getting heartily sick of it. And then, yesterday, Martin had started talking about Christmas dinner . . . sprouts, a bird, a pudding . . . and Polly had told them straight.

'I can't cook things like that,' she had wailed. 'And

I won't. You're a bunch of lazy moochers and if you don't help me more you'll go hungry so you will, because I won't cook so much as a spud for youse!'

'Temper, temper,' Martin said. 'Brogan told us to pull together, Polly, and he told you to mind me. Remember?'

Polly did remember, but that didn't make it any easier to bear.

'Don't care; shan't cook,' she had said succinctly. 'Nor I shan't light the fires, 'cos that last lot of turf you brought in was drippin' wet – soaked, it were. It's someone else's turn, and it'll be someone else's turn on Christmas Day, an' all.'

'We're workin' hard,' Donal said in an injured voice. 'You aren't even at school, Polly.'

Polly had volunteered to give up school until her mother returned and this, she had soon realised, was a tactical error of giant proportions. How often had she got out of an unpopular task with a cry of 'I've got to do me eckers!' But now such pretence was useless. Kids who aren't at school don't get homework, they have to listen to the excuses of others, knowing them to be excuses but powerless to do anything about it.

But now, Tad and Polly had drawn level with a fish stall, or rather with a basket-car full of fish. It smelt, but Tad pulled Polly to a halt.

'Holly an' mistletoe for Christmas! Sure an' the girl's a genius, so she is! Phoenix Park!'

'I thought we might go to the country,' Polly said uncertainly. 'We can catch a tram for quite a way, then we can walk.'

'Sure we could, but the big houses in Phoenix Park, they like holly hedges. It keeps the chisellers out, d'you see? So why not get some little, berried bits today, an' go out after mistletoe after Mass tomorrow? We could sell it for six bunches a penny . . . something like that. 'Tis all profit, after all.'

'All right, I'd do anythin' rather than housework,' Polly agreed rather bitterly. She had left the beds unmade, the porridge pan unscraped, the clothes unwashed, and she intended to keep it that way.

'Other girls raise *families* when their mammies are workin',' Martin had pointed out when she moaned at him that she was nothin' but a slave. 'Kids of seven do all the messages, bring up the babies, cook the food . . .'

''Tis a liar you are, Martin O'Brady!' Polly had yelled. 'I'm nine and I can't do all that. As for Ivan, sure and he's not a baby at all, he's a *fiend* so he is!'

The fiend, sitting on the hearthrug with a piece of paper and some stumps of pencil, looked up and grinned. He knew Polly hated him right now but he didn't much care. He got up when he felt like it and went out to play with his friends, bowling hoops down Thomas Street, chasing cats, cheeking shopkeepers. It was great sport and his mammy would never have allowed it, but Polly was just pleased to get him out of her hair now and then and seldom bothered to ask where he had been. And she fed him, so that was all right.

'So you're on, then?' Tad chuckled and rubbed his hands. 'We'll be rich by the time Christmas comes!'

'Rich and scratched to ribbons,' Polly moaned two hours later, as they wheeled their borrowed perambulator across the dusky meadows of Phoenix Park. But though her arms and hands smarted, she felt rather pleased with herself. The two of them had gone round the back of the President's house, the most important man in all Ireland, and they had hacked away with the breadknife at the holly bushes there and chucked their prickly spoil in the pram and now they were wheeling it home.

'We ought to see if the President would like to buy some to make a Christmas wreath for his door,' Tad whispered, and Polly had giggled, though she was secretly rather shocked. Fancy stealing holly off an important man and then selling it back to him!

But in fact, by the time their pram bulged with holly, they were too tired and it was too late for selling anything.

'Tomorrer we'll do the countryside an' get mistletoe,' Tad said, pushing beside her. 'After Mass, mind. I don't aim to imperil me immortal soul just for a few pennies.'

'Your immortal soul's in poor shape anyway, 'cos stealin' holly's a sin,' Polly said. She did feel rather ashamed of herself. Boxing the fox was one thing, that wasn't stealing exactly, even the police didn't call that stealing. But taking the presidential holly... well, that wasn't quite so straightforward.

'You can't steal holly,' Tad said impatiently, shoving away at the pram much harder than Polly was, so that they waltzed right across the sandy path and into the grass verge. 'Have a care where you're pushin', girl! No, you can't steal holly, because it's a wild tree, a woodland tree. You've sung *The Holly and the Ivy*, haven't you?'

'What's that got to do with it?' Polly asked. Her back was aching and her scratches burned like fire. Hell fire, she thought apprehensively. Oh, God love me, I didn't mean no harm, honest!

'Well, the holly and the ivy are Christmas things, and they grow wild in the woods. So you can't steal 'em. Nor mistletoe,' Tad said instructively. 'I swear to God, Poll, that I wouldn't lead you into stealin', because I promised Martin to see you was all right.

And it's fine holly, wouldn't you say? It's got a *grush* of berries. Have you seen the holly in the market? Not a berry, most of it. Oh aye, ours is good holly, we'll see our money back on that lot.'

'We didn't put any money out for it,' Polly said crossly. 'Oh, Tad, and when I get home there'll be no fire, no supper cooked, no washin' done. Oh, I want me mammy back mortal bad!'

Sara had met Peader in the Queen's Arms, so naturally, the next time she was collecting in the pub, she expected to see him, sitting in his corner seat with his friends around him. But he wasn't there. She was collecting of course, handing out the *War Cry* and rattling her tin to raise money for the Army's various charitable ventures, which meant that she could scarcely pop in next day to check that Peader hadn't merely been absent from his usual corner for the one night.

But a couple of weeks later she was in again and little Freddy Mack was there.

'I wonder, you're Irish, aren't you?' Sara said, having listened to his brogue for a few minutes. 'Do you know a fellow-countryman of yours called Peader O'Brady? I'm by way of being a – a friend of his son's, Brogan O'Brady, and I'm rather keen to get in touch.'

The small man looked at her pityingly.

'Peader O'Brady was hit by an express train, when he was laying detonators in fog,' he said. 'There's sorry I am, Miss, to be the one to tell you.'

'My God! Oh, I'm so sorry . . . you don't know what's happened to his son Brogan, do you? We were friends years ago, but I've not seen him for a long time. I'd like to send him my condolences.'

Freddy Mack shrugged.

'He's gone back to Dublin,' he said. 'He went a whiles ago; he'll be workin' over there now, taking care of his mammy and the young 'uns.'

'And – and you don't think he'll come back?' Sara said faintly. She felt as though she had stepped into a pit of darkness, which was absurd, because Brogan was only a friend after all, and she'd not seen him for a long while. 'Not at all? Not ever?'

'There's a young lady,' Freddy Mack said, wrinkling his brow. 'I can't be recallin' her name, now, but there was a young lady he spoke of from time to time. Likely he's marryin' her, Miss.'

'I see. Well, thank you, Mr Mack,' Sara said politely, through dry lips. It serves me right, she thought, never really trying to get in touch with him again, always assuming he'd turn up, cap in hand, and we'd pick up our friendship where we left off. Well, that won't happen now, Sara Cordwainer, so you'd better start wondering what you're going to do with the rest of your life! Resolutely, she moved away from Freddy Mack, her newspapers fanned out in front of her.

'Would anyone like a copy of the *War Cry*? Thank you, sir, that's very generous of you. God bless you, sir.'

And presently, when all her copies of the paper had gone, she made her way back to the Barracks with Clarrie and as they walked home through the chilly night air, she told her friend all about Peader O'Brady, and a little bit about Brogan, too. Because I've got to learn to accept it, and acceptance comes easier if you're frank about something, she told herself. I'm terribly sorry about Peader's death, but . . . oh, I'm going to miss Brogan so badly! I hated not seeing him, but at least, before, I knew, or thought I knew, that he was going to come back to me, one day.

'So finding that Peader was killed by a train is tragic, but it's a coincidence, too,' she ended thoughtfully. 'Because there was a similar tragedy years ago, it was how I came to know Peader and his son Brogan, actually. And that involved a train-death.'

'The young girl? And the baby that simply disappeared?' Clarrie said at once. 'Your gran told me that story when I first went to live with her, but I never realised your friend Brogan had anything to do with it. Did you ever ask him what he thought had happened to that baby?'

Sara nodded. 'Yes, that was the first thing I said to him, as I remember. But he couldn't tell me much, only that he was sure the baby was safe and happy, nothing else.' She paused, then took Clarrie's arm. 'I'll tell you something else, Clarrie. The first time I met Brogan I was running after a little girl who I honestly thought might be one of the Carberys. You see she came up to me as I was starting to eat a pastie I'd bought . . .'

The story was soon told and Clarrie eyed her friend thoughtfully. 'And you thought it was the sister who'd been ill and stayed at home when you met Jess and Mollie? I wonder if it really was her? It could have been just wishful thinkin', chuck.'

'I suppose,' Sara admitted cautiously. 'Anyway, Brogan was really nice to me, really kind, and we kept in touch for ages. Only then we moved away from Snowdrop Street . . . well, you know how it is.'

'I do,' Clarrie said. 'You like this feller, don't you?'

'Very much,' Sara said at once. 'Not in the way you mean, though! He's just a friend and someone I'm sad I've lost touch with. But if he's gone home, to Ireland, we'll probably never clap eyes on each other again.'

'Oh, I don't know,' Clarrie said. 'People who matter

to each other have a way of turning up. Just keep on living, and hoping, and you'd be surprised at the way God can turn things round. But to change the subject completely, chuck, are you comin' carol-singing round the wards at the Stanley on Christmas Eve? You've a pretty voice and we could do with a female soloist. You've been properly taught, what's more. Say you will!'

'Of course I will,' Sara said readily. 'It's a date then, Clarrie.'

But for the rest of the evening her mind felt sore with loss. Why hadn't she made more effort to keep in touch with Brogan? Mr Mack was undoubtedly right, if the poor chap was taking care of his entire family he would need a wife, so he'd marry some pretty little Irish colleen and never think of young Sara Cordwainer again.

And it serves me right, now I'll be a spinster all the days of my life and undoubtedly that is what I deserve, Sara told herself. I love children, but I'm a teacher, I don't have to have a family of my own. As for men . . . apart from Brogan, I've never met one I'd even consider marrying.

Not that I ever considered marrying him, either, she reminded herself hastily as she and Clarrie cycled through the quiet streets. But I did like him as a friend. Oh, if only I hadn't been so heedless, so careless! If only I'd gone straight back to the Queen's Arms, instead of waiting a whole month!

'What's on your mind, chuck?' Miss Boote said presently, as the silence between them stretched. 'You're very quiet all of a sudden.'

'I'm tired, I think,' Sara said. 'I'm really ready for my bed.'

But when she got there, it was a long while before she slept.

Chapter Thirteen

April 1934

'When one door closes another opens.' Sara had been hearing it all her life, particularly from Gran, and right now she needed to believe it, because things were not good. The job which she had valued was about to finish, through no fault of her own, and a fortnight earlier, Mrs Prescott had suffered a slight stroke. She had been cooking, and had pulled out a chair and climbed on to the seat to reach a high shelf on which were some spices they did not often use ... and the next thing Sara knew was the crash as Gran and the spices hit the kitchen floor together.

'She's one of the lucky ones,' Dr Pemberton had told her when he had examined Mrs Prescott and was having a quiet word with Sara in the kitchen. 'Look on it as a warning; if we all heed the warning and take care, she may well live out the rest of her life with no recurrence. And she's lost none of her faculties.' Dr Pemberton looked at Sara over the tops of his little gold-rimmed glasses. 'She could have been partially paralysed, she could have lost the power of speech, she could, at worst, have been little better than a cabbage. As it is, she's just very shaken and will take more care in future.'

'No trying to climb on chairs again, Gran,' Sara scolded her gently when she returned to the bedroom. 'It was my fault, but I never realised you'd try to get to the top of the cupboard with me around to reach it down for you.'

'I don't like being a nuisance,' Gran muttered. 'I feel odd . . . funny.'

'Of course you do! A fall like that isn't something to be treated lightly at your age,' Sara told her. 'But the doctor says a couple of days in bed and you'll be running around like a spring chicken again.'

'Wheeling around, you mean,' Mrs Prescott said, but she smiled at her granddaughter. 'Oh well, mustn't grumble, and I'll heed what the doctor says. I mustn't act like a ten-year-old, me bones won't stand for it.'

So now, making her way along the pavement towards the tram stop, Sara told herself that she was grateful for the warning and would take better care of Gran in future. For Gran was her rock, she could not imagine life without her. But she would have to do something quickly or she would be in no position to take care of anyone.

Miss Marks had explained to her why she was going to have to let her go at the end of term, but Sara had seen it coming. The school was a small private one, and as the Depression bit deeper so pupil numbers shrank. The last thing a man without work can do is pay school fees, however reasonable, when free schooling is available.

'With pupil numbers now so small, Miss Cordwainer, my sister and I can manage easily between us,' Miss Marks had said. 'I'm deeply sorry because you are an excellent teacher, but by saving your salary, at least our little school may continue, in a smaller way of course, to flourish.'

Sara understood completely and had taken her dismissal in good part, but that didn't mean she'd not been secretly dismayed. And now Gran's stroke had meant they were even more dependent upon the money brought in by herself and Clarrie. So without saying a word to anyone else, Sara decided to go and see her parents. After all, they might have talked about having to retrench when she first returned from Switzerland, but that hadn't stopped her mother from shopping at the most exclusive stores in Liverpool, nor her father from running an extremely expensive motor car. By now, their economies might well be over, and it would cost them very little to reinstate Gran's pension.

If it was just myself I wouldn't dream of asking, Sara told herself defiantly as she got off one tram and changed to another which would carry her the rest of the way to Aigburth Road. But Gran's different. She brought my mother up, loved her, spent money on her, and she's had a hard life. How can a Christian such as my mother professes herself to be turn round and refuse to help her own mother when she's in need?

The tram rattled on its way and when it reached the terminus at Croxteth Gate Sara got down and turned into Aigburth Road, aware, suddenly, that she felt nervous. But the die was cast, it was too late for regrets. She had never contacted her parents since the day they had left her in the house in Snowdrop Street; now circumstances had forced her to ask a favour from them, not for herself but for her grandmother. The worst they could do was refuse!

Sara walked on through the sweet and sunny afternoon; it was good to be away from the city centre, good to breathe fresh, clean air and to hear birdsong rather than the traffic's roar. She reached the house in its large grounds and stopped for a moment, looking rather apprehensively between the gateposts. The house, at any rate, seemed unchanged. The windows sparkled with cleanliness, the gravel was raked and weed-free. It was not the home of people who were having to count their pennies, Sara concluded, setting off along the curving drive, her shoes crunching on the thick gravel. If she stood on tiptoe she could just see the glasshouses where the gardener had once grown so many rare and delicious things. There, too, glass sparkled and she could see, through it, the healthy green of plants. There was no doubt about it, the place looked just the same, there were no signs of a shortage of money . . . she would really have to make the attempt.

She reached the front door and pulled the bell. She heard it jangle and realised that her heart was beating uncommonly loudly, almost loudly enough to compete with the bell in fact. Still, it was too late to retreat. She must go ahead, having undertaken the journey.

She had already decided to say nothing about losing her own job, though. She neither wanted nor needed help from either of her parents, not after the way they had treated her. I can cope, she told herself, standing on the doorstep. But Gran – she's a different kettle of fish. She's been quite ill, and she's reached an age when she should be looked after; I'll tell Mother that if she's difficult.

She heard the tread of someone approaching the door. It opened.

'Miss Sara!'

'Hello, Williams,' Sara said, smiling at the young man. Williams had been employed by her parents for years; some things, apparently, did not change. 'Is Mrs Cordwainer in?'

'Well, no, Miss. She and the master moved out the best part of a year ago. They went to Preston, I believe.' He looked at her curiously. 'They didn't tell you?'

'No. But I've neither seen nor heard from them since

I left,' Sara said quietly. 'Do you have their address, Williams?'

'No, Miss. But Mrs Arbuthnot might have. I'll go and ask her.'

'Wait, Williams! Who's Mrs Arbuthnot?'

Williams, who had turned away, turned back.

'Why, the Arbuthnots live here now, Miss. They took the staff over when they bought the house. They're very nice people, Miss, and I do believe the mistress does have an address for your parents.' He stood aside and waved her to go past him. 'Wait in the study, Miss, while I find out.'

But Sara shook her head.

'It's all right, Williams, I'll wait here. It's a lovely day, I prefer to be in the air. If you could just ask Mrs Arbuthnot to write the address on a piece of paper . . . and Williams, can you just say a friend wants it? I'd rather she didn't know it was me.'

'Of course, Miss,' Williams said at once. 'I shan't be a moment.'

He was back quickly, a sheet of blue writing paper in his hand. 'Here we are, Miss Sara . . . I trust you'll find it helpful, Mrs Arbuthnot's written down the telephone number, too.'

'That's wonderful,' Sara said gratefully, taking the paper. 'To tell you the truth, Williams, it's Nanny Prescott. I'm living with her now, and she's been ill, so I thought perhaps my mother should know.'

Williams looked concerned. 'I'm sorry to hear that, Miss. And if there's anything we could do, Miss . . . the staff, I mean . . . we were all very fond of Mrs Prescott.'

'Thank you, Williams. It's a kind offer, but we'll manage. Good day to you.'

Walking back to the tram with her hands shoved into her coat pockets and her collar turned up, Sara reflected that she was not really sorry she had not seen either of her parents. I was probably panicking too soon, she told herself. I've been very lucky with jobs in the past. First I got the job in Barringtons and when my mother spoiled that for me I found the laundry work, and then I got the teaching job . . . I'll be all right, I'm sure of it.

Yet despite the failure of her errand she realised, as she climbed aboard the tram, that she felt happier than she had done for days. The truth was she had decided to see her parents once more against her better judgement. Now, having tried and failed, she felt fully justified in not trying again. And since she'd not told anyone she was visiting Aigburth Road she would not have any explanations to make, either.

She had intended to go straight back to Florence Street, but she thought she might pop into Clarrie's bank before seeing Gran again. Clarrie had said she'd put the word about that Sara was looking for a job and you never knew, she might have heard of something suitable already. It would be best to check, Sara decided, before getting the tram back into the city centre after lunch to start on the office bureaux.

So when she climbed down off the tram on Walton Road, Sara went straight to the bank. She went past the long counter with the clerks sitting behind the grilles and knocked on the door to the offices. After a short pause a girl opened it.

'Can I help . . .' she began, and then, recognising Sara: 'Oh, hello, Miss Cordwainer; do you want to see Miss Boote?'

'Yes, please,' Sara said gratefully. 'Can I come through?'

The girl led her through to the small office where Clarrie sat with three other secretaries. Clarrie finished rattling away on her typewriter and then stood up and came over to her friend.

'How did your visit go?' Clarrie asked and for a moment Sara wondered how she had found out about her trip to Aigburth Road. Then she remembered that she had told Clarrie she was going to see whether there were any jobs on offer in the office bureaux.

'I've not been round the bureaux yet, to tell the truth. So rather than going into the city centre first, I've come here to see if you've heard of anything. You said you'd ask around amongst the Army . . . did you have any luck?'

Clarrie looked smug. 'Maybe. Miss Marks had a word with Major Ellis and there *is* a job, though from what I understand it isn't a permanent job, but it might tide you over. The major says it will probably last for six months or so. I know you'd rather have permanent work but the trouble is, everyone's cutting down. So I won't say any more, I'll leave the major to tell you what's on offer. He said he'd see you this evening, at the soup kitchen.'

'I hope it's something I can do,' Sara said. 'Because the rent bill and the fuel bill and the food bill all turn up with great regularity, needing to be settled. I suppose I could have a try for shop work, but I've been out of it for rather a long while. Still . . .'

'Cheer up,' Clarrie said bracingly. 'I think it's work you might enjoy . . . but I did give my word not to talk about it until it's been put to you. You haven't told Mrs Prescott your job's finished, I take it?'

'No point in worrying her,' Sara said. 'She would worry, too, though she'd never let us know it. No, as you say, something will turn up.'

Walking along Walton Road in the direction of their

flat however, Sara found herself wondering what on earth the job could be? The Army did employ people in large numbers, but she had not heard, on the grapevine, of a vacancy for a particular job, nor did she think that anyone had retired, or moved on, in the area. How will I wait until this evening to find out what it's all about? she asked herself, hurrying along the pavement. She had intended visiting the office bureaux in the city centre but with the possibility of a job connected with the Army, would not such a visit be a waste of time? She had just decided to suggest to her grandmother that they should go for a walk in Stanley Park and leave the bureaux until next day, when someone hailed her.

'Miss Cordwainer! *Just* the person I wanted to see!'

It was Major Ellis. He was a tall, commanding-looking man with a big white moustache, wavy white hair and very bright blue eyes. He approached Sara at a smart pace, then stopped and took both her hands in his.

'Such excitement, Miss Cordwainer! Have you got a minute? Would you like a cup of coffee, or tea, or – or a bun or something?'

'It's awfully kind of you, Major,' Sara said. 'I gather you wanted to speak to me about the possibility of some work? Only Clarrie wouldn't tell me anything, save that you wanted to talk to me. But she said there was no hurry; you'd see me this evening, at the soup kitchen.'

'Yes, but since we've bumped into one another, what's wrong with right now?' the major said. 'And – you aren't hurrying off anywhere? – only if you've a moment I think we really should talk.' He looked impatiently up and down the road. 'Ah, Andrews' Café – the very place.' He took her arm. 'Come with me,

Miss Cordwainer – Andrews' does delicious coffee and marvellous cakes!'

'Do tell me what this is all about, Major,' Sara begged as they hurried along the pavement. The major was clearly so anxious to get to the café that he was almost running and she, perforce, was almost running too since he had her elbow in a firm grip. 'And do slow down, people will think you're kidnapping me!'

'So I shall, so I shall,' the major said, mystifying Sara even more. '*Such* news, Sara – just wait until I tell you!'

And at last, seated in Andrews' Café with a pot of coffee and a plate of cream cakes before them, Sara discovered what it was all about.

'Some time ago we had a bequest, Miss Cordwainer,' the major said impressively. 'A good, kind woman who wanted to do her bit for those less fortunate left us a mansion! Yes, a mansion, in the Woolton area of the city. She suggested in her will that it became either a children's home or an eventide home, but we were able to do nothing until all the legal difficulties had been untangled.

'Well, it has taken time, but we are now free to go ahead, and we've decided – in fact the feeling was unanimous – that we should open the place as a home for children. It's ideal for them, it has wonderful grounds and is surrounded by countryside . . . ideal for kiddies. And there has been so much hardship amongst the young because of this Depression! We've done what we could, but we've not been able to put a roof over young heads. But now . . .' he rubbed his hands, beaming all over his face, ' . . . but now, Miss Cordwainer, our opportunity has arisen and we shall seize it with both hands! Work on the new premises will start in a week or so.'

'That's marvellous, Major,' Sara said warmly. She

took a bite out of her cake. 'Very good news. But – forgive me – I fail to see why you wanted to tell me!'

'Why, because we're going to need workers, Miss Cordwainer, hard workers! And at the meeting last night Miss Marks told us that she had been forced to ask for your resignation, which means, of course, that just at the present moment, you are not gainfully employed. Unless . . .' he raised his eyebrows quizzically, ' . . . unless you've already obtained another position?'

'Not yet, Major. Jobs are hard to find,' Sara said regretfully. Because it was the school holidays, no one had really noticed her being out of work, but she was, of course.

'Aha!' the major said triumphantly. 'Then would you consider working for the Army for six months or so? As you know, we have trained officers for the majority of our work, men and women who've been through the staff college, but this is a little different. The thing is, we need someone to oversee the changes and alterations which must be put in hand before we can open the house for destitute children. We want a person with practical experience of building matters and also someone who has been working with children and can advise on what will suit them best. A simple example is water closets – Miss Marks pointed out that for very young children a lower – er – position is more – er –'

'I understand,' Sara said quickly, smiling to herself. 'But I know nothing about construction work, I'm afraid. Isn't there someone who could do both, so to speak?'

'Oh, didn't I explain? Young Alderwood will oversee the builders, but he doesn't feel in any way qualified to give advice on the *planning* of a home for young people. And once the house is altered and we open up, we would hope, Miss Cordwainer, that you might come on the staff of the home as someone to help with the children, to make them feel wanted, cherished. Miss Marks says you have a very nice way with young people, so who better than yourself for such a task?'

'Well, Major, it s-sounds marvellous, but . . .' Sara stammered, almost overcome. A job in a million – and one she would delight in! She liked Robert Alderwood too, though he was fifty if he was a day, but she supposed that to the major, a man in his late seventies, fifty *was* young. And she would be helping the very children she had long felt guiltiest over, children like the Carberys, who lived in miserable penury, victims of society rather than members of it. 'If you think I could do the job . . .'

'I'm sure you could. As you know, we pay a fair salary to our employees though we cannot, of course, afford to throw our money about. I realise you have to support your grandmother, however . . .'

The sum he named seemed fair to Sara. She smiled at him.

'That would be fine, Major. When would I start?'

'Well, we thought next Monday, if that was all right. Now, any other questions?'

'Yes, one. Would I be expected to live on the premises whilst the alterations were in hand? Only as you know, my grandmother is crippled with arthritis and is in a wheelchair. Furthermore she has recently suffered a slight stroke. She could not possibly manage without my help.'

'At first, the house will probably be uninhabitable, but once the work is finished you might be expected to live in, though it may not be necessary,' the major said. 'Later we'll have a full-time matron, who will undoubtedly live in. At this stage, I'm not sure about the rest of the staff – but shall we cross that bridge when we come to it? Anything else?'

'No, I can't think of anything . . . oh, when can I see the house?'

'Tomorrow morning, at nine o'clock. We're all going to meet there, the Committee, yourself, young Alderwood and the head of the building firm which we hope will do the alterations. Is that all right? Can you join us at nine o'clock sharp?'

'Oh, *yes*,' Sara said at once, already looking forward to her first glimpse of this mansion. 'Certainly I can. I'll be there.'

'Good, good.' The major rose to his feet and Sara followed suit. 'Now I must get on, I've a great deal to do.'

Sara and her companion left the café, and outside, the major shook her hand.

'Until tomorrow, Miss Cordwainer,' he said. He sketched a salute and was several yards away when Sara suddenly remembered something.

'Major . . . wait! What's this mansion called?'

The major turned back, smiling, slapping his brow.

'I'll forget my own head next,' he said jovially. 'Of course, I haven't told you, have I? It's on Beaconsfield Road, Miss Cordwainer, and it's called Strawberry Field.'

Grace often wondered about the feller who had saved her life that night, but she didn't think he could be alive, still. Which meant he was with Jess. Wish I'd had a chance to talk to him, she thought as she roamed the streets, searching for food. I could have asked him to tell Jess all sorts – that the baby never was found, just for a start. That I'm still alive and makin' me way awright, as well. And that I think of her often – all the time, just about.

But that was daft thinking, because everyone knew you couldn't get messages across to them that had passed on. It just weren't possible. And the big man would have had other things than her sister on his mind as he approached the pearly gates. At least Grace imagined he would, though she knew herself to be ignorant about such matters. How could she be anything else? She had not attended school after she was seven or so; you had to have boots and decent clothes for school. She didn't go to church much, either, for the same reason. The priest tutted when he saw small boys with their little bums sticking out of their kecks and small girls with no knickers under brief, ragged skirts, and sent them home with instructions to their parents to see that they were properly clothed in future. And that, of course, made her da angry. It were bad enough round their place in the ordinary way, but when her da was angry it quickly became not only unbearable but dangerous.

So Grace and the other Carbery young had simply slithered out of the educational and religious net and had not particularly worried over their lack. Grace had loved school, the quiet orderliness of it, the intriguing lessons, but she knew better than to annoy her da.

Almost two years ago, he'd killed their mam. Oh, he'd never swing for it like he deserved, Grace knew that, but he'd killed her, nevertheless. A drunken argument, a fist in the face at the top of the stairs . . . Grace had heard her mam hittin' every step, just about, as she crashed down 'em. The scuffers were called – not by us, Grace thought, ashamed, but then they would have had to face their da after – and a doctor came with 'em. The doctor said Mrs Carbery had broken her neck in a fall and Mr Carbery, sobered by the mere sight of his wife with her head on at right-angles, said they'd been comin' back after a night on the ale and she'd slipped on a piece of orange peel at the top of the flight. When all the fuss was over and they'd taken Mam off to the hospital mortuary he'd threatened the kids with the beating of their life and instant strangulation if any of them ever breathed a peep about what had really happened.

But there was no point. Mam had never protected them from her bullying, baby-beating husband, had stood by and watched them being battered with an impassive face, so there had been no love lost. Grace knew that none of the kids felt any affection for the woman who had given birth to them and ignored them ever after. It would have been nice to have seen their father taken away by the law, but the truth was, they dreaded the workhouse. Da made sure they dreaded it – he said the workhouse had made him what he was today, and told them terrifying stories of unbelievable cruelties. And when he wasn't scaring the wits out of them he bullied them, screamed and shouted at them, took the food they brought in and any money they were unwise enough to have about their persons, and generally mistreated them, with the inevitable result.

They went. One by one, silently, a child would slip out of the door in the morning and not slip back in at night. At first the child would be gone a few days, but then it slid into weeks, months. And Stan Carbery bellowed that he'd kill 'em if he ever laid hands on 'em and bore down even harder on the ones that were left. Then he brought a fancy woman back and Grace, who had stuck it longest, slung her hook as well.

They became street children, dodging the scuffers and kindly but interfering adults, running like the wind the moment anyone in a uniform appeared on the street, begging, stealing, living from hand to mouth. They slept in the parks, in any public place left unlocked, under steps, in areas. If the wind was in the right direction Grace often scraped together a pile of cardboard boxes and newspapers and slept in a sheltered jigger.

There were eight of them when their mam died. The only other girl beside Grace, Addy, had left home a good deal earlier and after their mam's death Grace guessed she'd moved right away from the Pool. She'd had a feller . . . she'd had several fellers. She'd be with one of them, Grace supposed, and wished she could have gone with the older girl.

Then their da decided he could do with fewer kids and put the four youngest into the Father Berry Orphan Asylum, where doubtless they were a good deal better off than those still at home. Grace sometimes wondered why he hadn't got rid of them all to the orphanage, but imagined she and her three brothers were probably too old to be taken in. You four can work so you're workhouse fodder, their father had said gloatingly, when any one of them looked especially like rebelling. And he made them work for him, Grace toiling in their dirty rooms, the boys selling papers, nicking fruit, going messages. They never saw the money they earned, of course, and very soon realised that their only chance of staying alive was to escape, get out and stay out. And now, of the four who had deserted their father and kept out of institutions, Grace saw only her older brother Sid from time to time, and the truth was she didn't like him much. He was growing too like their father – a bullying lout of a lad quicker with a cuff than a kiss.

She avoided the second brother, too. Solly was smaller, not so aggressive, but he was a sharp, secretive kid. He did well on the streets, Grace was certain. He had joined a gang of hooligans who battened on anyone weaker than themselves, and Grace kept out of their way.

She hadn't seen Alf for a long time, probably more than a year. He was next to her in age, a sickly, whining boy. Grace thought he was probably either in hospital or dead. But there was nothing she could do about it; she had no means of finding out about Alf and, in any case, could not have helped him. It was all she could do to keep herself alive – and out of her father's way.

He wanted her back. She was a useful slave, a punch-bag, someone to send on messages and then to beat up if something went wrong. She feared him from the bottom of her heart and never went near the noisome court where he and his latest lady-friend drank and screamed at one another . . . and probably fought, Grace thought, knowing her father.

So no wonder she remembered with affection and gentleness the man who had saved her life at the expense of his own! She could still remember the look on his face, the feel of the hands which had seized and flung her to safety. She knew his name, too, because when she'd led the men back one of them had exclaimed: 'Dear God in Heaven, it's Peader O'Brady! He's dead, for sure.'

She'd run away then, unable to bear the guilt. She had as good as killed him – the scuffers would be after her, she'd been trespassing on railway property, she'd be in awful trouble, imprisoned, flogged . . . sent to the workhouse.

But the days passed, and the weeks, and nothing happened. If people stared at her in the street it was because of the state she was in. Unwashed, ragged, half-starved, cold even in warm weather, she was not a pretty sight. But a scavenging child must keep on the move or it will be taken into custody, and Grace dreaded that. She had no idea what the scuffers or the priests or the teachers did to kids who lived on the streets, who begged and stole, but it would be something unpleasant, she knew that all right. In her whole life, nothing that had happened to Grace Carbery had led her to expect fair treatment at the hands of adults. The only love she had ever received had been from her sister Jess . . . and Jess had died so long ago that Grace could scarcely remember her face, save that its expression had been sweet.

So now Grace had a new hero. Peader O'Brady, who had cared so much for a girl he did not even know that he had risked – lost – his life to save her. Grace had carried a heavy basket of shopping all the way from the Great Homer Street market to Wilbraham Street, a considerable distance, and the threepenny joe thus earned had been spent on a candle, which she had lit for Peader O'Brady. Grace knew nothing of purgatory, sin, the life hereafter; how could she? No one had ever taught her. But she knew folk lit candles when someone they loved died, or when they were grateful for something, and she loved Peader O'Brady, and was grateful for what he had done for her. Lighting a candle with money which would otherwise have been spent on food seemed a small enough price to pay. It never occurred to Grace for one moment that the people who came in and out of the church, telling beads, genuflecting, putting their money in the box and lighting up their candles, had none of them paid, penny for penny, anywhere near as much as she.

Because Grace Carbery, who had so little, had willingly given her all for that candle.

*

Brogan sat by the bed and held his daddy's hand and talked soothingly into his daddy's ear. Mrs Burt had let him have the small front bedroom so he could be near his mammy and he spent every hour that he was not working sitting by his father and talking to him.

Summer was upon them now, with its long, light evenings and warmer days. And Brogan had moved back to Liverpool. First as a fireman and only recently as a driver, he had learned the road between Crewe and Rugby, and then he had done his time on the road between Crewe and Liverpool until he knew every inch of the track, every light, every signal, every bump in the rails, indeed. And now, when he needed so desperately to be back in Liverpool, the Powers that Be on the LMSR line had put him to learning the Liverpool to Southport road, which meant, of course, that the move back to living, once more, in Liverpool was a natural one. It just showed that prayer worked, Brogan's mammy said triumphantly, when he told her he'd be staying in Liverpool now. She'd lit candles and prayed for her son's support and presence, and she had got it.

And now, by Peader's bed, his son continued his monologue.

'So then, Daddy, I walked along by the pier head and breathed in the good salt air of the sea, and thought about Dublin. Daddy, you know Mammy's here wit' you, longin' for you to be better? Well, it means the kids is by themselves so they are, and you know Polly's only a spalpeen, a baby almost. When you're better, Mammy will take you home ... oh, Daddy, can you not hear a word I say?'

'Talk to him,' the doctor had said. 'His body has healed but his mind's wheeling out there in limbo somewhere, waiting for something, or someone, to call him back. So talk, argue, laugh, cry, but keep doing it, and one day, he'll respond.'

Brogan picked up his father's hand, once so huge and gnarled, now so thin and white and pathetic somehow. He squeezed it.

'Daddy, I'm worried over Polly so I am! Can ye not hear me? She's only a little girl and she's tryin' her best to keep the family together whiles Mammy and I . . .' For a second Brogan's voice failed him; his father's eyelids had flickered and a slight frown had gathered on his pale brow! 'Daddy! Can ye hear me, Daddy?'

'A little gorl . . .' the words were whispered so faintly that Brogan could barely catch them. 'A little gorl . . .'

He had spoken and his words had made sense, for hadn't Brogan been talking about Polly and his worries concerning her only seconds before?

'That's right, Daddy, she's just a little girl,' he said excitedly. 'Can you take a drink now? There's a glass of barley water by your bed . . .'

'A little gorl . . .' the whisper faded to nothing but even as Brogan watched, he saw his father's lips frame the three words again.

A passing nurse found herself grabbed and hustled over to Peader's bed by his handsome young son who did not even seem to know he was handsome – nor to take any notice of even the prettiest and most forthcoming nurse.

'Sister, Sister, he spoke, me daddy spoke! I was talkin' about me little sister, and me daddy said *A little girl*! Honest to God, Sister, he spoke!'

'Talk about your sister some more, Mr O'Brady,' the nurse said, almost as excited as he. Peader had been gradually regaining his physical strength for weeks now. His wounds had healed up well, but his mind had refused to recognise any stimuli which had been offered. If only they could interest him, bring him back!

But though Brogan continued to talk to his father until the nurses on the night-shift turned him out, not another word passed his lips.

Everyone knew, soon enough, that Peader had spoken. Deirdre spent hours in church, on her knees, thanking God – and then demanding a repeat performance when she herself was present. She was a little hurt that Peader had responded to talk of Polly and not of herself but what did it really matter, after all? What mattered was that he had spoken, was on the road to recovery.

'Bring Polly in,' the doctor said next day when the incident was related to him. 'He's clearly very fond of the little girl; she must visit him, talk to him.'

'She's in Dublin . . . but I could go back, bring her over,' Brogan said excitedly. 'Oh, Mammy, we should have thought – Daddy always responded well to Polly.'

But there was no need, because that very same night, Peader spoke again. Deirdre and Brogan were by his bed, getting ready to say goodnight to him because the night-shift wanted them out. Deirdre bent over, kissed him on the brow and then, on impulse, recited a bit of a poem she sometimes said to the children.

Matthew, Mark, Luke and John,
The bed be blest that I lie on,
Four angels to my bed,
Four angels round my head,
One to watch and one to pray
And two to bear my soul away.

Deirdre was turning away from the bed, Brogan was taking her elbow, when Peader moved his head restlessly on the pillow, and spoke, his voice slow and rusty from disuse.

'That little gorl – is she an angel?' Peader said.

Meanwhile, things had reached a parlous state in the O'Brady place in Dublin. Mammy wrote regularly, Brogan intermittently, but the children hardly ever wrote back. Polly had decided that work must be evenly divided and drove poor Ivan into screaming fits by sitting him down with a bowl of spuds and telling him to 'scrub the dirt off that lot or I'll not let you play out for a week, young feller'.

The rooms were dirty, untidy, unwelcoming. Polly did more than her share but it seemed to Donal and Bevin that she spent an awful lot of time making them do household tasks which, they felt, were unsuited to the superior sex. And then the priest came round.

'How are ye managing?' he said jovially, entering the living room without knocking, the priests naturally having little respect for a handful of kids, Polly thought to herself, glancing hastily round the room. 'Oh, Mother of Jesus!'

Polly knew what had called forth the exclamation – but he didn't know how hard it was to manage when you were only just ten and hadn't ever been taught housekeeping skills. And then for a moment she saw the room through a stranger's eyes and was ashamed Dust everywhere, food lying about waiting to be eaten. dirty clothing scuffed into corners, clean clothing in rumpled, unironed heaps. And the hens.

Mammy would never have stood for the hens, but then she didn't have Polly's problems, and Tad had given her the hens, anyway. She had never asked where he'd got them because she suspected she might not like the answer . . . but she liked the hens. They got on well with Lionel the ginger tom-cat, with the tortoise-shell stray which Polly had lately acquired, and with Delilah the dog, though Delilah got angry when he found the hens pecking away at his half-chewed bones. And Lionel teased them sometimes by hiding on top of the dining table and then leaping on to a passing feathered back, which Tad said – and he, as the donor of the hens, should know – did not help egg production.

The eggs were lovely, though. You couldn't go into the country to collect eggs, but you could go and collect corn, and with the corn plus any old bits of rotting fruit or vegetables which the stallholders in Francis Street threw out at the end of the day, you fed the hens.

'Poultry, my child?' That was the priest, his voice faint with disbelief. 'In your mammy's good parlour?' his voice rose, gained a little strength. 'Oh, God save you, that one's drinkin' out of the holy water stoup so it is!'

'That's not the holy . . . oh, well, someone's stood it on the floor by mistake,' Polly muttered, red to her ears. 'Honest to God, father, they have a nice tin bowl for their water . . . the bloody dog must of kicked it under a chair.'

'Wha-aat?' roared Father Feeney, his voice coming back alarmingly suddenly. 'What did ye say, child?'

Polly, who never swore and had simply repeated what Martin had called Delilah when he had caught the dog thoughtfully chewing the stiff white collar to his best shirt, reddened still further, or at least she supposed she had because she felt as though she were on fire so she did.

'Oh! Sorry, Father . . . the naughty dog, I meant. The naughty dog must of kicked it under the chair.'

'Kicked what?' Father Feeney said. 'What the divil

are you talkin' about, child? What I'm sayin' is you've turned your mammy's lovely home into a madhouse! Dogs, cats, hens and dirt. It won't do, Polly, indeed it won't.'

'I know it won't, Father,' Polly said – and did the best thing she could have done. She bolted across the room and landed fair and square in Father Feeney's waistcoat, or where his waistcoat would have been had he been a man and not a priest. 'Oh, Father, it's so awful here wit'out me mammy!'

Polly, a regular attender at Sunday school, a buyer of candles and the owner of one of the sweetest, purest voices ever to be raised in John's Lane Church, knew herself to be one of Father Feeney's favourites, otherwise she would never have dared. Priests, the boys frequently complained, could hit harder than teachers or policemen, so they could. But Father Feeney, after the initial staggering back, put his arms round Polly's narrow shoulders and gave her a comforting squeeze.

'Sure and it's none of it your fault, alanna,' he said roundly. ''Tis the lads, wit'out a doubt. But 'tis a woman's hand that's lackin' here. I'll send someone round.'

A fortnight earlier Polly's heart might have sunk at the thought of adult interference, but not any more. All she wanted was another woman to come and take the responsibility off her shoulders. She gave a consenting mutter and hugged Father Feeney harder, causing him to sit down rather abruptly on the arm of the sofa. But he patted her soothingly, told Ivan to get off his bum and put the holy water stoup back where it belonged, out of that evil hen's reach, and then stood back, putting Polly gently away from him.

'Don't worry, girleen, we'll soon have this place

straight,' he told her. 'I'll send someone up at once. Is your mammy sending you money?'

'Brogan sends as much as he can,' Polly said, starting to try to shush the hens back into the kitchen. In a way it was a pity the priest had called; she and Tad had talked about acquiring a pig, but though pigs looked very sweet when they were small, she could imagine that one of the big ones could do a deal of damage in Mammy's nice parlour and besides, it might not like the cats and Delilah. 'Will I give the person you send money then, Father? Only we don't have much to spare . . . I'm not at school any more, which is a saving . . .'

'Not at school, alanna?' Father Feeney's voice had gone high again. Ah, God, I've give meself away, Polly thought. Priests an' teachers always stick together, don't they so? He'll tell me what's wrong wit' the National School so he will; he'll say what's to pay there?

'What's wrong wit' the National School?' the priest said, echoing Polly's thoughts. 'There's no money to pay there.'

'It's the time; I can't spare the time when I've all the housework an' the cookin' an' the messages to do,' Polly said plaintively, trying to ignore the glance which the priest sent around the room. Ivan, sitting on the floor scrubbing potatoes in a bowl of filthy water, said loudly: 'I do the messages, Poll – you make me.'

Polly waited until the priest had turned to stare at a peculiarly arrogant hen as it strutted in from the kitchen and then she aimed a kick at Ivan which landed rather neatly on his small bottom. Ivan yelled, then scrambled to his feet to kick back just as the priest said in an outraged voice: 'It's a cockerel!'

'What, that hen?' Polly said. 'What's a cockerel, Father?'

'It's a male hen, alanna. It – it's the daddy to the little yellow chicks. What in God's good name are ye doin' wit' a cockerel up here?'

'Tad said they'd make little chicks if we waited a while,' Polly said in a satisfied tone. You could trust Tad, she thought, he was almost always right. 'Oh, so that's the daddy, is it?' She examined the cockerel closely, but apart from the scarlet ribbon-thing on his head and the dangly red bobbles on each side of his beak he looked just like the other hens to her. 'So that's why he doesn't lay eggs, is it?' she added. 'He's the daddy, so the others are the mammies, and they're the ones that lay the eggs. Do I have it right, Father?'

'You do,' Father Feeney said in a strangled sort of voice. He put a hand into his collar and pulled it away from his neck as though it were too tight for him. 'Glory be to God, it's an education, this place.' He turned and opened the door on to the landing, then turned back. 'Polly, you'll be in school tomorrow, either at the Convent or the National School; is that clear?'

Polly had always known it was too good to last and besides, what with Brogan's money, Martin's earnings and the hens, they weren't too badly off financially. Summer was almost upon them and she and Tad had various plans for the summer. They included cockling at Booterstown, taking the pram out into the country and digging spuds (after dark, Tad had said evilly), working at fruit picking and rabbiting.

'Rabbit is grand so it is,' Tad had said. 'You'll love rabbit.'

Polly had agreed that she would, and it was not until she realised that they were talking at cross-purposes

– she of hutches, he of pots – that she vetoed that suggestion. And Tad had agreed, presumably because the thought of Polly lovingly rearing rabbits to eat the hens' corn was more than he could bear.

'You're nutty about animals so you are,' he grumbled, but made no further attempt to persuade her and suggested, instead, that they might dig worms for the hens. But Polly, thinking this was unsporting to say the least, said worms gave her the creeps so they did, so that one had been shelved, too.

'Polly!' the priest said warningly, now. 'Did ye hear what I said now? School on Monday; understand?'

'Yes, Father,' Polly said obediently. There were, after all, only another few weeks to the end of term. 'I'll be glad to go back so I will.'

After the priest had gone, however, she and Ivan began to try to tidy up.

'I don't like hen's shit,' Ivan whined, trying feebly to get it off the linoleum. 'It's sticky and stinky.'

'Shut up and scrub,' Polly ordered. Then, relenting: 'If you get it off, Ivan me little love, sure an' I'll give you an egg to your tea – two eggs.'

'An' bread an' Maggie Ryan?' Ivan said, scrubbing away. 'An' chewed apple?'

'It's *stewed* apple,' Polly said reprovingly. 'Do try and talk proper, me boy. Yes, you shall have two eggs, bread an' margarine, and stewed apple. Only you've got to get the lino clean first.'

She then set to herself, wondering rather apprehensively who the father would send, but presently there was a knock on the door and a gentle, very young voice said, 'Can I come in, now? The father sent me.'

'Come in an' welcome,' Polly said. 'Oh, Miren, 'tis glad I am to see you! I was wonderin' who Father

Feeney would send . . . don't be cross, but it's got a bit messy so it has.'

'Whoever knew me cross?' Miren said. 'Good Lord, hens! I *t'ought* I heard some funny sounds here, as I went past.'

Miren lived on the floor above and was a poor unfortunate, but everyone liked her and pitied her, too. She had come to Dublin as a housemaid and had become pregnant as had many another before her. Sacked and forbidden to go home, she had given birth to her baby and handed it over for adoption, and then she had done the only thing she knew, for no one wanted her, now, as a housemaid.

'Damaged goods they call the girls they've ruined, the so-called gentry do,' Mammy had said once, referring to the poor girls who shared a couple of rooms on the floor above their own. 'And many of those poor innocents have been murdered in their beds by men who take their pleasure and then won't pay for it.'

'Innocents?' the neighbour to whom the remark had been addressed said in a bemused tone. 'Sure an' that's not the right word I'm thinkin', Deirdre.'

'It is so,' Deirdre had asserted. 'Innocent they were when they came to this town despite what life has done to them and innocent they'll die, for they've no malice or evil in their souls.'

But now Miren was looking round the room and tutting gently so Polly put both arms round the older girl's waist and hugged her hard.

'I'm sorry, Miren, about the mess, but I'm only ten and . . .'

'Don't worry, little one,' Miren said. 'Help me and we'll have it clear and bright in two shakes of a . . . oh, my God, what's that doin' here?'

'He's a man-hen,' Polly said rather proudly. 'He's

goin' to help the other hens, the woman-hens, to make little yellow chicks; Father Feeney says so.'

'Oh, does he?' Miren said. She was laughing. 'Cockerels peck, or have you already found that out, alanna?'

'He doesn't peck me, I'm his friend. I give him corn an' cabbage an' turnip,' Polly said. 'Besides, I like him. My friend Tad gave me them.'

'Glory be! How many have you?'

'Seven hens and one man-hen,' Polly said. 'What did you say he was called?'

'A cockerel, alanna. Eh, it's like old times to see hens scrattin', but it's not the place for them, you know. Hens needs outside, they needs to peck an' croodle an' pick at fresh grass, worms . . .' Polly shuddered, ' . . . leaves, all sorts. You could get the boys to make you a run an' keep 'em in the courtyard.'

'No, indeed,' Polly said. 'They'd be stole an' ate. You know what folk are. Besides, they're happy in here really they are, Miren. They peck an' pick at the dirt between the floorboards in the kitchen, an' they eat their corn . . . they sit by the fire of an evenin', just like the cats, blinkin' at the flames. And the eggs is good . . . once we beat 'em in milk an' made a custard – it was the nicest thing!'

'Oh well, I'm a country girl meself,' Merin said philosophically. 'But what'll you do when they're old, past layin', child?'

'Get more, an' retire these,' Polly said. She turned to the nearest hen, which was thoughtfully tugging at a loose thread on the rag rug, doubtless under the impression that it had found a worm at last. 'You won't be ate, I promise,' she informed its indifferent back.

'That's cleared that up, then,' Miren said. 'And now, alanna, let's get on wit' our tidyin'!'

Chapter Fourteen

August–October 1934

The day the doctors officially agreed that Peader was out of danger, more, that he was going to get well, Deirdre lit an altar-full of candles and thanked God, his Holy Mother and all the saints. She stayed on her knees for an hour, thanking the whole of the heavenly host, just about, she even threw in a special little prayer of thanks to Polly's guardian angel, for sure and hadn't the angel done her work well? Deirdre had needed to concentrate wholly on her man, and though she had worried a little when Polly told her that Miren was now coming in daily to 'help out', the truth was that beside the crippling anxiety of a sick husband, every other worry paled into insignificance. But that particular worry was over, now, for the doctors, nurses and support staff were delighted with Peader's progress.

'He'll not work as a safety man again, but there's nothing to stop him doing a clerical job,' the doctor told Deirdre a couple of weeks before she took her husband home. 'And the railway has agreed that they'll find him something – a country station, probably, with a small ticket office which needs manning. Or a level crossing, because you'd have a little cottage, a garden . . . now that's a job you could help him with, my dear.'

A level crossing! From that moment on, Deirdre was all smiles. Her worries disappeared like frost in June at the mere prospect of a little cottage and a garden. She knew, now, that her strange attitude to Peader's suggestion of a move had been partly fear of the unknown and partly the change of life. The doctor, when consulted, had told her that the change of life was something with which she would learn to cope, that he could give her some pills, but that she probably would not need them now she knew the cause of her bad temper and depression. And because she loved Peader deeply, always had and always would, and wanted to be with him, she knew that she would be able to tackle this old change of life, to take it in her stride. She would conquer the bad temper and depression, not allow either to rule her. And, armed with this resolution, she found that her attacks of unhappiness and misery had all but disappeared. Love, and nearness, had won. She would cling to Peader wherever he was, whatever he did, and they would be all right.

She had acknowledged, both to herself and to Peader, that the letter had been dreadful, a terrible mistake. She had shown him the other letter, which had arrived soon after his accident, explained how she had regretted the first one as soon as it was in the box, begged his forgiveness. And Peader had smiled his faint smile and said what was there to forgive? She was here, wasn't she? She loved him, didn't she? Well, then!

And he was a hero. The fellers who had gone out and brought him back after the train had hit him hadn't told the whole story when they thought Peader was going to die; the little girl might have been in trouble and there would have been no point. But when they realised that he was going to recover, Trucker Jones blabbed it all over.

'Peader's a bleedin' 'ero,' he told everyone who

would listen. 'Fellers say 'e didn't 'ear the train in the fog – as though an old railwayman like Peader wouldn't 'ave 'ad 'is ears akimbo, strainin' to 'ear, let alone that 'e'd 'ave *felt* 'er approachin', same as we all do! No, it seems 'e saw this little girl, see, comin' towards him across the lines. 'E yelled 'er to gerrout the way but she didn't gerrit, went on a-comin'. So bein' the sort o' feller 'e was 'e ran towards 'er, grabbed 'er, threw 'er to safety . . . and left it too late to save 'imself.'

'Where's the little girl? Who was she?' folk asked, but neither Trucker nor his mates could tell them. The men all agreed she was young, light-haired, ragged, with a bit of a shawl round her shoulders and cracked boots several sizes too large on her feet. She had come out of the fog, screamed to them that there had been an accident, led them to the spot whilst telling them breathlessly what had happened . . . and disappeared.

The newspapers got hold of it, of course. It wasn't only the *Echo* which gave the 'mystery girl', as they were soon calling her, banner headlines. The nationals did, too. And when the Dublin papers realised Peader was a local they, too, published the story – with suitable embellishments, naturally.

Deirdre wrote to Polly that she and the boys should be terrible proud of their daddy and Polly wrote back that they were, so. And then Deirdre realised that Peader was actually worrying about that little girl.

'But, me darlin', you saved her life, everyone knows that,' she said gently, walking beside him in the grounds of the convalescent home to which he had been sent. 'You can't doubt that . . . and what else could you have done?'

Peader sighed. 'I'd have fed her,' he said, in the new slow, careful voice which had come to him after the accident. 'I'd feed 'em all, if I could, all the little gorls an' the chisellers an' the babes in arms who don't get enough to eat.'

Deirdre squeezed his arm. 'So would I, me darlin', so would I,' she agreed. 'And when the little girl comes forward, we'll see her right.' She smiled up into his face, her eyes unshadowed now. 'Brogan's coming to visit you this evening; you'll like that!'

Peader loved strolling with Brogan in the grounds of the convalescent home. He knew, now, that he was going to be offered a level crossing with a little house attached, that he would man the crossing, open and close the gates . . . it sounded idyllic. And there was a garden. Peader knew nothing about gardening but wasn't Brogan the expert there? Since he'd been in the convalescent home, furthermore, Peader had done a lot of talking to the gardeners and felt he was beginning to learn. He found he couldn't wait to get his hands on that garden . . . oh, the cabbage he would grow there, the magnificent crops of potatoes, the fine carrots and onions!

So naturally he was ready and waiting that evening, standing by the side door through which his son usually came. He would be out in a few days, going home to Dublin for a while. There, he would arrange for their possessions to be shipped to Liverpool. They would say goodbye to their friends and neighbours, walk out of the house in Swift's Alley, and journey back to England to take up his new job.

But he was worried about Polly. To bring her back here . . . was it asking for trouble? He knew what Polly meant to Deirdre and to the rest of them as well. He would never forgive himself if, by bringing her back, they lost her.

But it wasn't likely, was it? Deirdre knew about Polly's past, that her mother had not loved her children, that her father was a brute and a bully. She knew about Jess, too, and how, after Jess's death, Peader and Brogan had decided that bringing the baby back to Ireland was the only safe course. She had never questioned it – why should she? She knew her men, knew they wouldn't have lied to her.

And weren't we right? Peader reminded himself stoutly now. Decent food, fresh air and lots of love had turned his little girl into a beauty – if she'd been left in Liverpool, to drag herself up as best she could, Peader was sure she would look very different, now.

And he wanted to ask Brogan about the girl who had been pushed to safety from under the wheels of the train. For one confused moment, when he'd come round in hospital and heard Deirdre reciting the poem about angels which his children loved, he had thought that perhaps the girl on the tracks had been an angel. But he knew it wasn't so, of course. He could still feel the thin shoulders of her against the calloused palms of his hands, still feel the slight weight of her. And she wasn't a ghost, either, even though she seemed to have disappeared so completely. She was just another little stray cat of a child, unloved, uncherished, searching for the means to continue what passed for her life.

Brogan would find her, though, if anyone could. Brogan was kind, generous-spirited; a broth of a boy in fact. He shouldered burdens with never a frown, undertook anything asked of him, seldom argued, never complained. So if he, Peader, explained how important it was to him to find that scrawny little girl, asked Brogan to keep an eye out when he was anywhere near the marshalling yards, then there was a good chance his boy would come across her in the fullness of time.

Because once they were back from Ireland, the rest of the family wouldn't be seeing much of the city of Liverpool again. It would be straight out on to the Wirral, to their new home, and they would find out how country living suited them.

Peader gave a big, contented grin, he couldn't help himself. Just the thought of having all that loveliness around him brought his wonderful luck to mind and made him smile. Of course he would not be unscathed; he would walk with a stick for the rest of his life, feel pain from some of his wounds, never be able to do really heavy work. But what did that matter, when all was said and done? He could man his crossing, open and close his gate . . . and dig his garden, plant and hoe, weed and sow. What more could a man ask?

Brogan left the convalescent home that evening in a thoughtful frame of mind. That young girl – wasn't it an odd coincidence, now, that there had been two extremely dangerous accidents on the rails just there, both involving a young girl? When Jess Carbery had been killed there had been no one near enough to save her, but this time, his daddy had acted fast and the child had escaped unscathed.

Was she a Carbery? She couldn't possibly be, the family seemed to have disappeared. And it was hard, now, to remember exactly what Jess had talked about that evening in the draughty little shed so long ago. But she had mentioned another sister, a child, then, of three or four. Had she used her name? But that he truly could not remember, and in any event, since he had no idea what the child was called whose life had been saved by his daddy, remembering would do very little good.

And even if she was a Carbery, did it really matter, make any difference? His daddy had been shocked and distressed by the skinny waif wandering the railway and had wanted to help her no matter what her name was. So do I, Brogan told himself quickly. I want to help her, too. But if she is the missing Carbery daughter, wouldn't that be grand, now? The fellers say Jess haunts the track, searching for her little sister, but if she's in Heaven then she knows full well that the sister we've rechristened Polly is safer, and happier, with us than she ever could have been with her own family.

But if Jess was searching for the other sister and not Polly at all, it would make a sort of sense. She would be anxious about Grace, the child she'd left at home on that snowy Christmas Day. Now look at that, Brogan told himself, when you don't try sure and doesn't the name pop into your head as though it had never been forgot? Of course she was Grace, I remember now.

He had walked out of the convalescent home grounds and now he set off along the quiet and dusty roadway, meaning to head for civilisation and a tram stop, but it was such a nice evening that he thought he'd walk, instead. He reached the top of Beaconsfield Road, hesitated, then turned down it. He could pick up a tram on the main road, but the gardens and houses down here were marvellous, he often went this way after he'd left his father. And it was a perfect late summer evening, with sweet gusts of perfume blowing to him on the breeze and the birds singing their hearts out as the sun sank in the sky.

Brogan walked slowly, looking long and keenly into each garden as he passed. The convalescent home had once been a manor house of some description and the grounds were tended with care, but some of these houses had gardens almost unbelievable in their beauty. Brogan lingered more than ever, gazing at smooth lawns, flower-beds rich with roses, wisteria clambering over grey stone or russet brick, and of course at the wonders he could only guess at because they were imprisoned behind the glittering walls of glasshouses or conservatories.

But presently, about halfway down the hill – for Beaconsfield Road was on a steepish hill – he came to a house which was not surrounded by an impeccable garden. It was overgrown; fancy that! There was a tennis lawn with grass almost knee-high, weed-choked flower-beds and a gravel frontage which was not only weedy, it was also covered with piles of bricks, a concrete mixer, a great many long planks of wood and assorted tools connected with the building trade.

It's being rebuilt, or altered, at any rate, Brogan thought to himself, stopping to stare. It's going to be something different – I wonder what? And I wonder whether they'd be glad of a chap to help with the garden, in the evenings and on his days off? He missed his Crewe plot and Mrs Burt, kind though she was, could not conjure a garden out of thin air for him to help her with. She had a smelly little back yard where the only things which flourished were bits of old bicycles and a couple of washing lines. Allotments, though they did exist in the city, were all full and were passed on, Brogan gathered, from father to son. So if these people really could do with help, Brogan was the feller for them.

Pity he didn't know their name, though. But as he was about to pass regretfully on, he glanced at the big stone gateposts. *Strawberry Field* the legend on the gatepost ran. Brogan nodded to himself and committed it to memory, then walked on, a little faster now. Tomorrow he would begin to put out feelers to find the little girl his father felt he had lost. He would speak to the gangs who worked the marshalling yard because, like Peader, he suspected that the kid probably hung around there, hoping for scraps of some sort, using the sheds for shelter. And if that failed he could go round the schools when he had a couple of hours off, see whether he could find out from teachers or pupils if the 'mystery girl' was known to them. And then he could try churches, priests, parks and places of entertainment beloved of kids – the Saturday rush for example.

I'll find her in the end, Brogan told himself. I'll start tomorrow.

By the time September came round, Sara was beginning to see light out at the new children's home. She was a small cog in a fairly big wheel, but *how* she enjoyed herself! She had not realised how much she had taken in, without realising it, about the running of a large house and larger garden, and now, at last, such knowledge came in useful.

'Leave the garden surrounding the house itself until last,' she advised. 'Because whilst the alterations are going on it will only get trampled flat anyway. For now, let's put all our efforts into getting the house right – and into keeping the vegetable garden and the greenhouses producing. That way, we'll have a reasonable amount of fresh fruit and vegetables when the children come in.'

She was learning a lot, too – more than she taught, definitely. She learned how to plan rooms in which children can happily spend their days and nights, to make nurseries for very young children, bedrooms for others, playrooms, classrooms, sitting rooms – in fact she began to learn how to plan a house in which children and adults may live happily together.

She was still not living in, which was a blessing in a way, since her grandmother was becoming increasingly frail, even Sara's prejudiced eye could see it. Mrs Prescott enjoyed living in Florence Street and found it easy to get to the shops, but she went out less and less and relied more and more on Sara and Clarrie. However, she had become a cinema enthusiast and once a week a neighbour wheeled her round to the Victoria Picture Palace where she sampled everything they had on offer – comedies, horror, thrillers, cowboy and Indian films.

'You should come wi' me from time to time, queen,' she told her granddaughter. 'For one thing it takes you out of yourself, and for another, it entertains you. What's wrong wi' that, eh?'

Sara said politely that she was sure there was nothing wrong with that, and continued to spend her evenings planning, reading, or preparing for the coming day, apart from when she was on soup kitchen duty, or taking the *War Cry* round the pubs, of course. Because she was so absorbed in her work, indeed, even her Saturdays, once an oasis of rest and pleasure, became simply another day in which to plot and plan.

'We could do so many things, if we'd a mind,' Mrs Prescott said persuasively one fine evening in August when the breeze was mild and the air coming through the window sweet. 'There's the theatre, art galleries, all sorts. If you had more spare time, queen, we could get about a bit. And there's Sat'day night dances . . . you could wheel me in perched on me chair and I could watch all the gallivanting. My, I'd enjoy that.'

She had sounded wistful but Sara, though she would

have loved to take her grandmother about a bit, was firm.

'The Strawb needs me right now,' she said, with a sigh. 'Later, when it's up and running, I'll be able to relax a bit more, enjoy myself. But right now, Gran, I dare not let up, really. Will you forgive me for being so boring?'

'No, I shan't,' Mrs Prescott said, then chuckled and leaned across the table which divided them, taking Sara's hands in hers. 'My dear girl, you're a tower of strength . . . it's just that I don't want to see you growing into an old maid, looking after me for the rest of your life. I want you to get about more, meet people.'

'All work and no play makes Jack a dull boy,' Clarrie said, and later that same week she announced, after supper, that she was going to the cinema whether Sara liked it or not.

'Come with me, Sara. Mrs Prescott's right, a bit of an outing would do you good. Besides, it'll be much more fun if there's two of us eatin' peanuts and chuckin' the shells about in the sixpenny seats! I'd enjoy meself far better if you came along, honest I would. It's not as if there was anything wrong with the cinema; the Army approves!'

But Sara, though she laughed, still shook her head.

'Can't. I'm going along with the brigadier tomorrow to look at little desks. And I'm trying to produce a drawing of the ideal locker for a child's dormitory. What's on at the Vic, anyway?'

'I'm not going to the Vic, I'm going to the Astoria,' Clarrie told her. 'They're showin' Shirley Temple in *Little Miss Marker*. Do come, queen.'

'We-ell, I really ought to finish this drawing,' Sara said. 'Only I do love to watch the child stars. It's the teacher in me coming out, I suppose.' She laid down her paperwork and smiled at her friend. Oh, all right, you've persuaded me. I'll come.' She turned to her grandmother. 'Why don't you come as well, Gran? You said you wanted more exciting outings.'

'Well, I'm glad you're not turnin' into some boring little Goody-two-shoes,' Gran said unkindly from her seat by the window. 'But I've seen it – so I won't trouble you this evening. But if you're comin' past the fried fish shop when it's over, I'd like a penn'orth of chips, please! And if you'll pass over my knitting and turn the wireless on, I'll have another scarf finished by the time you get back!'

It was a good film, and Sara really enjoyed it. Coming past Platts fried fish shop on their way home, she remembered her grandmother's request and tugged Clarrie's arm.

'Gran wanted a penn'orth of chips, Clarrie. I wouldn't mind some myself, and a bit of fish. I wonder if they've got any haddock? Gran's fond of that.'

'I prefer cod,' Clarrie said. 'Oh, come on, let's treat ourselves. Fish an' chips all round, eh? And if we get indigestion, that's hard luck. It's our evenin' off, queen!'

So, armed with three portions of fish and chips wrapped in newspaper, they went back to the flat, letting themselves in through the back door straight into the tiny scullery and calling to Gran that they would be bringing her tea through just as soon as they'd got the food on to the plates.

'I like 'em best in the newspaper,' Clarrie said as she unwrapped. 'But I've gorra pretend to be a lady now and then. Good for Mrs P, the kettle's still hot. I'll just warm the pot . . . you take the grub through.'

Sara piled the food on a tray and carried it into the living room.

'Tan tara! A penn'orth of chips, Gran, *and* some fish, because we've decided to treat ourselves to a . . . Gran?'

Mrs Prescott was sitting in her chair by the window, but she had lolled over sideways at what looked like a very uncomfortable angle. She had obviously fallen asleep, for her knitting was on the floor at her feet and the wireless played on unregarded.

'Gran, we've bought fish and chips,' Sara said softly. She stood the tray down and went over to her grandmother's side. 'Well, fancy falling asleep when . . . oh, my God!'

'What's up?' Clarrie said, appearing in the doorway. 'Don't you want . . . oh, Sara, is she ill? I'll get the doctor at once . . . I'll run down the road to the telephone box . . .'

Sara stroked her grandmother's wispy grey hair back from her forehead and straightened her in the chair. Then she closed her fingers round her grandmother's wrist. Finally, she turned to Clarrie.

'Yes, do get the doctor,' she said quietly. 'But I think it's too late, Clarrie. I think she's already gone.'

'It's great you're comin' home wit' us, Brog,' Peader said as the ship drew nearer to Ireland's shore. 'Your mammy's very good, but she's got a lot on her mind. She'll stay wit' me, make sure I get down the gangplank an' so on, if you'll see to the cases.'

'I will, Daddy,' Brogan said equably. 'Is it excited you are to be seein' your native land after you've been so ill?'

'I'm more excited at the thought of the kids,' Peader admitted. 'They've been great, none could be better. I want to tell 'em so meself, Brog.'

'They have done well, especially Polly,' Brogan agreed. 'I don't suppose the boys did much in the house, knowing them, though I'm sure they carted coal, wood, water, that sort of thing. Poor Polly, she's only a baby, really.'

'She's ten years old and that's no baby,' Deirdre said rather sharply. She had been standing a short way away, gazing silently at the approaching coastline, but now she moved nearer them. 'But sure she's done well so she has. The father wrote, you know. A bit guarded, he was, but he seemed pleased wit' our girl.'

'And how'll they take the news that we're all movin'?' Brogan asked. 'Will they be pleased, d'you t'ink, Mammy?'

'Polly will be just thrilled,' Deirdre said happily. 'Because she's mad about animals so she is and the thought of livin' in the countryside and bein' able to have as many cats and dogs as she wants . . . that'll win her over if nothin' else does.'

'I *know* they're comin' home tomorrow, an' I *am* glad, sure I am, but I still don't want to send me hens away,' Polly said stubbornly. 'What's wrong wit' them, Miren? I'll keep 'em in the kitchen just for a day or so, if you like.'

'Polly, the bleedin' poultry must go,' Martin said severely from his seat by the fire. 'We've let you and them alone now for weeks – well, the eggs was worth a bit o' muck on the lino – but our mammy will go mad wit' you so she will. And you don't want that, do you, so she won't see them, is that clear? You can't keep hens in the house, that's what she'll say, and you'll spoil an' ruin her homecoming so you will.'

'I won't, so,' Polly said defiantly. 'Mammy's sensible; she'll love me hens.'

'She won't, because she isn't going to see them,' Martin repeated. 'Don't you defy me, alanna, or it's to bed you'll go straight away, and you'll not even see your hens when we let you up again.'

Polly's eyes rounded. Martin was as easy-going as Brogan and a good deal lazier; she'd had no trouble with him until this very moment, and she didn't like it one bit. Why, if he persisted, it would be he who ran the household and not her! But she did concede, having thought it over, that he had a point. Mammy might not be too thrilled to find her home overrun with hens.

'All right then,' she said sulkily after a moment. 'Say I send 'em away for a bit – where am I to send 'em? I won't let anyone lay a finger on 'em if they're thinkin' of roast fowl, Martin, 'cos they're me friends so they are.'

'Give them to someone in a ground-floor room, who's got a bit of space outside,' Martin said tactfully. Bevin, not nearly so tactful, said: 'Give them to old Halligan – no, sell them to him. He'd make good use of 'em.'

Mr Halligan was a butcher. Polly screamed.

'Don't you say that name where me hens can hear,' she shrieked. 'I'm warnin' ye, Bevin O'Brady, that I'll swing for you if you touch a feather of their heads.'

'No, no, he's only coddin' you,' Martin said, chuckling. 'What about Tad? There's plenty of space in Gardiners Lane for hens . . . doesn't he have a few of his own, come to think? You could let him take care of your hens, alanna, until Mammy and Daddy are settled again.'

'Tad's daddy might eat 'em,' Polly said with quivering lip. 'He kilt one of Tad's birds one day when he found her perched on his clean boots so he did. I won't have me birds kilt by that . . . that . . .'

'We'll have to tell Tad's daddy that they're ours,' Bevin said. He was doing his eckers sitting cross-legged on the hearthrug and now he threw down his book and smiled kindly up at his sister. 'I was coddin' you, alanna, and I'm sorry. I'll help you take 'em round to Tad, if you like. We'll go in an' see Mr Donoghue an' tell him they're our hens . . . we'll tell him we're payin' rent for 'em, then he won't dare to kill so much as a feather of 'em.'

'Well, all right,' Polly said at last, having tried – and failed – to think of a better solution. She didn't trust Tad's daddy, but she did trust Tad. He never let her down, no doubt if she explained the seriousness of the situation he would stand by her again.

So they put the hens in pillowcases and carried their squawking burdens down the stairs, across the courtyard, along Swift's Alley and into Francis Street, where some ribald remarks followed them from interested stallholders, and finally into Gardiners Lane. As luck would have it, Tad was mucking around in one of the ruined houses and called them over.

'Hello Poll, Bev,' he said cheerfully. 'What you got there, eh?'

'Me hens,' Polly said heavily. 'The ones you gave me, Tad. Martin says we can't have 'em in the rooms when Mammy and Daddy come home tomorrow. Can you keep 'em for us if we pay rent?'

'How much?' Tad said with all his usual bluntness. 'And will the rent include corn?'

'We'll give ye a tanner a week,' Polly said briskly, her interest aroused. A tanner sounded like a lot of money, but feeding the hens, Polly knew, was no sinecure, and Tad might not find it easy to beg scraps the way she did.

'A tanner! Make it a bob and we're in business.'

'Ninepence,' Polly offered, enjoying the huckstering now. 'Ninepence and not a penny more, Mr Donoghue.'

Tad laughed. 'Done!' he said. 'And you must help gather the corn, Poll, or it won't be fair.'

The arrival of Mammy, Daddy and Brogan, long anticipated, was every bit as good as Polly could have wished. Daddy's face had a long scar across one cheek, all purple and wrinkled still, and another across his forehead, thin and angry-looking. His hair had gone snowy white, but Polly thought it suited him, and he walked with a stick and slowly, at that, and he took his time getting in and out of chairs, and it had taken him a long, long while to mount the stairs, but other than that he was just the same. Her dearest daddy, with his slow speech, his slow smile, and his quick kindnesses.

Polly had done her best, aided by Miren, and thought that all traces of her feathered friends had been removed. To be sure, the first thing Mammy noticed was the crack in the big mirror, the second thing that the ornaments on the mantel were either gone or chipped. Polly, forewarned that she must not mention the hens at first, murmured that she'd been careless, she was sorry, and wished she had told the truth when Brogan took her aside later and asked her for the pawn tickets.

'For you surely had to take 'em down there,' he murmured, smiling at her. 'But you couldn't tell Mammy.'

'No, they are broke, truly,' Polly admitted in hushed tones. She lowered her voice still further. ''Twas me hens, only don't say a word to Mammy. At first they flew, 'cos their wings wasn't clipped. But Miren said Mammy mustn't know, you see, so I had to tell a fib.'

'It's possible she may guess, alanna,' Brogan said cautiously. 'There's corn in between the floorboards in the kitchen; I noticed it meself so I did. But she won't worry, because . . .'

He broke off and Polly, assuming that he thought they were about to be interrupted, returned to the kitchen, where she was making a meal for the family with quite a lot of help from Deirdre despite Polly constantly telling her, in a very motherly way, to 'go and sit yourself down, Mammy, an' have a nice crack wit' your sons!'

Teatime came. They were all round the table, even Martin having returned from his work, when Daddy broke the news. He sat back in his chair, took a sip of tea, cleared his throat and addressed them.

'You can see I'm well again, but not so spry. In fact the bosses have changed me job, because a safety man needs his full strength, and a deal of agility, too.' He laughed, but no one else even smiled. The accident was too close for that. 'Yes, well. So they've given me a crossing gate. It's in beautiful countryside. There's a cottage with a good garden, and we'll be able to grow a good deal of our own food, and we can keep hens . . .' Polly's ears pricked up, ' . . . pigs, all sorts. So what d'you think?'

'It sounds grand, Daddy,' Bevin said, grinning. 'Wait'll I tell the fellers!'

'Polly?' Peader spoke enquiringly, but he was smiling already.

'Oh, Daddy . . . hens and pigs! I'll look after 'em, I know all about hens.' She turned to her brother. 'Can I tell 'em now, Brogan?'

'Go ahead,' Brogan said. 'Mammy thought you'd be pleased.'

'I've been keepin' hens,' Polly disclosed. 'Only they

made me take 'em round to the ruins, where Tad keeps his. They said you'd not like hens in your parlour, Mammy.'

Deirdre nodded her head slowly. 'Me ornaments – and the corn between the floorboards,' she said ruefully. 'They were right, alanna. But hens in their proper place now, that's another thing altogether so it is.'

'You kept hens here, in our good rooms?' Peader said incredulously, 'Whatever next, alanna? And don't say pigs, because . . .'

'She wanted to have a pig,' Ivan said, placidly cramming half a round of bread and margarine into his mouth. 'But she was afraid it would eat the dog and the cats when it got big.'

'I never did . . . I only said . . .' Polly squeaked, very confused. She turned to her mother. 'Oh, Mammy, it's just . . . and anyway, we're goin' to live in the country! Oh, I'm so, *so* happy!'

And indeed, as soon as tea was over she begged leave to go round and tell Tad that his rent for the hens would not be coming in for long.

'We'll be away in a couple of weeks,' her father had said. 'We won't take the linoleum, but everything else will have to be packed.'

So off Polly trotted on the familiar round. Out of Swift's Alley, along Francis Street . . . and there was Tad, with a dirty old sack, grubbing in the gutters for damaged vegetables for the hens!

'Tad! Oh, Tad, you'll never guess what me daddy's telled us!' Polly gabbled, clutching his sleeve. 'He can't be a safety man no more, 'cos he was hurt bad so he was, but he's goin' to be a railway crossing man instead, wit' a cottage, an' a garden, an' pigs an' hens . . .' She stopped short. 'Tad? Aren't you pleased, now? You can come each day an' see the pigs, if you like.'

'Where?'

'What d'you mean, where? Where can you see the pigs? In their sty, when we've made them one.'

'No, Poll,' Tad said patiently. 'Where's this crossin'?'

'Oh, I see, but what does *where* matter? It'll be on the Howth Road, I bet . . . oh, I *hope* it's there, 'cos of the sea.'

'Ask your daddy,' Tad said in a very peculiar voice. If he hadn't been a chiseller, Polly would have thought he was upset, trying to hold back tears. 'I'll come back wit' you now an' you can ask him right away.'

'Sure I will,' Polly said stoutly, but for the first time, a niggling doubt crossed her mind. Why should the LMS give her daddy a crossing to take care of on a Southern Ireland line? She knew all about the LMS because Daddy and Brogan talked about it. But . . . but they wouldn't give him a line in *England*, surely, and him Irish through and through? She scowled at Tad but he wasn't looking at her. He was staring at his feet, bare and dust-coloured, as they padded along the pavement.

They reached the O'Bradys' door and Polly shoved it open and tugged Tad inside. Scarcely through the door she said loudly, 'Daddy, where's your crossin'? *Say* it isn't in England, *say* it isn't!'

Peader had been dozing in a chair by the fire whilst Deirdre cleared away the tea things and his daughter's abrupt entrance into the room had disturbed a rather pleasant dream. Now, he rubbed his eyes, then yawned fiercely. Deirdre must be washing up in the kitchen; he could hear the clatter as she brought the crocks out of the soapy water and stood them on the bit of a draining board he had made for her himself on his last visit home. She was singing a tune beneath her breath and sounded very happy. Peader sat up straight and tried to answer Polly's question.

'What? Me crossin', d'you mean? It's on the Wirral, alanna, that's a very pleasant part of the country, very pleasant indeed. You'll love it so you will.'

'It's in England, that Wirral, isn't it, Mr O'Brady?' Tad said in a hollow voice. 'You're takin' me pal to England!'

And before anyone could so much as say a word Tad had whipped round and could be heard thundering down the stairs.

'Oh dear,' Peader said inadequately. 'What's worryin' Tad then, alanna?'

Polly ignored the question. 'Daddy?' she said slowly. 'Daddy, Tad's not right, is he?'

'Me darlin', I t'ought you knew, t'ought you'd guess,' Peader said, all his happiness gone and guilt swamping him. He'd not thought of this one, not thought of the kids havin' to leave their pals! 'Of course it's in England, but that's . . .'

'Oh, Tad, Tad!' Polly burst into tears and before Peader could move she was out of the room and clattering down the stairs in Tad's wake.

Peader had got to his feet and was halfway across to the door when Deirdre popped her head into the room.

'I heard that,' she said reassuringly. 'Don't be in a worry, me darlin', 'twas bound to occur. She'll come round when we say Tad must come an' stay wit' us from time to time.'

'But a boy can't pop across the water just like that,' Peader said heavily. 'Oh, why didn't I *think*? She's heartbroken, so she is.'

'I know he won't come to stay, an' so do you, but 'tis a comfort for the child,' Deirdre said. 'She'll accept it better and by the time she realises he's not come over she'll have a dozen new friends an' a whole new life so she will. She's only ten, that's no age, and in England she'll have a better chance than she would here, didn't you say?'

'I did. There's factories, shops . . . yes, I'm sure she'll get work when she's old enough,' Peader said, returning to his chair. 'You're a good woman, Deirdre. When the young one comes back we'll comfort her wit' promises.'

'That's it,' Deirdre agreed. 'Now you sit and rest awhile; close your eyes.'

'Go back to sleep, you mean, like an ould feller,' Peader said, wryly, but he leaned back in the chair and closed his eyes.

It was a long while, however, before he could sleep.

Polly had stood in the stern of the ship and watched Ireland disappear, and now she was standing in the bows and watching Liverpool approach. It was huge so it was – and there were some grand and beautiful buildings. But although the sun was shining a pall of smoke hung over the city, greyish yellow smoke, and the voices which came to her ears both from the shore and from many of the sailors were harsh, with turns of phrase which were new to her.

Brogan was standing beside her and now he put an arm about her shoulders. 'Don't scowl so, Polly,' he said. 'Liverpool's a fine city, but you won't be stayin' there long. You'll be off to me daddy's new crossing in a matter of days. Now you'll like that, won't you?'

'I shall not,' Polly said firmly. 'I want to be wit' Tad so I do. I *like* the Liberties, an' Dublin, an' me school, an' me pals.' She shivered and pointed ahead of her, to where the big buildings were getting ever closer. 'What's *that*?'

'It's the Liver building. Them's the Liver birds, sittin' on them little tower things. English sailors who've travelled from all over the world know that when they can see the Liver birds, they're nearly home.'

Polly sniffed. Then she rubbed her eyes and sagged against Brogan's comforting arm.

'It's no use, is it, Brog? I can be as horrible as I like, but I'm still only ten years old. They won't let me go home, will they?'

'No, alanna, they won't let you go home,' Brogan said quietly. 'Not yet, not till you're a good deal older. But 'tis the same for all of us. Daddy and me, we have to stay to earn our livin', whether we will or no. The boys will have to stay too, until they're old enough to try for work over the water, that is. So you're in good company. We've all got to earn a crust, eh?'

'Martin and Donal stayed in Dublin. Why couldn't I stay wit' them?' Polly said, but she spoke without much conviction. She knows, poor kid, that what's done is done, Brogan thought, and felt, for a fleeting second, the helplessness of a child, carried hither and thither by the wishes of an adult world which she cannot really understand.

'You can't stay wit' Martin because he'll be workin' hard, wit' no time to take care of a little sister,' Brogan pointed out. 'Polly, love, you'll be happy in your new home, I promise you. Aren't your hens in the hold this minute, an' Delly, an' both cats? And won't you have new pets, more hens, pigs? And the whole of the lovely countryside to play in, what's more.'

'But not Tad,' Polly reminded him. 'Never Tad.'

'You must write often, two or three times a week,'

Brogan said. 'You must tell him every little thing that happens, and then, when you do meet again, it'll be as if you'd never been apart.'

'I will, so,' Polly said, cheering up a little. 'Daddy said yesterday I might be able to have a little horse of me own one day.'

Poor Daddy, Brogan thought, desperate to make up to this odd little daughter of his for taking her away from her playmate. Indeed, though he used the term 'playmate', he thought that she had behaved as though she and Tad had loved one another! And wit' her ten years old and the lad no more than twelve, that wasn't likely.

Was it?

Her grandmother's death changed Sara; she had always worked hard but now she seemed to have very little interest in what went on outside Strawberry Field. She and Mr Alderwood were determined to get everything right, and at last the day came when the major pronounced himself satisfied and brought the new matron along to inspect things. That lady pronounced herself delighted with everything and suggested that they should have an Open Day, at which friends, relatives and local dignitaries might see for themselves what a pleasant place the Strawberry Field Children's Home had become.

'Well, Clarrie, we'll be opening the place up in no time at all now, so the brigadier has decided to have an Open Day,' Sara said when she got back to the flat that night. She and Clarrie had kept the place on, though without Mrs Prescott's small pension – and warm presence – their ability to continue to pay the rent and stay there would probably not last. Besides, Sara had been offered a live-in post at the home and thought she would take it. 'You will come, won't you? All sorts of local dignitaries will be coming, and a great many high-ranking Salvationists of course. And when the Open Day is over we're going to have a little tea party – that is, the friends and relatives of everyone who's helped to make Strawberry Field what it is today – and you can all tell us what you think.'

'I just wish Mrs Prescott could have seen it,' Clarrie said with a sigh. 'But there, I expect she can in her way – she'll be rare proud of you, queen. And you must accept the job, you know. I'll find someone else to share here. And thanks for invitin' me to the Open Day – I'll do you credit, chuck. I'll go down to Zena's, get me hair set, and I'll wear me new suit – or should it be uniform?'

'The suit, I think,' Sara said. 'There are going to be an awful lot of uniforms about! And – and thanks, Clarrie.'

'What for? For comin' to a free do, where'll I gerra cuppa tea?'

'No, silly. For telling me to go ahead and take the job, which I'm longing to do. For making me feel it's all right to – well, to leave you in the lurch, in a way.'

Clarrie tutted. The two girls were in the living kitchen, both knitting away though with different measures of success; Clarrie had been taught to knit as a child, Sara had never mastered it.

'Well, a poor sort of friend I'd think meself if I didn't tell you to take the job, the way things are. And as for leavin' me in the lurch, you're doin' no such thing. I tell you, folk will be fallin' over theirselves to take a share of a place like this 'un. Now who's goin' to put the kettle on, you or me? 'Cos I'm dyin' for a nice cuppa.'

It was all very well to feel confident that the house was now fit for occupancy when you compared it with how it had looked six months ago, but when the Open Day dawned, Sara discovered that she was actually nervous. People who had never been up the drive before, let alone in at the big front door, were going to be staring, peering into cupboards, possibly even criticising. She went from room to room, tidying, straightening, trying to see it through the eyes of a stranger, but in the end she simply went into the big front hall and waited. It was too late for changing her mind, too late for adjustments, even. She must simply smile and accept whatever the visitors said.

It helped that she wasn't the only one who was nervous. The brigadier, who would be running the home, was nervous too. She tidied her study, went and changed the pink and white checked cloths in the dining room for blue and white, then changed them back again. She ran a finger along the banisters and couldn't find any dust, then she hurried into the kitchens to check that arrangements for the staff tea party were complete.

'Relax, Brigadier,' Sara said at last. 'I thought I was nervous, but you're so much worse that you've made me feel quite calm.'

'You won't have to explain to the Lord Mayor if he finds fault,' the brigadier said. 'Oh, is that them now? Lor, whose idea *was* this, anyway?'

'Yours, and a very good idea it was, too,' Mr Alderwood said, winking at Sara. 'Just stop fussing, Matron . . . I do believe I hear a car!'

It was only the major, but as he opened the door Clarrie appeared behind him, mounted on her bicycle. She got off, leaned the machine carefully against the house wall, and then came in, smiling broadly.

'Ah, Miss Boote,' the brigadier said, coming forward. 'Isn't this exciting? Would you like to come in and see what we've done on the ground floor, whilst we wait for the official party?'

'I'm early; but better early than late,' Clarrie said. 'Yes, I'd love to see what you've all been up to . . . ain't it a lovely big garden, though? I've never seen one so big, it's more like a blinkin' park!'

'But we can't start until the Lord Mayor arrives,' Sara hissed, only to be told the brigadier knew that but thought she would enjoy showing someone round who didn't make her nervous.

'Don't worry, the major and I will call the brigadier back the minute the official cars arrive,' Mr Alderwood said as Sara began to fuss. 'It's better that she has something to do other than worry whether everything's perfect. You go with her, my dear, we'll hold the fort here.'

The kitchens were wonderful, Clarrie said with all her usual enthusiasm. Large and airy, with beautiful modern cooking stoves, sinks at the right height so that those who worked at them would not be perpetually stooping and views of the garden from the large windows.

'My mam would love it,' Clarrie said, clearly setting the Boote seal of approval on the Children's Home.

The rest of the ground floor lived up to the kitchens, what was more. The dining room was very large, but it seemed cosy because it was designed with family life rather than institutions in mind. Small tables for four, six or eight were scattered around the room, there was a polished wood floor, rugs, pretty lampshades, ornaments on the mantel . . .

'It's homely, that's what it is,' Clarrie announced.

And the living rooms were pleasant, the playrooms well planned with furniture to fit children from two or three to fourteen or so, though they seemed a little bare with neither children nor toys yet in occupation. 'And them grounds, Brigadier – it's a paradise for kids.'

'We've not started on the gardens, yet,' the brigadier said rather evasively. They had disagreed over the gardens. She wanted velvet lawns, flower-beds, trees. There was already an orchard and a very good vegetable garden, though the orchard was full of elderly apple trees and the vegetable plot was just full of weeds. But Sara and Mr Alderwood thought that a beautiful, orderly garden would make the kids feel uncomfortable. They wanted it left as it was except for the front which, they agreed, would have to be made respectable as soon as possible.

'Well, you'll want to do some hedge-trimmin' an' lawn-cuttin', no doubt,' Clarrie agreed. 'But the rest . . . well, kids all want places they can climb trees an' swing on gates an' dig an' plant for theirselves. So why not leave it wildish, like?'

'It has been suggested,' the brigadier admitted. 'So you think it's a paradise for kids as it stands, eh, Miss Boote?'

'I do,' Clarrie said decidedly. 'Let the kids 'ave a say, Matron. Let 'em get their hands dirty, diggin' an' plantin'. There's nothin' kids like more.'

And indeed by the time the official party arrived all the brigadier's nerves had vanished under Miss Boote's soothing comments and she was able to show her distinguished visitors round and give them a running commentary on the work which had been done without a blush. She even told the party that the gardens would not be cleared and made beautiful; that was work the children themselves might undertake and plan.

Sara, following the party, winked at Clarrie. She was elated, walking on air. It was clear that these important, influential people approved of what had been done – better, they liked it. When the brigadier said they would be having their first destitute children in at the beginning of the month they offered help, money to be spent on clothing, food, playthings.

And finally the official party cut the length of ribbon which had been tied across the foot of the stairs and declared that the Strawberry Field Children's Home was open for business.

'Now all we want is the kids,' Sara said quietly to Mr Alderwood. 'This has been grand, but it's not what we're here for. We're here for the kids.'

Brogan was glad when the crossing was over; Polly hadn't enjoyed it, she'd been too busy staring back at Ireland and longing for Tad, and he had felt ridiculously guilty, as though he'd done wrong to take her to Ireland in the first place if he was then going to turn round and bring her back here again.

But he busied himself getting all their gear ashore and then to the tram stop, for the family were to stay tonight in a cheap hotel just off the Walton Road, and he would go back to his lodging with Mrs Burt, and then, tomorrow, he would go with his family to his daddy's new post – the level crossing with the cottage and the large garden.

He had thought getting them off the ship was bad enough, but getting them aboard the tram was worse. The conductor of the first tram to arrive refused even to consider having the crated hens aboard, and he didn't like the cat basket much, either, though he only sniffed when Delilah, ears flattened, eyes staring anxiously, was lugged aboard.

'I'll get a taxi to fetch the hens to Salop Street,' Brogan said. 'It won't tek me but a minute.' He climbed down off the tram-step, wondering what he'd done to deserve all this. Why the hell did they have to *bring* the bloody hens, he was thinking to himself. Hens were hens, Polly could have let Tad keep these; Brogan would have bought her some more when they were settled in, honest to God he would.

He lugged the hens, in their crate, over to the taxi rank. The first driver said he didn't carry freight and suggested, jeeringly, that Brogan should carry them on his head, as doubtless he carried them when trotting over his ancestral bog.

Brogan smiled at him and turned away, but his fist must have been thinking of something different, for instead of following his body it whammed the driver of the first taxi right on the nose, causing him to give a howl of mingled pain and rage. Brogan gave him a surprised glance and turned to the second driver. The second driver, oddly enough, was much more polite. He said that he, too, never carried freight and though he would like to oblige . . .

'I'd take 'em if I was you, pal,' Brogan said. 'Because I'm a big feller, tryin' to do right by me family, an' they're wantin' these hens so they are.'

The second driver, looking thoughtfully at his pal's scarlet and swollen nose, decided that he would oblige just this once. Brogan loaded the hens into the cab, called Bevin to come off the tram and travel in the cab with the hens, and gave his young brother some money.

'The driver's a grand feller so he is,' he told Bevin. 'He'll help you unload 'em, carry 'em to the door for you, very like. When you arrive give the door a knock an' when Mrs Burt comes, explain we'll not be long. Sure you'll be all right?'

Bevin said he would be grand, just grand, so Brogan rejoined the rest of his family aboard the tram, whose conductor was beginning to say he wouldn't wait any longer, not if it was for the King himself.

'Isn't this fun, Polly?' Deirdre said as Brogan sat wearily down by them and the tram jerked into motion. 'Did ye see the overhead railway when Brogan pointed it out? What about a train chuff-chuffin' along in the air, then? What about that, eh?'

'I – I don't know,' Polly said. She was staring all round her, and there was something in her attitude which worried Brogan. She didn't look like a totally confused stranger, she looked more like – like someone who half-recognises a place and doesn't want to do so. But that was impossible; Polly had been a babe in arms when she left the city, she'd been no more than nine months old!

'Sure an' of course you know,' Deirdre said bracingly. 'You like it . . . it's fun, isn't it? Ivan thinks it's fun, don't you, little feller?'

Ivan, bouncing in his seat, said yes, it was fun so it was, but Polly just sat, staring. Delilah gave a little moan and leaned against her legs. He didn't like the motion of the tram and several times made swallowing, gulping movements of his throat but to Brogan's immense relief, the dog didn't actually throw up. Perhaps we'll get back before anything else happens, he thought hopefully. Ah God, what are those bloody cats doin' now in the name of all that's wonderful?

The cat basket was rocking as the inmates apparently hurled themselves at each other, caterwauling loud enough to make the other passengers on the tram turn and stare. Peader grinned and made soothing noises in the direction of the wildly rocking basket but the conductor, who must have known a thing or two about cats, gave the wicker a good kick as he passed it. Shocked, Lionel and Samson stopped attacking each other and silence descended.

'Even the cats don't like all this,' Polly muttered, glaring darkly at the conductor's oblivious back. 'Even the cats t'ink we've run mad so they do. And poor Delly . . . oh Delilah, don't be sick, there's a good feller!'

Delilah swallowed, shivered, and then moved to lean against Peader's knee. He cast his eyes up at Peader with a pitiful expression; let's get off, he seemed to be saying, before I chuck me liver and lights on to the deck!

Brogan leaned across the dog. He took hold of Polly's hand and began to play with her fingers.

'Round an' round the garden, like a teddy bear . . .'

Polly had sunk back into her reverie but the childish game brought her mind back to the present. 'Stop that, you big Brogan, 'tis not a baby I am,' she said crossly, snatching her hand away. 'Oh . . . oh . . . where's *that*?'

'Nowhere in particular,' Brogan said, following her gaze. 'Oh, the market, you mean? We're goin' along Great Homer Street, there's always stalls an' that.'

'It looks a little bit like Francis Street,' Polly said wistfully. 'I wonder what Tad's doin' now? He's missin' me already. I can tell.'

Brogan sighed. 'Of course he is, alanna,' he said gently. 'But you're a big girl now, you just said so. You're here, wit' Mammy, Daddy, me, your brothers and all your animals . . . so stop lookin' backwards and look forwards, instead.'

Polly sighed but her hand gentled the dog's silky head and her eyes fell on the cat basket with affection. Brogan could see he'd made his point.

'I'll try, Brog,' she said resignedly. 'I really will try.'

Mrs Burt had a grand tea waiting for them and by the time they had left their bags at the Belvedere Guest House they were all in urgent need of tea.

'Those bloody hens,' Bevin said, 'One of 'em, the one wit' the red tassles on its head, squeezed t'rough the slats of the crate an' pecked the taxi driver on the back of the neck. He was *wild* so he was. He said words Mammy would have smacked his head for – words Brogan would have biffed him on the nose for!'

'Words you've never heard in all your born puff, I suppose,' Brogan said sarcastically. 'And who said you could swear at the hens, anyway?'

'I didn't swear at them, it was . . .'

'You said bloody hens,' Ivan said placidly. They were washing up for tea in Brogan's room and now Ivan began to slick his hair down with water. 'If Mammy was here she'd wash your mouth out so she would.'

'Oh, I see what you mean. But she'd do better to wash the taxi driver's mouth out. Honest to God, Brog, the language the feller used . . .'

'Wash your hands, never mind your mouth,' Brogan said. 'The hens is here now, so no point in moaning. Tomorrow we'll be takin' them to the country, where hens belong.'

'In a taxi cab?' Bevin said suspiciously. 'Or on a tram? Because I tell you, Brogan, you may be me big brother but I'll not travel wit' them hens again . . . not by meself I won't. They're Polly's birds, let her cart them around.'

'You liked the eggs,' Ivan said. Brogan regarded his little brother with new respect. You had to hand it to Ivan, he wasn't yet five but he didn't miss a trick. 'You can't have eggs wit'out hens, Bev.'

'I'm not sayin' all hens is bad, I'm not even sayin' hens isn't all right in their place, what I'm sayin' is . . .'

'Shut up, the pair of ye!' Brogan roared, suddenly losing his temper. 'I've heard enough of the bloody hens, d'you hear me? The subject's *closed*.'

He led his brothers down the stairs to the parlour where high tea awaited them, and grinned to himself when he heard Ivan whisper to Bevin: 'Did ye hear what Brogan said, Bev? He swore just like that taxi driver so he did!'

In the parlour, Peader, Deirdre and Polly waited for them whilst Mrs Burt presided over the pot.

'Tea for you all? Tea, boys?' she enquired affably. 'Help yourself to the loaf now . . . I've soused some herrin', there's a dish of baked potatoes, and Peader's goin' to carve some mutton for anyone who fancies a slice. Now . . . who's hungry?'

Polly ate her tea in a daze. It was very strange, one minute she hated this place so badly that she could have screamed, the next she felt a weird, tugging sort of affection for it. But she had never been here in her life before, she'd only heard tell of it from Daddy and Brogan, so why on earth did she feel this way?

She liked Mrs Burt, though. Mrs Burt had said Delilah was the handsomest dog she'd ever met and the cats were charming. She had shaken hands with Delilah and given the cats a saucer of milk. And what Mrs Burt called high tea was delicious, one of the nicest meals Polly had ever tasted. But food wasn't everything, and even the nicest food couldn't make up for being away from Tad.

'You'll make other friends,' Daddy had said, which just went to prove that grown-ups did not understand. Of *course* she would make other friends, she had had a *grush* of other friends in Dublin, always had had. But other friends weren't Tad. There could only be one Tad in her life.

So Polly ate her tea rather silently, then walked back to the guest house with Mammy, Daddy and her brothers. Delilah was staying with Brogan and so were the cats. The hens, still in their crate, were staying in the back yard, under the washing lines. Only people were allowed in guest houses, Mammy had explained, and Polly had tried hard to understand and be sensible.

She was sleeping with Mammy and Daddy too, in a tiny pull-out bed which was stowed away, during the day, under their big bed. The little bed was great fun, the nicest thing about the room which, otherwise, was pretty ordinary, though enormously large and extremely bare to one accustomed to the crowded, close-knit life of a Dublin tenement.

'You'd best go to bed now, alanna,' Mammy said about an hour after they'd finished their high tea. 'We've a full day tomorrow so we have, and you'll be wantin' all your energy to help wit' the move.'

'All right,' Polly said obediently. 'I am tired.'

She was tired, too. The only thing was, tired or not, she simply could not sleep. She lay in bed, staring at the ceiling, her mind filled with the most curious thoughts, until her parents came up to bed. And then she shut her eyes tight and pretended as hard as she could that she was asleep because if they knew she was awake they would only worry. And of course she listened to the conversation as her parents prepared for bed.

'Sure and she's fast off,' Mammy murmured quite soon after they entered the room. 'Poor little soul, she's wore out . . . what a day, Peader!'

'Aye, what wit' the cats, the dog, the hens . . .' he chuckled. 'Still, tomorrow we'll be in the country.'

He sounded infinitely content but Polly felt a pang of real distress. Tomorrow they would be in the country; so what was wrong with that? The country was nice, she knew because she and Tad had visited the country . . . oh, Tad, Tad, whatever will I do wit'out you and your lovin' ways?

'I shan't be sorry.' That was Mammy. 'The child was – was *odd*, didn't you think, when we were travellin' here, in the tram?'

'Odd? No, me love, she was just tired, puzzled and cross wit' me for bringin' you all here.'

'No, it's not that. It's being parted from Tad. But it was the way she stared around, Peader, as though she expected to recognise something . . . it worried me.'

'Why on earth? This is all new to her, alanna, a great city wit' stately buildings . . . it's all new, no wonder she stares.'

'No.' Mammy's voice was so low Polly had to strain to hear it. 'No, Peader, it's not new. She was here before – remember? Holy Mother, I'll be glad to leave this city behind so I will.'

'Deirdre, the child was a babe in arms, she'll not remember anything from that time. Dear God above, I hope wit' all my heart she remembers nothin', for what could she remember but hardship, hunger, and lovelessness?'

'The other one loved her.' Mammy's voice was lower, if anything. 'The other child worshipped her; you said it yourself, Peader.'

'Yes. But the other's gone from here. And I'm tellin' you, a babe that young could remember nothin' whatsoever of what happened, once, long ago.' The bedsprings creaked as Peader climbed between the sheets. 'Now stop your worryin', woman, and come to bed.'

Polly lay quiet and still in her own little bed, not daring to move, hardly daring to breathe. What did it all *mean*? Why should Mammy say that she, Polly, had been here before, when she knew, none better, that Polly had been born, bred and brought up in the Liberties? And why had Daddy said she would remember nothing but hardship, hunger and lovelessness? And who, in heaven's name, was the other child?

Polly lay and pondered and wondered, and watched the moon's slow progress across the sky through a gap in the curtains. And when the night was at its darkest she got out of her little bed, picked up her clothes from the chair by the window, and stole to the door.

The door was locked. The key was big and took some turning, but Polly turned it. She slid silently out of the room and outside in the dark corridor, she dressed herself by touch. She struggled into her clothing, pulled on her woollen stockings, her stout little lace-up shoes. She even put on her coat with the round navy buttons and her small, pudding-basin hat.

It was cold in the corridor, and frightening, too. As she fumbled with her fastenings, tried to tidy her hair with her hands, straightened the woollen stockings, her head ached from lack of sleep and from the mystery which she had sensed surrounding both herself and this city. Because in one way Mammy was right. She *had* felt a weird feeling of remembering rather than merely seeing as they had got off the ship at the Pierhead and made their way to the tram stop. And though she'd said that the market had reminded her of Francis Street, she was not at all sure she had really meant that. She had meant that it reminded her of – of somewhere she had once known.

However, fully dressed, she stole along the corridor, down the stairs, and after a struggle with another big key, out of the front door. She wished Delilah were with her, but Delly was staying at Mrs Burt's house with Brogan. Knowing her dog, she guessed that by now Delly would be hogging the lion's share of Brogan's bed and snoring loud enough to wake the dead. And if he had been at the guest house there was no saying he wouldn't have jumped and barked and roused the whole house, including her parents, who would not, she knew, approve of her actions. So she decided to be grateful that Delilah was far away and let herself quietly out of the front door.

Standing on the pavement, she considered. Did she mean to run off, to stow away aboard the next boat bound for Dublin? But she knew better than to try. A child can run away, protest, escape, but it will always be brought back in disgrace in the end. To return to Dublin would be an adventure, but if she did go back and move in with Martin and Donal, what sort of life would that be? They wouldn't want her but if she insisted they'd probably let her stay. She would have to work as she'd worked whilst Peader had been ill and she didn't fancy that, no sir! She would go back to Tad one day, when she was big, and they would get married, but until then it might be best to stay with Mammy and Daddy and her dear animals.

So what was she doing out in this great, strange city, with the stars still pricking at the dark, velvet blue of the night sky, and the lighter line on the eastern horizon all that was to show, yet, of the new day?

She didn't know, to tell the truth. But having got out, she did not intend to go back to the Belvedere Guest House yet. I'll explore, have a good look round, Polly thought to herself, and immediately realised that this was just what she needed to do. At some time, in some way, she had known this city. She had felt she knew it, but listening to Mammy and Daddy, she had realised she really did know it. She had been here before . . . how, why or where was what, she decided, she had escaped from the guest house to find out.

Which way, though? Which way? Polly stood in the middle of the pavement and spun round, spun and spun until she was giddy. Then, when she scarcely knew which way up she was, she set off, reeling along the pavement like a drunk. Luck would guide her, help her, sustain her. And in a few hours, perhaps, if she was very lucky before her parents were up, she would understand just what she had been doing in the city once, long, long ago.

Chapter Fifteen

Polly trotted along the pavement, under the hissing gas lamps. She could not have said that she knew where she was going, but she let her feet take her and that seemed to work quite well, because before day had anywhere near dawned, she was on a road which she felt was familiar to her. It was wide and though there were no trams about at this hour, there were tram-lines. A main road, then. She stood on the kerb, waiting, wondering, then crossed the road and turned into a narrow street which, she saw when she looked up at the name plate on the end house, was called Snowdrop Street.

Halfway down it she slowed, stopped. All the houses were identical, terraced houses with wooden front doors and bay windows yet Polly had the oddest feeling that she knew what was behind those primly closed front doors. Or one of them, at any rate. A parlour, with ragged curtains, a kitchen behind that . . . a girl stood in the kitchen, humming, stirring a pot. A half-naked baby played on a floor so dirty that it looked like hard-packed earth. In fact the place was dirtier than any house Polly had ever seen, save perhaps the Donoghue's home.

Polly closed her eyes, then opened them again. She only got that disturbing mental picture when she looked at one particular house, yet the house looked solid, reliable, not at all the sort of place where raggedy curtains and dirt reigned supreme. It isn't like that now, Polly finally concluded, but it must have been like that once. Long, long ago, when I was a baby. If I heard Mammy and Daddy right, that is. Unless I'm goin' off me head, of course, which seems likeliest.

She stood for some while, staring up at the house in the grey dawn light. Nothing stirred behind its respectable, dark-blue curtains, not a sound issued through its respectable, brown-painted door. Whatever it had once meant to her, if it had meant anything, it was all part of the past.

Moving like a sleepwalker now, Polly walked on. She stood on the corner of Snowdrop Street and there was another big, wide street – it was Commercial Road this time. A lorry rumbled past; doesn't he know it's the middle of the night and he should be in his bed so he should, Polly wondered rather crossly. She didn't mind a cat, stalking, yellow-eyed, along a house-wall, nor a dog trotting by, pressing close to the house-fronts . . . but lorries meant people and people could spell danger.

But the lorry made her look across the road to see what was over there, and she realised that there was a long, long view . . . no houses, in other words. Despite the fact that it was still dark she could, she thought, smell the sea . . . there were docks over the road, she was sure of it, and she liked docks. And nearer, glistening in the pale, unearthly before-dawn dark, she could just make out what looked like miles of railway lines – a marshalling yard? She remembered, suddenly, that Brogan had once mentioned that he lived near streets called after spring flowers . . . Snowdrop Street, of course, she had just traversed it!

Immediately, her attention was caught and held. Brogan worked for the railway, so did Daddy – was that why she had come here, then? Because at some time, long, long ago, Brogan and Daddy had . . . had brought her here? It didn't seem quite right, but it would have to do for now.

Polly crossed the road, dodging more tram-lines. She pressed her nose to a large gap in the fence and wondered at the sheer complexity of what lay beyond. It must be the hugest mass of railway lines in the world, she thought, all laid out like steel spaghetti, curving and joining, parting and rejoining. And there were sheds and shelters and big warehouses and little cabins and . . .

In Polly's mind, a picture was forming. She was in a small hut with an earth floor, there was a stove burning brightly, illuminating the smiling faces of the men who surrounded her . . . and then, when she looked around, she saw her angel! Was this why she had come down here, to the marshalling yards? Did her angel, for some reason, want her here?

The fencing which was between the road and the rails had been put up years ago to keep prowlers, children, stray dogs, off the tracks. Polly walked over to it. It would be quite simple just to wriggle through there, to go and find that hut . . .

She was small and neatly made, though her little red coat with its black velvet collar was a bulky garment. But she got through, anyway. She felt brave, adventurous . . . she wished devoutly, however, that Tad had been with her. Somehow, he took all the responsibility for their doings upon himself so that she could enjoy without guilt their various ploys. But he wasn't here, and anyway, she was, she felt, being guided. It was undoubtedly her guardian angel again, leading her to find . . .

Polly paused again. Leading her to find what? The hut, presumably, and the firelight, the men with smiling faces. Ah, then she would know just what her mammy and daddy had meant last night – because, in some mysterious way, she was more conscious of her angel's presence here than she had ever been.

Back in Dublin the kids in her class had learned a poem by some English feller called Alfred Lord Tennyson. It had a good old rhythm for shouting and declaiming and Polly and Tad rather liked it. But this was a quiet and secret place, a place where she was quite probably not allowed to be. So Polly stole forward, taking advantage of every patch of shadow, whilst whispering the words of the poem to bolster her up and give her courage.

Cannon to right of them
Cannon to left of them
Cannon in front of them
Volleyed and thundered.

She might have got the words wrong, it might not be appropriate, it might even seem stupid when you considered the silence which surrounded her, but Polly thought it helped. It conjured up Tad, going ahead of her, a hand behind him ready to grasp hers if she felt afraid. It conjured up confidence, courage.

She had not truly known which of the small huts she was heading for, but when she was hesitating something seemed to prompt her. *That way, that way!* She turned her head and thought she saw a slim shadow flickering between two particular huts. *That way, that way!* She was afraid and chilly and yet she knew, in a strange way, that she was in no danger. Am I sleeping, she thought suddenly, am I still in my bed? If so, there's nothing to be afraid of . . . come on, Polly . . . this way!

She headed for the shed which seemed, for some reason, likeliest, still keeping in deep shadow whenever she could, darting across great patches of silver moonlight and into black shade once more. The pre-dawn chill nipped at her, the colourless world of the night was suddenly unfriendly, threatening. But then she slid in through the doorway, and it was like stepping into a different world.

The first thing she noticed was the warmth, the smell of food and people, a homely, lived-in sort of smell. The second was that the hut was empty save for a couple of rough wooden benches, a coke burner and a blanket thrown down against one wall. Polly stole forward. It was nice in here, warm and hearteningly normal after being out for so long in the greys and silvers and blacks of the pre-dawn light. Furthermore the night had seemed threatening, it had made her aware that she was trespassing, but here in the hut Polly felt instantly at home. She sat unselfconsciously down on the floor in front of the coke burner and warmed her hands at the faint red glow. She looked around again and noticed, under the nearest bench, a number of tin mugs and plates and a canvas bag. The railway gangs come here to eat their carry-out, Polly thought triumphantly. Brogan and Daddy probably came here once; perhaps Brogan comes here still. I knew I should come here . . . Brogan will walk in presently, give me a cuddle and make me go home to me own bed. But first he'll tell me why I came here so he will.

Polly warmed her hands, then she reached for the blanket and wrapped it round herself. How cosy it was! If she wasn't careful she'd fall asleep so she would and then how Brogan would tease her when he found her!

She sat up straighter, then leaned against the bench.

It would not do any harm to close her eyes for ten minutes . . .

Polly woke when she heard an irritable voice shouting somewhere near at hand. It was a man's voice, irate, threatening.

'Gerrout of it, you thievin' little cat! Go on . . . if I catches you I'll teach you to come sneakin' round our shelters . . . go on, clear orf!'

There was a clatter and a cry. Polly sat up. Long experience of living with a family of brothers had made her familiar with the sounds. Someone was shouting at a child and throwing stones to get rid of that child. The clatter had been a sizeable stone hitting a rail – and probably bouncing off and then hitting the child.

Automatically, still more than half asleep, Polly reached out for Tad, and found herself grabbing empty air. Immediately her heart started to thump like a trip-hammer. Oh, Mary, Mother of Jesus, Tad wasn't here, she was trespassing on railway property all by her lonesome and someone, someone large and fierce and terrible, was just outside the hut, no doubt waiting to thump anyone handy who happened to be smaller than himself!

Polly tried to stand up but the blanket hampered her and she fell, skinning her knees on the hard floor. The pain, however, brought her to her senses. She stood with care, threw the blanket down more or less where she had found it, and sidled over to the door, peering out through the gap, for it was not completely shut.

It was still very dark but no moon or stars shone now; a drizzling rain was falling from the dark clouds overhead and the wet gleamed on the complex pattern of the rails and sleepers, on the huts and warehouses and engine sheds . . . and on a small group of men, one of whom was still poised in the classic throwing action – arm bent back, body angled, a stone held threateningly. And well away now, running across the rails with incredible fleetness, was a thin figure in a long, draggly skirt. Clearly a female figure.

'Go on, gerrout of it or I'll break every bone in your bleedin' body!'

The man broke into a lumbering run. Polly knew a bully when she saw one and she was so indignant that she came out of the shed at a run, shouting as she did so.

'Hey, leave her alone, will ye? A feller your size, chasin' a wee young wan . . . pick on someone your own size, you big moocher!'

The man swung round with a roar . . . and Polly was off, running like greased lightning. This is quite like old times, she told herself, skipping across the rails, heading at speed for the gap in the fence. Many's the time I've been keepin' nix for Tad whilst he did something evil, and ended up runnin' for me life. But the shouting man was between her and the hole in the fence, she would have to go a bit further along. Polly ran hard, bending low, and somewhere to her right she was conscious of the other figure . . . but then the fence loomed and she ran alongside it for a bit, searching for a gap . . . found one, was through it in one wiggle and dashing across the road, horribly aware that her pursuer had emerged on to the pavement behind her, was screaming after her . . .

She ignored him, doubling down the little roads and alleys until all sounds of pursuit had died, until at last she felt safe to stop and catch her breath.

Phew, Polly thought to herself, that was close! And then she looked around her, deciding which way . . .

She was in totally foreign territory. She had never

seen this road before, and when, presently, she began to try to retrace her steps, she realised that she had absolutely no idea where she was – worse, she had no idea where the guest house was. Worse still, she could not for the life of her remember the name of it, or the name of the street on which it was situated.

It was still dark, the houses were still curtained, not a soul stirred. Polly stood like a statue for a moment in the middle of the pavement whilst the rain fell, chill, on her. And then she put her hands over her face and began to cry.

When a voice spoke quite near her ear Polly jumped and almost ran again, but she was worn out and besides, the voice was gentle. So she put her hands down from her face and looked around her.

The speaker proved to be a young girl, thin, light-haired, wearing a draggly skirt much torn at the hem, and a cloak-thing around her shoulders. She was smiling down at Polly with the gentlest, sweetest expression on her face. Polly gasped. It was her guardian angel, she would have known that face anywhere!

'Wha's the marrer, chuck?' her angel said gently. 'By 'eck, but you can run. You're well away, though – we both are – so why's you cryin'?'

None of this made much sense to Polly, save for the last question. She gave a big gulp and then wiped her tears away with the heels of both hands. Then she took a deep breath and smiled at her companion.

'I'm lost,' she said baldly. 'I'm stayin' in a guest house but I d-don't remember what it's called nor where it is. And me mammy an' me daddy'll be in a takin' if they wake up an' I'm not in me bed!'

Her angel considered this. 'Why are you in a guest 'ouse?' she enquired after a moment's thought. 'And whar are you doin' 'ere? You're from Ireland, by the sound of it.'

'Me daddy's a railwayman; we're goin' to live at a level crossin' on the Wirral,' Polly explained. 'Me brother Brogan lives here, too, so he does.'

'Where does your brother Brogan live?'

Polly beamed. So it was that simple – but of course she didn't have the brains of her angel, or she'd have thought of it for herself.

'Brogan lives on Salop Road, off the Walton Road,' she said triumphantly. 'D'you know where that is?'

''Course. Come on, I'll walk with you.' The angel tucked her hands into her pockets and then fell companionably into step with Polly. 'You'll be 'ome before you knows it, chuck.'

Fortunately, Brogan was awake when the knocker sounded. He waited a moment, then rolled out of bed and headed for the stairs. His landlady would sleep through the last trump, she only woke when the alarm clock had been shrilling away for five minutes. So he pulled his trousers on and padded down the stairs, with Delilah close at his heels, and tugged the front door open.

'Yes? My God, Polly!'

'Oh, Brogan, 'tis glad I am to see you,' his small sister gabbled, clutching his hand whilst Delilah frisked around his little mistress, licking any bit of her he could reach. 'You'll never guess what's happened – I've met me angel!' She glanced behind her, but not as though she expected to see anyone. 'She's gone, I knew she wouldn't stay, but she found me when I was ever so lost, an' she brought me right to your door! Wasn't she good, Brog?'

'Yes, indeed,' Brogan said. 'And you've been bad . . . d'you know what time it is, alanna?'

'No.' Polly's eyes opened very wide. 'Sure an' how should I know the time, Brogan, an' me wit'out a watch? Is it early?'

'It's terrible early,' Brogan said, not mincing words. 'And what's all this talk of angels, Polly? Here, get indoors and get that coat off, you're soaked to the skin! I don't suppose Mammy and Daddy know where you are, eh?'

'Well, no-oo, but if you'll tell me how to get back there, Brogan, I can be into me bed an' snorin' before they know a thing! You see, I listened to Mammy an' Daddy talkin' last night when they came to bed, an' they talked about me, Brog, so they did! They said I'd been in Liverpool before an' they were right . . . I *knew* places, Brog, so I did, just as if – as if I'd lived there meself! So I had to find out, you see.'

Brogan pushed his small sister through the house and into the back kitchen where the fire, though damped down, soon burned up brightly after a prod or two with the poker.

'Let's be havin' that coat off you,' he said. 'And the hat, and them foolish shoes . . . oh Polly, your stockin's is drenched through so they are.'

Polly sat down in the chair nearest the fire, kicked off her shoes and peeled off her stockings. Then she ran a hand through her wet and tousled curls. 'Oh Brog, I'm glad to see you! But I think you ought to take me back to Mammy at once, or she'll worry sick so she will.'

'Get dry first,' Brogan said. He took the roller towel off the back of the door and threw it over to her. 'Go on, rub your hair hard. Well, you spalpeen, what in heaven's name am I goin' to do wit' you? Runnin' away, talkin' a lot of rubbish, tryin' to blame your angel for your behaviour . . .'

'I'm *not* tryin' to blame me angel,' Polly said immediately, her cheeks going pink. 'It wasn't her fault at all at all. She brought me back, Brogan, she helped me. Only she didn't know where the guest house was, so she brung me here.'

Brogan had been putting the kettle over the flame; now he looked thoughtfully at Polly. For the first time it occurred to him that bad though his little sister frequently was, she had never, so far as he knew, been a liar. If she thought she had seen an angel then who was he to disbelieve her? And what was more, he remembered Mammy saying that she believed Jess was Polly's guardian angel. So if someone really had got Polly out of a scrape . . . well, it could have been the living and not the dead sister – Grace, not Jess.

The kettle boiled and Brogan wet the pot, made the tea, poured a cup and stirred in two generous spoons of sugar.

'There you are; drink it up,' he said, handing Polly a cup. 'And tell me about this angel of yours, alanna.'

Polly told the story quickly and well. Clearly, she was totally convinced of the angelic nature of her rescuer. But it sounded, to Brogan, as though two naughty young girls had been trespassing on railway property, two girls had run away from the bad-tempered and bullying gang boss, and then one of the girls had found the other crying in the street and had brought her home. He put this point to Polly who thought about it and then admitted, reluctantly, that her angel had borne a fleeting resemblance to the girl the feller had thrown stones at, but only insofar as they were both thin and raggedy.

'Because I've seen me angel before, in Dublin, so I have,' she reminded her brother. 'If it wasn't me angel who rescued me but a real live girl, then how come I seed her in Dublin, on our stairs?'

Brogan had to admit this baffled him. Indeed, he said no more on the subject until Polly was warm, dry and had a cup of tea and a round of bread and jam inside her. Then he got his waterproof down off its hook and told Polly he was going to take her home on the back of his bicycle, snug under his waterproof.

'You'll be back in bed in no time, if you're lucky,' he told her. 'No need to worry Mammy and Daddy with your adventuring.'

He was watching Polly's face as he spoke and saw relief light her small face.

'Oh thank you, Brogan,' she said fervently. 'I wouldn't want to worry Mammy and Daddy and the boys, indeed I would not. So if you'll say nothing, me dearest brother, then I'll keep the secret too, I'll not say a word.'

'Well, good,' Brogan said heartily. 'And now you know you really were in Liverpool once, when you were just a baby, is that enough for you?'

Polly nodded. 'I don't want to know any more, I just wanted to know if I was right so I did,' she declared. 'It isn't important, is it, Brog?'

'No, it's not important. You were here as a wee one for a short time, that's all there is to it. Look, Poll, are you ready to go back to the guest house now? Because the night's wearin' on and it'll be morning before you know it.'

'Yes, I'm ready,' Polly said quickly, nodding her head until her curls bounced. 'I won't ask Mammy or Daddy any more questions and I won't try to get back to Ireland, either, not if you think me angel wouldn't like it. I'm lucky to have me family, and to be Polly O'Brady, even if I *was* in Liverpool once, when I was very small. It's strange, isn't it, that I don't want to know anything else? But I don't, I just want to live in this Wirral wit' me dog an' the cats an' me family, and I'll be happy as the day is long so I shall!'

'Well, that's grand,' Brogan said reassuringly. 'Now if I put me waterproof round me shoulders and you come underneath it . . .'

He lifted Polly on to the seat of his bicycle and wheeled it out of the house and across the pavement. Delilah whined hopefully but was left in the house whilst Brogan cycled slowly down the road, standing up on the pedals all the way from Salop Street to the Belvedere Guest House. And once there, he saw Polly indoors and then turned his bicycle round. But not in the direction of Salop Street. As soon as he was sure that Polly was safely out of the way he headed for the marshalling yard.

It was Grace, he told himself exultantly, pedalling as fast as he could now. That poor child is living rough around the yard, and now that I know it I can find her and see that she's looked after. And Jess, me love, he added, addressing the figure that had haunted his dreams for so long, Jess, me love, you'll be able to rest in peace at last.

As Polly slid inside the guest house she did grow rather anxious, but luck – or her guardian angel – was with her. No one stirred in the house, no door opened, no inquisitive nose poked out, anxious to discover who was around so early. Polly knew her missing coat would be bound to bring forth adverse comments later, when her parents and brother woke, but she hoped to be able to get round that. Brogan was going to try to bring her back the dry garments when he came to collect them, and that, she thought, would be time enough. Mammy would be in a good old state anyway, trying to get everyone ready for the next stage of their journey. Polly thought it might be quite possible to get into the coat and hat before anyone realised that they had spent a good deal of the night under Brogan's roof.

So she went upstairs, took off all her clothes except for her shift, and opened the door to the bedroom which had been allocated to her and to her parents. She put her head round it. Mammy and Daddy slumbered still, Daddy was actually snoring.

Polly had a bad moment as she climbed into bed, though; Daddy stopped snoring, gave a huge, deep sigh and leaned up on his elbow.

'You all right, alanna?' he said softly. 'It's terrible early still.'

'I just needed to go, Daddy,' Polly said primly, but with a bumping heart. She thanked her stars she had already laid her clothing on the chair before her father stirred.

'Well, back to sleep wit' you,' her father said, lying down again. 'We've a full day later, Polleen, so sleep while you can.'

Brogan didn't find anyone in the marshalling yard, but he did not let it depress him. For the first time, he felt sure Grace Carbery was still alive, because Polly's description of the girl who had brought her home was how he would have described Jess, eight or nine years ago. He knew that Polly believed in her guardian angel, and that Mammy thought the angel was there, guarding her beloved daughter, but Brogan did not think a guardian angel would flee across the rails, shout with pain when struck by a stone, and later come and take care of his little sister, talking all the while in a scouse accent which Polly had reconstructed pretty faithfully. No, Polly had come across Grace Carbery, which meant that sooner or later he, Brogan, would find her as well.

So when he'd searched the yard he returned to Salop Street, glanced at the clock, saw he was not due to get up for a couple of hours, and climbed back into bed And very soon, slept.

Brogan was dreaming. He dreamed that he was chasing Polly across miles and miles of countryside, she flitting over bog and round briar whilst he got stuck in the mud and constantly held up. He knew it was terribly important to catch her, that it might make the difference between life and death, but he didn't know why, so he ran and ran and his mouth dried out and he got terribly thirsty and terribly hot and he could hear his own panting breath . . .

The dream changed, as dreams will. Now he was pursuing Polly across miles and miles of railway track, stretching into the middle distance. There were no trains coming, yet he knew that there were engines in the vicinity, and not far distant, either. And she was only a little girl, she could not jump from rail to rail as he did, she was scrambling over the rails, then running on the hardcore between them, and he could tell by the way she ran that the hardcore hurt her feet, was slowing her down.

But at least it meant it should be easier for him to catch her up. So he put a spurt on . . . and felt, through the rails, the vibration of an approaching train.

Brogan went faster. With the breath sobbing in his throat he hurled himself across the rails . . . he was only a matter of feet behind Polly now, he would make it, he knew he would! He reached out, caught hold of her . . . and felt the hot breath of the mighty engine on the back of his neck, the screech of steam, the weight of it . . .

And it wasn't Polly. The girl he was holding wasn't Polly at all, it was another girl. He was going to die for a girl he didn't even know! Suddenly she turned in his grasp and it was Grace, he knew her at once. He had to save her, to throw her out of the train's path and get out himself . . .

Brogan woke. He was lying in his bed with Polly's dog sprawled across his chest, breathing hot breath into his face and whining plaintively, whilst any movement he tried to make was frustrated by the entangling, sweat-soaked sheets.

'Delly!' Brogan said, relieved beyond belief to find that he'd been dreaming. 'Get on the floor, will you, where dogs belong.'

He sat up, tipping the dog off his chest. What a nightmare! It must have been caused partly by the fact that he'd spent a good deal of the night either dealing with his little sister or searching for Grace, and Delilah's weight on him and the dog's hot breath in his face could not have helped. It was early, too, but Brogan didn't fancy going back to sleep, not if dreams like that lay in wait, so he swung his feet out of bed. He looked out of his bedroom window and the rain had gone, to be replaced by a milk-blue sky and frail, autumn sunshine. I'll dress and take the bloody dog for a walk, Brogan thought resignedly as Delilah, sensing an ally, began to caper. After all, it's not a bad morning and a walk will cool me off and calm me down.

Dressed, Brogan strolled down the stairs, out of the front door and along Salop Street. It was very early still, but there were people about. Men bound for an early start, newspaper delivery boys, girls travelling a long way to start work. Delilah, with a piece of rope round his neck, behaved quite well, unless you took exception to having to stop every six paces whilst he cocked a leg against the nearest stationary object.

'What are you *doing*?' Brogan demanded after half a mile had been traversed in this fashion. 'Markin' our trail, like they do in fairy stories? Because if so, I know me way home perfectly well so I do and since I'm not lettin' you off this rope you've no need to worry yourself.'

Delilah cocked a wise and knowing eye, but continued to try to lift his leg every six paces until Brogan got fed up and simply towed the dog along. Then Delilah trotted beside him without complaint, showing a lively interest in his surroundings but no longer bothering to mark.

I wonder if he ought to be off the rope for a bit, though? Brogan thought to himself as they walked. I don't remember Polly having him on a rope in Dublin. He just wandered along behind her. He looked at Delilah, who looked back with such limpid innocence that Brogan nearly let him off the rope then and there, only commonsense prevailed. It wouldn't hurt the dog to have a rope round his neck for half an hour, for the Lord's sake! And if it was grass Delilah was after, sure and wasn't Stanley Park just a stone's throw away? I'll go there and mebbe let him off for a few minutes if there's no one much about, Brogan decided. He can have a bit of a run and do what he has to do, then we'll go home for breakfast.

Brogan liked the park, with its bandstand, little shelters, glasshouses and, of course, its boating lake. A dog could have a run there without fear of the traffic... he could not bear to consider how he would behave should Delilah be hurt whilst in his charge. Polly would marmalise him, just for a start.

So Brogan and the dog walked to Stanley Park, which was quiet and pleasant in the very early sunshine. And Brogan let go the rope and Delilah behaved in an exemplary fashion, just sniffing round and running on the grass but coming back at once when Brogan called.

Until he saw something across the road, in Anfield Cemetery, and set off like a greyhound to investigate.

Brogan followed, of course. The pair of them tore across Priory Road and into the cemetery. It's a cat, Brogan thought. Oh, dear God, if Delly catches it an' hurts it what'll I do?

But then he remembered Lionel and Samson. It seemed unlikely that Delilah, who lived cheek by jowl with two members of the cat family, should suddenly turn round and chase one. Few canines knew better how sharp are a cat's claws, or how difficult they are to untangle from one's soft and unprotected nose.

But still, who knew? It might have been a rabbit, living on all the lovely grass in Stanley Park and in the cemetery. So Brogan ran and shouted and Delilah just ran . . . until their path was barred by a sturdy woman with a bunch of chrysanthemums in one hand.

'Look out!' Brogan roared, and grabbed the rope, which fortunately was stronger than it looked. Delilah skidded to a halt and yelped as the rope cut into his brawny neck, but Brogan almost had the woman off her feet, his shoulder catching hers and spinning her round, to crash quite hard on to the gravel path.

'Are you all right, missus? Be God, I'm awful sorry so I am,' Brogan gasped, lifting the woman gently to her feet. ''Twas the dog, divil take him! He's a lollopin' great fiend, so he is . . . are you hurt, now?'

The woman snorted, then smiled at Brogan.

'It takes more than a thump from a mad dog to kill me dead, young man,' she said. 'Tek me flowers for a minute, whiles I see if me leg's broke.'

'Broke? Oh, God love you, it can't be broke . . .' Brogan began, but the woman waggled her foot a couple of times and then pointed at the ankle.

'I were jokin', but be the look of it it's sprained. See that colour? And though I'm the last one to urge a young feller such as yourself to admire me legs, they don't usually 'ave one ankle twice the size of t'other.'

Brogan looked and indeed the ankle seemed to be swelling before his very eyes. Even through the woman's sensible stocking he could see the bruise coming out, purple and black and painful-looking. He swallowed uncomfortably. What a thing to do, and he was supposed to be taking Polly's coat round to the guest house as soon as he could. But this woman would not be able to get far under her own steam, one glance at the ankle convinced him of that.

'I can see you're right, missus. Will ye let me take you round to the Stanley Hospital? For you'll not be able to put weight on that ankle.' He cleared his throat self-consciously. 'I've a bicycle . . . if you'd not mind me wheeling you across the park then I'll go home and fetch it.'

The woman had tried her weight on the foot and had lost colour as a result. She leaned against the nearest object, which happened to be a gravestone, and tried to smile again, but it was a shaky effort.

'I'm sorry, I'm feelin' a bit strange . . . if I could sit down . . .'

Brogan let go Delilah's rope and assisted the woman to the nearest grave-kerb. She sank down on it and took a deep breath.

'Well! It's quite painful, but I'll be all right here whilst you fetches your bike. I wonder if you could put these flowers on that grave for me? There is a vase, it oughter have plenty of water in after the rain we had last night. It's the angel and the weepin' willow tree . . . that one.'

She pointed to the monument. Brogan took the chrysanthemums and went over to the vase. He took out the old, wilted flowers and put the fresh ones into the vase, then turned . . . to find Delilah, sniffing at the angel's feet in a way which immediately alerted him to the dog's intentions.

'Delilah . . . don't you dare do that now, or I'll crucify you so I will!'

Delilah, leg poised, thought better of it. He lowered the leg and cast Brogan a long, reproachful look. The woman sitting on the kerb laughed, though it was a rather short, wheezy sort of laugh.

'Ah, dogs don't 'ave no respect, chuck,' she told Brogan. 'Me paternal grandfather, Elias Boote, was a merchant prince, or thought 'e was, which accounts for the monument. To tell you the truth I bring the flowers to please me mam. Left to meself I'd sooner give the old skinflint a piece of me mind . . . or your dog could do it for me.'

Very relieved, Brogan picked up the rope once more and turned back to his victim. 'There, now, he kept himself to himself when I shouted, thank the good God,' he said piously. 'So we've saved your grandfather's angel from a wettin', that's for sure. If you'll wait here for five minutes, Miss Boote, I'll fetch me bicycle and we'll have you in the Stanley Casualty Department in a trice so we will.'

'And the dog? Will you take 'im or leave 'im wi' me, Mr . . . I'm afraid I don't know your name.'

'Me name's O'Brady, and I'll be takin' the dog,'

Brogan said grimly. 'I'll leave him wit' me landlady just while I get you to the Stanley. She'll not mind that.'

'Very good, Mr O'Brady,' Miss Boote said. She leaned back against the gravestone. 'A bit of a rest won't hurt me, so don't break your neck rushin' back.'

'I won't,' Brogan promised. 'Come on, Delly, let's see you run now!'

Brogan was back with his bicycle in no time at all, and lifted his second passenger in a couple of hours on to the saddle with great care and tenderness.

'Sure an' if you can balance there, you'll be safe in the Stanley in less than thirty minutes,' he promised her. 'What a day this has been already . . . oh, is there anyone waitin' on you who should be told you're at the hospital?'

'Only a friend who works at the Strawberry Field Children's Home,' Miss Boote said. 'I'll telephone her from the hospital, explain what's happened. She'll come down when she can . . . but they won't keep me in, not for a sprained ankle.'

'Strawberry Field,' Brogan said thoughtfully. Where had he heard that name before? 'That's a familiar sort of name.'

'It's a big old house out on Beaconsfield Road,' Miss Boote told him. 'It's only recently been converted into a home for destitute children – me friend's a worker there.'

'I know it. Huge grounds, but they've been allowed to go wild,' Brogan said triumphantly after a moment. ''Tis a keen gardener I am, and I thought, at one time, I might offer me services to get the place tidied up. But what wit' one thing an' another I've never got round to it. And now, wit' winter all but upon us . . .'

'They'd be that pleased if you did, Mr O'Brady,' Miss

Boote said earnestly. 'It was left to the Army, you see – the Salvation Army – in the old lady's will. They've put a mint o' money into it already . . . any help would be grand. Even in winter there's work to be done, or so they say. I believe me dad says heavy diggin's best done when there's frost to break up the soil.'

'That's true; and does the Strawberry Field home only take Salvationist children?' Brogan asked presently, turning his bicycle, complete with passenger, neatly on to Stanley Road. 'Are they full?'

Miss Boote snorted on a laugh. 'Children are children, when they're destitute they don't know if they're Catholic, Protestant or heathen, all they know is they're hungry, weary, cold and unloved. Strawberry Field is for any child – and it's only been open a matter of weeks so it's not full be a long chalk. Why d'you ask, Mr O'Brady?'

'Oh . . . I know a child, I've seen her wanderin' the streets so I have. I'm a single feller, livin' in lodgings, but I'd like to see the child settled somewhere.'

'Well, tell her about the Strawb,' Miss Boote said decidedly. 'She'll be welcome there. Me friend was a teacher and she's very good wi' kids. Yes, Mr O'Brady, if you find your little wanderer, send her along. Or bring her yourself for that matter. Then you could tek a look at the garden at the same time.'

'I'll do that,' Brogan said. 'Here we are, Miss Boote – the Stanley Hospital. They'll have you right in a trice, never you fret!'

Sara heard with some dismay about her friend's unfortunate collision with a young Irishman and his dog in the cemetery, but though Miss Boote was obviously shaken by the experience, she sounded quite capable and cheerful when she rang Sara that evening from a public call box on Walton Road.

'I'm goin' to ask you a favour, queen,' she said earnestly. 'Could you do my stint with the *War Cry* for a week or so? I wouldn't ask but I know you're still quiet out at the home, and I'll not be doin' much walkin' for a while, wi' this ankle. You've got your own bicycle still, I know, otherwise you could borry mine.'

'I'd be pleased to give a hand,' Sara said at once. Truth to tell, now that the excitement of getting the home ready for occupation had worn off, she often felt herself to be useless, at a loose end. The onset of winter hadn't helped, of course; the short damp days and long, chilly evenings were enough to depress anyone. Matron told her that she would look back nostalgically on these first few weeks once they were up and running but right now, Sara had too much time on her hands, too much time to think.

She could not forget that when she had decided to take a night off, behave like a normal girl again and go to the cinema with Clarrie Boote, her grandmother had died. Nor that Mrs Prescott had longed for more of her granddaughter's company. If I'd been at home, she kept telling herself, I'd have spotted the signs, fetched the doctor, got her into hospital . . . she might be alive today. If I'd taken her about more, pushed her wheelchair up to the dances she wanted to attend . . . if I'd not been so selfish . . . Why, if I'd not decided to buy fish and chips all round, waited in the queue, I might have got back in time to revive her.

A part of her mind knew that this was foolish, that it could have happened at any time; when she was working, when she was taking the *War Cry* round the pubs, which could scarcely be considered light entertainment, when she was shopping . . . anything. Naturally she regretted not spending more time on the older woman, but she was sensible enough to know that her grandmother could not be brought back to life by vain regrets. But the knowledge did not stop her moping.

And she had not succeeded in finding either Grace or Mollie. She had kept her eyes open and asked around but there was no trace of the Carbery family; they might have disappeared off the face of the earth. Like Brogan had. Oh, she knew he'd really only disappeared back to Ireland, but she missed him badly, thought about him often. He had made her feel young and carefree, pretty even. She had known when she was in his company that she was valued. Though there were several very nice young men anxious to take his place, she could find none of them even slightly attractive. When young Mr Briscoe had asked her to go to a dance she had gone . . . and seen Brogan's dark hair and eyes every time she caught Mr Briscoe's sad, spaniel gaze.

So in a way, taking the *War Cry* round was a good idea; it would take her out of herself. And Matron was very understanding.

'You go, my dear,' she said earnestly. 'You've grown pale and thin of late, you're working too hard and worrying too much. You've not even been working in the soup kitchen as you used, and though I know it's a long way to go, I'd rather you were active, cheerful. You'll be much better for the children if you're more involved in the ordinary life of the Liverpool poor.' She smiled at her colleague. 'You might even find us some customers,' she added. 'Our two little inmates would welcome additions to the fold.'

Sara bicycled down to the Barracks, explained that her

friend was temporarily out of commission and picked up Clarrie's newspapers. Then she left her bicycle round the back of the hall, where it would be safe from thieves. Since the Army girls always went into pubs in pairs she was happy to see that she would be working with Miss Chadwick, who was a slum officer during the day but sometimes came and sold newspapers in the evening.

Miss Chadwick was a brisk, efficient young woman in her mid-twenties and she and Sara had always got on well.

'Good evening, Miss Cordwainer, good to see you again,' she said as soon as she set eyes on Sara. 'Of course I see you on Sundays . . . but not for long, just for the morning service. Are you busy, out at the Strawb?'

'Not really. That's the trouble,' Sara admitted. 'Half the time we're just polishing furniture and lighting fires in the rooms to keep them aired. It all seems . . . oh, I don't know, I suppose it makes me feel as if all our labour was for nothing.'

'It takes time,' Miss Chadwick said soothingly. 'Surely Matron's told you that?'

'Yes, she has, of course. But somehow, I expected we'd be full in a week. There are so many unfortunate children . . .'

'Yes, but a good few of them, having escaped from their parents, simply want to keep clear of all authority, all adults,' Miss Chadwick pointed out placidly. 'But they'll gradually come in, fill the place. Then you'll look back on these early weeks as a halcyon period when you had time to think! Now, which pub shall we try first?'

'The Queen's Arms?' Sara suggested. She still had a fondness for that particular pub since it had been

Peader O'Brady's local once. She remembered meeting Brogan's father there one winter evening. They had talked about his son . . . she could still remember the pleasure the chance meeting had given her, the hope.

But it wouldn't have been the same now, anyway, she reminded herself as Miss Chadwick said no, not tonight. Tonight, it seemed, they were going further afield . . . to the pubs on Commercial Road.

'We'll start at the Eagle and go on to the Union, then we'll cross over and do the Great Mersey, the Evelyn, the Midland and the Sandhills, I think,' Miss Chadwick decided. 'It's a cold night, so at least we'll keep warm inside the pubs, and we should do well – I find people buy more willingly coming up to Christmas.'

So off they set, with their bonnets pulled on at a determined angle and every hair smoothed out of sight, their stocking seams straight, their shoes polished. They might be visiting rough areas, where the coin which tinkled most frequently into their collecting tins would be a ha'penny, but that did not mean they should not be spruce, tidy, polite.

It paid off, too. Folk treated the Army lasses with respect because the Army lasses respected them, and they bought the *War Cry* because they knew the Army did a great deal for people like them. So Sara and Miss Chadwick walked briskly along the frosty pavements, with their metal-tipped heels striking sparks as they marched, heading for their first call.

There was a brawl outside the Great Mersey when they reached it, however, so Miss Chadwick decreed that they should continue on to the Evelyn, and return when things had calmed down somewhat. Sara agreed; they were having a good evening, the money which tinkled into her tin was mounting up and the pile of newspapers in her arms was shrinking in a very satisfactory manner. What was more, folk were so friendly – she had forgotten that in the six or seven months she'd not been handling the *War Cry*.

But although all the Irishmen – and railwaymen – they met made her think of Brogan she did not recognise any of them and besides, what was the point of asking for news of him? She knew he was in Ireland, so why make herself unhappy by hearing someone reiterate the fact?

And presently, with full tins and only a couple of newspapers apiece left, Miss Chadwick suggested that they return to their headquarters.

'For we've both left our bicycles at the Barracks and you've a long way to go, my dear Miss Cordwainer,' she said. 'It's several miles out to Woolton; it was good of you to come into the city to help me out.'

Sara said, politely, that it was a pleasure but added that she supposed they really ought to go back to the Great Mersey, because it was a generous pub with a generous landlady. 'We'll get rid of the last of our papers there,' she said positively. 'Mrs Boyce will see we do so.'

'Well, if you don't mind a late bicycle ride . . .' Miss Chadwick said. 'Come along, then, best foot foremost!'

Grace was hovering near the pub, waiting as she did most nights, for closing time. She was quite pleased with life right now. She came to the pub out of habit and because the landlady still fed her, but it wasn't cold enough yet to be offered shelter and besides, she had a good place up beside a bakery. The bakers came in early, at around three o'clock in the morning, and from the moment they started work warmth and a delicious smell of bread began to drift through the narrow windows above Grace's head. One of the best things about her retreat was its narrowness; only a child, and a skinny child at that, could crawl along the narrow passage-like entrance between the wall of the next building and the bakery itself. So tucked up in her blanket and lying on a thick pad of old newspapers, Grace felt both secure and comfortable.

But now, still waiting outside the pub for closing time, Grace saw the Army lasses coming and hid, because she did not know them. The girls went into the pub and Grace stole back to huddle close to the bright lights. She never went in, of course; kids didn't go into public houses, but she enjoyed being in the vicinity of warmth, laughter, happiness.

After a while, she grew careless. She leaned against the wall, then slid down beside it. She could feel the lovely warmth of the pub from here, it was soothing, it made her sleepy . . .

She woke when someone said: 'Are you all right, my love?'

She looked up and a beautiful, concerned face was only inches from her own. A dark bonnet framed the face – it was one of the Army lasses, she'd been caught!

Somehow, she managed to get to her feet and move back, gabbling something, saying she was sorry, she'd just dropped asleep . . .

'You don't have to apologise, dear,' the beautiful girl said. 'But you aren't very old . . . isn't it time you were at home in bed? Or are you waiting for your father – is he in the pub?'

'I 'ope to God 'e's not,' Grace said fervently, forgetting herself for a moment. 'I 'ope to God 'e's a long way from 'ere.'

'Where's your mother, then? Do you live near here?'

She was so pretty, so concerned, but . . . *danger,*

danger, Grace's mind said. *She'll take you away, put you in the work'ouse – tell 'er something, anything, but gerraway before she teks you in!*

'Me mam? Oh, at 'ome, I daresay,' Grace said. She moved back a little further. 'You're right, Miss, she's be a-waitin' for me. I'd best be gerrin' off 'ome.'

She half turned, but she didn't really want to leave. Presently the drinkers would go off home and Mrs Boyce would come out, show her Kitty, now a great strong animal with a coat so thick and soft that, come winter, Grace would envy him, and then bring Grace out some food. They would chat a little, Grace keeping a bit of distance between them, as though she were a wild animal and Mrs Boyce a zoo-keeper, and then Grace would say goodnight and return to her bakery.

'Don't let me drive you away, dear,' the Army lass said. Her voice was gentle, persuasive. 'You've a perfect right to stay here as long as you want. But look . . . can you read?'

'A bit,' Grace said. She wasn't going to admit that she could not remember how to read at all, having seldom attended school.

'Very well, then. I'm going to write my name and address down on a bit of paper,' the Army lass said. 'And I'll give it to you. If you ever need a roof over your head, or any sort of help, you can always come to me. D'you think you can read a name and address?'

'Dunno,' Grace said. 'It's awright, I'm awright, I don't need nothin' . . . I don't need nobody!'

The Army lass sighed; she sounded discouraged. 'Well, if you don't need any help . . . but suppose you met someone who *did* need help? Then you could pass my name and address on, couldn't you? Not everyone is independent, you see. Not everyone has good parents, either.'

Grace was frightened and wary of anyone who addressed her directly, but she was inherently kind. She had heard the distress in the girl's voice when she had more or less thrown her offer back in her face and was ashamed of herself. It would not, after all, hurt her to take the piece of paper. She came forward and took the page the girl was offering and tucked it into one of her disgraceful pockets.

'Thanks, Miss,' she said. 'I'll keep it by me.'

And then, feeling that she had done more than her duty, she turned and made off into the night.

'What did you do that for, Miss Cordwainer?' Miss Chadwick asked curiously as they made their way home through the streets, humming now with men leaving the pubs as they closed. 'I daresay her father *was* in the Great Mersey for all she denied it. And her mother was quite likely laid out insensible, clutching a gin bottle, in some dreadful slum room somewhere. Children of such parents often find it politic to stay away from home for a night or two.'

'I know,' Sara said. 'But if she was ever in need . . .'

'You're very right, I'd not thought of it quite like that,' Miss Chadwick said, nodding. 'You gave her the Strawberry Field address?'

'I did. After all, we've a great many places still to fill . . .'

Miss Chadwick chuckled. 'Touting for business, eh, Miss Cordwainer? Well, I think you've done a kind and sensible thing, let us hope your little waif turns up on your doorstep – if she's really in need. And now we'd best hurry back to the Barracks and fetch our bicycles.'

'I wonder if she really can read?' Sara said as the two of them reached the Barracks, reclaimed their bicycles, and began to cycle down Walton Road. 'She said *a bit*, which could mean anything.'

'I doubt it,' Miss Chadwick said. 'But never mind, dear, you've done your best.'

Sara sighed and cycled on. She had no idea why she had suddenly wanted to give her name and address to the ragged child outside the pub, but she was glad she had done it. Even if the kid couldn't read, she would know someone who could. And presently, what with the cold and the moonlight and the distance she had to travel, Sara stopped conjecturing and put her heart and soul into her pedalling.

Grace crawled up to her bakery bedroom and lay down on the newspapers, then pulled the blanket up round her and sniffed, in great contentment, the smell of new bread which came floating out of the bakery's half-open window.

What an odd sort of day it had been! First she'd found that pretty, nicely dressed little girl a-bawlin' her eyes out in the middle of the road, shortly after she herself had been chased across the marshalling yard by a bullying beast of a foreman. She'd felt really sorry for the kid, lost and alone in a big city like Liverpool. So she'd offered her help and taken her home.

And this evening the Army lass had tried to do her a good turn. She'd been suspicious, but she should have realised that no one belonging to the Army would have hurt her. Why, didn't they give her soup and bread from their kitchens, supply her from time to time with a nice bit of blanket, new shoes, stockings, even? She never kept these nice things long, either they were stolen from her by street kids with more brawn or more cunning, or she had to pop 'em at the pawnshop. Well, not the soup or the bread, of course, she downed them as soon as they were offered, but the clothes and shoes . . . nice though they were, eating was nicer.

Mrs Boyce had given her a chunk of cheese and some bread tonight. She had eaten most of it – you couldn't go off to sleep with bread and cheese about your person or you'd wake up and find yourself being investigated by stray cats or rats. Now, Grace drew out of the pocket of her dirty jacket the last bit of bread and just as she was about to eat it, noticed the piece of paper fluttering to the floor.

Sighing, she bent and picked it up, spread it out, looked at it.

There was writing on it. Well, she supposed it was writing, at any rate. It was all sort of *joined*, though, so even if she could have managed the letters, she doubted that she could ever have read the words.

Not that it mattered. She supposed the Army lass had meant she could get soup, or a pair of new shoes, if she went to her. She thought that was about all the Army could do for you.

She thought about throwing the paper away, then changed her mind and tucked it into her pocket. Might as well keep it, you never knew.

The bread was still uneaten and Grace realised she really wasn't particularly hungry so she pushed it under her makeshift newspaper pillow, heaved her blanket up over her shoulders and curled up on the newspapers; very soon she slept.

She woke because something was rustling. She opened her eyes and saw a lean grey body only inches from her face – it was a rat, investigating the bread under her pillow. Grace gave a squeak and tried to grab at the rat, meaning to throw it away from her, but unfortunately the rat, cornered by her body, gave a horrid squeal, launched itself at her, and fastened its teeth in her cheek.

It was all over in a minute. Grace grabbed the rat and pulled. The rat, probably already terrified, let go of her cheek and wriggled out of her grip, running in a horrid, slithery sort of way towards the hole in the wall which led, she assumed, into the cellars of the bakery, its long, scaly tail disappearing last.

Grace sat up. Her head was throbbing and she knew, with real dismay, that she would never want to sleep here again. Not if rats were going to attack her. She had always known there were rats on the streets, they shared her scavenging life, but she had never before been attacked by one and was astonished at her own disgust and despair. It was a horrible, horrible thing, and her face really hurt. She put her fingers to her cheek and they came away wet with blood. She could feel the tear marks where the rat had tried to hang on like a little bulldog before finally releasing her.

Presently she got up, shook herself, sorted out her bedding and crawled to the end of her retreat. She picked up her blanket, which she usually left behind for the next night, feeling worse than she had when her father had first made it imperative that she left her home. She glanced back, once, at her cosy nook, then straightened up. Best get to a tap – there were taps on the street in various places – and clean up a bit, get rid of the blood for a start. Folk didn't like a child with a bloody face, they feared it was a sign of disease and either chucked a stone to keep you off or called the scuffers.

Twenty minutes later, washed, with her hair damp and slicked down, Grace made her way to the marshalling yards. There was a good shed there where she could decide what best to do now that the bakery was lost to her.

She reached the shed and sat down on her blanket and thought. Twice, she got out the piece of paper and perused it thoughtfully. Mrs Boyce could read, she could take it along there . . . or she could go to the Barracks, see if they knew the Army lass. But the trouble was her face hurt and her head was throbbing and she didn't really feel like doing too much. She really felt like catching up on the sleep she had lost last night. Presently she lay down. She might as well get some rest whilst she could. She slept.

The taxi driver never even saw where she came from. One moment Commercial Road was clear and he was driving at a steady pace along it, the next there was this creature staggering in front of him. A skinny bit of a girl she was, with a raw, suppurating wound in one cheek and nothing but rags on her back.

'I didn't touch 'er, officer,' he told the policeman who appeared almost as magically as the girl had done. Trust a scuffer, the driver thought sourly, to appear when he was least wanted. 'She sorta stumbled out into the roadway an' fell over . . . she's gorra fever on 'er, be the looks.'

'Hmm. Been hidin' out in the marshallin' yard, I daresay,' the policeman said. 'Catch a holt of 'er feet, we'll get 'er out of the roadway for a start.'

She weighed nothing, you had to say that for her, the taxi driver thought, picking up her shoulders and lifting too high, then steadying her. They carried her to the side of the road but when the driver would have laid her on the pavement the policeman shook his head.

'No, we can't leave 'er on the roadway, like a sack

o' spuds. Put 'er in the back of your taxi; I'll thank you to take the pair of us up to the Stanley, get 'er sorted.'

But in the taxi, she came round. The driver saw her eyelids flicker, then lift. She frowned, struggled to sit up, then collapsed back on to the seat.

'What's goin' on?' she asked weakly. 'Where am I? Where's you takin' me? I ain't done nothin' wrong... I jest want to go 'ome.'

The scuffer was good with her, you had to say that, even the taxi driver admitted it, and he was fond of neither scuffers nor stray kids.

'It's awright, queen,' the policeman said placidly. 'You come over queer, like, in the roadway. I was goin' to tek you along to the 'ospital, but if you'll tell me where you live I'll get this feller to run you home.'

The girl hesitated, then plunged a hand into her pocket and produced a sheet of blue paper. She handed it to the scuffer, then stared – almost glared – at him.

'That's it, that's me address,' she said. 'Can you take me there?'

'Miss Sara Cordwainer... is that you, queen?' the policeman said. 'Strawberry Field Children's Home, Beaconsfield Road... and then there's a telephone number. Ah, I *see*.'

The taxi driver saw, too. She'd run off from some children's home and hidden up in the shed on the marshalling yard. Probably in trouble at the place... though he'd heard good things about the Strawb as he went about his business. It was run by the Sally Army, and he had time for them. It was a real good place for kids to be from all accounts. But before he could comment aloud the policeman leaned forward and spoke.

'Did you 'ear that, cabby? The Strawberry Field Children's Home, on Beaconsfield Road, pronto!'

The taxi driver turned in his seat, stunned.

'*Beaconsfield Road?* Are you mad, constable? That's miles out . . . I ain't made o' money, you know! Wharrabout me fare? I've gorra livin' to make, you know!'

'We'll talk about your fare later,' the policeman said soothingly. 'Just do it if you please, cabby. Strawberry Field, as soon as you like!'

Sara was making a frieze for the nursery when the knock came at the door. She and Matron were both in the staff room, working away, because Christmas was coming and they wanted to be ready. Matron was embroidering hankies with great care and dedication and Sara's frieze was to be a selection of teddy bears, golliwogs and other toys, to be drawn, painted and cut out.

'Drat, I wonder who that is?' Matron said, her needle poised for a moment. 'Are you very busy, Sara, because if so . . .'

The home was not yet fully staffed, which meant that Sara and Matron were doing most of the work. Sara, who had just finished drawing a particularly cuddly bunny rabbit, jumped to her feet.

'I'll go. It'll be that man to see about the chimney in the dining room.'

She hurried to the door, and flung it open. A policeman stood on the doorstep and beside him stood a small girl. Sara frowned. The child looked vaguely familiar; an ex-pupil, perhaps? Or a neighbour? But the child was pulling a face at her, an urgent, entreating sort of face, and the policeman was speaking.

'Afternoon, Miss. We found this young person collapsed in the street – she says she lives here.'

'That's right,' Sara said, thinking rapidly. Where on *earth* had she seen the child before? 'Yes, that's right . . . come inside, dear, and wait there, I want a word with you.' She turned back to the policeman. 'She's not in any sort of trouble, I trust?'

'None in the world, Miss,' the policeman said gallantly. 'A good child... though the clothes she's wearin' don't look much like the sorta thing...'

'They aren't. We haven't kitted her out yet,' Sara said. 'Oh, of course!'

She had remembered the child outside the pub, the name and address scribbled on a sheet of cheap blue writing paper. Well, well, the poor little thing! When faced with authority and a demand for her address she had immediately thought of Sara. A clear case of man's extremity being God's opportunity, Sara supposed.

'Of course what, Miss?'

'Oh! Of course she must have slipped away from a – a group of children being taken shopping,' Sara said wildly. 'Thank you, officer, for bringing her back home. Do we owe you anything?'

The policeman touched his helmet and turned away. 'No Miss, nothing at all. Any time, Miss. You do good work here, everyone knows it, I'm glad to be of help.'

As soon as the policeman had climbed back into the taxi, Sara turned back into the hall. Her unexpected guest stood at bay by the stairs, looking frightened out of her wits... and somehow defiant, too. The wound on her face looked livid against the extreme pallor of her skin, Sara thought, eyeing the dirt which was liberally smeared over the child's face. The other night she had scarcely noticed the child's condition, but now she realised she had never seen anyone quite so dirty, nor so battered. Poor kid, she had been in the wars! Sara walked towards her, a hand held out.

'My dear child, I'm so very glad you came to me when you felt you needed a friend. If you'll come through into the kitchen I'll get you something to eat and drink. There's plenty of milk and some really delicious scones . . . but we'll take a look in the pantry, shall we, see what you fancy?'

The girl looked rather wildly round, then stared up into Sara's face. After a moment the doubt which had filled her eyes seemed to clear and she said in a low, rather hoarse voice, 'Awright. I – I like milk, I does.'

As Sara and her charge passed the staff room door on the way to the kitchen Matron emerged. She smiled placidly at them both.

'Ah, another inmate, I see. I don't imagine that this young lady came from one of the other homes, so I suppose it was our friends the police? Can you manage, Miss Cordwainer? Anything I can do?'

'Yes, a policeman brought her,' Sara said. She realised that Matron had guessed the child had not come from another home by the state of her. Their other inmates had come from reception centres where they had been cleaned up before being sent on to the Strawb. 'We'll manage, thanks Matron.' She turned to the child once more. 'Here's the kitchen, dear . . . bless me, I never asked you your name!'

'Matty,' the child said without a second's hesitation. 'Matty Brown.'

'Nice to meet you, Matty,' Sara said. She smiled and held out her hand and after a long moment, the child took it in a scratched and filthy paw. 'I'm Miss Cordwainer, I'm Matron's assistant here. And now let's fetch milk and scones and see how you feel after you've had a meal.'

Sara took it very gently, wooing the child, talking about the other children who lived at the home but who were going round the Walker Art Gallery this afternoon, and when the child had eaten as much as Sara thought she ought, she took her upstairs to the pleasant bedroom with six beds, only two of which were claimed so far.

'Would you like a bed by the window?' she asked. 'Or would you prefer to sleep on the other side, which is perhaps a bit warmer?'

'Winder,' Matty muttered. 'Only – only I telled a lie to that scuffer. I only come 'ere 'cos I 'ad your address in me pocket. I di'n't want 'im to take me to the work'ouse, that was why.'

'Well, dear, I'm glad you came to me, by however circuitous a route,' Sara said cheerfully, walking towards the long cupboard at the end of the room. 'There are quite a lot of clothes in here, I'm sure we'll find something to fit you. What about these?' She took down a blue woollen skirt and cardigan, a white blouse and some white woolly vests and knickers. 'They look as if they'd fit – shall we try them?'

'But I aren't . . . I don't . . . this ain't my 'ome,' the girl said desperately. 'I can't take them clothes – it ain't like food.'

'No, I agree clothes aren't much like food, but this is a children's home, Matty. We want to help children and – forgive me – you look as if you could do with some help. So won't you give us a chance? See how you like us, how you fit in?'

The child's eyes filled with tears and she turned her head away, scrubbing at them surreptitiously with both hands. Then she turned back.

'Awright, I'll try them clothes,' she said gruffly. 'If – if you're sure.'

'Good.' Sara gathered up the nice new clothes then headed out of the room again, knowing without having to check that the child was close on her heels. 'Then I think perhaps a bath, with something nice and freshening in the water . . . what d'you say to that? Only you wouldn't want to put clean clothes on a dirty body, would you?'

To judge from her expression Matty had no objection to such behaviour herself, but she agreed, obediently, that it would not do and the two of them went into the bathroom. It was large and rather old-fashioned, but the big tub looked comfortable and there were clean towels over a clothes rail in one corner.

'Would you like to take your things off?' Sarah asked. 'A bath's better for getting you clean all over, a wash is a bit hit and miss, wouldn't you say?'

'I'd sooner wash,' Matty said. 'Just me 'ands an' face.'

'I think a bath would be best, love. Because if you're going to be putting on lovely clean new clothes . . .'

Matty, it seemed, had never washed all over and did not fancy starting now. But when Sara ran warm water into the bath, splashed disinfectant and got out a bar of carbolic soap, Matty, with a shudder, began to undress.

She got her jacket off easily, and threw it across the cork-topped bathroom stool, but the filthy shift beneath seemed almost glued to her skin. Sara tried to get it off and realised that it wouldn't come. Dirt and dried blood had welded the garment to the child's body . . . and her hair was definitely verminous.

'Look, your – your shift could do with a wash,' Sara said finally. 'I think if you hop into the water . . .'

She picked Grace up, appalled by the lightness of the little body in her arms, and dumped her, shift and all, in the bath. Then, whilst Grace was still gasping from the shock, Sara held her torso gently beneath the water until the shift could be pulled painlessly from the child's grey, bruised flesh.

'Hair too, dear,' Sara said, reaching for the jug which

stood handy. 'I'll just wet it, then work up a nice lather . . .'

Matty was very good, all things considered. Sara had heard stories from Army officers of how children would fight to protect themselves from a bath, how they howled and shrieked when they felt soap stinging wounds and eyes, but Matty did all she could to help, even rubbing away at her blackened knees with a soapy flannel and letting Sara pour the jug of water repeatedly over her filthy, matted hair.

But at last the job was done. Matty stepped out of the water clean, with every bite, scratch, bruise and abrasion now clearly etched on her pale skin and her little hip bones standing out from her almost concave stomach. Sara, helping her to dry herself, asked her what the marks were, though she could guess. The child glanced down at the red bumps and the scratches and bruises, then shrugged indifferently.

'Dunno. Bed-bugs, fleas . . . some are from fights, old ones, some's where me dad battered me. Oh, and a rat bit me cheek.'

Sara shuddered, she could not help herself.

'It'll have to have some antiseptic on it, dear, or it may go bad. It's festering already. In fact you've got several nasty wounds. But we can soon set them to rights; I expect you'll not mind if the stuff I put on stings a bit.'

Sara fetched antiseptic, cleaned and dressed the wounds, then took Matty, now paler than ever, back into the bedroom. She gave her the clothing she had already selected, as well as some long black stockings and a pair of lace-up shoes which proved to be a bit too big.

'But it's better than too small,' Sara said cheerfully. 'Shall I plait your hair, Matty? It'll be lovely smooth hair one of these days, such a pretty light-brown colour, too. But for now perhaps it's best tied back. I've got a nice piece of scarlet ribbon somewhere . . .'

She found the ribbon, tied the child's hair back, and then gestured to the pathetic little pile of rags which Matty had brought through from the bathroom.

'What shall I do with your old clothes, love? Only you've got all this nice, new stuff, you won't need your other things, will you? We'll keep them if you wish, of course, but if not, perhaps we might throw them away?'

Matty looked doubtful. One did not cast aside perfectly good clothes, her expression said. But then she looked round the room, at the flowered wallpaper, the pretty curtains, the beds with their white coverlets.

'That's my bed, izzit?'

'Yes, that's your bed.'

'An' these are me clothes, eh? No one else won't take 'em off me?'

'They're yours for as long as they fit you, and when you grow bigger, you'll be given new clothes.'

Matty gave the pile of rags a disdainful flick with her toe. It said a lot, Sara thought.

'Chuck 'em out,' Matty said. 'Oh . . . wait on; there's suffin' . . .' She delved into the pocket of the torn old jacket she had worn and produced a small, round object. It was greyish-white, soft and fluffy. That's all I want to keep,' she said rather shyly. 'Them were me sister's. It's the only thing of 'ers I've got, see?'

'What is it?' Sara asked idly. 'Is it a ball? It's a bit dirty, isn't it?'

'Yes, it's filthy,' the child agreed. 'But it's not a ball.' She pulled at the object, which became two. 'See?'

Sara held her hand out wonderingly and took both small objects in the palm of her hand. She looked at the once-white angora gloves for a long, long moment. Then she looked up.

'Grace,' she said quietly. 'Oh, my dear, you're not Matty Brown, you're Grace Carbery – and these are the little gloves I gave to Jess!'

Miss Boote had been right; the hospital strapped up her ankle, lent her some crutches, and sent her off home. Brogan, who had had to move his family out to their new home later that day, visited her there as soon as he got back. Miss Boote lived in a neat ground-floor flat in Florence Street, just up the road from his own lodgings in Salop Street.

'How are you feelin' now, Miss Boote?' he asked her when she came to the door in answer to his knock. 'I've been thinkin' about you for two days, worryin' in case the ankle got worse. But you look fine an' fit, so you do.'

'Do come in, Mr O'Brady, and thanks for the compliment,' Miss Boote said, ushering him into her living kitchen. 'Sorry it's a bit untidy, but four of us share the place and sometimes we could do with more space round us. Did you manage your move all right?'

Brogan had told her, whilst they waited in casualty, about his family's move out of the city, and now he grinned reminiscently, remembering that awful day, the complications caused by Polly's behaviour and the way her livestock had behaved.

'We managed very well in the end, if you don't count the cockerel gettin' loose and scarin' the livin' daylights out of the guard on the train, and Delly bein' sick as . . . as a dog. Heaven knows what he'd ate but it must have been an unsavoury meal. And Lionel takin' a dislike to the cat basket and tryin' to claw his way out of it. When I got back to the city I had to start work again of course, me holiday bein' up, but if all holidays are as exhaustin' as that one, I'll be more relaxed in the cab of me engine.'

Miss Boote laughed. She went over to a small gas stove and lit it, then pulled the kettle over the flame.

'You do cheer me up, Mr O'Brady! Sit down, I'll make us a nice cup of tea.'

And presently, with the tea-tray before her, she began to ask Brogan about himself and what he intended to do with the rest of his life.

'Because you mentioned giving a hand in the garden out at Strawberry Field,' she said. 'I've not said too much, in case you felt you'd better things to do with your time – after all, for all I knew you might have decided to stay with your family – but I did say I knew someone who liked gardening and I was told to send you along whenever you had a moment to spare.'

'Well, now that I've me family settled, I've a moment to spare,' Brogan decided. 'I'll go along there now so I will. I'll go back home and fetch me bike . . . I don't use the tram much – and I can be there in half an hour.' He drained his teacup and then stood up. 'Thanks, Miss Boote – you say I cheered you up – you don't know how much better I feel. First I know you're comin' on nicely so you are, and next I've the prospect of gettin' me hands on some gardenin' again!'

Miss Boote beamed. She stood up as well and accompanied him to the door.

'And you're going to do a good turn,' she said exuberantly. 'There's nothin' like doin' a good turn to cheer a person up. And you never know, Mr O'Brady – sometimes when you do something for someone else it's you that actually benefit.'

'Uh?' Brogan said, rather bemused.

Miss Boote laughed again. 'I didn't put it very well,

did I? What I meant was that doing good sometimes brings unexpected rewards.'

'Oh, I see,' Brogan said. 'Well, I'll be off if you don't mind, Miss Boote. It's a nice day for once, I might get some diggin' done this afternoon!'

When she had seen her visitor off, Miss Boote returned to her favourite chair and carefully put her injured ankle up on a small footstool. Then she reached for her book, but though she turned the pages at intervals she did not read a word. Her mind was far away, with Sara at Strawberry Field. She had deliberately reminded Mr O'Brady of his offer to do some gardening because she had a feeling that he might be that friend of Sara's who had gone back to Ireland to take care of his family. She could be wrong, of course, she acknowledged that. Or Sara might be no longer interested in her old friend. Nevertheless, there was a good chance, Miss Boote thought, that she had actually done something to bring two very nice people together.

I've never seen meself as a matchmaker, Miss Boote told herself at last, getting up from her chair and limping over to the kettle to make more tea. But even if I'm not successful, even if it isn't the same feller, there's no harm in gettin' a gardener for free!

Chapter Sixteen

Brogan got off his bicycle at soon as he reached the Strawberry Field drive and pushed it the rest of the way up to the front door. Then he swerved round to the side of the house, because a would-be gardener would scarcely approach the front door in so brazen a manner. Besides, it gave him a chance for a good look around.

The garden was in a state all right, he told himself, eyeing the beds, many of them trampled flat by builders and decorators, some simply winter-bare, but all lacking the clean, tilled look of a well-kept garden. There were roses in need of pruning, shrubs and bushes in need of cutting back, lawns positively begging for draining, cleaning, nurturing. Yes, Strawberry Field could do with someone, and he very much hoped it could be him. I'd start off with a series of bonfires, he told himself, looking disparagingly at the paths, almost hidden beneath a carpet of fallen leaves, hedges straggling across them, a paved patio mossy and puddled where it was not mounded up with dead leaves. Yes, I'd start with bonfires, then I'd go on by doing some good, old-fashioned double-digging. And then I'd get a few cartloads of farmyard muck and spread it all around . . . the place would begin to benefit by the spring.

He reached the back door. He could hear muted sounds from beyond it so he knocked politely, then stood back and waited.

*

'Oh dear, every time I put pen to paper someone either rings up or comes to the door,' Sara grumbled, putting her pen down and jumping to her feet. 'I'd only just seen the children off for their cinema trip, thankful for at least two hours' peace and quiet, when Mr Reid arrived, asking about the new geyser for the staff bathroom. Still, if this is the gardener Miss Boote asked to call, he can't come soon enough. Oh, Matron, I do wonder how I'll cope when all the children arrive, considering I'm finding three such hard work!'

'When the place is full there'll be someone else to answer the door,' the matron said placidly. The two women were in the staff sitting room, Sara trying to catch up with her paperwork and the matron knitting for Christmas. So far she had made each of their three resident children a scarlet woolly jumper, a pom-pom hat and a pair of brightly coloured mittens. Sara, entrusted with the scarves, had barely got halfway up – or down – the first. 'Off you go, Miss Cordwainer. And since you're so busy I'll do a bit of your knitting, shall I? I seem to have finished mine.'

'Oh, I *would* be grateful,' Sara said, pausing for a moment. 'I'm afraid I'm not a very good knitter. Gran did try to teach me, but she gave up because I kept producing a different number of stitches, though goodness knows how. I really don't understand it at all, to tell you the truth.'

'That's clear,' the matron said, surveying the uneven piece of knitting which dangled from Sara's needles. 'Are those holes part of the pattern, then?'

'Umm . . . I'm not sure. I'll just . . .'

Sara hurried from the room, glad to escape the difficult task. Matron, who clearly took knitting quite complex patterns in her stride, seemed to expect her assistant to be similarly gifted, which wasn't helping either. I'm good at other things, Sara told herself defensively now, crossing the hallway with a quick, impatient step. I do the books and amuse the children, do quite a lot of the cooking when Cook is on her day off or otherwise engaged, I teach Sunday school . . .

She reached the back door and flung it open.

'Good aftern . . .' Sara stopped short. 'Brogan! Oh, Brogan!'

She had told herself he was only a friend, but she did not treat him like one. She simply flew across the short distance which separated them and hugged him. And Brogan hugged her back, hugged her hard, and began kissing any bit of her that he could reach, which was entirely unexpected and entirely lovely, so far as Sara was concerned. Locked in each other's arms, they both knew the sheer bliss of reunion, and Sara felt tears form in her eyes and begin to trickle down her cheeks because *this* was where she wanted to be, *this* was where she belonged! She had thought a life of caring for children was all she could possibly desire, now she knew she was wrong. More than anything else, she wanted to be with Brogan. It was, in the end, that simple.

Brogan's face was shining. He hadn't said a word so far, but finally he held her away from him, his eyes fixed lovingly on her face.

'Sara? Dear God above, I've missed you so bad! But I'd given you up, after they told me you'd got a feller, an Army feller.'

'An *Army* feller? Who on earth told you that? I've never had a feller at all, if you want to know the truth. Oh, and Brogan, I'm so sorry about your father's death; what a terrible thing to happen.'

'Indeed,' Brogan said solemnly. 'Me father was hit by a train, it near kilt him so it did, but he recovered.

Now he's fit an' well, and livin' on the Wirral, mindin' a crossin' for the LMS. Boote, your feller's name was, accordin' to your neighbour, in Snowdrop Street.' He grinned suddenly. 'God love you, Sara, it wouldn't be Miss Boote she was meanin', would it? The young woman me sister's dog knocked over?'

'That's right, or I think it is . . . certainly Clarrie was knocked down in Anfield Cemetery by a dog . . . Oh, Brogan, was *that* why you never came calling? Because you thought Miss Boote was my – my intended? She was our lodger, that's all! And Peader's fit and well, you say? That's wonderful news, Brog. A little feller in the Queen's Arms told me you'd gone back to Ireland to look after your family because your father had died. He said he thought you'd be getting married over there. Honestly, what a fool I was not to check up!'

'We've been a pair of fools, both believin' whatever we were told about the other,' Brogan said. 'And what d'you think you've done to me, hidin' yourself away like this? Ah God, an' the last time we met sure an' wasn't I a tongue-tied idiot! But you were so grand, so special . . . I had no words to tell you the things I wanted you to know . . . ah, Sara, why in God's name didn't I just hug you?'

'I don't know,' Sara said. She knew her own eyes were shining, she could feel the tears building. 'Brogan . . . this is madness! Last time we met we almost quarrelled . . . We've believed all sorts of silly things about the other one . . . oh, Brog, I've missed you!'

'Not so bad as I've missed you,' Brogan said tenderly. 'But why the uniform?'

Sara looked down at herself as though she didn't know what he was talking about, then laughed.

'Oh, that. I'm a Salvationist, Brog, the same as my

friend Clarrie is. Didn't you know that Strawberry Field is a Salvation Army children's home? I joined the Army a while back, when Clarrie took me up to the Barracks and showed me the sort of work they did. I knew that if I joined them I'd be able to help the people who needed it most, especially children – it gave me a purpose in life. So I'm working here now, as an assistant to the matron.'

Brogan frowned. 'You're a Salvationist, then? I never guessed, never t'ought... you said you'd met the Carbs for the first time outside a church, you see. Not that it matters, one way or t'other, alanna.' But then he began to smile. 'So we've both been livin' here, believin' the other to be out of reach! And there was me, searchin' for the Carbery young wan, and never thinkin' to ask about yourself!'

'And there was me...' Sara broke off. 'We had a new child in recently, Brog; someone you know. Grace, her name is. Grace Carbery. The baby never put in an appearance, Grace spent years searching for her, but at least we know Grace herself is safe, now.'

'What about the parents?' Brogan asked. 'The mother died fallin' on the stairs, I read that somewhere. But what's become of the father? I take it he's not in full cry after gettin' Grace back again?'

Sara shook her head.

'No, we found out that he was killed in a drunken brawl outside the Great Mersey public house on Commercial Road a month or two back. The Army was able to trace him, once Grace admitted who she really was. She was so relieved... she cried with joy, which sounds terrible, but the things he'd done to her .. he was a wicked man and the best thing he could do for his kids was to die, believe me.'

'I believe you,' Brogan said fervently. 'Look, my

darlin' girl, can you come out wit' me for a while? Because we've a deal of talkin' to do, and I can't talk freely before anyone but you. And Sara, I'm not lettin' you out of me sight again until we've had this talk, so you'd best agree to it or I'll be makin' up me bed on your doorstep so I shall.'

'I'll come with you, but first you'd best come in and meet Matron and have a word about the garden,' Sara said. 'Oh, Brog, I can't tell you how relieved I was when I realised we'd found young Grace. Nor – nor how wonderful it is to see you again.'

'Ditto,' Brogan said briefly. 'I hope you'll still think it's nice to know me when I tell you . . . what I've got to tell you. But first, let's be meetin' this matron of yours.'

They took themselves off to Calderstones Park in the end. It was a cold afternoon, but the refreshment rooms were open, so the two of them chose a table in the window, ordered tea and cakes and proceeded to tell each other everything which had happened to them, both lately and long ago.

Sara, watching Brogan's face as he studied the menu, wondered how she had managed without him for so long. He was downright beautiful, with his thick, black hair which shone like coal, his expressive dark-brown eyes, and the slow smile which warmed those eyes, lit that strong, intelligent face. She knew, now, that she loved him, had probably loved him right from the start. But she did not know whether he loved her or simply liked her as a friend.

But this time I'll find out, she vowed, as they took their places on opposite sides of the small window-table. I'll find out . . . and if it's the right answer, I'm not going to pretend. I'm going to tell him I want to be with him for always, no matter how forward and bad it seems.

When their tea arrived Sara poured and Brogan insisted that she choose her cake first. Then he smiled at her, his eyes alight with affection.

'Who's goin' to start? Ladies first, I'm thinkin'.'

So Sara started, with the story of the child calling herself Matty Brown who had arrived on the doorstep at Strawberry Field. She gave Brogan a blow-by-blow account right up to the moment when Grace had brought the little grey fluffy ball out of her pocket, and Sara had recognised the gloves as the ones she herself had given to Jess on that snowy Christmas morning long ago.

It was tempting to leave it at that, to forget the other, darker side, but having decided to make a clean breast of it Sara took the plunge.

'I think the truth was, Brogan, that because my parents were indifferent to me I felt a real kinship for those other girls whose parents were indifferent, too. The Carberys, I mean. I know the circumstances were not the same, but at the root of it, the Carbery girls and myself all knew what it was to be unloved.

'So Jess touched me in a way which is probably a bit difficult to understand. It – it wasn't just the poverty, you see, it went deeper than that. But I could do so little; only give her what I had myself, which was the shilling and the white angora gloves, and of course what I gave her hadn't helped at all, not really. Indeed, for a while I actually felt I'd almost caused her death.

'My grandmother – and you – talked me out of a good deal of the guilt, but I did know how lucky I was. I had Gran, for a start, and she truly loved me. And though my parents didn't love me, they gave me things the Carbery kids would have given their eye-teeth for – food, clothing, education, self-confidence – compared to the kids from the slums, I was rich! So I decided to find the Carbery girls, who were having to fend for themselves now, and help them in any way I could.

'But it wasn't easy. I only visited Gran in the school holidays, and by the time the spring term was over and I went back to Snowdrop Street, the Carbs had been kicked out for not paying their rent and seemed to have disappeared.

'And then of course I was sent away to school in Switzerland and when I came back the first time I showed any sympathy for the poor, my parents disowned me. So back I came to Snowdrop Street, to earn my own living, help my grandmother . . . and try to find Grace and Mollie.

'Then Clarrie took me to the Barracks for the first time, and it was a revelation. There were people actually *doing* the things I'd thought about, talked about. They were working for the poor in a way I'd never imagined. They didn't just collect money, or say things should be different, they worked their fingers to the bone making sure that things *were* different. If a woman was too ill to come to the soup kitchen, the Army went to her. If a child was beaten and abused, the police brought the child to one of the Army shelters and the kid was cleaned up, taken to hospital if necessary, and found somewhere safe to sleep at nights. Old people who'd lost their homes, men who'd lost their jobs, lost hope, were all picked up, dusted down, and set on the path to recovery. I can't tell you, Brog, all the Army does because I don't know myself, yet. But I suppose in a way I wanted a share of all that shining faith, all that generosity. I admired them more than words can say and I saw that to become one of them, to work as they did, was not just a good way of helping people like the Carbs, it was the best way of helping, full stop. The Army net spreads wide, you see. Even if I, personally, wasn't able to help Grace and Mollie, others might well be doing so, and I was helping *them*.' She stopped talking, putting both hands to her hot cheeks. 'Oh, Brogan, do I sound an awful little prig? My mother called me a prig once. But I must try to explain what the Army did for me, and why I value it so!'

'I understand, alanna,' Brogan said quietly. 'And you aren't the only one to admire the Army, even though I don't share their faith. And now that you've Grace under your wing, is the guilt dead? What more could you have done, indeed?'

'I still wonder about Mollie,' Sara confessed. 'She was such a pretty child. I'd hate to think of her growing pale and indifferent, slouching around the street, begging . . . But what about you, Brogan? I remember the very first time we met you said you carried your burden of guilt, too.'

'I think I stopped feeling guilty when my mammy looked at the baby I'd got tucked under me donkey jacket, and fell in love wit' her,' Brogan said thoughtfully. 'Because I knew I was doin' what young Jess wanted. And now, every time I set eyes on our young'un . . .'

'*You* took her? Brogan O'Brady, don't say you've known where Mollie was all these years and never breathed a word to me? Oh, and I've worried myself sick, sometimes, at what I'd done.'

'Once she was wit' me mammy it wasn't my secret, you see,' Brogan said humbly. 'If it had been my secret, Sara love, you'd have known first go off so you would. But you were only a child yourself then; I couldn't risk you tellin' someone. Polly's whole life was at stake.'

'Polly? Don't you mean . . .' Sara stopped short with a gasp. 'Your little sister! She's ten years old, the only girl . . . Oh, Brogan, and whenever you've talked about her I've thought what a natural, happy child she seemed. You were right; it wasn't your secret to give away. But thank you, thank you, for telling me now!'

'I feel better for tellin' you, so I do,' Brogan assured her. 'You aren't the only one who's felt bad about those young wans. And you do understand, alanna, that I'd have told you if I could? Because – because I was fond of you from the first, so I was, and there was nothing I'd have liked better than to take the worry over the baby's whereabouts from your shoulders. But it wasn't possible, me darlin' girl.'

Brogan leaned across the little table and took both her hands in his. Then he turned them palm upwards and kissed them, starting at the wrists and moving across her palms and down to the tips of her fingers. Sara's heart did an enormous double-thump and then settled to a rapid, noisy rhythm. He loved her – didn't he? She realised she had no idea how young men behaved when they were in love, nor how young women behaved, come to that. The Army had taught her a great deal, but there were still some things she simply had to learn for herself.

'Brog? When you kissed my hands like that I felt very peculiar,' Sara whispered bashfully. 'It – it's an exciting sort of feeling. Is it wrong to feel – to feel that I'd like you to – to go on kissing me?'

'No, it's not wrong, darlin',' Brogan said. 'Sure an' isn't it how I've wanted and waited for you to feel this past decade? Look, we've sorted out what's happened to Grace and Polly, now d'you t'ink we might sort ourselves out, too? Because it's you I'm wantin' to spend the rest of me life wit', Sara Cordwainer. I know there's difficulties . . .'

'I don't see any,' Sara murmured. She could feel her cheeks begin to flame at the mere thought of what she was about to say. 'Because that's how I feel too, Brogan.'

'Oh, my love!' Brogan leaned forward ardently . . . and tipped the milk jug over. Sara jumped to her feet, perhaps a little relieved that the excitement and tension of the last few moments had so abruptly dissipated, and fetched a cloth. Laughing, she mopped up the milk, then went and fetched more. He had proposed to her – hadn't he? Was it a proposal when a man told a girl that he wanted to spend the rest of his life with her? She suspected that it was and her heart beat faster at the thought. To be with Brogan for always, as man and wife! It was what she wanted most out of life, she realised, though she had never even put it into thoughts, let alone words.

'So what are these difficulties?' Sara said presently, when order had been restored and they both had a fresh cup of tea before them. To her, the path stretched ahead, rose-strewn, sunny. 'Are you a married man, Brogan O'Brady, with a dozen kids hidden away somewhere?'

He laughed, shaking his head. 'No, indeed. But I'm a Catholic, darlin' Sara, and you're an Army lass. Liverpool may not be as bad as Dublin for mixed marriages . . .'

'It is,' Sara said. 'Oh, why didn't I *think*? But love . . . love can't be ordered and paid for, can it, Brog? You can't help who you fall in love with.'

'No, indeed, and our love's already stood the test of time so it has. Well, we'll see. I'm goin' back to the crossing cottage at the weekend, I'll see what's said when I tell them I'm marryin' the best, prettiest, most lovin' girl in the whole of Liverpool. But they'll expect such a one to be a good Cat'olic girl and raise a good Cat'olic family, and to be honest, alanna, it never crossed me mind, until you opened the door to me earlier, that you weren't a good Cat'olic girl!'

'I never was, even as a child,' Sara admitted. 'I was Church of England, Brog, before I joined the Army. And you really think your parents will disapprove? That they won't like me, because I'm a Salvationist? Not even when you point out the good we do, the work . . .'

'We won't judge them,' Brogan said. 'Wait and see. But if the worst comes to the worst, alanna, there's always America.'

'America? But why, Brog?'

'Because my brother Niall went there a while back and so I've been readin' up about the country, the prospect there. I'm an engine driver as you know, but because I'm young still there's no question, in England or Ireland, of me havin' an express, or doin' the more important lines, for another twenty years at least. I'll be doddlin' up and down branch lines or drivin' goods trains for years so I will. But if I go to the States, wit' the experience I've already had and me exam results, Niall says I'd be driving the transcontinental locomotives wit'in a year or two, but quite early on I'd be taking out the freights. Imagine it, Sara – to be a hogger on a freight train, travelling the high iron between Marshall and Dallas, and me not yet t'irty!'

'Imagine,' breathed Sara, who did not even know what he was talking about. 'And if . . . if two people of different religions were to marry in America, Brogan, would they be ostracised, made to feel guilty?'

'No, alanna. No one would give a tinker's cuss, so long as they didn't frighten the horses!'

And then Brogan leaned across the table and gathered Sara into his arms. Crockery crashed, milk jugs spilt, cakes became crumbs. But Sara, finding herself in the one place she most wanted to be, was indifferent.

'Oh, Brogan, we'll be so happy just to be together,' she murmured against his mouth. 'Can we go and see your parents *soon*?'

'Very soon. But . . . you've no regrets, alanna? What about Grace? Strawberry Field? Your friends?'

'Grace is happy, though I'd feel bad to leave her,' Sara admitted, sitting back in her seat once more. 'But we may not need to go to the States, not if your parents take to me. Then I wouldn't have to leave the Strawb, would I?'

'My parents will love you! But you know there'll be disapproval . . . mixed marriages are frowned on; even the Salvationists would prefer you to marry within the Army, I daresay. Because I'd want me children brought up in the faith so I would. If you'd agree?'

'I'd like my children to have the freedom to choose,' Sara said after a moment. 'Would that be unfair, Brog? After all, religion's an important thing, it's not like saying "I support Liverpool, or Everton," it's a way of life. Serving God is serving God, whether you do it as a Catholic or a Salvationist. Choice is important.'

'I agree. But we'll leave that problem until after we're married,' Brogan said. 'Only I doubt that Salvationists would want you workin' on at the Strawb if you were married to a Catholic.'

'Oh? And they wouldn't want a Catholic for a gardener, I suppose?'

Brogan laughed and threw up his hands in the immortal gesture of surrender. 'Pax, pax! You're right and I'm wrong, me darlin'. And when the babies come along it isn't workin' at the Strawb you'd be anyway. You'd be taking care of me and them!'

'That sounds wonderful,' Sara murmured. 'But what about Grace? She's tremendously happy at the Strawb, but there's no doubt her sister is having a more – more normal sort of life with your family out at the level-crossing cottage.'

'Me family will want to meet her, no doubt,' Brogan said cautiously. 'But I'm not plannin' on tellin' either Grace or Polly what happened all those years ago, if that's what you were thinkin'. What I did was illegal even if 'twas for the best, I'd be t'rown in prison, very like, if it came out. And they're only kids, the young Carbs. I wouldn't be puttin' the responsibility of knowin' such t'ings on their shoulders.'

'True,' Sara agreed. 'All right, suppose we offered to have Grace to live with us, Brogan? Would you like that?'

'Look, sweetheart, stop anticipatin'. Let's take it one step at a time, shall we? And the first step is for me to go down to the cottage and break the news that we're engaged to be wed. Then I'll take you to meet them and we'll go on from there. Agreed?'

'No! If we're engaged to be wed the first thing to do is buy me a ring,' Sara said. 'Just a little, cheap one, you know, but a real engagement ring.'

Brogan got up from the table and, as Sara rose too, kissed her quickly on the side of her mouth. 'You're right; we'll take a tram into the city centre tomorrow morning, first thing,' he said buoyantly. 'You're a girl who gets her priorities right, Miss Cordwainer, I can tell that!'

Brogan walked up from the station to the crossing

cottage, a heavy bag full of small Christmas gifts slung over his shoulder. The cottage was on the telephone, and Deirdre had rung him a couple of times, once to ask if he could do some shopping for them.

'Wit' only ten days to go before the holiday we're havin' our work cut out to get the place straight,' she had shouted into the mouthpiece. 'You're in the city, me boy, so if I read you a list out, could you do me messages and bring 'em wit' you, next time you come?'

'I could and I will, Mammy,' Brogan assured her. 'But the telephone's a wonderful invention, it carries your voice to me by the electric – you don't have to bellow like that, you know.'

'Who's bellowin'?' Deirdre said, still at full volume. ''Twon't take no heed of a whisper, that I *do* know. Did ye hear me?'

'I heard,' Brogan said patiently. 'I'll do your messages then, Mammy, and see you in a week, so I will.'

And now he was walking up the lane, the hedges winter-bare but bright with berries, the grass of the verge dry and white after the long summer. Over the gates he passed, Brogan could see the clean line of plough, a field of winter cabbage growing well, pasture dotted with cattle or sheep. Trees overhung the lane, trees which, in summer, would cast a delightful shade, though now they, like the hedges, were bare of leaves, and when the lane deepened, running between high banks, Brogan could see by the foliage that when spring came there would be wild strawberries here, and violets, primroses.

'It's just like heaven,' Polly had written to him only last week. 'I love it best in the world, so I do. But I wish Tad were here too.'

And the crossing cottage was nice as well. Long and low, with the bedroom ceilings slanted, the windows set in the warm red tiles so that the house looked as though it was perpetually raising its eyebrows, it crouched midway between the track and the lane, its whitewashed walls cool to the touch in summer, warm in winter. There was an airy living room which overlooked the railway line so the family could watch the trains as they thundered past, and a large kitchen overlooking the garden where the cats strolled elegantly or sneaked on their bellies after the birds, and the borders, even at this time of year, were gay with late roses, chrysanthemums, and autumn crocus.

Brogan hitched his bag a bit higher on his shoulder and strode on. His family were happy and settled already, the boys and Polly enjoying the village school, his parents almost unable to believe the rural peace by which they were surrounded. To be sure, Deirdre had complained at first that she could not sleep at nights for the trains, whilst Peader, sheepishly, had said that the long silences between trains kept him awake. But it hadn't lasted. They had grown accustomed; indeed, Peader now said that if a train was late he was likely to wake because it hadn't gone through, though the roar of its normal progress disturbed him not at all.

There were only two trains through between the hours of ten at night and six the next morning, and now that they were settled, Deirdre had offered to do them every other night so that Peader could sleep straight through.

'But I like to wake and see to me gate,' her husband had assured her. ''Tis a pleasure to me, alanna, and no pain. And I'm fast asleep five minutes after she's gone through, you know that.'

The hens had settled as well as the rest of the family, and Delilah was in his element. Though not the meekest or most biddable of dogs, he was well content with the large garden in which he could wander, and the nearby meadows where cows grazed and willows overhung the small streams. There was a river, too. The boys went fishing with their homemade rods and Polly spent hours hanging over the water with a flour-bag on a split cane and came home with pinkeens galore, though the local children told her they were stickleback, and assured her that she would find more exciting things in the streams than that when spring came.

Brogan came alongside the cottage garden, or rather the orchard. He looked through the hedge at the old trees standing in the long, whitened grass, and thought that he and Peader really ought to start off some new stock. And then as he drew level with the vegetable patch he saw his father. Peader wore old corduroys and a much-patched shirt. His head was bare and despite the cold, his shirt was rolled up above the elbows. He was digging over a patch of ground which had not been cultivated for years but he must have heard Brogan's footsteps for he straightened, a hand in the small of his back, and turned, then gave a broad, welcoming smile.

'Brogan! Good to see you, son.'

'Good to see you, Daddy,' Brogan said, putting down his haversack for a moment. Grinning, they shook hands over the hedge, then Brogan hefted his bag once more and set off again, Peader keeping pace with him on the other side of the hedge. 'I've done all Mammy's messages, and a couple for you, as well. And I've some news for you; I hope you'll t'ink it good.'

'Sure we shall, boy,' Peader said heartily. He held open the gate, gesturing Brogan inside. 'Your mammy's got the kettle on and some oat cakes warmin'. Let's go in for a bit, it's time I had a break.'

Brogan had known, in his heart, that it was not going to be a picnic, telling his family about Sara. But he had not been prepared for the downright antagonism. Peader and the boys hadn't been so bad, but his Mammy! She had wept and wailed and said he'd go to hell so he would for marryin' an Army lass, no matter how good, sweet or high-principled.

'Sure an' even the child here would know better than to consort wit' such people,' Deirdre had said at one point, putting a protective hand on Polly's curly head. 'Doesn't she go to a school now which is *crawling* wit' Proddies, but does she bring 'em home or tell me she's goin' to wed one of 'em? Of course not; she's got more sense!'

Polly looked hunted; Brogan guessed that the religion of her schoolmates simply had not, until this moment, entered her head. Poor little creature, he thought compassionately, what a fuss about nothing, when you had to bring a child of ten into it!

'But, Mammy, Sara's a lovely person...' Brogan began, only to be overridden. Lovely people, it appeared, were very fine if they stayed on their own side of the fence. If they trespassed, then they were no longer lovely people. A lovely Proddy, his mother assured him, was incapable of falling in love wit' a decent Catholic boy. And, she added with a glare, a lovely Catholic boy would never demean himself by even considerin' marriage to a Protestant, let alone a Salvationist.

'But they're in love, Deirdre,' Peader pointed out, when his wife had paused momentarily in her lamentations. 'Love's not somethin' you can switch on or off like a tap, you know. D'you t'ink I'd have walked away from you if you'd been an Army lass – or a heathen Chinee, for that matter?'

'But you didn't mix wit' those sort of people,' Deirdre reminded him truthfully. 'Our boy's been mixin' wit' the wrong sort, that's the trouble. I tell you, decent Catholic boys don't even t'ink of Proddy girls in that sort of way. Why, a decent Catholic lad would as soon marry a cow in the meadow as a Proddy! If we'd been back in Dublin, now . . .'

'Oh, if, if! Don't ever condemn love, alanna. I'm tellin' you, if you'd had a ring t'rough your nose and worshipped a totem pole, I'd still have wed ye!'

'The more fool you, Peader O'Brady,' Deirdre had muttered darkly. 'I'd sooner dance at the weddin' of a cat wit' a mouse than a decent Catholic boy wit' a Proddy.'

Brogan, still annoyed at the suggestion that Sara was as marriageable as a cow, cast his mother a dark look and she scowled back at him, muttered something about scheming hussies in black stockings who were no better than they ought to be, and stamped out of the living room and back to her kitchen sink, leaving Peader and Brogan to stare helplessly at each other.

Polly, sitting on the windowsill ostensibly watching for the 16.05, turned and stared at them with big, puzzled eyes.

'Daddy, what's *wrong* wit' Proddies? I didn't know me school was crawlin' wit' them at all at all.'

'Oh hell,' Peader said helplessly. He never swore. 'Oh hell, alanna, don't you let such talk take root. There's nothin' wrong wit' Proddies, nothin' at all. Mammy didn't mean it, it's just . . . Brogan's her eldest boy now, and she doesn't want to lose him.'

'But she wouldn't lose you, would she, Brog?' Polly said eagerly. 'The Proddy wouldn't take you away from us, would she? She'd come here as well – I'd like that.'

'Well, don't tell Mammy,' Brogan growled. 'If she

t'ought I'd influenced you to think well of a Salvationist sure me head would be on a spike on the crossin' gate, instead of on me shoulders. I was goin' to bring Sara to meet you next weekend . . .'

'Better not,' Peader advised. 'Leave it a week or two. Come over wit' her in the New Year. Your mammy won't be rude . . .'

'Oh, no, she'll just tell Sara she's as marriageable as a cow and a scheming hussy in black stockings,' Brogan said bitterly. 'How can I bring me innocent girl here, Daddy, when there's talk like that?'

'I'll make sure Deirdre's polite and welcoming,' Peader said grimly. 'Polly, go out an' play!'

'It's cold out,' Polly whined. 'I'm waitin' on the 16.05, the driver's me friend, he waves!'

'He's a Proddy, you'd better not wave back,' Brogan said, just as his mother re-entered the room. She coloured hotly, but ignored the remark, holding out her hand to Polly.

'Come into the kitchen, alanna. I'm bakin' scones, you can put a few extra currants in, make them wit' laughin' faces.'

'I don't want to,' Polly muttered. 'Mammy, I *like* the kids at school, I didn't know they were Proddies.'

'No, well, 'tis a small village, alanna, we can't choose . . .' Deirdre began, only to be interrupted.

Peader jumped to his feet, his face turning scarlet and veins beginning to bulge on his forehead. He slammed both fists down on the small table, and shouted at his wife.

'I won't have you turnin' the child into a mass of blind prejudice so I won't! Now tell us all you spoke out of turn and when the New Year comes we'll meet Brogan's young lady and judge for ourselves. D'you understand me, Deirdre O'Brady?'

Deirdre, looking stunned, muttered that she supposed it would be all right if that was his attitude and held out an appealing hand to Polly, who continued to shake her head.

'Go wit' your mammy, Polleen,' Peader said quietly. 'And in ten minutes or so we'll all have a nice cup of tay and one of those scones she was talkin' about. And the first weekend after the New Year, Brogan shall bring Miss Cordwainer to visit us. I'm the master in me own house and I say who's welcome here!'

Brogan had to tell Sara, of course. He went round to the Strawb and waited until she had put the children to bed and finished work for the day. Then he announced that he was going to do some digging and would be grateful for her company. Sara accordingly put on her thick grey worsted coat and her red tam o'shanter and went and stood beside him whilst he double-dug the vegetable patch.

'Well?' she asked impatiently after a few moments. 'What did they say? Was it bad, Brog?'

'It was,' Brogan said, not mincing matters. 'Me daddy was fair; he always is. Me mammy wasn't. But we expected it, didn't we?'

'Ye-es,' Sara said doubtfully. 'Then what are we to do, Brog? You don't want to marry in the face of your mother's objections, I suppose, and I can understand it because your mother's always been good to you. Honestly, if you . . .'

'I'm to take you round to the cottage in the New Year,' Brogan said. 'We'll sort it all out then. When Mammy sees you . . .'

But even to his own ears his words did not have that air of confidence which he wanted to convey.

'Shall we take Grace, as well?' Sara suggested presently. Brogan could see her self-confidence had taken a nasty knock and stopped digging for a moment to reach across and give her hand a squeeze. 'No, it's all right, you did say it might be difficult. It's just that because I'm so happy I can't see how anything like two different religions could possibly matter. If we do as we said – turn and turn about – what's wrong with that? Only you'll have to take them to Mass and Confession, because I – well, I'm a Salvationist when all's said and done.'

'We don't have any children yet, me darlin',' Brogan reminded her with a smile. 'So that's a matter between us, for the future. And we won't take Grace when we go to the crossing cottage, not the first time. I've a feelin' we'll have our work cut out to make me family see reason wit'out addin' Grace to the party.'

Because Grace liked to garden, she spent a lot of time with Brogan, sweeping leaves, tidying hedges, making bonfires, and with every day her self-confidence – and her naughtiness – grew. Brogan applauded this, but did not fancy having to cope with it at the crossing cottage.

'I thought she might take their minds off me, that's all,' Sara said meekly. 'What'll I wear? Not uniform?'

'Definitely not uniform,' Brogan said quickly. His mammy would go mad if she saw how very beautiful Sara's legs looked in the despised black stockings, or how becomingly the bonnet framed her lovely face! 'Somethin' warm, alanna, because – because we'll maybe take a walk after dinner. And somethin' pretty, because I'm proud of you.'

'Oh, Brogan,' Sara said. 'Oh, Brogan, I do love you!'

Sara had known meeting Brogan's family would be

an ordeal, but in fact it was worse than her wildest imaginings. First, they walked into the cottage to meet a positive barrage of eyes. Not just Deirdre, Peader, Polly, Bevin and Ivan, but Donal, too, because he had come over for a job interview and was spending a day with his family at the same time.

Then, having been introduced all round, Sara was invited, by Deirdre, to take a moment to tidy up, which meant going upstairs with her hostess and trying to make light conversation with someone, whilst combing her hair and hanging up her coat, who simply said nothing but let her eyes roam insultingly over her.

Finally, of course, Sara had been stung into speech.

'Mrs O'Brady, I know you can't be too pleased that your son has brought a Salvationist home . . .' she began, to be swiftly interrupted.

'Pleased? Is it pleased I should be that me eldest, dearest son has broke me heart wit' his selfishness and gone against family tradition? But there, Miss Cordwainer, he's a handsome feller, I'll grant you that, and likely to earn good money by and by. I shouldn't be after blamin' you for seizin' the chance of him.'

Sara opened her mouth, closed it, opened it again, then turned on her heel and made for the stairs. She was hot with rage – according to her hostess she was, in addition to being a Proddy, a fortune hunter as well! But down in the living room, she decided on a plan of action. From being tongue-tied and diffident, she became, once more, Miss Cordwainer of Aigburth Road. She talked amusingly about her work, the children in her care, the soup kitchens of the inner city. She showed a great interest in Peader's garden and insisted that he take her round it. She went up to the boys' room and admired the view, their pictures, the stories they told her. She did not have to woo Polly, who was frankly delighted to find that Brogan's young lady thought her dog a fine fellow, her cats beautiful, her hens useful and her rabbits sweet. She deferred constantly to Deirdre, tried to help her with the meal, admired her possessions and said the cottage was the prettiest house she had ever visited. Deirdre sniffed, snubbed her, turned the conversation, but she could not have complained about Sara's manners.

And by the time Brogan was helping Sara into her coat so that they would be in good time for their train, she knew she had won. They liked her! Well, everyone except Deirdre, and her mother-in-law, Sara thought sadly, was a lost cause. But the others would come to the wedding, though it would have to be a register office ceremony. They would wish her happy, even though they also wished her Catholic. It was the most she could hope for.

Christmas at Strawberry Field had been the happiest so far in Grace's entire life. She had loved every minute of it, from the excitement of Christmas Eve to the wonderful moment, on Christmas morning, when they had been taken to the Barracks to see the crib, and to join the rest of the congregation in praising God and singing their hearts out. And there was Christmas dinner – so much wonderful food – and present-giving round the tree, then Christmas tea – more wonderful food – and finally, stories round the fire before bed. The only disappointment, in fact, had been that Brogan was spending Christmas with his family.

Soon after Grace arrived at the Strawb, Peader had come into the city specially to see her, and it had been an emotional moment. Grace had stammered a few words of thanks, had muttered that it was her fault that he'd almost been killed . . . and Peader had enveloped her in a bear-hug, told her that the boot was on the other foot – if she'd not run like the very dickens he'd have been long dead, so he would – and invited her to visit him and his family at the crossing cottage, just as soon as it could be arranged.

Grace was absolutely delighted to find that she loved Peader just as much as she loved Brogan. 'They're goin' to ax me to stay,' she told Sara, beaming. 'They've gorra gel, you know, norra lot younger'n me – Polly she's called. If we gets on . . . well, it'll be nice, eh? Wish we was there now, Sara.'

Sara agreed, and admitted she missed Brogan too, which made Grace cast her a rather thoughtful look. She understood that she was a child and Sara was a young woman, so of course Sara spent more time with Brogan than she did, but she did hope Sara was not going to get ideas about Brogan. The Irishman was Grace's ideal and she had every intention of marrying him just as soon as she was old enough. But of course she had not told Brogan this, not yet. His surprise and delight she took for granted, but she wanted to be beautiful for him and that meant putting on more weight, brushing her hair – and teeth – with horrible and boring regularity, and taking baths.

Grace was not particularly keen on baths. Being in the warm water was nice enough, but she was secretly afraid of slipping beneath the surface and drowning, and she did hate getting out and having to rub herself dry. But Sara told her that young men like young ladies to be extremely clean, so Grace, gritting her teeth, bathed.

Not that Sara was right all the time. Grace knew a great many men who had married thoroughly dirty women – her father was one – and seemed to find clean ones daunting, not attractive at all. She said as much to Sara one evening when Sara had come back from a day out rather subdued. They were in the bathroom and Sara was getting earth out from under Grace's nails with a small object called an orange stick. Grace was complaining that she'd not have a finger-end left to bless herself with if Sara kept on digging like that and they were both laughing when Sara finished Grace's right hand – she had already done the left one – and stood back.

'There! Lovely nails, nice clean hair, and your skin's all pink and white now, after all this washing! And whatever you may say the nicest men all value cleanliness next to godliness . . . it isn't just a biblical thing, love, it's actually true. And since you are becoming such a very pretty girl, I want to ask a favour of you.'

'Ask away, queen,' Grace said loftily. 'I'd do jest about anythin' for you, Sara, after all you done for me.'

'Well, I'm getting married, dear, and I'd love you to be a bridesmaid. It won't be a white wedding, it's going to take place in a register office because as you know I'm a Salvationist and Brogan's a Catholic, but . . .'

'Brogan? Wharrever does it matter if Brogan's a Catholic or a Sally Ann?' Grace asked. 'He ain't bein' a bridesmaid too, I suppose?'

She meant it jokingly; she knew fellers weren't bridesmaids. Sara smiled, but it was perfunctorily.

'Oh, Grace, you know very well he isn't going to be a bridesmaid! He's the bridegroom, of course.'

There was a horrid silence. Grace, unable to believe her ears, tried to tell herself that a bridegroom was probably a male attendant to the feller Sara was marrying, but an awful suspicion had entered her mind.

'Bridegroom? Brogan? You do mean *our* Brogan, Sara? Brogan O'Brady?'

'That's it. We're getting married in a few weeks. I'm afraid his family aren't terribly pleased because . . .'

'No!' Grace was so indignant that her voice came out as a squeak. 'No! I don't believe it!'

She meant she didn't – couldn't – believe that Brogan, *her* Brogan, had actually asked Sara to marry him. Oh, she knew they were *engaged*, whatever that might imply, but being married was different. Being married was for life, and she wanted to marry Brogan herself, they were well-suited, anyone could see that! But Sara immediately got hold of the wrong end of the stick.

'It's true. His family aren't very pleased because they want him to marry a Catholic. But we don't think it matters, Brogan and I, so . . .'

Grace was dressed in her nightgown. Now she jammed her slippers on to her feet and flapped towards the door. 'I didn't mean . . . I meant I won't be a bleedin' bridesmaid,' she called back over her shoulder. Her voice, to her horror, was distinctly wobbly. 'If 'e's so bleedin' stupid . . . after all, it must ha' been clear . . . why the *devil* couldn't 'e 'ave waited . . . Well, I'm *not* goin' to be a bleedin' bridesmaid, no matter what you say!'

And she tore out of the bathroom, slamming the door so hard behind her that it echoed like a cannon shot.

Sara, thoroughly upset, ran out of the bathroom and, after a second's hesitation, into Grace's bedroom. It appeared to be empty, so she hurried down the stairs and into the kitchen. No Grace. Sara was about to try another room when the back door opened and Brogan, in his stockinged feet, came gingerly into the room.

'I've done the marrow bed . . .' he was beginning,

when he saw Sara's face. He crossed the kitchen in a couple of strides and took her in his arms. 'What's the matter, me love? Who's upset you?'

'Oh, Brog, I asked Grace to be my bridesmaid and she said no, and rushed out of the room,' Sara wailed, clutching him. 'I don't know what I've done wrong I'm sure; she's always seemed to like me, but . . .'

'I'll have a word,' Brogan said grimly. 'How can she upset you so, alanna, and you askin' her to stand by you on your weddin' day! Where's she gone?'

'I don't know,' Sara said, clinging on. 'Don't go after her, she's done nothing wrong, it's just . . . I really don't understand!'

'Nor me. Did she say anything else?' Brogan asked. 'Or did she just say *no* and leave the room?'

'She swore a bit, and said why couldn't he have waited, I think,' Sara said, having given the matter some thought. 'I don't know what she meant by that, but . . .'

'Oh dear,' Brogan said helplessly. 'Oh dear . . . I think I may know. I'd best have a word, love. Can you fetch her out – and then leave us for a few minutes?'

'Of course,' Sara said. She dried her eyes, blew her nose, then left the kitchen, to return presently with a defiant but red-eyed Grace, who marched into the room and sat herself down on the table edge, saying as she did so: 'She says you want a word wi' me, Brogan. I were 'avin' a quiet moment to meself, but she come and dug me out.'

'She was under her bed,' Sara said. 'Hiding! Really, Grace, I don't know what I've done, but . . .'

'I'm goin' to sort that out,' Brogan said soothingly. 'You go and finish your work, Miss Cordwainer, whilst Grace and I have a bit of a crack.' He waited until Sara had left the room, then turned to Grace, perching on the edge of the kitchen table and looking, even to Brogan's unaccustomed eyes, extremely defiant. 'Now, Grace, Miss Cordwainer told you she and I plan to marry quite soon, and she asked you to be her bridesmaid. I understand you turned us down.'

'Us? Well, yes, but you di'n't ask me, did you?' Grace said belligerently. 'You never even telled me you was gettin' wed! You could of telled me!'

'Yes, I could. I'm sorry, Grace, if I hurt your feelings, but you see Sara and I have known each other for years, and you and I are quite new acquaintances, wouldn't you say?'

'I'd say friends,' Grace muttered, very red about the gills.

'All right, we're quite new friends, then. Isn't that so? Sara and I have known each other for ten years, you see.'

'I daresay,' Grace said. Her lip, to Brogan's alarm, first jutted and then trembled. 'But, Brogan, you're me best, me very best pal! I thought mebbe, one day . . .'

So I was right, Brogan thought, dismayed. The poor kid's gone and got a crush on me so she has. Now what am I to do?

'Sure an' you're me best pal too, Grace,' he said, playing for time. 'But when I first met Sara she was your age . . . about twelve. I've waited ten years . . .'

He let his voice trail into silence. Grace studied her hands, the scone dough, the floor at her feet. But when she did speak, her voice was gentle.

'Waitin's hard, ain't it, Brogan? Is that what you're tryin' to say? If you did . . . if you did wait, you'd be real old – is that it?'

Crossing his fingers for the half-lie, Brogan nodded. 'That's it, Grace. A feller can't wait for ever. And besides, in ten years' time you'll mebbe have met a nice young feller . . .'

'No I shan't,' Grace said. But she didn't sound fierce any more, just forlorn. 'I won't ever meet anyone like you, Brog.'

'No, you'll meet someone better,' Brogan assured her. 'Grace, will you please, please, be our bridesmaid? You'd make us both very happy, so you would.'

'Will I 'ave to wear flowers in me 'air?' Grace said suspiciously. 'I don't want the other kids mockin' me.'

'You'll wear whatever you're comfortable in,' Brogan assured her. 'Sara's goin' to buy you somethin' really nice – a dress, shoes, the lot. Look, alanna, I'm goin' to let you into a really big secret, something that not even Sara knows yet. Do you promise you won't tell?'

'I promise,' Grace said eagerly. Already her woes were lessening at the prospect of new clothes; now there was a secret, too.

'After we're wed, Sara an' me may be goin' to America to live. There's a better life there for a train driver, or so I've been told. And because you're goin' to be our bridesmaid we'd like you to come an' visit us there, in a year or so, when you're old enough for the journey.'

'America!' Before his eyes the small, pale face lit up, the grey eyes glowed. 'Oh, Brogan, will you write to me? I can save the stamps . . . you can tell me all sorts about wharrit's like over there. Ooh, think of the fillum stars you'll meet!'

The crisis was over, peace was restored. Brogan, promising to write to Grace as often as he possibly could, was thankful to have got over heavy ground so lightly.

And presently, when it was time for Brogan to leave and Sara walked him down to the gate, he was able to put an arm round her, give her a squeeze, and explain what had been the matter.

''Tis an odd thing when a child of twelve or thirteen thinks she's in love wit' a feller so it is,' he said. 'But I think she's over it, now.'

'What's odd about it?' Sara demanded, standing on tiptoe to kiss his cheek. 'I was a child of twelve or so when I first met you, and I fell in love then. Didn't you realise it, Brogan? Ah, what a modest soul you are!'

'I know,' Brogan said. 'I've a delightful nature so I have. And now I'd better love you and leave you, alanna, or I'll miss me tram.'

Chapter Seventeen

'But why won't you come, Mammy? You've always loved a wedding so you have and Sara's goin' to look a picture, Brogan says so. And the boys are comin', all the people from the Strawb... you'll miss out, Mammy!'

Polly's voice was pleading, but loud. She was standing before her mirror putting the finishing touches to her new dark-green coat and matching hat and Deirdre was in her own room across the landing. It was necessary to shout or the two could not have heard one another, and Polly felt that it was important to keep begging her mother to accompany them right up to the last moment. Peader had given up days ago and it had caused a rift between the two of them but Polly was sure that, given the chance, her mother would change her mind.

Polly had been looking forward to this wedding ever since Brogan had told them that it was to take place in early March and though she was not to be bridesmaid after all – Mammy had forbidden it – she was going to give the bride a lucky horseshoe before the happy couple got into the cab which would take them down to the docks. And this had meant a new coat and hat, new shoes and a great deal of fuss and excitement.

But from her mother's bedroom there came a low reply to Polly's shout. 'I'm not comin' to see me boy tied to a Proddy,' Deirdre said, with more than a trace of tears in her voice. 'Your daddy said I needn't, if I didn't want to, and I don't want to, so I'm not comin', and there's an end to it.'

Polly sighed. 'You're spoilin' our day, Mammy,' she said truthfully. 'It won't be the same wit'out you. Please, please come to the weddin'. If you don't, Brogan will be heartbroken so he will.'

This time, there was a snort.

'Oh, yes? Well, 'tis heartbroken his mammy is, I'm tellin' you. Darin' to tell me I was cruel to spoil that Proddy madam's big day . . . I only wish I might!'

Polly sighed again, gave a last glance in the mirror, and headed for the stairs. 'All right, Mammy,' she said kindly. 'You stay at home and be miserable. Daddy says I may hold his arm like a grown-up lady, and at the hooley afterwards I'm to have a sip of wine and a big piece of weddin' cake.'

Silence.

'Ivan's wearin' his white carnation already,' Polly went on as she descended the stairs. 'He looks a proper little man, Mammy. Oh . . . you won't forget to feed Delly and the cats? And me hens, me rabbits . . . best check on the eggs, because the speckled hen kicks them out of the nest if you aren't careful.' Polly reached the hall where the rest of the family waited. They were to catch an early train into the city centre. She raised her voice. 'Bye, Mammy. Have a nice day, now!'

Silence.

'Never mind, alanna,' Peader said, seeing his little daughter's face fall as her mother failed to so much as come to the head of the stairs to wave them off. 'We're goin' to have a grand day so we are. My goodness, don't you look a sight for sore eyes?'

'She's not so dusty,' Ivan said. He was very conscious of his new suit and the huge buttonhole which tickled against his chin. 'Aw, c'mon, Poll, don't keep lookin' over your shoulder! We've a good walk to get to the station, remember.'

Sara was crying. Now that it had come to it, she was realising how much she'd miss the Strawb, the other staff, the children. And though she longed to be Brogan's wife, she hadn't really thought that they would have to go off to the United States of America as soon as the knot was tied. But things were difficult, she acknowledged that. Folk were so tight-lipped, so disapproving of their union, as though the fact that Sara was a Salvationist and Brogan a Catholic should have made their love – and their marriage – unthinkable.

'Sara, me love, we'd be very uncomfortable livin' in the centre of Liverpool, wit' such strong disapproval all around us, to say nothin' of bricks t'rough the winders an kids shoutin' in the street,' Brogan had said when he had told her they would be having their honeymoon aboard a transatlantic liner bound for the port of New York. 'I took you home once, and Mammy wasn't kind to you. And when the babies come, what d'you t'ink folk will say then, eh? We're best out of it.'

'But what'll we live on, until we find work?' Sara had said, stalling desperately. 'Can't we just try it here first, Brog?'

'We'll live on my wages as an engineer,' Brogan said, trying not to sound proud with a total lack of success. 'I've got a job to go to, alanna. I had me certificates copied in a fair hand and I listed all me experience, got some good references, and I sent the whole lot off to Niall. He got me a job wit' a railroad company, starting two weeks after we land. So what about that, eh?'

She had had to say it was wonderful, that he was

wonderful, and it *was*. But America was a long way away and she was giving up her career, her home . . .

'The Army's waiting for you across the water,' the brigadier said comfortingly when Sara tried to explain how she felt. 'You can go on with your career over there if you wish to do so, or you can simply continue to worship with your fellow Salvationists. My poor child, you won't be lonely or left out, not if you go to the nearest citadel and tell them you're an Army lass.'

But it was a big step, and one that Sara was reluctant to take whilst Brogan and his mother were still at odds with one another. So yesterday she had telephoned to the crossing cottage and spoken to Peader.

'We're going so far away, Mr O'Brady,' she had said. 'Can't you persuade your wife to come along, just to bid us goodbye? Brogan can't believe she'll let him down when she's been such a wonderful mother to him.'

But Peader had told her that he'd been forced to agree that Deirdre should stay at home.

'Better that than spoilin' your weddin' wit' a long face,' he'd said heavily. 'I'm disappointed in Mrs O'Brady, I am indeed. But the rest of us will be there to wish you well.'

So be thankful for small mercies and stop behaving like a spoilt baby, Sara scolded herself, carefully wiping her tears away on a small linen handkerchief. Grace will be here any moment and I don't want to show her a long face. She really would tell me off, since I'm the happiest, luckiest person on earth today!

And presently Grace came knocking on the door, resplendent in a smart pink coat with a black velvet collar, a lovely furry muff and patent leather strap shoes. Sara, eyeing her appreciatively, thought her a far cry from the draggly, raggedy orphan-child who, only months before, had been begging outside the Great Mersey public house.

'You look lovely, Miss Cordwainer,' Grace said shyly, coming fully into the room. 'Wharrabout me, eh? Awright, am I?'

'You're a picture, Grace,' Sara said warmly. 'Is it time to go down yet?'

'I reckon. The brig called out the car's 'ere, anyroad.'

'Right.' Sara took one last, long look at herself in her mirror. She saw a slender, pale young woman in a cream-coloured dress with a leaf-green coat over it. Her hair was piled on top of her head in a coronet of dark curls and she was carrying a bouquet of spring flowers. 'Off we go then, Grace!'

Polly found the wedding service disappointing, but then Daddy had warned her it wouldn't be like a proper church wedding. Still, it didn't take long, that was one advantage, and afterwards they went back to the Strawb for a bit of a hooley and then it was into the cars and down to the docks. Polly had watched Grace being a bridesmaid enviously and as soon as the ceremony was over the two girls got together and started chattering for all the world, Peader said, as though they'd known each other for ever.

'You must come and stay wit' us at our cottage out in the country, alanna,' he said to Grace. 'Our Polleen would like that, wouldn't you, Poll? And then you can talk until the cows come home.'

Polly said she would like that and Grace, her whole face brightening, said it would be prime. 'I ain't never been in the country, norrin the 'ole of me life,' she told Polly. 'But I reckon I'll like it more'n any old city. I could 'elp Mr O'Brady in your garden – I'm a dab 'and at gardenin' thanks to Brogan.'

e party made its way down to the docks od together, both with hands plunged ckets so that they could bombard the vith confetti as they arrived to board was wildly excited but she knew tears not far distant, and she saw that Grace was similarly affected. Oh, I suppose she loves Miss Cordwainer – Sara – like I love Brogan, Polly thought to herself. And poor Grace must hate the thought of her going off, perhaps for ever, to another country, like I hate Brogan leaving. It was all very well for her daddy to say Polly could go and visit him there, but that was what they said about Tad and it hadn't happened; she doubted that it ever would.

And then the bride and groom arrived, and the confetti was thrown and there were huggings and kissings and quite a lot of crying. And then Brogan, with his arm round Sara, led her up the gangplank and on to the ship and the O'Bradys stood and waved and waved and Polly felt tears begin to slide down her cheeks and saw, beside her, that Grace was crying too.

Deirdre had told Peader that she would take care of his crossing for him, so she was rather indignant when a tall young man with very pale skin and bright ginger hair turned up about half an hour after the party had left and informed her that he was her husband's stand-in.

'I'm to stay until the weddin' party gets home,' he said. 'Mr O'Brady said there would be a dinner standin' by the oven waitin' to be popped inside, an' I've gorra list of all the trains. So any time you like to leave, Mrs O'Brady . . .'

I couldn't stay, after that, Deirdre told herself, changing hastily into her best coat and hat and putting on her smartest shoes. I might as well just walk d the village, I might do a bit of shopping, wa meet the train . . .

Lime Street station is an enormous, echoing place when you're by yourself, but by now, Deirdre had acknowledged that she would go down to the docks. She would make sure no one saw her, but she would watch Brogan and that stuck-up little madam going off on the liner. And later she'd find Peader and the others and perhaps, because she had journeyed this far, Peader would stop being tight-lipped over her behaviour.

Because I'm right, I know I am, Deirdre told herself, emerging from Lime Street and gazing across at St George's Plain. 'Tis a wrong thing for a Catholic to marry someone who isn't, and they can't say different. Why, even the Army folk must be disappointed that the girl hasn't found herself a feller in their ranks.

Having crossed the busy roadway, Deirdre found herself by the statue of a huge black horse with an old-fashioned-looking woman on its back. Close to the statue taxi cabs stood waiting for fares and on impulse, Deirdre jumped into the nearest. The driver slid back the glass pane which separated them and asked her where she wanted to go. His accent, to Deirdre's pleasure, was warmly Irish.

'Me son's off to America this afternoon, I'm not sure . . .' she began, but apparently this was enough.

'The docks, right? Sure and I'll take you as near as I can get you, missus.' He drove for a short way through the bustling streets, then half-turned to say conversationally, 'Your son'll be on the SS *Europa*, I daresay? We'll 'ave to make it snappy, she sails on the tide.'

Sara got out of the taxi and crossed the dock to the

gangplank which she would presently ascend, then turned to the wedding party, who, unencumbered by luggage, had arrived at the quayside first. She kissed her brand-new father-in-law, her brothers-in-law and her pretty little sister-in-law and told them she would write often. Then she hugged Grace and thanked her for being such an excellent bridesmaid, and thanked Clarrie for giving her away – lacking a relative wishing to do the job she had appealed to Clarrie and her friend had obliged. Then she shook hands with the other staff members who had come to see her off, and took Brogan's hand. There was a great bustle aboard the ship which, she assumed, meant that they should be aboard so with a final round of goodbyes she and Brogan began to ascend the gangplank. Halfway up Sara had an urge to change her mind to return to the quayside, but Brogan, apparently guessing how she felt, slid a strong arm about her waist, his calm, loving presence reassuring her that she was doing the right thing.

They reached the deck.

'I told the family not to come aboard, I said parting once was bad enough,' Brogan whispered in her ear. 'Daddy's goin' to get them all back to the Strawb, where Matron's goin' to give them a supper before they get their train. We'll go below presently and take a look at our cabin, but not until we've waved them off.'

The two of them stood by the rail and waved until their family and friends had all gone, then Brogan turned to her. He smiled and squeezed her hand.

'Come on, let's find the cabin.'

It was a nice cabin, an outside one, which meant that they could look down on to the quay, far below. Brogan took off his heavy coat and hung it in the tiny wardrobe, then put a cautious hand on the bed.

'Nice and soft,' he said. 'We're all right there!'

Sara knew she should have laughed, made some joking reply, but she felt silly, unsure. Deep in the bowels of the ship the engines were rumbling, and the huge craft was beginning to sway slightly. It would not be long now before they sailed, she supposed, and felt vulnerable, uneasily aware that her whole life had now changed. She was in Brogan's charge and he was in hers. Oh, dear God, let us make a success of this strange thing called marriage, she prayed confusedly as she took off her coat and hat. She hung them up, then wandered over to the mirror. Standing before it, she smoothed her hair with shaking hands, then began to fiddle with the string of beads round her throat. Trying to keep her voice steady she said as brightly as she could: 'Are we about to sail, Brog? Should we go on deck?'

'I thought you might prefer a quiet...' Brogan began, then nodded, with so much loving understanding in his eyes that Sara could have wept all over again, except that she was determined to do no such thing. 'Yes, why not? Come on then, Mrs O'Brady!'

They left the cabin, climbed the companionway and crossed the crowded deck. They managed to find a spot by the rail and Brogan put his arm around her as though it belonged there. His head was so close to hers that she could feel his breath on her cheek, stirring her hair.

'All right, sweetheart? Are you goin' to give the old Liver birds a wave, then, to say goodbye? Any moment now the gangplank will be wound in and they'll cast off and – ' He broke off. 'Mary Mother of Jesus... what's goin' on?'

Someone was running up the gangplank, they could see it bouncing from where they stood. There were shouts from the deck – the sailors had been hurrying about, clearly intending to cast off – but the figure continued to come doggedly on.

'Someone nearly missed the boat,' Sara said, trying to make a joke of it. 'Oh, Brogan, it looks like . . .'

'Mammy!' Brogan said. He seized Sara exuberantly round the waist and almost carried her towards where his mother was arguing animatedly with the seamen at the top of the gangplank. 'She's come after all so she has!'

They reached the gangplank breathless, beaming. Deirdre took one look at them and then suddenly she was in Brogan's arms, reaching out a hand, pulling Sara, too, into her embrace.

'I'm sorry I didn't make the weddin',' Deirdre panted. 'I – I just wanted to say goodbye and to wish you happy!' And before either Sara or Brogan could say a word she had reached up and kissed her daughter-in-law heartily on the cheek. 'Now be good to me son,' she instructed, her voice tear-filled but determined. 'Sure an' you'll make him a broth of a wife so you will!'

'Madam, are you a passenger on this ship?' The officer who had spoken took Deirdre's arm in a firm grip. 'You really must go, visitors were asked to leave some while ago, we're about to set sail, you know.'

'It's all right, officer, I'll go quietly now I've said goodbye to me son and his new wife,' Deirdre said soothingly. She turned back to Sara and gave her, for the first time ever, a clear-eyed glance and a gentle, affectionate smile. 'Take care of him, me dear girl,' she said softly. 'And may God bless you both.'

When they could see no land, when the bounding ocean lay all around them, Brogan and Sara returned to their cabin and walked straight into each other's arms. For a moment they just hugged, wordlessly, tightly, then Brogan held her back from him and kissed her brow, her eyelids, her tear-wet cheeks.

'Darlin' Sara, 'tis a big step we're takin', but we're takin' it together and it's an adventure, so it is. All right?'

Sara smiled at him. 'All right, Brog,' she said. 'I can't think of anyone I'd rather have beside me on an adventure, either. Shall we find the dining room and get ourselves some dinner?'

Brogan sat down on the bed and pulled her down beside him. Then, very gently, he began to kiss the side of her neck, her face, her small, rosy ear. 'Sara?' he murmured. 'Are you sure you're wantin' your dinner now?'

Sara sighed tremulously. 'Well, I daresay I could wait for a bit, if you aren't too hungry,' she said.

Outside the cabin the sun sank in the west and the seabirds hawked and called. On deck the lights came on, passengers made their way to the dining room, to the bars and lounges. But in their small cabin, holding each other close, Brogan and Sara were oblivious. Dinner was forgotten, Liverpool might have happened in another life, America was just a dream. Brogan O'Brady and his new wife were learning to love one another.

Epilogue

It was two days since the wedding and life in the crossing cottage was returning to normal after all the excitement. And in the little bedroom overlooking the railway line, Polly lay on her tummy and, with considerable pauses for thought, wrote a letter.

Dear Tad,

Well, it was a wonderful wedding so it was and the hooley after was grand, too. I met a girl called Grace, she was nice, and all the other people were nice as well. We went and waved to Brogan and Sara and Mammy wasn't there then, but she went after. I've already told you about me animals and how happy we all are. Only I would rather be back in the Liberties, with you. I go to a nice school in a nice village and I have found some nice friends. Mammy says they're Proddies but they are all right, you'd like 'em. Only they are none of them as nice as you. There isn't a church too near so we can't go every Sunday which is great, but when I do go it is just like home in there and I think about you. You would like it here, honest to God you would, Tad. There is so much countryside, you have no idea, it stretches for miles and miles. I can pick blackers every day if I like and paddle in the brook which is just like the canal only not so big and a lot wigglier. My teacher is pretty, she says I read and write good for my age, she says I might go to the grammar school if I work hard.

Polly paused, sucking the end of her pencil. The trouble was, the only words she had were words which Tad, in his wisdom, would probably think soppy. But there you were. She would have to say them, it was the whole reason she was writing.

Mammy and Daddy like it here and so do the boys. It is fun to open and close the gate so's the cars and lorries and tractors can get by. The farm hands call me 'Ginger' and tease me but they bring me fruit and sweets so I don't mind. I could box the fox every day if I wanted but I don't, because we have apple trees and a pear tree and two plum trees of our own – think of that, Tad!

Polly paused again and gave her pencil another chew. She had written to Tad three times already and hadn't had a single reply. She had better threaten him a little.

This is me third letter to you, Tad, where is yours to me? she enquired laboriously. He wouldn't like it, but you needed a reply now and then else you got discouraged and gave up. *I can't write for ever when I don't know if you're getting the letters. And Tad, please don't forget we're going to get married when we're big. Because . . .* Could she say it? Could she risk either his wrath or his mirth? But she knew she would have to, because Brogan had told her how he'd nearly lost his Sara through being afraid to speak out, and she did not intend to lose Tad, not she! . . . *Because I love you, Tad Donoghue,* she wrote at last, then rolled over on to her back and read the letter through, word by word, right down to the very end where she had bared her soul, her heart . . . ah, if that bloody Tad Donoghue laughed . . . didn't reply . . .

She signed off. *Please write back quick. Your loving Polly O'Brady.* Then she got off her bed and went over to the windowseat. If she looked far into the distance and let her eyes go all unfocussed she could imagine she was looking right across the country, across the sea . . . yes, there it was, way, way in the distance.

Dublin. The Liberties. Tad Donoghue.

You could go a long way for someone you loved, Polly mused, turning away from the window. Look at Brogan now, going all the way to the United States of America so that he and his Sara could be together without fighting and argument. So if she was serious about Tad, and she was, she would go back for him. Or possibly he would come over here for her. It didn't much matter, so long as they ended up together.

Polly crossed the bedroom and went out on to the small landing. Spring was coming and outside a sweet breeze blew in through the tiny open window which looked out over miles and miles of rolling countryside, to the hills of Wales beyond. Polly glanced down the stairwell; if she wanted to go for a run with Delilah before tea was served she would have to get a move on.

With the letter in her hand she began to descend the stairs and when she reached the bottom she closed both eyes and prayed. Let Tad get my letter, and let him write back, she begged. And then she addressed herself to her guardian angel. If you love me, could you just fly off to Dublin for a bit, an' keep an eye on Tad Donoghue for me? He's a naughty chiseller, but his heart's in the right place so it is, and I'm none too sure he's got an angel of his own. But I've got so much, me mammy, me daddy, me friends and me home. So please, Angel, wherever you are, give a t'ought to Tad.

Polly opened her eyes and just for an instant, in the darkness of the downstairs hallway, she thought she saw someone . . . something. Faint as mist, gentle as the spring breeze, her guardian angel smiled on Polly O'Brady.

To find out more about Katie Flynn why not join the Katie Flynn Readers' Club and receive a twice-yearly newsletter.

To join our mailing list to receive the newsletter and other information* write with your name and address to:

Katie Flynn Readers' Club
The Marketing Department
Arrow Books
20 Vauxhall Bridge Road
London
SW1V 2SA

Please state whether or not you would like to receive information about other Arrow saga authors.

*Your details will be held on a database so we can send you the newsletter(s) and information on other Arrow authors that you have indicated you wish to receive. Your details will not be passed to any third party. If you would like to receive information on other Random House authors please do let us know. If at any stage you wish to be deleted from our Katie Flynn Readers' Club mailing list please let us know.